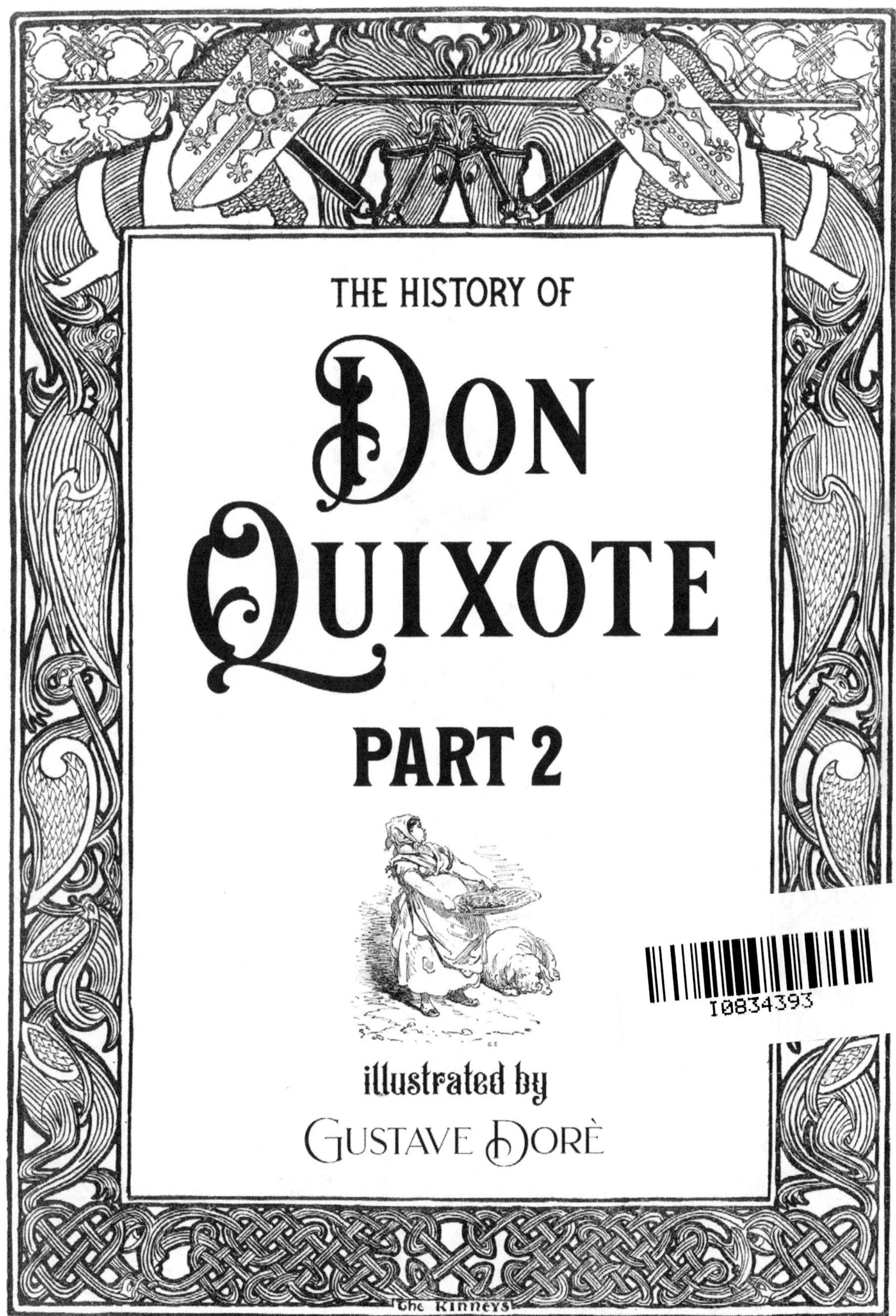

THE HISTORY OF

DON QUIXOTE

PART 2

illustrated by

GUSTAVE DORÈ

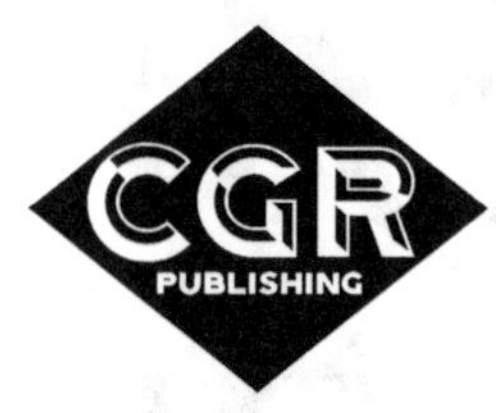

The History of Don Quixote Part 2:
Gustave Doré Restored Special Edition

By Cervantes
Illustrations by Gustave Doré
Edited by F.W. Clark
Cover design by Mark Bussler

www.CGRpublishing.com

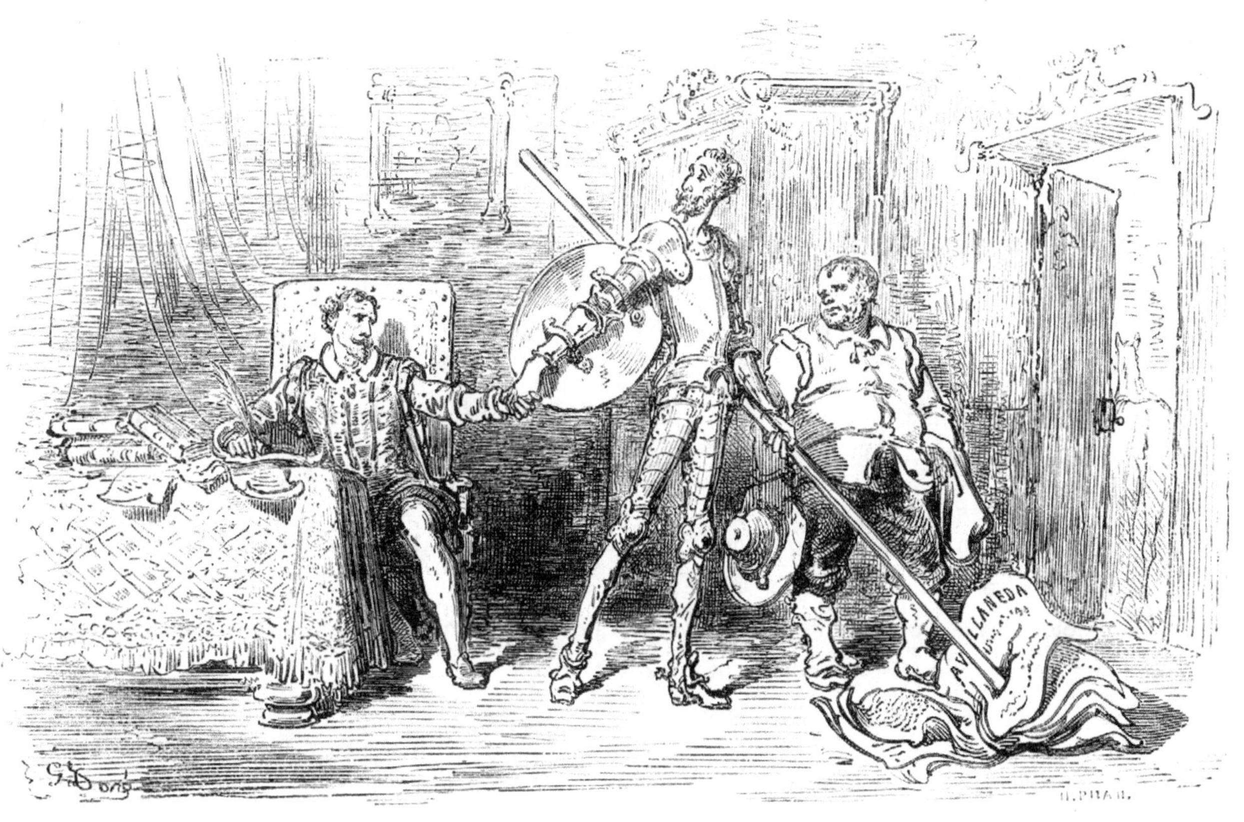

DON QUIXOTE.

PART II.

PROLOGUE.—TO THE READER.

VERILY, gentle or it may be simple reader, with what impatience must you now be waiting for this prologue, expecting to find in it resentments, railings, and invectives against the author of the second Don Quixote. But in truth, it is not my design to give you that satisfaction; for, though injuries are apt to awaken choler in the humblest breasts, yet in mine this rule must admit of an exception. You would have me, perhaps, call him ass, madman, and coxcomb; but I have no such design. Let his own sin be his punishment; let him eat it with his food, and much good may it do him.

What I cannot forbear resenting is, that he upbraids me with my age, and with having lost my hand, as if it were in my power to have hindered time from passing over my head, or as if my injury had been got in some drunken quarrel at a tavern, and not on the noblest occasion that past or present ages have seen, or future can ever hope to see. If my wounds do not reflect a lustre in the eyes of those who barely behold them, they will, however, be esteemed by those who know how I came by them; for a soldier makes a better figure dead in battle, than alive and at liberty in running away. I am so firmly of this opinion, that could an impossibility be rendered practicable, and the same opportunity be recalled, I would rather be again present in that prodigious action, than whole and sound without having shared the glory of it. The scars a soldier shows in his face and breast are stars which guide others to the haven of honour and the desire of just praise. And it must be observed that men do not write with grey hairs, but with the understanding which is usually improved by years.

Say no more to him, nor will I say more to you. Only I will let you know that this second part of "Don Quixote," which I offer you, is cut by the same hand, and out of the same piece, as the first. Herein I present you with Don Quixote at his full length, and at last fairly dead and buried, that no one may presume to bring fresh accusation against him, those already being enough. Let it suffice also that a writer of some credit has given an account of his ingenious follies, resolving not to take up the subject any more. Too much even of a good thing lessens it in our esteem, and scarcity, even of an indifferent, makes it of some estimation.

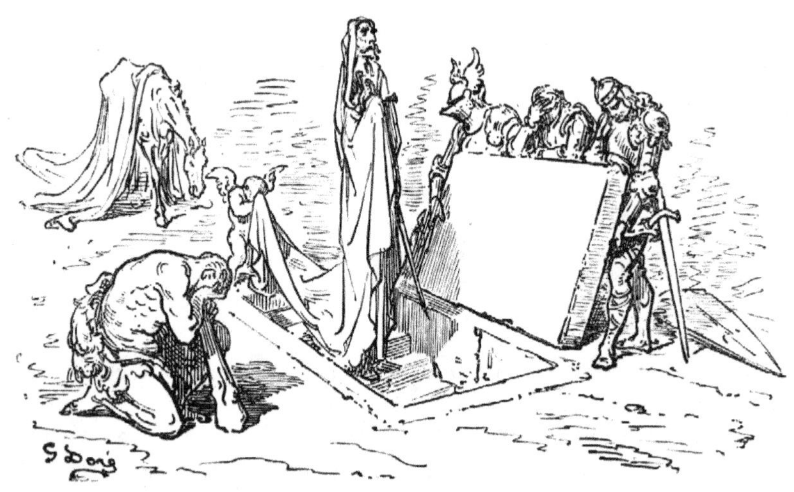

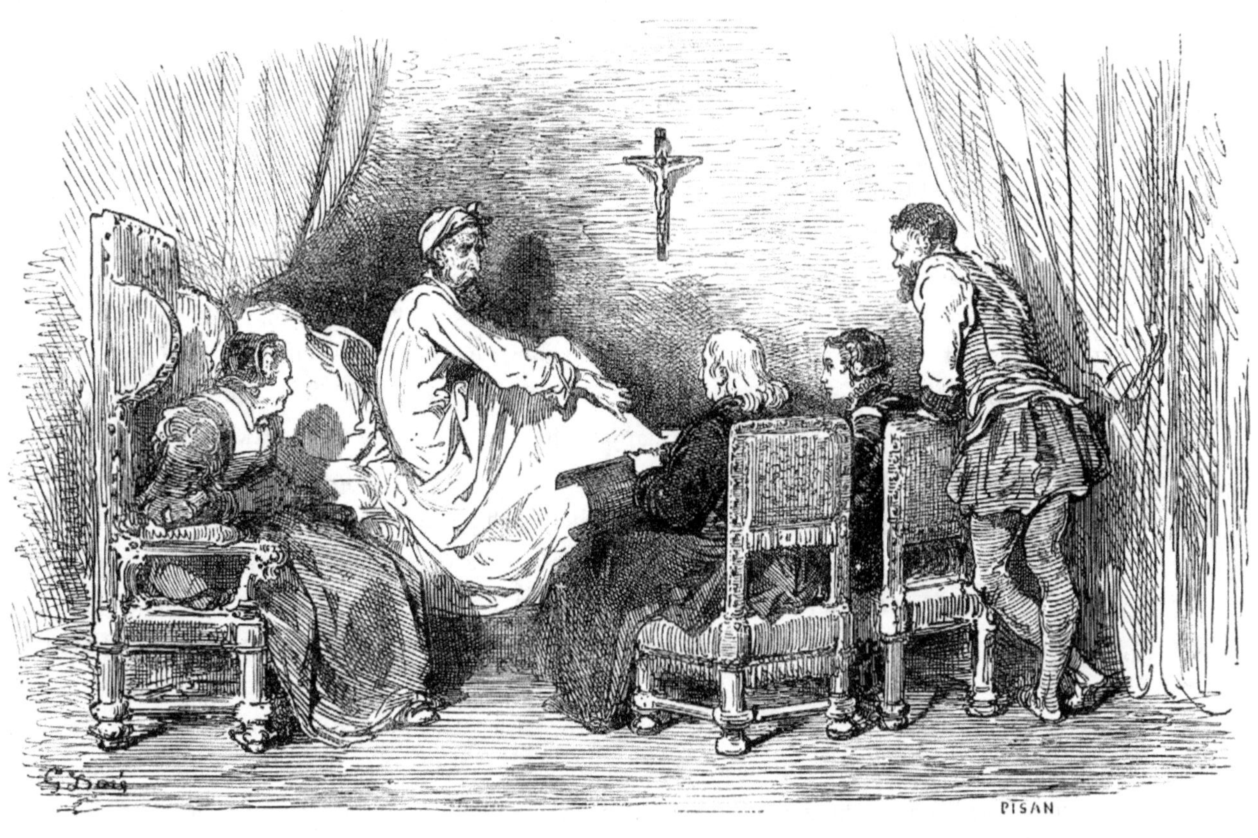

CHAPTER I.

WHAT PASSED BETWEEN THE CURATE, THE BARBER, AND DON QUIXOTE, CONCERNING HIS INDISPOSITION.

CID HAMET BENENGELI relates in the second part of this history, and Don Quixote's third sally, that the curate and the barber were almost a whole month without paying him a visit, lest, calling to mind his former extravagances, he might take occasion to renew them. However, they failed not every day to see his niece and his housekeeper, whom they charged to treat and cherish him with great care, and to give him such diet as might be most proper to cheer his heart, and comfort his brain, whence, in all likelihood, his disorder wholly proceeded. They answered that they did so, and would continue it to their utmost power; the rather, because they observed that sometimes he seemed to be in his right senses. This news was very welcome to the curate and the barber, who looked on this amendment as an effect of their contrivance in bringing him home in the enchanted wagon, as it is recorded in the last chapter of the first part of this most important and no less faithful history. Thereupon they resolved to pay him a visit, and make trial themselves of the progress of a cure, which they thought almost impossible. They also agreed not to speak a word of knight-errantry, lest they should endanger a wound so lately closed, and so tender. In short, they went to see him, and found him sitting up in his bed, in a waistcoat of green baize, and a red Toledo cap on his head; but the poor gentleman was so withered and wasted, that he looked like a mere mummy. He received them very civilly, and when they inquired of his health, gave them an account of his condition, expressing himself very handsomely, and with a great deal of judgment. After they had discoursed a while of several matters, they fell at last on state affairs and forms of government, correcting this grievance and condemning that; reforming one custom, rejecting another, and establishing new laws, as if they had been the Lycurguses or Solons of the age, till they had refined and new modelled the commonwealth at such a rate, that they seemed to have clapped it into a forge, and drawn it out wholly different from what it was before. Don Quixote reasoned with so much discretion on every subject, that his two visitors now undoubtedly believed him in his right senses.

His niece and housekeeper were present at these discourses, and hearing him give so many marks of sound understanding, thought they could never return Heaven sufficient thanks for so extraordinary a blessing. But the curate, who wondered at this strange amendment, being resolved to try whether Don Quixote was perfectly recovered, thought fit to alter the resolution he had taken to avoid entering into any discourse of knight-errantry, and therefore began to talk to him of news, and, among the rest, that it was credibly reported at court, that the Grand Seignior was advancing with a vast army, and nobody knew where the tempest would fall; that all Christendom was alarmed, as it used to be almost every year; and that the king was providing for the security of the coasts of Sicily and Naples, and the island of Malta.

"His majesty," said Don Quixote, "acts the part of a most prudent warrior, in putting his dominions betimes in a posture of defence, for by that precaution he prevents the surprises of the enemy; but yet, if my counsel were to be taken in this matter, I would advise another sort of preparation, which, I fancy, his majesty little thinks of at present."

"Now Heaven assist thee, poor Don Quixote!" said the curate to himself, hearing this; "I am afraid thou art now tumbling from the top of thy madness to the very bottom of simplicity."

Thereupon the barber, who had presently made the same reflection, desired Don Quixote to communicate to them this mighty project of his; "for," said he, "who knows but, after all, it may be one of those that ought only to find a place in the list of impertinent admonitions usually given to princes?"

"No, Goodman Shaver," answered Don Quixote, "my projects are not impertinent, but highly advisable."

"I meant no harm in what I said, sir," replied the barber; "only we generally find most of those projects that are offered to the king are either impracticable or whimsical, or tend to the detriment of the king or kingdom."

"But mine," said Don Quixote, "is neither impossible nor ridiculous; far from that, it is the most easy, the most thoroughly weighed, and the most concise, that ever can be devised by man."

"Methinks you are too long before you let us know it, sir," said the curate.

"To deal freely with you," replied Don Quixote, "I should be loth to tell it you here now, and have it reach the ear of some privy-councillor to-morrow, and so afterwards see the fruit of my invention reaped by somebody else."

"As for me," said the barber, "I give you my word here, and in the face of Heaven, 'never to tell it, either to king, queen, rook, pawn, or knight, or any earthly man'—an oath I learned out of the romance of the curate, in the preface of which he tells the king who it was that robbed him of his hundred doubloons and his ambling mule."

"I know nothing of the story," said Don Quixote, "but I have reason to be satisfied with the oath, because I am confident Master Barber is an honest man."

"Though he were not," said the curate, "I will be his surety in this matter, and will engage for him that he shall no more speak of it than if he were dumb, under what penalty you please."

"And who shall answer for you, Master Curate?" asked Don Quixote.

"My profession," replied the curate, "which binds me to secresy."

"Bless me, then!" cried Don Quixote, "what has the king to do more but to cause public proclamation to be made, enjoining all the knights-errant that are dispersed in this kingdom to make their personal appearance at court upon a certain day? For though but half a dozen should meet, there may be some one among them who, even alone, might be able to destroy the whole united force of Turkey. For pray observe well what I say, gentlemen, and take me along with ye. Do you look upon it as a new thing for one knight-errant alone to rout an army of 200,000 men, with as much ease as if all of them joined together had but one throat, or were made of sugar-paste? You know how many histories are full of these wonders. Were but the renowned Don Belianis living now, or some knight of the innumerable race of Amadis de Gaul, and he met with these Turks, what a woful condition would they be in! However, I hope Providence will in pity look down upon his people, and raise up, if not so prevalent a champion as those of former ages, at least some one who may perhaps rival them in courage. Heaven knows my meaning; I say no more."

"Alas!" said the niece, hearing this, "I will lay my life my uncle has still a hankering after knight-errantry."

"I will die a knight-errant," cried Don Quixote; "and so let the Turks land where they please, how they please, and when they please, and with all the forces they can muster; once more I say, Heaven knows my meaning."

"Gentlemen," said the barber, "I beg leave to tell you a short story of something that happened at Seville; indeed, it falls out as pat as if it had been made for our present purpose, and so I have a great desire to tell it."

Don Quixote gave consent, the curate and the rest of the company were willing to hear; and thus the barber began:—

"A certain person being distracted, was put into the madhouse at Seville by his relations. He had studied the civil law, and taken his degrees at Ossuna, though, had he taken them at Salamanca, many are of opinion that he would have been mad too. After he had lived some years in this confinement, he was pleased to fancy himself in his right senses, and, upon this conceit, wrote to the archbishop, beseeching him, with great earnestness, and all the colour of reason imaginable, to release him out of his misery by his authority, since, by the mercy of Heaven, he was wholly freed from any disorder in his mind; only his relations, he said, kept him in still, to enjoy his estate, and designed, in spite of the truth, to have him mad to his dying day. The archbishop, persuaded by many letters which he wrote to him on that subject, all penned with sense and judgment, ordered one of his chaplains to inquire of the governor of the house into the truth of the matter, and also to discourse with the party, that he might set him at large, in case he found him free from distraction. Thereupon the chaplain went, and having asked the governor what condition the graduate was in, was answered that he was still mad; that sometimes, indeed, he would talk like a man of excellent sense, but presently after he would relapse into his former extravagances, which, at least, balanced all his rational talk, as he might find if he pleased to discourse with him. The chaplain, being resolved to make the experiment, went to the madman, and conversed with him above an hour, and in all that time could not perceive the least disorder in his brain; far from that, he delivered himself with so much sedateness, and gave such direct and pertinent answers to every question, that the chaplain was obliged to believe him sound in his understanding; nay, he went so far as to make a plausible complaint against his keeper, alleging that, for the lucre of those presents which his relations sent him, he represented him to those who came to see him as one who was still distracted, and had only now and then lucid intervals; but that, after all, his greatest enemy was his estate, the possession of which his relations being unwilling to resign, they would not acknowledge the mercy of Heaven, that had once more made him a rational creature. In short, he pleaded in such a manner, that the keeper was suspected, his relations were censured as covetous and unnatural, and he himself was thought master of so much sense, that the chaplain resolved to take him along with him, that the archbishop might be able to satisfy himself of the truth of the whole business. In order to this, the credulous chaplain desired the governor to give the graduate the habit which he had brought with him at his first coming. The governor used all the arguments which he thought might dissuade the chaplain from his design, assuring him that the man was still frantic and disordered in his brain. But he could not prevail with him to leave the madman there any longer, and therefore was forced to comply with the archbishop's order, and returned the man his habit, which was neat and decent.

"Having now put off his madman's weeds, and finding himself in the garb of rational creatures, he begged of the chaplain, for charity's sake, to permit him to take leave of his late companions in affliction. The chaplain told him he would bear him company, having a mind to see the mad folks in the house. So they went up-stairs, and with them some other people that stood by. Presently the graduate came to a kind of cage, where lay a man that was outrageously mad, though at that instant still and quiet; and addressing himself to him—'Brother,' said he, 'have you any service to command me? I am just going to my own house, thanks be to Heaven, which, of its infinite goodness and mercy, has restored me to my senses. Be of good comfort, and put your trust in the Father of Wisdom, who will, I hope, be as merciful to you as he has been to me. I will be sure to send you some choice victuals, which I would have you eat by all means; for I must needs tell you that I have reason to imagine, from my own experience, that all our madness proceeds from keeping our stomachs empty of food, and our brains full of wind. Take heart, then, my friend, and be cheerful; for this desponding in misfortunes impairs our health, and hurries us to the grave.'

"Just over against that room lay another madman, who, having listened with an envious attention to all this discourse, starts up from an old mat on which he lay. 'Who is that,' cried he aloud, 'that is going away so well recovered and so wise?'

"'It is I, brother, that am going,' replied the graduate; 'I have now no need to stay here any longer; for which blessing I can never cease to return my humble and hearty thanks to the infinite goodness of Heaven.'

"'Doctor,' quoth the madman, 'have a care what you say, and let not the devil delude you. Stir not a foot, but keep snug in your old lodging, and save yourself the vexation of being brought back to your kennel.'

"'Nay,' answered the other, 'I will warrant you there will be no occasion for my coming hither again; I know I am perfectly well.'

"'You well!' cried the madman; 'we shall soon see that. Farewell; but by the sovereign Jupiter, whose majesty I represent on earth, for this very crime alone that Seville has committed in setting thee at large, affirming that thou art sound in thy intellects, I will take such a severe revenge on the whole city, that it shall be remembered with terror from age to age, for ever and aye. Amen. Dost thou know, my poor brainless thing in a gown, that this is in my power—I that am the thundering Jove, that grasp in my hands the red-hot bolts of Heaven, with which I keep the threatened world in awe, and might reduce it all to ashes? But stay, I will commute the fiery punishment, which this ignorant town deserves, into another: I will only shut up the flood-gates of the skies, so that there shall not fall a drop of rain upon this city, nor on all the neighbouring country round about it, for three years together, to begin from the very moment that gives date to this my inviolable execration. Thou free! thou well, and in thy senses! and I here mad, distempered, and confined! By my thunder, I will no more indulge the town with rain than I would hang myself.'

"As every one there was attentive to these loud and frantic threats, the graduate turned to the chaplain, and taking him by the hand, 'Sir,' said he, 'let not that madman's threats trouble you. Never mind him; for, if he be Jupiter, and will not let it rain, I am Neptune, the parent and god of the waters; and it shall rain as often as I please, whenever necessity shall require it.'

"'However,' answered the chaplain, 'good Mr. Neptune, it is not convenient to provoke Mr. Jupiter; therefore be pleased to stay here a little longer, and some other time, at convenient leisure, I may chance to find a better opportunity to wait on you, and bring you away.'

"The keeper and the rest of the company could not forbear laughing, which put the chaplain almost out of countenance. In short, Mr. Neptune was disrobed again, stayed where he was, and there is an end of the story."

"Well, Master Barber," said Don Quixote, "and this is your tale which you said came so pat to the present purpose, that you could not forbear telling it? Ah! Goodman Cut-beard, Goodman Cut-beard! how blind must he be that cannot see through a sieve! Is it possible your pragmatical worship should not know that the comparisons made between wit and wit, courage and courage, beauty and beauty, birth and birth, are always odious and ill taken? I am not Neptune, the god of the waters, good Master Barber: neither do I pretend to set up for a wise man when I am not so. All I aim at is only to make the world sensible how much they are to blame, in not labouring to revive those most happy times in which the order of knight-errantry was in its full glory. But, indeed, this degenerate age of ours is unworthy the enjoyment of so great a happiness, which former ages could boast, when knights-errant took upon themselves the defence of kingdoms, the protection of damsels, the relief of orphans, the punishment of pride and oppression, and the reward of humility. Most of your knights, now-a-days, keep a greater rustling with their sumptuous garments of damask, gold brocade, and other costly stuffs, than with the coats of mail, which they should glory to wear. No knight now will lie on the hard ground in the open field, exposed to the injurious air, from head to foot enclosed in ponderous armour. Where are those now, who, without taking their feet out of the stirrups, and only leaning on their lances, like the knights-errant of old, strive to disappoint invading sleep, rather than indulge it? Where is that knight, who, having first traversed a spacious forest, climbed up a steep mountain, and journeyed over a dismal barren shore, washed by a turbulent, tempestuous sea, and finding on the brink a little skiff, destitute of sails, oars, mast, or any kind of tackling, is yet so bold as to throw himself into the boat with an undaunted resolution, and resign himself to the implacable billows of the main, that now mount him to the skies, and then hurry him down to the most profound recesses of the waters; till with his insuperable courage, surmounting at last the hurricane, even in its greatest fury, he finds himself above three thousand leagues from the place where he first embarked, and, leaping ashore in a remote and unknown region, meets with adventures that deserve to be recorded, not only on parchment but on Corinthian brass? But now, alas! sloth and effeminacy triumph over vigilance and labour; idleness over industry; vice over virtue; arrogance over valour, and the theory of arms over the practice—that true practice, which only lived and flourished in those golden days, and among those professors of chivalry. For where shall we hear of a knight more valiant and more honourable than the renowned Amadis de Gaul? Who more discreet than Palmerin of England? Who more affable and complaisant than Tirante the White? Who more gallant than Lisuarte of Greece? Who more cut and hacked, or a greater cutter and hacker, than Don Belianis? Who more intrepid than Perion of Gaul? Who more daring than Felixmarte of Hyrcania? Who more sincere than Esplandian? Who more courteous than Ciriongilio of Thrace? Who more brave than Rodomont? Who more prudent than King Sobrino? Who more desperate than Rinaldo? Who more invincible than Orlando? And who more agreeable or more affable than Rogero, from whom (according to Turpin, in his cosmography) the Dukes of Ferrara are descended? All these champions, Master Curate, and a great many more that I could mention, were knights-errant, and the very light and glory of chivalry. Now, such as these are the men I would advise the king to employ; by which means his majesty would be effectually served, and freed from a vast expense, and the Turk would tear his very beard for madness. For my part, I do not design to stay where I am, because the chaplain will not fetch me out; though, if Jupiter, as Master Barber said, will send no rain, here stands one that will and can rain, when he pleases. This I say, that Goodman Basin here may know I understand his meaning."

"Truly, good sir," said the barber, "I meant no ill; Heaven is my witness, my intent was good: and therefore I hope your worship will take nothing amiss."

"Whether I ought to take it amiss or no," replied Don Quixote, "is best known to myself."

"Well," said the curate, "I have hardly spoken a word yet; and before I go I would gladly be eased of a scruple, which Don Quixote's words have started within me, and which grates and gnaws my conscience."

"Master Curate may be free with me in greater matters," said Don Quixote, "and so may well tell his scruple; for it is no pleasure to have a burden upon one's conscience."

"With your leave then, sir," said the curate, "I must tell you, that I can by no means prevail with myself to believe that all this multitude of knights-errant, which your worship has mentioned, were ever real men of this world, and true, substantial flesh and blood; but rather that whatever is said of them is all fable and fiction, lies and dreams, related by men rather half asleep than awake."

"This is indeed another mistake," said Don Quixote, "into which many have been led, who do not believe there ever were any of those knights in the world. And in several companies I have many times had occasion to vindicate that manifest truth from the almost universal error that is entertained to its prejudice. Sometimes my success has not been answerable to the goodness of my cause, though at others it has; being supported on the shoulders of truth, which is so apparent, that I dare almost say I have seen Amadis de Gaul with these very eyes. He was a tall, comely personage, of a good and lively complexion; his beard well ordered, though black; his aspect at once awful and affable: a man of few words, slowly provoked, and quickly pacified. And as I have given you the picture of Amadis, I fancy I could readily delineate all the knights-errant that are to be met with in history: for once apprehending, as I do, that they were just such as their histories report them, it is an easy matter to guess their features, statures, and complexions, by the rules of ordinary philosophy, and the account we have of their achievements and various humours."

"Pray, good sir," quoth the barber, "how tall then might the giant Morgante be?"

"Whether there ever were giants or no," answered Don Quixote, "is a point much controverted among the learned. However, Holy Writ, that cannot deviate an atom from truth, informs us there were some, of which we have an instance in the account it gives us of that huge Philistine, Goliath, who was seven cubits and a half high, which is a prodigious stature. Besides, in Sicily thigh-bones and shoulder-bones have been found of so immense a size, that from thence of necessity we must conclude, by the certain rules of geometry, that the men to whom they belonged were giants, as big as huge steeples. But, for all this, I cannot positively tell you how big Morgante was; though I am apt to believe he was not very tall, and that which makes me inclinable to believe so is, that in the history which gives us a particular account of his exploits we read that he often used to lie under a roof. Now, if there were any house that could hold him, it is evident he could not be of an immense bigness."

"That must be granted," said the curate, who took some pleasure in hearing him talk at that strange rate, and therefore asked him what his sentiments were of the faces of Rinaldo of Montalban, Orlando, and the rest of the twelve peers of France, who had all of them been knights-errant.

"As for Rinaldo," answered Don Quixote, "I dare venture to say he was broad-faced, of a ruddy complexion, his eyes sparkling and large, very captious, extremely choleric, and a favourer of robbers and profligate fellows. As for Rolando, Rotolando, or Orlando (for all these several names are given him in history), I am of opinion, and assure myself, that he was of the middling stature, broad-shouldered, somewhat bandy-legged, brown-visaged, red-bearded, surly-looked, no talker, but yet very civil and good-humoured."

"If Orlando was no handsomer than you tell us," said the curate, "no wonder the fair Angelica slighted him, and preferred the brisk, pretty, charming young Moor before him; neither was she to blame to neglect the one for the other."

"That Angelica, Mr. Curate," said Don Quixote, "was a dissolute damsel, a wild, flirting, wanton creature, and somewhat capricious to boot. She left the world as full of her impertinences as of the fame of her beauty. She despised a thousand princes, a thousand of the most valiant and discreet knights in the world, and took up with a paltry page, that had neither estate nor honour, and who could lay claim to no other reputation but that of being grateful, when he gave a proof of his affection to his friend Dardinel. And, indeed, even that great extoller of her beauty, the celebrated Ariosto, either not daring, or rather not desiring, to rehearse what happened to Angelica, after her disgraceful intrigue (which passages doubtless could not be very much to her reputation), that very Ariosto, I say, dropped her character quite, and left her with these lines :

'Perhaps some better lyre shall sing,
How love and she made him Cataya's king.'

And without doubt that was a kind of a prophecy; for the denomination of Vates, which signifies a prophet, is common to those whom we otherwise call poets. Accordingly, indeed, this truth has been made evident; for in process of time, a famous Andalusian poet wept for her, and celebrated her tears in verse; and another eminent and choice poet of Castile made her beauty his theme."

"But pray, sir," said the barber, "among so many poets that have written in that lady Angelica's praise, did none of them ever write a satire upon her?"

"Had Sacripante or Orlando been poets," answered Don Quixote, "I make no question but they would have mentioned her to some purpose; for there is nothing more common than for poets, when disdained by their feigned or false mistresses, to revenge themselves with satires and lampoons—a proceeding certainly unworthy a generous spirit. However, I never yet did hear of any defamatory verses on the Lady Angelica, though she made so much mischief in the world."

"That is a miracle indeed," cried the curate. But here they were interrupted by a noise below in the yard, where the niece and the housekeeper, who had left them some time before, were very obstreperous, which made them all hasten to know what was the matter.

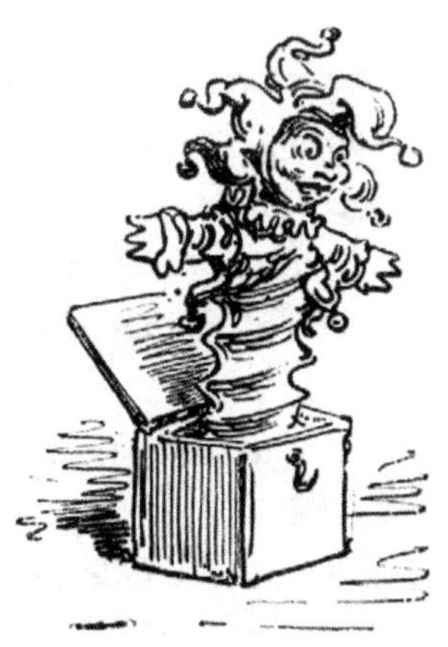

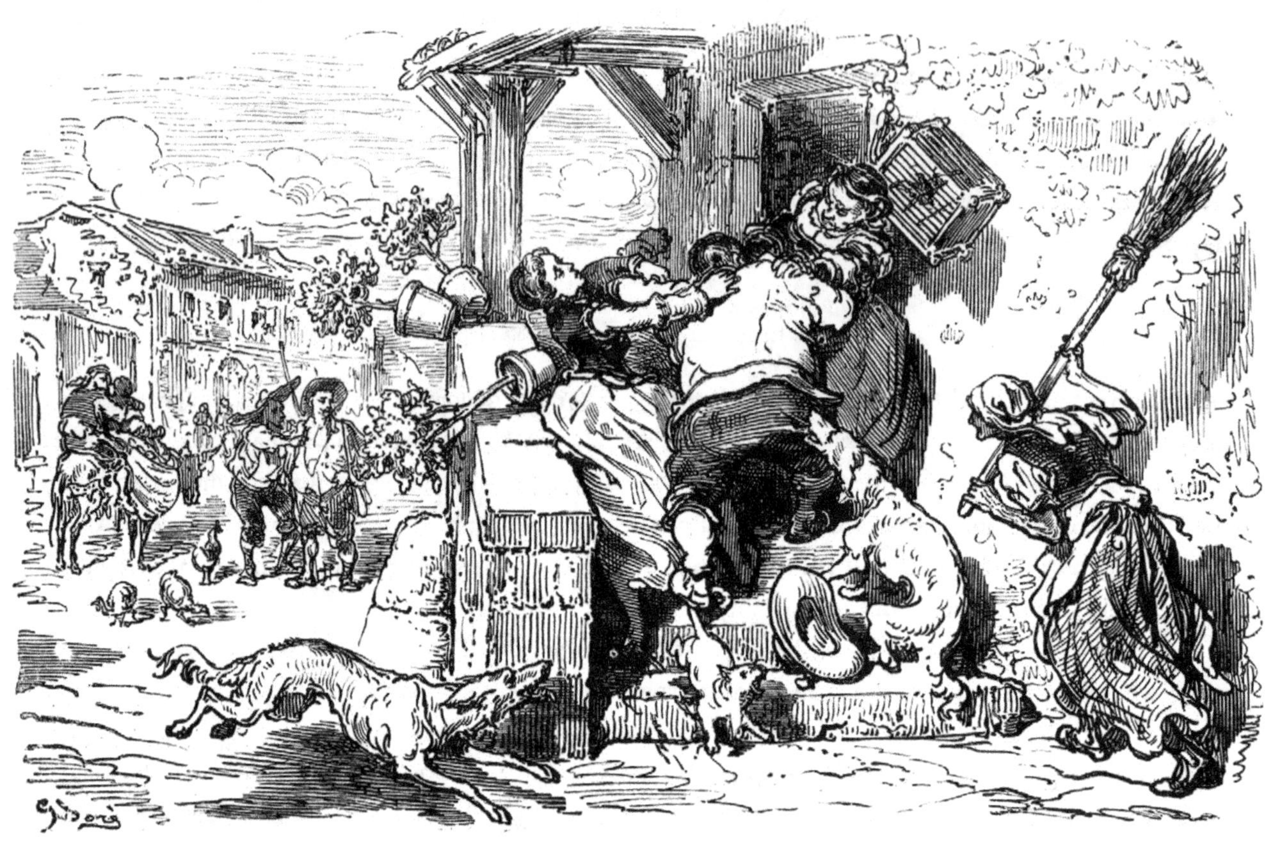

CHAPTER II.

OF THE MEMORABLE QUARREL BETWEEN SANCHO PANZA AND DON QUIXOTE'S NIECE AND HOUSEKEEPER; WITH OTHER PLEASANT PASSAGES.

THE history informs us that the occasion of the noise which the niece and housekeeper made was Sancho Panza's endeavouring to force his way into the house, while they at the same time held the door against him to keep him out.

"What have you to do in this house?" cried one of them. "Go, go, keep to your own home, friend. It is all because of you, and nobody else, that my poor master is distracted, debauched, and carried a-rambling all the country over."

"What next?" replied Sancho; "it is I that am distracted, debauched, and carried a-rambling, and not your master! It was he led me the jaunt; so you are wide of the matter. It was he that inveigled me from my house and home with his talk, promising he would give me an island, which is not come yet, and I still wait for."

"Mayest thou be filled with thy islands!" cried the niece. "And what are your islands? anything to eat, ha?"

"Hold you there!" answered Sancho, "they are not to eat, but to govern; and better governments than any four cities, or as many heads of the king's best corporations."

"For all that," quoth the housekeeper, "thou comest not within these doors, thou bundle of wickedness, and sackful of roguery! Go, govern your own house! Work, you lazy rogue! To the plough, and never trouble your head about islands."

The curate and barber had a great deal of pleasure in hearing this dialogue. But Don Quixote fearing lest Sancho should not keep within bounds, but blunder out some discoveries prejudicial to his reputation, while he ripped up a pack of little foolish slander, called him in, and enjoined the women to be silent. Sancho entered, and the curate and the barber took leave of Don Quixote, despairing of his cure, considering how deep his folly was rooted in his brain, and how bewitched he was with his silly knight-errantry.

"Well, neighbour," said the curate to the barber, "now do I expect nothing better of our gentleman than to hear shortly he is gone upon another ramble."

"Nor I neither," answered the barber; "but I do not wonder so much at the knight's madness as at the silliness of the squire, who thinks himself so sure of the island, that I fancy all the art of man can never beat it out of his skull."

"Heaven mend them!" said the curate. "In the meantime let us observe them; we shall see what will be the event of the extravagance of the knight, and the foolishness of the squire. One would think they had been cast in one mould; and indeed the master's madness without the man's impertinence were not worth a rush."

"Right," said the barber. "And now they are together, I long to know what passes between them. I do not doubt but the two women will be able to give an account of that, for they are not of a temper to withstand the temptation of listening."

Meanwhile, Don Quixote having locked himself up with his squire, they had the following colloquy:—

"I take it very ill," said he, "Sancho, that you should report, as you do, that I enticed you out of your paltry hut, when you know that I myself left my own mansion-house. We set out together, continued together, and travelled together. We ran the same fortune, and the same hazards together. If thou hast been tossed in a blanket once, I have been battered and bruised a hundred times; and that is all the advantage I have had above thee."

"And reason good," answered Sancho; "for you yourself used to say that ill-luck and cross-bitings are oftener to light on the knights than on the squires."

"Thou art mistaken, Sancho," replied Don Quixote; "for the proverb will tell thee that *quando caput dolet*, &c."

"Nay," quoth Sancho, "I understand no language but my own."

"I mean," said Don Quixote, "that when the head aches, all the members partake of the pain. So then, as I am thy master, I am also thy head; and as thou art my servant, thou art one of my members; it follows, therefore, that I cannot be sensible of pain, but thou, too, oughtest to be affected with it; and likewise, that nothing of ill can befall thee, but I must bear a share."

"Right," quoth Sancho; "but when I, as a limb of you, was tossed in a blanket, my head was pleased to stay at the other side of the wall, and saw me frisking in the air, without taking part in my bodily trouble."

"Thou art greatly mistaken, Sancho," answered Don Quixote, "if thou thinkest I was not sensible of thy sufferings. For I was then more tortured in mind than thou wast tormented in body; but let us adjourn this discourse till some other time, which doubtless will afford us an opportunity to redress past grievances. I pray thee tell me now, what does the town say of me? What do the neighbours, what do the people think of me? What say the gentry, and the better sort? How do the knights discourse of my valour, my high feats of arms, and my courteous behaviour? What thoughts do they entertain of my design to raise from the grave of oblivion the order of knight-errantry, and restore it to the world? In short, tell me freely and sincerely whatever thou hast heard, neither enlarged with flattering commendations or lessened by any omission of my dispraise; for it is the duty of faithful servants to lay truth before their masters in its honourable nakedness. And I would have thee know, Sancho, that if it were to appear before princes in its native simplicity, and disrobed of the odious disguise of flattery, we should see happier days; this age would be changed into an age of gold, and former times, compared to this, would be called the iron age. Remember this, and be advised, that I may hear thee impart a faithful account of these matters."

"That I will, with all my heart," answered Sancho, "so your worship will not take it amiss, if I tell what I have heard, just as I heard it, neither better nor worse."

"Nothing shall provoke me to anger," answered Don Quixote; "speak freely, and without any circumlocution."

"Why, then," quoth Sancho, "first and foremost you are to know that the common people take you for a downright madman, and me for one who has not much good in his brains. The gentry say, that not being content to keep within the bounds of gentility, you have taken upon you to be a Don, and set up for a knight and a right worshipful, with a small vineyard and two acres of land, a tatter before and another behind. The knights, forsooth, take pepper in the nose, and say they do not like to have your small gentry think themselves as good as they, especially your old-fashioned country squires, who mend and lamp-black their own shoes, and darn their old black stockings themselves with a needleful of green silk."

"All this does not affect me," said Don Quixote, "for I always wear good clothes, and never have them patched. It is true, they may be a little torn sometimes, but that is more with my armour than by long wearing."

"As for what relates to your prowess," said Sancho, proceeding, "together with your feats of arms, your courteous behaviour, and your undertaking, there are several opinions about it. Some say, 'He is mad, but a pleasant sort of a madman;' others say, 'He is valiant, but his luck is naught;'

others say, He is courteous, but sometimes rude.' And thus they pass so many verdicts upon you, and take us both so to pieces, that they leave neither you nor me a sound bone in our skins."

"Consider, Sancho," said Don Quixote, "that the more eminently virtue shines, the more it is exposed to the persecution of envy. Few or none of those famous heroes of antiquity could escape the venomous arrows of calumny. Julius Cæsar, that most courageous, prudent, and valiant captain, was marked as being ambitious, and neither so clean in his apparel nor in his manners as he ought to have been. Alexander, whose mighty deeds gained him the title of 'the Great,' was charged with being addicted to drunkenness. Hercules, after his many heroic labours, was accused of voluptuousness and effeminacy. Don Galaor, the brother of Amadis de Gaul, was taxed with being quarrelsome, and his brother himself with being a whining, blubbering lover. And, therefore, my Sancho, since so many worthies have not been free from the assaults of detraction, well may I be content to bear my share of that epidemical calamity, if it be no more than thou hast told me now."

"Ah!" quoth Sancho, "there is the business; but they don't stop here."

"Why," said Don Quixote, "what can they say more?"

"More!" cried Sancho; "you have yet to hear the worst. You have had nothing yet but apple-pies and sugar-plums. But if you have a mind to hear all those slanders and back-bitings that are about town concerning your worship, I will bring you one anon that shall tell you every kind of thing that is said of you, without bating you an ace on it! Bartholomew Carrasco's son, I mean, who has been a scholard at the 'versity of Salamanca, and is got to be a bachelor of arts. He came last night, you must know, and as I went to bid him welcome home, he told me that your worship's history is already in books, by the name of the most renowned Don Quixote de la Mancha. He says I am in too, by my own name of Sancho Panza, and also my Lady Dulcinea del Toboso; nay, and many things that passed betwixt nobody but us two, which I was amazed to hear, and could not imagine how he that set them down could have come by the knowledge of them."

"I dare assure thee, Sancho," said Don Quixote, "that the author of our history must be some sage enchanter, and one of those from whose universal knowledge none of the things which they have a mind to record can be concealed."

"How should he be a sage and an enchanter?" quoth Sancho. "The bachelor Samson Carrasco—for that is the name of my tale's master—tells me he that wrote the history is called Cid Hamet Berengenas."

"That is a Moorish name," said Don Quixote.

"Like enough," quoth Sancho; "your Moors are great lovers of berengenas."

"Certainly, Sancho," said Don Quixote, "thou art mistaken in the surname of that cid; that lord, I mean; for cid, in Arabic, signifies lord."

"That may very well be," answered Sancho; "but if you will have me fetch you the young scholard, I will fly to bring him hither."

"Truly, friend," said Don Quixote, "thou wilt do me a particular kindness; for what thou hast already told me has so filled me with doubts and expectations, that I shall not eat a bit that will do me good till I am informed of the whole matter."

"I will go and fetch him," said Sancho. With that, leaving his master, he went to look for the bachelor, and having brought him along with him a while after, they all had a very pleasant dialogue.

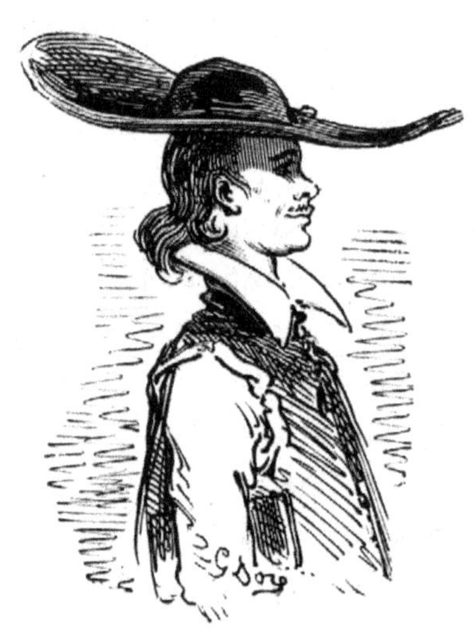

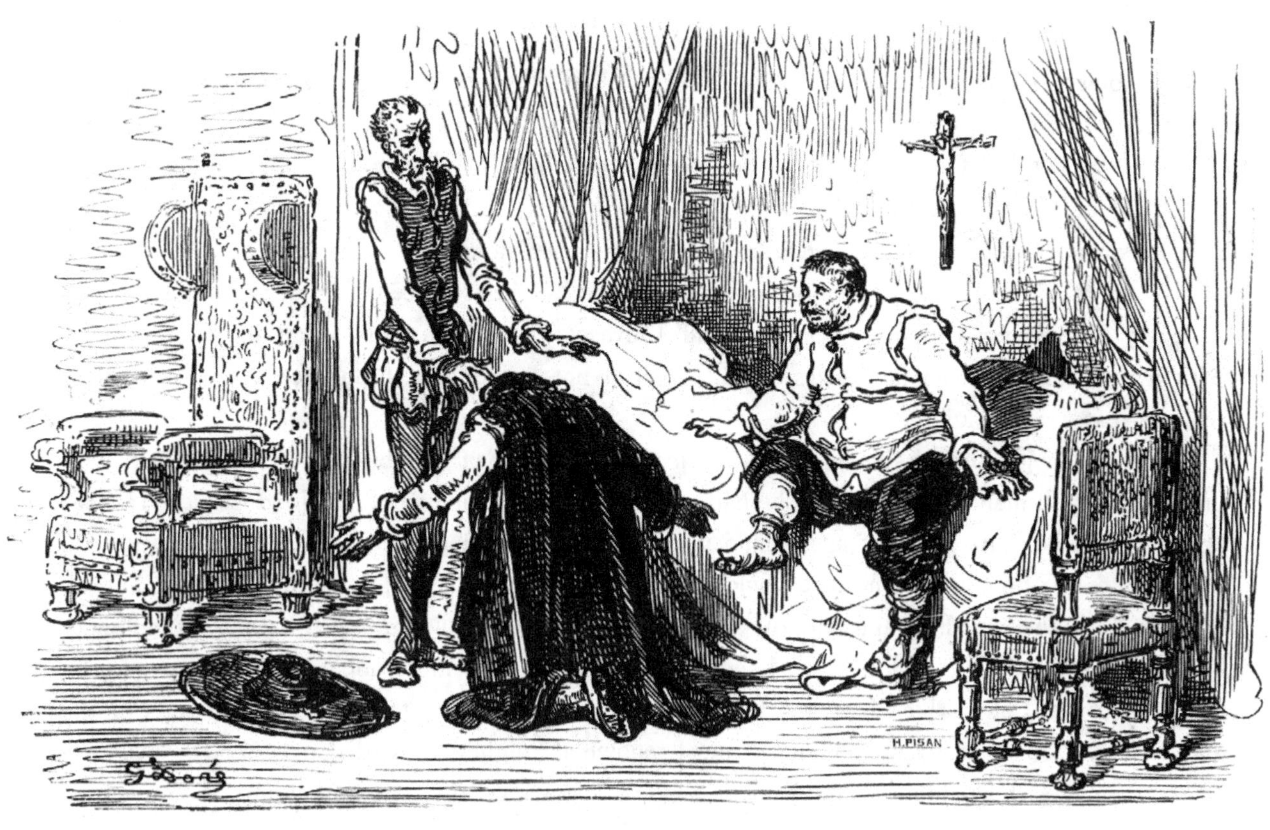

CHAPTER III.

THE PLEASANT DISCOURSE BETWEEN DON QUIXOTE, SANCHO PANZA, AND THE BACHELOR SAMSON CARRASCO.

DON QUIXOTE remained strangely pensive, expecting the bachelor Carrasco, from whom he hoped to hear news of himself, recorded and printed in a book, as Sancho had informed him. He could not be persuaded that there was such a history extant, while yet the blood of those enemies he had cut off had scarce done reeking on the blade of his sword ; so that they could not have already finished and printed the history of his mighty feats of arms. However, at last he concluded that some learned sage had, by the way of enchantment, been able to commit them to the press, either as a friend, to extol his heroic achievements above the noblest performances of the most famous knights-errant, or as an enemy, to sully and annihilate the lustre of his great exploits, and debase them below the most inferior actions that ever were mentioned of any of the meanest squires. "Though," thought he to himself, "the actions of squires were never yet recorded ; and, after all, if there were such a book printed, since it was the history of a knight-errant, it could not choose but be pompous, lofty, magnificent, and authentic."

This thought yielded him a while some small consolation ; but then he relapsed into melancholic doubts and anxieties when he considered that the author had used the title of cid, and consequently must be a Moor—a nation from whom no truth could be expected, they all being given to impose on others with lies and fabulous stories, to falsify and counterfeit, and very fond of their own chimeras.

He was not less uneasy lest that writer should have been too lavish in treating of his amours, to the prejudice of his Lady Dulcinea del Toboso's honour. He earnestly wished that he might find his own inviolable fidelity celebrated in the history, and the reservedness which he had always so religiously observed in his passion for her; slighting queens, empresses, and damsels of every degree for her sake. Sancho and Carrasco found him thus agitated and perplexed with a thousand melancholic fancies, which yet did not hinder him from receiving the stranger with a great deal of civility.

This bachelor, though his name was Samson, was none of the biggest in body, but a very great man at all manner of drollery; he had a pale and bad complexion, but good sense. He was about four-and-twenty years of age, round visaged, flat nosed, and wide mouthed—all signs of a malicious disposition, and of one that would delight in nothing more than in making sport for himself by ridiculing others, as he plainly discovered when he saw Don Quixote. For, falling on his knees before him, "Admit me to kiss your honour's hand," cried he, "most noble Don Quixote; for by the habit of St. Peter, which I wear—though, indeed, I have as yet taken but the four first of the holy orders—you are certainly one of the most renowned knights-errant that ever was, or ever will be, through the whole extent of the habitable globe. Blest may the sage Cid Hamet Benengeli be for enriching the world with the history of your mighty deeds; and more than blest that curious virtuoso, who took care to have it translated out of the Arabic into our vulgar tongue, for the universal entertainment of mankind!"

"Sir," said Don Quixote, making him rise, "is it then possible that my history is extant, and that it was a Moor, and one of the sages, that penned it?"

"It is so notorious a truth," said the bachelor, "that I do not in the least doubt but at this day there have already been published above twelve thousand copies of it. Portugal, Barcelona, and Valencia, where they have been printed, can witness that, if there were occasion. It is said that it is also now in the press at Antwerp. And I verily believe there is scarce a language into which it is not to be translated."

"Truly, sir," said Don Quixote, "one of the things that ought to yield the greatest satisfaction to a person of eminent virtue, is to live to see himself in good reputation in the world, and his actions published in print. I say in good reputation; for otherwise there is no death but would be preferable to such a life."

"As for a good name and reputation," replied Carrasco, "your worship has gained the palm from all the knights-errant that ever lived: for both the Arabian, in his history, and the Christian, in his version, have been very industrious to do justice to your character, your peculiar gallantry, your intrepidity and greatness of spirit in confronting danger, your constancy in adversities, your patience in suffering wounds and afflictions, your modesty and continence in that amour, so very platonic, between your worship and my Lady Donna Dulcinea del Toboso."

"Heyday!" cried Sancho; "I never heard her called so before. That donna is a new name; for she used to be called only my Lady Dulcinea del Toboso: in that, the history is out already."

"That is no material objection," said Carrasco.

"No, certainly," added Don Quixote; "but pray, good Mr. Bachelor, on which of all my adventures does the history seem to lay the greatest stress of remark?"

"As to that," answered Carrasco, "the opinions of men are divided according to their taste: some cry up the adventure of the windmills, which appeared to your worship so many Briareuses and giants. Some are for that of the fulling-mills; others stand up for the description of the two armies, that afterwards proved two flocks of sheep. Others prize most the adventure of the dead corpse that was carrying to Segovia. One says, that none of them can compare with that of the galley-slaves; another, that none can stand in competition with the adventure of the Benedictine giants and the valorous Biscayner."

"Pray, Mr. Bachelor," quoth Sancho, "is there nothing said of that of the Yanguesians, an please you, when our precious Rozinante was so mauled?"

"There is not the least thing omitted," answered Carrasco. "The sage has inserted all, with the nicest punctuality imaginable; so much as the capers which honest Sancho fetched in the blanket."

"I fetched none in the blanket," quoth Sancho, "but in the air; and that, too, oftener than I could have wished, and more to my sorrow."

"In my opinion," said Don Quixote, "there is no manner of history in the world where you shall not find variety of fortune, much less any story of knight-errantry, where a man cannot always be sure of good success."

"However," said Carrasco, "some who have read your history wish that the author had spared himself the pains of registering some of that infinite number of drubs which the noble Don Quixote received."

"There lies the truth of the history," quoth Sancho.

"Those things in human equity," said Don Quixote, "might very well have been omitted; for actions that neither impair nor alter the history ought rather to be buried in silence than related, if they redound to the discredit of the hero of the history. Certainly Æneas was never so pious as Virgil represents him, nor Ulysses so prudent as he is made by Homer."

"I am of your opinion," said Carrasco; "but it is one thing to write like a poet, and another thing to write like an historian. It is sufficient for the first to deliver matters as they ought to have been, whereas the last must relate them as they were really transacted, without adding or omitting anything upon any pretence whatever."

"Well," quoth Sancho, "if this same Moorish lord be once got into the road of truth, a hundred to one but among my master's rib-roastings he has not forgot mine: for they never took measure of his worship's shoulders, but they were pleased to do as much for my whole body: but it was no wonder; for it is his own rule that if once his head aches, every limb must suffer too."

"Sancho," said Don Quixote, "you are an arch, unlucky knave. Upon my honour you can find memory when you have a mind to have it."

"Nay," quoth Sancho, "though I were minded to forget the rubs and drubs I have suffered, the bumps and tokens that are yet fresh on my ribs would not let me."

"Hold your tongue," said Don Quixote, "and let the learned bachelor proceed, that I may know what the history says of me."

"And of me too," quoth Sancho; "for they tell me I am one of the top parsons in it."

"Persons, you should say, Sancho," said Carrasco, "and not parsons."

"Heyday!" quoth Sancho; "have we got another corrector of hard words? If this be the trade, we shall never have done."

"I assure you," said Carrasco, "that you are the second person in the history, honest Sancho; nay, and some there are who had rather hear you talk than the best there; though some there are again that will say you were horribly credulous, to flatter yourself with having the government of that island which your master here present promised you."

"While there is life there is hope," said Don Quixote: "when Sancho is grown mature with time and experience, he may be better qualified for a government than he is yet."

"Well, sir," quoth Sancho, "if I be not fit to govern an island at these years, I shall never be a governor, though I live to the years of Methusalem; but there the mischief lies: we have brains enough, but we want the island."

"Come, Sancho," said Don Quixote, "hope for the best; trust in Providence; all will be well, and, perhaps, better than you imagine: but know, there is not a leaf on any tree that can be moved without the permission of Heaven."

"That is very true," said Carrasco; "and I dare say Sancho shall not want a thousand islands to govern, much less one; that is, if it be Heaven's will."

"Why not?" quoth Sancho; "I have seen governors in my time who, to my thinking, could not come up to me passing the sole of my shoes, and yet, forsooth, they called them 'your honour,' and they eat their victuals all in silver."

"Ay," said Carrasco, "but these were none of your governors of islands, but of other easy governments: why, man, these ought, at least, to know their grammar."

"Trust me for that," quoth Sancho; "give me but a grey mare once, and I shall know her well enough, I'll warrant ye. But leaving the government in the hands of him that will best provide for me, I must tell you, Master Bachelor Samson Carrasco, I am very glad that, as your author has not forgot me, so he has not given an ill character of me; for by the faith of a trusty squire, had he said anything that did not become an old Christian as I am, I had rung him such a peal that the deaf should have heard me."

"That were a miracle," said Carrasco.

"Miracle or no miracle," cried Sancho, "let every man take care how he talks, or how he writes of other men, and not set down at random, higgle-de-piggledy, whatever comes into his noddle."

"Now," said Don Quixote, "I perceive that he who attempted to write my history is not one of the sages, but some ignorant, prating fool, who would needs be meddling, and set up for a scribbler without the least grain of judgment to help him out; and so he has done like Orbaneja, the painter of Ubeda, who, being asked what he painted, answered, 'As it may hit;' and when he had scrawled out a mis-shapen cock, was forced to write underneath, in Gothic letters, 'This is a cock.' At this rate, I believe, he has performed in my history, so that it will require a commentary to explain it."

"Not at all," answered Carrasco; "for he has made everything so plain, that there is not the least thing in it but what any one may understand. Children handle it, youngsters read it, grown men understand it, and old people applaud it. In short, it is universally so thumbed, so gleaned, so studied, and so known, that if the people do but see a lean horse they presently cry, 'There goes Rozinante.' But none apply themselves to the reading of it more than your pages; there is never a nobleman's ante-chamber where you shall not find a 'Don Quixote.' No sooner has one laid it down but another takes it up. One asks for it here, and there it is snatched up by another. In a word, it is esteemed the most pleasant and least dangerous diversion that ever was seen, as being a book that does not betray the least indecent expression, nor so much as a profane thought."

"To write after another manner," said Don Quixote, "were not to write truth, but falsehood; and those historians who are guilty of that should be punished like those who counterfeit the lawful coin. But I cannot conceive what could move the author to stuff his history with foreign novels and adventures, not at all to the purpose, while there was a sufficient number of my own to have exercised his pen. But, without doubt, we may apply the proverb, 'With hay or with straw,' &c.: for verily, had he altogether confined himself to my thoughts, my sighs, my tears, my laudable designs, my adventures, he might yet have swelled his book to as great a bulk, at least, as all Tostatus's works. I have also reason to believe, Mr. Bachelor, that to compile a history, or write any book whatsoever, is a more difficult task than men imagine. There is need of a vast judgment, and a ripe understanding. It belongs to none but great geniuses to express themselves with grace and elegance, and to draw the manners and actions of others to the life. The most artful part in a play is the fool's, and therefore a fool must not attempt to write it. On the other side, history is in a manner a sacred thing, so far as it contains truth; for where truth is, the supreme Father of it may also be said to be, at least, in as much as concerns truth. However, there are men that will make you books, and turn them loose into the world, with as much dispatch as they would do a dish of fritters."

"There is no book so bad," said the bachelor, "but something good may be found in it."

"That is true," said Don Quixote; "yet it is quite a common thing for men who have gained a very great reputation by their writings, before they printed them, to lose it afterwards quite, or at least the greatest part."

"The reason is plain," said Carrasco; "their faults are more easily discovered after their books are printed, as being then more read, and more narrowly examined, especially if the author had been much cried up before, for then the severity of the scrutiny is so much the greater. All those that have raised themselves a name by their ingenuity—great poets and celebrated historians—are most commonly, if not always, envied by a sort of men who delight in censuring the writings of others, though they never publish any of their own."

"That is no wonder," said Don Quixote; "for there are many divines that would make but very dull preachers, and yet are very quick at finding faults and superfluities in other men's sermons."

"All this is truth," replied Carrasco; "and therefore I could wish these censurers would be more merciful and less scrupulous, and not dwell ungenerously upon small spots, that are in a manner but so many atoms on the face of the clear sun, which they murmur at. And if *aliquando bonus dormitat Homerus*, let them consider how many nights he kept himself awake to bring his noble works to light as little darkened with defects as might be. Nay, many times it may happen that what is censured for a fault is rather an ornament, like moles that sometimes add to the beauty of the face. And when all is said, he that publishes a book runs a very great hazard, since nothing can be more impossible than to compose one that may secure the approbation of every reader."

"Sure," said Don Quixote, "that which treats of me can have pleased but few."

"Quite contrary," said Carrasco; "for as *Stultorum infinitus est numerus*, so an infinite number have admired your history. But some there are who have taxed the author with want of memory or sincerity, because he forgot to give an account of who it was that stole Sancho's Dapple, for that particular is not mentioned there: only we find, by the story, that it was stolen; and yet, by-and-by, we find him riding the same ass again, without any previous light given us into the matter. Then they say that the author forgot to tell the reader what Sancho did with those hundred pieces of gold he found in the portmanteau in the Sierra Morena; for there is not a word said of them more; and many people have a great wish to know what he did with them, and how he spent them; which is one of the most material points in which the work is defective."

"Master Samson," quoth Sancho, "I am not now in a condition to call up the accounts; for I am taken ill of a sudden with such a fainting feeling, and find myself so mawkish, that if I do not see and alter it with a sup or two of good drink, I shall waste like the snuff of a farthing candle. I have that cordial at home, and my wife stays for me. When I have had my dinner, I am for you, and will satisfy you, or any man that wears a head, about anything in the world, either as to the loss of the ass or the laying out of those same pieces of gold."

This said, without a word more, or waiting for a reply, away he went. Don Quixote desired and entreated the bachelor to stay and do penance with him. The bachelor accepted his invitation and stayed. A couple of pigeons were got ready to mend their commons. All dinner time they discoursed about knight-errantry, Carrasco humouring him all the while. After they had slept out the heat of the day, Sancho came back, and they renewed their former discourse.

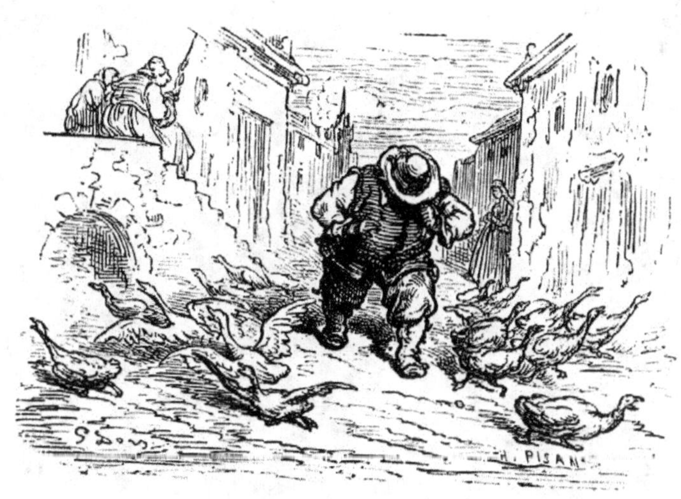

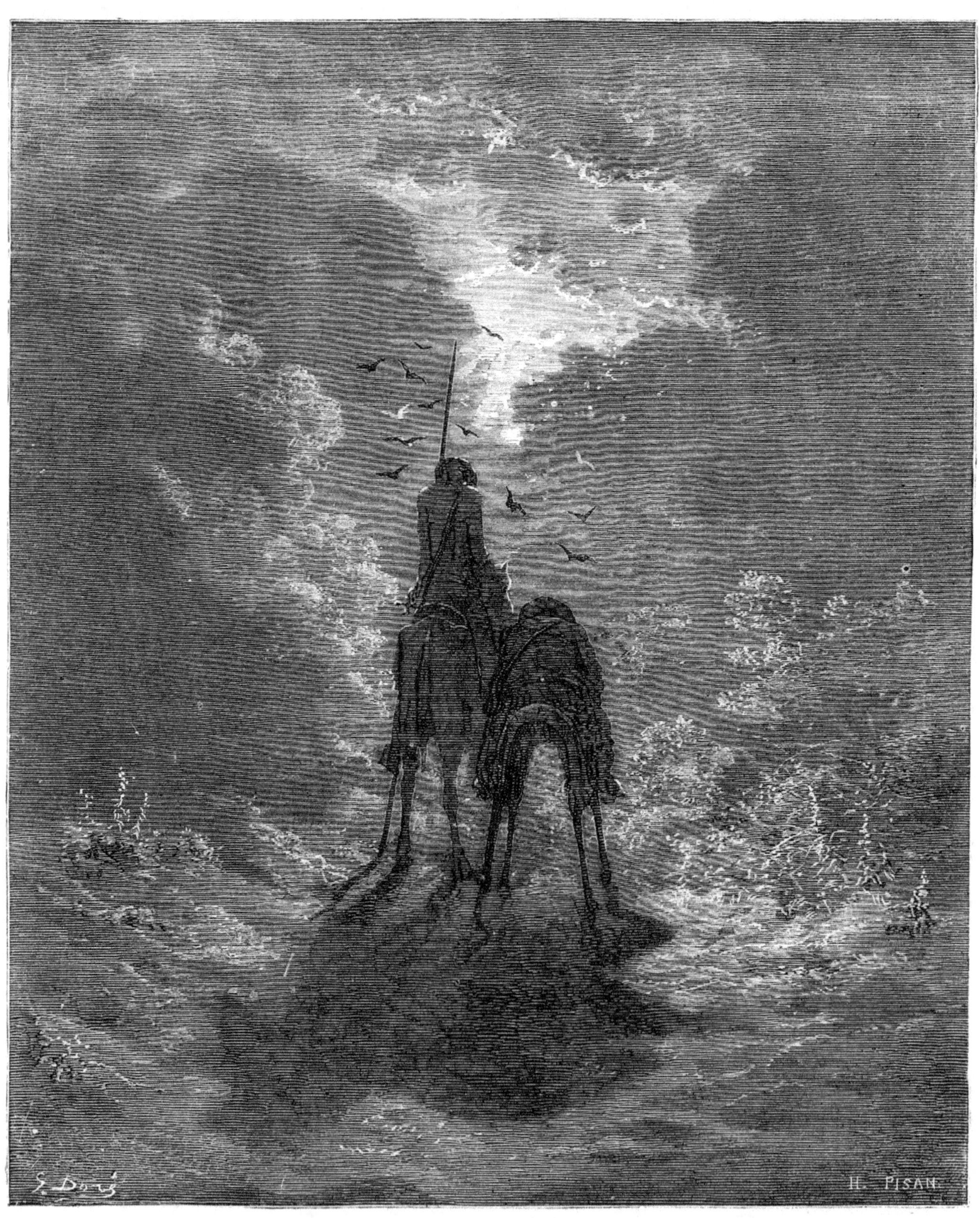

"We slept as soundly as if we had four feather-beds under us."

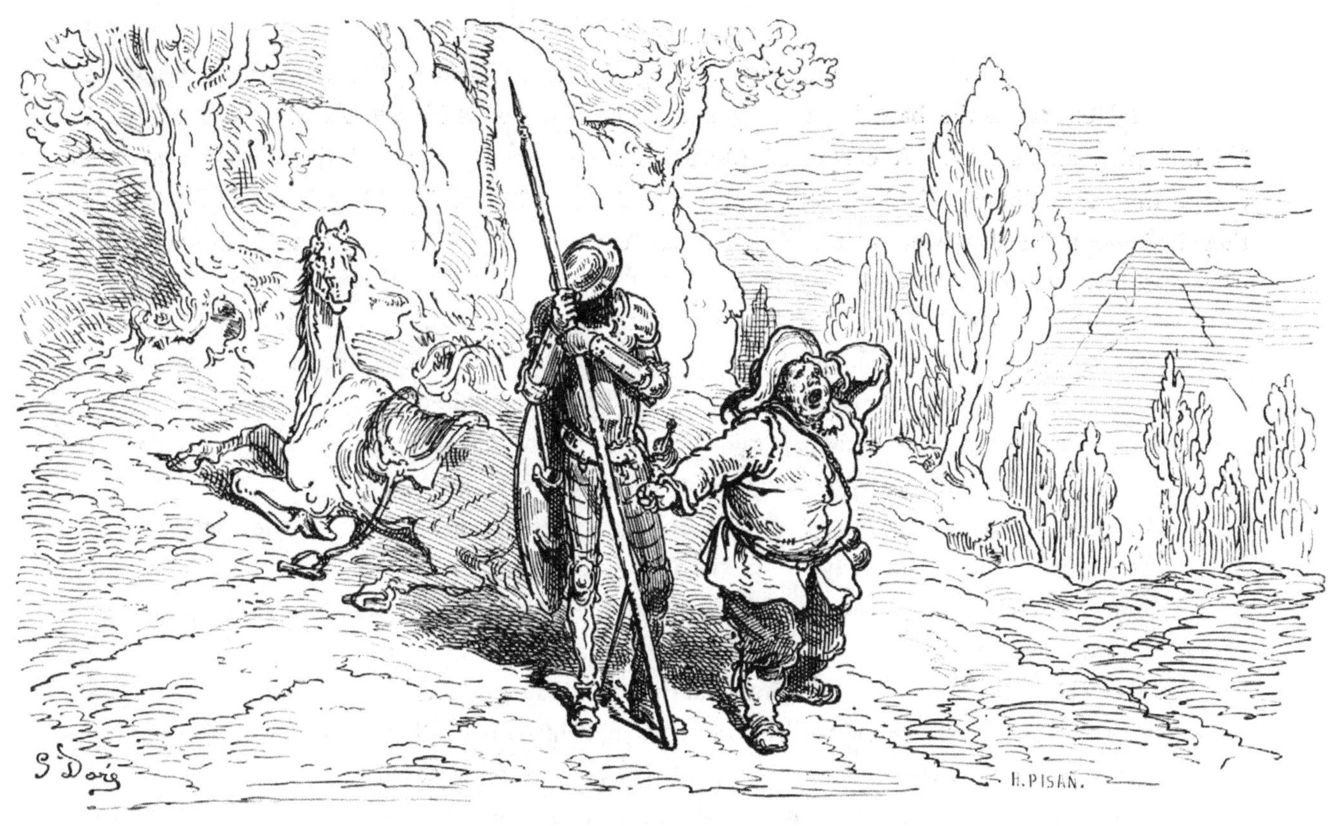

CHAPTER IV.

SANCHO PANZA SATISFIES THE BACHELOR, SAMSON CARRASCO, IN HIS DOUBTS AND QUERIES; WITH OTHER PASSAGES FIT TO BE KNOWN AND RELATED.

SANCHO returned to Don Quixote's house, and beginning again where he left off, "Now," quoth he, "as to what Master Samson wanted to know—that is, when, where, and by whom my ass was stolen. I answer that the very night that we marched off to the Sierra Morena, to avoid the hue and cry of the holy brotherhood, after the rueful adventure of the galley slaves, and that of the dead body that was carrying to Segovia, my master and I slunk into a wood, where he, leaning on his lance, and I, without alighting from Dapple, both sadly bruised and tired with our late skirmishes, fell fast asleep, and slept as soundly as if we had four feather-beds under us; but I especially was as serious at it as any dormouse; so that the thief, whoever he was, had leisure enough to clap four stakes under the four corners of the pack-saddle, and then, leading away the ass from between my legs, without being perceived by me in the least, there he fairly left me mounted."

"This is no new thing," said Don Quixote; "nor is it difficult to be done. With the same stratagem Sacrepante had his steed stolen from under him by that notorious thief, Brunelo, at the siege of Albraca."

"It was broad day," said Sancho, going on, "when I, half awake and half asleep, began to stretch myself in my pack-saddle; but with my stirring, down came the stakes, and down came I flat, with a confounded blow, on the ground. Presently I looked for my ass, but no ass was to be found. Oh, how thick the tears trickled from my eyes, and what a piteous moan I made! If he that made our history has forgot to set it down word for word, I would not give a rush for his book, I will tell him that. Some time after—I cannot just tell you how long it was—as we were going with my lady, the Princess Micomicona, I knew my ass again, and he that rid him, though he went like a gipsy; and who should it be, do you think, but Gines de Passamonte, that son of mischief, that crack rope, whom my master and I saved from the galleys?"

"The mistake does not lie there," said Carrasco; "but that the author sets you upon the same ass that was lost, before he gives an account of his being found."

"As to that," replied Sancho, "I do not know very well what to say. If the man made a blunder, who can help it? But, mayhap, it was a fault of the printer."

"I make no question of that," said Carrasco; "but pray what became of the hundred pieces? Were they sunk?"

"I fairly spent them on myself," quoth Sancho, "and on my wife and children: they helped me to lay my spouse's clack, and made her take so patiently my rambling and trotting after my master, Don Quixote; for had I come back with my pockets empty, and without my ass, I must have looked for a rueful greeting. And now, if you have any more to say to me, here am I, ready to answer the king himself; for what has anybody to meddle or make whether I found or found not, or spent or spent not? If the knocks and swaddlings that have been bestowed on my carcase in our jaunts were to be rated but at three maravedis apiece, and I to be satisfied ready cash for every one, a hundred pieces of gold more would not pay for half of them; and therefore let every man lay his finger on his mouth, and not run hand over head, and mistake black for white, and white for black; for every man is as Heaven made him, and sometimes a great deal worse."

"Well," said the bachelor, "if the author prints another edition of the history, I will take special care he shall not forget to insert what honest Sancho has said, which will make the book as good again."

"Pray, good Mr. Bachelor," asked Don Quixote, "are there any emendations requisite to be made in this history?"

"Some there are," answered Carrasco, "but none of so much importance as those already mentioned."

"Perhaps the author promises a second part?" said Don Quixote.

"He does," said Carrasco; "but he says he cannot find it, neither can he discover who has it: so that we doubt whether it will come out or no, as well for this reason as because some people say that second parts are never worth anything; others cry, 'There is enough of Don Quixote already:' however, many of those that love mirth better than melancholy cry out, 'Give us more Quixotery let but Don Quixote appear, and Sancho talk, be it what it will, we are satisfied.'"

"And how stands the author affected?" said the knight.

"Truly," answered Carrasco, "as soon as ever he can find out the history, which he is now looking for with all imaginable industry, he is resolved to send it immediately to the press, though more for his own profit than through any ambition of applause."

"What!" quoth Sancho, "does he design to do it to get a penny by it? Nay, then we are like to have a rare history indeed; we shall have him botch and whip it up, like your tailors on Easter Eve, and give us a huddle of flim flams that will never hang together; for your hasty work can never be done as it should be. Let Mr. Moor take care how he goes to work: for, my life for his, I and my master will stock him with such a heap of stuff, in matter of adventures and odd chances, that he will not have enough only to write a second part, but a hundred. The poor fellow, belike, thinks we do nothing but sleep on a hay-mow; but let us once put foot into the stirrup, and he will see what we are about: this, at least, I will be bold to say, that if my master would be ruled by me, we had been in the field by this time, undoing of misdeeds and righting of wrongs, as good knights-errant used to do."

Scarce had Sancho made an end of his discourse, when Rozinante's neighing reached their ears. Don Quixote took it for a lucky omen, and resolved to take another turn within three or four days. He discovered his resolution to the bachelor, and consulted him to know which way to steer his course. The bachelor advised him to take the road of Saragosa, in the kingdom of Aragon, a solemn tournament being shortly to be performed at that city on St. George's Festival; where, by worsting all the Aragonian champions, he might win immortal honour, since to out-tilt them would be to out-rival all the knights in the universe. He applauded his noble resolution, but withal admonished him not to be so desperate in exposing himself to dangers, since his life was not his own, but theirs who in distress stood in want of his assistance and protection.

"That is it now," quoth Sancho, "that makes me sometimes ready to run mad, Mr. Bachelor; for my master makes no more to set upon a hundred armed men, than a young hungry tailor to swallow half a dozen of cucumbers. Bless me! Mr. Bachelor, there is a time to retreat, as well as a time to advance. 'Saint Jago and forward, Spain!' must not always be the cry; for I have heard somebody say, and, if I am not mistaken, it was my master himself, that valour lies just between rashness and cow-heartedness; and if it be so, I would not have him run away without there is a reason for it, nor would I have him fall on when there is no good to be got by it. But above all things I would have him to know, if he has a mind I should go with him, that the bargain is he shall fight for us both, and that I am tied to nothing but to look after him and his victuals and clothes: so far as this comes to, I will fetch and carry like any water-spaniel; but to think I will lug out my sword, though it be but against poor rogues, and sorry shirks, and hedge-birds, y'troth I must beg his diversion. For my part, Mr. Bachelor, it is not the fame of being thought valiant that I aim at, but that of being deemed the very best and trustiest squire that ever followed the heels of a knight-errant. And if, after all my services, my master Don Quixote will be so kind as to give me one of those many islands which his worship says he shall light on, I shall be much beholden to him; but if he does not, why then I am born, do ye see, and one man must not live to rely on another, but on his Maker. Mayhaps the bread I shall eat without government will go down more savourily than if I were a governor; and what do I know but that some one is providing me one of those governments for a stumbling-block, that I may stumble and fall, and so break my jaws, and knock out my butter-teeth? I was born Sancho, and Sancho I mean to die; and yet for all that, if fairly and squarely, with little trouble and less danger, Heaven would bestow on me an island, or some such like matter, I am no such fool neither, do ye see, as to refuse a good thing when it is offered me. No; I remember the old saying, 'When the ass is given thee, run and take him by the halter; and when good luck knocks at the door, let him in, and keep him there.' "

"My friend Sancho," said Carrasco, "you have spoken like any university professor. However, trust in Heaven's bounty, and the noble Don Quixote, and he may not only give thee an island, but even a kingdom."

"One as likely as the other," quoth Sancho; "and yet let me tell you, Mr. Bachelor, the kingdom which my master is to give me you shall not find thrown into an old sack; for I have felt my own pulse, and find myself sound enough to rule kingdoms and govern islands; I have told my master as much before now."

"Have a care, Sancho," said Carrasco; "honours change manners; perhaps, when you come to be a governor, you will scarce know your own mother."

"This," said Sancho, "may happen to those that were born in a ditch, but not to those whose souls are covered, as mine is, four fingers thick with good old Christian fat. No; do but think how good-conditioned I be, and then you need not fear I should do badly to any one."

"Grant it, good Heaven!" said Don Quixote; "we shall see when the government comes, and methinks I have it already before my eyes."

After this he desired the bachelor, if he were a poet, to oblige him with some verses on his designed departure from his mistress, Dulcinea del Toboso; every verse to begin with one of the letters of her name, so that, joining every first letter of every verse together, they might make Dulcinea del Toboso. The bachelor told him that though he were none of the famous poets of Spain, who, they say, were but three and a half, he would endeavour to make that acrostic; though he was sensible this would be no easy task, there being seventeen letters in the name; so that if he made four stanzas of four verses apiece, there would be a letter too much; and if he made his stanzas of five lines, so as to make a double Decima or a Redondilla, there would be three letters too little; however, he would strive to drown a letter, and so take in the whole name in sixteen verses."

"Let it be so by any means," said Don Quixote; "for no woman will believe that those verses were made for her where her name is not plainly to be discerned."

After this it was agreed they should set out within a week. Don Quixote charged the bachelor not to speak a word of all this, especially to the curate, Mr. Nicolas the barber, his niece, and his housekeeper, lest they should obstruct his honourable and valorous design. Carrasco gave him his word, and having desired Don Quixote to send an account of his good or bad success at his conveniency, immediately took his leave, and Sancho went to get everything ready for his journey.

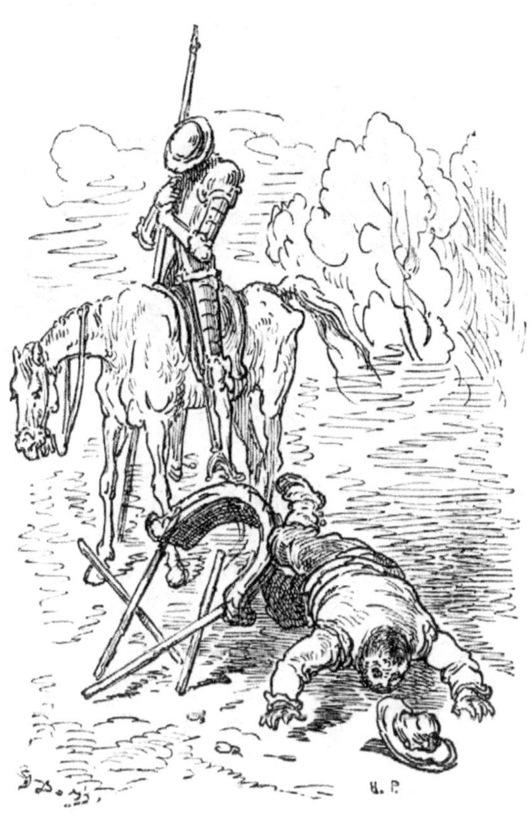

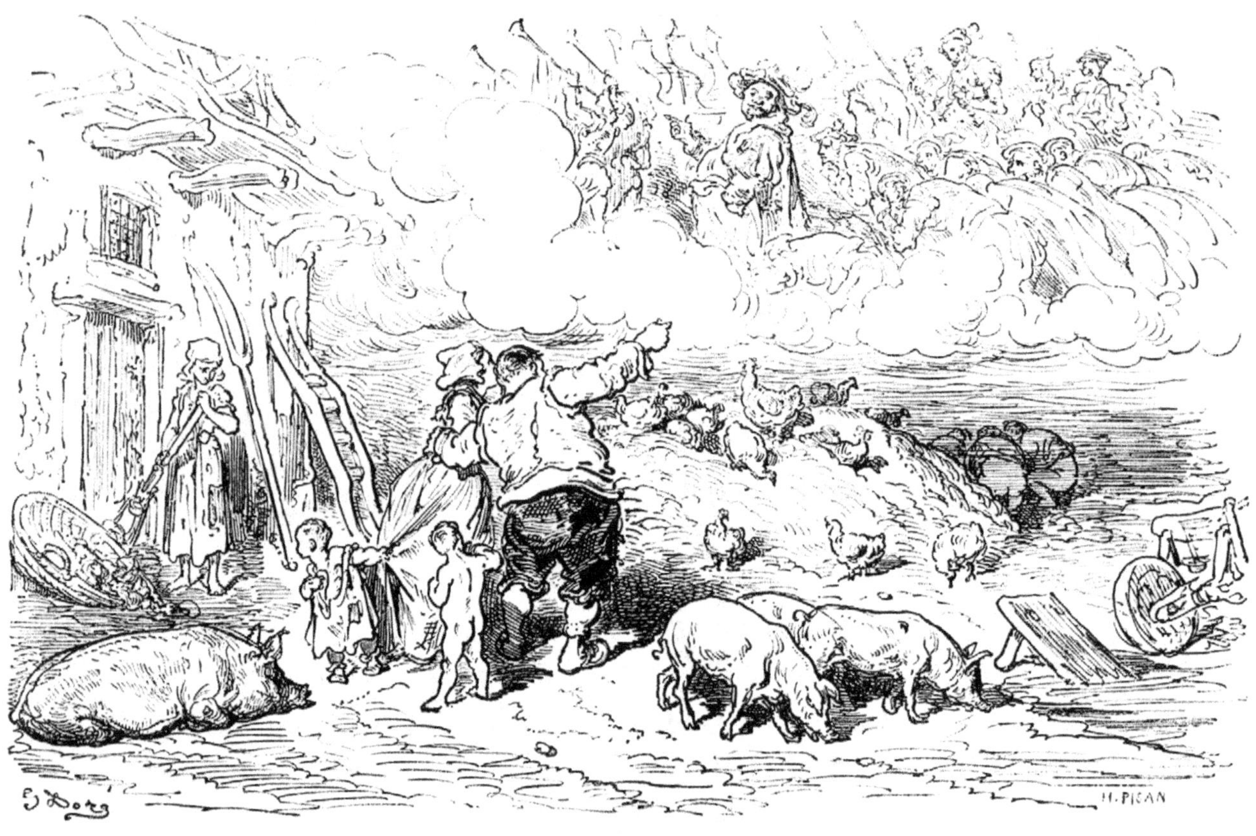

CHAPTER V.

THE WISE AND PLEASANT DIALOGUE BETWEEN SANCHO PANZA AND TERESA PANZA, HIS WIFE: TOGETHER WITH OTHER PASSAGES WORTHY OF HAPPY MEMORY.

THE translator of this history, being come to this fifth chapter, thinks fit to inform the reader that he holds it to be apocryphal, because it introduces Sancho speaking in another style than could be expected from his slender capacity, and saying things of so refined a nature that it seems impossible he could do it. However, he thought himself obliged to render it in our tongue, to maintain the character of a faithful translator, and therefore he goes on in this manner.

Sancho came home so cheerful and so merry, that his wife read his joy in his looks a bow-shot off. Being impatient to know the cause, "My dear," cried she, "what makes you so merry?"

"I should be more merry, my dear," quoth Sancho, "would but Heaven so order it that I were not so well pleased as I seem to be."

"You speak riddles, husband," quoth she; "I don't know what you mean by saying you should be more merry if you were not so well pleased; for, though I am silly enough, I cannot think a man can take pleasure in not being pleased."

"Look ye, Teresa," quoth Sancho, "I am merry because I am once more going to serve my master, Don Quixote, who is resolved to have another frolic, and go a-hunting after adventures, and I must go with him; for he needs must run whom fortune drives. What should I lie starving at home for? The hopes of finding another parcel of gold like that we spent rejoices my heart: but then it grieves me to leave thee, and those sweet babes of ours; and would Heaven but be pleased to let me live at home dry-shod, in peace and quietness, without gadding over hill and dale, through brambles and briars, why then it is a clear case that my mirth would be more firm and sound, since my present gladness is mingled with a sorrow to part with thee. And so I think I have made out what I have said, that I should be merrier if I did not seem so well pleased."

"Look you, Sancho," quoth the wife, "ever since you have been a member of a knight-errant, you talk so round about the bush that nobody can understand you."

"It is enough," quoth Sancho, "that he understands me who understands all things; and so scatter no more words about it, spouse. But be sure you look carefully after Dapple for these three days, that he may be in good case and fit to bear arms; double his pittance, look out his pannel and all his harness, and let everything be set to rights; for we are not going to a wedding, but to roam about the world, and to have now and then a set-to with giants, and dragons, and hobgoblins, and to hear nothing but hissing, and yelling, and roaring, and howling, and bellowing; all which would be but sugar-plums, if we were not to meet with the Yanguesian carriers and enchanted Moors."

"Nay, as for that, husband," quoth Teresa, "I am apt enough to think you squire-errants don't eat their masters' bread for nothing; and therefore it shall be my daily prayer, that you may quickly be freed from that plaguy trouble."

"Troth, wife," quoth Sancho, "were I not in hopes to see myself ere long governor of an island, o' my conscience I should drop down dead on the spot."

"Not so," quoth the wife. "Do thou live, and let all the governments in the world go. Thou camest into the world without government, thou hast lived hitherto without government, and thou mayest be carried to thy long home without government, when it shall please the Lord. How many people in this world live without government, yet do well enough, and are well looked upon! There is no sauce in the world like hunger, and as the poor never want that, they always eat with a good stomach. But look ye, my precious, if it should be thy good luck to get a government, pr'ythee do not forget thy wife and children. Take notice that little Sancho is already full fifteen, and it is high time he went to school, if his uncle the abbot mean to leave him something in the Church. Then there is Mary Sancho, your daughter; I dare say she longs as much to be well married as you do for a government."

"I' good sooth! wife," quoth Sancho, "if it be Heaven's blessed will that I get anything by government, I will see and match Mary Sancho so well, that she shall, at least, be called 'my lady.'"

"By no means, husband," cried the wife; "let her match with her match: if from clouted shoes you set her upon high heels, and from her coarse russet coat you put her into a fardingale, and from plain 'Moll' and 'thee' and 'thou,' go to call her 'madam,' and 'your ladyship,' the poor girl won't know how to behave herself, but will every foot make a thousand blunders, and show her homespun country breeding."

"Tush! fool," answered Sancho; "it will be but two or three years' 'prenticeship; and then you will see how strangely she will alter; 'your ladyship' and keeping of state will become her, as if they had been made for her; and suppose they should not, what is it to anybody? Let her be but a lady, and let what will happen."

"Good Sancho," quoth the wife, "don't look above yourself; I say, keep to the proverb, that says, 'Birds of a feather flock together.' It would be a fine thing, e'trow! for us to go and throw away our child on one of your lordlings, or right worshipfuls, who, when the toy should take him in the head, would find new names for her, and call her 'country Joan,' 'plough-jobber's bearn,' and 'spinner's web.' No, no, husband, I have not bred the girl up as I have done to throw her away at that rate, I will assure ye. Do thee but bring home money, and leave me to get her a husband. Why, there is Lope Tocho, old Joan Tocho's son, a hale, jolly young fellow, and one whom we all know; I have observed he casts a sheep's eye at the wench; he is one of our inches, and will be a good match for her; then we shall always have her under our wings, and be all as one, father and mother, children and grandchild, and Heaven's peace and blessing will always be with us. But never talk to me of marrying her at your courts and great men's houses, where she will understand nobody, and nobody will understand her."

"Why, thou good-for-nothing," cried Sancho, "thou wife of Barabbas, why dost thou hinder me from marrying my daughter to one whose grandchildren may be called 'your honour' and 'your lordship?' Have I not always heard my betters say, that

'He who will not when he may,
When he will he shall have nay?

When good luck is knocking at our door, is it fit to shut him out? No, no, let us 'make hay while the sun shines,' and spread our sails before this prosperous gale."

[This mode of allocution, and the following huddle of reflections and apophthegms, said to have been spoken by Sancho, made the translator of this history say he held this chapter apocryphal.]

"Canst thou not perceive, thou senseless animal," said Sancho, going on, "that I ought to venture over head and ears to light on some good, gainful government, that may free our ankles from the clogs of necessity, and marry Mary Sancho to whom we please? Go to, let us have no more of this; little Sancho shall be a countess in spite of thy teeth, I say."

"Well, well, husband," quoth the wife, "have a care what you say, for I fear me these high kicks will be my Molly's undoing. Yet do what you will, make her a duchess or a princess, but I will never give my consent. Look ye, yoke-fellow, for my part I ever love to see everything upon the square, and cannot abide to see folks take upon them when they should not. I was christened plain Teresa without any fiddle-faddle, or addition of 'madam,' or 'your ladyship.' My father's name was Cascajo; and because I married you they call me Teresa Panza, though indeed by right I should be called Teresa Cascajo. But where the kings are, there are the laws, and I am e'en contented with that name without a flourish before it, to make it longer and more tedious than it is already; neither will I make myself anybody's laughing-stock. I will give them no cause to cry, when they see me go like a countess, or a governor's madam, 'Look, look, how Madam Hog-wash struts along! It was but the other day she'd tug ye a distaff, capped with hemp, from morning till night, and would go to mass with her coat over her head for want of a hood; yet now, look how she goes in her fardingale, and her rich trimmings and fallals, no less than a whole tradesman's shop about her back, as if everybody did not know her.' No, husband, if it please Heaven but to keep me in my seven senses, or my five, or as many as I have, I will take care to tie up people's tongues from setting me out at this rate. You may go, and be a governor, or an islander, and look as big as bull-beef an you will; but by my grandmother's daughter, neither I nor my girl will budge a foot from our thatched house, for the proverb says—

'The wife that expects to have a good name,
Is always at home, as if she were lame;
And the maid that is honest, her chiefest delight
Is still to be doing from morning to night.'

March you and your Don Quixote together, to your islands and adventures, and leave us here to our sorry fortune; I will warrant you Heaven will better it, if we live as we ought to do. I wonder, though, who made him a Don; neither his father nor his grandsire ever had that feather in their caps."

"Heaven help thee, woman!" quoth Sancho; "what a heap of stuff hast thou twisted together without head or tail! What have thy Cascajos, thy fardingales and fallals, thy old saws, and all this tale of a roasted horse, to do with what I have said? Hark thee me, Gammer Addlepate—for I can find no better name for thee, since thou art such a blind buzzard as to miss my meaning, and stand in thy own light—should I have told thee that my girl was to throw herself head foremost from the top of some steeple, or to trot about the world like a gipsy, as the Infanta Donna Urraca did, then thou mightest have some reason not to be of my mind. But if, in the twinkling of an eye, and while one might toss a pancake, I can equip her with a Don and a Ladyship; if I fetch her out of her straw, to sit under a stately bed's tester, and squat her down on more velvet cushions than there are Almohadas in Morocco, why shouldest thou be against it, and not be pleased with what pleases me?"

"I do not understand you, husband," quoth Teresa; "even follow your own inventions, and do not puzzle my brains with your harangues and retricks. If you are so devolved to do as ye say——"

"Resolved, you should say, wife," quoth Sancho, "and not devolved."

"Pr'ythee, husband," said Teresa, "let us have no words about that matter: I speak as Heaven is pleased I should; and for hard words, I give my share to the curate. All I have to say now is this, if you hold still in the mind of being a governor, pray even take your son

Sancho along with you, and henceforth train him up to your trade of governing; for it is but fitting that the son should be brought up to the father's calling."

"When once I am governor," quoth Sancho, "I will send for him by the post, and I will send thee money withal; for I dare say I shall want none; there never wants those that will lend governors money when they have none. But then be sure you clothe the boy so, that he may look not like what he is, but like what he is to be."

"Send you but money," quoth Teresa, "and I will make him as fine as a May-day garland."

"So then, wife," quoth Sancho, "I suppose we are agreed that our Moll shall be a countess."

"The day I see her a countess," quoth Teresa, "I reckon I lay her in her grave. However, I tell you again, even follow your own inventions; you men will be masters, and we poor women are born to bear the clog of obedience, though our husbands have no more sense than a cuckoo."

Here she fell a-weeping as heartily as if she had seen her daughter already dead and buried. Sancho comforted her, and promised her, that though he was to make her a countess, yet he would see and put it off as long as he could. Thus ended their dialogue, and he went back to Don Quixote, to dispose everything for a march.

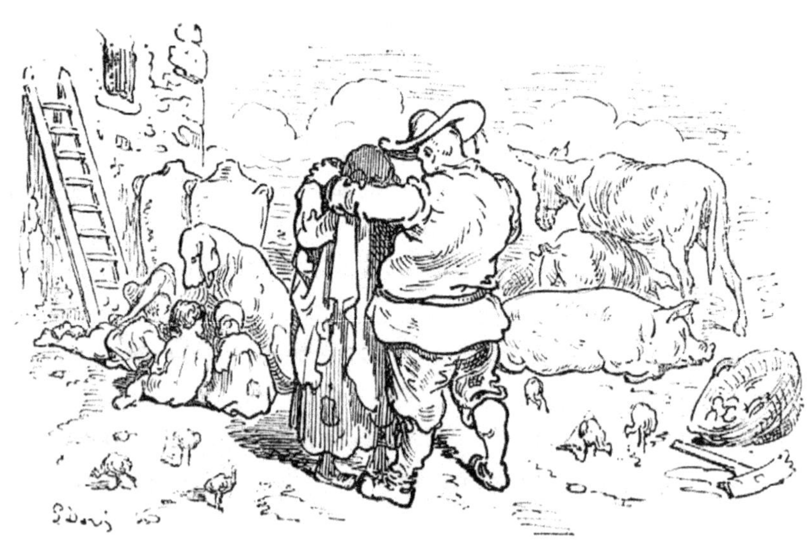

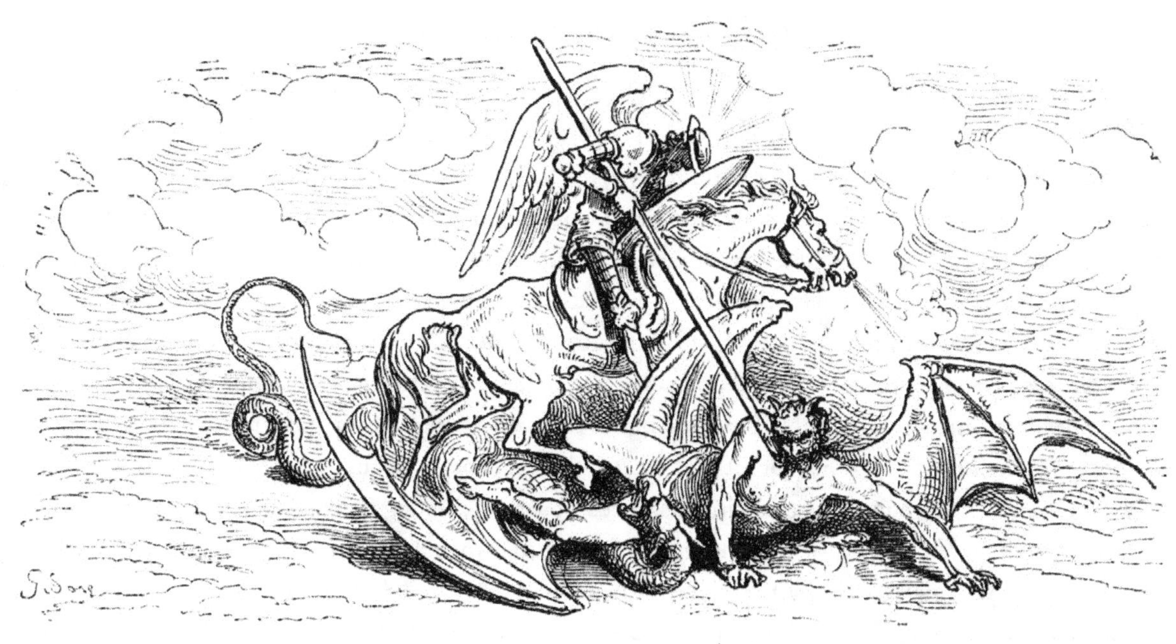

CHAPTER VI.

WHAT PASSED BETWEEN DON QUIXOTE, HIS NIECE, AND THE HOUSEKEEPER: BEING ONE OF THE MOST IMPORTANT CHAPTERS IN THE WHOLE HISTORY.

WHILE Sancho Panza and his wife, Teresa Cascajo, had the foregoing important dialogue, Don Quixote's niece and housekeeper were not idle, guessing by a thousand signs that the knight intended a third sally. Therefore they endeavoured by all possible means to divert him from his foolish design, but all to no purpose; for this was but preaching to a rock, and hammering cold stubborn steel. But among other arguments, "In short, sir," quoth the housekeeper, "if you will not be ruled, but will needs run wandering over hill and dale, seeking for mischief, for so I may well call the hopeful adventures which you go about, I will never leave complaining to Heaven and the king, till there is a stop put to it some way or other."

"What answer Heaven will vouchsafe to give thee, I know not," answered Don Quixote; "neither can I tell what return his majesty will make to thy petition. This I know, that were I a king I would excuse myself from answering the infinite number of impertinent memorials that disturb the repose of princes. I tell thee, woman, among the many other fatigues which royalty sustains, it is one of the greatest to be obliged to hear every one, and to give answer to all people. Therefore, pray trouble not his majesty with anything concerning me."

"But pray, sir, tell me," replied she, "are there not a many knights in the king's court?"

"I must confess," said Don Quixote, "that for the ornament, the grandeur, and the pomp of royalty, many knights are, and ought to be, maintained there."

"Why, then," said the woman, "would it not be better for your worship to be one of those brave knights, who serve the king their master on foot in his court?"

"Hear me, sweetheart," answered Don Quixote, "all knights cannot be courtiers, nor can all courtiers be knights-errant. For your courtiers, without so much as stirring out of their chambers, or the shade and shelter of the court, can journey over all the universe in a map, without the expense and fatigue of travelling, without suffering the inconveniences of heat, cold, hunger, and thirst; while we who are the true knights-errant, exposed to those extremities, and all the inclemencies of heaven, by night and by day, on foot as well as on horseback, measure the whole surface of the earth with our own feet. Nor are we only acquainted with the pictures of our enemies, but with their very persons, ready upon all occasions and at all times to engage them, without standing upon trifles, or the ceremony of measuring weapons, stripping, or examining whether our opponents have any holy relics or other secret charms about them, whether the sun be duly divided, or any other punctilios and circumstances observed among private duelists—things which thou understandest not, but I do, and must further let thee know that the true knight-errant, though he met ten giants, whose tall aspiring heads not only touch but overtop the clouds, each of them stalking with prodigious legs like huge towers, their sweeping arms like masts of mighty ships, each eye as large as a mill-wheel, and more fiery than a glass furnace, yet he is so far from being afraid to meet them, that he must encounter them with a gentle countenance and an undaunted courage, assail them, close with them, and if possible vanquish and destroy them all in an instant; nay, though they came armed with the scales of a certain fish, which they say is harder than adamant, and instead of swords had dreadful sabres of keen Damascus steel, or mighty maces with points of the same metal, as I have seen more than a dozen times."

"Ah! sir," said the niece, "have a care what you say; the stories of knights-errant are nothing but a pack of lies and fables; and if they are not burnt, they ought at least to wear a *sanbenito*, the badge of heresy, or some other mark of infamy, that the world may know them to be wicked, and perverters of good manners."

"Now, by the powerful sustainer of my being," cried Don Quixote, "wert thou not so nearly related to me, wert thou not my own sister's daughter, I would take such revenge for the blasphemy thou hast uttered, as would resound through the whole universe. Who ever heard of the like impudence? What would Sir Amadis have said, had he heard this? But he undoubtedly would have forgiven thee, for he was the most courteous and complaisant knight of his time, especially to the fair sex, being a great protector of damsels; but thy words might have reached the ears of some that would have sacrificed thee to their indignation; for all knights are not possessed of civility or good nature; some are rough and revengeful; and neither are all those that assume the name of a disposition suitable to the function. Some indeed are of the right stamp, but others are either counterfeit or of such an alloy as cannot bear the touchstone, though they deceive the sight. Inferior mortals there are, who aim at knighthood, and strain to reach the height of honour; and high-born knights there are, who seem fond of grovelling in the dust, and being lost in the crowd of inferior mortals. The first raise themselves by ambition or by virtue; the last debase themselves by negligence or by vice; so that there is need of a distinguishing understanding to judge between these two sorts of knights, so nearly allied in name, and so different in actions."

"Bless me! dear uncle," cried the niece, "that you should know so much as to be able, if there was occasion, to get up into a pulpit, or preach in the streets, and yet be so strangely mistaken, so grossly blind of understanding, as to fancy a man of your years and infirmity can be strong and valiant; that you can set everything right, and force stubborn malice to bend, when you yourself stoop beneath the burden of age; and what is yet more odd, that you are a knight, when it is well known you are none! For though some gentlemen may be knights, a poor gentleman can hardly be so, because he cannot buy it."

"You say well, niece," answered Don Quixote; "and as to this last observation, I could tell you things that you would wonder at, concerning families; but because I will not mix sacred things with profane, I waive the discourse. However, listen both of you, and for your farther instruction know that all the lineages and descents of mankind are reducible to these four heads:—First, those who, from a very small and obscure beginning, have raised themselves to a spreading and prodigious magnitude. Secondly, those who, deriving their greatness from a noble spring, still preserve the dignity and character of their original splendour. A third are those who, though they had large foundations, have ended in a point like a pyramid, which by little and little dwindles, as it were, into nothing, or next to nothing, in comparison of its basis. Others there are (and those are the bulk of mankind) who have neither had a good beginning nor a rational continuance, and whose ending shall therefore be obscure; such are the common people, the plebeian race. The Ottoman family is an instance of the first sort, having derived their present greatness from the poor beginning of a base-born shepherd. Of the second sort, there are many princes who, being born such, enjoy their dominions by inheritance, and leave them to their successors without addition or diminution. Of the third sort there is an infinite number of examples: for all the Pharaohs and Ptolemies of Egypt, your Cæsars of Rome, and all the swarm (if I may use that word) of princes, monarchs, lords—Medes, Assyrians, Persians, Greeks, and barbarians—all these families and empires have ended in a point, as well as those who gave rise to them: for it were impossible at this day to find any of their descendants; or if we could find them, it would be in a poor, grovelling condition. As for the vulgar, I say nothing of them, more than that they are thrown in as ciphers to increase the number of mankind, without deserving any other praise. Now, my good-natured souls, you may at least draw this reasonable inference from what I have said of this promiscuous dispensation of honours, and this uncertainty and confusion of descent, that virtue and liberality in the present possessor are the most just and indisputable titles to nobility; for the advantages of pedigree, without these qualifications, serve only to make vice more conspicuous. The great man that is vicious will be greatly vicious, and the rich miser is only a covetous beggar; for, not he who possesses, but who spends and enjoys his wealth, is the rich and the happy man; nor he neither who barely spends, but who does it with discretion. The poor knight, indeed, cannot show he is one by his magnificence; but yet by his virtue, affability, civility, and courteous behaviour, he may display the chief ingredients that enter into the composition of knighthood; and though he cannot pretend to liberality, wanting riches to support it, his charity may recompense that defect; for an alms of two maravedis cheerfully bestowed upon an indigent beggar, by a man in poor circumstances, proves him as liberal as the larger donative of a vain-glorious rich man before a fawning crowd. These accomplishments will always shine through the clouds of fortune, and at last break through them with splendour and applause. There are two paths to dignity and wealth—arts and arms. Arms I have chosen; and the influence of the planet Mars, that presided at my nativity, led me to that adventurous road: so that all your attempts to shake my resolution are in vain; for in spite of all mankind, I will pursue what Heaven has fated, fortune ordained, reason requires, and (which is more) my inclination demands. I am sensible of the many troubles and dangers that attend the prosecution of knight-errantry, but I also know what infinite honours and rewards are the consequences of the performance. The path of virtue is narrow, and the way of vice easy and open; but their ends and resting-places are very different. For I know, as our great Castilian poet expresses it, that

'Through steep ascents, through strait and rugged ways,
Ourselves to glory's lofty seats we raise:
In vain he hopes to reach the bless'd abode,
Who leaves the narrow path for the more easy road.'"

"Alack a-day!" cried the niece, "my uncle is a poet, too! He knows everything. I will lay my life he might turn mason in case of necessity. If he would but undertake it, he could build a house as easy as a bird-cage."

"Why truly, niece," said Don Quixote, "were not my understanding wholly involved in thoughts relating to the exercise of knight-errantry, there is nothing which I durst not engage to perform; no curiosity should escape my hands, especially bird-cages and tooth-picks."

By this somebody knocked at the door, and being asked who it was, Sancho answered it was he; whereupon the housekeeper slipped out of the way, not wishing to see him, and the niece let him in. Don Quixote received him with open arms; and locking themselves both in the closet, they had another dialogue as pleasant as the former.

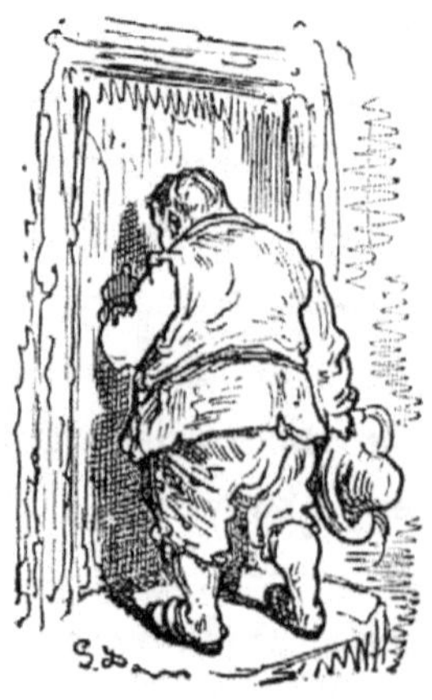

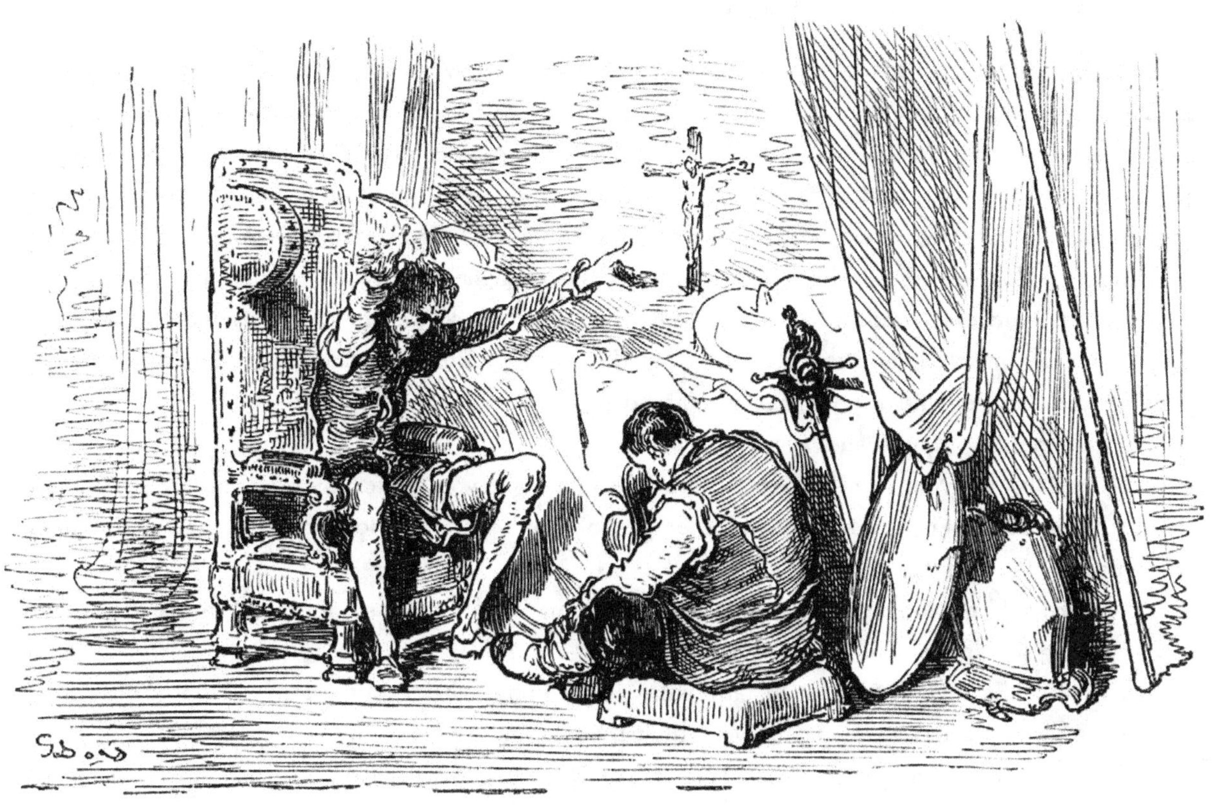

CHAPTER VII.

AN ACCOUNT OF DON QUIXOTE'S CONFERENCE WITH HIS SQUIRE, AND OTHER MOST FAMOUS PASSAGES.

THE housekeeper no sooner saw her master and Sancho locked up together, but she presently surmised the drift of that close conference, and concluding that no less than villanous knight-errantry and another sally would prove the result of it, she flung her veil over her head, and, quite cast down with sorrow and vexation, trudged away to seek Samson Carrasco, the bachelor of arts; depending on his wit and eloquence to persuade his friend Don Quixote from his frantic resolution. She found him walking in the yard of his house, and fell presently on her knees before him in a cold sweat, and with all the marks of a disordered mind.

"What is the matter, woman?" said he, somewhat surprised at her posture and confusion; "what has befallen you, that you look as if you were ready to give up the ghost?"

"Nothing," said she, "dear sir, but that my master is departing! he is departing, that is most certain."

"How!" cried Carrasco, "what do you mean? Is his soul departing out of his body?"

"No," answered the woman, "but all his wits are quite and clean departing. He means to be gadding again into the wide world, and is upon the spur now the third time to hunt after ventures, as he calls them, though I don't know why he calls those chances so. The first time he was brought home was athwart an ass, and almost cudgelled to pieces. The other bout he was forced to ride home in a wagon, cooped up in a cage, where he would make us believe he was enchanted; and the poor soul looked so dismally, that his own mother would scarcely have known hei child—so meagre, wan, and withered, and his eyes so sunk and hid in the utmost nook and corner of his brain, that I am sure I used about six hundred eggs to fatten him up again; ay, and more too, as Heaven and all the world is my witness; and the hens that laid them cannot deny it."

"That I believe," said the bachelor, "for your hens are so well bred, so fat, and so good, that they won't say one thing and think another for the world. But is this all? Has no other ill luck befallen you, besides this of your master's intended ramble?"

"No other, sir," quoth she.

"Then trouble your head no farther," said he, "but get you home; and as you go, say me the prayer of St. Apollonia, if you know it; then get me some warm bit for breakfast, and I will come to you presently, and you shall see wonders."

"Dear me!" quoth she, "the prayer of St. Polonia! Why, it is only good for the toothache; but his ailing lies in his skull."

"Mistress," said he, "do not dispute with me: I know what I say. Have I not commenced bachelor of arts at Salamanca, and do you think there is any *bachelorising* beyond that?"

With that away she goes, and he went presently to find the curate, to consult with him about what shall be declared in due time.

When Sancho and his master were locked up together in the room, there passed some discourse between them, of which the history gives a very punctual and impartial account.

"Sir," quoth Sancho to his master, "I have at last reluced my wife to let me go with your worship wherever you will have me."

"Reduced, you would say, Sancho," said Don Quixote, "and not reluced."

"Look you, sir," quoth Sancho; "if I am not mistaken, I have wished you once or twice not to stand correcting my words, if you understand my meaning: if you do not, why then do but say to me, 'Sancho,' or what you please, 'I understand thee not;' and if I do not make out my meaning plainly, then take me up; for I am so forcible ——"

"I understand you not," said Don Quixote, interrupting him; "for I cannot guess the meaning of your forcible."

"Why, so forcible," quoth Sancho, "is as much as to say, forcible; that is, I am so and so, as it were."

"Less and less do I understand thee," said the knight.

"Why, then," quoth Sancho, "there is an end of the matter; it must even stick there for me, for I can speak no better."

"Oh! now," quoth Don Quixote, "I fancy I guess your meaning; you mean *docible*, I suppose, implying that you are so ready and apprehensive, that you will presently observe what I shall teach you."

"I will lay any even wager now," said the squire, "you understood me well enough at first, but you had a mind to put me out, merely to hear me put your fine words out o' joint."

"That may be," said Don Quixote, "but pr'ythee tell me what says Teresa."

"Why, an't please you," quoth Sancho, "Teresa bids me make sure work with your worship, and that we may have 'less talking and more doing;' that 'a man must not be his own carver;' that 'he who cuts does not shuffle;' that 'it is good to be certain;' that 'paper speaks when beards never wag;' that 'a bird in hand is worth two in the bush.' 'One hold-fast is better than two I will give thee.' Now, I say, a woman's counsel is not worth much, yet he that despises it is no wiser than he should be."

"I say so too," said Don Quixote; "but pray, good Sancho, proceed; for thou art in an excellent strain; thou talkest most sententiously to-day."

"I say," quoth Sancho, "as you know better yourself than I do, that we are all mortal men, here to-day and gone to-morrow; 'as soon goes the young lamb to the spit as the old wether;' no man can tell the length of his days; for Death is deaf, and when he knocks at the door, mercy on the porter! He is in post-haste; neither fair words nor foul, crowns nor mitres, can stay him, as the report goes, and as we are told from the pulpit."

"All this I grant," said Don Quixote; "but what would you infer from hence?"

"Why, sir," quoth Sancho, "all I would be at is, that your worship allow me so much a month for my wages, whilst I stay with you, and that the aforesaid wages be paid me out of your estate. For I will trust no longer to rewards, that mayhaps may come late, and mayhaps not at all. I would be glad to know what I get, be it more or less. 'A little in one's own pocket is better than much in another man's purse.' 'It is good to keep a nest egg.' 'Many little makes a mickle.' 'While a man gets he never can lose.' Should it happen, indeed, that your worship should give me this same island, which you promised me, though it is what I dare not so much as hope for, why then I aint such an ungrateful nor so unconscionable a muckworm, but that I am willing to strike off upon the income, for what wages I receive, cantity for cantity."

"Would not quantity have been better than cantity?" asked Don Quixote.

"Ho! I understand you now," cried Sancho: "I dare lay a wager I should have said quantity and not cantity: but no matter for that, since you knew what I meant."

"Yes, Sancho," quoth the knight, "I have dived to the very bottom of your thought, and understand now the aim of all your numerous shot of proverbs. Look you, friend Sancho, I should never scruple to pay thee wages, had I any example to warrant such a practice. Nay, could I find the least glimmering of a precedent through all the books of chivalry that ever I read, for any yearly or monthly stipend, your request should be granted. But I have read all, or the greatest part of the histories of knights-errant, and find that all their squires depended purely on the favour of their masters for a subsistence, till by some surprising turn in the knight's fortune, the servants were advanced to the government of some island, or some equivalent gratuity; at least, they had honour and a title conferred on them as a reward. Now, friend Sancho, if you will depend on

B B

these hopes of preferment, and return to my service, it is well; if not, get you home, and tell your impertinent wife that I will not break through all the rules and customs of chivalry, to satisfy her sordid diffidence and yours; and so let there be no more words about the matter, but let us part friends; and remember this, that if there be vetches in my dove-house, it will want no pigeons. 'Good arrears are better than ill pay;' and 'a fee in reversion is better than a farm in possession.' Take notice too, there is proverb for proverb, to let you know that I can pour out a volley of them as well as you. In short, if you will not go along with me upon courtesy, and run the same fortune with me, Heaven be with you, and make you a saint; I do not question but I shall get me a squire, more obedient, more careful, and less saucy and talkative than you."

Sancho hearing his master's firm resolution, it was cloudy weather with him in an instant; he was struck dumb with disappointment, and down sunk at once his heart to his girdle; for he verily thought he could have brought him to any terms, through a vain opinion that the knight would not for the world go without him. While he was thus dolefully buried in thought, in came Samson Carrasco and the niece, very eager to hear the bachelor's arguments to dissuade Don Quixote from his intended sally. But Samson, who was a rare comedian, presently embracing the knight, and beginning in a high strain, soon disappointed her. "Oh, flower of chivalry!" cried he, "refulgent glory of arms, living honour and mirror of our Spanish nation, may all those who prevent the third expedition which thy heroic spirit meditates be lost in the labyrinth of their perverse desires, and find no thread to lead them to their wishes!" Then turning to the housekeeper, "You have no need now to say the prayer of St. Apollonia," said he, "for I find it written in the stars that the illustrious champion must no longer delay the prosecution of glory; and I should injure my conscience should I presume to dissuade him from the benefits that shall redound to mankind by exerting the strength of his formidable arm, and the innate virtues of his heroic soul. Alas! his stay deprives the oppressed orphans of a protector, damsels of a deliverer, champions of their honour, widows of an obliging patron, and married women of a vigorous comforter; nay, also delays a thousand other important exploits and achievements, which are the duty and necessary consequences of the honourable order of knight-errantry. Go on then, my graceful, my valorous Don Quixote, rather this very day than the next; let your greatness be upon the wing, and if anything be wanting towards the completing of your equipage, I stand forth to supply you with my life and fortune, and ready, if it be thought expedient, to attend your excellence as a squire—an honour which I am ambitious to attain."

"Well, Sancho," said Don Quixote, hearing this, and turning to his squire, "did I not tell thee I should not want squires? behold who offers me his service! the most excellent bachelor of arts, Samson Carrasco, the perpetual darling of the Muses, and glory of the Salamanca schools, sound and active of body, patient of labour, inured to abstinence, silent in misfortune, and, in short, endowed with all the accomplishments that constitute a squire. But forbid it, Heaven! that to indulge my private inclinations I should presume to weaken the whole body of learning, by removing from it so substantial a pillar, so vast a repository of sciences, and so eminent a branch of the liberal arts. No, my friend, remain thou another Samson in thy country; be the honour of Spain, and the delight of thy ancient parents; I shall content myself with any squire, since Sancho does not vouchsafe to go with me."

"I do, I do," cried Sancho, relenting with tears in his eyes; "I do vouchsafe; it shall never be said of Sancho Panza, 'No longer pipe, no longer dance.' Nor have I heart of flint, sir; for all the world knows, and especially our town, what the whole generation of the Panzas has ever been. Besides, I well know, and have already found by many good turns, and more good words, that your worship has had a good will towards me all along; and if I have done otherwise than I should, in standing upon wages or so, it was merely to humour my wife, who, when once she is set upon a thing, stands digging and hammering at a man, like a cooper at a tub, till she clinches the point. But I am the husband, and will be her husband; and she is but a wife, and shall be a wife. None can deny but I am a man every inch of me, wherever I am, and I will be a man at home, in spite of anybody; so that you have no more to do but to make your will and testament; but be sure you make the conveyance so firm that it cannot be rebuked, and then let us be gone as soon as you please, that Master Samson's soul may be at rest; for he says his conscience won't let him be quiet till he has set you upon another journey through the world; and I here again offer myself to follow your worship, and promise to be faithful and loyal, as well, nay, and better, than all the squires that ever waited on knights-errant."

The bachelor was amazed to hear Sancho Panza express himself after that manner; and though he had read much of him in the first part of his history, he could not believe him to be so pleasant a fellow as he is there represented. But hearing him now talk of rebuking instead of revoking testaments and conveyances, he was induced to credit all that was said of him, and to conclude him one of the oddest compounds of the age; nor could he imagine that the world ever saw before so extravagant a couple as the master and man.

Don Quixote and Sancho embraced, becoming as good friends as ever; and so, with the approbation of the grand Carrasco, who was then the knight's oracle, it was decreed that they should set out at the expiration of three days; in which time all necessaries should be provided, especially a whole helmet, which Don Quixote said he was resolved by all means to purchase. Samson offered him one which he knew he could easily get of a friend, and which looked more dull with the mould and rust, than bright with the lustre of the steel. The niece and the housekeeper made a woful outcry; they tore their hair, scratched their faces, and howled like common mourners at funerals, lamenting the knight's departure, as if it had been his real death, and cursing Carrasco most unmercifully, though his behaviour was the result of a contrivance plotted between the curate, the barber, and himself. In short, Don Quixote and his squire having got all things in readiness, the one having pacified his wife, and the other his niece and housekeeper, towards the evening, without being seen by anybody but the bachelor, who would needs accompany them about half a league from the village, they set forward for Toboso. The knight mounted his Rozinante, and Sancho his trusty Dapple, his wallet well stuffed with provisions, and his purse with money, which Don Quixote gave him to defray expenses. At last Samson took his leave, desiring the champion to give him, from time to time, an account of his success, that, according to the laws of friendship, he might sympathise in his good or evil fortune. Don Quixote made him a promise, and then they parted; Samson went home, and the knight and squire continued their journey for the great city of Toboso.

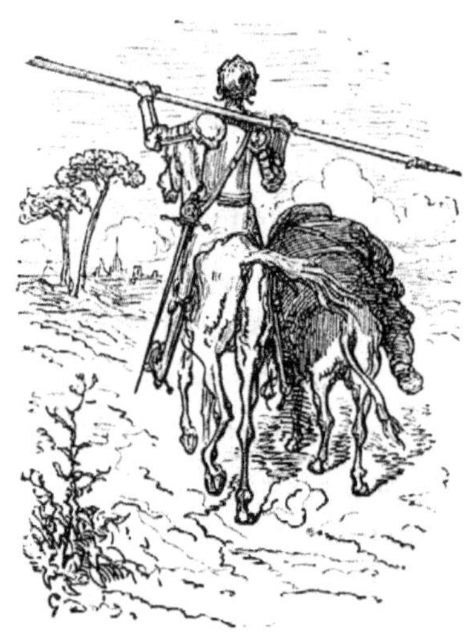

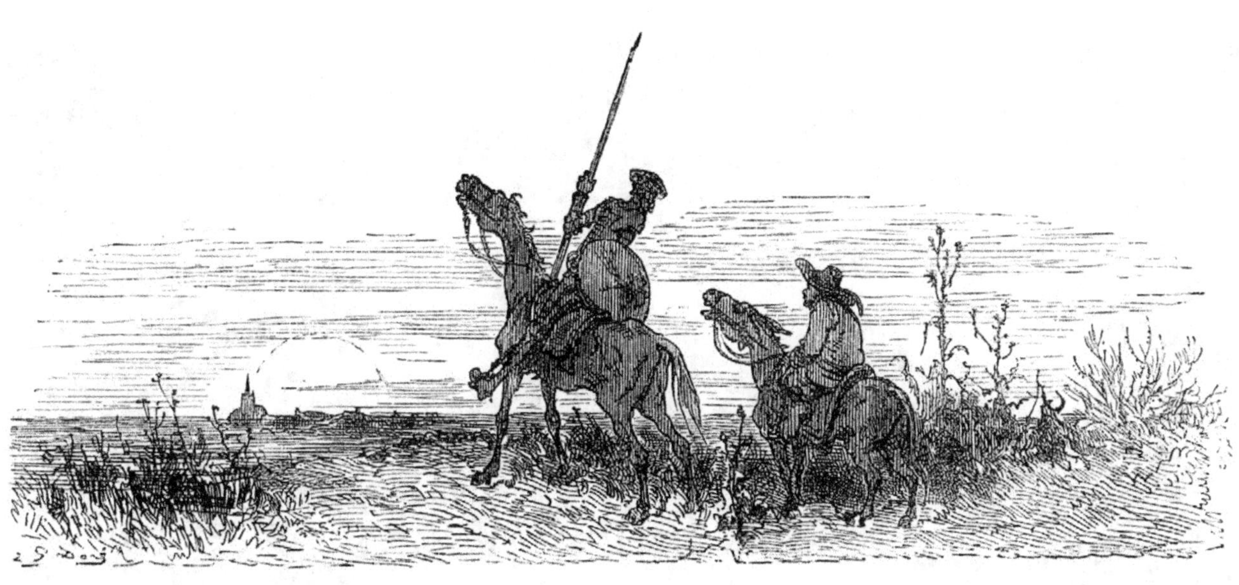

CHAPTER VIII.

DON QUIXOTE'S SUCCESS IN HIS JOURNEY TO VISIT THE LADY DULCINEA DEL TOBOSO.

BLESSED be the mighty Allah!" says Hamet Benengeli, at the beginning of his eighth chapter; "blessed be Allah!" which ejaculation he thrice repeated, in consideration of the blessing that Don Quixote and Sancho had once more taken the field again, and that from this period the readers of their delightful history may date the knight's achievements and the squire's pleasantries; and he entreats them to forget the former heroical transactions of the wonderful knight, and fix their eyes upon his future exploits, which take birth from his setting out for Toboso, as the former began in the fields of Montiel. Nor can so small a request be thought unreasonable, considering what he promises, which begins in this manner.

Don Quixote and his squire were no sooner parted from the bachelor, but Rozinante began to neigh, and Dapple to bray; which both the knight and the squire interpreted as good omens, and most fortunate presages of their success; though the truth of the story is, that as Dapple's braying exceeded Rozinante's neighing, Sancho concluded that his fortune should out-rival and eclipse his master's; which inference I will not say he drew from some principles in judicial astrology, in which he was undoubtedly well grounded, though the history is silent in that particular; however, it is recorded of him that oftentimes upon the falling or stumbling of his ass, he wished he had not gone abroad that day, and from such accidents prognosticated nothing but dislocation of joints and breaking of ribs; and notwithstanding his foolish character, this was no bad observation. "Friend Sancho," said Don Quixote to him, "I find the approaching night will overtake us ere we can reach Toboso, where, before I enter upon any expedition, I am resolved to pay my vows, receive my benediction, and take my leave of the peerless Dulcinea; being assured after that of happy events, in the most dangerous

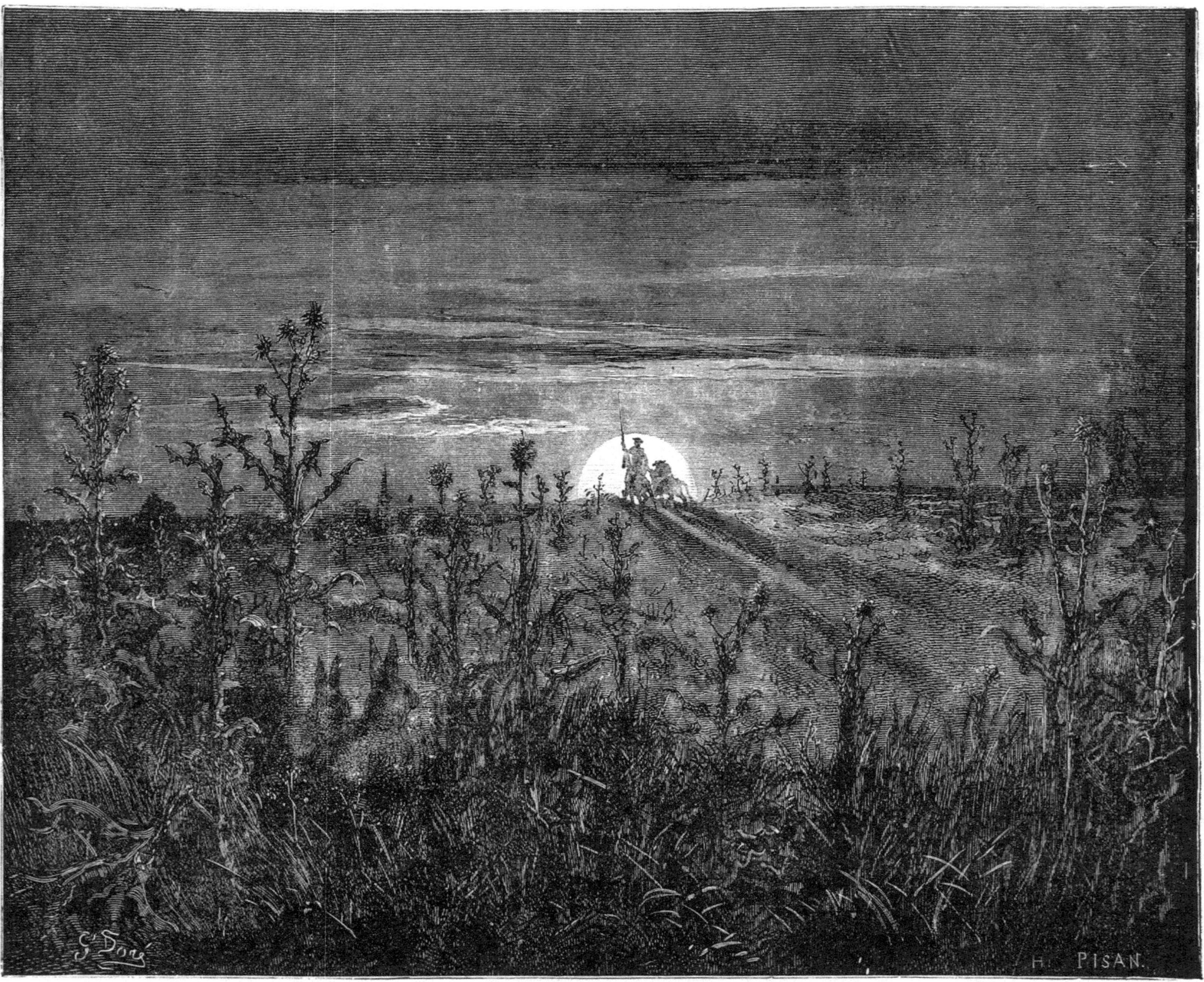

"Friend Sancho," said Don Quixote, "I find the approaching night will overtake us ere we can reach Toboso."

adventures; for nothing in this world inspires a knight-errant with so much valour as the smiles and favourable aspects of his mistress."

"I am of your mind," quoth Sancho: "but I am afraid, sir, you will hardly come at her, to speak with her, at least not to meet her in a place where she may give you her blessing, unless she throw it over the mud wall of the yard, where I first saw her, when I carried her the news of your mad pranks in the midst of Sierra Morena."

"Mud wall! dost thou say?" cried Don Quixote: "mistaken fool! that wall could have no existence but in thy muddy understanding: it is a mere creature of thy dirty fancy; for that never-duly-celebrated paragon of beauty and gentility was then undoubtedly in some court, in some stately gallery or walk, or, as it is properly called, in some sumptuous and royal palace."

"It may be so," said Sancho, "though, so far as I can remember, it seemed to me neither better nor worse than a mud wall."

"It is no matter," replied the knight, "let us go thither; I will visit my dear Dulcinea; let me but see her, though it be over a mud wall, through a chink of a cottage, or the pales of a garden, at a lattice, or anywhere; which way soever the least beam from her bright eyes reaches mine, it will so enlighten my mind, so fortify my heart, and invigorate every faculty of my being, that no mortal will be able to rival me in prudence and valour."

"Troth, sir," quoth Sancho, "when I beheld that same sun of a lady, methought it did not shine so bright as to cast forth any beams at all; but, mayhaps, the reason was, that the dust of the grain she was winnowing raised a cloud about her face, and made her look somewhat dull."

"I tell thee again, fool," said Don Quixote, "thy imagination is dusty and foul. Will it never be beaten out of thy stupid brain, that my Lady Dulcinea was winnowing? Are such exercises used by persons of her quality, whose recreations are always noble, and such as display an air of greatness suitable to their birth and dignity? Canst thou not remember the verses of our poet, when he recounts the employments of the four nymphs at their crystal mansions, when they advanced their heads above the streams of the lovely Tagus, and sat upon the grass, working those rich embroideries, where silk and gold, and pearl embossed, were so curiously interwoven, and which that ingenious bard so artfully describes? So was my princess employed when she blessed thee with her sight; but the envious malice of some base necromancer fascinated thy sight, as it represents whatever is most grateful to me in different and displeasing shapes. And this makes me fear that if the history of my achievements, which they tell me is in print, has been written by some magician who is no well-wisher to my glory, he has undoubtedly delivered many things with partiality, and misrepresented my life, giving a hundred falsehoods for one truth, and diverting himself with the relation of idle stories, foreign to the purpose, and unsuitable to the continuation of a true history. Oh, envy! envy! thou gnawing worm of virtue, and spring of infinite mischiefs! there is no other vice, my

Sancho, but pleads some pleasure in its excuse; but envy is always attended by disgust, rancour, and distracting rage."

"I am much of your mind," said Sancho; "and I think, in the same book which neighbour Carrasco told us he had read of our lives, the story makes bold with my credit, and has handled it in a strange manner, dragging it about the kennels, as a body may say. Well, now, as I am an honest man, I never spoke an ill word of a magician in my born days; and I think they need not envy my condition so much. The truth is, I am somewhat malicious; I have my roguish tricks now and then; but I was ever counted more fool than knave, for all that, and so indeed I was bred and born; and if there were nothing else in me but my religion—for I firmly believe whatever our holy Roman Catholic Church believes, and I hate the Jews mortally—these same historians should take pity on me, and spare me a little in their books. But let them say on to the end of the chapter; naked I came into the world, and naked must go out. It is all a case to Sancho; I can neither win nor lose by the bargain: and so my name be in print, and handed about, I care not a fig for the worst they can say of me."

"What thou sayest, Sancho," answered Don Quixote, "puts me in mind of a story. A celebrated poet of our time wrote a very scurrilous and abusive lampoon upon all the intriguing ladies of the court, forbearing to name one, as not being sure whether she deserved to be put into the catalogue or no; but the lady, not finding herself there, was not a little affronted at the omission, and made a great complaint to the poet, asking him what he had seen in her, that he should leave her out of his list; desiring him, at the same time, to enlarge his satire, and put her in, or expect to hear further from her. The author obeyed her commands, and gave her a character with a vengeance, and, to her great satisfaction, made her as famous for infamy as any other. Such another story is that of Diana's Temple, one of the seven wonders of the world, burnt by an obscure fellow merely to eternise his name; which, in spite of an edict that enjoined all people never to mention it, either by word of mouth or in writing, yet is still known to have been Erostratus. The story of the great Emperor Charles V., and a Roman knight, upon a certain occasion, is much the same. The emperor had a great desire to see the famous temple once called the Pantheon, but now more happily the Church of All Saints. It is the only entire edifice remaining of heathen Rome, and that which best gives an idea of the glory and magnificence of its great founders. It is built in the shape of a half orange, of a vast extent, and very lightsome, though it admits light but at one window, or, to speak more properly, at a round aperture on the top of the roof. The emperor being got up thither, and looking down from the brink upon the fabric, with a Roman knight by him, who showed all the beauties of that vast edifice, after they were gone from the place, the knight said, addressing the emperor, 'It came into my head a thousand times, sacred sir, to embrace your majesty, and cast myself, with you, from the top of the church to the bottom, that I might thus purchase an immortal name.'

'I thank you,' said the emperor, 'for not doing it; and for the future, I will give you no opportunity to put your loyalty to such a test. Therefore I banish you my presence for ever;' which done, he bestowed some considerable favour on him. I tell thee, Sancho, this desire of honour is a strange, bewitching thing. What dost thou think made Horatius, armed at all points, plunge headlong from the bridge into the rapid Tiber? What prompted Curtius to leap into the profound flaming gulf? What made Mutius burn his hand? What forced Cæsar over the Rubicon, spite of all the omens that dissuaded his passage? And to instance a more modern example, what made the undaunted Spaniards sink their ships, when under the most courteous Cortez, but that, scorning the stale honour of this so often conquered world, they sought a maiden glory in a new scene of victory? These and a multiplicity of other great actions are owing to the immediate thirst and desire of fame, which mortals expect as the proper price and immortal recompense of their great actions. But we that are Christian catholic knights-errant must fix our hopes upon a higher reward, placed in the eternal and celestial regions, where we may expect a permanent honour and complete happiness; not like the vanity of fame, which, at best, is but the shadow of great actions, and must necessarily vanish, when destructive time has eaten away the substance which it followed. So, my Sancho, since we expect a Christian reward, we must suit our actions to the rules of Christianity. In giants we must kill pride and arrogance: but our greatest foes, and whom we must chiefly combat, are within. Envy we must overcome by generosity and nobleness of soul; anger, by a reposed and easy mind; riot and drowsiness, by vigilance and temperance; lasciviousness, by our inviolable fidelity to those who are mistresses of our thoughts; and sloth, by our indefatigable peregrinations through the universe, to seek occasions of military as well as Christian honours. This, Sancho, is the road to lasting fame, and a good and honourable renown."

"I understand passing well every tittle you have said," answered Sancho; "but, pray now, sir, will you dissolve me of one doubt, that is just come into my head——"

"Resolve, thou wouldst say, Sancho," replied Don Quixote: "well, speak, and I will endeavour to satisfy thee."

"Why, then," quoth Sancho, "pray tell me these same Julys, and these Augusts, and all the rest of the famous knights you talk of that are dead, where are they now?"

"Without doubt," answered Don Quixote, "the heathens are in hell. The Christians, if their lives were answerable to their profession, are in heaven."

"So far so good," said Sancho; "but pray tell me, the tombs of these lordlings, have they any silver lamps still burning before them, and are their chapel walls hung about with crutches, winding-sheets, old periwigs, legs, and wax-eyes? or with what are they hung?"

"The monuments of the dead heathens," said Don Quixote, "were for the most part sumptuous pieces of architecture. The ashes of Julius Cæsar were deposited on the top of an obelisk, all of one stone of a prodigious bigness, which is now called Aguglia di San Pietro—St. Peter's Needle. The Emperor Adrian's sepulchre was a vast structure as big as an ordinary village, and called Moles Adriani, and now the castle of St. Angelo in Rome. Queen Artemisia buried her husband Mausolus in so curious and magnificent a pile, that his monument was reputed one of the seven wonders of the world. But none of these, nor any other of the heathen sepulchres, were adorned with any winding-sheets, or other offering, that might imply the persons interred were saints."

"Thus far we are right," quoth Sancho; "now, sir, pray tell me, which is the greatest wonder—to raise a dead man, or kill a giant?"

"The answer is obvious," said Don Quixote; "to raise a dead man, certainly."

"Then, master, I have nicked you," saith Sancho; "for he that raises the dead, makes the blind see, the lame walk, and the sick healthy, who has lamps burning night and day before his sepulchre, and whose chapel is full of pilgrims, who adore his relics on their knees—that man, I say, has more fame in this world and in the next than any of your heathenish emperors or knights-errant ever had, or will ever have."

"I grant it," said Don Quixote.

"Very good," quoth Sancho; "I will be with you anon. This fame, these gifts, these rights, privileges, and what do you call them, the bodies and relics of these saints have; so that by the consent and good liking of our holy mother, the Church, they have their lamps, their lights, their winding-sheets, their crutches, their pictures, their heads of hair, their legs, their eyes, and I know not what else, by which they stir up people's devotion, and spread their Christian fame. Kings will vouchsafe to carry the bodies of saints or their relics on their shoulders, they will kiss the pieces of their bones, and spare no cost to set off and deck their shrines and chapels."

"And what of all this?" said Don Quixote; "what is your inference?

"Why, truly, sir," quoth Sancho, "that we turn saints as fast as we can, and that is the readiest and cheapest way to get this same honour you talk of. It was but yesterday or the other day, or I cannot tell when—I am sure it was not long since—that two poor bare-footed friars were sainted; and you cannot think what a crowd of people there is to kiss the iron chains they wore about their waists instead of girdles, to humble the flesh. I dare say they are more reverenced than Orlando's sword, that hangs in the armoury of our sovereign lord the king, whom Heaven grant long to reign! So that for aught I see, better it is to be a friar, though but of a beggarly order, than a valiant errant-knight; and a dozen or two of sound lashes, well meant, and as well laid on, will obtain more of Heaven than two thousand thrusts with a lance, though they be given to giants, dragons, or hobgoblins."

"All this is very true," replied Don Quixote, "but all men cannot be friars; we have different parts allotted us, to mount to the high seat of eternal felicity. Chivalry is a religious order, and there are knights in the fraternity of saints in heaven."

"However," quoth Sancho, "I have heard say there are more friars there than knights-errant."

"That is," said Don Quixote, "because there is a greater number of friars than of knights."

"But are there not a great many knights-errant too?" said Sancho.

"There are many indeed," answered Don Quixote, "but very few that deserve the name."

In such discourses as these the knight and squire passed the night, and the whole succeeding day, without encountering any occasion to signalise themselves; at which Don Quixote was very much concerned. At last, towards evening the next day, they discovered the goodly city of Toboso, which revived the knight's spirits wonderfully, but had quite a contrary effect on his squire, because he did not know the house where Dulcinea lived, no more than his master. So that the one was mad till he saw her, and the other very melancholic and disturbed in mind, because he had never seen her; nor did he know what to do, should his master send him to Toboso. However, as Don Quixote would not make his entry in the day time, they spent the evening among some oaks not far distant from the place, till the prefixed moment came; then they entered the city, where they met with adventures indeed.

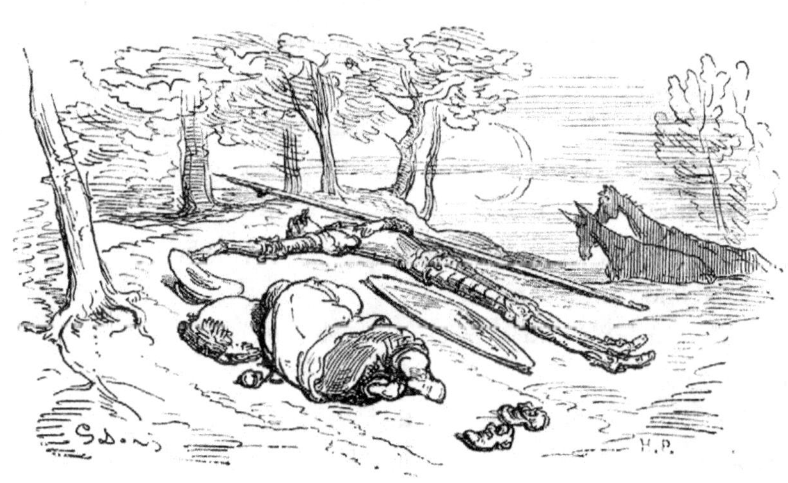

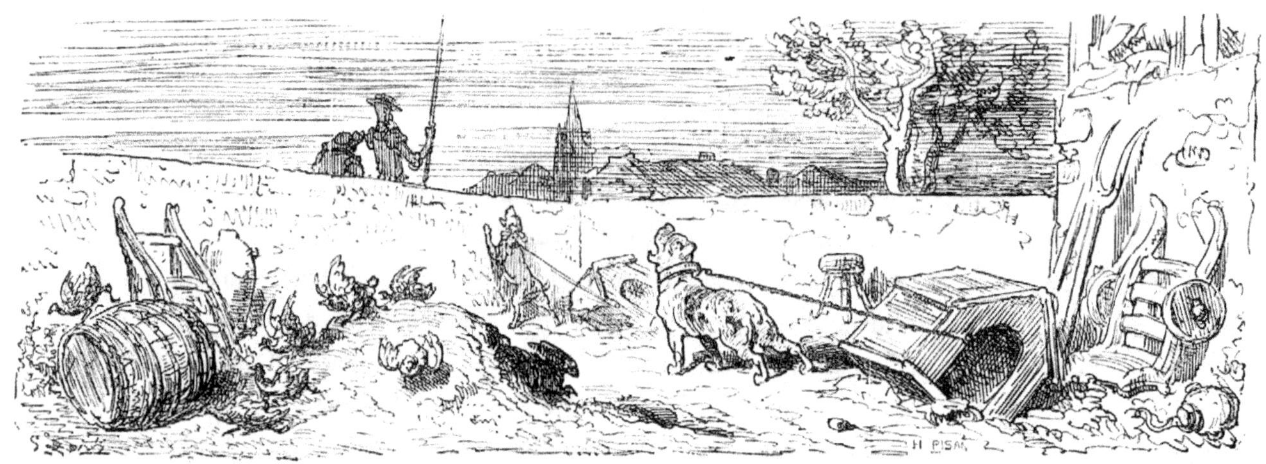

CHAPTER IX.

THAT GIVES AN ACCOUNT OF THINGS WHICH YOU WILL KNOW WHEN YOU READ IT.

THE sable night had spun out half her course, when Don Quixote and Sancho descended from a hill, and entered Toboso. A profound silence reigned over all the town, and all the inhabitants were fast asleep, and stretched out at their ease. The night was somewhat clear, though Sancho wished it dark, to hide his master's folly and his own. Nothing disturbed the general tranquillity, but now and then the barking of dogs, that wounded Don Quixote's ears, but more poor Sancho's heart. Sometimes an ass brayed, hogs grunted, cats mewed; which jarring mixture of sounds was not a little augmented by the stillness and serenity of the night, and filled the enamoured champion's head with a thousand inauspicious chimeras. However, turning to his squire, "My dear Sancho," said he, "show me the way to Dulcinea's palace; perhaps we shall find her still awake."

"Bless me," cried Sancho, "what palace do you mean? When I saw her highness, she was in a little paltry cot."

"Perhaps," replied the knight, "she was then retired into some corner of the palace, to divert herself in private with her damsels, as great ladies and princesses sometimes do."

"Well, sir," said Sancho, "although it must be a palace whether I will or no, yet can you think this a time of night to find the gates open, or a seasonable hour to thunder at the door, till we raise the house and alarm the whole town? Are we going to a lodging-house, think you, like your travellers, that can rap at a door any hour of the night, and knock people up when they list?"

"Let us once find the palace," said the knight, "and then I will tell thee what we ought to do. But stay! either my eyes delude me, or that lofty, gloomy structure which I discover yonder is Dulcinea's palace."

"Well, lead on, sir," said the squire; "and yet, though I were to see it with my eyes, and feel it with my ten fingers, I should believe it even as much as I believe it is now noon-day."

The knight led on, and having rode about two hundred paces, came at last to the building which he took for Dulcinea's palace, but found it to be the great church of the town.

"We are mistaken, Sancho," said he; "I find this is a church."

"I see it is," said the squire; "and I pray Heaven we have not found our graves; for it is a plaguy ill sign to haunt churchyards at this time of night, especially when I told you, if I am not mistaken, that this lady's house stands in a little blind alley, without any thoroughfare."

"A curse on thy distempered brain!" cried Don Quixote. "Where, blockhead, where didst thou ever see royal edifices and palaces built in a blind alley, without a thoroughfare?"

"Sir," said Sancho, "every country has its several fashions; and, for aught you know, they may build their great houses and palaces in blind alleys at Toboso: and therefore, good your worship, let me alone to hunt up and down in what by-lanes and alleys I may strike into—mayhap in some nook or corner we may light upon this same palace. Would any one had it for me, for leading us such a jaunt, and plaguing a body at this rate!"

"Sancho," said Don Quixote, "speak with greater respect of my mistress's concerns. Be merry and wise, and do not throw the helve after the hatchet."

"Cry mercy, sir," quoth Sancho; "but would it not make any mad, to have you put me upon finding readily our dame's house at all times, which I never saw but once in my life?—nay, and to find it at midnight, when you yourself cannot find it, that have seen it a thousand times!"

"Thou wilt make me desperately angry," said the knight. "Hark you, heretic! have I not repeated it a thousand times that I never saw the peerless Dulcinea, nor ever entered the portals of her palace; but that I am in love with her purely by hearsay, and upon the great fame of her beauty and rare accomplishments?"

"I hear you say so now," quoth Sancho; "and since you say you never saw her, I must needs tell you I never saw her either."

"That is impossible," said Don Quixote; "at least, you told me you saw her winnowing wheat, when you brought me an answer to the letter which I sent by you."

"That is neither here nor there, sir," replied Sancho; "for, to be plain with you, I saw her but by hearsay too, and the answer I brought you was by hearsay as well as the rest, and I know the Lady Dulcinea no more than the man in the moon."

"Sancho! Sancho!" said Don Quixote, "there is a time for all things; unseasonable mirth always turns to sorrow. What! because I declare that I have never seen nor spoken to the mistress of my soul, is it for you to trifle and say so too, when you are so sensible of the contrary?"

Here their discourse was interrupted, a fellow with two mules happening to pass by them; and, by the noise of the plough which they drew along, they guessed it might be some country labourer going out before day to his husbandry; and so, indeed, it was. He went singing the doleful ditty of the defeat of the French at Roncesvalles: "Ye Frenchmen! all must rue the woful day."

"Let me die," said Don Quixote, hearing what the fellow sung, "if we have any good success to-night. Dost thou hear what this peasant sings, Sancho?"

"Ay, marry do I," quoth the squire. "But what is the rout at Roncesvalles to us? it concerns us no more than if he had sung the ballad of 'Colly my Cow:' we shall speed neither the better nor the worse for it."

By this time, the ploughman being come up to them—"Good morrow, honest friend!" cried Don Quixote to him. "Pray, can you inform me which is the palace of the peerless princess, the Lady Dulcinea del Toboso?"

"Sir," said the fellow, "I am a stranger, and but lately come into this town; I am ploughman to a rich farmer. But here, right over against you, live the curate and the sexton; they are the likeliest to give you some account of that lady princess, as having a list of all the folks in town, though I fancy there is no princess at all lives here. There be, indeed, a power of gentle-folk, and each of them may be a princess in her own house for aught I know."

"Perhaps, friend," said Don Quixote, "we shall find the lady for whom I inquire among those."

"Why, truly, master," answered the ploughman, "as you say, such a thing may be, and so speed you well! 'Tis break of day." With that, switching his mules, he stayed for no more questions.

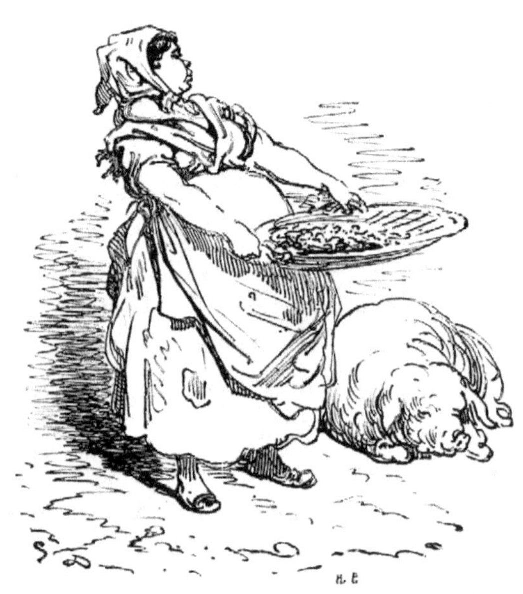

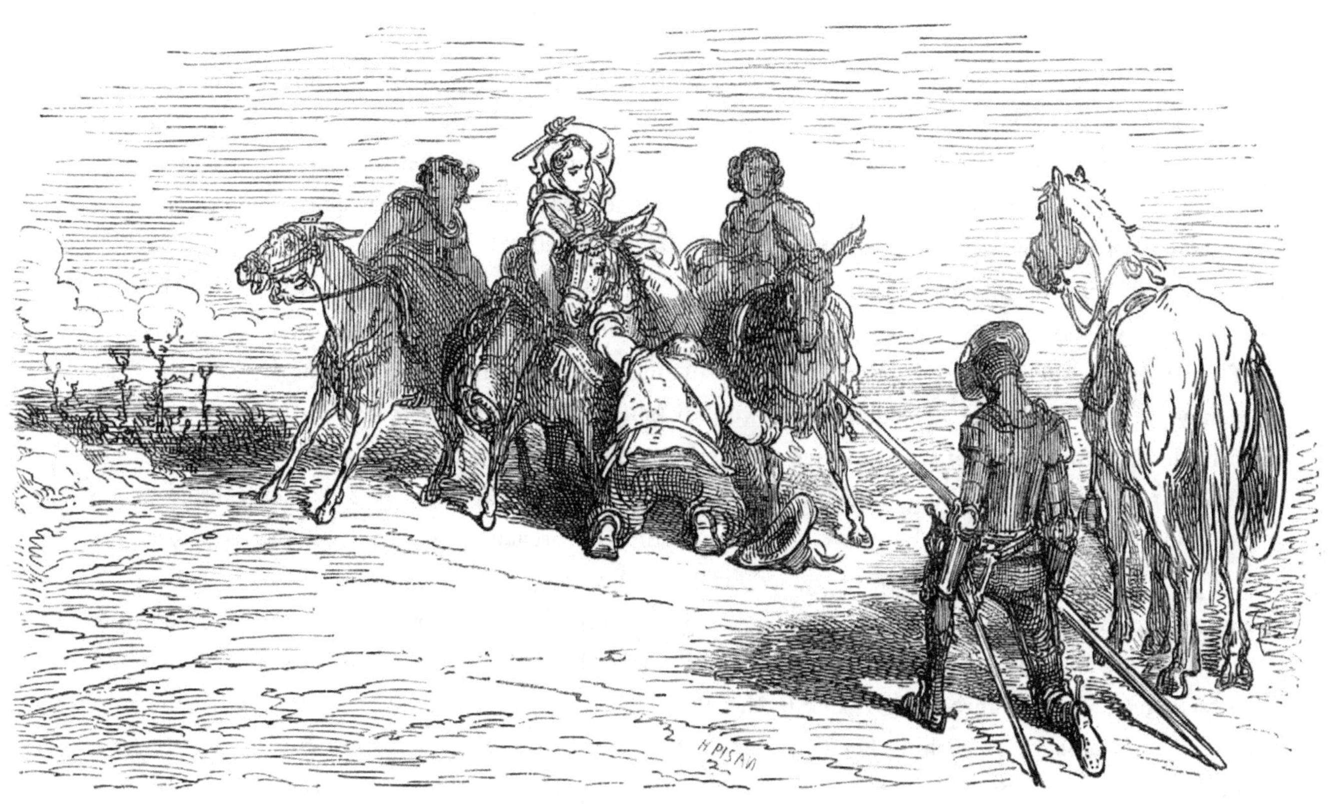

CHAPTER X.

HOW SANCHO CUNNINGLY FOUND OUT A WAY TO ENCHANT THE LADY DULCINEA, WITH OTHER PASSAGES NO LESS CERTAIN THAN RIDICULOUS.

SANCHO, perceiving his master in suspense and not very well satisfied, "Sir," said he, "the day comes on apace, and I think it will not be very handsome for us to stay to be stared at, and sit sunning ourselves in the street. We had better slip out of town again, and betake ourselves to some wood hard by, and then I will come back and search every hole and corner in town for this same house, castle, or palace of my lady's, and it will go hard if I do not find it out at long run; then will I talk to her highness, and tell her how you do, and how I left you hard by, waiting her orders and instructions about talking with her in private, without bringing her name in question."

"Dear Sancho," said the knight, "thou hast spoke and included a thousand sentences in the compass of a few words. I approve and lovingly accept thy advice. Come, my child; let us go and in some neighbouring grove find out a convenient retreat; then, as thou sayest, thou shalt return to seek, to see, and to deliver my embassy to my lady, from whose discretion and most courteous mind I hope for a thousand favours that may be counted more than wonderful."

Sancho sat upon thorns till he had got his master out of town, lest he should discover the falsehood of the account he brought him in Sierra Morena, of Dulcinea's answering his letter; so, hastening to be gone, they were presently got two miles from the town into a wood, where Don Quixote took covert, and Sancho was dispatched to Dulcinea, in which negotiation some accidents fell out that require new attention and a fresh belief.

The author of this important history being come to the matters which he relates in this chapter, says he would willingly have left them buried in oblivion, in a manner despairing of his reader's belief. For Don Quixote's madness flies here to so extravagant a pitch, that it may be said to have outstripped, by two bow-shots, all imaginable credulity. However, notwithstanding this mistrust, he has set down every particular, just as the same was transacted, without adding or diminishing the least atom of truth through the whole history, not valuing in the least such objections as may be raised to impeach him of breach of veracity—a proceeding which ought to be commended; for truth, indeed, rather alleviates than hurts, and will always bear up against falsehood, as oil does above water. And so, continuing his narration, he tells us that when Don Quixote was retired into the wood or forest, or rather into the grove of oaks near the Grand Toboso, he ordered Sancho to go back to the city, and not to return to his presence till he had an audience of his lady, beseeching her that it might please her to be seen by her captive knight, and vouchsafe to bestow her benediction on him, that by the virtue of that blessing he might hope for a prosperous event in all his onsets and perilous attempts and adventures. Sancho undertook the charge, engaging him as successful a return of this as of his former message.

"Go, then, child," said the knight, "and have a care of being daunted when thou approachest the beams of that refulgent sun of beauty. Happy thou, above all the squires of the universe! Observe and engrave in thy memory the manner of thy reception; mark whether her colour changes upon the delivery of thy commission; whether her looks betray any emotion or concern when she hears my name; whether she does not seem to sit on her cushion with a strange uneasiness, in case thou happenest to find her seated on the pompous throne of her authority. And if she be standing, mind whether she stands sometimes upon one leg, and sometimes on another; whether she repeats three or four times the answer which she gives thee, or changes it from kind to cruel, and then again from cruel to kind; whether she does not seem to adjust her hair, though every lock appears in perfect order. In short, observe all her actions, every motion, every gesture; for by the accurate relation which thou givest of these things, I shall divine the secrets of her breast, and draw just inferences in relation to my amour. Go, then, my trusty squire! thy own better stars, not mine, attend thee, and meet with a more prosperous event than that which in this doleful desert, tossed between hopes and fears, I dare expect."

"I will go, sir," quoth Sancho, "and I will be back in a trice: meanwhile cheer up, I beseech you; come, sir, comfort that little heart of yours, no bigger than a hazel-nut! Don't be cast down, I say; remember the old sayings, 'Faint heart never won fair lady;' 'Where there is no hook, to be sure there will hang no bacon;' 'The hare leaps out of the bush where we least look for her.' I speak this to give you to understand that though we could not find my lady's castle in the night, I may light on it when I least think on it now it is day; and when I have found it, let me alone to deal with her."

"Well, Sancho," said the knight, "thou hast a rare talent in applying thy proverbs; Heaven give thee better success in thy designs!"

This said, Sancho turned his back, and switching his Dapple, left the Don on horseback, leaning on his lance, and resting on his stirrups, full of melancholy and confused imaginations. Let us leave him too, to go along with Sancho, who was no less uneasy in his mind.

No sooner was he got out of the grove, but turning about, and perceiving his master quite out of sight, he dismounted, and laying himself down at the foot of a tree, thus began to hold a parley with himself.

"Friend Sancho," quoth he, "pray let me ask you whither your worship is a-going? Is it to seek some ass you have lost?" "No, by my troth." "What is it, then, thou art hunting after?" "Why, I am looking, you must know, for a thing of nothing, only a princess, and in her the sun of beauty, forsooth, and all heaven together." "Well, and where dost thou think to find all this, friend of mine?" "Where? why, in the great city of Toboso." "And pray, sir, who set you to work?" "Who set me to work? There is a question! Why, who but the most renowned Don Quixote de la Mancha? he that rights the wrong, that gives drink to the hungry, and meat to those that are dry." "Very good, sir; but pray dost know where she lives?" "Not I, indeed; but my master says it is somewhere in a king's palace or stately castle." "And hast thou ever seen her, trow?" "No, marry, han't I; why, my master himself never set eyes on her in his life." "But tell me, Sancho, what if the people of Toboso should know that you are come to inveigle their princesses, and make their ladies run astray, and should baste your carcase handsomely, and leave you never a sound rib—do you not think they would be mightily in the right on it?" "Why, troth, they would not be much in the wrong, though methinks they should consider, too, that I am but a servant, and sent on another body's errand, and so I am not at all in fault." "Nay, never trust to that, Sancho, for your people of La Mancha are plaguy hot and toucheous, and will endure no tricks to be put upon them: bless me! if they but touch thee, they will maul thee after a strange rate." "No, no; 'fore-warned, fore-armed.' Why do I go about to look for more feet than a cat has for another man's maggot? Besides, when all is done, I may perhaps as well look for a needle in a bottle of hay, or for a scholar at Salamanca, as for Dulcinea all over the town of Toboso. Well, it is mischief, and nothing else, that has put me upon this troublesome piece of work."

This was the dialogue Sancho had with himself; and the consequence of it was the following soliloquy: "Well, there is a remedy for all things but death, which will be sure to lay us flat one time or other. This master of mine, by a thousand tokens I have seen, is a downright madman, and I think I come within an inch of him; nay, I am the greatest cod's-head of the two to serve and follow him as I do, if the proverb be not a liar—'Show me thy company, I will tell thee

CC

what thou art;' and the other old saw, 'Birds of a feather flock together.' Now, then, my master being mad, and so very mad as to mistake sometimes one thing for another, black for white, and white for black—as when he took the windmills for giants, the friars' mules for dromedaries, and the flock of sheep for armies, and much more to the same tune—I guess it will be no hard matter to pass upon him the first country wench I shall meet with for the Lady Dulcinea. If he won't believe it, I will swear it; if he swear again, I will out-swear him; and if he be positive, I will be more positive than he, and stand to it, and outface him in it, come what will on it; so that when he finds I won't flinch, he will either resolve never to send me more of his sleeveless errands, seeing what a lame account I bring him, or he will think some one of those wicked wizards who, he says, owe him a grudge, has transmogrified her into some other shape out of spite."

This happy contrivance helped to compose Sancho's mind, and now he looked on his grand affair to be as good as done. Having, therefore, stayed till the evening, that his master might think he had employed so much time in going and coming, things fell out very luckily for him; for as he arose to mount his Dapple, he spied three country wenches coming towards him from Toboso, upon three young asses; whether male or female, the author has left undetermined, though we may reasonably suppose they were she asses, such being most frequently used to ride on by country lasses in those parts. But this being no very material circumstance, we need not dwell any longer upon the decision of that point. It is sufficient they were asses, and discovered by Sancho; who thereupon made all the haste he could to get to his master, and found him breathing out a thousand sighs and amorous lamentations.

"Well, my Sancho!" said the knight, immediately upon his approach, "what news? are we to mark this day with a white or a black stone?"

"Even mark it rather with red ochre," answered Sancho, "as they do church chairs, that everybody may know who they belong to."

"Why, then," said Don Quixote, "I suppose thou bringest good news."

"Ay, marry do I," quoth Sancho; "you have no more to do but to clap spurs to Rozinante, and get into the open fields, and you will see my Lady Dulcinea del Toboso, with a brace of her damsels, coming to see your worship."

"Blessed heavens!" cried Don Quixote, "what art thou saying, my dear Sancho? Take heed, and do not presume to beguile my real grief with a delusive joy."

"Bless me, sir!" said Sancho, "what should I get by putting a trick upon you, and being found out the next moment? Seeing is believing, all the world over. Come, sir! put on, put on, and you will see our lady princess coming, dressed up and bedecked like her own sweet self indeed. Her damsels and she are all one spark of gold; all pearls, all diamonds, all rubies, all cloth of gold above ten inches high; their hair spread over their shoulders like so many sunbeams, and dangling and dancing in the wind; and what is more, they ride upon three gambling hags; there is not a piece of horseflesh can match them in three kingdoms."

"Ambling nags, thou meanest, Sancho," said Don Quixote.

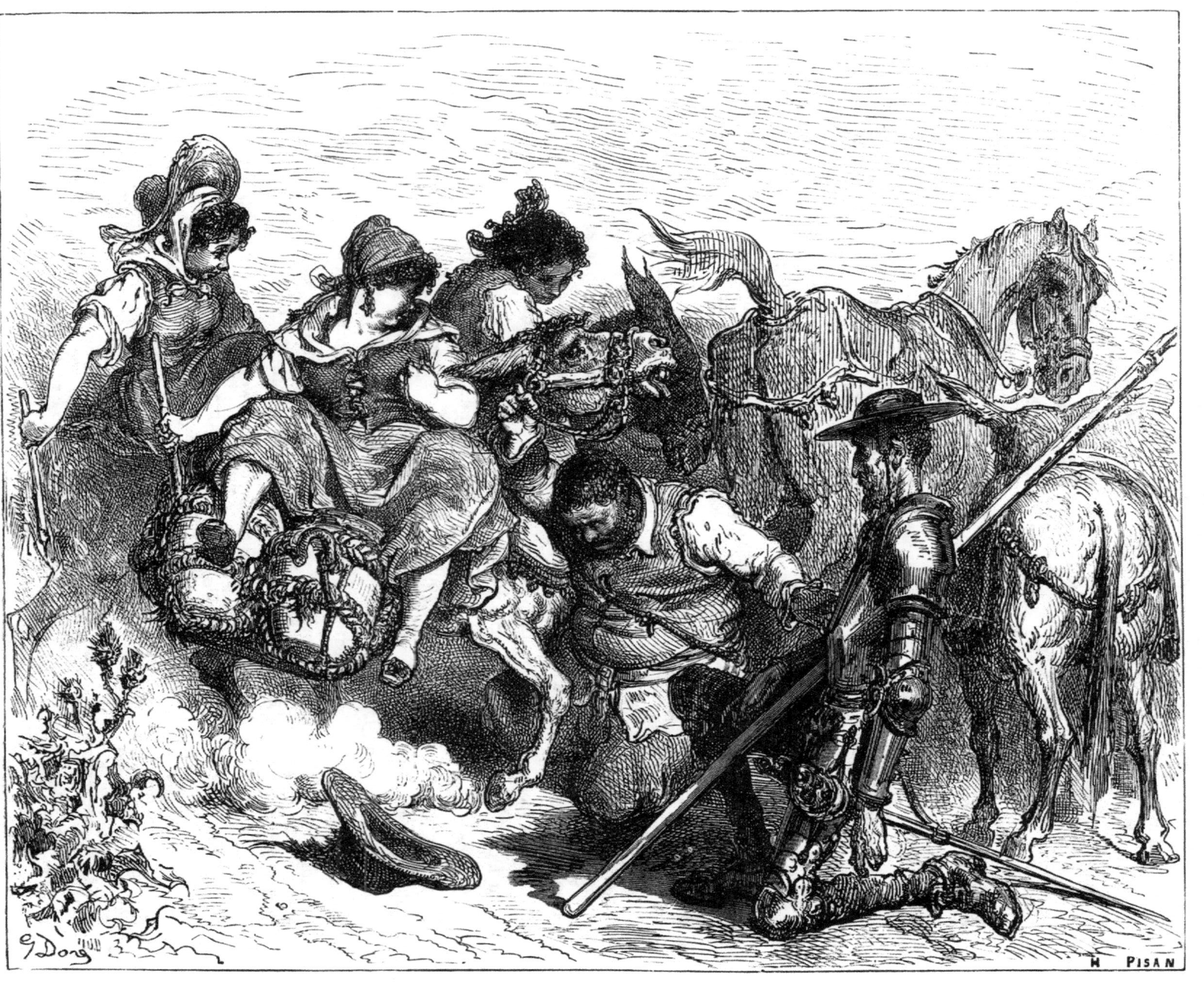

"Don Quixote gazed with dubious and disconsolate eyes on the creature whom Sancho called queen and lady."

"Gambling hags, or ambling nags," quoth Sancho, "there is no such difference methinks; but be they what they will, I am sure I never set eyes on finer creatures than those that ride upon their backs, especially my lady Dulcinea; it would make one swoon away but to look upon her."

"Let us move, then, my Sancho," said Don Quixote, "and as a gratification for these unexpected happy tidings, I freely bestow on thee the best spoils the next adventure we meet with shall afford; and if that content thee not, take the colts which my three mares thou knowest of are now ready to foal on our town common."

"Thank you for the colts," said Sancho; "but as for the spoils, I am not sure they will be worth anything."

They were now got out of the wood, and discovered the three country lasses at a small distance. Don Quixote casting his eyes toward Toboso, and seeing nobody on the road but the three wenches, was strangely troubled in mind; and turning to Sancho, asked him whether the princess and her damsels were come out of the city when he left them.

"Out of the city!" cried Sancho; "why, where are your eyes? are they in your heels, in the name of wonder, that you cannot see them coming towards us, shining as bright as the sun at noon-day?"

"I see nothing," returned Don Quixote, "but three wenches upon as many asses."

"Now heaven deliver me from all evil!" quoth Sancho. "Is it possible your worship should mistake three what d'ye-call-ems—three ambling nags, I mean, as white as driven snow, for three ragged ass colts? I will even pull off my beard by the roots an't be so."

"Take it from me, friend Sancho," said the knight; they are either he or she asses, as sure as I am Don Quixote and thou Sancho Panza; at least, they appear to be such."

"Come, sir," quoth the squire, "do not talk at that rate, but snuff your eyes, and go pay your homage to the mistress of your soul, for she is near at hand." And so saying, Sancho hastens up to the three country wenches; and, alighting from Dapple, took hold of one of the asses by the halter, and falling on his knees, "Queen and princess, and duchess of beauty! an't please your haughtiness and greatness," quoth he, "vouchsafe to take into your good grace and liking yonder knight, your prisoner and captive, who is turned of a sudden into cold marble stone, and struck all of a heap, to see himself before your high and mightiness. I am Sancho Panza, his squire, and he himself the wandering, weather-beaten knight, Don Quixote de la Mancha, otherwise called the Knight of the Woful figure."

By this time, Don Quixote, having placed himself down on his knees by Sancho, gazed with dubious and disconsolate eyes on the creature whom Sancho called queen and lady; and, perceiving her to be no more than a plain country wench, so far from being well-favoured that she was blubber-cheeked and flat-nosed, he was lost in astonishment, and could not utter one word. On the other side, the wenches were no less surprised to see themselves stopped by two men in such different outsides, and on their knees. But at last, she whose ass was held by Sancho took courage, and broke silence in an angry tone.

"Come," cried she, "get out of our way, and let us go about our business, for we are in haste."

"Oh, princess, and universal Lady of Toboso!" answered Sancho, "why does not that great heart of yours melt to see the post and pillar of knight-errantry fall down before your high and mighty presence?"

"Heyday!" quoth another of the females, hearing this, "what is here to do? Look how your small gentry come to jeer and flout poor country girls, as if we could not give them as good as they bring. Go, get about your business, and let us go about ours, and speed you well!"

"Rise, Sancho," said Don Quixote, hearing this, "for I am now convinced that my malicious stars, not yet satisfied with my past misfortunes, still shed their baleful influence, and have barred all the passages that could convey relief to my miserable soul in this frail habitation of animated clay. Oh, thou extremity of all that is valuable, masterpiece of all human perfection, and only comfort of this afflicted heart, thy adorer, though now a spiteful enchanter persecutes me and fascinates my sight, hiding with mists and cataracts from me, and me alone, those peerless beauties under the foul disguise of rustic deformity, if he has not transformed thy faithful knight into some ugly shape, to make me loathsome to thy sight, look on me with a smiling, loving eye; and in the submission and genuflection which I pay to thy beauty, even under the fatal cloud that obscures it, read the humility with which my soul adores thee."

"Tittle-tattle!" quoth the country wench; "spare your breath to cool your porridge, and rid me of your idle gibberish. Get you on, sir, and let us go; and we shall think it a kindness."

This said, Sancho made way for her, and let her pass, overjoyed his plot had succeeded so well. The imaginary Dulcinea was no sooner at liberty, but punching her ass with the end of a staff which she had in her hand, she began to scour along the plain; but the angry beast, not being used to such smart instigations, fell a-kicking and wincing at such a rate, that down came my Lady Dulcinea. Presently, Don Quixote ran to help her up, and Sancho to re-settle and gird her pack-saddle, that hung under the ass's belly; which being done, the knight, very courteously, was going to take his enchanted mistress in his arms, to set her on her saddle; but she, being now got on her legs, took a run, and clapping her hands upon the ass's crupper, at one jump leaped into her pannel as swift as a hawk, and there she sat.

"Well, I declare!" quoth Sancho, "our lady mistress is as nimble as an eel. Let me be hanged if I don't think she might teach the best jockey in Cordova or Mexico to mount on horseback. At one jump she was vaulted into the saddle, and, without spurs, makes her nag smoke it away like a greyhound! her damsels are notable whipsters too; they don't come much short of her, for they fly like the wind."

Indeed, he said true, for when Dulcinea was once mounted, they both made after her full speed, without so much as looking behind them for above half a league.

Don Quixote followed them, as far as he could, with his eyes; and when they were quite out of sight, turning to his squire, "Now, Sancho," said he, "what thinkest thou of this matter?

Are not these base enchanters inexorable? How extensive is their spite, thus to deprive me of the happiness of seeing the object of my wishes in her natural shape and glory! Sure, I was doomed to be an example of misfortunes, and the mark against which those caitiffs are employed to shoot all the arrows of their hatred. But tell me, Sancho, that saddle, which appeared to me to be the pannel of an ass, was it a pillion or side saddle?"

"It was a pad saddle," answered Sancho, "with a field covering, and so rich that it might purchase half a kingdom."

"And could not I see all this?" cried Don Quixote. "Well, I have said it, and must repeat it a thousand times: I am the most unfortunate man in the universe."

The cunning rogue of a squire, hearing his master talk at that rate, could hardly keep his countenance and refrain from laughing, to see how admirably he had fooled him. At last, after a great deal of discourse of the same nature, they both mounted again, and took the road for Saragosa, designing to be present at the most celebrated festivals and sports that are solemnised every year in that noble city. But they met with many accidents by the way, and those so extraordinary, and worthy the reader's information, that they must not be passed over unrecorded nor unread, as shall appear from what follows.

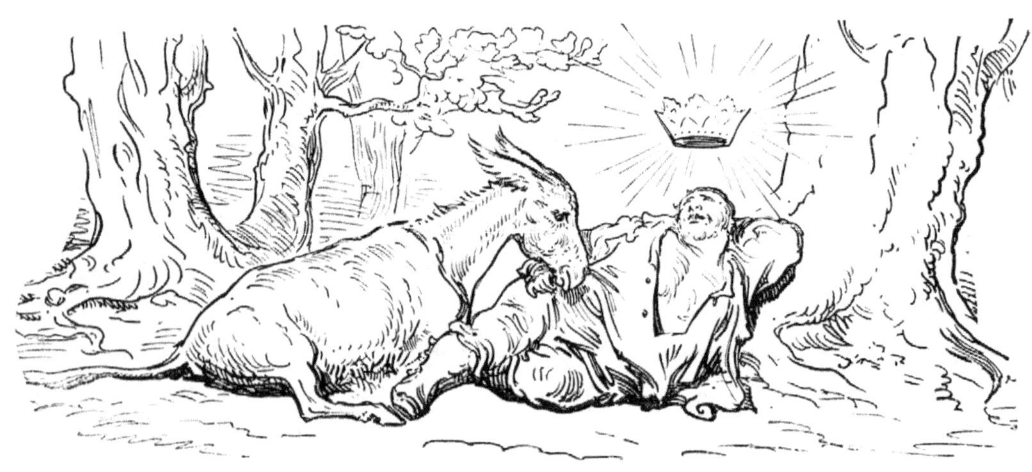

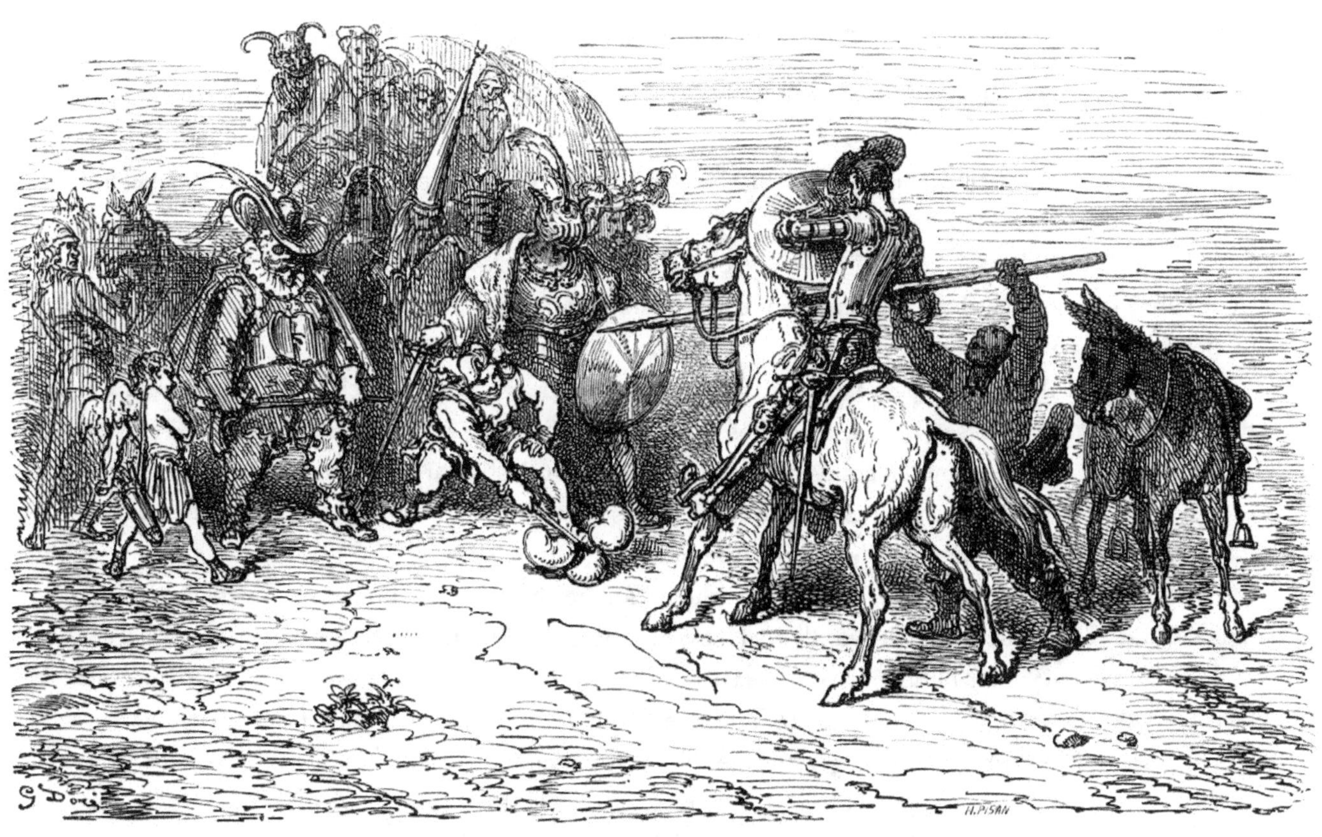

CHAPTER XI.

OF THE STUPENDOUS ADVENTURE THAT BEFELL THE VALOROUS DON QUIXOTE, WITH THE CHARIOT OR CART OF THE COURT OR PARLIAMENT OF DEATH.

DON QUIXOTE rode on very melancholic; the malice of the magicians, in transforming his Lady Dulcinea, perplexed him strangely, and set his thoughts upon the rack how to dissolve the enchantment, and restore her to her former beauty. In this disconsolate condition, he went on abandoned to distraction, carelessly giving Rozinante the reins; and the horse, finding himself at liberty, and tempted by the goodness of the grass, took the opportunity to feed very heartily; which Sancho perceiving, "Sir," said he, rousing him from his waking dream, "sorrow was never designed for beasts, but men; but yet, let me tell you, if men give way to it too much, they make beasts of themselves. Come, sir, awake, awake by any means! pull up the reins, and ride like a man; cheer up, and show yourself a knight-errant. What is it that ails you? Was ever a man so moped? 'Are we here, or are we in France?' as the saying is. Let all the Dulcineas in the world be doomed to poverty, rather than one single knight-errant be cast down at this rate."

"Hold, Sancho!" cried Don Quixote, with more spirit than one would have expected "hold, I say! not a detracting word against that beauteous enchanted lady; for all her mis fortunes are chargeable on the unhappy Don Quixote, and flow from the envy which those necromancers bear to me."

"So say I, sir," replied the squire; "for would it not vex any one that had seen her before to see her now. as you saw her?"

"Ah! Sancho," said the knight, "thy eyes were blessed with a view of her perfections in their entire lustre; thou hast reason to say so. Against me—against my eyes only—is the malice of her transformation directed. But now I think on it, Sancho, thy description of her beauty was a little absurd in that particular of comparing her eyes to pearls. Sure, such eyes are more like those of a whiting or a sea-bream, than those of a fair lady; and in my opinion, Dulcinea's eyes are rather like two verdant emeralds, railed in with two celestial arches, which signify her eyebrows. Therefore, Sancho, you must take your pearls from her eyes, and apply them to her teeth, for I verily believe you mistook the one for the other."

"Troth, sir, it might be so," replied Sancho; "for her beauty confounded me as much as her ugliness did you. But let us leave all to Heaven, that knows all things that befall us in this vale of misery—this wicked, troublesome world, where we can be sure of nothing without some spice of knavery or imposture. In the meantime, there is a thing comes into my head that puzzles me plaguily. Pray, sir, when you get the better of any giant or knight, and send them to pay homage to the beauty of your lady and mistress, how will the poor knight or giant be able to find this same Dulcinea? I cannot but think how they will have to seek, how they will saunter about, gaping and staring all over Toboso town; and if they should meet her full butt in the middle of the king's highway, yet they will know her no more than they can know my father."

"Perhaps, Sancho," answered Don Quixote, "the force of her enchantment does not extend so far as to debar vanquished knights and giants from the privilege of seeing her in her unclouded beauties. I will try the experiment on the first I conquer, and will command them to return immediately to me, to inform me of their success."

"I like what you say main well," quoth Sancho; "we may chance to find out the truth by this means: and if so be my lady is only hid from your worship, she has not so much reason to complain as you may have. But when all comes to all, so our mistress be safe and sound, let us make the best of a bad market, and even go seek adventures. The rest we will leave to time, which is the best doctor in such cases—nay, in worse diseases."

Don Quixote was going to return an answer, but was interrupted by a cart that was crossing the road. He that drove it was a hideous being, and the cart being open, without either tilt or boughs, exposed a number of the most surprising and different shapes imaginable. The first figure that appeared to Don Quixote was no less than Death itself, though with a human countenance. On the one side of Death stood an angel, with large wings of different colours; on the other side was placed an emperor, with a crown that seemed to be of gold; at the feet of Death lay Cupid, with his bow, quiver, and arrows, but not blindfold. Next to these a knight appeared, completely armed except his head; on which, instead of a helmet, he wore a hat, whereon was mounted a large plume of party-coloured feathers. There were also several other persons in strange and various dresses. This strange appearance at first somewhat surprised Don Quixote, and frighted the poor squire out of his wits; but presently the knight cleared up on second thoughts, imagining it some rare and hazardous adventure that called on his courage. Pleased with his conceit, and armed with a resolution able to confront any danger, he placed himself in the middle of the road, and with a loud and menacing voice, "You carter, coachman, or whatever you be," cried he, "let me know immediately whence you come, and whither you go, and what strange figures are those which load that carriage, which, by the freight, rather seems to be Charon's boat than any terrestrial vehicle."

"Sir," answered the man very civilly, stopping his cart, "we are strolling players, that belong to Angulo's company, and it being Corpus-Christi tide, we have this morning acted a tragedy, called *The Parliament of Death,* in a town yonder behind the mountain, and this afternoon we are to play it again in the town you see before us; which being so near, we travel to it in the same clothes we act in, to save the trouble of new dressing ourselves. That young man plays Death; that other an angel; this woman, sir, plays the queen; there is one acts a soldier; he next to him an emperor; and I myself play the evil one: and you must know, that is the best part in the play. If you desire to be satisfied in anything else, I will resolve you."

"Now, by the faith of my function," said Don Quixote, "I find we ought not to give credit to appearances, before we have made the experiment of feeling them; for at the discovery of such a scene, I would have sworn some strange adventure had been approaching. I wish you well, good people. Drive on to act your play, and if I can be serviceable to you in any particular, believe me ready to assist you with all my heart; for in my very childhood I loved shows, and have been a great admirer of dramatic representations from my youthful days."

During this friendly conversation, it unluckily fell out that one of the company, antiquely dressed, being the fool of the play, came up frisking with his morrice bells, and three full-blown cows' bladders fastened to the end of a stick. In this odd appearance he began to flourish his stick in the air, and bounce his bladders against the ground just at Rozinante's nose. The jingling of the bells and the rattling noise of the bladders so startled and affrighted the quiet creature, that Don Quixote could not hold him in; and having got the curb betwixt his teeth, away the horse hurried his unwilling rider up and down the plain, with more swiftness than his feeble bones seemed to promise. Sancho, considering the danger of his master's being thrown, presently alighted, and ran as fast as he could to his assistance; but before he could come up to him, Rozinante had made a false step, and laid his master and himself on the ground, which was, indeed, the common end of Rozinante's mad tricks and presumptuous racing. On the other side, the fool no sooner saw Sancho slide off to help his master, but he leaped upon poor Dapple, and rattling his bladders over the terrified animal's head, made him fly through the field towards the town where they were to play.

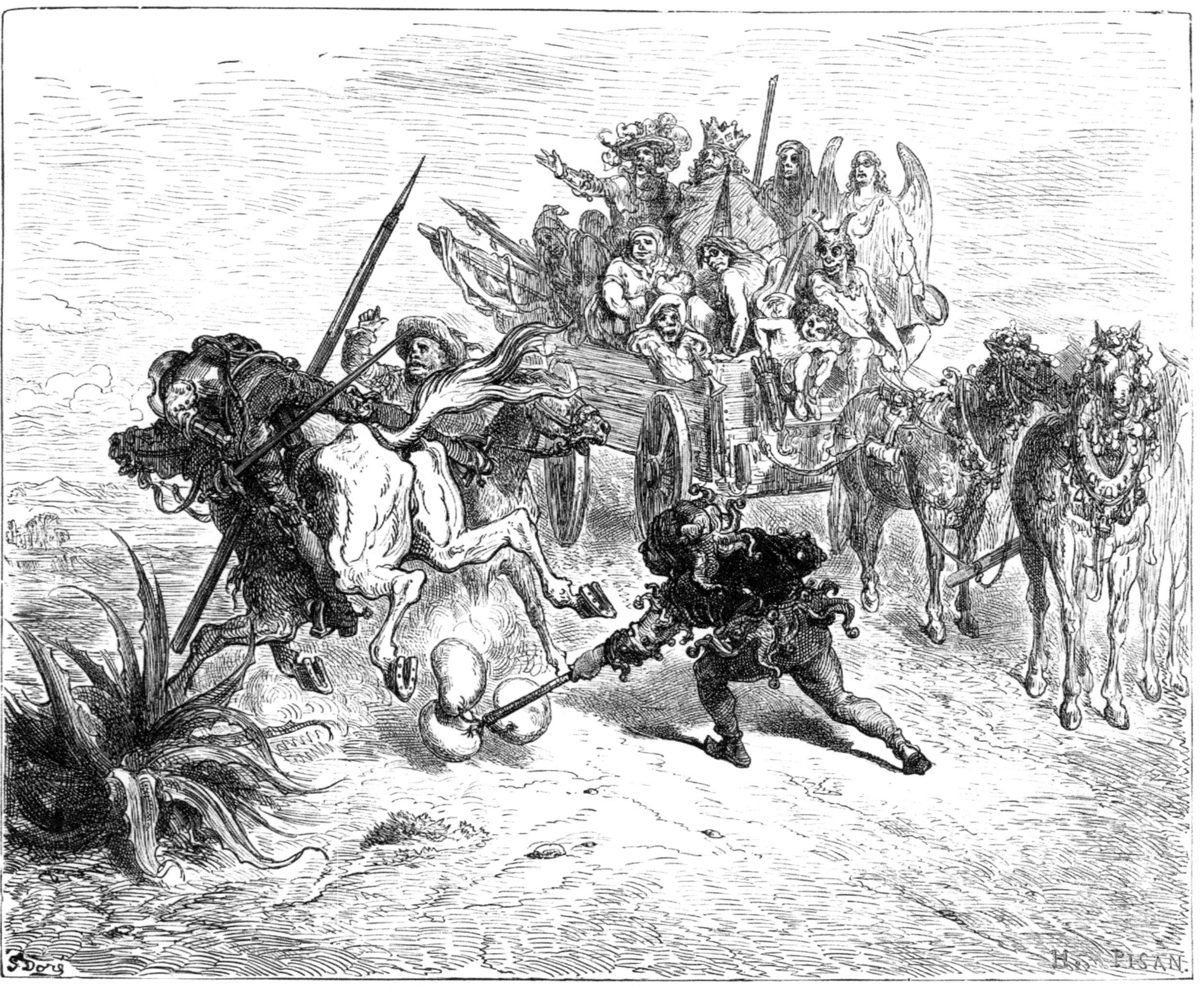

"The fool of the play came up frisking with his morrice bells."

Sancho beheld his master's fall and his ass's flight at the same time, and stood strangely divided in himself, not knowing which to assist first, his master or his beast. At length, the duty of a good servant and a faithful squire prevailing, he ran to his master, though every obstreperous bounce with the bladders upon Dapple's hind-quarters struck him to the very soul, and he could have wished every blow upon his own eye-balls rather than on the least hair of his ass's tail. In this agony of spirits he came to Don Quixote, whom he found in far worse circumstances than the poor knight could have wished; and helping him to re-mount, "Oh, sir!" cried he, "the fool is run away with Dapple."

"What fool?" asked Don Quixote.

"The one with the bladders," answered Sancho.

"No matter," said Don Quixote; "I will force the traitor to restore him, though he were to lock him up in the most profound and gloomy caverns of earth. Follow me, Sancho; we may easily overtake the wagon, and the mules shall atone for the loss of the ass."

"You need not be in such haste now," quoth Sancho, "for I perceive the fool has left Dapple already, and is gone his ways."

What Sancho said was true, for both ass and man tumbled for company, in imitation of Don Quixote and Rozinante; and Dapple, having left his new rider to walk on foot to the town, now came himself running back to his master.

"All this," said Don Quixote, "shall not hinder me from revenging the affront put upon us by that unmannerly fellow, at the expense of some of his companions, though it were the emperor himself."

"Oh, good your worship!" cried Sancho; "never mind it. I beseech you take my counsel, sir: never meddle with players, there is never anything to be got by it; they are a sort of people that always find many friends. I have known one of them taken up for two murders, yet escape the gallows. You must know that, as they are a parcel of merry wags, and make sport wherever they come, everybody is fond of them, and is ready to stand their friend, especially if they be the king's players, or some of the noted gangs, who go at such a tearing rate that one might mistake some of them for gentlemen or lords."

"I care not," said Don Quixote; "though all mankind unite to assist them, that buffooning fellow shall never escape unpunished, to make his boast that he has affronted me." Whereupon, riding up to the wagon, which was now got pretty near the town, "Hold, hold!" he cried; "stay, my pretty sparks! I will teach you to be civil to the beast that is entrusted with the honourable burden of a squire to a knight-errant."

This loud salutation having reached the ears of the strolling company, though at a good distance, they presently understood what it imported; and resolving to be ready to entertain him, Death presently leaped out of the cart; the emperor, the driver, and the angel immediately followed; and even the queen and the god Cupid, as well as the rest, having taken up their share of flints, stood ranged in battle array, ready to receive their enemy as soon as he should come within stone-cast. Don Quixote, seeing them drawn up in such excellent order, with their arms lifted up and ready to let fly at him a furious volley of shot, made a halt to consider in what quarter he might attack this dreadful battalion with least danger to his person.

Thus pausing, Sancho overtook him, and seeing him ready to charge, "For goodness' sake, sir," cried he, "what d'ye mean? Are you mad, sir? There is no fence against the players' bullets, unless you could fight with a brazen bell over you. Is it not rather rashness than true courage, think you, for one man to offer to set upon a whole army? where Death is too, and where emperors fight in person—nay, and where good and bad angels are against you? But if all this weighs nothing with you, consider, I beseech you, that though they seem to be kings, princes, and emperors, yet there is not so much as one knight-errant among them all."

"Now thou hast hit upon the only point," said Don Quixote, "that could stop the fury of my arm; for, indeed, as I have often told thee, Sancho, I am bound up from drawing my sword against any below the order of knighthood. It is thy business to fight in this cause, if thou hast a just resentment of the indignities offered to thy ass; and I from this post will encourage and assist thee with salutary orders and instructions."

"No, I thank you, sir," quoth Sancho; "I hate revenge. A true Christian must forgive and forget; and as for Dapple, I don't doubt but to find him willing to leave the matter to me, and stand to my verdict in the case, which is to live peaceably and quietly as long as Heaven is pleased to let me."

"Nay, then," said Don Quixote, "if that be thy resolution, good Sancho, prudent Sancho, Christian Sancho, downright Sancho, let us leave these idle apparitions, and proceed in search of more substantial and honourable adventures, of which, in all probability, this part of the world will afford us a wonderful variety."

So saying, he wheeled off, and Sancho followed him. On the other side, Death, with all his flying squadron, returned to their cart and went on their journey.

Thus ended the most dreadful adventure of the chariot of Death, much more happily than could have been expected, thanks to the laudable counsels which Sancho Panza gave his master, who, the day following, had another adventure no less remarkable, with one that was a knight-errant and a lover too.

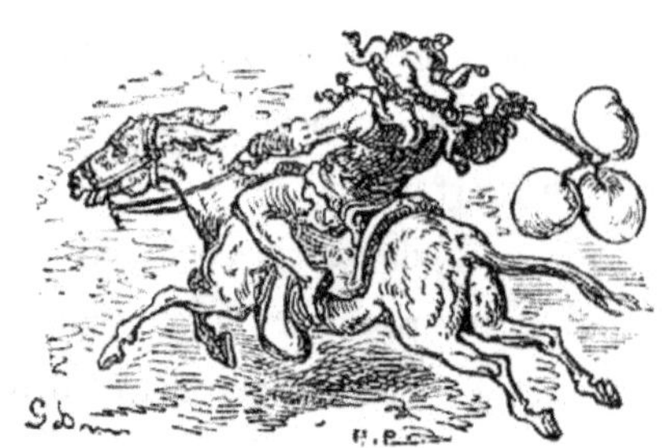

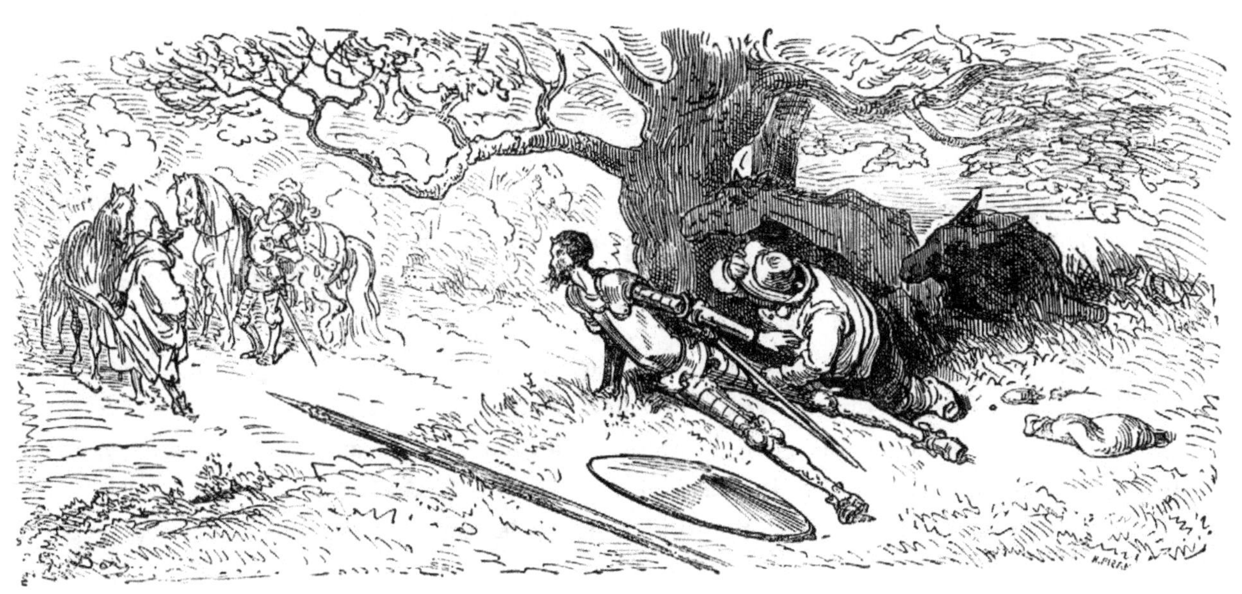

CHAPTER XII.

THE VALOROUS DON QUIXOTE'S STRANGE ADVENTURE WITH THE BOLD KNIGHT OF THE MIRRORS.

DON QUIXOTE passed the night that succeeded his encounter with Death under the covert of some lofty trees; where, at Sancho's persuasion, he refreshed himself with some of the provisions which Dapple carried. As they were at supper, "Well, sir," quoth the squire, "what a rare fool I had been, had I chosen for my good news the spoils of your first venture, instead of the breed of the three mares! Troth! commend me to the saying, 'A bird in hand is worth two in the bush.'"

"However," answered Don Quixote, "hadst thou let me fall on, as I would have done, thou mightest have shared at least the emperor's golden crown, and Cupid's painted wings; for I would have plucked them off, and put them into thy power."

"Ah! but," said Sancho, "your strolling emperors' crowns and sceptres are not of pure gold, but tinsel and copper."

"I grant it," said Don Quixote; "nor is it fit the decorations of the stage should be real, but rather imitations, and the resemblance of realities, as the plays themselves must be; which, by the way, I would have you love and esteem, Sancho, and consequently those that write and also those that act them; for they are all instrumental to the good of the commonwealth, and set before our eyes those looking-glasses that reflect a lively representation of human life—nothing being able to give us a more just idea of Nature, and what we are or ought to be, than comedians and comedies. Prithee tell me, hast thou never seen a play acted, where kings, emperors, prelates, knights, ladies, and other characters are introduced on the stage? One acts a ruffian, another a soldier; this man a cheat, and that a merchant; one plays a designing fool, and another a foolish lover: but the play done, and the actors undressed, they are all equal, and as they were before."

"All this I have seen," quoth Sancho.

"Just such a comedy," said Don Quixote, "is acted on the great stage of the world, where some play the emperors, others the prelates, and, in short, all the parts that can be brought into a dramatic piece; till death, which is the catastrophe and end of the action, strips the actors of all their marks of distinction, and levels their quality in the grave."

"A rare comparison," quoth Sancho, "though not so new but that I have heard it over and over. Just such another is that of a game at chess, where, while the play lasts, every piece has its particular office; but when the game is over, they are all mingled and huddled together, and clapped into a bag, just as, when life is ended, we are laid in the grave."

"Truly, Sancho," said Don Quixote, "thy simplicity lessens, and thy sense improves every day."

"And good reason why," quoth Sancho; "some of your worship's wit must needs stick to me; for your dry, unkindly land, with good dunging and tilling, will in time yield a good crop. I mean, sir, that your conversation being thrown on the barren ground of my wit, together with the time I have served your worship and kept you company, which is, as a body may say, the tillage, I must needs bring forth blessed fruit at last, so as not to shame my master, but keep in the paths of good manners, which you have beaten into my sodden understanding."

Sancho's affected style made Don Quixote laugh, though he thought his words true in the main; and he could not but admire his improvement. But the fellow never discovered his weakness so much as by endeavouring to hide it, being most apt to tumble when he strove to soar too high. His excellence lay chiefly in a knack of drawing proverbs into his discourse, whether to the purpose or not, as any one that has observed his manner of speaking in this history must have perceived.

In such discourses they passed a great part of the night, till Sancho wanted to drop the portcullices of his eyes, which was his way of saying he had a mind to go to sleep. Thereupon he unharnessed Dapple, and set him grazing; but Rozinante was condemned to stand saddled all night, by his master's injunction and prescription, used of old by all knights-errant, who never unsaddled their steeds in the field, but took off their bridles and hung them at the pummel of the saddle. However, he was not forsaken by faithful Dapple, whose friendship was so unparalleled and inviolable, that unquestioned tradition has handed it down from father to son that the author of this true history composed particular chapters of the united affection of these two beasts, though, to preserve the decorum due to so heroic a history, he would not insert them in the work. Yet sometimes he cannot forbear giving us some new touches on that subject; as when he writes that the two friendly creatures took a mighty pleasure in being together, to scrub and lick one another; and when they had had enough of that sport, Rozinante would gently lean his head at

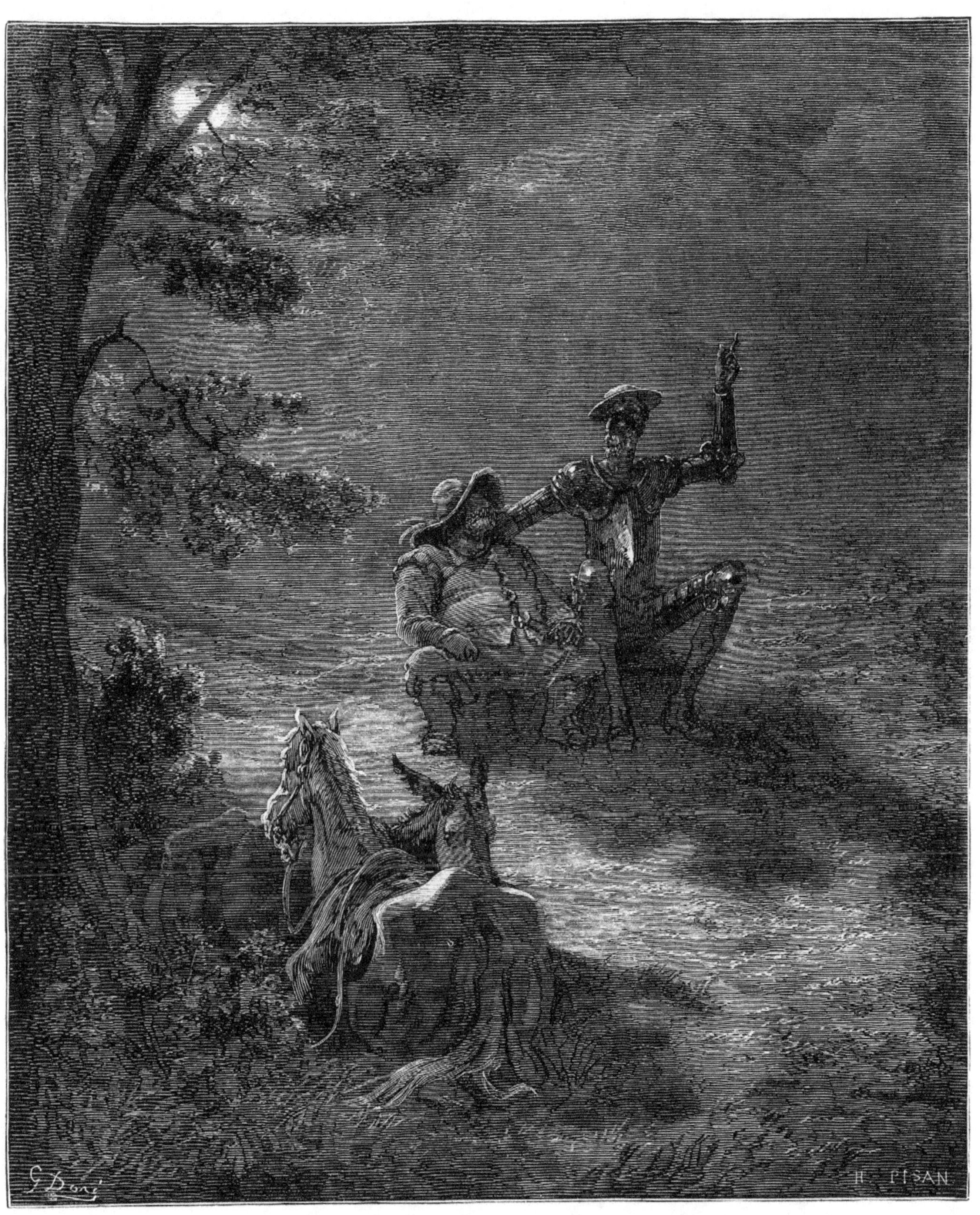

"In such discourses they passed a great part of the night,"

least half a yard over Dapple's neck, and so they would stand very lovingly together, looking wistfully on the ground for some time, unless somebody made them leave that contemplative posture, or hunger compelled them to a separation. Nay, I cannot pass by what is reported of the author, how he left in writing that he had compared their friendship to that of Nisus and Euryalus, and that of Pylades and Orestes, which, if it were so, deserves universal admiration; the sincere affection of these quiet animals being a just reflection on men, who are so guilty of breaking their friendship to one another. From hence came the sayings, "There is no friend, all friendship is gone;" "Now men hug, then fight anon;" and that other, "Where you see your friend, trust to yourself." Neither should the world take it ill that the cordial affection of these animals was compared by our author to that of men, since many important principles of prudence and morality have been learnt from irrational creatures. The crane gave mankind an example of vigilance; the ant, of providence; the elephant, of honesty; and the horse, of loyalty.

At last, Sancho fell asleep at the root of a cork-tree, and his master went to slumber under a spacious oak. But it was not long ere he was disturbed by a noise behind him, and starting up he looked and hearkened on the side whence he thought the voice came, and discovered two men on horseback, one of whom, letting himself carelessly slide down from the saddle, and calling to the other—"Alight, friend," said he, "and unbridle your horse, for methinks this place will supply them plentifully with pasture, and me with silence and solitude to indulge my amorous thoughts."

While he said this, he laid himself down on the grass; in doing which, the armour he had on made a noise—a sure sign—that gave Don Quixote to understand he was some knight-errant. Thereupon going to Sancho, who slept on, he plucked him by the arm, and having waked him with much ado—"Friend Sancho," said he, whispering him in his ear, "here is an adventure."

"Heaven grant it be a good one!" quoth Sancho. "But where is that same lady adventure's worship?"

"Where! dost thou ask, Sancho? why, turn thy head, man, and look yonder. Dost thou not see a knight-errant there lying on the ground? I have reason to think he is in melancholy circumstances, for I saw him fling himself off from his horse, and stretch himself on the ground in a disconsolate manner, and his armour clashed as he fell."

"What of all that?" quoth Sancho. "How do you make this to be an adventure?"

"I will not yet affirm," answered Don Quixote, "that it is an adventure; but a very fair rise to one as ever was seen. But, hark! he is tuning some instrument, and by his coughing and spitting he is clearing his throat to sing."

"Troth now, sir," quoth Sancho, "it is even so in good earnest; and I fancy it is some knight that is in love."

"All knight-errants must be so," answered Don Quixote: "but let us hearken, and if he sings, we shall know more of his circumstances presently, 'for out of the abundance of the heart the mouth speaketh.'"

Sancho would have answered, but that the Knight of the Wood's voice, which was but indifferent, interrupted him with the following

SONG.

I.

Bright queen, how shall your loving slave
Be sure not to displease?
Some rule of duty let him crave:
He begs no other ease.

II.

Say, must I die, or hopeless live?
I'll act as you ordain:
Despair a silent death shall give,
Or Love himself complain.

III.

My heart, though soft as wax, will prove
Like diamonds firm and true:
For what th' impression can remove
That's stamp'd by love and you?

The Knight of the Wood concluded his song with a sigh, that seemed to be fetched from the very bottom of his heart; and after some pause, with a mournful and disconsolate voice, "Oh, most beautiful, but most ungrateful of womankind," cried he, "how is it possible, most serene Casildea de Vandalia, your heart should consent that a knight who idolises your charms should waste the flower of his youth, and kill himself with continual wanderings and hard fatigues? Is it not enough that I have made you to be acknowledged the greatest beauty in the world by all the knights of Navarre, all the knights of Leon, all the Tartesians, all the Castilians, and, in fine, by all the knights of La Mancha?"

"Not so neither," said Don Quixote then; "for I myself am of La Mancha, and never acknowledged, nor ever could nor ought to acknowledge, a thing so injurious to the beauty of my mistress; therefore, Sancho, it is a plain case, this knight is out of his senses. But let us hearken; perhaps we shall discover something more."

"That you will, I warrant you," quoth Sancho, "for he seems in tune to moan a month together."

But it happened otherwise; for the Knight of the Wood overhearing them, ceased his lamentations, and raising himself on his feet, in a loud but courteous tone called to them "Who is there? What are ye? Are ye of the number of the happy or the miserable?"

"Of the miserable," answered Don Quixote.

"Repair to me then," said the Knight of the Wood, "and be assured you have met misery and affliction itself." Upon so moving and civil an invitation, Don Quixote and Sancho drew near to him; and the mournful knight taking Don Quixote by the hand, "Sit down," said he, "Sir Knight; for that your profession is chivalry I need no other conviction than to have found you in this retirement, where solitude and the cold night dews are your companions, and the proper stations and reposing places of knights-errant."

D D

"I am a knight," answered Don Quixote, "and of the order you mention; and though my sorrows, and disasters, and misfortunes usurp the seat of my mind, I have still a heart disposed to entertain the afflictions of others. Yours, as I gather by your complaints, is derived from love, and, I suppose, owing to the ingratitude of that beauty you now mentioned."

While they were thus parleying, they sat close by one another on the hard ground, very peaceably and lovingly, and not like men that by break of day were to break one another's heads.

"And is it your fortune to be in love?" asked the Knight of the Wood.

"It is my misfortune," answered Don Quixote; "though the reflection of having placed our affections worthily sufficiently balances the weight of our disasters, and turns them to a blessing."

"This might be true," replied the Knight of the Wood, "if the disdain of some mistresses were not often so galling as to inspire us with something like the spirit of revenge."

"For my part," said Don Quixote, "I never felt my mistress's disdain."

"No, truly," quoth Sancho, who was near them; "for my lady is as gentle as a lamb."

"Is that your squire?" said the Knight of the Wood.

"It is," answered Don Quixote.

"I never saw a squire," said the Knight of the Wood, "that durst presume to interrupt his master when he was speaking himself. There is my fellow, yonder; he is as big as his father, and yet no man can say he was ever so saucy as to open his lips when I spoke."

"Well, well," quoth Sancho, "I have talked, and may talk again, and before as, and perhaps—but I have done."

At the same time the Squire of the Wood, pulling Sancho by the arm, "Come, brother," said he, "let us two go where we may chat freely by ourselves, like downright squires as we are, and let our masters get over head and ears in the stories of their loves."

"With all my heart," quoth Sancho; "and then I will tell you who I am and what I am, and you shall judge if I am not fit to make one among the talking squires."

With that the two squires withdrew, and had a dialogue as comical as that of their masters was serious.

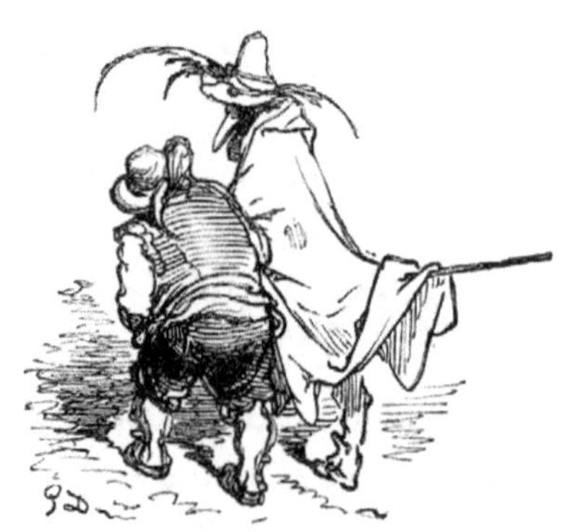

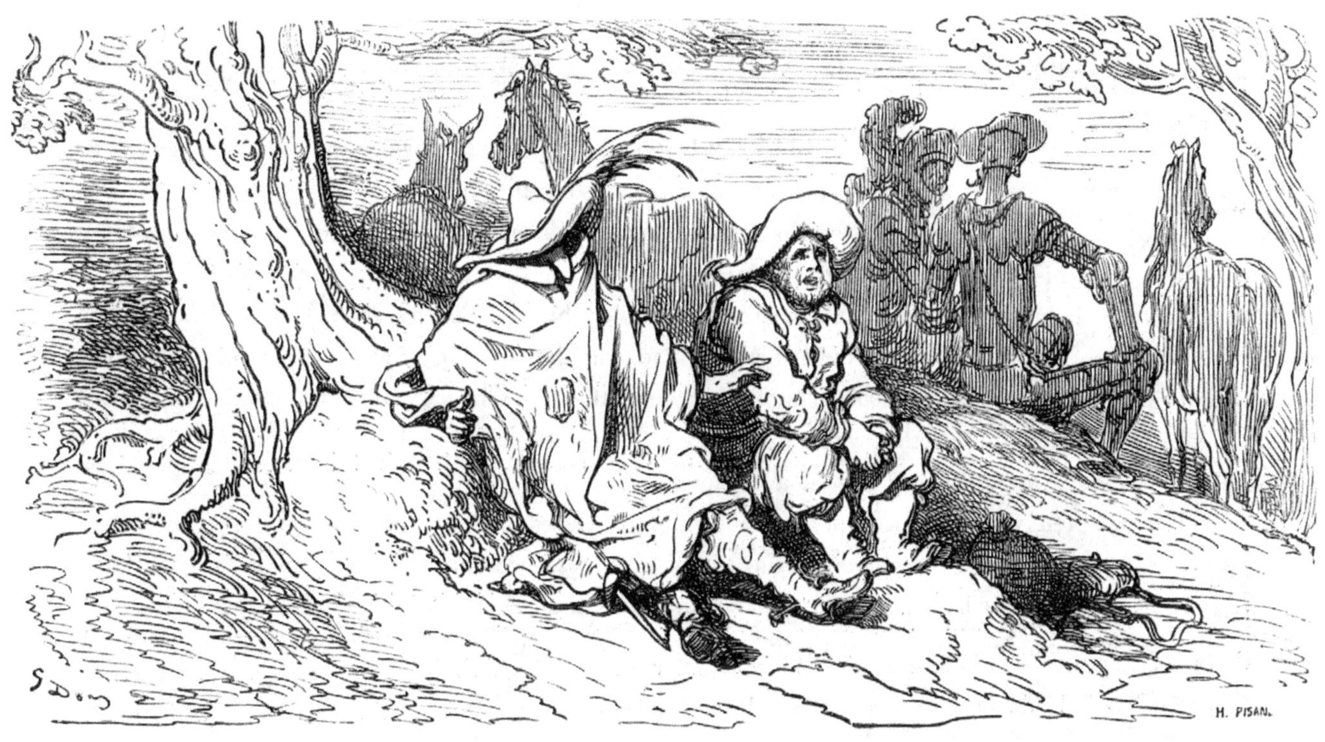

CHAPTER XIII.

THE ADVENTURE WITH THE KNIGHT OF THE WOOD CONTINUED, WITH THE WISE, RARE, AND PLEASANT DISCOURSE THAT PASSED BETWEEN THE TWO SQUIRES.

THE knights and their squires thus divided—the latter to tell their lives, and the former to relate their amours—the story begins with the Squire of the Wood.

"Sir," said he to Sancho, "this is a troublesome kind of life that we squires of knights-errant lead. Well may we say we eat our bread with the sweat of our brows, which is one of the curses laid on our first parents."

"Well may we say, too," quoth Sancho, "we eat it with a cold shivering of our bodies; for there are no poor creatures that suffer more by heat or cold than we do. Nay, if we could but eat at all, it would never vex one, for 'good fare lessens care;' but sometimes we shall go a day or two, and never so much as breakfast, unless it be upon the wind that blows."

"After all," said the Squire of the Wood, "we may bear with this, when we think of the reward we are to expect; for that same knight-errant must be excessively unfortunate that has not, some time or other, the government of some island, or some good, handsome earldom, to bestow on his squire."

"As for me," quoth Sancho, "I have often told my master I would be contented with the government of any island; and he is so noble and free-hearted, that he has promised it over and over."

"For my part," quoth the other squire, "I should think myself well paid for my services with some good canonry, and I have my master's word for it too."

"Why, then," quoth Sancho, "belike your master is some church-knight, and may bestow such livings on his good squires. But mine is purely laic; some of his wise friends, indeed (no thanks to them for it), once upon a time counselled him to be an archbishop—I fancy they wished him no good—but he would not, for he will be nothing but an emperor. I was plaguily afraid he might have had a hankering after the Church, and so have spoiled my preferment, I not being gifted that way; for between you and me, though I look like a man in a doublet, I should make but an ass in a cassock."

"Let me tell you, friend," quoth the Squire of the Wood, "that you are out in your politics; for these island governments bring more cost than worship; there is 'a great cry, but little wool;' the best will bring more trouble and care than they are worth, and those that take them on their shoulders are ready to sink under them. I think it were better for us to quit this confounded slavery, and e'en jog home, where we may entertain ourselves with more delightful exercises, such as fishing and hunting, and the like; for he is a sorry country squire indeed that wants his horse, his couple of hounds, or his fishing-tackle, to live pleasantly at home."

"All this I can have at will," quoth Sancho; "indeed, I have never a nag, but I have an honest ass here worth two of my master's horses any day in the year. A bad Christmas be my lot, and may it be the next, if I would change beasts with him, though he gave me four bushels of barley to boot—no, marry would not I. Laugh as much as you will at the value I set on my Dapple; for Dapple, you must know, is his colour. Now, as for hounds, we have enough to spare in our town; and there is no sport like hunting at another man's cost."

"Faith and troth! brother squire," quoth the Squire of the Wood, "I am fully set upon it. These vagrant knights may e'en seek their mad adventures by themselves; for me, I will home, and bring up my children, as it behoves me; for I have three, as precious as three orient pearls."

"I have but two," quoth Sancho, "but they might be presented to the Pope himself, especially my girl, that I bring up to be a countess (Heaven bless her!) in spite of her mother's teeth."

"And how old, pray," said the Squire of the Wood, "may this same young lady countess be?"

"Why, she is about fifteen," answered Sancho, "a little over or a little under; but she is as tall as a pike, as fresh as an April morning, and strong as a porter."

"With these parts," quoth the other, "she may set up not only for a countess, but for one of the wood-nymphs!"

"Heaven send me once more to see them!" quoth Sancho, in a grumbling tone; "and deliver me out of this mortal sin of squire-erranting, which I have been drawn into a second time by the wicked bait of a hundred ducats, which the tempter threw in my way in Sierra Morena, and which he still haunts me with, and brings before my eyes here and there and everywhere. Oh, that plaguy purse! it is still running in my head; methinks I am counting such another over and over. Now I hug it, now I carry it home, now I am buying land with it; now I let leases, now I am receiving my rents, and live like a prince. Thus I pass away the time, and this lulls me on to drudge on to the end of the chapter, with this dunder-headed master of mine, who, to my knowledge, is more a madman than a knight."

"Truly," said the Squire of the Wood, "this makes the proverb true, 'Covetousness breaks the sack.' And now you talk of madmen, I think my master is worse than yours; for he is one of those of whom the proverb says, 'Fools will be meddling;' and 'Who meddles with another man's business, milks his cows into a sieve.' In searching after another knight's wits, he loses his own, and hunts up and down for that which may make him rue the finding.'"

"And is not the poor man in love?" quoth Sancho.

"Ay, marry," said the other, "and with one Casildea de Vandalia, one of the oddest pieces in the world; she will neither roast nor boil, and is neither fish, flesh, nor good red-herring. But that is not the thing that plagues his noddle now. He has some other crotchets in his crown, and you will hear more of it ere long."

"There is no way so smooth," quoth Sancho, "but it has a hole or rub in it to make a body stumble. In some houses they boil beans, and in mine are whole kettles full. So madness has more need of good attendants than wisdom. But if this old saying be true, that 'it lightens sorrow to have companions in our grief,' you are the fittest to comfort me—you serve one fool, and I another."

"My master," quoth the Squire of the Wood, "is more stout than foolish, but more knave than either."

"Mine is not like yours, then," quoth Sancho; "he has not one grain of knavery in him; he is as dull as an old cracked pitcher, hurts nobody, does all the good he can to everybody; a child may persuade him it is night at noon-day; and he is so simple, that I cannot help loving him with all my heart and soul, and cannot leave him, in spite of all his follies."

"Have a care, brother!" said the Squire of the Wood; "when the blind leads the blind, both may fall into the ditch. It is better to wheel about fair and softly, and steal home again to our own firesides."

Here the Squire of the Wood observing that Sancho spoke as if he was very dry, "I fancy, brother," said he, "that our tongues stick to the palates of our mouths with talking; but to cure that disease I have something that hangs to the pommel of my saddle, as good as ever was tipped over tongue." Then he went and took down a leather bottle of wine, and a cold pie at least half a yard long; which is no fiction, for Sancho himself, when he laid his hands on it, took it rather for a baked goat than a kid, though it was indeed but an overgrown rabbit.

"What!" said Sancho, at the sight, "did you bring this too abroad with you?"

"What d'ye think?" said the other; "do you take me for one of your fresh-water squires? I'd have you know, I carry as good provisions at my horse's crupper as any general upon his march."

Sancho did not stay for an invitation, but fell to in the dark, cramming down morsels as big as his fist. "Ay, marry, sir," said he, "you are a squire, every inch of you, a true and trusty, round and sound, noble and free-hearted squire. This good cheer is a proof of it, which I do not say jumped hither by witchcraft, but one would almost think so. Now, here sits poor wretched I, that have nothing in my knapsack but a crust of cheese—so hard, a giant might break his grinders in 't—and a few acorns, walnuts, and filberts; a shame on my master's niggardly temper, in fancying that all knights-errant must be content to live on a little dried fruit and salads!"

"Well, well, brother," replied the Squire of the Wood, "our masters may diet themselves by rules of chivalry, if they please; your thistles and your herbs and roots do not at all agree with my stomach; I must have good meat, i' faith, and this bottle here still at hand at the pommel of my saddle. It is my joy, my life, the comfort of my soul; I hug and kiss it every moment, and now recommend it to you as the best friend in the world."

Sancho took the bottle, and rearing it to his thirsty lips, with his eyes fixed upon the stars, kept himself in that happy contemplation for a puarter of an hour together. At last, when he had taken his draught, with a deep groan, a nod on one side, and a cunning leer, "Now, by the remembrance of her you love best, pr'ythee, tell me, is not this your right Ciudad Real wine?

"Thou hast a rare palate," answered the Squire of the Wood; "it is the very same, and of a good age too."

"I thought so," said Sancho; "but is it not strange now, that turn me but loose among a parcel of wines, I shall find the difference? Ah! sir, I no sooner clap my nose to any kind of wine, but I can tell the place, the grape, the flavour, the age, the strength, and all the qualities of the parcel; and all this is natural to me, sir, for I had two relations, by the father's side, that were the nicest tasters that were known for a long time in La Mancha, of which two I will relate you a story that makes good what I said. It fell out on a time that some wine was drawn fresh out of a hogshead, and given to these same friends of mine to taste; and they were asked their opinions of the condition, the quality, the goodness, the badness of the wine, and all that. The one tried it with the tip of his tongue; the other only smelled it. The first said the wine tasted of iron; the second said it rather had a tang of goat's leather. The vintner swore his vessel was clean, and the wine neat, and so pure that it could have no taste of any such thing. Well, time ran on, the wine was sold, and when the vessel came to be emptied, what do you think, sir, was found in the cask? A little key, with a bit of leathern thong tied to it. Now, judge you by this whether he that comes of such a generation has not reason to understand wine?"

"More reason than to understand adventures," answered the other; "therefore, since we have enough, let us not trouble ourselves to look after more, but e'en jog home to our little cots, where Heaven will find us, if it be its will."

"I intend," said Sancho, "to wait on my master till we come to Saragosa, but then I will turn over a new leaf."

To conclude: the two friendly squires having talked and drank, and held out almost as long as their bottle, it was high time that sleep should lay their tongues and assuage their thirst, for to quench it was impossible. Accordingly, they soon fell fast asleep, both keeping their hold on their almost empty bottle, where we shall for a while leave them to their rest, and see what passed between their masters.

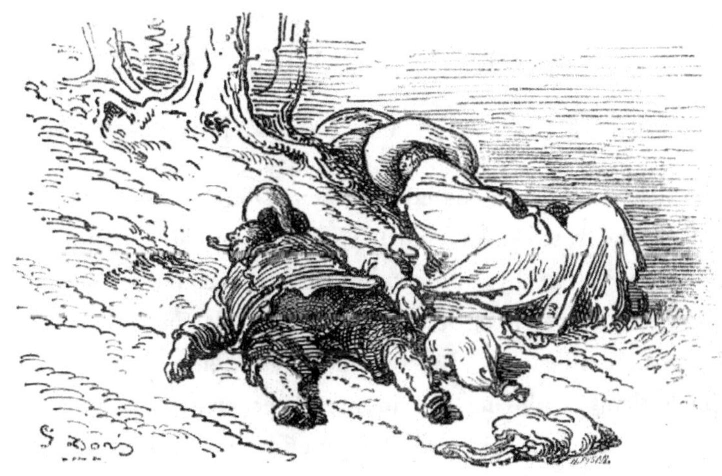

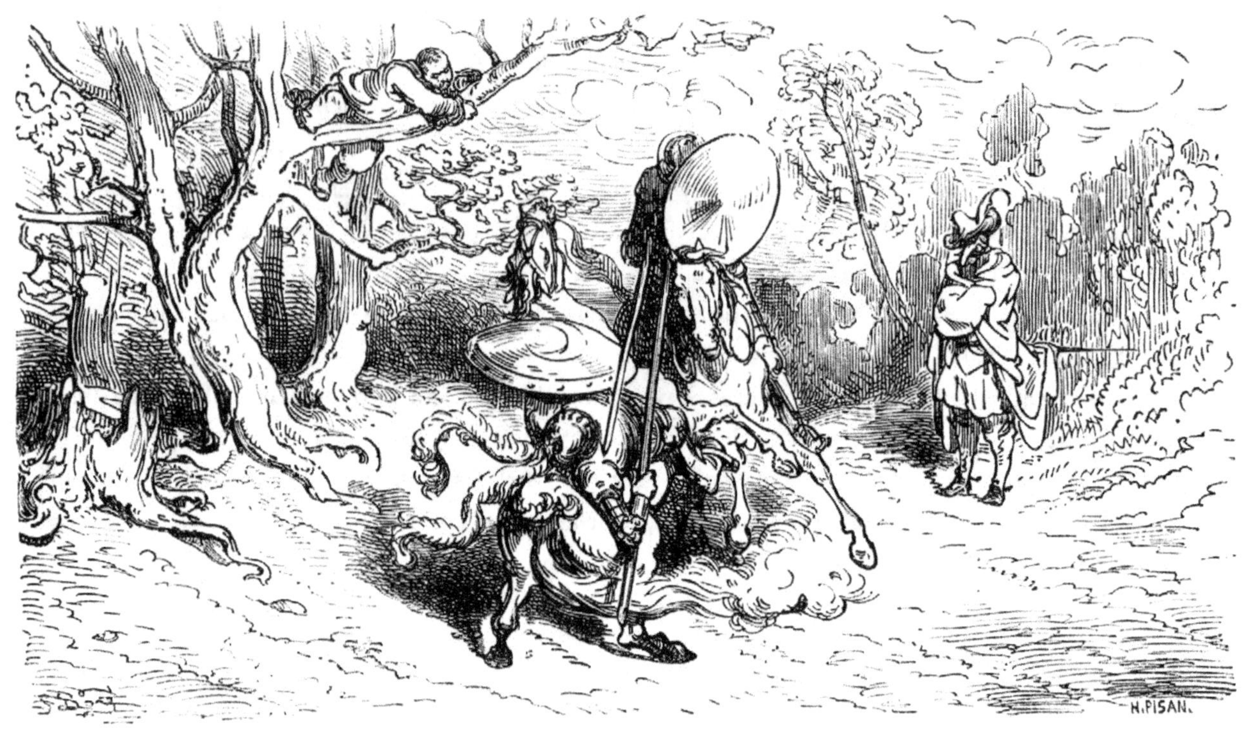

CHAPTER XIV.

A CONTINUATION OF THE ADVENTURE OF THE KNIGHT OF THE WOOD.

MANY were the discourses that passed between Don Quixote and the Knight of the Wood; amongst the rest, "You must know, Sir Knight," said the latter, "that by the appointment of Fate, or rather by my own choice, I became enamoured of the peerless Casildea de Vandalia. I call her peerless, because she is singular in the greatness of her stature, as well as in that of her state and beauty. But this lady has been pleased to take no other notice of my honourable passion than employing me in many perilous adventures, like Hercules' step-mother; still promising me, after I had put an happy end to one, that the performance of the next should put me in possession of my desires. But after a succession of numberless labours, I do not know which of her commands will be the last and will crown my lawful wishes. Once, by her particular injunction, I challenged that famous giantess, La Giralda of Seville, who is as strong and undaunted as one that is made of brass, and who, without changing place, is the most changeable and inconstant woman in the world. I went, I saw, and overcame; I made her stand still, and fixed her in a constant point, for the space of a whole week, no wind having blown in the skies during all that time but the north. Another time she enjoined me to remove the ancient stones of the sturdy bulls of Guisando, a task more suitable to the arms of porters than those of knights. Then she commanded me to descend and dive into the cavern or den of Cabra (a terrible and unheard-of attempt), and to bring her an account of all the wonders in that dismal profundity. I stopped the motion of La Giralda; I weighed the bulls of Guisando; and, with a precipitated fall, plunged and brought to light the darkest secrets of Cabra's black abyss. But still, ah! still my hopes are dead. How dead? How! because her disdain still lives, still lives to enjoin me new labours, new exploits; for, lastly, she has ordered me to traverse the remotest provinces of Spain, and exact a confession from all the knights-errant that roam about the land that her beauty alone excels that of all other women, and that I am the most valiant and most enamoured knight in the world. I have already journeyed over the greatest part of Spain on this expedition, and overcome many knights who had the temerity to contradict my assertion. But the perfection of my glory is the result of my victory over the renowned Don Quixote de la Mancha, whom I conquered in single combat, and compelled to submit his Dulcinea's to my Casildea's beauty. And now I reckon the wandering knights of the whole universe all vanquished by my prowess; their fame, their glory, and their honours being all vested in this great Don Quixote, who had before made them the spoils of his valorous arm, though now they must attend the triumphs of my victory, which is the greater, since the reputation of the victor rises in proportion to that of the vanquished, and all the latter's laurels are transferred to me."

Don Quixote was amazed to hear the knight run on at this rate, and had the lie ready at his tongue's end to give him a thousand times; but designing to make him own his falsity with his own mouth, he strove to contain his choler; and arguing the matter very calmly, "Sir Knight," said he, "that your victories have extended over all the knights in Spain, and perhaps over the whole world, I will not dispute; but that you have vanquished Don Quixote de la Mancha you must give me leave to doubt. It might be somebody like him, though he is a person whom but very few can resemble."

"What do ye mean?" answered the Knight of the Wood. "By yon spangled canopy of the skies, I fought Don Quixote hand to hand, vanquished him, and made him submit. He is a tall, wither-faced, leathern-jaw fellow, scragged, grizzle-haired, hawk-nosed, and wears long, black, lank mustachios; he is distinguished in the field by the title of the Knight of the Woful Figure; he has for his squire one Sancho Panza, a labouring man; he bestrides and manages that far-famed courser Rozinante, and has for the mistress of his affection one Dulcinea del Toboso, sometimes called Aldonsa Lorenzo; as mine, whose name was Casildea, and who is of Andalusia, is now distinguished by the denomination of Casildea de Vandalia; and if all these convincing marks be not sufficient to prove this truth, I wear a sword that shall force even incredulity to credit it."

"Not so fast, good Sir Knight," said Don Quixote; "pray, attend to what I shall deliver upon this head. You must know that this same Don Quixote is the greatest friend I have in the world, insomuch that I may say I love him as well as I do myself. Now, the tokens that you have described him by are so agreeable to his person and circumstances, that one would think he should be the person you subdued. On the other hand, I am convinced, by the more powerful argument of undeniable sense, that it cannot be he. But thus far I will allow you, as there are many enchanters that are his enemies, especially one whose malice hourly persecutes him, perhaps one of them has assumed his likeness, thus, by a counterfeit conquest, to defraud him of the glory contracted by his signal chivalry over all the universe. In confirmation of which, I can farther tell you it is but two days ago that these envious magicians transformed the figure and the person of the beautiful Dulcinea del Toboso into the base and sordid likeness of a rustic wench. And if this will not convince you of your error, behold Don Quixote himself in person, that here stands ready to maintain his words with his arms, either a-foot or on horse-back, or in what other manner you may think convenient."

As he said this, up he started, and laid his hand on his sword, waiting the motions and resolutions of the Knight of the Wood. But with a great deal of calmness, "Sir," said he, "a good pay-master grudges no surety; he that could once vanquish Don Quixote when transformed needs not fear him in his proper shape. But since darkness is not proper for the achievements of knights, but rather for robbers and ruffians, let us await the morning light, that the sun may be witness of our valour. The conditions of our combat shall be, that the conquered shall be wholly at the mercy of the conqueror, who shall dispose of him at discretion; provided always he abuses not his power by commanding anything unworthy the honour of knighthood."

"Content," said Don Quixote. "I like these terms very well."

With that they both went to look out their squires, whom they found snoring very soundly in just the same posture as when they first fell asleep. They roused them up, and ordered them to get their steeds ready, for the first rays of the rising sun must behold them engage in a fearful and unparalleled single combat.

This news thunder-struck Sancho, and put him to his wits' end for his master's danger, having heard the Knight of the Wood's courage strangely magnified by his squire. However, without the least reply, he went with his companion to seek their beasts, who by this time had found out one another, and were got lovingly together.

"Well, friend," said the squire to Sancho, as they went, "I find our masters are to fight; so you and I are like to have a brush too; for it is the way among us Andalusians not to let the seconds stand idly by, with arms across, while their friends are at it."

"This," said Sancho, "may be a custom in your country; but, let me tell you, it is a foolish custom, Sir Squire, and none but ruffians and evil-minded fellows would stand up for it; but there is no such practice among squires-errant, else my master would have minded me of it ere this, for he has all the laws of knight-errantry by heart. But suppose there be such a law, I will not obey it, that is flat; I will rather pay the penalty that is laid on such peaceable squires. I do not think the fine can be above two pounds of wax, and that will cost me less than the lint would to make tents for my skull, which, methinks, is already cleft down to my chin. Besides, how would you have me fight? I have ne'er a sword, nor ever wore any."

"No matter," quoth the Squire of the Wood; "I have a cure for that sore. I have got here a couple of linen bags, both of a size; you shall take one, and I the other, and so we will let drive at one another with these weapons, and fight at bag-blows."

"Ay, ay, with all my heart," quoth Sancho; "this will dust our jackets purely, and won't hurt our skins."

"Not so neither," replied the Squire of the Wood; "for we will put half a dozen of smooth stones into each bag, that the wind may not blow them to and fro, and they may play the better, and so we may brush one another's coats cleverly, and yet do ourselves no great hurt."

"Smooth stones, indeed!" quoth Sancho; "what soft sable fur, what dainty carded cotton and lamb's wool he crams into the bags, to hinder our making pap of our brains and touch-wood of our bones! But I say again and again, I am not in a humour to fight, though they were only full of silk balls. Let our masters fight, and hear on't hereafter; but let us drink and live while we may; for why should we strive to end our lives before their time and season, and be so eager to gather the plums that will drop of themselves when they are ripe?"

"Well," said the Squire of the Wood, "for all that, we must fight half an hour or so."

"Not a minute," replied Sancho; "I havn't the heart to quarrel with a gentleman with whom I have been eating and drinking. I aint angry with you in the least, and were I to be hanged for it, I could never fight in cold blood."

"Nay, if that be all," said the Squire of the Wood, "you shall be angry enough, I'll warrant you; for before we go to it, d'ye see, I'll walk up very handsomely to you, and lend your worship three or four sound slaps o' the chaps, and knock you down, which will be sure to waken your choler, though it slept as sound as a dormouse."

"Nay, then," quoth Sancho, "I have a trick for your trick, if that be all, and you shall have as good as you bring; for I will take me a pretty middling lever (you understand me), and before you can awaken my choler, will I lay yours asleep so fast, that it shall never wake more. 'Let every man look before he leaps;' 'many come for wool that go home shorn;' no man knows what another can do; so, friend, let every man's choler sleep with him. 'Blessed are the peace-makers,' and cursed are the peace-breakers. 'A baited cat may turn as fierce as a lion.' Who knows, then, what I, that am a man, may turn to if I am provoked? Take it, therefore, for a warning from me, squire, that all the mischief you may be hatching in this manner shall lie at your door."

"Well," said the other, "it will be day anon, and then we shall see what is to be done."

And now a thousand sorts of pretty birds began to warble in the trees, and with their various cheerful notes seemed to salute the fresh Aurora, who then displayed her rising beauties through the gates and arches of the east, and gently shook from her dewy locks a shower of liquid pearls, sprinkling and enriching the verdant meads with that reviving treasure which seemed to spring and drop from the bending leaves. The willows distilled their delicious manna, the rivulets fondly murmured, the fountains smiled, the woods were cheered, the fields enriched, at her approach. But no sooner had the dawning light recalled distinction, than the first thing that presented itself to Sancho's view was the Squire of the Wood's nose, which was so big, that it overshadowed almost his whole body. In short, it is said to have been of a monstrous size, crooked in the middle, studded with warts and carbuncles, tawny as a russet-pippin, and hanging down some two fingers below his mouth. The unreasonable bulk, dismal hue, protuberancy, and crookedness of that nose so disfigured the squire, that Sancho was seized with a trembling at the sight, like a child in convulsions.

As for Don Quixote, he fixed his eyes upon his antagonist; but as his helmet was on, and he had pulled down the beaver, his face could not be seen; however, he observed him to be strong-limbed, though not very tall. Over his armour he wore a coat that looked like cloth of gold, overspread with looking-glasses (mirrors), cut into half-moons, which made a very glittering show; a large plume of yellow, green, and white feathers waved about his helmet; and his lance, which he had set up against a tree, was very thick and long, with a steel head a foot in length. Don Quixote surveyed every particular, and, from his observations, judged him to be a man of great strength. But all this was so far from daunting his courage, like Sancho, that, with a gallant deportment, "Sir Knight of the Mirrors," said he, "if your eager desire of combat has not made you deaf to the entreaties of civility, be pleased to lift up your beaver a while, that I may see whether the gracefulness of your face equals that of your body."

"Whether you be vanquished or victorious in this enterprise," answered the Knight of the Mirrors, "you shall have leisure enough to see my face. I cannot at present satisfy your curiosity; for every moment of delay is a wrong done to the beautiful Casildea de Vandalia."

"However," replied Don Quixote, "while we get a-horseback, you may tell me whether I be the same Don Quixote whom you pretend to have overcome?"

"To this I answer you," said the Knight of the Mirrors, "you are as like the knight I vanquished as one egg is like another. But considering what you tell me, that you are persecuted by enchanters, I dare not affirm that you are the same."

"It is enough," said Don Quixote, "that you believe you may be in error; but that I may entirely rid your doubts, let us to horse; for if Providence, my mistress, and my arm assist me, I will see your face in less time than it would have cost you to have lifted up your beaver, and make you know that I am not the Don Quixote whom you talked of having vanquished."

This said, they mounted. Don Quixote wheeled about with Rozinante, to take ground for the career; the Knight of the Mirrors did the like. But before Don Quixote had rode twenty paces, he heard him call to him. So meeting each other half way, "Remember, Sir Knight," cried he, "the condition on which we fight; the vanquished, as I told you before, shall be at the mercy of the conqueror."

"I grant it," answered Don Quixote, "provided the victor imposes nothing on him that derogates from the laws of chivalry."

"I mean no otherwise," replied the Knight of the Mirrors.

At the same time Don Quixote happened to cast his eyes on the squire's strange nose, and wondered no less at the sight of it than Sancho, taking him to be rather a monster than a man. Sancho, seeing his master set out to take so much distance as was fit to return on his enemy with greater force, would not trust himself along with Squire Nose, fearing the greater should be too hard for the less, and either that or fear should strike him to the ground. This made him run after his master, till he had taken hold of Rozinante's stirrup-leathers; and when he thought him ready to turn back to take his career, "Good your worship," cried he, "before you run upon your enemy, help me to get up into yon cork tree, where I may better see your brave battle with the knight."

"I rather believe," said Don Quixote, "thou wantest to be perched up yonder as on a scaffold, to see the bull-baiting without danger."

"To tell you the truth," quoth Sancho, "that fellow's unconscionable nose has so frighted me, that I dare not stay within his reach."

"It is, indeed, such a sight," said Don Quixote, "as might affect with fear any other but myself, and therefore come, I will help thee up."

Now, while Sancho was climbing the tree with his master's assistance, the Knight of the Mirrors took as much ground as he thought proper for his career; and imagining Don Quixote had done the same, he faced about, without expecting the trumpet's sound or any other signal for a charge, and with his horse's full speed, which was no more than a middling trot, he went to encounter his enemy; but seeing him busy in helping up his squire, he held in his steed, and stopped in middle career, for which the horse was mightily obliged to him, being already scarce able to stir a foot farther.

Don Quixote, who thought his enemy was flying upon him, set spurs to Rozinante, and so wakened his mettle, that the story says this was the only time he was known to gallop a little, for at all others downright trotting was his best. With this unusual fury, he soon got to the place where his opponent was striking his spurs into his horse's sides up to the very rowels, without being able to make him stir an inch from the spot. Now, while he was thus goading him on, and at the same time encumbered with his lance, either not knowing how to set it in the rest, or wanting time to do it, Don Quixote, who took no notice of his disorder, encountered him without danger so furiously, that the Knight of the Mirrors was hurried, in spite of his teeth, over his horse's crupper, and was so hurt with falling to the ground, that he lay without motion or any sign of life. Sancho no sooner saw him fallen, but down he comes sliding from the tree and runs to his master, who, having dismounted, was got upon the Knight of the Mirrors, and was unlacing his helmet, to see if he were dead or alive, and give him air But who can relate what he saw when he beheld the face of the Knight of the Mirrors, without raising wonder, amazement, or astonishment in those that shall hear it?

"He saw," says the historian, "in that face the very visage, the very aspect, the very physiognomy, the very make, the very features, the very effigy of the bachelor Samson Carrasco!"

"Come, Sancho!" cried he, as he saw it, "come hither, look, and admire what thou mayest see, yet not believe! Haste, my friend, and mark the power of magic—what sorcerers and enchanters can do!"

Sancho drew near, and seeing the bachelor Samson Carrasco's face, began to cross himself a thousand times, and bless himself as many more.

The poor defeated knight all this while gave no sign of life.

"Sir," quoth Sancho to his master, "if you will be ruled by me, make sure work. Right or wrong, e'en thrust your sword down this fellow's throat that is so like the bachelor Samson Carrasco, and so mayhap in him you may chance to murder one of those bitter dogs—those enchanters that haunt you so."

"That thought is not amiss," said Don Quixote; and with that, drawing his sword, he was going to put Sancho's advice in execution, when the knight's squire came running without the nose that so disguised him before, and calling to Don Quixote, "Hold, noble Don Quixote!" cried he; "take heed! beware! 'tis your friend Samson Carrasco that now lies at your worship's mercy; and I am his squire."

"And where is your nose?" quoth Sancho, seeing him now without disguise.

"Here, in my pocket," answered the squire; and, so saying, he pulled out the nose of a varnished pasteboard vizard, such as it has been described.

Sancho having more and more stared him in the face with great earnestness, "Blessed Virgin, defend me!" quoth he; "who is this? Thomas Cecial, my friend and neighbour!"

"The same, friend Sancho," quoth the squire. "I will tell you anon by what tricks and wheedles he was inveigled to come hither. Meanwhile desire your master not to misuse, nor slay, nor meddle in the least with the knight that now lies at his mercy, for there is nothing more sure than that it is our ill-advised countryman, Samson Carrasco, and nobody else."

By this time the Knight of the Mirrors began to come to himself, which, when Don Quixote observed, setting the point of his sword to his throat, "Thou diest, knight," cried he, "if thou refuse to confess that the peerless Dulcinea del Toboso excels thy Casildea de Vandalia in beauty. Besides this, thou shalt promise (if thou escape with life from this combat) to go to the city of Toboso, where, as from me, thou shalt present thyself before the mistress of my desires, and resign thy person to her disposal; if she leaves thee to thy own, then thou shalt come back to me (for the track of my exploits will be thy guide), and thou shalt give me an account of the transaction between her and thee."

"I do confess," said the discomfited knight, "that the Lady Dulcinea del Toboso's ripped and dirty shoe is preferable to the clean, though ill-combed locks of Casildea; and I promise to go to her, and come from her presence to yours, and bring you a full and true relation of all you have enjoined me."

"You shall also confess and believe," added Don Quixote, "that the knight you vanquished neither was nor could be Don Quixote de la Mancha, but somebody else in his likeness; as I, on the other side, do confess and believe that though you seem to be the bachelor Samson Carrasco, you are not he, but some other, whom my enemies have transformed into his resemblance, to assuage the violence of my wrath, and make me entertain with moderation the glory of my victory."

"All this I confess, believe, and allow," said the knight; "and now, I beseech you, let me rise; for I find myself very much bruised."

Don Quixote helped him to rise, by the aid of his squire, Thomas Cecial, on whom Sancho fixed his eyes all the while, asking him a thousand questions, the answers to which convinced him that he was the real Thomas Cecial, as he said, though the conceit of what was told him by his master, that the magicians had transformed the Knight of the Mirrors into Samson Carrasco, had made such an impression on his fancy, that he could not believe the testimony of his own eyes. The Knight of the Mirrors and his squire, much out of humour and much out of order, left Don Quixote, to go to some town where he might get some ointments and plaisters for his ribs. Don Quixote and Sancho continued their progress for Saragosa, where the history leaves them, to relate who the Knight of the Mirrors and his squire were.

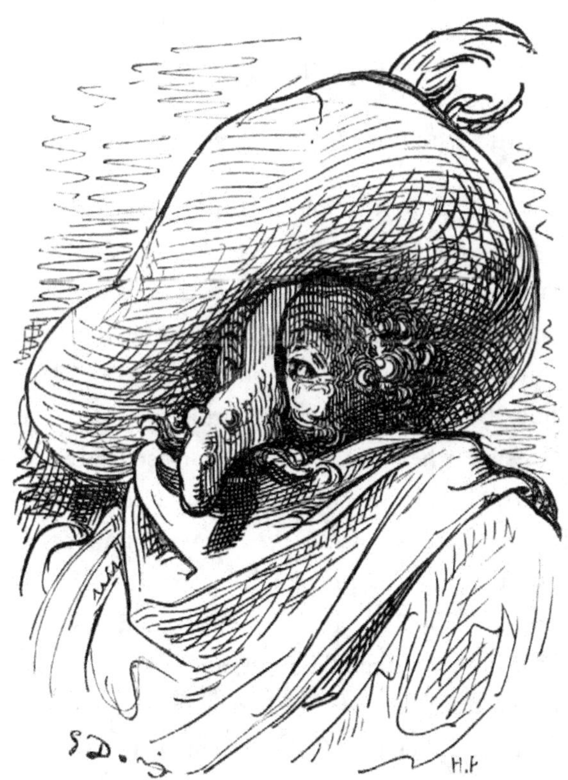

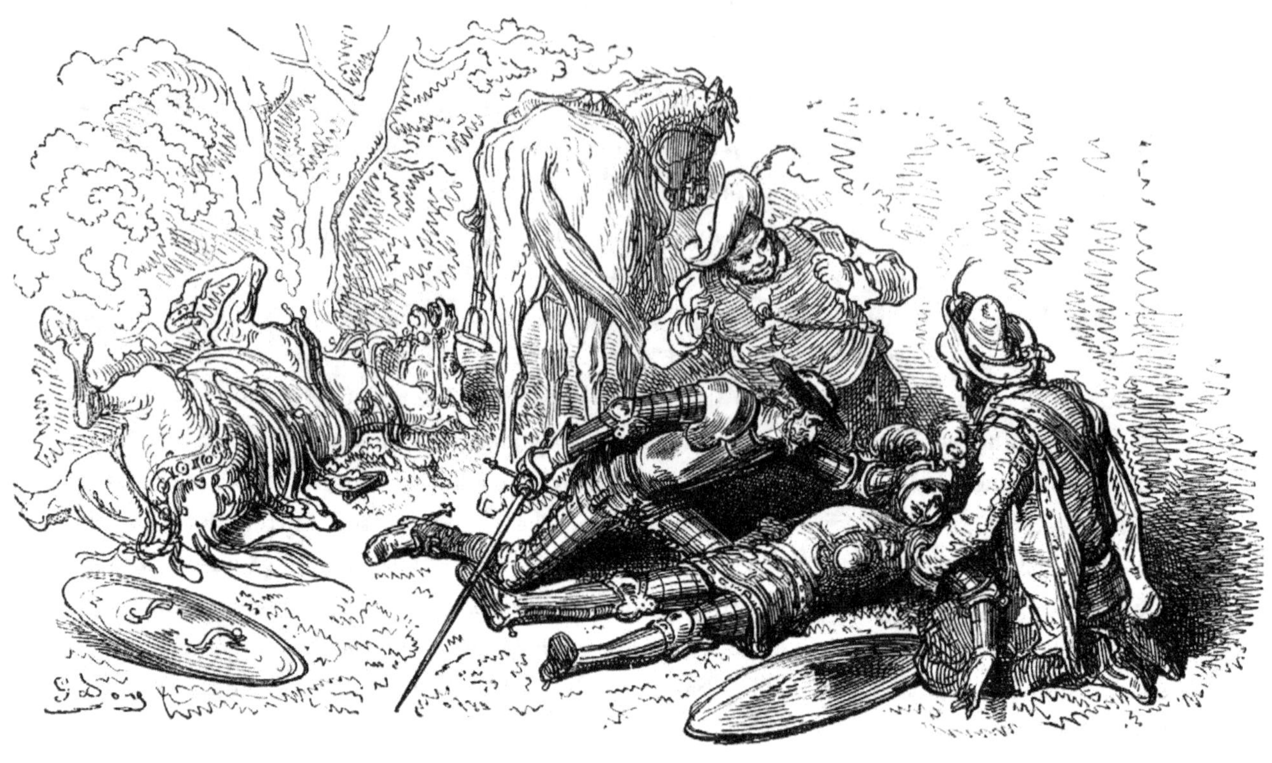

CHAPTER XV.

GIVING AN ACCOUNT WHO THE KNIGHT OF THE MIRRORS AND HIS SQUIRE WERE.

DON QUIXOTE went on extremely pleased and joyful, glorying in the victory he had got over so valiant a knight as the Knight of the Mirrors, and relying on his parole of honour, that he would return to give him an account of his reception, by which means he expected to hear whether his mistress continued under the bonds of enchantment. But Don Quixote dreamed of one thing, and the Knight of the Mirrors thought of another—his only care for the present was how to get cured of his bruises.

Here the history relates that when the bachelor Carrasco advised Don Quixote to proceed in his profession of knight-errantry, it was the result of a conference which he had with the curate and the barber about the best means to prevail with him to stay at home, for Carrasco thought, and so did the rest, that it was in vain to pretend to hinder him from going abroad again, and therefore the best way would be to let him go, and that he should meet him by the way, equipped like a knight-errant, and should fight and overcome him, which he might easily do; first making an agreement that the vanquished should submit to the victor's discretion; so that, after the bachelor had vanquished him, he should command him to return to his house, and not offer to depart thence for two years, without permission; which it was not doubted but Don Quixote would religiously observe, for fear of infringing the laws of chivalry; and in this time they hoped he might be weaned of his frenzy, or they might find some means to cure him of his madness. Carrasco undertook this task, and Thomas Cecial, a brisk, pleasant fellow, Sancho's neighbour and gossip, proffered to be his squire. Samson equipped himself, as you have heard, and Thomas Cecial fitted a huge pasteboard nose to his own, that his gossip Sancho might not know him when they met. Then they followed Don Quixote so close, that they had like to have overtaken him in the midst of his adventure with the Chariot of Death; and at last, they found him in the wood that was the scene of their encounter, which might have proved more fatal to the bachelor, and had spoiled him for ever from taking another degree, had not Don Quixote been so obstinate, in not believing him to be the same man.

And now Thomas Cecial, seeing the ill success of their journey, "By my troth," said he, "Master Carrasco, we have been served well enough. It is easy to begin a business, but a hard matter to go through. Don Quixote is mad, and we think ourselves wise; yet he is gone away sound, and laughing in his sleeve; and your worship is left here well banged, and in the dumps. Now, pray, who is the greatest madman? he that is so because he cannot help it, or he that is so for his pleasure?"

"The difference is," answered the bachelor, "that he that cannot help being mad will always be so; but he that only plays the fool for his fancy may give over when he pleases."

"Well, then," quoth Cecial, "I, who was pleased to play the fool in going a squire-erranting with your worship, for the selfsame reason will give it over now, and even make the best of my way home again."

"Do as you will," replied Carrasco, "but it is a folly to think I ever will go home till I have thoroughly paid that madman. It is not that he may recover his wits neither; no, it is pure revenge now, for the pain in my bones won't give me leave to have any manner of charity for him."

Thus they went on discoursing, till at last they got to a town, where, by good fortune they met with a bone-setter, who gave the bruised bachelor some ease. Thomas Cecial left him, and went home, while the other stayed to meditate revenge. In due time the history will speak of him again, but must not now forget to entertain you with Don Quixote's joy.

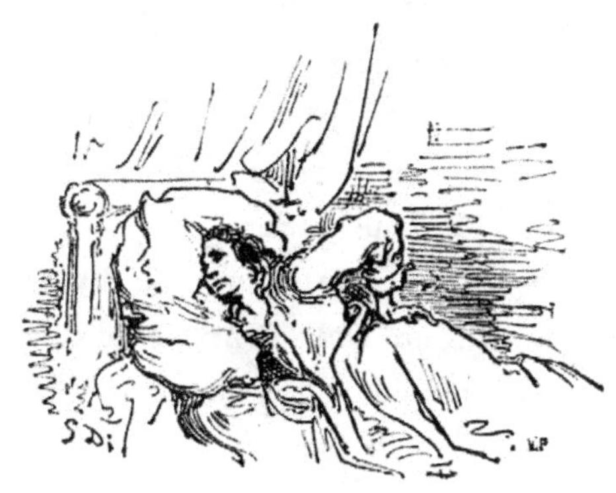

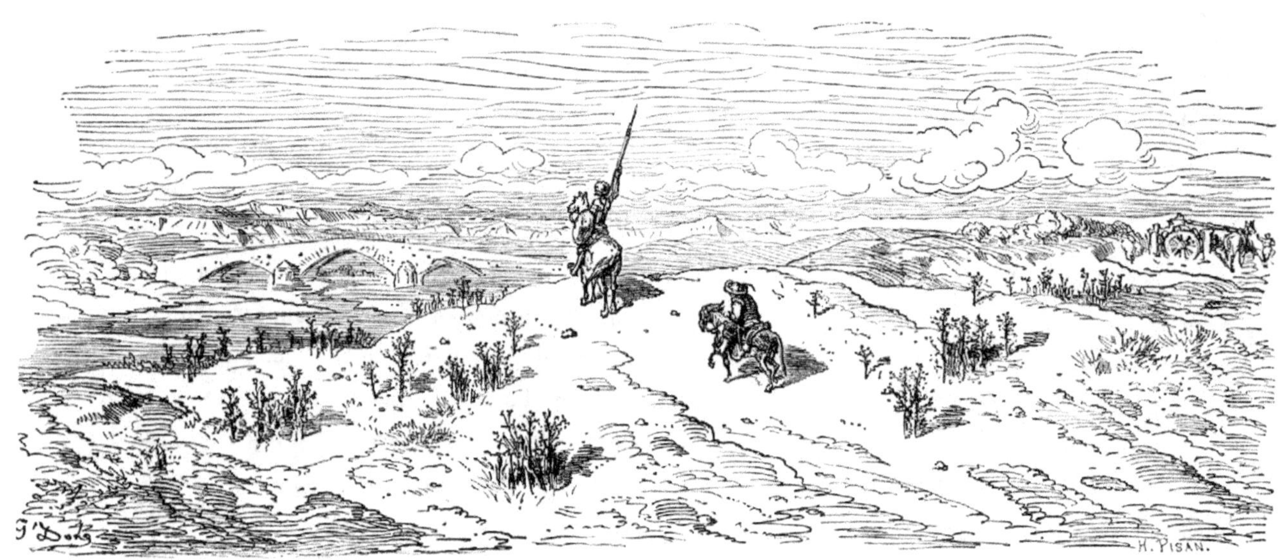

CHAPTER XVI.

WHAT HAPPENED TO DON QUIXOTE WITH A SOBER GENTLEMAN OF LA MANCHA.

DON QUIXOTE pursued his journey, full, as we said before, of joy and satisfaction; his late victory made him esteem himself the most valiant knight-errant of the age. He counted all his future adventures as already finished and happily achieved. He defied all enchantments and enchanters. No longer did he remember the innumerable blows he had received in the course of his errantry, nor the shower of stones that had dashed out half of his teeth, nor the ingratitude of the galley-slaves, nor the insolence of the Yanguesian carriers, who had so abominably battered his ribs with their pack-staves. In short, he concluded with himself, that if he could but by any manner of means dissolve the enchantment of his adored Dulcinea, he should have no need to envy the greatest felicity that ever was or could be attained by the most fortunate knight in the habitable globe.

While he was wholly employed in these pleasing imaginations, "Sir," quoth Sancho to him, "is it not a strange thing that I cannot, for the life of me, put out of my mind that unconscionable nose of Thomas Cecial, my gossip?"

"How! Sancho," answered Don Quixote, "dost thou still believe that the Knight of the Mirrors was the bachelor Carrasco, and that Thomas Cecial was his squire?"

"I do not know what to say to it," quoth Sancho, "but this I am sure of, that nobody but he could give me those items of my house, and of my wife and children, as he did. Besides, when his huge nose was off, he had Tom Cecial's face to a hair. I ought to know it, I think; I have seen it a hundred and a hundred times, for we are but next door neighbours; and then he had his speech to a tittle."

"Come on," returned Don Quixote; "let us reason upon this business. How can it enter into any one's imagination, that the bachelor Samson Carrasco should come armed at all points like a knight-errant, on purpose to fight with me? Have I ever been his enemy, or given him any occasion to be mine? am I his rival? or has he taken up the profession of arms, in envy of the glory which I have purchased by my sword?"

"Ay, but then," replied Sancho, "what shall we say to the resemblance between this same knight, whoever he be, and the bachelor Carrasco, and the likeness between his squire and my gossip? If it is an enchantment, as your worship says, were there no other people in the world but they two, to make them like?"

"All, all," cried Don Quixote, "is the artifice and delusion of those malevolent magicians that persecute me, who, foreseeing that I should get the victory, disguised their vanquished property under the resemblance of my friend the bachelor, that at the sight my friendship might interpose between the edge of my sword, and moderate my just resentment, and so rescue him from death, who basely had attempted my life. But thou, Sancho, by experience, which could not deceive thee, knowest how easy a matter it is for magicians to transmute the face of any one into another resemblance, fair into foul, and foul again into fair; since, not two days ago, with thine own eyes thou beheldest the peerless Dulcinea in her natural state of beauty and proportion, when I, the object of their envy, saw her in the homely disguise of a country wench. Why, then, shouldest thou wonder so much at the frightful transformation of the bachelor and thy neighbour Cecial? But, however, this is a comfort to me, that I got the better of my enemy, whatsoever shape he assumed."

"Well," quoth Sancho, "Heaven knows the truth of all things."

This was all the answer he thought fit to make; for as he knew that the transformation of Dulcinea was only a trick of his own, he was willing to waive the discourse, though he was the less satisfied in his master's chimeras; but feared to drop some word that might have betrayed his roguery.

While they were in this conversation, they were overtaken by a gentleman, mounted on a very fine mare. He had on a riding-coat of beautiful green cloth, faced with murrey-coloured velvet, and a hunter's cap of the same. The furniture of his mare was country-like, and after the jennet fashion, and also murrey and green. By his side hung a Moorish scimitar in a large belt of green and gold. His buskins were of the same work with his belt; his spurs were not gilt, but burnished so well with a certain green varnish, that they looked better to suit with the rest of his equipage than if they had been of pure gold. As he came up with them, he very civilly saluted them, and, clapping spurs to his mare, began to leave them behind him. Thereupon Don Quixote called to him: "Sir, if you are not in too much haste, we should be glad of the favour of your company, so far as you travel this road."

Upon this the traveller stopped his mare, and did not a little gaze at the figure and countenance of our knight, who rode without his helmet, which, like a wallet, hung at the saddle-bow of Sancho's ass. If the gentleman in green gazed on Don Quixote, Don Quixote looked no less on him, judging him to be some man of consequence. His age seemed about fifty; he had some grey hairs, a sharp look, and a grave yet pleasing aspect. In short, his mien and appearance spoke him a man of quality. When he looked on Don Quixote, he thought he had never beheld before such a strange appearance of a man. He could not but wonder at the lankness of his horse; he considered then the long-backed, raw-boned thing that bestrid him; his wan, meagre face; his air, his gravity, his arms and equipage; such a figure as perhaps had not been seen in that country time out of mind.

Don Quixote observed how intent the travelling gentleman had been in surveying him, and reading his desire in his surprise, as he was the very pink of courtesy, and fond of pleasing every one, without staying till he should question him, he thought fit to prevent him.

"Sir," said he, "that you are surprised at this figure of mine, which appears so new and exotic, I do not wonder in the least; but your wonder will cease when I have informed you that I am one of those knights who go in quest of adventures. I have left my country, mortgaged my estate, quitted my pleasures, and thrown myself into the arms of fortune. My design was to give a new life to knight-errantry, that so long has been lost to the world; and thus, after infinite toils and hardships, sometimes stumbling, sometimes falling, casting myself headlong in one place and rising again in another, I have compassed a great part of my desire—relieving widows, protecting damsels, assisting married women and orphans, the proper and natural office of knights-errant; and so, by many valorous and Christian-like achievements, I have merited the honour of being in print in almost all the nations of the world. Thirty thousand volumes of my history have been printed already, and thirty thousand millions more are like to be printed, if Heaven prevent not. In short, to sum up all in one word, know I am Don Quixote de la Mancha, otherwise called the Knight of the Woful Figure. I own it lessens the value of praise to be the publisher of its own self, yet it is what I am sometimes forced to when there is none present to do me justice. And now, good sir, no longer let this steed, this lance, this shield, this armour, this squire, the paleness of my looks, nor my exhausted body, move your wonder, since you know who I am and the profession I follow."

Having said this, Don Quixote was silent, and the gentleman in green, by his delaying to answer him, seemed as if he did not intend to make any return. But at last, after some pause, "Sir Knight," said he, "you were sensible of my curiosity by my looks, and were pleased to say my wonder would cease when you had informed me who you were; but I must confess, since you have done that, I remain no less surprised and amazed than ever. For is it possible there should be at this time any knights-errant in the world, or that there should be a true history of a living knight-errant in print? I cannot persuade myself there is anybody now upon earth that relieves widows, protects damsels, or assists married women and orphans; and I should still have been of the same mind, had not my eyes afforded me a sight of such a person as yourself. Now, Heaven be praised! for this history of your true and noble feats of arms, which you say is in print, will blot out the memory of all those idle romances of pretended knights-errant that have so filled and pestered the world, to the detriment of good education, and the prejudice and dishonour of true history."

"There is a great deal to be said," answered Don Quixote, "for the truth of histories of knight-errantry, as well as against it."

"How?" returned the gentleman in green; "is there anybody living who makes the least scruple but that they are false?"

"Yes, sir; myself for one," said Don Quixote. "But let that pass; if we continue any time together on the road, I hope to convince you that you have been to blame in suffering yourself to be carried away with the stream of mankind, who generally disbelieve them."

The traveller, at this discourse, began to have a suspicion that Don Quixote was distracted, and expected the next words would confirm him in that opinion; but before they entered into any further conversation, Don Quixote begged him to acquaint him who he was, since he had given him some account of his own life and condition.

"Sir Knight of the Woful Figure," answered the other, "I am a gentleman, born at a village, where, God willing, we shall dine by-and-by. My name is Don Diego de Miranda. I have a reasonable competency; I pass my time contentedly with my wife, my children, and my friends; my usual diversions are hunting and fishing, yet I keep neither hawks nor hounds, but some tame partridges and a ferret; I have about three or four score books—some Spanish, some Latin, some of history, others of divinity; but for books of knight-errantry, none ever came within my doors. I am more inclinable to read those that are profane than those of devotion, if they be such as yield an innocent amusement, and are agreeable for their style, and surprising for their invention, though we have but few of them in our language. Sometimes I eat with my neighbours and friends, and often I invite them to do the like with me. My treats are clean and handsome, neither penurious nor superfluous. I am not given to murmur and backbite, nor do I love to hear others do it. I am no curious inquirer into the lives and actions of other people. Every day I hear divine service, and give to the poor, without making a show of it, or presuming on my good deeds, lest I should give way to hypocrisy and vain-glory—enemies that too easily possess themselves of the best guarded hearts. I endeavour to reconcile those that are at variance. I pay my devotions to the blessed Virgin, and ever trust in Heaven's infinite mercy."

Sancho listened with great attention to this relation of the gentleman's way of living; and believing that a person who had led so good and pious a life was able to work miracles, he jumped in haste from his ass, and catching hold of his right stirrup, with tears in his eyes and devotion in his heart, fell to kissing his foot.

"What is the matter, friend?" cried the gentleman, wondering at his proceeding; "what is the meaning of this kissing?"

"Oh, good sir!" quoth Sancho, "let me kiss that dear foot of yours, I beseech you; for you are certainly the first saint on horseback I ever saw in my born days."

"Alas!" replied the gentleman, "I am no saint, but a great sinner; you, indeed, friend, I believe, are a good soul, as appears by your simplicity."

With that Sancho returned to his pack-saddle, having by this action provoked the profound gravity of his master to smile, and caused new admiration in Don Diego. And now Don Quixote inquired of him how many children he had, telling him, at the same time, that among the things in which the ancient philosophers, who had not the true knowledge of God, made happiness consist, as the advantages of nature and fortune, one was, to have many friends and a numerous and virtuous offspring.

"I have a son, Sir Knight," answered the gentleman; "and perhaps if I had him not I should not think myself the more unhappy; not that he is so bad neither, but because he is not so good as I would have him. He is eighteen years of age; the last six he has spent at Salamanca, to perfect himself in his Latin and Greek. But when I would have him to have proceeded to the study of other sciences, I found him so engaged in that of poetry, if it may be called a science, that it was impossible to make him look either to the study of the law, which I intended him for, or of divinity, the noblest part of all learning. I was in hopes he might have become an honour to his family, living in an age in which good and virtuous literature is highly favoured and rewarded by princes; for learning without virtue is like a pearl upon a dunghill. He now spends whole days in examining whether Homer, in such a verse of his 'Iliad,' says well or no; whether such an epigram in Martial ought not to be expunged; and whether such and such verses in Virgil are to be taken in such a sense or otherwise. In short, his whole converse is with the celebrated poets—with Horace and Persius, Juvenal and Tibullus. But as for modern rhymers, he has but an indifferent opinion of them. And yet for all this disgust of Spanish poetry, he is now breaking his brain upon a paraphrase or gloss on four verses that were sent him from the university, and which, I think, are designed for a prize."

"Sir," replied Don Quixote, "children are the flesh and blood of their parents, and whether good or bad, are to be cherished as part of ourselves. It is the duty of a father to train them up from their tenderest years in the path of virtue, in good discipline and Christian principles, that when they advance in years they may become the staff and support of their parents' age, and the glory of their posterity. But as for forcing them to this or that study, it is a thing I do not so well approve. Persuasion is all, I think, that is proper in such a case; especially when they are so fortunate as to be above studying for bread, they ought, in my opinion, to be indulged in the pursuit of that science to which their own genius gives them the most inclination. For though the art of poetry is not so profitable as delightful, yet it is none of those that disgrace the ingenious professor. Poetry, sir, in my judgment, is like a tender virgin in her bloom, beautiful and charming to amazement; all the other sciences are so many virgins, whose care it is to enrich, polish, and adorn her; as she is to make use of them all, so are they all to have from her a grateful acknowledgment. But this virgin must not be roughly handled, nor dragged along the streets, nor exposed at every market-place and corner of great men's houses. A good poet is a kind of an alchymist, who can turn the matter he prepares into the purest gold and an inestimable treasure. But he must keep his muse within the rules of decency, and not let her prostitute her excellency in lewd satires and lampoons, nor in licentious sonnets. She must not be mercenary, though she need not give away the profits she may claim for heroic poems, deep tragedies, and pleasant and artful comedies. She is not to be attempted by buffoons, nor by the ignorant vulgar, whose capacity can never reach to a due sense of the treasures that are locked up in her. And know, sir, that when I mention the vulgar, I do not mean only the common rabble; for whoever is ignorant, be he lord or prince, is to be reckoned in the number of the vulgar. But whoever shall apply himself to the muses with those qualifications which, as I said, are essential to the character of a good poet, his name shall be famous, and valued in all the polished nations of the world. And as to what you say, sir, that your son does not much esteem our modern poetry, in my opinion, he is somewhat to blame; and my reason is this: Homer never wrote in Latin, because he was a Grecian; nor did Virgil write in Greek, because Latin was the language of his country. In short, all your ancient poets wrote in their mother-tongue, and did not seek other languages to express their lofty thoughts. And thus it would be well that custom should extend to every nation; there being no reason that a German poet should be despised, because he writes in his own tongue, or a Castilian or Biscayan, because they write in theirs. But I suppose your son does not mislike modern poetry, but such modern poets as have no tincture of any other language or science, that may adorn, awaken, and assist their natural impulse. Though even in this, too, there may be error. For it is believed, and not without reason, that a poet is naturally a poet from his birth, and that with the talent which Heaven has infused into him, without the help of study or art, he may produce those compositions that verify that saying, *Est Deus in nobis*, &c. Not but that a natural poet, who improves himself by art, shall be much more accomplished, and have the advantage of him that has no title to poetry but by his knowledge in the art; because art cannot go beyond nature, but only adds to its perfection: from which it appears that the most perfect poet is he whom nature and art combine to qualify. Let, then, your son proceed and follow the guidance of his stars, for being so good a student as I understand he is, and already gone up the first step of the sciences—the knowledge of the learned tongues—he will easily ascend to the pinnacle of learning, which is no less an honour and an ornament to a gentleman than a mitre is to a bishop, or the long robe is to a civilian. Should your son write satires to lessen the reputation of any person, you would do well to take him to task, and destroy his defamatory rhymes; but if he studies to write such discourses in verse, to ridicule and explode vice in general, as Horace so elegantly did, then encourage him: for a poet's pen is allowed to inveigh against envy and envious men, and so against other vices, provided it aim not at particular persons. But there are poets so abandoned to the love of scurrility, that rather than lose a villanous jest, they will venture being banished to the islands of Pontus. If a poet is modest in his manners, he will be so in his verses. The pen is the tongue of the mind; the thoughts that are formed in the one, and those that are traced by the other, will bear a near resemblance. And when kings and princes see the wonderful art of poetry shine in prudent, virtuous, and solid subjects, they honour, esteem, and enrich them, and even crown them with leaves of that tree which is never offended by the thunderbolt, as a token that nothing shall offend those whose brows are honoured and adorned with such crowns."

The gentleman, hearing Don Quixote express himself in this manner, was struck with so much admiration, that he began to lose the bad opinion he had conceived of his understanding. As for Sancho, who did not much relish this fine talk, he took an opportunity to slink aside in the middle of it, and went to get a little milk of some shepherds that were hard by, keeping their sheep. Now when the gentleman was going to renew his discourse, mightily pleased with these judicious observations, Don Quixote, lifting up his eyes, perceived a wagon on the road, set round with little flags, that appeared to be the king's colours; and believing it to be some new adventure, he called out to Sancho to bring him his helmet. Sancho hearing him call aloud, left the shepherds, and, clapping his heels vigorously to Dapple's sides, came trotting up to his master, to whom there happened a most terrifying and desperate adventure.

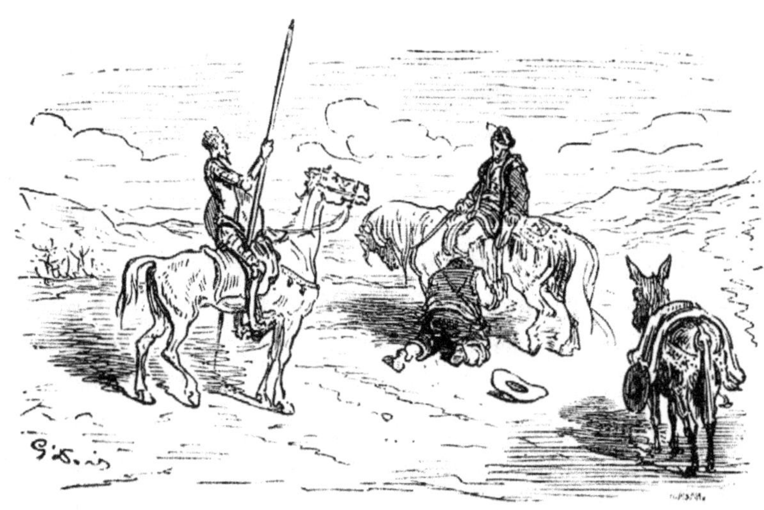

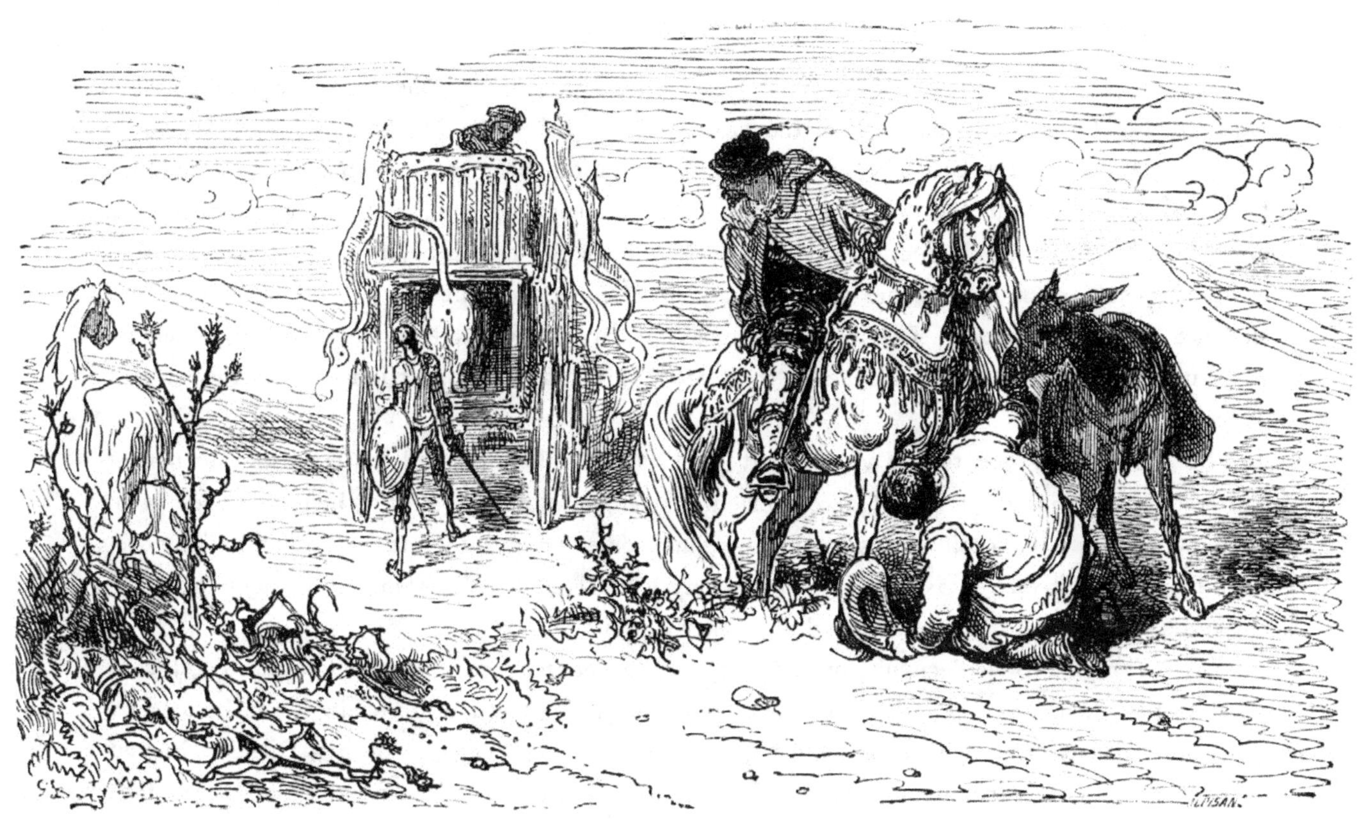

CHAPTER XVII.

WHERE YOU WILL FIND SET FORTH THE HIGHEST AND UTMOST PROOF THAT GREAT DON QUIXOTE EVER GAVE, OR COULD GIVE, OF HIS INCREDIBLE COURAGE, WITH THE SUCCESSFUL ISSUE OF THE ADVENTURE OF THE LIONS.

THE history relates that Sancho was chaffering with the shepherds for some curds, when Don Quixote called to him; and finding that his master was in haste, he did not know what to do with them, nor what to bring them in; yet loth to lose his purchase (for he had already paid for them), he bethought himself at last of clapping them into the helmet, where having them safe, he went to know his master's pleasure. As soon as he came up to him, "Give me that helmet, friend," said the knight, "for if I understand anything of adventures, I descry one yonder that obliges me to arm."

The gentleman in green, hearing this, looked about to see what was the matter, but could perceive nothing but a wagon, which made towards them; and by the little flags about it, he judged it to be one of the king's carriages, and so he told Don Quixote. But his head was too much possessed with notions of adventures to give any credit to what the gentleman said. "Sir," answered he, "'forewarned, forearmed;' a man loses nothing by standing on his guard. I know by experience that I have enemies visible and invisible, and I cannot tell when or where, or in what shape they may attack me." At the same time he snatched the helmet out of Sancho's hands, before he could discharge it of the curds, and clapped it on his head, without examining the contents. Now, the curds being squeezed between his bare crown and the iron, the whey began to run all about his face and beard, which so surprised him, that, calling to Sancho in great disorder, "What's this," cried he, "Sancho? What's the matter with me? Sure, my skull is growing soft, or my brains are melting, or else I sweat from head to foot! But if I do, I am sure it is not for fear. This certainly must be a very dreadful adventure that is approaching. Give me something to wipe my face if thou canst, for I am almost blinded with the torrent of sweat."

Sancho did not dare to say a word, but giving him a cloth, blessed his stars that his master had not found him out. Don Quixote dried himself, and taking off the helmet to see what it should be that felt so cold on his head, perceiving some white stuff, and putting it to his nose, soon found what it was. "Now, by the life of my Lady Dulcinea Toboso," cried he, "thou hast put curds in my helmet, vile traitor, and unmannerly squire!"

"Nay," replied Sancho cunningly, and keeping his countenance, "if they be curds, good your worship, give them me hither, and I will eat them. But hold, now I think on it, I had better not, for some enchanter must have put them there. What! I offer to do such a trick! Do you think I have no more manners? As sure as I am alive, sir, I have got my enchanters too, that owe me a grudge, and plague me as a limb of your worship; and I warrant they have put that stuff there on purpose to set you against me, and make you fall foul on my bones. But I hope they have missed their aim this time, i' troth! My master is a wise man, and must needs know that I had neither curds nor milk, nor anything of that kind; and if I had met with curds, I should sooner have put them in my mouth than his helmet."

"Well," said Don Quixote, "there may be something in that."

The gentleman had observed these passages, and stood amazed, but especially at what immediately followed; for the knight-errant, having put on the helmet again, fixed himself well in the stirrups, tried whether his sword were loose enough in his scabbard, and rested his lance. "Now," cried he, "come what will come; here am I, who dare encounter any enchanter *in propria persona*." By this time the wagon was come up with them, attended only by the carter, mounted on one of the mules, and another man who sat on the forepart of the wagon. Don Quixote making up to them, "Whither go ye, friends?" said he. "What wagon is this? What do you convey in it? And what is the meaning of these colours?"

"The wagon is mine," answered the wagoner: "I have there two brave lions, which the general of Oran is sending to the king our master, and these colours are to let the people understand that what goes here belongs to him."

"And are the lions large?" inquired Don Quixote.

"Very large," answered the man in the forepart of the wagon: "there never came bigger from Africa into Spain. I am their keeper," added he, "and have had charge of several others, but I never saw the like of these before. In the foremost cage is a lion, and in the other behind a lioness. By this time they are very hungry, for they have not eaten to-day; therefore, pray, good sir, ride out of the way, for we must make haste to get to the place where we intend to feed them."

"What!" said Don Quixote, with a scornful smile, "lion whelps against me! Against me, those puny beasts! And at this time of day? Well, I will make those gentlemen, that sent their lions this way, know whether I am a man to be scared with lions. Get off, honest fellow; and since you are the keeper, open their cages and let them both out; for, despite of those enchanters that have sent them to try me, I will make the creatures know, in the midst of this very field, who Don Quixote de la Mancha is."

"So," thought the gentleman to himself, "now has our poor knight discovered what he is; the curds, I find, have softened his skull, and mellowed his brains."

While he was making this reflection, Sancho came up to him, and begged him to dissuade his master from his rash attempt. "Oh, good, dear sir!" cried he, "for pity sake, hinder my master from falling upon these lions, by all means, or we shall be torn in pieces."

"Why," said the gentleman, "is your master so arrant a madman then, that you should fear he would set upon such furious beasts?"

"Ah, sir!" said Sancho, "he is not mad, but very venturesome."

"Well," replied the gentleman, "I will take care there shall be no harm done;" and with that, advancing to Don Quixote, who was urging the lion-keeper to open the cage, "Sir," said he, "knights-errant ought to engage in adventures from which there may be some hopes of coming off with safety, but not in such as are altogether desperate; for that courage which borders on temerity is more like madness than true fortitude. Besides, these lions are not come against you, but are sent as a present to the king, and therefore it is not the best way to detain them, or stop the wagon."

"Pray, sweet sir," replied Don Quixote, "go and amuse yourself with your tame partridges and your ferrets, and leave every one to his own business. This is mine, and I know best whether these worthy lions are sent against me or no." Then turning about to the keeper, "Sirrah! you rascal you," said he, "open your cages immediately, or I vow I will pin thee to the wagon with this lance."

"Good sir," cried the wagoner, seeing this strange apparition in armour so resolute, "for mercy's sake, do but let me take out our mules first, and get out of harm's way as fast as I can, before the lions get out; for if they should once set upon the poor beasts, I should be undone for ever, as that cart and they are all I have in the world to get a living with."

"Thou man of little faith!" said Don Quixote, "take them out quickly then, and go with them where thou wilt; though thou shalt presently see that thy precaution was needless, and thou mightest have spared thy pains."

The wagoner on this made all the haste he could to take out his mules, while the keeper cried out as loud as he was able, "Bear witness, all ye that are here present, that it is against my will I am forced to open the cages and let loose the lions; and I protest to this gentleman here, that he shall be answerable for all the mischief and damage they may do, together with the loss of my salary and fees. And now, sirs, shift for yourselves as fast as you can, before I open the cages; for as for myself, I know the lions will do me no harm."

Once more the gentleman tried to dissuade Don Quixote from doing so mad a thing, telling him that he tempted Heaven, in exposing himself without reason to so great a danger.

To this Don Quixote made no other answer but that he knew what he had to do.

"Consider, however, what you do," replied the gentleman, "for it is most certain that you are very much mistaken."

"Well, sir," said Don Quixote, "if you care not to be spectator of an action which you think is likely to be tragical, e'en put spurs to your mare and provide for your safety."

Sancho, hearing this, came up to his master with tears in his eyes, and begged him not to go about this fearful undertaking, to which the adventure of the windmills and the fulling-mills, and all the brunts he had ever borne in his life, were but children's play. "Good your worship," cried he, "do but mind; here is no enchantment in the case, nor anything like it. Alack-a-day! sir, I peeped even now through the grates of the cage, and I am sure I saw the claw of a true lion, and such a claw as makes me think the lion that owns it must be as big as a mountain."

"Alas! poor fellow!" said Don Quixote, "thy fear will make him as big as half the world. Retire, Sancho, and leave me; and if I chance to fall here, thou knowest our old agreement; repair to Dulcinea—I say no more." To this he added some expressions, which cut off all hopes of his giving over his mad design.

The gentleman in green would have opposed him; but, considering the other much better armed, and that it was not prudence to encounter a madman, he even took the opportunity, while Don Quixote was storming at the keeper, to march off with his mare, as Sancho did with Dapple, and the carter with his mules, every one making the best of his way to get as far as he could from the wagon, before the lions were let loose. Poor Sancho at the same time made sad lamentations for his master's death; for he gave him up for lost, not questioning but the lions had already got him in their clutches. He cursed his ill fortune, and the hour he came again to his service; but for all his wailing and lamenting, he punched on poor Dapple, to get as far as he could from the lions.

The keeper, perceiving the persons who fled to be at a good distance, fell to arguing and entreating Don Quixote as he had done before. But the knight told him again that all his reasons and entreaties were in vain, and bid him say no more.

Now while the keeper took time to open the foremost cage, Don Quixote stood debating with himself whether he had best make his attack on foot or on horseback; and upon mature deliberation, he resolved to do it on foot, lest Rozinante, not used to lions, should be put into disorder. Accordingly he quitted his horse, threw aside his lance, grasped his shield, and drew his sword; then advancing with a deliberate motion, and an undaunted heart, he posted himself just before the door of the cage, commending himself to Heaven, and afterwards to his Lady Dulcinea.

Here the author of this faithful history could not forbear breaking the thread of his narration, and raised by wonder to rapture and enthusiasm, makes the following exclamation: "Oh, thou most magnanimous hero! Brave and unutterably bold Don Quixote de la Mancha! Thou mirror and grand exemplar of valour! Thou second and new Don Emanuel de Leon, the late glory and honour of all Spanish cavaliers! What words, what colours shall I use to express, to paint in equal lines, this astonishing deed of thine? What language shall I employ to convince posterity of the truth of this thy more than human enterprise? What praises can be coined, and eulogies invented, that will not be outvied by thy superior merit, though hyperboles were piled on hyperboles? Thou, alone, on foot, intrepid and magnanimous, with nothing but a sword, and that none of the sharpest, with thy single shield, and that none of the brightest, stoodest ready to receive and encounter the savage force of two huge lions, as fierce as ever roared within the Lybian deserts. Then let thy own unrivalled deeds, that best can speak thy praise, amaze the world, and fill the mouth of fame, brave champion of La Mancha; while I am obliged to leave off the high theme, for want of vigour to maintain the flight." Here ended the author's exclamation, and the history goes on.

The keeper observing the posture Don Quixote had put himself in, and that it was not possible for him to prevent letting out the lions, without incurring the resentment of the desperate knight, set the door of the foremost cage wide open; where, as I have said, the male lion lay, who appeared of a monstrous bigness, and of a hideous, frightful aspect. The first thing he did was to roll and turn himself round in his cage; in the next place, he stretched out one of his paws, put forth his claws, and roused himself. After that he gaped and yawned for a good while, and showed his dreadful fangs, and then thrust out half a yard of broad tongue, and with it licked the dust out of his eyes and face. Having done this, he thrust his head quite out of the cage, and stared about with his eyes, which looked like two live coals of fire; a sight and motion enough to have struck terror into temerity itself

But Don Quixote only regarded the lion with attention, wishing his grim adversary would leap out of his hold, and come within his reach, that he might exercise his valour, and cut the monster piecemeal. To this height of extravagance had his folly transported him; but the generous lion, more gentle than arrogant, taking no notice of him, after he had looked about him awhile, turned his tail, and very contentedly lay down again in his apartment.

Don Quixote, seeing this, commanded the keeper to rouse him with his pole, and force him out, whether he would or no.

"Not I indeed, sir," answered the keeper; "I dare not do it for my life; for if I provoke

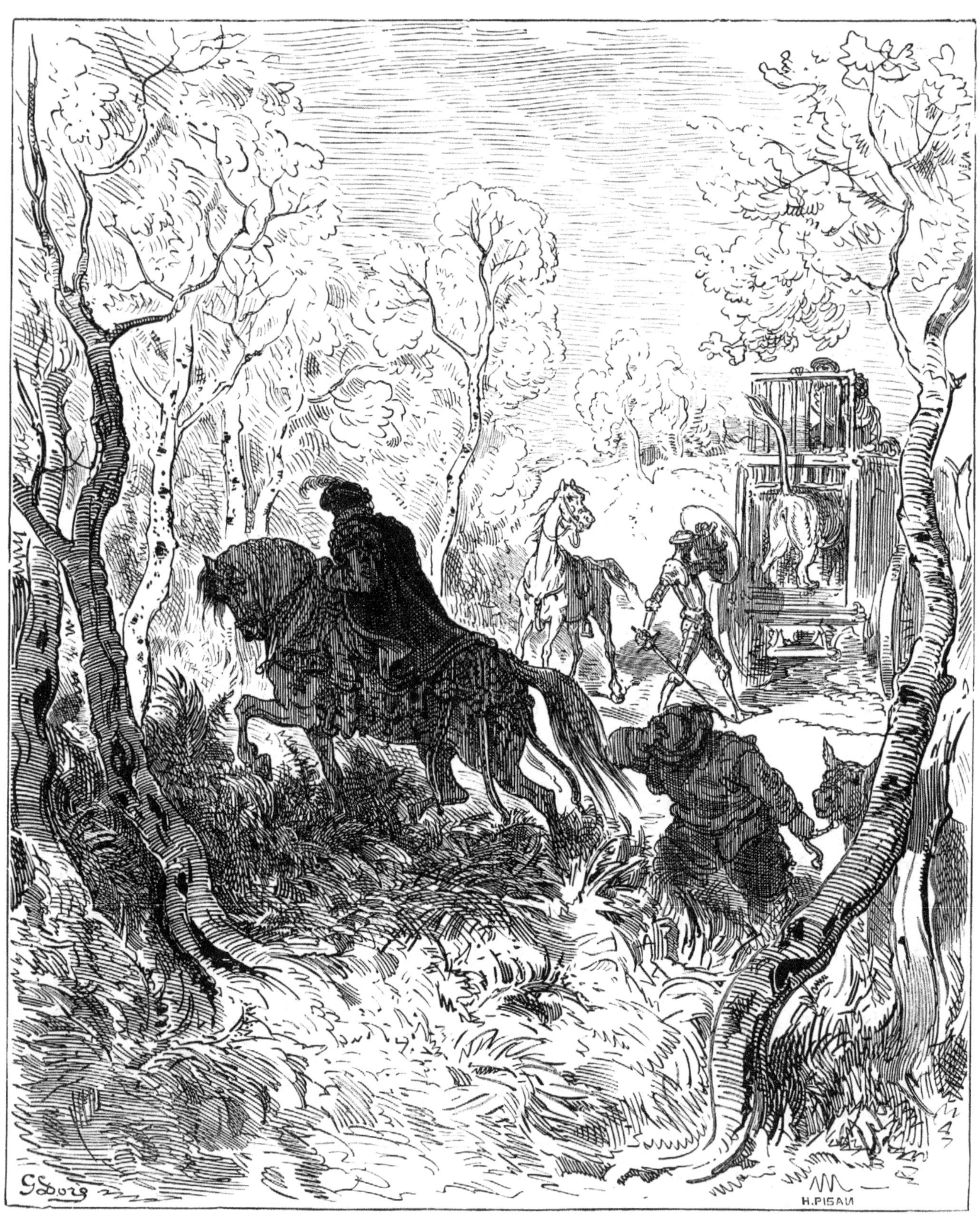

"He posted himself just before the door of the cage."

him, I am sure to be the first he will tear to pieces. Let me advise you, sir, to be satisfied with your day's work. 'Tis as much as the bravest that wears a head can pretend to do. Then pray go no farther, I beseech you. The door stands open, the lion is at his choice, whether he will come out or no. You have waited for him, you see he does not care to look you in the face; and since he did not come out at the first, I dare engage he will not stir out this day. You have shown enough the greatness of your courage. No man is obliged to do more than challenge his enemy, and wait for him in the field. If he comes not, that is his own fault, and the scandal is his, as the honour the challenger's."

"'Tis true," replied Don Quixote. "Come, shut the cage-door, honest friend, and give me a certificate under thy hand, in the amplest form thou canst devise, of what thou hast seen me perform; how thou didst open the cage for the lion; how I expected his coming, and he did not come out; how, upon his not coming out then, I stayed his own time, and instead of meeting me, he turned tail and lay down. I am obliged to do no more. So, enchantments avaunt! and Heaven prosper truth, justice, and knight-errantry!"

The keeper obeyed, and Don Quixote clapping on the point of his lance the handkerchief, with which he had wiped off the curds from his face, waved it in the air, and called as loud as he was able to the fugitives, who fled nevertheless, looking behind them all the way, and trooped on in a body, with the gentleman in green at the head of them.

At last Sancho observed the signal of the white flag, and calling out to the rest, "Hold," cried he, "my master calls to us; I will be hanged if he has not got the better of the lions."

At this they all faced about, and perceived Don Quixote flourishing his ensign; whereupon recovering a little from their fright, they leisurely rode back, till they could plainly distinguish Don Quixote's voice; and then they came up to the wagon. As soon as they were got near it—

"Come on, friend," said he to the carter; "put thy mules to the wagon again, and pursue thy journey; and, Sancho, do thou give him two ducats for the lion-keeper and himself, to make them amends for the time I have detained them."

"Ay, that I will with all my heart," quoth Sancho; "but what is become of the lions? Are they dead or alive?"

Then the keeper very formally related the whole action, not failing to exaggerate, to the best of his skill, Don Quixote's courage; how at his sight alone the lion was so terrified, that he neither would nor durst quit his stronghold, though for that end his cage-door was kept open for a considerable time; and how at length, upon his remonstrating to the knight, who would have had the lion forced out, that it was presuming too much upon Heaven, he had permitted, though with great reluctance, that the lion should be shut up again.

"Well, Sancho," said Don Quixote to his squire, "what dost thou think of this? Can enchantment prevail over true fortitude? No; these magicians may perhaps rob me of success, but never of my invincible greatness of mind."

In short, Sancho gave the wagoner and the keeper the two pieces. The first harnessed his mules, and the last thanked Don Quixote for his noble bounty, and promised to acquaint the king himself with his heroic action when he came to court.

"Well," said Don Quixote, "if his majesty should chance to inquire who the person was that did this thing, tell him it was the Knight of the Lions, a name I intend henceforth to take up, in lieu of that which I hitherto assumed—the Knight of the Woful Figure; in which proceeding I do but conform to the ancient custom of knights-errant, who changed their names as often as they pleased, or as it suited with their advantage."

After this the wagon made the best of its way, as Don Quixote, Sancho, and the gentleman in green did of theirs. The latter for a great while was so taken up with making his observations on Don Quixote, that he had not time to speak a syllable; not knowing what opinion to have of a person in whom he discovered such a mixture of good sense and extravagance. "For," said he to himself, "can there be anything more foolish than for this man to put on his helmet full of curds, and then believe them conveyed there by enchanters; or anything more extravagant than forcibly to endeavour to fight with lions?"

In the midst of this soliloquy, Don Quixote interrupted him.

"Without doubt, sir," said he, "you take me for a downright madman, and, indeed, my actions may seem to speak me no less. But for all that, give me leave to tell you I am not so mad, nor is my understanding so defective, as I suppose you may fancy. What a noble figure does the gallant knight make who, in the midst of some spacious place, transfixes a furious bull with his lance in the view of his prince! What a noble figure makes the knight who, before the ladies, at a harmless tournament, comes prancing through the lists enclosed in shining steel; or those court champions who, in exercises of martial kind, show their activity; and though all they do is merely but for recreation, are thought the ornament of a prince's court! But a much nobler figure is the knight-errant who, fired with the thirst of a glorious fame, wanders through deserts, through solitary wildernesses, through woods, through cross-ways, over mountains and valleys, in quest of perilous adventures, resolved to bring them to a happy conclusion. Yes, I say, a nobler figure is a knight-errant succouring a widow in some depopulated place, than the court-knight making his addresses to the city dames. Every knight has his particular employment. Let the courtier wait on the ladies; let him with splendid equipage adorn his prince's court, and with a magnificent table support poor gentlemen; let him give birth to feasts and tournaments, and show his grandeur, and liberality, and munificence, and especially his piety: in all these things he fulfils the duties of his station. But as for the knight-errant, let him search into all the corners of the world, enter into the most intricate labyrinths, and every hour be ready to attempt impossibility itself; let him in desolate wilds baffle the rigour of the weather, the scorching heat of the sun's fiercest beams, and the inclemency of winds and snow; let lions never fright him, dragons daunt him, nor evil spirits deter him. Since, then, my stars have decreed me to be one of those adventurous knights, I think myself obliged to attempt everything that seems to come within the verge of my profession. This, sir, engaged me to encounter those lions just now; and in attempting adventures, believe me, Signor Don Diego, it is better to exceed the bounds a little, and overdo rather than underdo the thing; because it sounds better in people's ears to hear it said how that such a knight is rash and hardy, than such a knight is dastardly and timorous."

"For my part, sir," answered Don Diego, "I think all you have said and done is agreeable to the exactest rules of reason; and I believe, if the ordinances of knight-errantry were lost, they might be all recovered from you, your breast seeming to be the safe repository where they are lodged. But it grows late; let us make a little more haste to get to our village, and to my habitation, where you may rest yourself after the fatigues which doubtless you have sustained, if not in body, at least in mind, whose pains often afflict the body too."

"Sir," answered Don Quixote, "I esteem your offer as a singular favour." And so, pushing on a little faster, about two in the afternoon they got to the house of Don Diego, whom now Don Quixote called the Knight of the Green Coat.

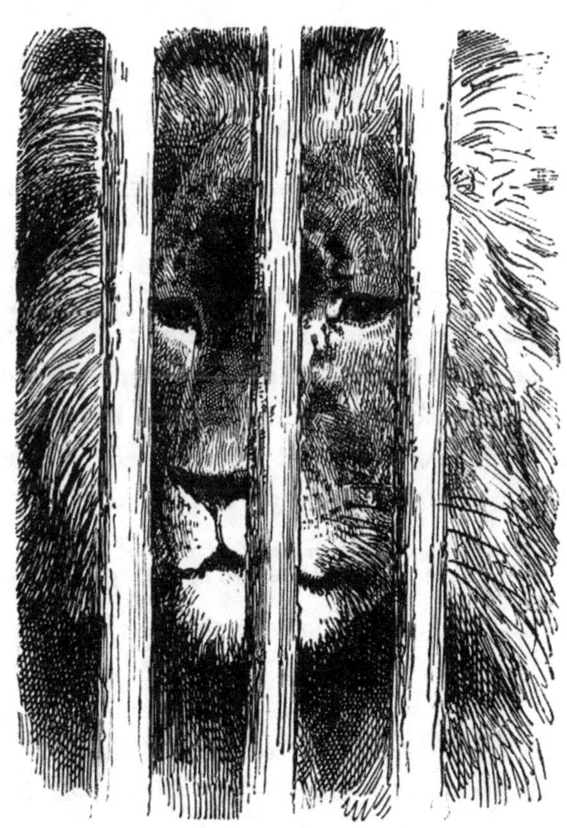

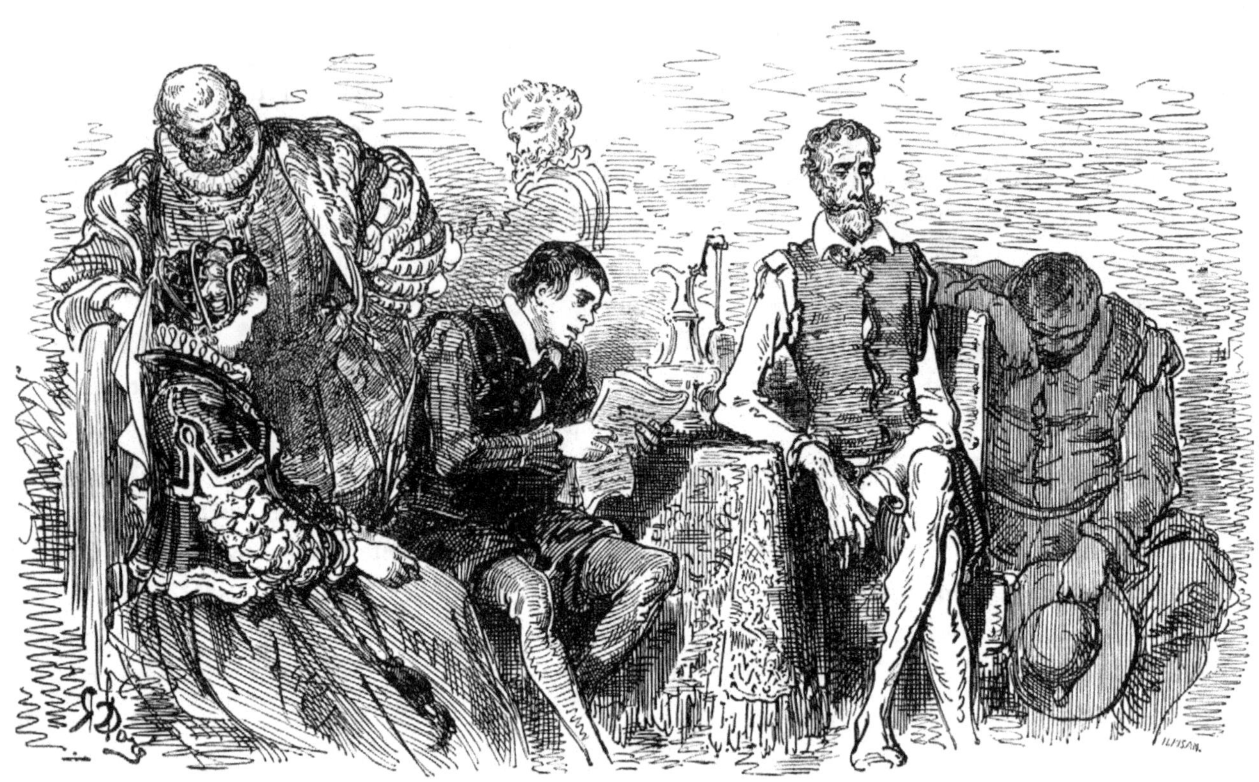

CHAPTER XVIII.

HOW DON QUIXOTE WAS ENTERTAINED AT THE CASTLE OR HOUSE OF THE KNIGHT OF THE GREEN COAT, WITH OTHER EXTRAVAGANT PASSAGES.

DON QUIXOTE found that Don Diego de Miranda's house was spacious, after the country manner. The arms of the family were over the gate in rough stone, the buttery in the fore-yard, the cellar under the porch, and all around several great jars of that sort commonly made at Toboso; the sight of which bringing to his remembrance his enchanted and transformed Dulcinea, he heaved a deep sigh, and neither minding what he said, nor who was by, broke out into the following exclamation :—

"'Oh, pledges! once my comfort and relief,
Though pleasing still, discovered now with grief.'

Oh, ye Tobosian urns! that awaken in my mind the thoughts of the sweet pledge of my most bitter sorrows!"

Don Diego's son, who, as it has been said, was a student and poetically inclined, heard these words as he came with his mother to welcome him home, and, as well as she, was not a little surprised to see what a strange creature his father had brought with him. Don Quixote alighted from Rozinante, and very courteously desired to kiss her ladyship's hands. "Madam," said Don Diego. "this gentleman is the noble Don Quixote de la Mancha, the

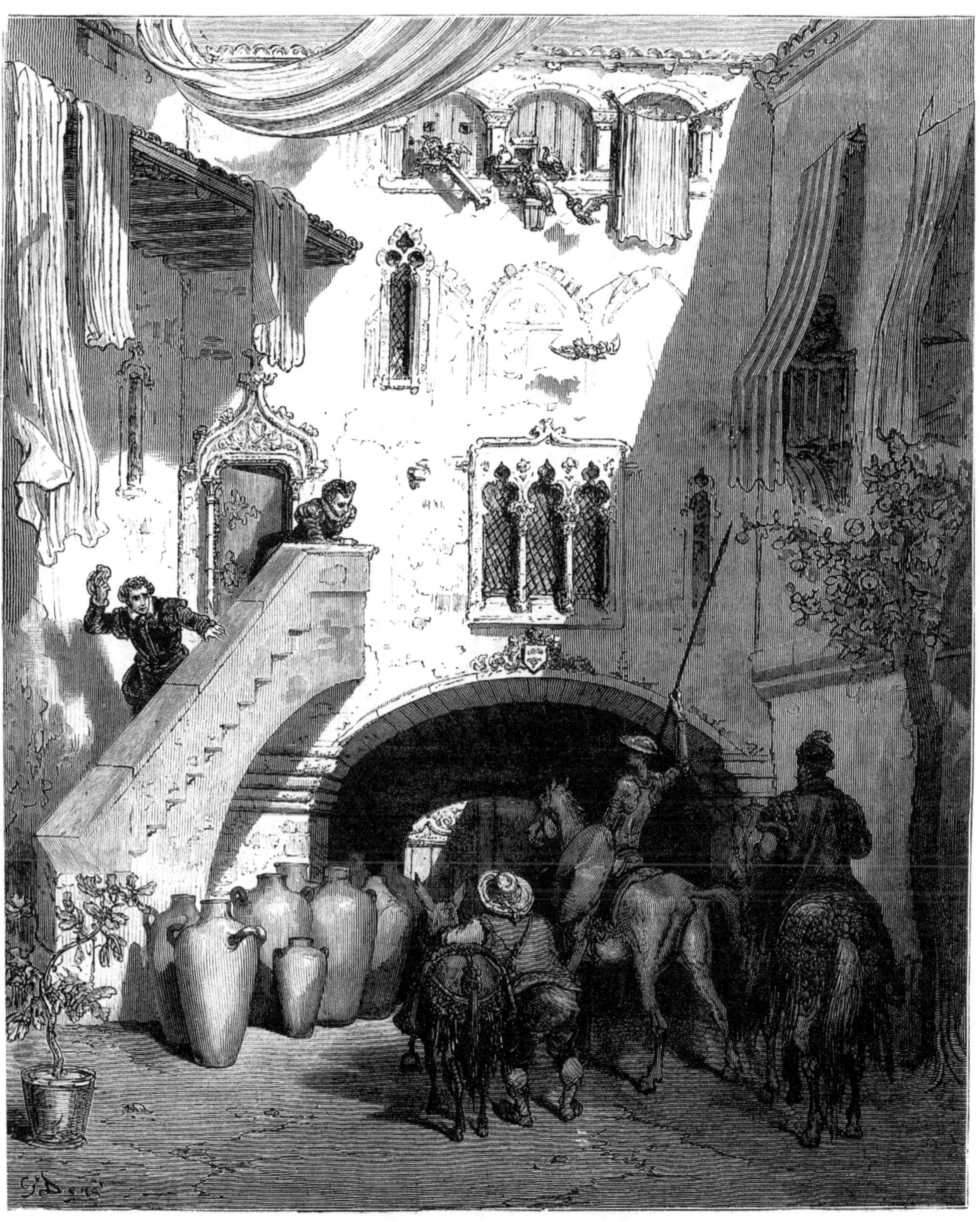

"Oh, ye Tobosian urns! that awaken in my mind the thoughts of the sweet pledge of my most bitter sorrows!"—*p.* 482.

wisest and most valiant knight-errant in the world; pray let him find a welcome suitable to his merit and your usual civility."

Thereupon Donna Christina (for that was the lady's name) received him very kindly, and with great marks of respect, to which Don Quixote made a proper and handsome return; and then almost the same compliments passed between him and the young gentleman, whom Don Quixote judged by his words to be a man of wit and sense.

Here the author inserts a long description of every particular in Don Diego's house, giving us an inventory of all the goods and chattels and every circumstance peculiar to the house of a rich country gentleman. But the translator presumed that it would be better to omit these little things and such like insignificant matters, being foreign to the main subject of this history, which ought to be more grounded on material truth than cold and insipid digressions.

Don Quixote was brought into a fair room, where Sancho took off his armour, and then the knight appeared in a pair of close breeches and a doublet of chamois-leather, all besmeared with the rust of his armour. About his neck he wore a plain band, unstarched, after the manner of a student; about his legs, sad-coloured spatterdashes; and on his feet, a pair of wax-leather shoes. He hung his trusty sword by his side in a belt of a sea-wolf's skin, which makes many of opinion he had been long troubled with a pain in the kidneys. Over all this he clapped on a long cloak of good russet-cloth. But first of all, he washed his head and face in five kettlefuls of water, if not in six (for as to the exact number there is some dispute), and it is observable that the water still retained a tincture of whey, thanks to Sancho's gluttony, which had made him clap into his master's helmet those dismal curds that so contaminated his awful head and face.

In this dress the knight, with a graceful and sprightly air, walked into another room, where Don Lorenzo, the young gentleman whom we have already mentioned, waited his coming, to keep him company till the cloth was laid; the mistress of the house being gone, in the meantime, to provide a handsome entertainment, that might convince her guest she understood how to make those welcome that came to her house. But before the knight was ready, Don Lorenzo had leisure to talk with his father about him.

"Pray, sir," said he, "who is the gentleman you have brought with you? Considering his name, his aspect, and the title of knight-errant which you give him, neither my mother nor I can tell what to think of him."

"Truly, son," answered Don Diego, "I do not know what to say to you. All that I can inform you of is that I have seen him play the maddest pranks in the world, and yet say a thousand sensible things that contradict his actions. But talk with him yourself, and feel the pulse of his understanding; make use of your sense to judge of his, though, to tell you the truth, I believe his folly exceeds his discretion."

Don Lorenzo then went to entertain Don Quixote, and after some discourse had passed between them, "Sir," said the knight, "I am not wholly a stranger to your merit; Don Diego de Miranda, your father, has given me to understand you are a person of excellent parts, and especially a great poet."

"Sir," answered the young gentleman, "I may perhaps pretend to poetry, but never to be a great poet. It is true, I am somewhat given to rhyming, and love to read good authors, but I am very far from deserving to be thought one of their number."

"I do not mislike your modesty," replied Don Quixote; "it is a virtue not often found among poets, for almost every one of them thinks himself the greatest in the world."

"There is no rule without an exception," said Don Lorenzo; "and it is not impossible but there may be one who may deserve the name, though he does not think so himself."

"That is very unlikely," replied Don Quixote. "But, pray, sir, tell me what verses are those that your father says you are so puzzled about? If it should be what we call a gloss or a paraphrase, I understand something of that way of writing, and should be glad to see it. If the composition be designed for a poetical prize, I would advise you only to put in for the second; for the first always goes by favour, and is rather granted to the great quality of the author than to his merit; but as to the next, it is adjudged to the most deserving; so that the third may in a manner be esteemed the second, and the first no more than the third, according to the methods used in our universities of giving degrees. And yet, after all, it is no small matter to gain the honour of being called the first."

"Hitherto all is well," thought Don Lorenzo to himself; "I cannot think thee mad yet; let us go on." With that, addressing himself to Don Quixote, "Sir," said he, "you seem to me to have frequented the schools; pray, what science has been your particular study?"

"That of knight-errantry," answered Don Quixote, "which is as good as that of poetry, and somewhat better, too."

"I do not know what sort of science that is," said Don Lorenzo, "nor, indeed, did I ever hear of it before."

"It is a science," answered Don Quixote, "that includes in itself all the other sciences in the world, or at least the greatest part of them. Whoever professes it, ought to be learned in the laws, and understand distributive and commutative justice, in order to right all mankind. He ought to be a divine, to give a reason of his faith and vindicate his religion by dint of argument. He ought to be skilled in physic, especially in the botanic part of it, that he may know the nature of simples, and have recourse to those herbs that can cure wounds; for a knight-errant must not expect to find surgeons in the woods and deserts. He must be an astronomer, to understand the motions of the celestial orbs, and find out by the stars the hour of the night, and the longitude and latitude of the climate in which fortune throws him; and he ought to be well instructed in all the other parts of the mathematics, that science being of constant use to a professor of arms, on many accounts, too numerous to be related. I need not tell you that all the divine and moral virtues must centre in his mind. To descend to less material qualifications: he must be able to swim like a fish, know how to shoe a horse, mend a saddle or bridle, and, returning to higher matters, he ought to be inviolably devoted to Heaven and his mistress, chaste in his thoughts, modest in words, liberal and valiant in deeds, patient in afflictions, charitable to the poor, and, finally, a maintainer of truth, though it cost him his life to defend it. These are the endowments to constitute a good knight-errant; and now, sir, be you a judge whether the professors of chivalry have an easy task to perform, and whether such a science may not stand in competition with the most celebrated and best of those that are taught in colleges."

"If it be so," answered Don Lorenzo, "I say it deserves the pre-eminence over all other sciences."

"What do you mean, sir, by that 'if it be so?'" cried Don Quixote.

"I mean, sir," cried Don Lorenzo, "that I doubt whether there are now, or ever were, any knights-errant, especially with so many rare accomplishments."

"This makes good what I have often said," answered Don Quixote; "most people will not be persuaded there ever were any knights-errant in the world. Now, sir, because I verily believe that, unless Heaven will work some miracle to convince them that there have been, and still are, knights-errant, those incredulous persons are too much wedded to their opinion to admit such a belief, I will not now lose time to endeavour to let you see how much you and they are mistaken; all I design to do is only to beseech Heaven to convince you of your being in an error, that you may see how useful knights-errant were in former ages, and the vast advantages that would result in ours from the assistance of men of that profession. But now effeminacy, sloth, luxury, and ignoble pleasures triumph, for the punishment of our sins."

"Now," said Lorenzo to himself, "our gentleman has already betrayed his blind side; but yet he gives a colour of reason to his extravagance, and I were a fool should I think otherwise."

Here they were called to dinner, which ended the discourse. And at that time Don Diego, taking his son aside, asked him what he thought of the stranger.

"I think, sir," said Don Lorenzo, "that it is not in the power of all the physicians in the world to cure his distemper. He is mad past recovery, but yet he has lucid intervals."

In short, they dined, and their entertainment proved such as the old gentleman had told the knight he used to give his guests—neat, plentiful, and well-ordered. But that which Don Quixote most admired was the extraordinary silence he observed through the whole house, as if it had been a monastery of mute Carthusians.

The cloth being removed, grace said, and hands washed, Don Quixote earnestly desired Don Lorenzo to show him the verses he had written for the poetical prize.

"Well, sir," answered he, "because I will not be like those poets that are unwilling to show their verses when entreated to do it, but will tire you with them when nobody desires it, I will show you my gloss or paraphrase, which I did not write with a design to get a prize, but only to exercise my muse."

"I remember," said Don Quixote, "a friend of mine, a man of sense, once told me he would not advise any one to break his brains about that sort of composition; and he gave me this reason for it, that the gloss or comment could never come up to the theme; so far from it, that most commonly it left it altogether, and ran contrary to the thought of the author. Besides, he said that the rules to which custom ties up the composers of those elaborate amusements are too strict, allowing no interrogations, no such interjections as 'said he,' or 'shall I say,' no changing of nouns into verbs, nor any altering of the sense; besides several other confinements that cramp up those who puzzle their brains with such a crabbed way of glossing, as you yourself, sir, without doubt, must know."

"Really, Signior Don Quixote," said Don Lorenzo, "I would fain catch you tripping, but you still slip from me like an eel."

"I do not know, sir," replied Don Quixote, "what you mean by your slipping."

"I will tell you another time," answered the young gentleman; "in the meanwhile be pleased to hear the theme and paraphrase, which is this:—

THE THEME.

"Could I recall departed joy,
Though barr'd the hopes of greater gain,
Or now the future hours employ,
That must succeed my present pain!"

THE GLOSS, OR PARAPHRASE.

I.

"All Fortune's blessings disappear,
She's fickle as the wind;
And now I find her as severe,
As once I thought her kind.
How soon the fleeting pleasure's past!
How long the lingering sorrows last!
Unconstant goddess, through thy hate,
Do not thy prostrate slave destroy,
I'd ne'er complain, but bless my fate,
Could I recall departed joy.

II.

"Of all thy gifts I beg but this,
Glut all mankind with more;
Transport them with redoubled bliss,
But only mine restore.
With thought of pleasure once possess'd,
I'm now as curst as I was bless'd;
Oh, would the charming hour return,
How pleased I'd live, how free from pain!
I ne'er would pine, I ne'er would mourn,
Though barr'd the hopes of greater gain.

III.

But, oh! the blessing I implore,
Not fate itself can give,
Since time elapsed exists no more,
No power can bid it live.
Our days soon vanish into nought,
And have no being but in thought.
Whate'er began must end at last;
In vain we twice would youth enjoy;
In vain would we recall the past,
Or now the future hours employ.

IV.

"Deceived by hope, and rack'd by fear,
No longer life can please;
I'll then no more its torments bear,
Since death so soon can ease.
This hour I'll die!—But let me pause—
A rising doubt my courage awes.
Assist, ye powers, that rule my fate!
Alarm my thoughts, my rage refrain,
Convince my soul there's yet a state
That must succeed my present pain."

As soon as Don Lorenzo had read over his paraphrase, Don Quixote rose from his seat, and taking him by the hand, "By the highest mansions in the universe," cried the knight aloud, "noble youth! you are the best poet in the world, and deserve to be crowned with laurel, not at Cyprus or Gaeta, as a certain poet said—whom Heaven forgive!—but at the University of Athens, were it still in being, and at those of Paris, Bologna, and Salamanca. May those judges that deny you the honour of the first prize, be shot with arrows by the god of verse, and may the Muses abhor to come within their houses! Pray, sir, if I may beg that favour, let me hear you read one of your loftiest productions, for I desire to have a full taste of your admirable genius."

I need not tell you that Don Lorenzo was mightily pleased to hear himself praised by Don Quixote, though he believed him to be mad; so bewitching and welcome a thing is adulation, even from those we at other times despise. Don Lorenzo verified this truth by his ready compliance with Don Quixote's request, and recited to him the following sonnet, on the story of Pyramus and Thisbe:—

PYRAMUS AND THISBE.

A SONNET.

See how, to bless the loving boy,
The nymph, for whom he burns with equal fires,
Pierces the wall that parts them from their joy,
While hovering love prompts, gazes, and admires.

"The trembling maid in whispers and in sighs
Dares hardly breathe the passion she betrays:
But silence speaks, and love through ravish'd eyes,
Their thoughts, their flames, their very souls conveys.

"Wild with desires, they sally out at last,
But quickly find their ruin in their haste:
And rashly lose all pleasure in despair.

"Oh, strange mischance! But do not fortune blame;
Love join'd them first, then death, the grave, and fame;
What loving wretch a nobler fate would share?"

"Now, Heaven be praised!" said Don Quixote, when Don Lorenzo had made an end. "Among the infinite number of insipid men of rhyme, I have at last found a man of rhyme and reason, and, in a word, an absolute poet."

Don Quixote stayed four days at Don Diego's house, and, during all that time, met with a very generous entertainment. However, he then desired his leave to go, and returned him a thousand thanks for his kind reception; letting him know that the duty of his profession did not admit of his staying any longer out of action, and therefore he designed to go in quest of adventures, which he knew were plentifully to be found in that part of Spain; and that he would employ his time in that till the tilts and tournaments began at Saragosa, to which place it was now his chief intent to go. However, he would first go to the cave of Montesinos, about which so many wonderful stories were told in those parts; and there he would endeavour to explore and discover the source and original springs of the seven lakes, commonly called the lakes of Ruydera. Don Diego and his son highly commended his noble resolution, and desired him to command whatever their house afforded, assuring him he was sincerely welcome to do it; the respect they had for his honourable profession, and his particular merit, obliging them to do him all manner of service.

In short, the day of his departure came, a day of joy and gladness to Don Quixote, but of grief and sadness to poor Sancho, who had no mind to change his quarters, and liked the good cheer and plenty at Don Diego's house much better than his short hungry commons in forests and deserts, or the sorry pittance of his ill-stored wallets, which he, however, crammed with what he thought could best make the change of his condition tolerable.

And now Don Quixote taking his leave of Don Lorenzo, "Sir," said he, "I do not know whether I have already said it to you, but if I have, give me leave to repeat it once more, that if you are ambitious of climbing up to the difficult, and in a manner inaccessible, summit of the Temple of Fame, your surest way is to leave the narrow path of poetry, and follow the narrower track of knight-errantry, which in a trice may raise you to an imperial throne." With these words Don Quixote seemed to have summed up the whole evidence of his madness. However, he could not conclude without adding something more. "Heaven knows," said he, "how willingly I would take Don Lorenzo with me, to instruct him in those virtues that are annexed to the employment I profess, to spare the humble, and crush the proud and haughty. But since his tender years do not qualify him for the hardships of that life, and his laudable exercises detain him, I must rest contented with letting you know that one way to acquire fame in poetry is to be governed by other men's judgment more than your own: for it is natural to fathers and mothers not to think their own children ugly; and this error is no where so common as in the offspring of the mind."

Don Diego and his son were again surprised to hear this medley of good sense and extravagance, and to find the poor gentleman so strongly bent on the quest of these unlucky adventures, the only aim and object of his desires.

After this, and many compliments and mutual reiterations of offers of service, Don Quixote having taken leave of the lady of the castle, he on Rozinante, and Sancho on Dapple, set out and pursued their journey.

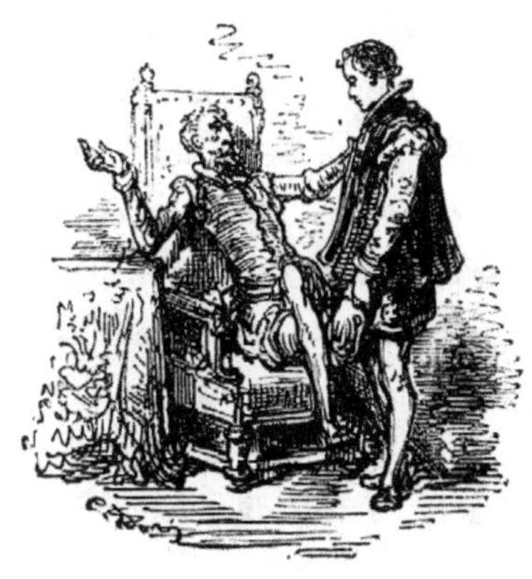

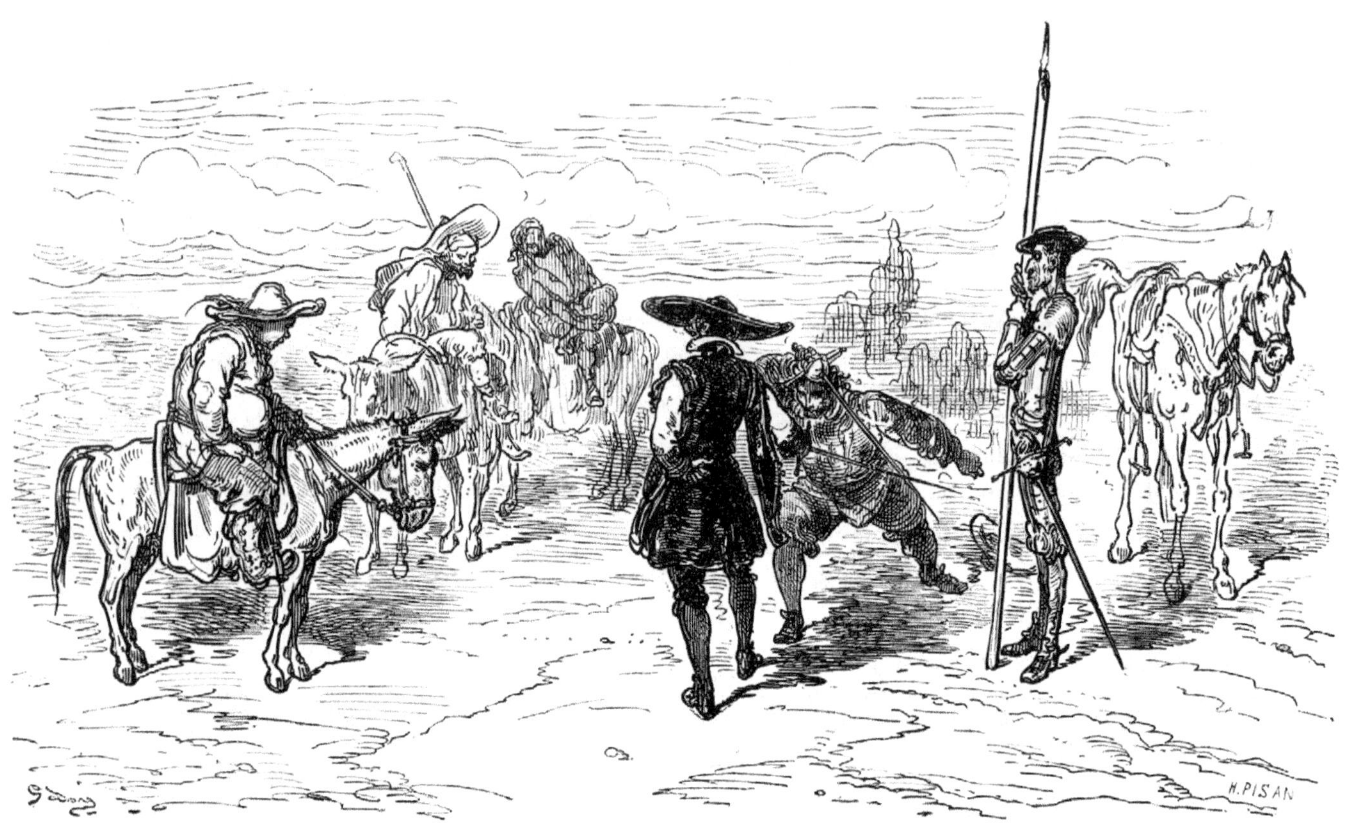

CHAPTER XIX.

THE ADVENTURE OF THE AMOROUS SHEPHERD, AND OTHER TRULY COMICAL PASSAGES.

DON QUIXOTE had not travelled far, when he was overtaken by two men that looked like students or ecclesiastics, with two farmers, all mounted upon asses. One of the scholars had behind him a small bundle of linen and two pairs of stockings, trussed up in green buckram like a portmanteau; the other had no other luggage but a couple of foils and a pair of fencing pumps. And the husbandmen had a parcel of other things, which showed that having made their market at some adjacent town, they were now returning home with their ware. They all wondered (as indeed all others did that ever beheld him) what kind of a fellow Don Quixote was, seeing him make a figure so different from anything they had ever seen. The knight saluted them, and perceiving their road lay the same way, offered them his company, entreating them, however, to move an easier pace, because their asses went faster than his horse; and to engage them the more, he gave them a hint of his circumstances and profession—that he was a knight-errant, travelling round the world in quest of adventures; that his proper name was Don Quixote de la Mancha, but his titular denomination the Knight of the Lions.

All this was Greek, or pedlar's French, to the countrymen; but the students presently found out his blind side. However, with a respectful distance, "Sir Knight," said one of them, "if you are not fixed to any set stage, as persons of your function seldom are, let us beg the honour of your company; and you shall be entertained with one of the finest and most sumptuous weddings that ever was seen, either in La Mancha or many leagues round it."

"The nuptials of some young prince, I presume?" said Don Quixote.

"No, sir," answered the other, "but of a yeoman's son and a neighbour's daughter; he the richest in all this country, and she the handsomest you ever saw. The entertainment at the wedding will be new and extraordinary; it is to be kept in a meadow near the village where the bride lives. They call her Quiteria the Handsome, by reason of her beauty; and the bridegroom Camacho the Rich, on account of his wealth. They are well matched as to age, for she draws towards eighteen, and he is about two-and-twenty, though some nice folks, that have all the pedigrees in the world in their heads, will tell ye that the bride comes of a better family than he; but that is not minded now-a-days, for money, you know, will hide many faults. And, indeed, this same Camacho is as free as a prince, and designs to spare no cost upon his wedding. He has taken a fancy to get the meadow shaded with boughs, that are to cover it like an arbour, so that the sun will have much ado to peep through and visit the green grass underneath. There are also provided for the diversion of the company several sorts of antics and morrice-dancers, some with swords, and some with bells; for there are young fellows in his village can manage them cleverly. I say nothing of those that play tricks with the soles of their shoes when they dance, leaving that to the judgments of their guests. But nothing that I have told or might tell you of this wedding is like to make it so remarkable as the things which I imagine poor Basil's despair will do. This Basil is a young fellow that lives next door to Quiteria's father. Hence love took occasion to give birth to an amour, like that of old between Pyramus and Thisbe; for Basil's love grew up with him from a child, and she encouraged his passion with all the kind return that modesty could grant; insomuch, that the mutual affection of the two little ones was the common talk of the village. But Quiteria coming to years of maturity, her father began to deny Basil the usual access to his house; and to cut off his further pretence, declared his resolution of marrying her to Camacho, who is indeed his superior in estate, though far short of him in all other qualifications; for Basil, to give him only his due, is the cleverest fellow we have; he will pitch ye a bar, wrestle, or play at tennis with the best in the country; he runs like a stag, leaps like a buck, plays at nine-pins so well you would think he tips them down by witchcraft; sings like a lark; touches a guitar so skilfully, he even makes it speak; and to complete his perfections, he handles a sword like a fencer."

"For that very single qualification," said Don Quixote, "he deserves not only Quiteria the Handsome, but a princess; nay, Queen Guinever herself, were she now living, in spite of Sir Lancelot and all that would oppose it."

"Well," quoth Sancho, who had been silent and listening all the while, "my wife used to tell me she would have every one marry with their match. 'Like to like,' quoth one to the collier, and 'every sow to her own trough,' as the other saying is. As for my part, all I would have is, that honest Basil e'en marry her; for, methinks, I have a huge liking to the young man; and so Heaven bless them together, say I, and a murrain seize those that will spoil a good match between those that love one another!"

"Nay," said Don Quixote, "if marriage should be always the consequence of mutual love, what would become of the prerogative of parents, and their authority over their children? If young girls might always choose their own husbands, we should have the best families intermarry with coachmen and grooms, and young heiresses would throw themselves away upon the first wild young fellows, whose promising outsides and assurance make them set up for fortunes, though all their stock consists in impudence. For the understanding, which alone should distinguish and choose in these cases as in all others, is apt to be blinded or biassed by love and affection; and matrimony is so nice and critical a point, that it requires not only our own cautious management, but even the direction of a superior power to choose right. Whoever undertakes a long journey, if he be wise, makes it his business to find out an agreeable companion. How cautious, then, should he be who is to take a journey for life, whose fellow-traveller must not part with him but at the grave; his companion at bed and board, and sharer of all the pleasures and fatigues of his journey, as the wife must be to the husband! She is no such sort of ware that a man can be rid of when he pleases. When once that is purchased, no exchange, no sale, no alienation can be made; she is an inseparable accident to man. Marriage is a noose, which, fastened about the neck, runs the closer and fits more uneasy by our struggling to get loose: it is a Gordian knot, which none can untie, and, being twisted with our thread of life, nothing but the scythe of death can cut it. I could dwell longer on this subject, but that I long to know from the gentleman whether he can tell us anything more of Basil."

"All I can tell you," said the student, "is, that he is in the case of all desperate lovers. Since the moment he heard of this intended marriage, he has never been seen to smile or talk rationally; he is in a deep melancholy, that might indeed rather be called a dozing frenzy; he talks to himself, and seems out of his senses; he hardly eats or sleeps, and lives like a savage in the open fields—his only sustenance a little fruit, and his only bed the hard ground; sometimes he lifts up his eyes to heaven, then fixes them on the ground, and in either posture stands like a statue. In short, he is reduced to that condition that we who are his acquaintance verily believe that this wedding to-morrow will be attended by his death."

"Heaven forbid, marry and amen!" cried Sancho. "Who can tell what may happen? 'He that gives a broken head can give a plaister.' 'This is one day, but to-morrow is another,' and 'strange things may fall out in the roasting of an egg.' 'After a storm comes a calm.' Many a man that went to bed well has found himself dead in the morning when he awaked. 'Who can put a spoke in Fortune's wheel?' nobody here, I am sure. Between a woman's yea and nay, I would not engage to put a pin's point, so close they be one to another. If Mrs. Quiteria love Mr. Basil, she will give Camacho the bag to hold: for this same love, they say, looks through spectacles that make copper like gold, a cart like a coach, and a shrimp like a lobster."

"Whither, in the name of ill-luck, art thou running now, Sancho?" said Don Quixote. "When thou fallest to threading thy proverbs and old wives' sayings, it is impossible for any one to stop thee. What dost thou know, poor animal, of Fortune, or her wheel, or anything else?"

"Why, truly, sir," quoth Sancho, "if you don't understand me, no wonder if my sentences be thought nonsense. But let that pass, I understand myself; and I am sure I have not talked so much like a ninny. But you, forsooth, are so sharp a cricket."

"A critic, blockhead!" said Don Quixote, "thou confounded corrupter of human speech!"

"By yea and by nay," quoth Sancho, "what makes you so angry, sir? I was never brought up at school nor 'varsity, to know when I murder a hard word. I was never at court to learn to spell, sir. Some are born in one town, some in another; one at St. Jago, another at Toledo; and even there all are not so nicely spoken."

"You are in the right, friend," said the student: "those natives of that city, who live among the tanners, or about the market of Zocodover, are confined to mean conversation, and cannot speak so well as those that frequent the polite part of the town, and yet they are all of Toledo. But propriety, purity, and elegance of style may be found among men of breeding and judgment, let them be born where they will; for their judgment is in the grammar of good language, though practice and example will go a good way. As for my part, I have had the happiness of good education; it has been my fortune to study the civil law at Salamanca, and I have made it my business all along to express myself properly, neither like a rustic nor a pedant."

"Ay, ay, sir," said the other student, "your parts might have qualified you for a master of arts degree, had you not misemployed them in minding so much those foolish foils you carry about with you, and that make you lag behind your juniors."

"Look you, good Sir Batchelor," said the other, "your mean opinion of these foils is erroneous and absurd; for I can deduce the usefulness of the art of fencing from several undeniable axioms."

"Pshaw," said Corchuelo, for so was the other called, "don't talk of axioms. I will fight you, sir, at your weapons. Here am I that understand neither quart nor tierce; but I have an arm, I have strength, and I have courage. Give me one of your foils, and in spite of all your distances, circles, falsifies, angles, and all other terms of your art, I will show you there is nothing in it, and will make reason glitter in your eyes. That man breathes not vital air that I will turn my back on; and he must have more than human force that can stand his ground against me."

"As for standing ground," said the artist, "I won't be obliged to it. But have a care, sir, how you press upon a man of skill, for ten to one, at the very first advance, but he is in your body up to the hilt."

"I will try that presently," said Corchuelo; and springing briskly from his ass, snatched one of the foils which the student carried.

" Hold, hold, sir," said Don Quixote, " I will stand judge of the field, and see fair play on both sides;" and interposing with his lance, he alighted, and gave the artist time to put himself in his posture and take his distance.

Then Corchuelo flew at him like a fury, helter-skelter, cut and thrust, back-stroke and fore-stroke, single and double, and laid on like any lion. But the student stopped him in the middle of his career with such a blow in the teeth, that he made Corchuelo foam at the mouth. He made him kiss the button of his foil, as if it had been a relic, though not altogether with so much devotion, In short, he told all the buttons of his short cassock with pure clean thrusts, and made the skirts of it hang about him in rags like fish-tails. Twice he struck off his hat, and in fine so mauled and tired him, that through perfect vexation Corchuelo took the foil by the hilt, and hurled it from him with such violence, that one of the countrymen that were by, happening to be a notary-public, has it upon record to this day, that he threw it almost three-quarters of a league; which testimony has served and yet serves to let posterity know that strength is overcome by art.

At last Corchuelo, puffing and blowing, sat down to rest himself, and Sancho, coming up to him, " Mr. Batchelor," quoth he, " henceforward take a fool's advice, and never challenge a man to fence, but to wrestle or pitch the bar; you seem cut out for those sports : but this fencing is a ticklish point, sir; meddle no more with it, for I have heard some of your masters of the science say they can hit the eye of a needle with the point of a sword."

Corchuelo acknowledged himself convinced of an error by experience, and embracing the artist, they became the better friends for this tilting. So, without staying for the notary that went for the foil, and could not be back in a great while, they put on to the town where Quiteria lived, they all dwelling in the same village.

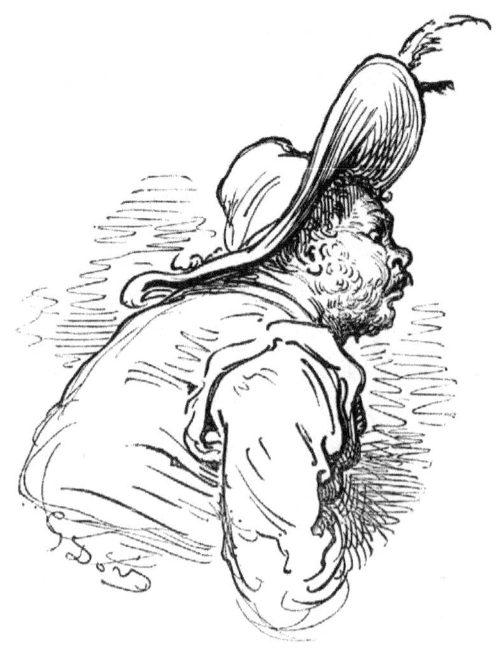

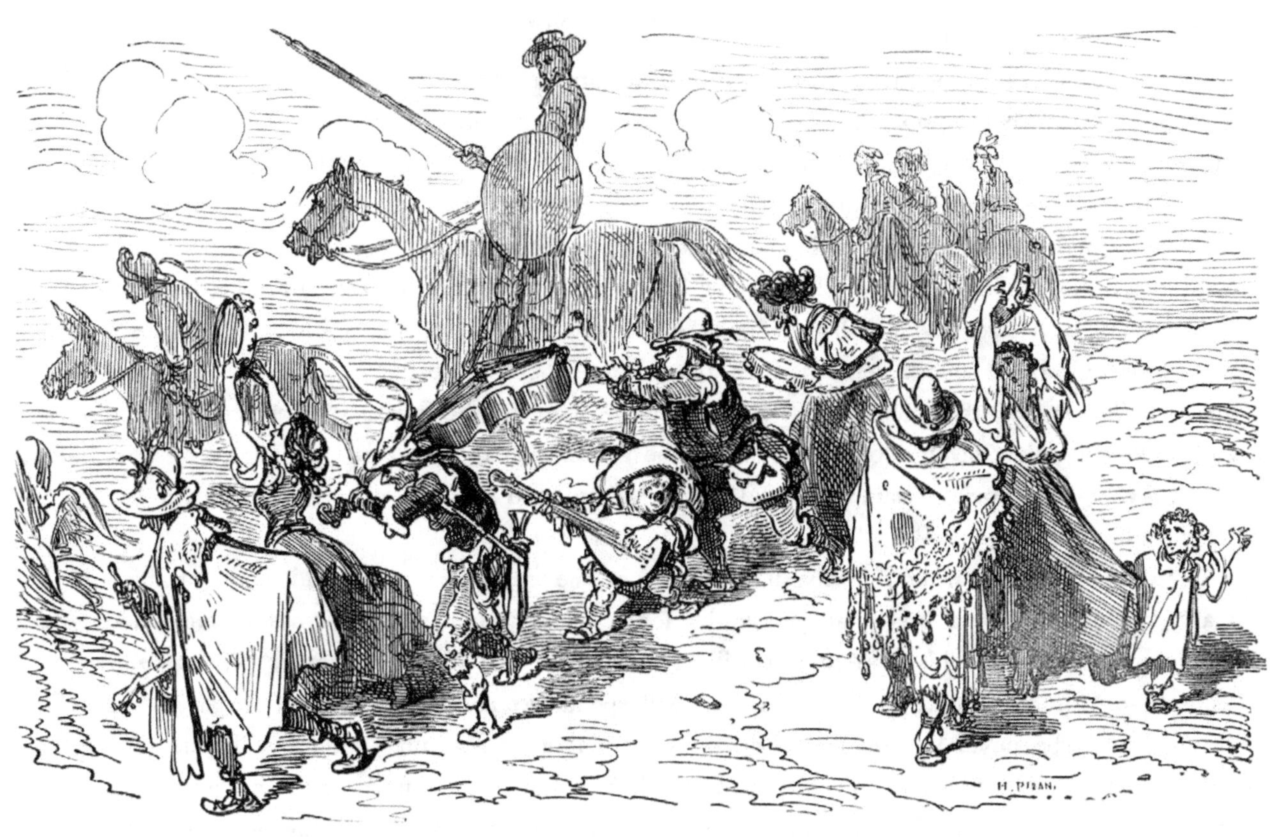

CHAPTER XX.

AN ACCOUNT OF RICH CAMACHO'S WEDDING, AND WHAT BEFELL POOR BASIL.

SCARCE had the fair Aurora given place to the refulgent ruler of the day, and allowed him time, with the heat of his prevailing rays, to dry the liquid pearls on his golden locks, when Don Quixote, shaking off sluggish sleep from his drowsy limbs, arose and called his squire; but finding him still snoring, " Oh, thou most happy mortal upon earth," said he, " how sweet is thy repose! envied by none, and envying no man's greatness, secure thou sleepest, thy soul composed and calm; no power of magic persecutes thee, nor are thy thoughts affrighted by enchantments. Sleep on, sleep on, a hundred times, sleep on. Those jealous cares that break a lover's heart do not extend to thee; neither the dread of craving creditors, nor the dismal foresight of inevitable want, or care of finding bread for a helpless family, keep thee waking. Ambition does not make thee uneasy, the pomp and vanity of this world do not perplex thy mind; for all thy care's extent reaches but to thy ass. Thy person and thy welfare thou hast committed to my charge—a burden imposed on masters by nature and custom, to weigh and counterpoise the offices of servants. Which is the greatest slave? The servant's business is performed by a few manual duties, which only reconcile him more to rest, and make him sleep more sound; while the anxious master has not leisure to close his eyes, but must labour day and night to make provision for the subsistence of his servant, not only in time of abundance, but even when the heavens deny those kindly showers that must supply this want."

To all this fine expostulation Sancho answered not a word, but slept on, and was not to be waked by his master's calling, or otherwise, till he pricked him with the sharp end of his lance. At length, opening his eyelids half way, and rubbing them, after he had gaped and yawned, and stretched his drowsy limbs, he looked about him, and sniffing up his nose, "I am much mistaken," quoth he, "if from this same arbour there come not a pure steam of a good broiled rasher, that comforts my nostrils more than all the herbs and rushes hereabouts; and a wedding that begins so savourly must be a dainty one."

"Away, cormorant!" said Don Quixote; "rouse, and let us go see it, and learn how it fares with the disdained Basil."

"Fare!" quoth Sancho; "why, if he be poor, he must e'en be so still, and not think to marry Quiteria. It is a pretty fancy, i' faith! for a fellow who has not a cross, to run madding after what is meat for his betters. I will lay my neck that Camacho covers this same Basil from head to foot with white sixpences, and will spend ye more at a breakfast than the other is worth, and be never the worse. And do you think that Madam Quiteria will quit her fine rich gowns and petticoats, her necklaces of pearl, her jewels, her finery and bravery, and all that Camacho has given her, and may afford to give her, to marry a fellow with whom she must knit or spin for her living? What signifies his bar-pitching and fencing? Will that pay for a pint of wine at a tavern? If all those rare parts won't go to market, and make the pot boil, any one may take them for me: though where they light on a man that has wherewithal, may I never stir if they do not set him off rarely. With good materials on a good foundation, a man may build a good house, and money is the best foundation in the world."

"For Heaven's sake, dear Sancho," said Don Quixote, "bring thy tedious harangue to a conclusion. For my part, I believe, wert thou let alone when thy clack is once set a going, thou wouldest scarce allow thyself time to eat or sleep, but wouldest prate on to the end of the chapter."

"Troth, master," replied Sancho, "your memory must be very short not to remember the articles of our agreement before I came this last journey with you. I was to speak what I would and when I would, provided I said nothing against my neighbour or your worship's authority; and I don't see that I have broken my indentures yet."

"I remember no such article," said Don Quixote; "and though it were so, it is my pleasure you now be silent and attend me; for the instruments we heard last night begin to cheer the valleys, and doubtless the marriage will be solemnised this morning, ere the heat of the day prevent the diversion."

Thereupon Sancho said no more, but saddled Rozinante, and clapped his pack-saddle on Dapple's back; then, both mounting, away they rode fair and softly into the arbour. The

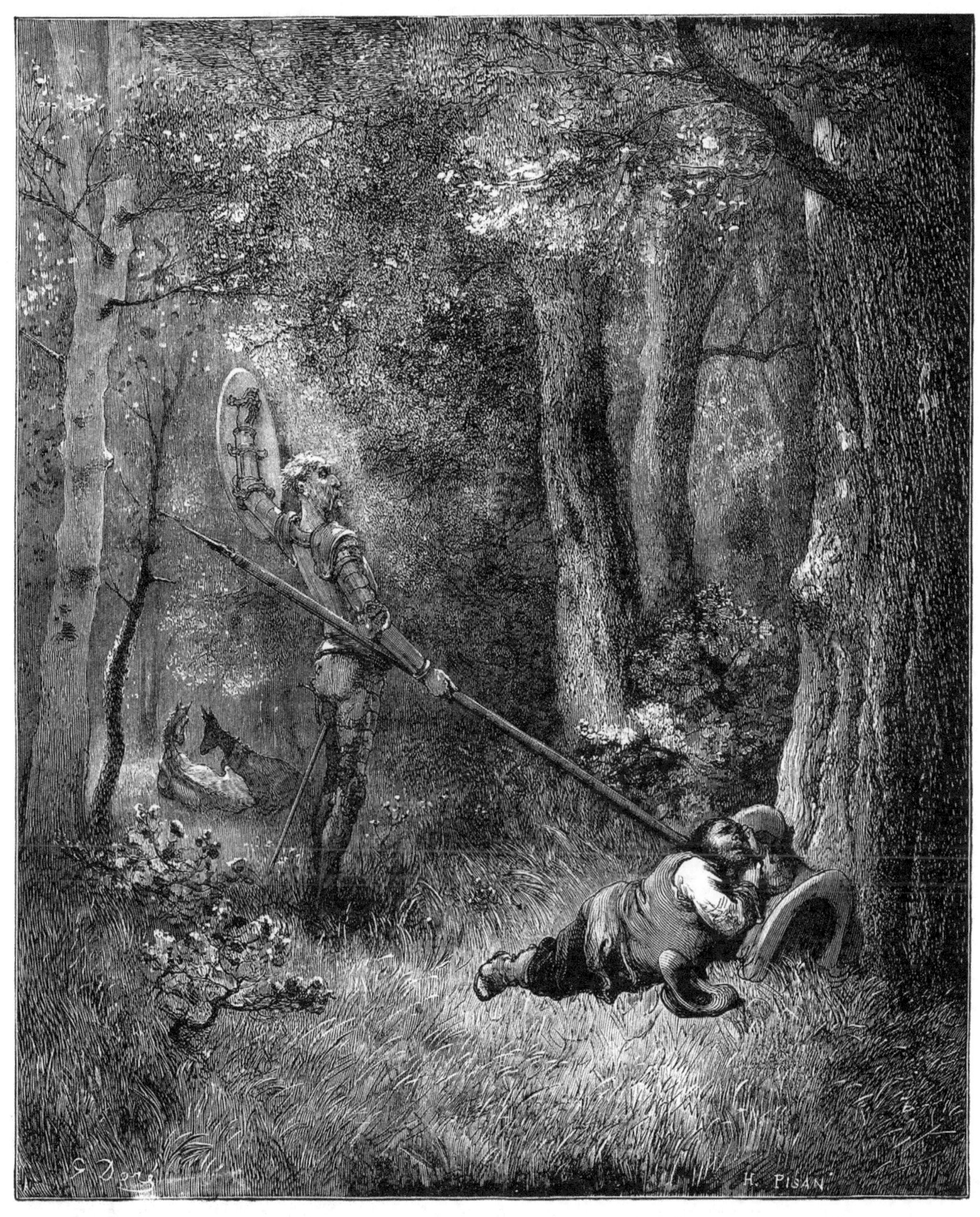

"To all this fine expostulation Sancho answered not a word."

first thing that blessed Sancho's sight there was a whole steer spitted on a large elm, before a mighty fire made of a pile of wood, that seemed a flaming mountain. Round this bonfire were placed six capacious pots, cast in no common mould, or rather six ample coppers, every one containing a whole shamble of meat, and entire sheep were sunk and lost in them, and soaked as conveniently as pigeons. The branches of the trees round were all garnished with an infinite number of cased hares and plucked fowls of several sorts: and then for drink, Sancho counted above threescore skins of wine, each of which contained above two arrobas, and, as it afterwards proved, sprightly liquor. A goodly pile of white loaves made a large rampart on the one side, and a stately wall of cheeses, set up like bricks, made a comely bulwark on the other. Two pans of oil, each bigger than a dyer's vat, served to fry their pancakes, which they lifted out with two strong peels when they were fried enough, and then they dipped them in as large a kettle of honey prepared for that purpose. To dress all this provision, there were above fifty cooks, men and women, all cleanly, diligent, and cheerful. In the ample belly of the steer, they had stewed up twelve little sucking pigs embowelled, to give it the more savoury taste. Spices of all sorts lay about in such plenty, that they appeared to be bought by wholesale. In short, the whole provision was indeed country-like, but plentiful enough to feast an army.

Sancho beheld all this with wonder and delight. The first temptation that captivated his senses was the goodly pots; his bowels yearned, and his mouth watered at the dainty contents: by-and-by he fell desperately in love with the skins of wine; and lastly, his affections were fixed on the frying-pans, if such honourable kettles may accept of the name. The scent of the fried meat put him into such a commotion of spirit, that he could hold out no longer, but accosting one of the busy cooks with all the smooth and hungry reasons he was master of, he begged his leave to sop a luncheon of bread in one of the pans.

"Friend," quoth the cook, "no hunger must be felt near us to-day, thanks to the founder. Light, 'light, man, and if thou canst find ever a ladle there, skim out a pullet or two, and much good may they do you."

"Alack-a-day!" quoth Sancho, "I see no ladle, sir."

"Blood and suet!" cried the cook, "what a silly, helpless fellow thou art! Let me see." With that he took a kettle, and sousing it into one of the pots, he fished out three hens and a couple of geese at one time. "Here, friend," said he to Sancho, "take this, and make shift to stay your stomach with that till dinner be ready."

"Heaven reward you!" cried Sancho, "but where shall I put it?"

"Here," answered the cook, "take ladle and all, and thank the founder, once more, I say; nobody will grudge it thee."

While Sancho was thus employed, Don Quixote saw twelve young farmers' sons, all dressed very gay, enter upon stately mares, as richly and gaudily equipped as the country could afford, with little bells fastened to their furniture. These, in a close body, made several

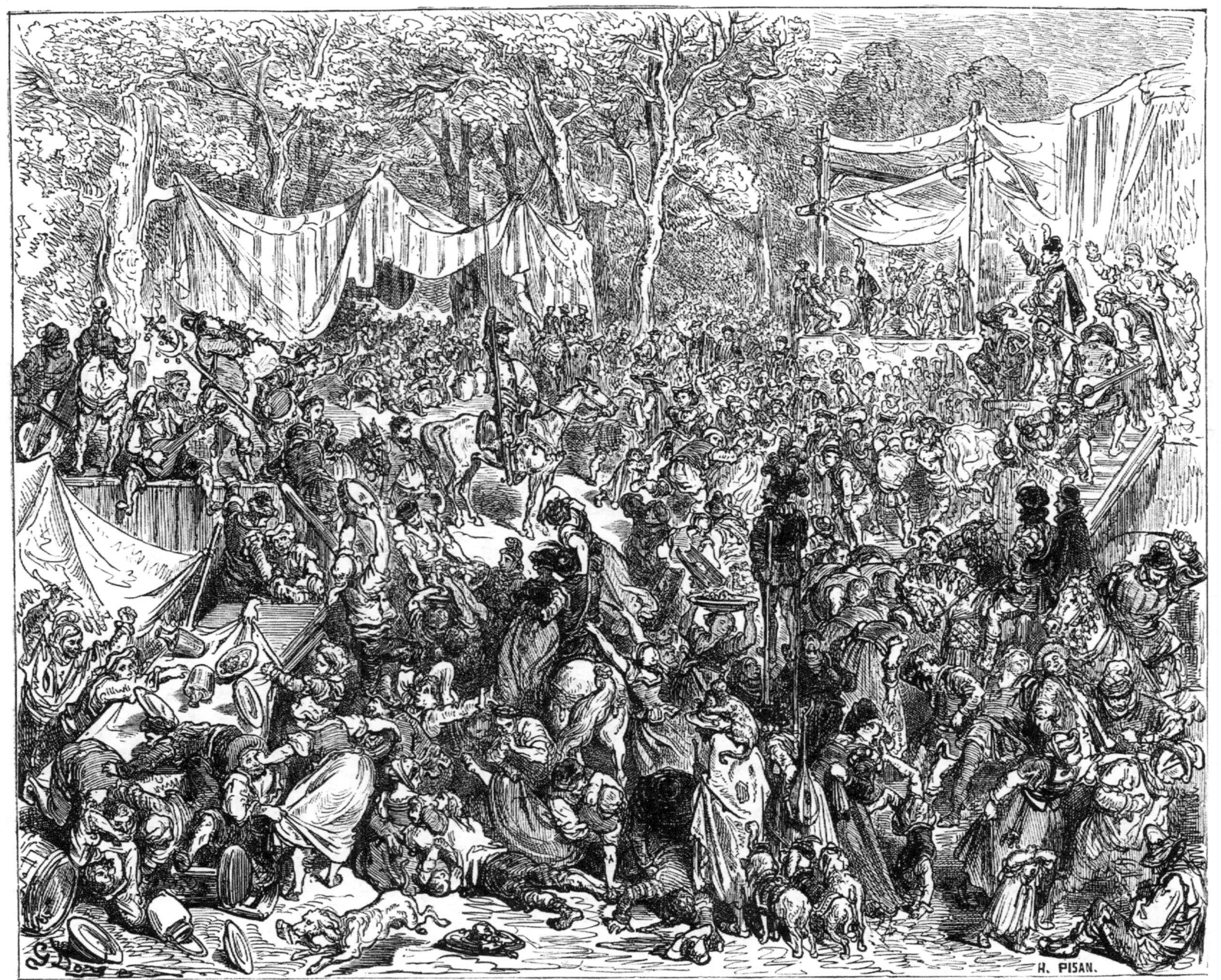

ARRIVAL OF DON QUIXOTE AT THE WEDDING OF CAMACHO AND QUITERIA.

careers up and down the meadow, merrily shouting and crying out, "Long live Camacho and Quiteria! he as rich as she is fair, and she the fairest in the world!"

"Poor ignorants!" thought Don Quixote, overhearing them, "you speak as you know; but had you ever seen my Dulcinea del Toboso, you would not be so lavish of your praises here."

In a little while, at several other parts of the spacious arbour entered a great number of dancers, and, amongst the rest, twenty-four young active country-lads, in their fine holland shirts, with their handkerchiefs wrought with several colours of fine silk, wound about their heads, each of them with sword in hand. They danced a military dance, and skirmished with one another, mixing and intermixing with their naked swords, with wonderful sleight and activity. without hurting each other in the least.

This dance pleased Don Quixote mightily, and though he was no stranger to such sort of dances, he thought it the best he had ever seen. There was another he also liked very well, performed by most beautiful young maids, between fourteen and eighteen years of age, clad in light green, with their hair partly filleted up with ribbons, and partly hanging loose about their shoulders, as bright and lovely as the sun's golden beams. Above all they wore garlands of roses, jasmine, amaranth, and honeysuckles. They were led up by a reverend old man and a matronly woman, both much more light and active than their years seemed to promise. They danced to the music of Zamora bagpipes; and such was the modesty of their looks, and the agility of their feet, that they appeared the prettiest dancers in the world.

After these came in an artificial dance or masque, consisting of eight nymphs, cast into two divisions, of which Love led one, and Wealth the other; one with his wings, his bow, his arrows, and his quiver; the other arrayed in several gaudy colours of gold and silk. The nymphs of Cupid's party had their names inscribed in large characters behind their backs. The first was Poesy, Prudence was the next, the third Nobility, and Valour was the fourth. Those that attended Wealth were Liberality, Reward, Treasure, and Peaceable Possession. Before them came a pageant representing a castle drawn by four savages clad in green, covered over with ivy, and grim surly vizards on their faces, so to the life that they had almost frightened Sancho. On the frontispiece, and on every quarter of the edifice, was inscribed, "The Castle of Wise Reservedness." Four expert musicians played to them on pipe and tabor. Cupid began the dance, and, after two movements, he cast up his eyes and bent his bow against a virgin that stood upon the battlements of the castle, addressing himself in this manner:—

"My name is Love, supreme my sway;
The greatest good and greatest pain.
Air, earth, and seas my power obey,
And gods themselves must drag my chain.

"In every heart my throne I keep,
Fear ne'er could daunt my daring soul:
I fire the bosom of the deep,
And the profoundest hell control."

Having spoken these verses, Cupid shot an arrow over the castle, and retired to his station. Then Wealth advanced and performed two movements; after which the music stopped, and he expressed himself thus:—

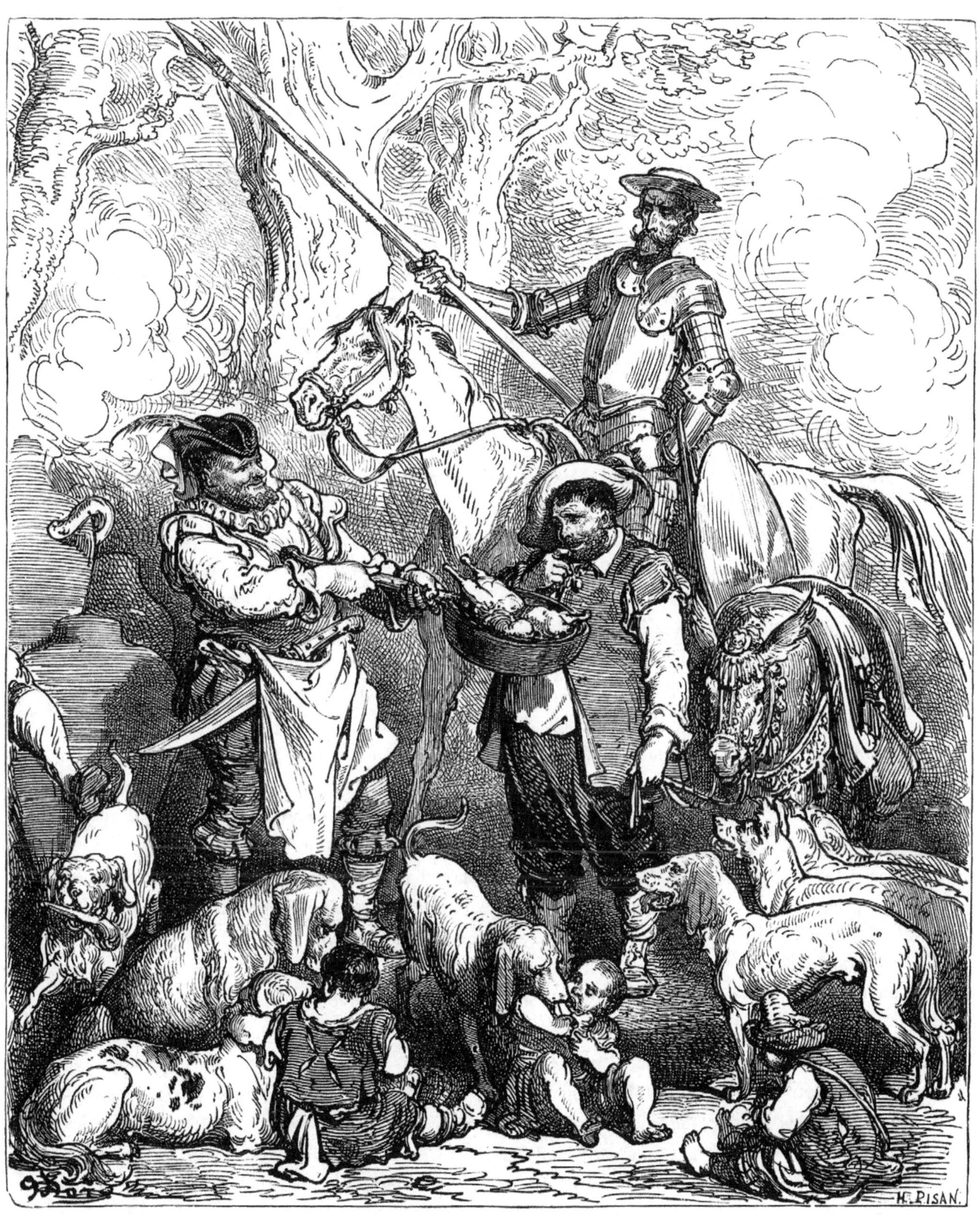

"Make shift to stay your stomach with that till dinner be ready."

"Love's my incentive and my end,
But I'm a greater power than Love;
Though earthly born, I earth transcend,
For Wealth's a blessing from above.

"Bright maid, with me receive and bless
The surest pledge of all success;
Desired by all, used right by few,
But best bestow'd, when graced by you."

Wealth withdrew, and Poesy came forward, and after she had performed her movements like the rest, fixing her eyes upon the lady of the castle, repeated these lines:—

"Sweet Poesy in moving lays
Love into hearts, sense into souls conveys;
With sacred rage can tune to bliss or woe,
Sways all the man, and gives him heaven below.

"Bright nymph, with every grace adorn'd,
Shall noble verse by thee be scorn'd?
'Tis wit can best thy beauty prize;
Then raise the Muse, and thou by her shalt rise."

Poesy retired, and Liberality advanced from Wealth's side, and, after the dance, spoke thus:—

'Behold that noble golden mien
Betwixt the sparing and profuse!
Good sense and merit must be seen
Where Liberality's in use.

"But I for thee will lavish seem;
For thee profuseness I'll approve:
For, where the merit is extreme,
Who'd not be prodigal of love?"

In this manner all the persons of each party advanced and spoke their verses, of which some were pretty and some foolish enough. Then the two divisions joined into a very pretty country-dance; and still as Cupid passed by the castle, he shot a flight of arrows, and Wealth battered it with golden balls; then drawing out a great purse of Roman cat's-skin, that seemed full of money, he threw it against the castle, the boards of which were presently disjointed, and fell down, leaving the virgin discovered without any defence. Thereupon Wealth immediately entered with his party, and throwing a golden chain about her neck, made a show of leading her prisoner. But then Cupid with his attendants came to her rescue; and both parties engaging, were parted by the savages, who joined the boards together, enclosing the virgin as before; and all was performed with measure and to the music that played all the while.

When all was over, Don Quixote asked one of the nymphs who it was that composed the entertainment. She answered that it was a certain clergyman who lived in their town.

"I dare lay a wager," said Don Quixote, "he was more a friend to Basil than to Camacho, and knows better what belongs to a play than a prayer-book. He has expressed Basil's parts and Camacho's estate very naturally in the design of your dance."

"God bless the king and Camacho! say I," quoth Sancho, who heard this.

"Well, Sancho," said Don Quixote, "thou art a white-livered rogue to change parties as thou dost; thou art like the rabble, which always cry, 'Long live the conqueror!'"

"I know not what I am like," replied Sancho; "but this I know, that this kettleful of geese and hens is a bribe for a prince. Camacho has filled my belly, and therefore has won my heart. When shall I ladle such dainty scum out of Basil's porridge-pots?" added he, showing his master the meat, and falling on lustily; "therefore, a fig for his abilities say I. As he sows so let him reap, and as he reaps so let him sow. My old grandam was wont to say there were but two families in the world—Have-Much and Have-Little; and she had ever a great kindness for the family of the Have-Much. A doctor gives

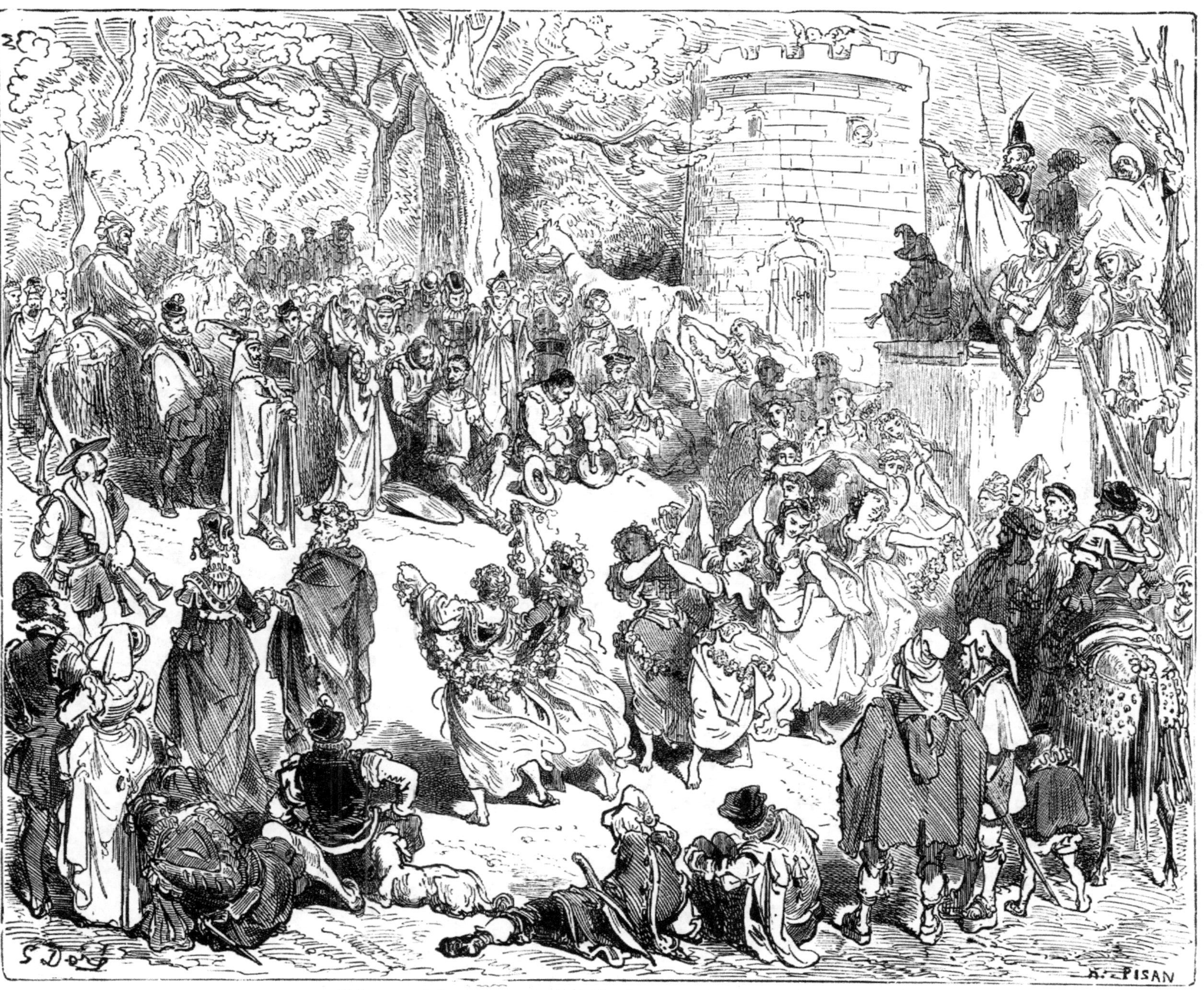

"They were led up by a reverend old man and a matronly woman."—*p.* 500.

his advice by the pulse of your pocket ; and an ass covered with gold looks better than a horse with a pack-saddle; so, once more I say, Camacho for my money!"

"Well!" said Don Quixote, "thou wilt never be silent till thy mouth is full of clay; when thou art dead, I hope I shall have some rest."

"Faith and troth, now, master!" quoth Sancho, "you did ill to talk of death; Heaven bless us! it is no child's play. Death eats up all things, both the young lamb and old sheep; and I have heard our parson say, 'Death values a prince no more than a clown;' all is fish that comes to his net; he throws at all, and sweeps stakes; he is no mower that takes a nap at noon-day, but drives on, fair weather or foul, and cuts down the green grass as well as the ripe corn."

"Hold, hold!" cried the knight, "go no farther, for thou art come to a very handsome period. Thou hast said as much of death, in thy home-spun cant, as a good preacher could have done. Thou hast got the knack of preaching, man! I must get thee a pulpit and benefice."

"He preaches well that lives well," quoth Sancho; "that is all the divinity I understand."

"Thou hast divinity enough," said the Don; "only I wonder at one thing: it is said the beginning of wisdom proceeds from the fear of Heaven; how happens it, then, that thou, who fearest a lizard more than Omnipotence, shouldst be so wise?"

"Pray, sir," said Sancho, "judge you of your knight-errantry, and don't meddle with other men's fears, for I am as pretty a fearer of Heaven as any of my neighbours; and so let me dispatch this scum, and much good may it do thee, honest Sancho!"

With that he attacked it with so courageous an appetite, that he sharpened his master's, who would certainly have kept him company, had he not been prevented by that which necessity obliges me to relate this instant.

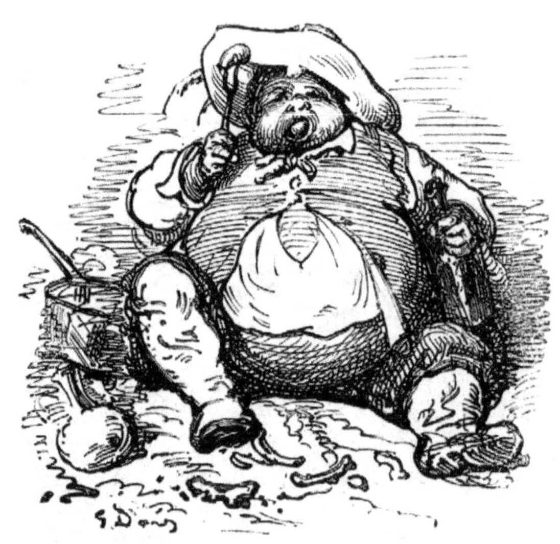

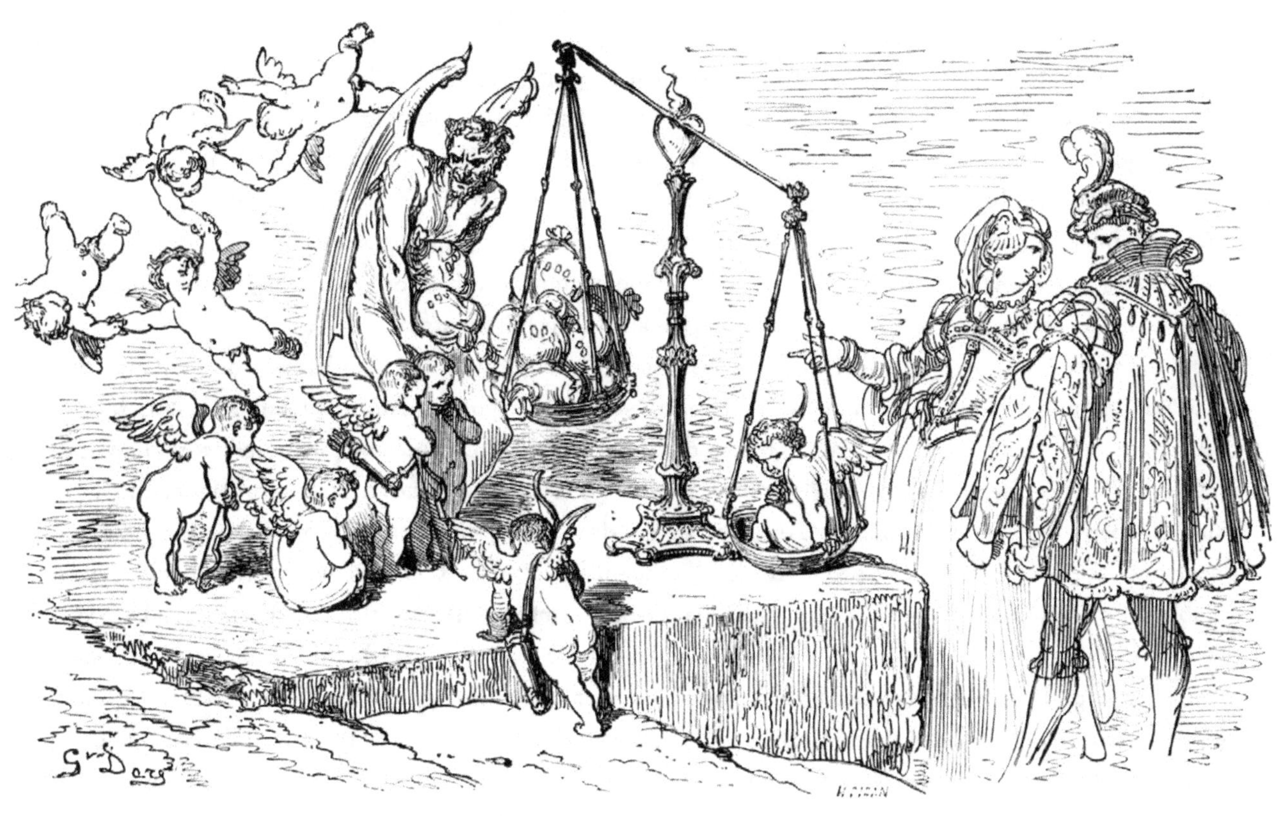

CHAPTER XXI.

THE PROGRESS OF CAMACHO'S WEDDING, WITH OTHER DELIGHTFUL ACCIDENTS.

WHILE Don Quixote and Sancho were discoursing, as the former chapter has told you, they were interrupted by a great noise of joy and acclamations raised by the horsemen, as, shouting and galloping, they went to meet the young couple, who, surrounded by a thousand instruments and devices, were coming to the arbour, accompanied by the curate, their relations, and all the better sort of the neighbourhood, set out in their holiday clothes.

"Hey-day!" quoth Sancho, as soon as he saw the bride; "what have we here? Ah! this is no country lass, but a fine court lady, all in her silks and satins, I declare! Look, look ye, master! see if, instead of glass necklaces, she have not on fillets of rich coral, and instead of green serge of Cuencha, a thirty-piled velvet. I'll warrant her lacing is white linen, too; but hold, may I never squint if it be not satin! Bless us! see what rings she has on her fingers! no jet, no pewter baubles—pure, beaten gold, as I am a sinner! and set with pearls, too! if every pearl be not as white as a syllabub, and each of them as precious as an eye! How she is bedizened, and glistens from top to toe! And now, yonder again, what fine long locks the girl has got! if they be not false, I never saw longer in my born days. Well, I say no more, but happy is the man that has thee!"

Don Quixote could not help smiling to hear Sancho set forth the bride after his rustic way, though, at the same time, he beheld her with admiration, thinking her the most beautiful woman he had ever seen, except his mistress Dulcinea. However, the fair Quiteria appeared somewhat pale, probably with the ill rest which brides commonly have the night before their marriage, in order to dress themselves to advantage. There was a large scaffold erected on one side of the meadow, and adorned with carpets and boughs, for the marriage ceremony, and the more convenient prospect of the shows and entertainments.

The procession was just arrived to this place, when they heard a piercing outcry, and a voice calling out, "Stay, rash and hasty people, stay!" Upon which all turning about, they saw a person coming after them in a black coat, bordered with crimson, powdered with flames of fire. On his head he wore a garland of mournful cypress, and a large truncheon in his hand, headed with an iron spike. As soon as he drew near, they knew him to be the gallant Basil, and the whole assembly began to fear some mischief would ensue, seeing him come thus unlooked-for and with such an outcry and behaviour. He came up, tired and panting, before the bride and bridegroom; then, leaning on his truncheon, he fixed his eyes on Quiteria, turning pale and trembling at the same time, and, with a fearful, hollow voice, "Too well you know," cried he, "unkind Quiteria, that, by the ties of truth and law of that Heaven which we all revere, while I have life you cannot be married to another. You, forgetting all the ties between us, are going now to break them, and give my right to another, whose large possessions, though they can procure him all other blessings, I had never envied if they had not purchased you. But no more. The Fates have ordained it, and I will further their design, by removing this unhappy obstacle out of your way. Live, rich Camacho, live happy with the ungrateful Quiteria many years, and let the poor, the miserable Basil die, whose poverty has clipped the wings of his felicity, and laid him in the grave!"

Saying these last words, he drew out of his supposed truncheon a short tuck that was concealed in it, and setting the hilt of it to the ground, he fell upon the point in such a manner, that it came out all bloody at his back, the poor wretch weltering on the ground in blood. His friends, confounded by this strange accident, ran to help him, and Don Quixote, forsaking Rozinante, made haste to his assistance, and taking him up in his arms, found there was still life in him. They would fain have drawn the sword out of his body, but the curate urged it was not convenient till he had made confession and prepared himself for death, which would immediately attend the effusion of blood, upon pulling out the tuck.

While they were debating this point, Basil seemed to come a little to himself, and calling on the bride, "O Quiteria!" said he, with a faint and doleful voice, "now, now, in this last and departing minute of my life, even in this dreadful agony of death, would you but vouchsafe to give me your hand and own yourself my wife, I would die contented."

The curate hearing this, very earnestly recommended to him the care of his soul's health, which at the present juncture was more proper than any gratification of his outward

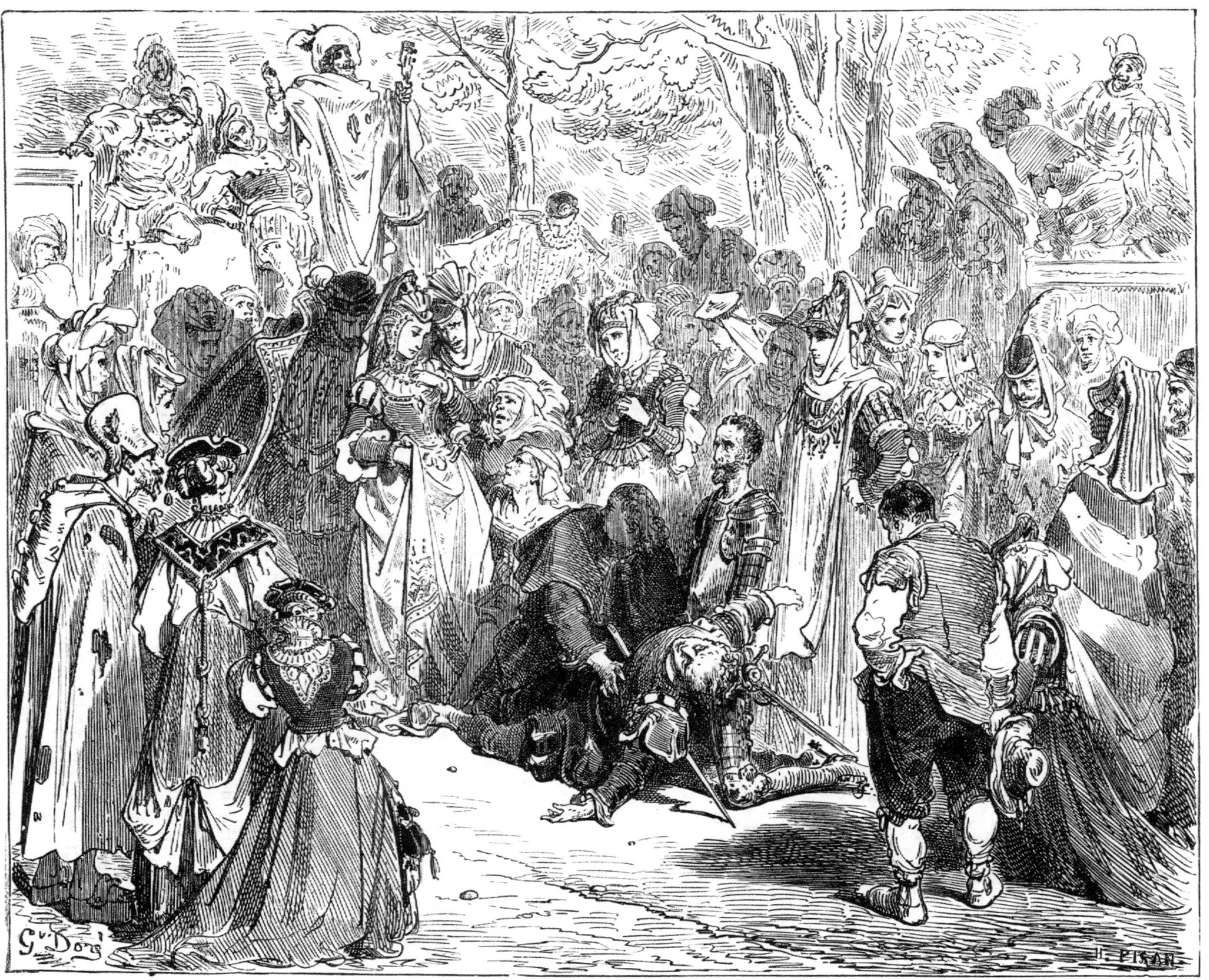

"The poor virgin, trembling and dismayed, without speaking a word, came to poor Basil."—*p.* 508.

man; that his time was but short, and he ought to be very earnest with Heaven, in imploring its mercy and forgiveness for all his sins, but especially for this last desperate action. To which Basil answered that he could think of no happiness till Quiteria yielded to be his; but if she would do it, that satisfaction would calm his spirits, and dispose him to confess himself heartily.

Don Quixote, hearing this, cried out aloud that Basil's demand was just and reasonable, and Signior Camacho might as honourably receive her as the worthy Basil's widow as if he had received her at her father's hands. "Say but the word, madam," continued he; "pronounce it once, to save a man from despair; you will not be long bound to it, since the only bed of this bridegroom must be the grave." Camacho stood all this while strangely confounded, till, at last, he was prevailed on, by the repeated importunities of Basil's friends, to consent that Quiteria should humour the dying man, knowing her own happiness would thereby be deferred but a few minutes longer. Then they all bent their entreaties to Quiteria, some with tears in their eyes, others with all the engaging arguments their pity could suggest. She stood a long time inexorable, and did not return any answer, till at last the curate came to her and bid her resolve what she would do, for Basil was just ready to give up the ghost. But then the poor virgin, trembling and dismayed, without speaking a word, came to poor Basil, who lay gasping for breath, with his eyes fixed in his head, as if he were just expiring. She kneeled down by him, and, with the most manifest signs of grief, beckoned to him for his hand. Then Basil, opening his eyes, and fixing them on her, "O Quiteria!" said he; "your heart at last relents, when your pity comes too late. Thy arms are now extended to relieve me, when those of death draw me to their embraces; and they, alas! are much too strong for thine. All I desire of thee, oh, fatal beauty! is this: let not that fair hand deceive me now, as it has done before, but confess that what you do is free and voluntary, without constraint, or in compliance to any one's commands; declare me openly thy true and lawful husband; thou wilt not, sure, dissemble with one in death, and deal falsely with his departing soul, that all his life has been true to thee?"

In the midst of this discourse he fainted away, and all the bystanders thought him gone. The poor Quiteria, with a blushing modesty, a kind of violence upon herself, took him by the hand, and with a great deal of emotion, "No force," said she, "could ever work upon my will to this degree; therefore, believe it purely my own free will and inclination that I here publicly declare you my only lawful husband; here is my hand in pledge, and I expect yours as freely in return, if your pains and this sudden accident have not yet bereft you of all sense."

"I give it you," said Basil, "and here I own myself thy husband."

"And I thy wife," said she, "whether thy life be long or whether from my arms they bear thee this instant to the grave."

"Methinks," quoth Sancho, "this young man talks too much for a man in his condition. Pray, advise him to leave off his wooing, and mind his soul's health."

Now, when Basil and Quiteria had thus plighted their faith to each other, while yet their hands were joined together, the tender-hearted curate, with tears in his eyes, poured on them both the nuptial blessing, beseeching Heaven, at the same time, to have mercy on the new-married man's soul, and in a manner mixing the burial service with the matrimonial.

As soon as the benediction was pronounced, up starts Basil briskly from the ground, and, with an unexpected activity, whips the sword out of his body, and caught his dear Quiteria close in his arms. All the spectators stood amazed, and some of the simpler sort stuck not to cry out, "A miracle! a miracle!"

"No, no!" cried Basil; "no miracle, no miracle, but a stratagem, a stratagem!"

The curate, more astonished and concerned than all the rest, came with both his hands to feel the wound, and discovered that the sword had nowhere passed through the cunning Basil's body, but only through a tin pipe full of blood artfully fitted to his body, and, as it was afterwards known, so prepared, that the blood could not congeal. In short, the curate, Camacho, and the company, found they had all been egregiously imposed upon. As for the bride, she was so far from being displeased, that, hearing it urged that the marriage could not stand good in law because it was fraudulent and deceitful, she publicly declared that she again confirmed it to be just, and by the free consent of both parties.

Camacho and his friends, judging by this that the trick was premeditated, and that she was privy to the plot, enraged at this horrid disappointment, had recourse to a stronger argument, and, drawing their swords, set furiously on Basil, in whose defence almost as many were immediately unsheathed. Don Quixote immediately mounting, with his lance couched, and covered with his shield, led the van of Basil's party, and falling in with the enemy, charged clear through the gross of their battalia. Sancho, who never liked any dangerous work, resolved to stand neuter, and so retired under the walls of the mighty pot whence he had got the precious skimmings, thinking that would be respected whatever side gained the battle.

Don Quixote, addressing himself to Camacho's party, "Hold, gentlemen!" cried he; "it is not just thus with arms to redress the injuries of love. Love and war are the same thing, and stratagems and policy are as allowable in the one as in the other. Quiteria was designed for Basil, and he for her, by the unalterable decrees of Heaven. Camacho's riches may purchase him a bride and more content elsewhere. Those whom Heaven has joined let no man put asunder. Basil had but this one lamb. Let none, therefore, offer to take his single delight from him, though presuming on his power; for here I solemnly declare, that he who first attempts it must pass through me, and this lance through him." At which he shook his lance in the air with so much vigour and dexterity, that he cast a sudden terror into those that beheld him.

In short, Don Quixote's words, the good curate's diligent mediation, together with Quiteria's inconstancy, brought Camacho to a truce; and he then discreetly considered that, since Quiteria loved Basil before marriage, it was probable she would love him afterwards, and that therefore he had more reason to thank Heaven for so good a riddance than to repine at losing her. This thought, improved by some other considerations, brought both parties to a fair accommodation; and Camacho, to show he did not resent the disappointment, blaming rather Quiteria's levity than Basil's policy, invited the whole company to stay and take share of what he had provided. But Basil, whose virtues, in spite of his poverty, had secured him many friends, drew away part of the company to attend him and his bride to her own town, and among the rest, Don Quixote, whom they all honoured as a person of extraordinary worth and bravery. Poor Sancho followed his master with a heavy heart; he could not be reconciled to the thoughts of turning his back so soon upon the good cheer and jollity at Camacho's feast. So he sullenly paced on after Rozinante, very much out of humour, though he had just filled his belly.

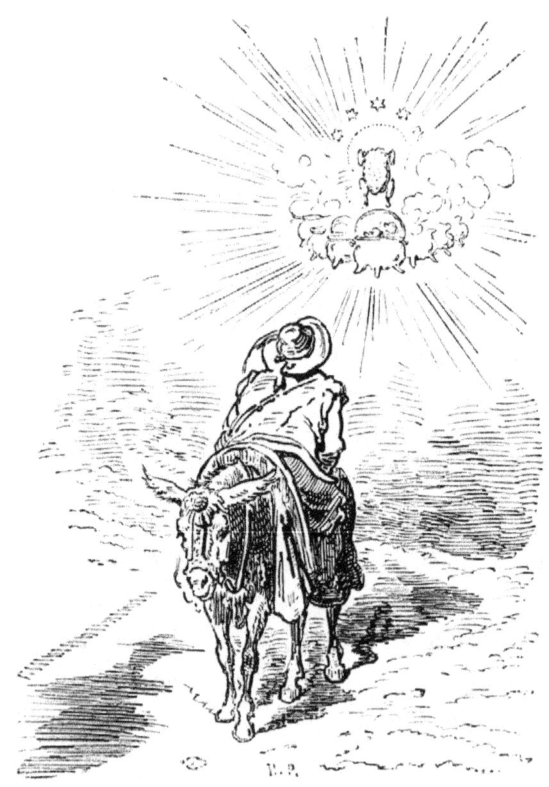

"Poor Sancho followed his master with a heavy heart."—*p.* 510.

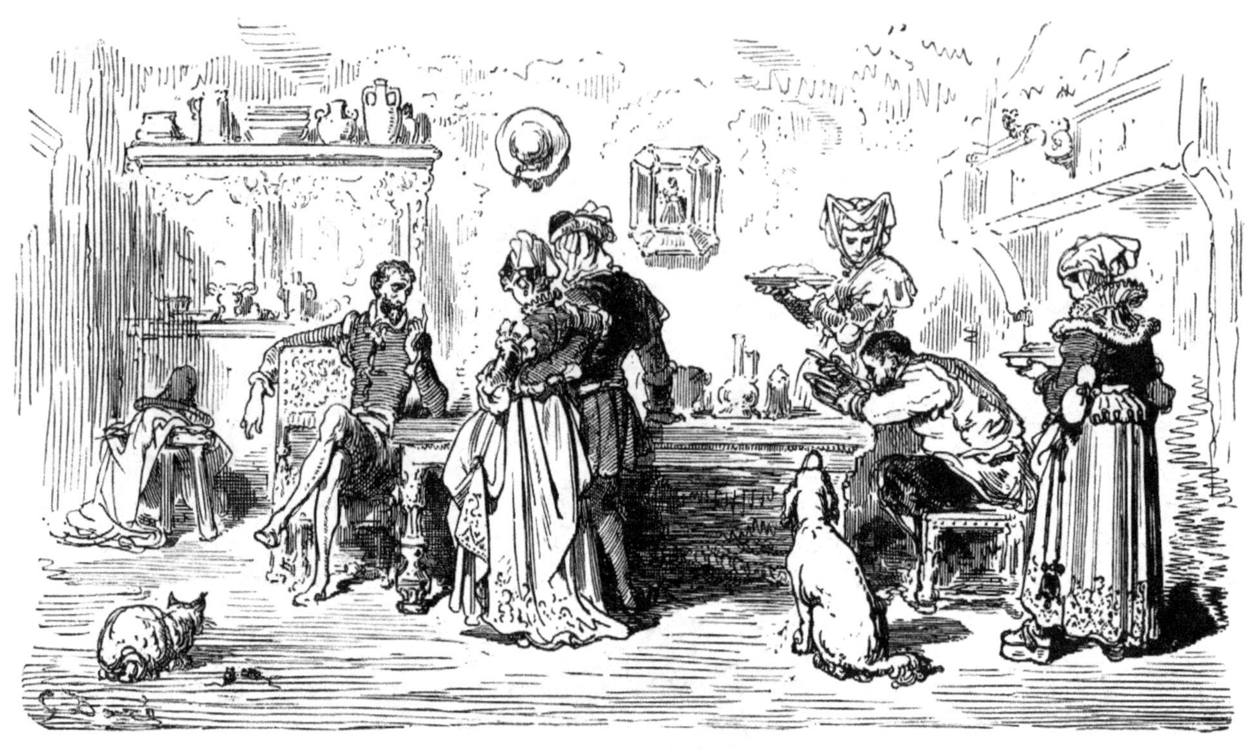

CHAPTER XXII.

AN ACCOUNT OF THE GREAT ADVENTURE OF THE CAVE OF MONTESINOS, SITUATED IN THE HEART OF LA MANCHA, WHICH THE VALOROUS DON QUIXOTE SUCCESSFULLY ACHIEVED

THE new-married couple entertained Don Quixote very nobly, in acknowledgment of his readiness to defend their cause; they esteemed his wisdom equal to his valour, and thought him both a Cid in arms and a Cicero in arts. Honest Sancho, too, recruited himself to the purpose, during the three days his master stayed, and so came to his good humour again. Basil then informed them that Quiteria knew nothing of his stratagem; but being a pure device of his own, he had made some of his nearest friends acquainted with it, that they should stand by him if occasion were, and bring him off upon the discovery of the deceit.

"It deserves a handsomer name," said Don Quixote, "since conducive to so good and honourable an end as the marriage of a loving couple. By the way, sir, you must know that the greatest obstacle to love is want and a narrow fortune; for the continual bands and cements of mutual affection are mirth, content, satisfaction, and jollity. These, managed by skilful hands, can make variety in the pleasures of wedlock, preparing the same thing always with some additional circumstance to render it new and delightful. But when pressing necessity and indigence deprive us of those pleasures that prevent satiety, the yoke of matrimony is often found very galling, and the burden intolerable."

These words were chiefly directed by Don Quixote to Basil, to advise him, by the way,

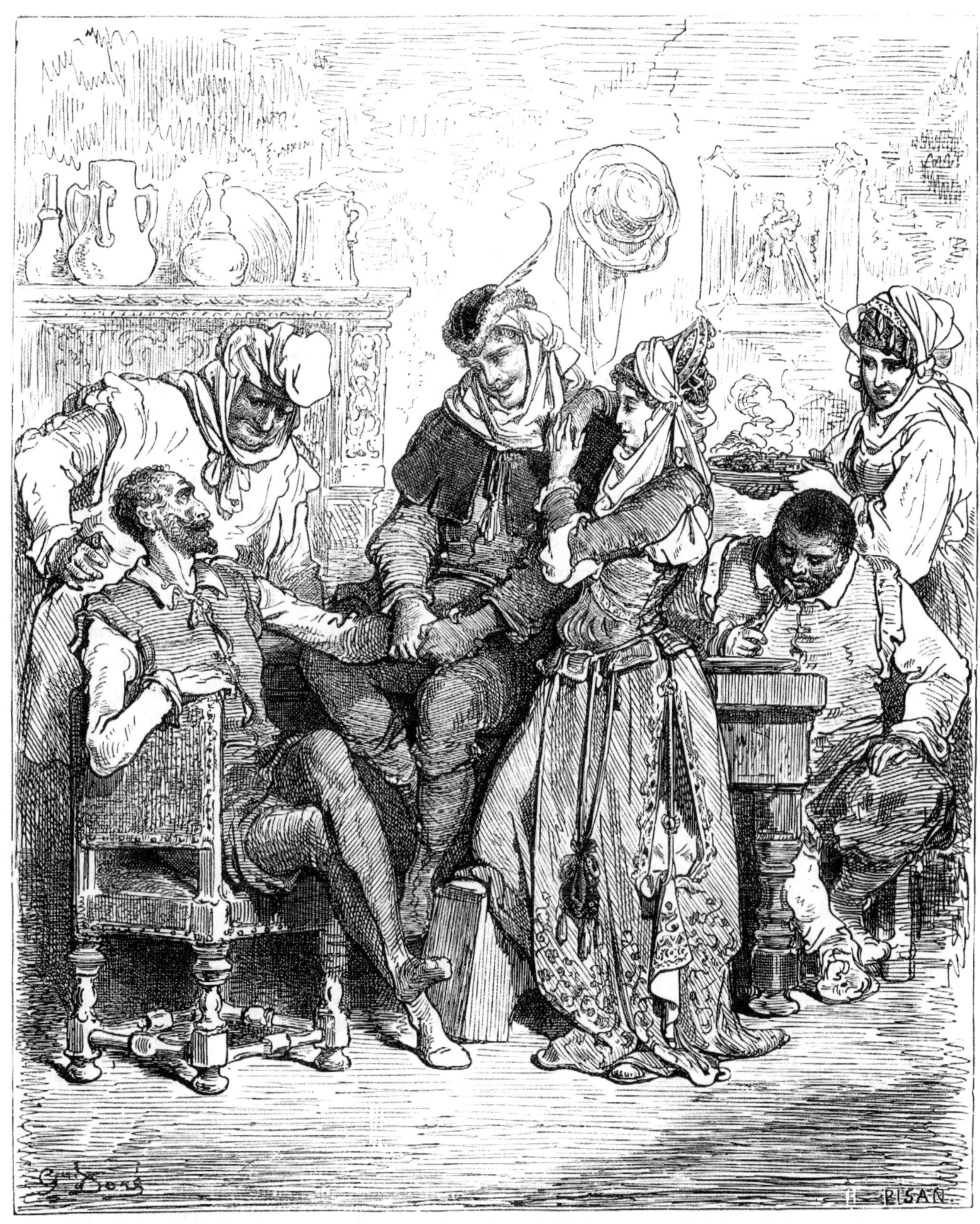

"Sancho and his master tarried three days with the young couple, and were entertained like princes."—*p.* 514.

II 11

to give over those airy sports, which, indeed, might feed his youth with praise, but not his old age with bread, and to bethink himself of some grave and substantial employment, that might afford him a competency for his declining years. Then, pursuing his discourse, "The honourable poor man," said he, "when he has a beautiful wife, is blessed with a jewel. He that deprives him of her robs him of his honour, and may be said to deprive him of his life. The woman that is beautiful, and keeps her honesty when her husband is poor, deserves to be crowned with laurel, as the conquerors were of old. Beauty is a tempting bait, that attracts the eyes of all beholders, and the princely eagles and the most high-flown birds stoop to its pleasing lure. But when they find it in necessity, then kites, and crows, and other ravenous birds, will all be grappling with the alluring prey. She that can withstand these dangerous attacks well deserves to be the crown of her husband. However, sir, take this along with you, as the opinion of a wise man, whose name I have forgot: he said, there was but one good woman in the world; and his advice was, that every married man should think his own wife was her, as being the only way to live contented. For my own part, I need not make the application to myself, for I am not married, nor have I as yet any thoughts that way; but if I had, it would not be a woman's fortune, but her character, should recommend her; for public reputation is the life of a lady's virtue, and the outward appearance of modesty is, in one sense, as good as the reality; since a private sin is not so prejudicial in this world as a public indecency. If you bring an honest woman to your home, it is easy keeping her so, and perhaps you may improve her virtues. If you take an unchaste partner, it is hard mending her; for the extremities of vice and virtue are so great in a woman, and their points so far asunder, that it is very improbable, I won't say impossible, they should ever be reconciled."

Sancho and his master tarried three days with the young couple, and were entertained like princes. On taking his leave, Don Quixote entreated the student, who fenced so well, to help him to a guide that might conduct him to the cave of Montesinos, resolving to go down into it, and prove by his own eyesight the wonders that were reported of it round the country. The student recommended a cousin-german of his for his conductor, who, he said, was an ingenious lad, a good scholar, and a great admirer of books of knight-errantry, and could show him the famous lake of Ruydera, too; adding that he would be very good company for the knight, as being one that wrote books for the booksellers, in order to dedicate them to great men. Accordingly, the learned cousin came, mounted on an ass with foal; his pack-saddle covered with an old carpet or coarse packing-cloth. Thereupon, Sancho having got ready Rozinante and Dapple, well stuffed his wallet, and the student's knapsack to boot, they all took their leave, steering the nearest course to the cave of Montesinos.

To pass the time on the road, Don Quixote asked the guide to what course of study he chiefly applied himself.

"Sir," answered the scholar, "my business is writing, and copy-money my chief study. I have published some things with the general approbation of the world, and much to my own advantage. Perhaps, sir, you may have heard of one of my books, called 'The Treatise of Liveries and Devices,' in which I have obliged the public with no less than seven hundred and three sorts of liveries and devices, with their colours, mottoes, and ciphers, so that any courtier may furnish himself there, upon any extraordinary appearance, with what may suit his fancy or circumstances, without racking his own invention to find what is agreeable to his inclination. I can furnish the jealous, the forsaken, the disdained, the absent, with what will fit them to a hair. Another piece, which I now have on the anvil, I design to call 'The Metamorphosis; or, The Spanish Ovid,' an invention very new and extraordinary; it is, in short, Ovid burlesqued, wherein I discover who the Giralda of Seville was; who the angel of Magdalen; I tell ye what was the pipe of Vecinguerra of Cordova, what the bulls of Guisando, the Sierra Morena, the fountains of Laganitos and Lavapies at Madrid; not forgetting that of Piojo, nor those of the golden pipe, and the abbey; and I embellish the fables with allegories, metaphors, and translations, that will both delight and instruct. Another work, which I soon design for the press, I call 'A Supplement to Polydore Virgil,' concerning the invention of things; a piece, I will assure you, sir, that shows the great pains and learning of the compiler, and perhaps in a better style than the old author."

Sancho having hearkened with great attention all this while, "Pray, sir," quoth he to him, "so Heaven guide your right hand in all you write, let me ask you who was the first man that scratched his head?"

"Scratched his head, friend?" answered the author.

"Ay, sir, scratched his head," quoth Sancho. "Sure, you that know all things can tell me that. What think you of old father Adam?"

"Old father Adam?" answered the scholar; "let me see. Father Adam had a head, he had hair, he had hands, and he could scratch; but father Adam was the first man—*ergo*, father Adam was the first man that scratched his head. It is plain you are in the right."

"Oh, ho! am I so, sir?" quoth Sancho. "Another question, by your leave, sir. Who was the first tumbler in the world?"

"Truly, friend," answered the student, "that is a point I cannot resolve you without consulting my books; but, as soon as ever I get home, I will study night and day to find it out."

"For two fair words," quoth Sancho, "I will save you that trouble."

"Can you resolve that doubt?" asked the author.

"Ay, marry, can I," said Sancho. "The first tumbler in the world was Lucifer; when he was cast out of heaven he tumbled into hell."

"You are positively in the right," said the scholar.

"Where did you get that, Sancho?" said Don Quixote; "for I dare swear it is none of your own."

"Mum!" quoth Sancho. "In asking of foolish questions, and selling of bargains, let Sancho alone, quoth I; I do not want the help of my neighbours."

"Truly," said Don Quixote, "thou hast given thy question a better epithet than thou art aware of; for there are some men who busy their heads, and lose a world of time in making discoveries, the knowledge of which is good for nothing upon the earth, unless it be to make the discoverers laughed at."

With these, and such diverting discourses, they passed their journey, till they came to the cave the next day, having lain the night before in an inconsiderable village on the road. There they bought a hundred fathoms of cordage to hang Don Quixote by, and let him down to the lowest part of the cave, he being resolved to go to the very bottom. The mouth of it was inaccessible, being quite stopped up with weeds, bushes, brambles, and wild fig-trees, though the entrance was wide and spacious. Don Quixote was no sooner come to the place, but he prepared for his expedition into that under world, telling the scholar that he was resolved to reach the bottom; and all having alighted, the squire and his guide accordingly girt him fast with a rope.

While this was doing, "Good, sweet sir," quoth Sancho, "consider what you do. Do not venture into such a black hole! Look before you leap, sir, and be not so wilful as to bury yourself alive. Do not hang yourself like a bottle or a bucket, that is let down to be soused in a well. Alack-a-day! sir, it is none of your business to pry thus into every hole."

"Peace, coward," said the knight, "and bind me fast; for surely for me such an enterprise as this is reserved."

"Pray, sir," said the student, "when you are in, be very vigilant in exploring and observing all the rarities in the place. Let nothing escape your eyes; perhaps you may discover there some things worthy to be inserted in my 'Metamorphoses.'"

"Let him alone," quoth Sancho; "he will go through with it, I will warrant you."

Don Quixote being well bound, not over his armour, but his doublet, bethought himself of one thing they had forgot.

"We did ill," said he, "not to provide ourselves with a little bell, that I should have carried down with me, to ring for more or less rope as I may have occasion for, and inform you of my being alive. But since there is no remedy, Heaven prosper me!" Then, kneeling down, he in a low voice recommended himself to the Divine Providence for assistance and success in an adventure so strange, and, to all appearance, so dangerous. Then, raising his voice, "Oh, thou mistress of my life and motions!" cried he, "most illustrious and peerless Dulcinea del Toboso! if the prayers of an adventurous absent lover may reach the ears of the far distant object of his wishes, by the power of thy unspeakable beauty I conjure thee to grant me thy favour and protection in this plunge and precipice of my fortune. I am now going to cast myself into this dismal profundity, that the world may know nothing can be impossible to him who, influenced by thy smiles, attempts, under the banner of thy beauty, the most difficult task."

This said, he got up again, and approaching the entrance of the cave, he found it stopped

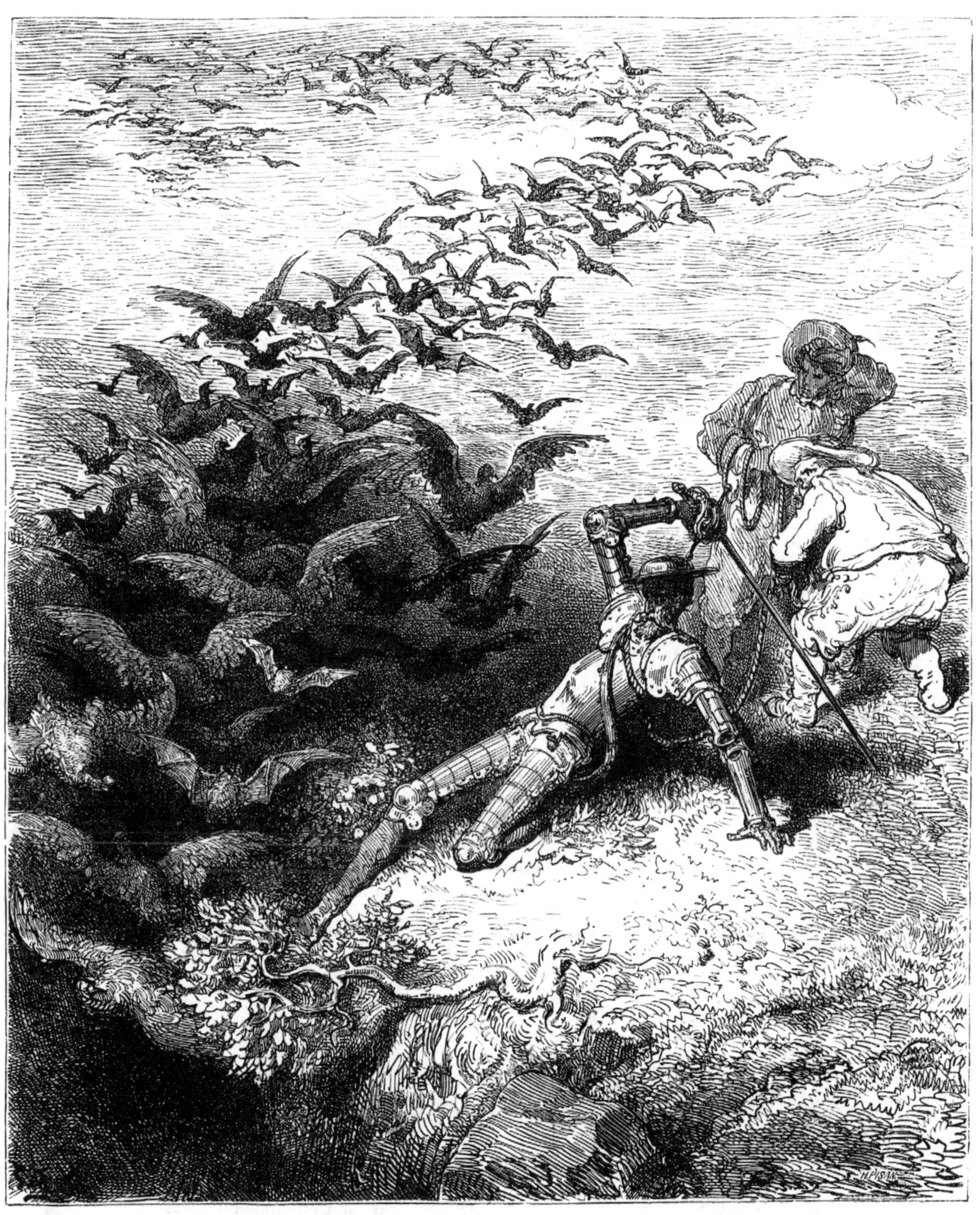

"An infinite number of overgrown crows and daws came rushing and fluttering out of the cave."

up with brakes and bushes, so that he must make his way by force. Whereupon, drawing his sword, he began to cut and slash the brambles that stopped up the mouth of the cave, when presently an infinite number of overgrown crows and daws came rushing and fluttering out of the cave about his ears, so thick, and with such an impetuosity, as overwhelmed him to the ground. He was not superstitious enough to draw any ill omen from the flight of the birds; besides, it was no small encouragement to him that he spied no bats nor owls, nor other ill-boding birds of night among them. He therefore rose again with an undaunted heart, and committed himself to the black and dreadful abyss. But Sancho first gave him his benediction and making a thousand crosses over him, "Heaven be thy guide!" quoth he, "and our Lady of the Rock in France, with the Trinity of Gaeta, thou flower and cream of all knights-errant! Go thy ways, thou hackster of the world, heart of steel, and arms of brass! and mayest thou come back sound out of this dreadful hole which thou art running into, once more to see the warm sun which thou art now leaving."

The scholar, too, prayed to the same effect for the knight's happy return. Don Quixote then called for more rope, which they gave him by degrees, till his voice was drowned in the winding of the cave, and their cordage was run out. That done, they began to consider whether they should hoist him up again immediately or no; however, they resolved to stay half an hour, and then they began to draw up the rope, but were strangely surprised to find no weight upon it, which made them conclude the poor gentleman was certainly lost. Sancho, bursting into tears, made a heavy lamentation, and began hauling up the rope as fast as he could, to be thoroughly satisfied. But after they had drawn up about fourscore fathoms, they felt a weight again, which made them take heart; and at length they plainly saw Don Quixote.

"Welcome!" cried Sancho to him, as soon as he came in sight; "welcome, dear master! I am glad you are come back again; we were afraid you had been pawned for the reckoning."

But Sancho had no answer to his compliment; and when they had pulled the knight quite up, they found that his eyes were closed, as if he had been fast asleep. They laid him on the ground, and unbound him, yet he made no sign of waking; and all their turning and shaking was little enough to make him come to himself.

At last he began to stretch his limbs, as if he had woke out of the most profound sleep, and staring wildly about him, "Heaven forgive you, friends!" cried he, "for you have raised me from one of the sweetest lives that ever mortal led, and most delightful sights that ever eyes beheld. Now I perceive how fleeting are all the joys of this transitory life; they are but an imperfect dream, they fade like a flower, and vanish like a shadow. Oh, ill-fated Montesinos! oh, Durandarte, unfortunately wounded! oh, unhappy Belerma! oh, deplorable Guadiana! and you the distressed daughters of Ruydera, whose flowing waters show what streams of tears once trickled from your lovely eyes!"

These expressions, uttered with great passion and concern, surprised the scholar and Sancho, and they desired to know his meaning, and what he had seen in that dreadful place.

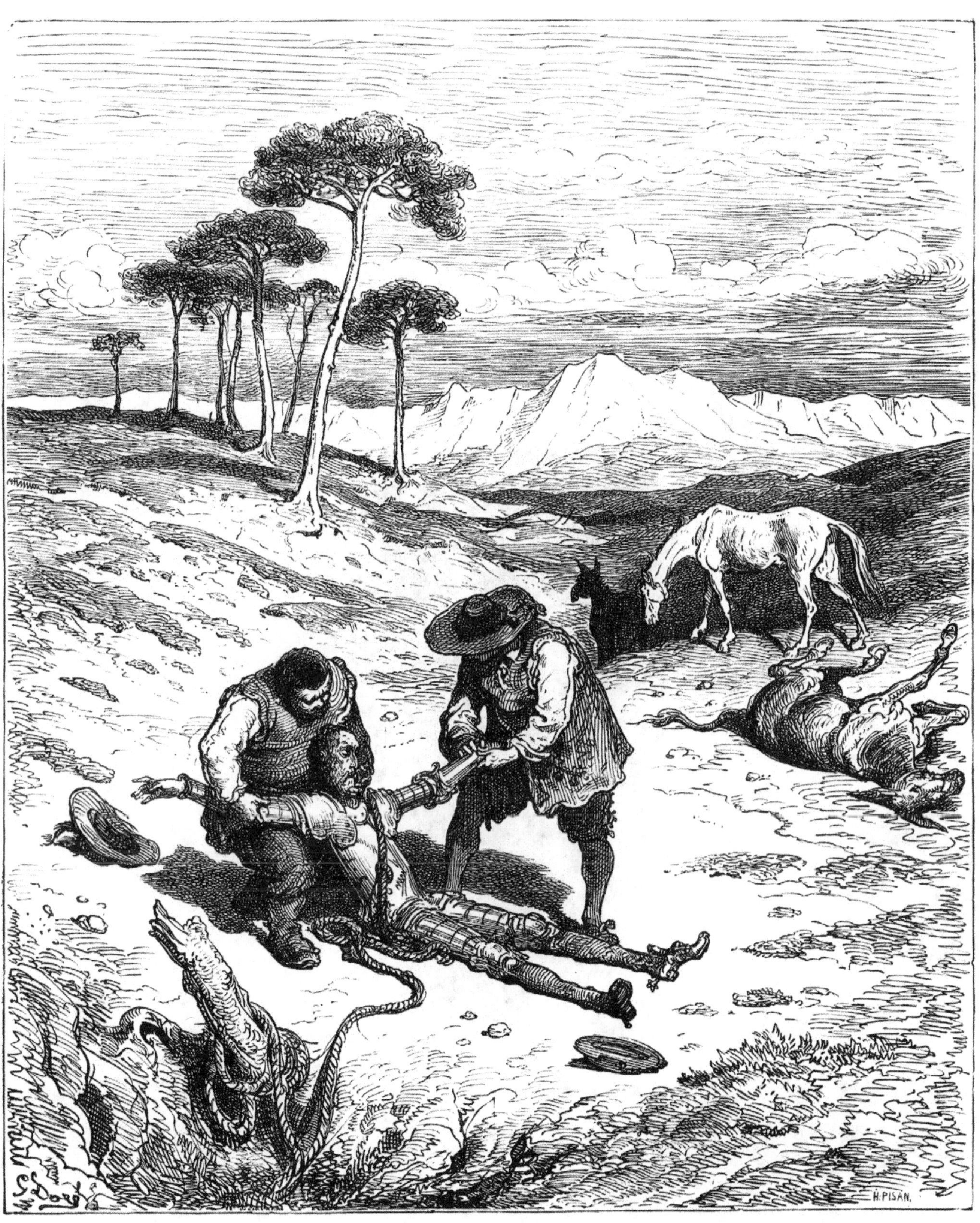

"They found that his eyes were closed, as if he had been fast asleep."—*p.* 518.

"Call it not that," answered Don Quixote, "for it deserves a better name, as I shall soon let you know. But first give me something to eat, for I am prodigiously hungry."

They then spread the scholar's coarse saddle-cloth for a carpet; and examining their old cupboard, the knapsack, they all three sat down on the grass, and ate heartily together, like men who were a meal or two behind-hand. When they had done, "Let no man stir," said Don Quixote; "sit still, and hear me with attention."

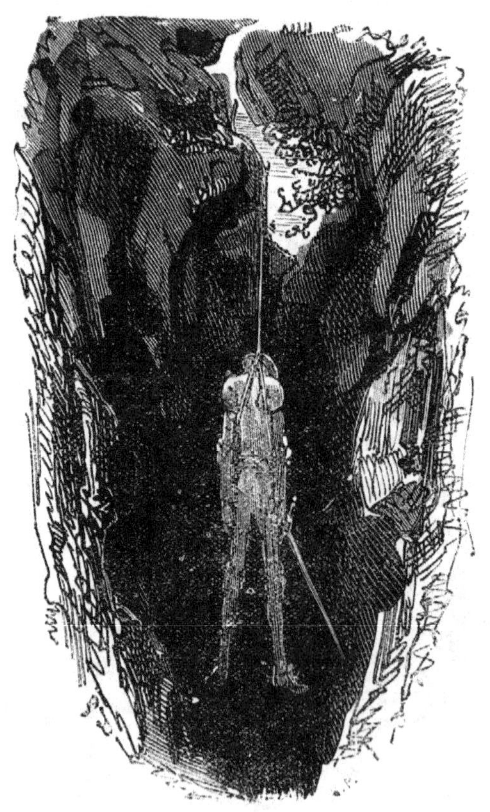

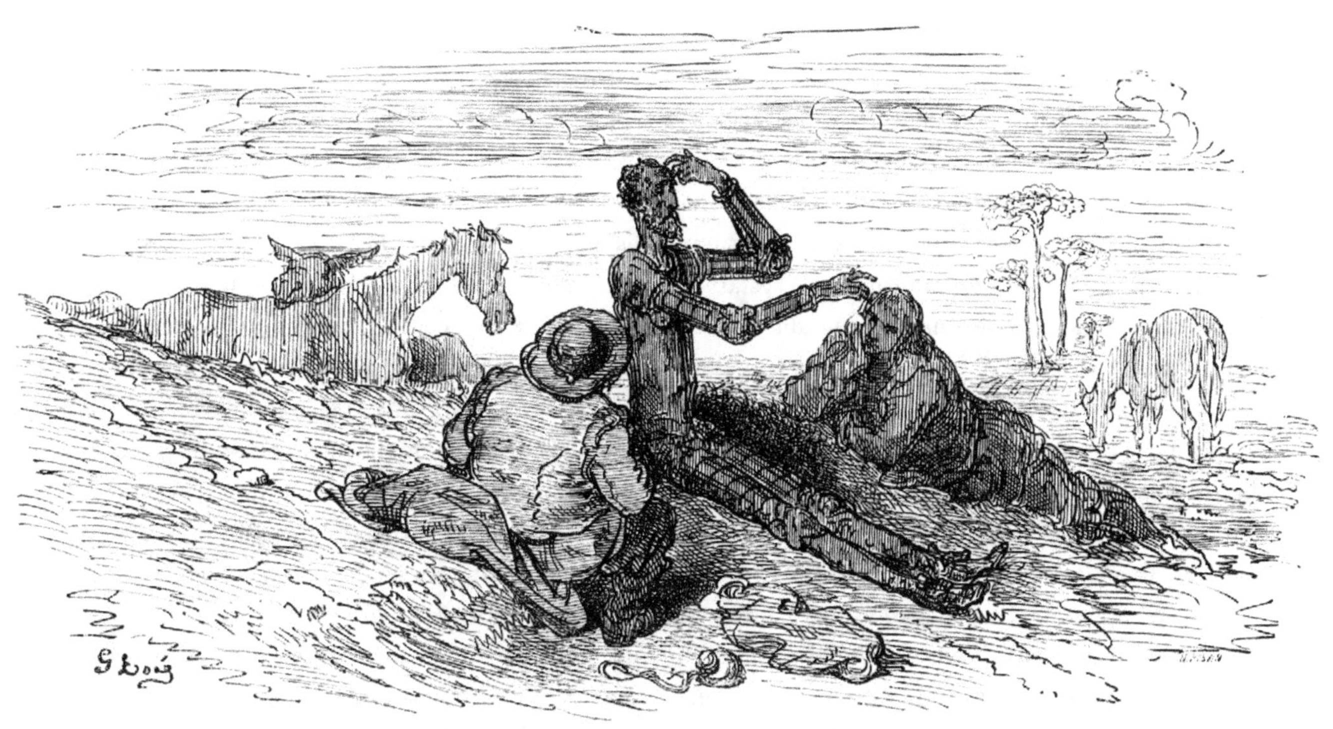

CHAPTER XXIII.

OF THE WONDERFUL THINGS WHICH THE UNPARALLELED DON QUIXOTE DECLARED HE HAD SEEN IN THE DEEP CAVE OF MONTESINOS, THE GREATNESS AND IMPOSSIBILITY OF WHICH MAKES THIS ADVENTURE PASS FOR APOCRYPHAL.

IT was now past four in the afternoon, and the sun was opportunely hid behind the clouds which, interposing between his rays, invited Don Quixote, without heat or trouble, to relate to his illustrious auditors the wonders he had seen in the cave of Montesinos.

"About twelve or fourteen men's depth," said he, "in the profundity of this cavern, on the right hand there is a concavity wide enough to contain a large wagon, mules and all. This place is not wholly dark, for through some chinks and narrow holes, that reach to the distant surface of the earth, there comes a glimmering light. I discovered this recess, being already weary of hanging by the loins, discouraged by the profound darkness of the region below me, destitute of a guide, and not knowing whither I went: resolving therefore to rest myself there a while, I called to you to give me no more rope, but it seems you did not hear me. I therefore entered, and coiling up the cord, sat upon it very melancholy, and thinking how I should most conveniently get down to the bottom, having nobody to guide or support me. While thus I sat pensive and lost in thought, insensibly, without any previous drowsiness, I found myself surprised by sleep; and after that, not knowing how nor which way I wakened. I unexpectedly found myself in the finest, the sweetest, and most delightful meadow that ever

Nature adorned with her beauties, or the most inventive fancy could ever imagine. Now, that I might be sure this was neither a dream nor an illusion, I rubbed my eyes, felt several parts of my body, and convinced myself that I was really awake, with the use of all my senses, and all the faculties of my understanding sound and active as at this moment.

"Presently I discovered a royal and sumptuous palace, of which the walls and battlements seemed all of clear and transparent crystal. At the same time, the spacious gates opening, there came out towards me a venerable old man, clad in a sad-coloured robe, so long that it swept the ground; on his breast and shoulders he had a green satin tippet after the manner of those worn in colleges. On his head he wore a black Milan cap, and his broad hoary beard reached down below his middle. He had no kind of weapon in his hands, but a rosary of beads about the bigness of walnuts, and his credo beads appeared as large as ordinary ostrich-eggs. The awful and grave aspect, the pace, the port and goodly presence of this old man, each of them apart, and much more all together, struck me with veneration and astonishment. He came up to me, and, without any previous ceremony, embracing me close, 'It is a long time,' said he, 'most renowned knight, Don Quixote de la Mancha, that we who dwell in this enchanted solitude have hoped to see you here; that you may inform the upper world of the surprising prodigies concealed from human knowledge in this subterranean hollow, called the cave of Montesinos: an enterprise reserved alone for your insuperable heart, and stupendous resolution. Go with me, then, thou most illustrious knight, and behold the wonders enclosed within the transparent castle, of which I am the perpetual governor and chief warden, being the same individual Montesinos, from whom this cavern took its name.'

"No sooner had the reverend old man let me know who he was, but I entreated him to tell me whether it was true or no that, at his friend Durandarte's dying request, he had taken out his heart with a small dagger the very moment he expired, and carried it to his mistress Belerma, as the story was current in the world. 'It is literally true,' answered the old gentleman, 'except that single circumstance of the dagger; for I used neither a small nor a large dagger on this occasion, but a well-polished poniard, as sharp as an awl.'"

"I will be hanged," quoth Sancho, "if it was not one of your Seville poniards, of Raymond de Hoze's making."

"That cannot be," said Don Quixote, "for that cutler lived but the other day, and the battle of Roncesvalles, where this accident happened, was fought many ages ago; but this is of no importance to the story."

"You are in the right, sir," said the student, "and pray go on, for I hearken to your relation with the greatest satisfaction imaginable."

"That, sir," said the knight, "increases my pleasure in telling it. But to proceed: the venerable Montesinos, having conducted me into the crystal palace, led me into a spacious ground-room, exceeding cool, and all of alabaster. In the middle of it stood a stately marble tomb, that seemed a masterpiece of art, upon which lay a knight extended all at length, not

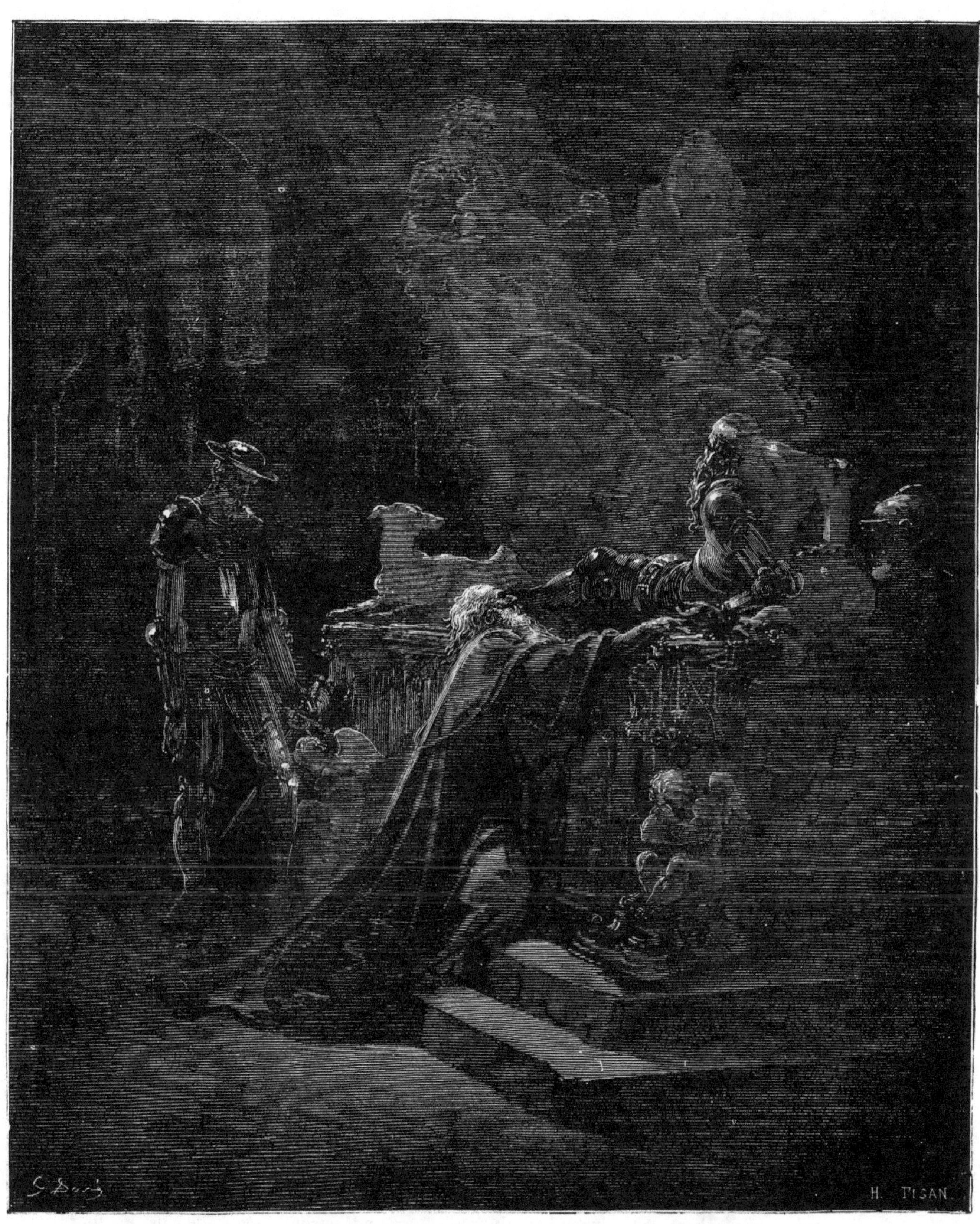

"The venerable Montesinos fell on his knees before the afflicted knight."

of stone or brass, as on other monuments, but pure flesh and bones. He covered the region of his heart with his right hand, which seemed to me somewhat hairy and very full of sinews —a sign of the great strength of the body to which it belonged. Montesinos, observing that I viewed this spectacle with surprise, 'Behold,' said he, 'the flower and mirror of all the amorous and valiant knights of his age, my friend Durandarte, who, together with me and many others of both sexes, are kept here enchanted by Merlin, that British magician, who, they say, was the son of the devil, though I cannot believe it; only his knowledge was so great, that he might be said to know more than the devil. Here, I say, we are enchanted, but how and for what cause no man can tell, though time, I hope, will shortly reveal it. But the most wonderful part of my fortune is this: I am as certain as that the sun now shines, that Durandarte died in my arms, and that with these hands I took out his heart, by the same token that it weighed above two pounds—a sure mark of his courage; for, by the rules of natural philosophy, the most valiant men have still the biggest hearts. Nevertheless, though this knight really died, he still complains and sighs sometimes as if he were alive.'

"Scarce had Montesinos spoke these words, but the miserable Durandarte cried out aloud, 'Oh, cousin Montesinos! the last and dying request of your departing friend was to take my heart out of my breast with a poniard or a dagger, and carry it to Belerma.' The venerable Montesinos, hearing this, fell on his knees before the afflicted knight, and with tears in his eyes, 'Long, long ago,' said he, 'Durandarte, thou dearest of my kinsmen, have I performed what you enjoined me on that bitter, fatal day when you expired. I took out your heart with all imaginable care, not leaving the least particle of it in your breast; I gently wiped it with a laced handkerchief, and posted away with it to France, as soon as I had committed your dear remains to the bosom of the earth, having shed tears enough to have washed my hands clear of the blood they had gathered by plunging in your entrails. To confirm this truth yet farther, at the first place where I stopped from Roncesvalles, I laid a little salt upon your heart, to preserve it from putrefaction, and keep it, if not fresh, at least free from any ill smell, till I presented it into the hands of Belerma, who, with you and me, and Guadiana your squire, as also Ruydera (the lady's woman) with her seven daughters, her two nieces, and many others of your friends and acquaintance, is here confined by the necromantic charms of the magician Merlin; and though it be now above five hundred years since we were first conveyed into this enchanted castle, we are still alive, except Ruydera, her daughters, and nieces, who, by the favour of Merlin that pitied their tears, were turned into so many lakes, still extant in the world of the living, and in the province of La Mancha, distinguished by the name of the Lakes of Ruydera; seven of them belonged to the kings of Spain, and the two nieces to the Knights of the Most Holy Order of St. John. Your squire Guadiana, lamenting his hard fate, was in like manner metamorphosed into a river that bears his name, yet still so sensible of your disaster, that when he first arose out of the bowels of the earth to flow along its surface, and saw the sun in a strange hemisphere, he plunged again under ground, striving to hide his melting

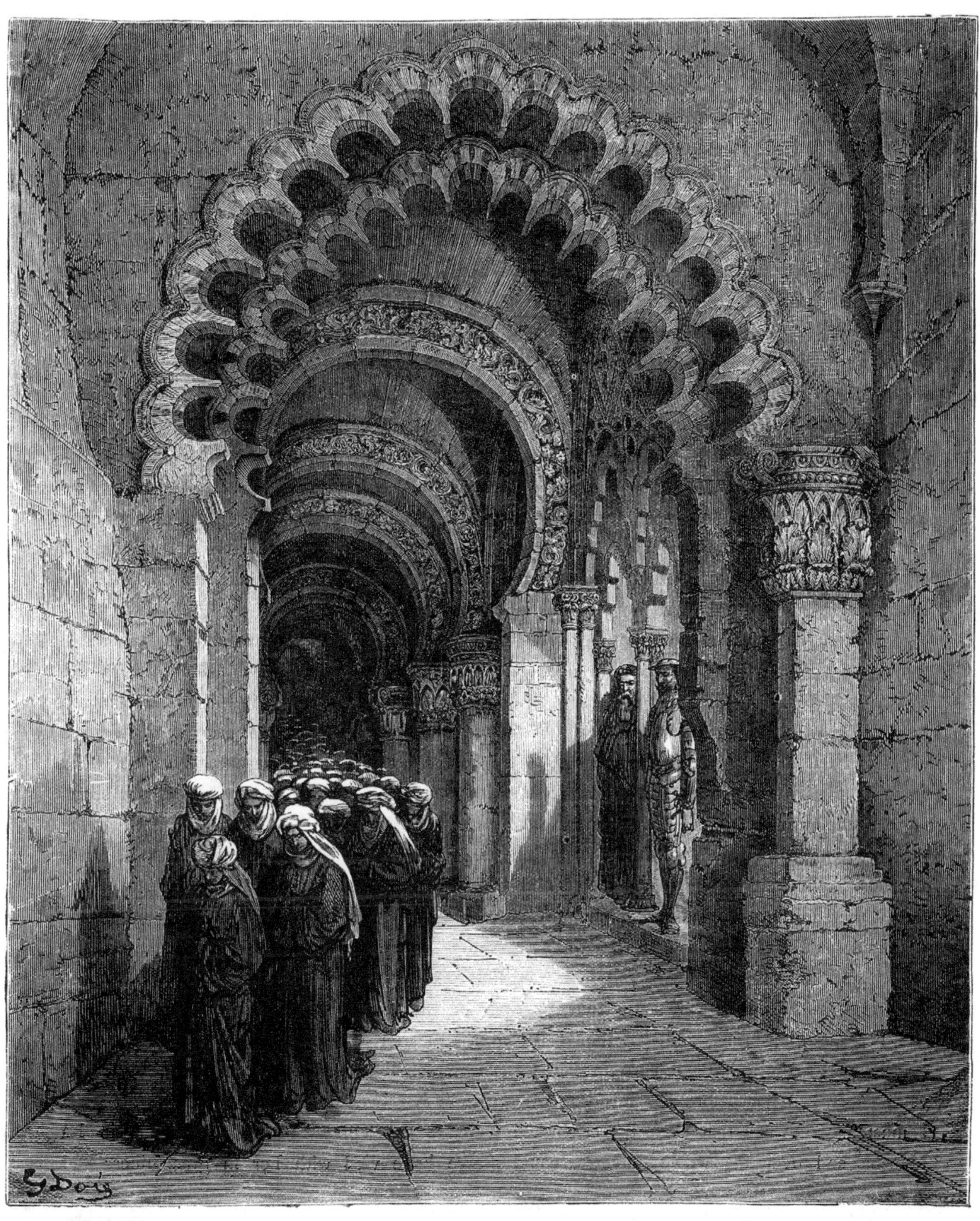

"I saw a mournful procession of most beautiful damsels, all in black."—*p.* 526.

sorrows from the world; but the natural current of his waters forcing a passage up again, he is compelled to appear where the sun and mortals may see him. Those lakes mixing their waters in his bosom, he swells, and glides along in sullen state to Portugal, often expressing his deep melancholy by the muddy and turbid colour of his streams, which, as they refuse to please the sight, so likewise deny to indulge mortal appetite by breeding such fair and savoury fish as may be found in the golden Tagus. All this I have often told you, my dearest Durandarte; and since you return me no answer, I must conclude you believe me not, or that you do not hear me, for which (witness it, Heaven!) I am extremely grieved. But now I have other news to tell ye, which, though perhaps it may not assuage your sorrows, yet, I am sure, it will not increase them. Open your eyes, and behold in your presence that mighty knight of whom Merlin the sage has foretold so many wonders—that Don Quixote de la Mancha, I mean, who has not only restored to the world the function of knight-errantry that has lain so long in oblivion, but advanced it to greater fame than it could boast in former ages, the nonage of the world. It is by his power we may expect to see the fatal charm dissolved that keeps us here confined; for great performances are properly reserved for great personages.' 'And should it not be so?' answered the grieving Durandarte, with a faint and languishing voice. 'Should it not be so, I say? Oh, cousin! patience, and shuffle the cards.' Then turning on one side, without speaking a word more, he relapsed into his usual silence.

"After this I was alarmed with piteous howling and crying, which, mixed with lamentable sighs and groans, obliged me to turn about, to see whence it proceeded. Then through the crystal wall I saw a mournful procession of most beautiful damsels, all in black, marching in two ranks, with turbans on their heads after the Turkish fashion; and last of all came a majestic lady, dressed also in mourning, with a long white veil, that reached from her head down to the ground. Her turban was twice as big as the biggest of the rest; she was somewhat beetle-browed, her nose was flattish, her mouth wide, but her lips red; her teeth, which she sometimes discovered, seemed to be thin and snaggy, but indeed as white as blanched almonds. She held a fine handkerchief, and within it I could perceive a heart of flesh, so dry and withered, that it looked like mummy. Montesinos informed me that the procession consisted of Durandarte's and Belerma's servants, who were enchanted there with their master and mistress: but that the last was Belerma herself, who, with her attendants, used four days in the week constantly thus to sing, or rather howl their dirges over the heart and body of his cousin; and that though Belerma appeared a little haggard at that juncture, occasioned by the grief she bore in her own heart for that which she carried in her hand, yet had I seen her before her misfortunes had sunk her eyes and tarnished her complexion, I must have owned that even the celebrated Dulcinea del Toboso herself, so famous in La Mancha, and over the whole universe, could scarce have vied with her in gracefulness and beauty.

"'Hold there. good Signior Don Montesinos,' said I. 'You know that comparisons are odious, therefore no more comparing, I beseech you; but go on with your story. The peerless Dulcinea del Toboso is what she is, and the lady Belerma is what she is, and has been: so no more upon that subject.' 'I beg your pardon,' answered Montesinos, 'Signior Don Quixote: I might have guessed indeed that you were the Lady Dulcinea's knight, and therefore I ought to have bit my tongue off, sooner than to have compared her to anything lower than heaven itself.' This satisfaction, which I thought sufficient from the great Montesinos, stifled the resentment I else had shown, for hearing my mistress compared to Belerma."

"Nay, marry," quoth Sancho, "I wonder you did not catch the old doating hunks by the weasand, and maul and thresh him thick and three-fold! How could you leave one hair on his chin?"

"No, no, Sancho," answered Don Quixote, "there is always a respect due to our seniors, though they be no knights; but most when they are such, and under the impression of enchantment. However, I am satisfied that in what discourse passed between us I took care not to have anything that looked like an affront fixed upon me."

"But, sir," asked the scholar, "how could you see and hear so many strange things in so little time? I cannot conceive how you could do it."

"How long," said Don Quixote, "do you reckon that I have been in the cave?"

"A little above an hour," answered Sancho.

"That is impossible," said Don Quixote, "for I saw morning and evening, and evening and morning, three times since; so that I could not be absent less than three days from this upper world."

"Ay, ay," quoth Sancho, "my master is in the right; for these enchantments, that have the greatest share in all his concerns, may make that seem three days and three nights to him which is but an hour to other people."

"It must be so," said Don Quixote.

"I hope, sir," said the scholar, "you have eaten something in all that time."

"Not one morsel," replied Don Quixote, "neither have had the least desire to eat, or so much as thought of it all the while."

"Do not they that are enchanted sometimes eat?" asked the scholar.

"They never do," answered Don Quixote, "though it is not unlikely that their nails, their beards, and hair still grow."

"Do they never sleep neither?" said Sancho.

"Never," said Don Quixote; "at least, they never closed their eyes while I was among them, nor I neither."

"This makes good the saying," quoth Sancho, "'Tell me thy company, and I will tell thee what thou art.' Troth! you have all been enchanted together. No wonder if you neither eat nor slept, since you were in the land of those that always watch and fast. But, sir, would you have me speak as I think? and pray do not take it in ill part, for if I believe one word of all you have said——"

"What do you mean, friend?" said the student. "Do you think the noble Don Quixote would be guilty of a lie? and if he had a mind to stretch a little, could he, think you, have had leisure to frame such a number of stories in so short a time?"

"I do not think that my master would lie neither," said Sancho.

"What do ye think then, sir?" said Don Quixote.

"Why truly, sir," quoth Sancho, "I do believe that this same cunning man, this Merlin, that bewitched, or enchanted, as you call it, all that rabble of people you talk of, may have crammed and enchanted into your noddle, some way or other, all that you have told us, and have yet to tell us."

"It is not impossible but such a thing may happen," said Don Quixote, "though I am convinced it was otherwise with me; for I am positive that I saw with these eyes, and felt with these hands, all I have mentioned. But what will you think when I tell you, among many wonderful things, that I saw three country wenches, leaping and skipping about those pleasant fields like so many wild goats; and at first sight knew one of them to be the peerless Dulcinea, and the other two the very same we spoke to not far from Toboso? I asked Montesinos if he knew them. He answered in the negative; but imagined them some enchanted ladies, who were newly come, and that the appearance of strange faces was no rarity among them, for many of the past ages and the present were enchanted there, under several disguises; and that, among the rest, he knew Queen Guinever and her woman Quintaniona, that officiated as Sir Lancelot's cup-bearer, as he came from Britain."

Sancho, hearing his master talk at this rate, had like to have forgot himself, and burst out a-laughing; for he well knew that Dulcinea's enchantment was a lie, and that he himself was the chief magician, and raiser of the story; and thence, concluding his master stark mad, "In an ill hour," quoth he, "dear master of mine, and in a woful day, went your worship down to the other world; and in a worse hour met you with that plaguy Montesinos, that has sent you back in this rueful pickle. You went hence in your right senses; could talk prettily enough now and then; had your handsome proverbs and wise sayings every foot, and would give wholesome counsel to all that would take it; but now, bless me! you talk as if you had left your brains in the cave."

"I know thee, Sancho," said Don Quixote, "and therefore I regard thy words as little as possible."

"And I yours," replied Sancho: "nay, you may cripple, lame, or kill me, if you please, either for what I have said or mean to say; I must speak my mind, though I die for it. But before your blood is up, pray, sir, tell me how did you know it was your mistress? Did you speak to her? What did she say to you? and what did you say to her?"

"I knew her again," said Don Quixote, "by the same clothes she wore when thou showedst her to me. I spoke to her; but she made no answer, but suddenly turned away, and fled from me like a whirlwind. I intended to have followed her, had not Montesinos told me it would be to no purpose; warning me, besides, that it was high time to return to the upper air; and, changing the discourse, he told me that I should hereafter be made acquainted with the means of disenchanting them all. But while Montesinos and I were thus talking together, a very odd accident, the thoughts of which trouble me still, broke off our conversation. For, as we were in the height of our discourse, who should come to me but one of the unfortunate Dulcinea's companions, and, before I was aware, with a faint and doleful voice, 'Sir, said she, 'my Lady Dulcinea del Toboso gives her service to you, and desires to know how you do; and, being a little short of money at present, she desires you, of all love and kindness, to lend her six reals upon this new fustian petticoat, or more or less, as you can spare it, sir, and she will take care to redeem it very honestly in a little time.'

"The message surprised me strangely; and therefore, turning to Montesinos, 'Is it possible, sir,' said I, 'that persons of quality, when enchanted, are in want?' 'Oh! very possible, sir,' said he; 'poverty rages everywhere, and spares neither quality enchanted nor unenchanted; and therefore, since the Lady Dulcinea desires you to lend her these six reals, and the pawn is a good pawn, let her have the money; for sure it is very low with her at this time.' 'I scorn to take pawns,' said I; 'but my misfortune is, that I cannot answer the full request; for I have but four reals about me;' and that was the money thou gavest me the other day, Sancho, to distribute among the poor. However, I gave her all I had, and desired her to tell her mistress I was very sorry for her wants; and that if I had all the treasures which Crœsus possessed, they should be at her service; and withal, that I died every hour for want of her reviving company; and made it my humble and earnest request, that she would vouchsafe to see and converse with her captive servant, and weather-beaten knight. 'Tell her,' continued I, 'when she leasts expects it, she will come to hear how I made an oath, as the Marquis of Mantua did, when he found his nephew Baldwin ready to expire on the mountain, never to eat upon a table-cloth, and several other particulars, which he swore to observe, till he had revenged his death; so, in the like solemn manner will I swear never to desist from traversing the habitable globe, and ranging through all the seven parts of the world, more indefatigably than ever was done by Prince Pedro of Portugal, till I have freed her from her enchantment.' 'All this and more you owe my mistress,' said the damsel; and then, having got the four reals, instead of dropping me a curtsey, she cut me a caper in the air two yards high."

"Now, Heaven defend us!" cried Sancho. "Who could ever have believed that these enchanters and enchantments should have so much power as to bewitch my master at this rate, and craze his sound understanding in this manner? Alas! sir, for the love of Heaven, take care of yourself. What will the world say of you? Rouse up your dozing senses, and do not dote upon those whimsies that have so wretchedly cracked that rare headpiece of yours."

II

"Well," said Don Quixote, "I cannot be angry at thy ignorant tittle-tattle, because it proceeds from thy love towards me. Thou thinkest, poor fellow! that whatever is beyond the sphere of thy narrow comprehension must be impossible; but, as I have already said, there will come a time when I shall give thee an account of some things I have seen below, that will convince thee of the reality of those I told thee now, the truth of which admits of no dispute."

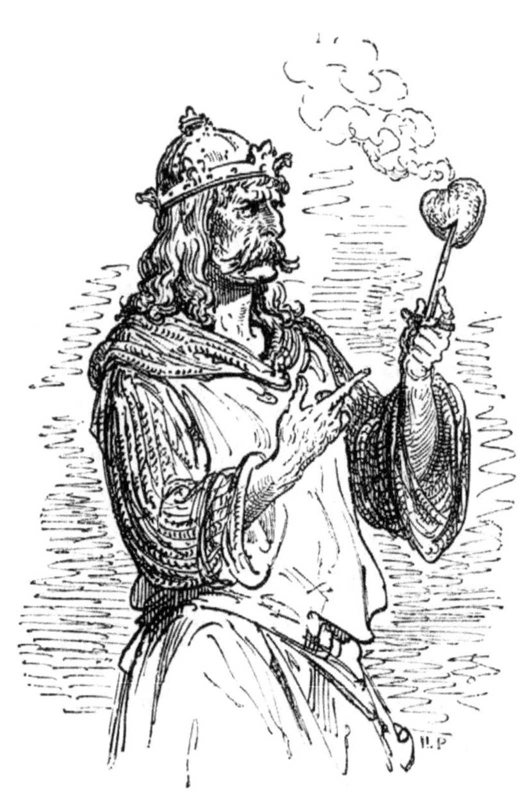

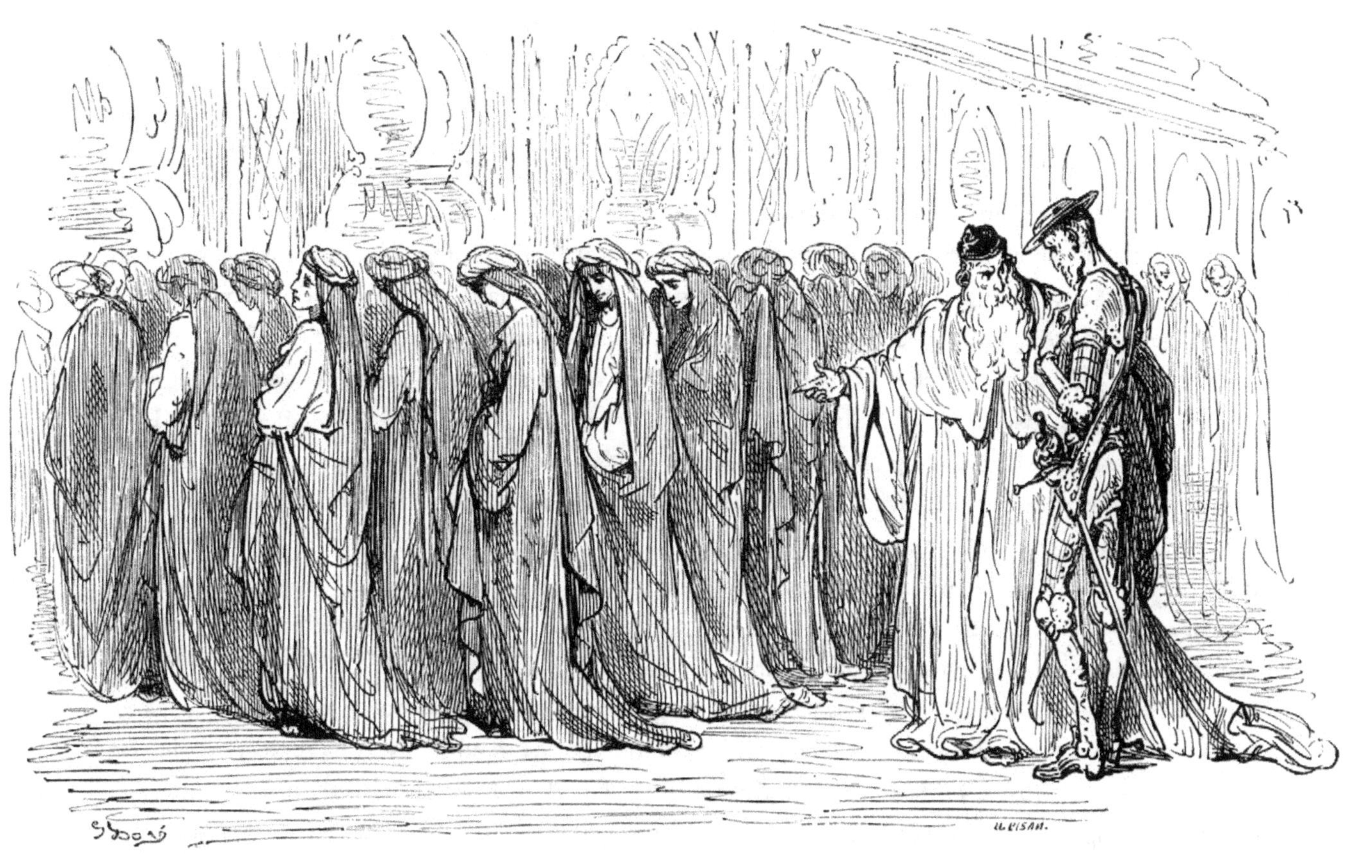

CHAPTER XXIV.

WHICH GIVES AN ACCOUNT OF A THOUSAND FLIMFLAMS AND STORIES, AS IMPERTINENT AS NECESSARY TO THE RIGHT UNDERSTANDING OF THIS GRAND HISTORY.

THE translator of this famous history declares that, at the beginning of the chapter which treats of the adventure of the cave of Montesinos, he found a marginal annotation, written with the Arabian author's own hand, in these words:—

"I cannot be persuaded, nor believe, that all the wonderful accidents said to have happened to the valorous Don Quixote in the cave, so punctually befell him as he relates them; for the course of his adventures hitherto has been very natural, and bore the face of probability, but in this there appears no coherence with reason, and nothing but monstrous incongruities. But, on the other hand, if we consider the honour, worth, and integrity of the noble Don Quixote, we have not the least reason to suspect he would be guilty of a lie, but rather that he would sooner have been transfixed with arrows. Besides, he has been so particular in his relation of that adventure, and given so many circumstances, that I dare not declare it absolutely apocryphal; especially when I consider that he had not time enough to invent such a cluster of fables. I therefore insert it among the rest, without offering to determine whether it is true or false, leaving it to the discretion of the judicious reader; though I must acquaint him, by the way, that Don Quixote, upon his death-bed, utterly disowned this adventure, as a perfect fable, which, he said, he had invented purely to please his humour, being suitable to such as he had formerly read in romances." And so much by way of digression.

The scholar thought Sancho the most saucy servant, and his master the calmest madman, that ever he saw, though he attributed the patience of the latter to a certain good humour and easiness of temper, infused into him by the sight of his mistress Dulcinea, even under enchantment; otherwise he would have thought his not checking Sancho a greater sign of madness than his discourse. "Noble Don Quixote," said he, "for four principal reasons I am extremely pleased with having taken this journey with you. First, it has procured me the honour of your acquaintance, which I shall always esteem a singular happiness. In the second place, sir, the secrets of the cave of Montesinos, and the transformations of Guadiana and Ruydera's lakes have been revealed to me, which may look very great in my Spanish Ovid. My third advantage is, to have discovered the antiquity of card-playing, which I find to have been a pastime in use even in the Emperor Charles the Great's time, as may be collected from the words of Durandarte, who, after a long speech of Montesinos', said, as he waked, 'Patience, and shuffle the cards,' which vulgar expression he could never have learned in his enchantment. It follows, therefore, that he must have heard it when he lived in France, which was in the reign of that emperor; which observation is nicked, I think, very opportunely for my supplement to Polydore Virgil, who, as I remember, has not touched upon card-playing. The fourth part of my good fortune is to know the certain and true source of the river Guadiana, which has hitherto disappointed all human inquiries."

"There is a great deal of reason in what you say," answered Don Quixote; "but, under favour, sir, pray tell me, should you happen to get a licence to publish your book, which I somewhat doubt, whom will you pitch upon for your patron?"

"Oh, sir," answered the author, "there are grandees enough in Spain, sure, that I may dedicate to."

"Truly, not many," said Don Quixote; "there are, indeed, several whose merits deserve the praise of a dedication, but very few whose generosity will reward the pains and civility of the author. I must confess, I know a prince whose generosity may make amends for what is wanting in the rest, and that to such a degree, that, should I make bold to come to particulars, and speak of his great merits, it would be enough to stir up a noble emulation in above four generous breasts; but more of this some other time—it is late now, and therefore convenient to think of a lodging."

"Hard by us here, sir," said the author, "is a hermitage, the retirement of a devout person, who, as they say, was once a soldier, and is looked upon as a good Christian, and so charitable, that he has built there a little house at his own expense, purely for the entertainment of strangers."

"But does he keep hens there, trow?" asked Sancho.

"Few hermits in this age are without them," said Don Quixote; "for their way of living now falls short of the strictness and austerity of those in the deserts of Egypt, who went clad only with palm-leaves, and fed on the roots of the earth. Now, because I speak well of those of old, I would not have you think I reflect on the others. No, I only mean that their penances are not so severe as in former days; yet this does not hinder but that the hermits of the present age may be good men. I look upon them to be such; at least their dissimulation secures them from scandal; and the hypocrite that puts on the form of holiness does certainly less harm than the barefaced sinner."

As they went on in their discourse, they saw a man following them at a great pace on foot, and switching up a mule laden with lances and halberts. He presently overtook them, gave them the time of the day, and passed by.

"Stay, honest fellow!" cried Don Quixote, seeing him go so fast, "make no more haste than is consistent with good speed."

"I cannot stay, sir," said the man; "for these weapons that you see must be used to-morrow morning; so, sir, I am in haste—good bye—I shall lodge to-night at the inn beyond the hermitage; if you chance to go that way, there you may find me, and I will tell you strange news; so, fare ye well." Then, whipping his mule, away he moved forwards; so fast, that Don Quixote had not leisure to ask him any more questions.

The knight, who had always an itching ear after novelties, to satisfy his curiosity, immediately proposed their holding straight on to the inn, without stopping at the hermitage, where the scholar designed to have stayed all night. Well, they all consented, and made the best of their way; however, when they came near the hermitage, the scholar desired Don Quixote to call with him for a moment, and drink a glass of wine at the door. Sancho no sooner heard this proposed, but he turned Dapple that way, and rode thither before; but, to his grief, the hospitable hermit was abroad, and nobody at home but the hermit's companion, who, being asked whether he had any liquor within, made answer that he could not come at any, but as for water, he might have plenty.

"Bless me!" quoth Sancho, "were mine a water-thirst, or had I a liking to your cold comfort, there are wells enough upon the road where I might have taken my fill. Oh, the good cheer of Don Diego's house, and the savoury scum at Camacho's wedding! when shall I find your fellow?"

They now spurred on towards the inn, and soon overtook on the road a young fellow, beating it on the hoof pretty leisurely. He carried his sword over his shoulder, with a bundle of clothes hanging upon it, which, to all outward appearance, consisted of a pair of breeches, a cloak, and a shirt or two. He had on a tattered velvet jerkin, with a ragged satin lining, and his shirt hung out. His stockings were of silk, and his shoes square at the toes, after the court fashion. He seemed about eighteen or nineteen years of age, a good, pleasant-looking lad, and of a lively and active disposition. To pass the fatigue of his journey the best he could, he sung all the way; and, as they came near him, was just ending the last words of a ballad, which the scholar got by heart, and were these:—

"A plague on ill luck! now my ready's all gone,
To the wars poor pilgarlick must trudge;
Though had I but money to rake as I've done,
The devil a foot would I budge."

"So, young gentleman," said Don Quixote to him, "methinks you go very light and airy. Whither are you bound, I pray you, if a man may be so bold?"

"I am going to the wars, sir; and for my travelling thus, heat and poverty will excuse it."

"I admit the heat," replied Don Quixote; "but why poverty, I beseech you?"

"Because I have no clothes to put on but what I carry in this bundle; and if I should wear them out upon the road, I should have nothing to make a handsome figure with in any town; for I have no money to buy new ones till I overtake a regiment of foot that lies some twelve leagues off, where I design to enlist myself, and then I shall not want a conveniency to ride with the baggage till we come to Carthagena, where, I hear, they are to embark; for I had rather serve the king abroad than any beggarly courtier at home."

"But pray," said the scholar, "have not you laid up something while you were there?"

"Had I served any of your grandees," said the young man, "I might have done well enough, and have had a commission by this time; for their foot-boys are presently advanced to captains and lieutenants, or some other good post; but, sir, it was always my ill fortune to serve pitiful upstarts and younger brothers; and my allowance was commonly so ill paid and so small, that the better half was scarce enough to wash my linen; how then should a poor page come to any good in such a miserable service?"

"But," said Don Quixote, "how comes it about that in all this time you could not get yourself a whole livery?"

"Alack-a-day, sir," answered the lad, "I had a couple; but my masters dealt with me as they do with novices in monasteries; if they go off before they profess, the fresh habit is taken from them, and they return them their own clothes. For you must know that such as I served only buy liveries for a little ostentation; so, when they have made their appearance at court, they sneak down into the country, and then the poor servants are stripped, and must even betake themselves to their rags again."

"A sordid trick!" said Don Quixote. "However, you need not repine at leaving the court, since you do it with so good a design; for there is nothing in the world more commendable than to serve God in the first place, and the king in the next, especially in the profession of arms, which, if it does not procure a man so much riches as learning, may at least entitle him to more honour. It is true that more families have been advanced by the gown, but yet your gentlemen of the sword, whatever the reason of it is, have always I know not what advantage above the men of learning; and something of glory and splendour attends them that makes them outshine the rest of mankind.

But take my advice along with you, child; if you intend to raise yourself by military employment, I would not have you be uneasy with the thoughts of what misfortunes may befall you; the worst can be but to die, and if it be an honourable death, your fortune is made, and you are certainly happy. Julius Cæsar, that valiant Roman emperor, being asked what kind of death was best, 'That which is sudden and unexpected,' said he; and though his answer had a relish of paganism, yet, with respect to human infirmities, it was very judicious; for suppose you should be cut off at the very first engagement by a cannon-ball, or the spring of a mine, what matters it? it is all but dying, and there is an end of the business. As Terence says, 'a soldier makes a better figure dead in the field of battle, than alive and safe in flight.' The more likely he is to rise in fame and preferment, the better discipline he keeps; the better he obeys, the better he will know how to command: and pray observe, my friend, that it is more honourable for a soldier to smell of gunpowder than of musk and amber; or if old age overtakes you in this noble employment, though all over scars, though maimed and lame, you will still have honour to support you and secure you from the contempt of poverty, nay, from poverty itself, for there is care taken that veterans and disabled soldiers may not want; neither are they to be used as some men do their negro slaves, who, when they are old and past service, are turned naked out of doors, under pretence of freedom, to be made greater slaves to cold and hunger; a slavery from which nothing but death can set the wretches free. But I will say no more to you on this subject at this time. Get up behind me, and I will carry you to the inn, where you shall sup with me, and to-morrow make the best of your way; and may Heaven prosper your good designs!"

The page excused himself from riding behind the knight, but accepted of his invitation to supper very willingly. In a short time they arrived at the inn, where Don Quixote alighting, asked presently for the man with the lances and halberts.

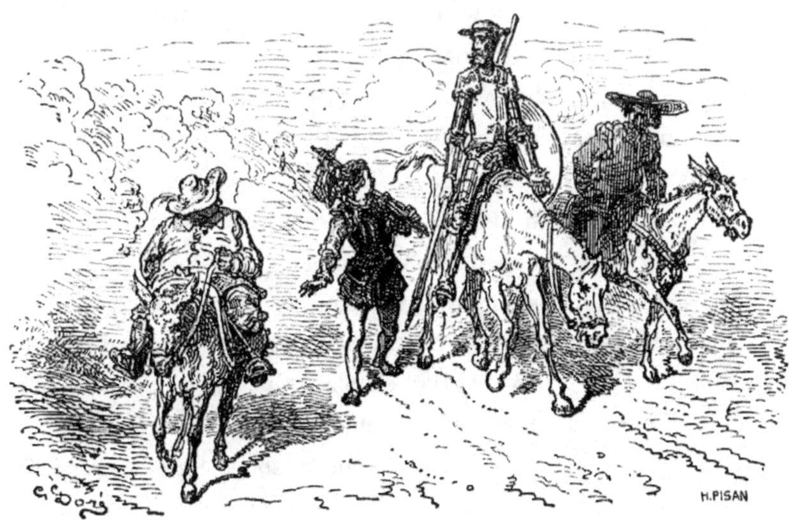

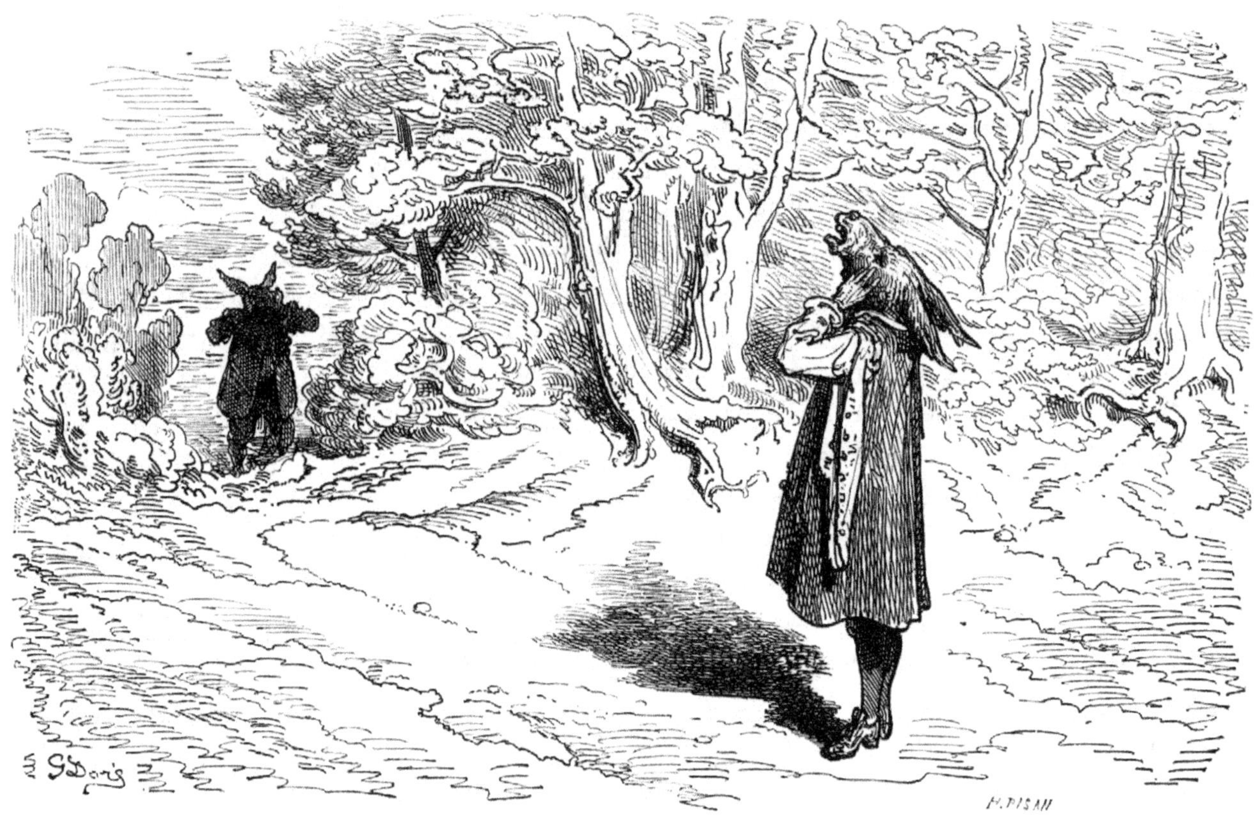

CHAPTER XXV.

WHERE YOU FIND THE GROUNDS OF THE BRAYING ADVENTURES, THAT OF THE PUPPET-PLAYER, AND THE MEMORABLE DIVINING OF THE FORTUNE-TELLING APE.

DON QUIXOTE was on thorns to know the strange story that the fellow upon the road engaged to tell him; so that, going into the stable, he reminded him of his promise, and pressed him to relate the whole matter to him that moment.

"My story will take up some time," quoth the man, "and is not to be told standing: have a little patience, master of mine; let me make an end of serving my mule, then I will serve your worship, and tell you such things as will make you stare."

"Do not let that hinder you," replied Don Quixote, "for I will help you myself."

And so saying, he lent him a helping hand, cleansing the manger, and sifting the barley, which humble compliance obliged the fellow to tell his tale the more willingly; so that, seating himself upon a bench, with Don Quixote, the scholar, the page, Sancho, and the innkeeper about him, for his full auditory, he began in this manner:—

"It happened on a time, that, in a borough about some four leagues and a half from this place, one of the aldermen lost his ass. They say it was by the roguery of a waggish jade that was his maid; but that is neither here nor there—the ass was lost and gone, that is certain; and what is more, it could not be found neither high nor low. This same ass had been missing about a fortnight, some say more, some less, when another alderman of the same town, meeting this same losing alderman in the market-place, 'Brother,' quoth he, 'pay me well, and I will tell you news of your ass.'

"'Troth,' replied the other, 'that I will; but then let me know where the poor beast is.'

"'Why,' answered the other, 'this morning what should I meet upon the mountains yonder but he, without either pack-saddle or furniture, and so lean that it grieved my heart to see him; but yet so wild and skittish, that when I would have driven him home before me, he ran away and got into the thickest of the wood. Now, if you please, we will both go together and look for him; I will but step home first and put up this ass, then I will come back to you, and we will about it out of hand.'

"'Truly, brother,' said the other, 'I am mightily beholden to you, and will do as much for you another time.'

"The story happened neither more nor less, but such as I tell you, for so all that know it relate it word for word. In short, the two aldermen, hand-in-hand, trudged afoot up the hills, and hunted up and down; but after many a weary step, no ass was to be found. Upon which quoth the alderman that had seen him to the other, 'Hark you me, brother, I have a device in my noddle to find out this same ass of yours, though he were under ground, as you shall hear. You must know I can bray to admiration, and if you can but bray but never so little, the job is done.'

"'Never so little!' cried the other; 'bless me, I won't vail my bonnet at braying to e'er an ass or alderman in the land.'

"'Well, we shall try that,' quoth the other, 'for my contrivance is, that you go on one side of the hill, and I on the other; sometimes you shall bray, and sometimes I; so that, if your ass be but thereabouts, my life for yours, he will be sure to answer his kind, and bray again.'

"'Well done, brother,' quoth the other; 'a rare device! let you alone for plotting.'

"At the same time they parted according to agreement, and when they were far enough off, they both fell a-braying so perfectly well, that they cheated one another; and meeting, each in hopes to find the ass, 'Is it possible, brother,' said the owner of the ass, 'that it was not my ass that brayed?'

"'No, marry, that it was not; it was I,' answered the other alderman.

"'Well, brother,' cried the owner, 'then there is no manner of difference between you and an ass, as to matter of braying; I never heard anything so natural in my life.'

"'Oh, fie! sir,' quoth the other, 'I am nothing to you: you shall lay two to one against the best brayer in the kingdom, and I will go you halves. Your voice is lofty, and of a great compass; you keep excellent time, and hold out a note rarely, and your cadence is full and ravishing. In short, sir, I knock under the table, and yield you the bays.'

"'Well then, brother,' answered the owner, 'I shall always have the better opinion of myself for this one good quality; for though I knew I brayed pretty well, I never thought myself so great a master before.'

"'Well,' quoth the other, 'thus you see what rare parts may be lost for want of being known; and a man never knows his own strength till he puts it to a trial.'

"'Right, brother,' quoth the owner; 'for I should never have found out this wonderful gift of mine, had it not been for this business in hand; and may we speed in it, I pray."

"After these compliments they parted again, and went braying, this on one side of the hill, and that on the other; but all to no purpose, for they still deceived one another with their braying, and, running to the noise, met one another as before.

"At last they agreed to bray twice one after another, that by that token they might be sure it was not the ass, but they that brayed; but all in vain—they almost brayed their hearts out, but no answer from the ass. And indeed, how could he, poor creature! for they found him at last in the wood, half-eaten by the wolves.

"'Alack-a-day! poor Grizzle,' cried the owner; 'I do not wonder now he took so little notice of his loving master. Had he been alive, as sure as he was an ass, he would have brayed again. But let him go; this comfort I have at least, brother, though I have lost him, I have found out that rare talent of yours, that has greatly solaced me under this affliction.'

"'The glass is in a good hand, Mr. Alderman,' quoth the other, 'and if the abbot sings well, the young monk is not much behind him.'

"With this these same aldermen, very much down in the mouth, and very hoarse, went home and told all their neighbours the whole story, word for word; one praising the other's skill in braying, and the other returning the compliment. In short, one got it by the end, and the other got it by the end; the boys got it, and all the idle fellows got it, and there was such a brawling and such a braying in our town, that one would have thought madmen were broke loose among us. But to let you see now how mischief never lies dead in a ditch, but catches at every foolish thing to set people by the ears, our neighbouring towns had it up; and when they saw any of our townsfolks, they fell a-braying, hitting us in the teeth with the braying of our aldermen. This made ill blood between us; for we took it in mighty dudgeon, as well we might, and came to words upon it, and from words to blows; for the people of our town are well known by this, as the beggar knows his dish, and are apt to be jeered wheresoever they go; and then to it they go, ding dong, hand over head, in spite of law or gospel. And they have carried the jest so far, that I believe to-morrow, or next day, the men of our town, to wit, the brayers, will be in the field against those of another town about two leagues off, that are always plaguing us. Now, that we should be well provided, I have brought these lances and halberts that you saw me carry. So this is my story, gentlefolks, and if it be not a strange one, I am greatly mistaken."

Here the honest man ended; when presently enters a fellow dressed in trousers and doublet all of chamois leather, and calling out, as if he were somebody, "Landlord, have you any lodgings? for here comes the fortune-telling ape, and the puppet-show of Melisandra's deliverance."

"Bless me!" cried the innkeeper, "who's here? Master Peter! We shall have a merry night, faith! Honest Master Peter, you are welcome with all my heart; but where is the ape and the show, that I cannot see them?"

"They will be here presently; I only came before to see if you had any lodgings."

"Lodging! man," said the innkeeper; "I would turn out the Duke of Alva himself, rather than Master Peter should want room. Come, come, bring in your things, for here are guests in the house to-night that will be good customers to you, I warrant you."

"That is a good hearing," said Peter; "and to encourage them I will lower my prices; and if I can but get my charges to-night, I will look for no more; so I will hasten forward the cart." This said, he ran out of the door again.

I had forgot to tell you that this same Master Peter wore over his left eye and half his cheek a patch of green taffeta, by which it was supposed that something ailed that side of his face.

Don Quixote inquired who this Master Peter was, and what his ape and his show.

"Why, sir," answered the innkeeper, "he has strolled about the country this great while with a curious puppet-show, which represents the play of Melisandra and Don Gayferos, one of the best shows that has been acted time out of mind in this kingdom. Then he has an ape: bless us, sir, it is such an ape!—but I will say no more—you shall see, sir. It will tell you everything you did in your life. The like was never seen before. Ask it a question, it will listen to you, and then, whip! up it leaps on its master's shoulder, and whispers first in his ear what it knows, and then Master Peter tells you. He tells you what is to come as well as what is past: it is true, he does not always hit so pat what is to come; but after all, he is seldom in the wrong, which makes us apt to think some one helps him at a dead lift. Two reals is the price for every question he answers, or his master for him, which is all one, you know; and that will mount to money at the year's end, so that it is thought the rogue is well to pass; and, indeed, much good may it do him, for he is a notable fellow, and leads the merriest life in the world; talks for six men, and drinks for a dozen; and all this he gets by his tongue, his ape, and his show."

By this time Master Peter came back with his puppet-show and his ape in a cart. The ape was pretty lusty, without any tail, and his back bare as a felt; yet he was not very ugly neither. Don Quixote no sooner saw him, but coming up to him, "Mr. Fortune-Teller," said he, "will you be pleased to tell us what fish we shall catch, and what will become of us? and here is your fee." Saying this, he ordered Sancho to deliver Master Peter two reals.

"Sir," answered Peter, "this animal gives no account of things to come; he knows something, indeed, of matters past, and a little of the present."

"Oh, indeed!" quoth Sancho; "I would not give a brass jack to know what is past, for who knows that better than myself? I am not so foolish as to pay for what I know already: but since you say he has such a knack at guessing the present, let goodman ape tell me what my wife Teresa is doing, and here are my two reals."

"I will have nothing of you beforehand," said Master Peter; so, clapping himself on his left shoulder, up skipped the ape thither at one frisk, and, laying his mouth to his ear, grated his teeth; and having made apish grimaces, and a chattering noise, for a minute or two, with another skip down he leaped upon the ground. Immediately upon this, Master Peter ran to Don Quixote, fell on his knees, and, embracing his legs, "Oh, glorious restorer of knight-errantry," cried he, "I embrace these legs as I would the pillars of Hercules! Who can sufficiently extol the great Don Quixote de la Mancha, the reviver of drooping hearts, the prop and stay of the falling, the raiser of the fallen, and the staff of comfort to the weak!"

At these words Don Quixote stood amazed, Sancho quaked, the page wondered, the brayer blessed himself, the innkeeper stared, and the scholar was in a brown study, all astonished at Master Peter's speech, who then, turning to Sancho, exclaimed, "And thou, honest Sancho Panza, the best squire to the best knight in the world, bless thy stars, for thy good spouse Teresa is a good house-wife, and is at this instant dressing a pound of flax; by the same token, she has standing by her, on her left hand, a large broken-mouth jug, which holds a pretty scantling of wine, to cheer up her spirits."

"By yea and nay," quoth Sancho, "that is likely enough; for she is a true soul, and a jolly soul: were it not for a spice of jealousy that she has now and then, I would not change her for the giantess Andondona herself, who, as my master says, was as clever a piece of woman's flesh as ever went upon two legs. Well, much good may it do thee, honest Teresa; thou art resolved to provide for one, I find, though thy heirs starve for it."

"Well," said Don Quixote, "great is the knowledge procured by reading, travel, and experience. What on earth but the testimony of my own eyes could have persuaded me that apes had the gift of divination! I am indeed the same Don Quixote de la Mancha, mentioned by this ingenious animal, though I must confess somewhat undeserving of so great a character as it has pleased him to bestow on me; but nevertheless I am not sorry to have charity and compassion bear so great a part in my commendation, since my nature has always disposed me to do good to all men, and hurt to none."

"Now had I but money," said the page, "I would know of Mr. Ape what luck I should have in the wars."

"I have told you already," said Master Peter, who was got up from before Don Quixote, "that this ape does not meddle with what is to come; but if he could, it should cost you nothing, for Don Quixote's sake, whom to oblige I would sacrifice all the interest I have in the world; and as a mark of it, gentlemen, I freely set up my show, and give all the company in the house some diversion gratis."

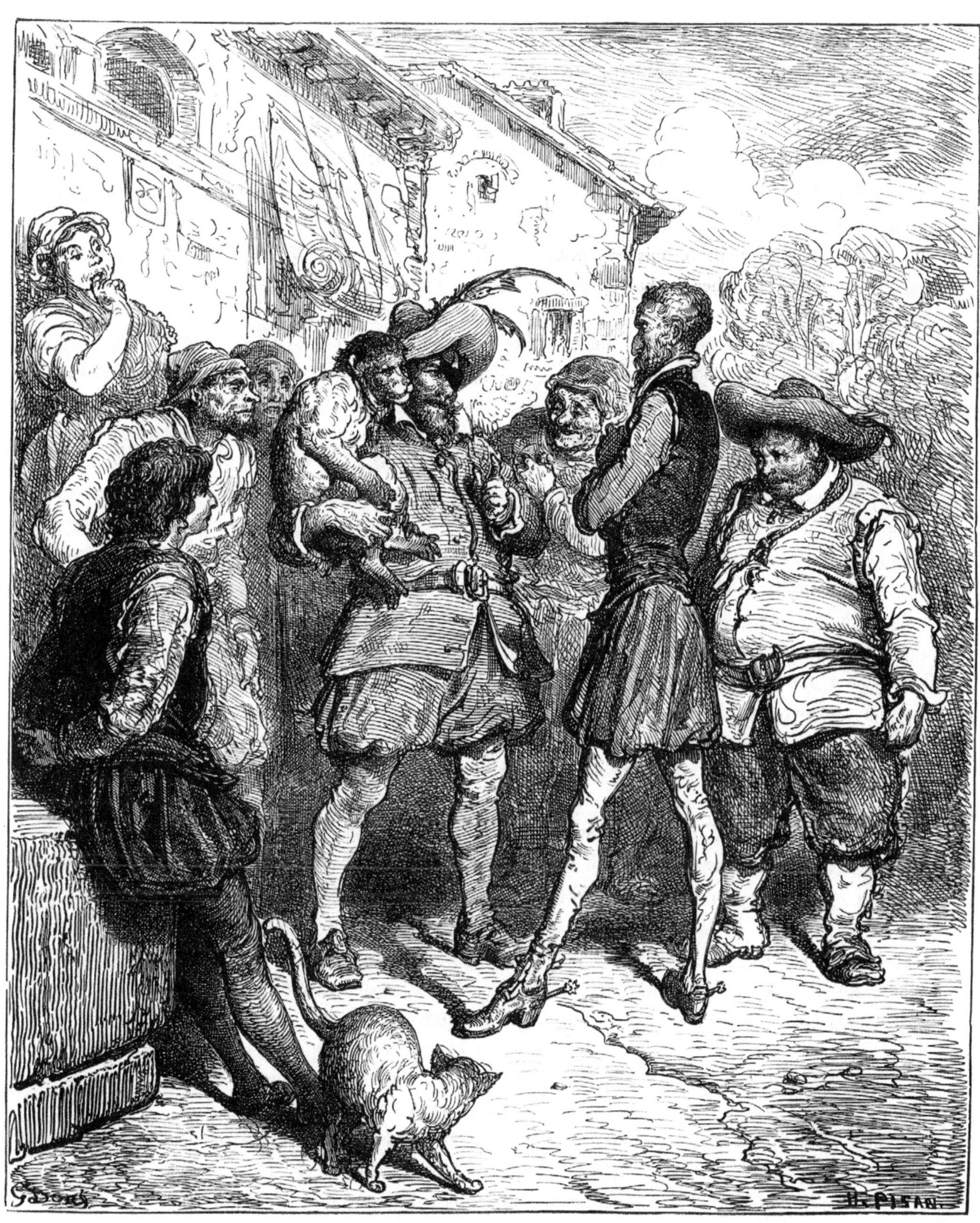

"At these words Don Quixote stood amazed."—*p.* 540.

The innkeeper, hearing this, was overjoyed, and ordered Master Peter a convenient room to set up his motion, and he immediately went about it.

In the meantime Don Quixote, who could not bring himself to believe that an ape could do all this, taking Sancho to a corner of the stable, "Look ye, Sancho," said he, "I have been weighing and considering the wonderful gifts of this ape, and find, in short, that Master Peter must have made a secret compact with the devil."

"Nay," quoth Sancho, misunderstanding the word *compact*, "if the devil and he have packed anything together in hugger-mugger, it is a pack of roguery, to be sure, and they are a pack of knaves for their pains, and let them e'en pack together, say I."

"Thou dost not apprehend me," said Don Quixote; "I mean, the devil and he must have made an agreement together, that Satan should infuse his knowledge into the ape, to purchase the owner an estate; and, in return, the last has certainly engaged his soul to this destructive seducer of mankind; for the ape's knowledge is exactly of the same proportion with the devil's, which only extends to the discovery of things past and present, having no insight into futurity, but by such probable conjectures and conclusions as may be deduced from the former working of antecedent causes; true prescience and prediction being the sacred prerogative of God, to whose all-seeing eyes all ages, past, present, and to come, without the distinction of succession and termination, are always present. From this, I say, it is apparent that this ape is but the organ through which the devil delivers his answers to those that ask it questions; and this same rogue should be put into the Inquisition, and have the truth pressed out of his bones. For sure neither the master nor his ape can lay any pretence to judicial astrology, nor is the ape so conversant in the mathematics, I suppose, as to erect a scheme. Though I must confess that creatures of less parts, as foolish, illiterate women, footmen, and cobblers, pretend now-a-days to draw certainties from the stars, as easily and as readily as they shuffle a pack of cards, to the disgrace of the sublime science, which they have the impudence to profess."

"For all that," said Sancho, "I would have you ask Master Peter's ape whether the passages you told us concerning the cave of Montesinos be true or no; for, saving the respect I owe your worship, I take them to be no better than fibs and idle stories, or dreams at least."

"You may think what you will," answered Don Quixote; "however, I will do as you would have me, though I confess my conscience somewhat scruples to do such a thing."

While they were thus engaged in discourse, Master Peter came and told Don Quixote the show was ready to begin, and desired him to come and see it, for he was sure his worship would like it.

The knight told him he had a question to put to his ape first, and desired he might tell him whether certain things that happened to him in the cave of Montesinos were dreams or realities, for he doubted they had something of both in them.

Master Peter fetched his ape immediately, and, placing him just before the knight and his squire, "Look you," said he, "Mr. Ape, this worthy knight would have you tell him whether some things which happened to him in the cave of Montesinos are true or no." Then, upon the usual signal, the ape, jumping upon Master Peter's left shoulder, chattered his answer into his ear, which the interpreter delivered thus to the inquirer:—"The ape, sir, says that part of those things are false, and part of them true, which is all he can resolve ye as to this question; and now his virtue has left him, and won't return till Friday next. If you would know any more you must stay till then, and he will answer as many questions as you please."

"Look you there now!" quoth Sancho; "did not I tell you that all you told us of the cave of Montesinos would not hold water?"

"That the event will determine," replied the knight, "which we must leave to process of time to produce, for it brings everything to light, though buried in the bowels of the earth. No more of this at present: let us now see the puppet-show; I fancy we shall find something in it worth seeing."

"Something!" said Master Peter; "sir, you shall see a thousand things worth seeing. I tell you, sir, I defy the world to show such another. I say no more: *Operibus credite, et non verbis.* But now let us begin, for it grows late, and we have much to do, say, and show."

Don Quixote and Sancho complied, and went into the room where the show stood with a good number of small wax-lights glimmering round about, that made it shine gloriously. Master Peter got to his station within, being the man that was to move the puppets; and his boy stood before to tell what the puppets said, and, with a white wand in his hand, to point at the several figures as they came in and out, and explain the mystery of the show. Then, all the audience having taken their places, Don Quixote, Sancho, the scholar, and the page, being preferred to the rest, the boy, who was the mouth of the motion, began a story, that shall be heard or seen by those who will take the pains to read or hear the next chapter.

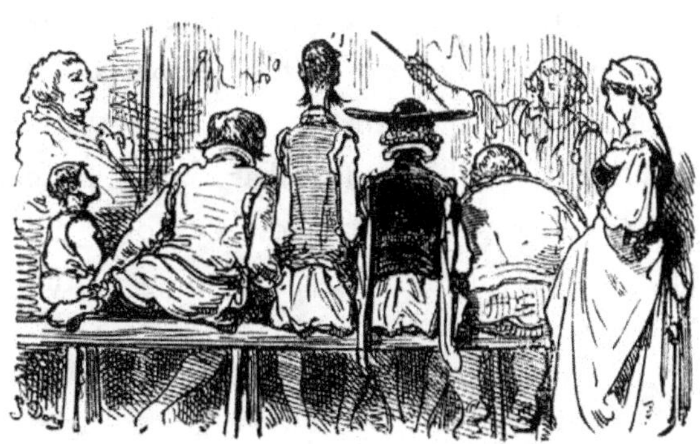

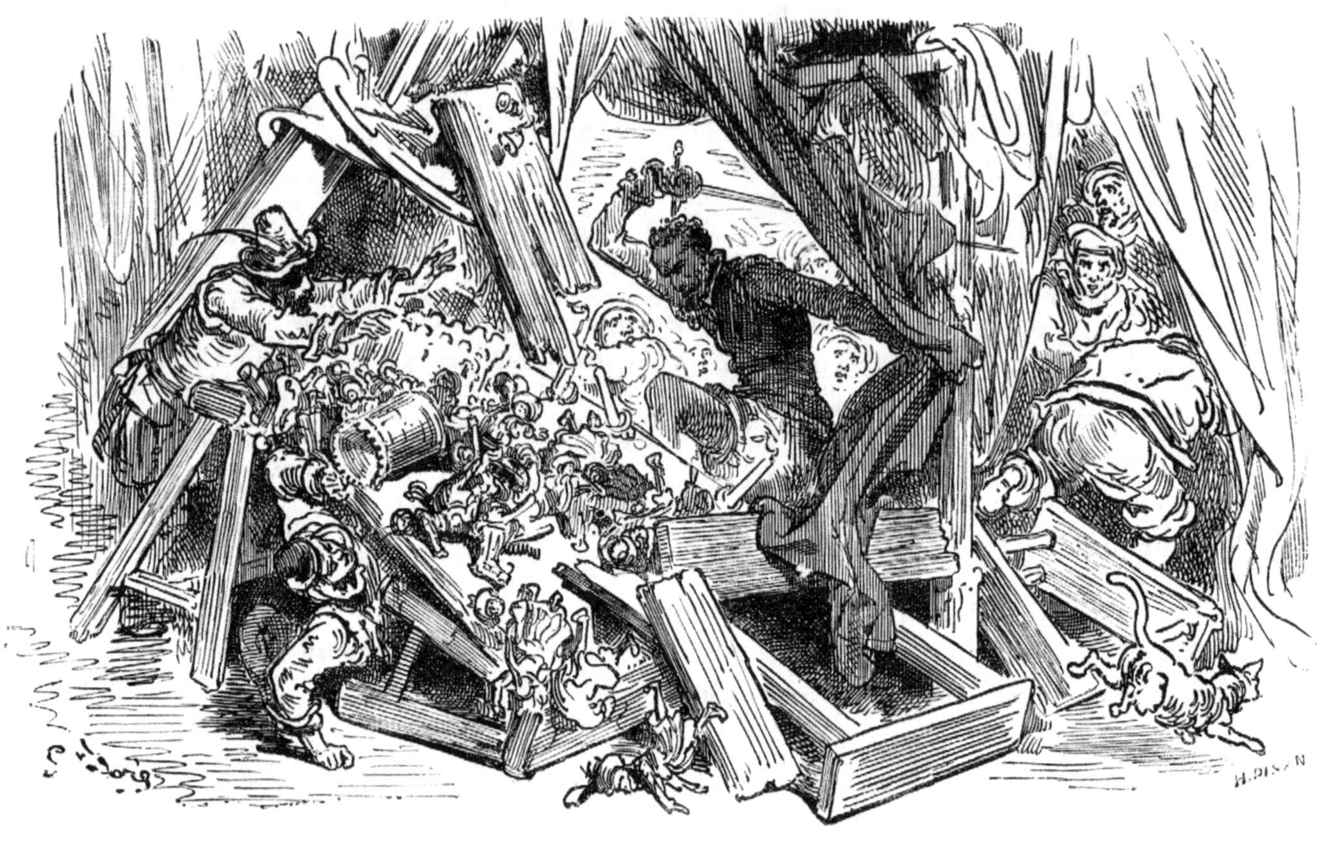

CHAPTER XXVI.

A PLEASANT ACCOUNT OF THE PUPPET-PLAY, WITH OTHER VERY GOOD THINGS TRULY.

THE Tyrians and the Trojans were all silent; that is, the ears of all the spectators hung on the mouth of the interpreter of the show, when, in the first place, they heard a loud flourish of kettle-drums and trumpets within the machine, and then several discharges of artillery; which prelude being soon over, "Gentlemen," cried the boy, raising his voice, "we present you here with a true history, taken out of the Chronicles of France, and the Spanish ballads, sung even by the boys about the streets, and in everybody's mouth; it tells you how Don Gayferos delivered his wife Melisandra, that was a prisoner among the Moors in Spain, in the city of Sansuena, now called Saragosa. Now, gallants, the first figure we present you with is Don Gayferos playing at tables, according to the ballad:

"'Now Gayferos the live-long day,
Oh! arrant shame, at draughts does play;
And, as at court most husbands do,
Forgets his lady fair and true.'

"Gentlemen, in the next place, mark that personage that peeps out there with a crown on his head and a sceptre in his hand; it is the Emperor Charlemagne, the fair Melisandra's reputed father, who, vexed at the idleness and negligence of his son-in-law, comes to chide him; and pray observe with what passion and earnestness he rates him, as if he had a mind to lend him half a dozen sound raps over the pate with his sceptre; nay, some authors do not stick to tell ye he gave him as many, and well laid on too. And after he had told him how his honour lay a-bleeding till he had delivered his wife out of durance, among many other pithy sayings, 'Look to it,' quoth he to him as he went, 'I will say no more.' Mind how the emperor turns his back upon him, and how he leaves Don Gayferos nettled, and in the dumps. Now see how he starts up, and, in a rage, dings the tables one way, and whirls the men another; and, calling for his arms with all haste, borrows his cousin-german Orlando's sword, Durindana, who withal offers to go along with him in this difficult adventure; but the valorous enraged knight will not let him, and says he is able to deliver his wife himself without his help, though they kept her down in the very centre of the earth. And now he is going to put on his armour, in order to begin his journey.

"Now, gentlemen, cast your eyes upon yon tower; you are to suppose it one of the towers of the castle of Saragosa, now called the Aljaferia. That lady whom you see in the balcony there in a Moorish habit is the peerless Melisandra, that casts many a heavy look towards France, thinking of Paris and her husband, the only comfort in her imprisonment. But now!—silence, gentlemen, pray silence—here is an accident wholly new, the like perhaps never heard of before. Don't you see that Moor, who comes a-tiptoe, creeping and stealing along, with his finger in his mouth, behind Melisandra? Hear what a smack he gives her on her sweet lips, and see how she spits, and wipes her mouth with her white sleeve; see how she takes on, and tears her lovely hair for very madness, as if it were to blame this affront. Next, pray observe that grave Moor that stands in the open gallery; that is Marsilius, the king of Sansuena, who, having been an eye-witness of the sauciness of the Moor, ordered him immediately to be apprehended, though his kinsman and great favourite; to have two hundred lashes given him; then to be carried through the city, with criers before to proclaim his crime, the rods of justice behind. And look how all this is put in execution sooner almost than the fact is committed; for among Moors, ye must know, there is no citation of the party, nor copies of the process, nor delay of justice, as among us."

"Child, child," said Don Quixote, "go on directly with your story, and don't keep us here with your excursions and ramblings out of the road. I tell you there must be a formal process, and legal trial, to prove matters of fact."

"Boy," said the master from behind the show, "do as the gentleman bids you. Don't run so much upon flourishes, but follow your plain song, without venturing on counter-points, for fear of spoiling all."

"I will, sir," quoth the boy, and so proceeding: "Now, sirs, he that you see there a-horse back, wrapped up in the Gascoigne cloak, is Don Gayferos himself, whom his wife, now revenged

JJ

on the Moor for his impudence, seeing from the battlements of the tower, takes him for a stranger, and talks with him as such, according to the ballad,

> 'Quoth Melisandra, If perchance,
> Sir Traveller, you go for France,
> For pity's sake, ask when you're there
> For Gayferos, my husband dear.'

"I omit the rest, not to tire you with a long story. It is sufficient that he makes himself known to her, as you may guess by the joy she shows; and accordingly, now see how she lets herself down from the balcony, to come at her loving husband, and get behind him; but unhappily, alas! one of the skirts of her gown is caught upon one of the spikes of the balcony, and there she hangs and hovers in the air miserably, without being able to get down. But see how Heaven is merciful, and sends relief in the greatest distress! Now Don Gayferos rides up to her, and, not fearing to tear her rich gown, lays hold on it, and at one pull brings her down; and then at one lift sets her astride upon his horse's crupper, bidding her to sit fast, and clap her arms about him, that she might not fall; for the Lady Melisandra was not used to that kind of riding.

"Observe now, gallants, how the horse neighs, and shows how proud he is of the burden of his brave master and fair mistress. Look now how they turn their backs, and leave the city, and gallop it merrily away towards Paris. Peace be with you, for a peerless couple of true lovers! may ye get safe and sound into your own country, without any let or ill chance in your journey, and live as long as Nestor, in peace and quietness among your friends and relations."

"Plainness, boy!" cried Master Peter, "none of your flights, I beseech you, for affectation is unbearable."

The boy answered nothing, but going on, "Now, sirs," quoth he, "some of those idle people, that love to pry into everything, happened to spy Melisandra as she was making her escape, and ran presently and gave Marsilius notice of it: whereupon he straight commanded to sound an alarm; and now mind what a din and hurly-burly there is, and how the city shakes with the ring of the bells backwards in all the mosques!"

"There you are out, boy," said Don Quixote: "the Moors have no bells; they only use kettle-drums, and a kind of shawms, like our waits or hautboys; so that your ringing of bells in Sansuena is a mere absurdity, good Master Peter."

"Nay, sir," said Master Peter, giving over ringing, "if you stand upon these trifles with us, we shall never please you. Don't be so severe a critic: are there not a thousand plays that pass with great success and applause, though they have many greater absurdities, and nonsense in abundance? On, boy, on! let there be as many impertinences as motes in the sun, no matter, so I get the money."

"Well said," answered Don Quixote.

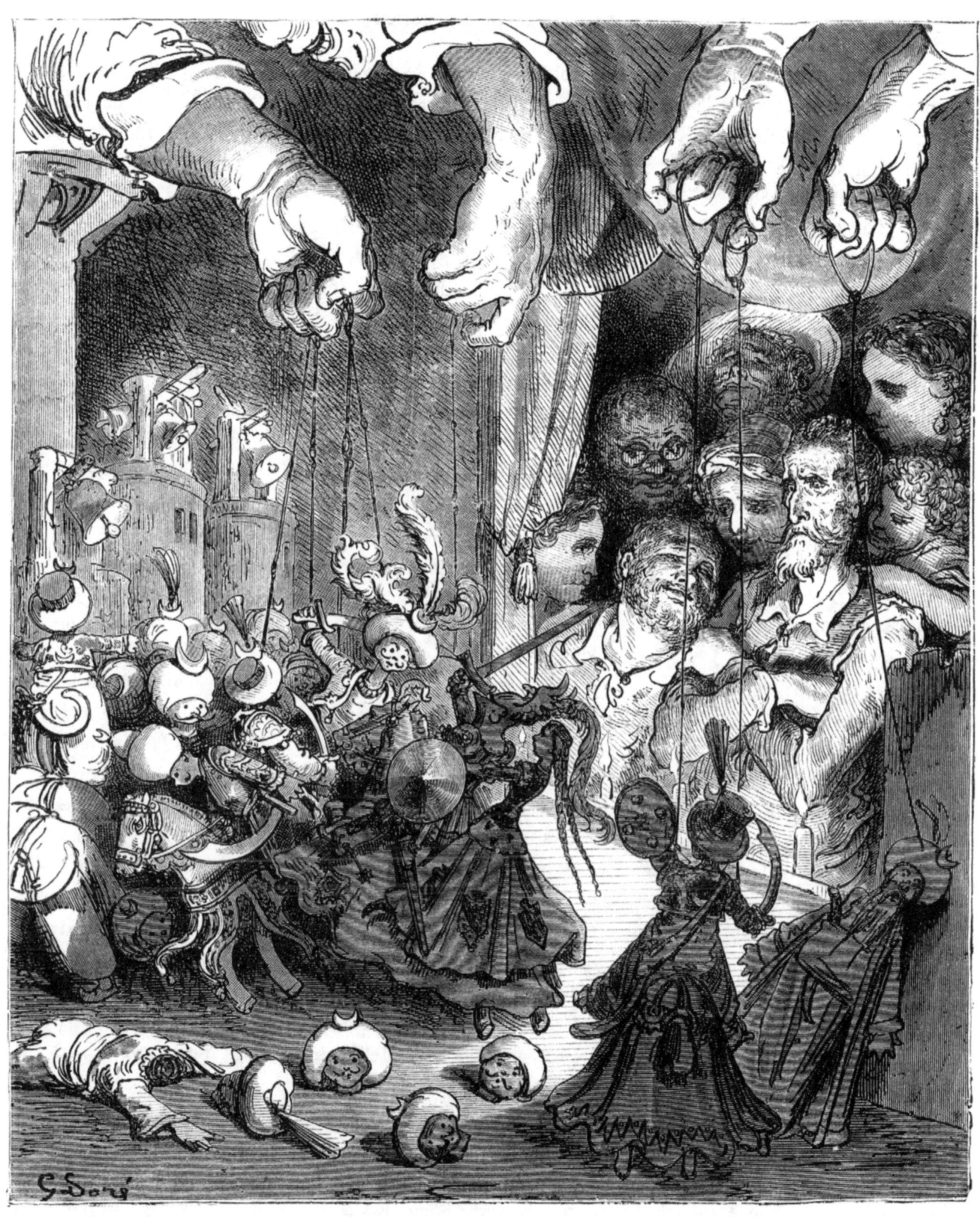

"Observe what a vast company of glittering horse comes pouring out of the city, in pursuit of the Christian lovers."—*p.* 548.

"And now, sirs," quoth the boy, "observe what a vast company of glittering horse comes pouring out of the city, in pursuit of the Christian lovers; what a dreadful sound of trumpets, and clarions, and drums, and kettle-drums there is in the air. I fear they will overtake them, and then will the poor wretches be dragged along most barbarously at the tails of their horses, which would be sad indeed."

Don Quixote, seeing such a number of Moors, and hearing such an alarm, thought it high time to assist the flying lovers; and starting up, "It shall never be said while I live," cried he aloud, "that I suffered such a wrong to be done to so famous a knight and so daring a lover as Don Gayferos. Forbear, then, your unjust pursuit, ye base-born rascals! Stop, or prepare to meet my furious resentment!"

Then drawing out his sword, to make good his threats, at one spring he gets to the show, and with a violent fury lays at the Moorish puppets, cutting and slashing in a most terrible manner; some he overthrows, and beheads others; maims this, and cleaves that in pieces. Among the rest of his merciless strokes, he thundered one down with such a mighty force, that had not Master Peter luckily ducked and squatted down, it had certainly chopped off his head as easily as one might cut an apple.

"Hold, hold, sir!" cried the puppet-player, after the narrow escape; "hold, for pity's sake! What do you mean, sir? These are no real Moors that you cut and hack so, but poor harmless puppets made of pasteboard. Think of what you do; you ruin me for ever! Oh, that ever I was born! you have broke me quite."

But Don Quixote, without minding his words, doubled and redoubled his blows so thick, and laid about him so outrageously, that in less than two credos he had cut all the strings and wires, mangled the puppets, and spoiled and demolished the whole motion. King Marsilius was in a grievous condition. The Emperor Charlemagne's head and crown were cleft in two. The whole audience was in a sad consternation. The ape scampered off to the top of the house. The scholar was frightened out of his wits; the page was very uneasy, and Sancho himself was in a terrible fright; for, as he said after the hurricane was over, he had never seen his master in such a rage before.

The general rout of the puppets being over, Don Quixote's fury began to abate; and with a more pacified countenance turning to the company, "Now," said he, "I could wish all those incredulous persons here who slight knight-errantry might receive conviction of their error, and behold undeniable proofs of the benefit of that function: for how miserable had been the condition of poor Don Gayferos and the fair Melisandra by this time, had I not been here and stood up in their defence! I make no question but those infidels would have apprehended them, and used them barbarously. Well, when all is done, long live knight-errantry; long let it live, I say, above all things whatsoever in this world!"

"Ay, ay," said Master Peter in a doleful tone, "let it live long for me, so I may die; for why should I live so unhappy as to say with King Roderigo, 'Yesterday I was lord of

Spain, to-day have not a foot of land I can call mine?' It is not half an hour, nay, scarce a moment, since I had kings and emperors at command. I had horses in abundance, and chests and bags full of fine things; but now you see me a poor sorry undone man, quite and clean broke and cast down, and in short a mere beggar. What is worst of all, I have lost my ape too, who I am sure will make me sweat ere I catch him again; and all through the rash fury of this Sir Knight here, who they say protects the fatherless, redresses wrongs, and does other charitable deeds, but has failed in all these good offices to miserable me, Heaven be praised for it. Well may I call him the Knight of the Woful Figure, for he has put me and all that belongs to me in a woful case."

The puppet-player's lamentations moving Sancho's pity, "Come," quoth he, "don't cry, Master Peter; thou break'st my heart to hear thee take on so; don't be cast down, man, for my master's a better Christian, I am sure, than to let any poor man come to loss by him: when he comes to know he has done you wrong, he will pay you for every farthing of damage, I will engage."

"Truly," said Master Peter, "if his worship would but pay me for the fashion of my puppets he has spoiled I will ask no more, and he will discharge a good conscience; for he that wrongs his neighbour, and does not make restitution, can never hope to be saved, that is certain."

"I grant it," said Don Quixote; "but I am not sensible how I have in the least injured you, good Master Peter."

"No, sir! not injured me?" cried Master Peter. "Why, these poor relics that lie here on the cold ground cry out for vengeance against you. Was it not the invincible force of that powerful arm of yours that has scattered and dismembered them so? And whose were those bodies, sir, but mine? and by whom was I maintained, but by them?"

"Well," said Don Quixote, "now I am thoroughly convinced of a truth which I have had reason to believe before, that those cursed magicians that daily persecute me do nothing but delude me, first drawing me into dangerous adventures by the appearances of them as really they are, and then presently after changing the face of things as they please. Really and truly, gentlemen, I vow and protest before you all that hear me, that all that was acted here seemed to be really transacted *ipso. facto* as it appeared. To me Melisandra appeared to be Melisandra, Don Gayferos was Don Gayferos, Marsilius was Marsilius, and Charlemagne was the real Charlemagne; which being so, I could not contain my fury, and acted according to the duties of my function, which obliges me to take the injured side. Now, though what I have done proves to be quite contrary to my good design, the fault ought not to be imputed to me, but to my persecuting foes; yet I own myself sorry for the mischance, and will condemn myself to pay the costs. Let Master Peter see what he must have for the figures that are damaged, and I will pay it him now in good and lawful money on the nail."

"Heaven bless your worship!" cried Master Peter, with a profound cringe; "I could expect no less from the wonderful Christianity of the valorous Don Quixote de la Mancha, the sure relief and bulwark of all miserable wanderers. Now let my landlord and the great Sancho be mediators and appraisers between your worship and myself, and I will stand to their award."

They agreed; and presently Master Peter, taking up Marsilius, King of Saragosa, that lay by on the ground with his head off, "You see, gentlemen," said he, "it is impossible to restore this king to his former dignity; and therefore, with submission to your better judgments, I think that for his destruction, and to get him a successor, seven-and-twenty pence is little enough on conscience."

"Proceed," said Don Quixote.

"Then for this that is cleft in two," said Master Peter, taking up the Emperor Charlemagne, "I think he is richly worth one-and-thirty pence halfpenny."

"Not so richly, neither," quoth Sancho.

"Truly," said the innkeeper, "I think it is pretty reasonable; but we will make it even money—let the poor fellow have half a crown."

"Come," said Don Quixote, "let him have his full price. We will not stand haggling for so small a matter in a case like this; so make haste, Master Peter, for it is near supper-time, and I have some strong presumptions that I shall eat heartily."

"Now," said Master Peter, "for this figure here that is without a nose, and blind with one eye, being the fair Melisandra, I will be reasonable with you: give me fourteen pence; I would not take less from my brother."

"Nay," said Don Quixote, "I am mistaken if Melisandra be not by this time, with her husband, upon the frontiers of France at least, for the horse that carried them seemed to me rather to fly than to gallop; and now you tell me of a Melisandra here without a nose, forsooth, when it is ten to one she is in France. Come, come, friend, Heaven help every man to his own; let us have fair dealing; so proceed."

Master Peter, finding that the knight began to harp upon the old string, was afraid he would fly off; and making as if he had better considered of it, "Cry ye mercy, sir," said he, "I was mistaken. This could not be Melisandra, indeed, but one of the damsels that waited on her; and so I think fivepence will be fair enough for her." In this manner he went on, setting his price upon the dead and wounded, which the arbitrators moderated to the content of both parties; and the whole sum amounted to forty reals and three quarters, which Sancho paid him down; and then Master Peter demanded two reals more, for the trouble of catching his ape.

"Give it him," said Don Quixote, "and set the monkey to catch the ape; and now would I give two hundred more to be assured that Don Gayferos and the Lady Melisandra were safely arrived in France among their friends."

"Nobody can better tell than my ape," said Master Peter, "though no one will be able to catch him if hunger or his kindness for me do not bring us together again to night

However, to-morrow will be a new day, and when it is light we will see what is to be done."

The whole disturbance being appeased, to supper they went lovingly together, and Don Quixote treated the whole company, for he was liberality itself.

Before day the man with the lances and halberts left the inn, and some time after the scholar and the page came to take leave of the knight; the first to return home, and the second to continue his journey, towards whose charges Don Quixote gave him twelve reals. As for Master Peter, he knew too much of the knight's humour to desire to have anything to do with him, and therefore, having picked up the ruins of the puppet-show, and got his ape again, by break of day he packed off to seek his fortune. The innkeeper, who did not know Don Quixote, was as much surprised at his liberality as at his madness. In fine, Sancho paid him very honestly by his master's order, and mounting a little before eight o'clock, they left the inn, and proceeded on their journey; where we will leave them, that we may have an opportunity to relate some other matters very requisite for the better understanding of this famous history.

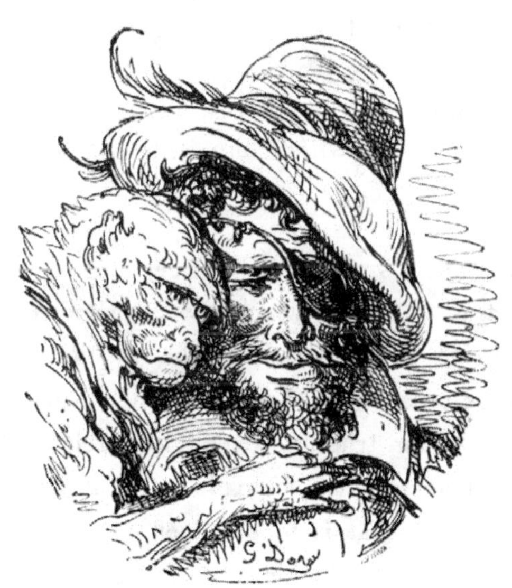

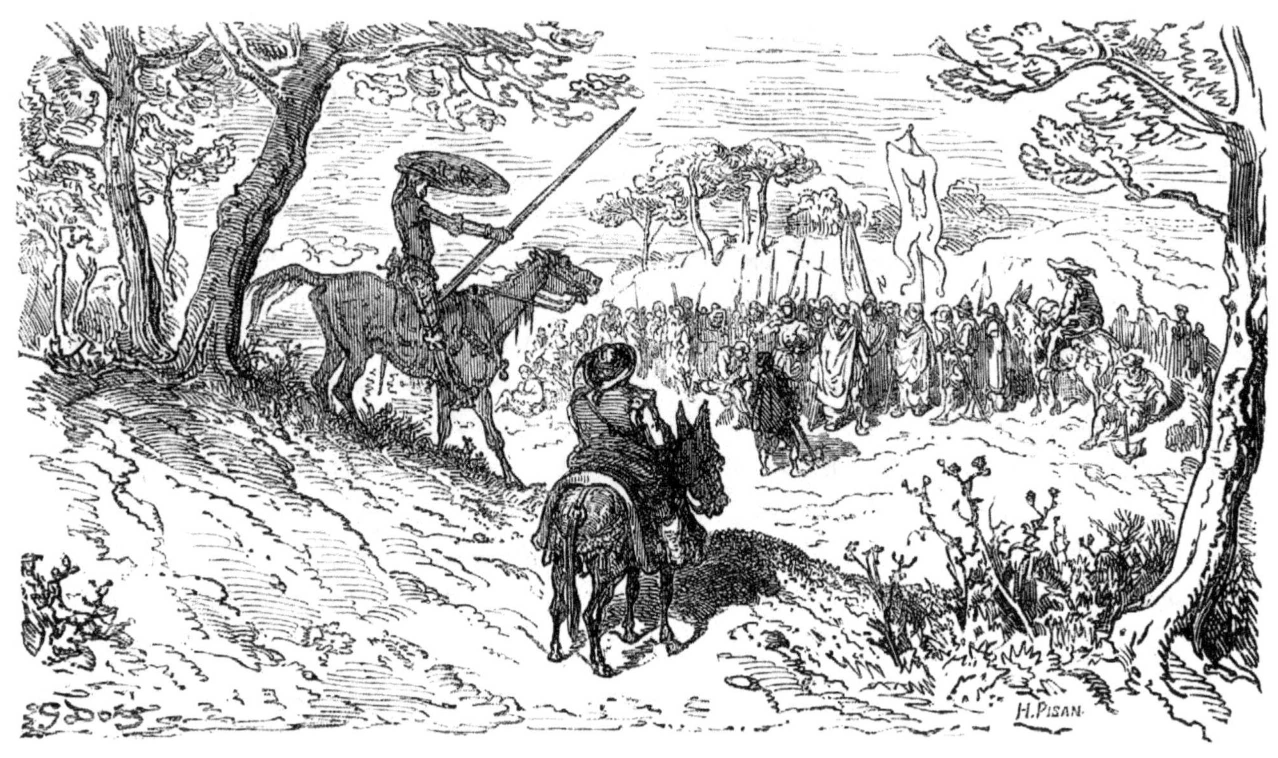

CHAPTER XXVII.

WHEREIN IS DISCOVERED WHO MASTER PETER WAS, AND HIS APE; AS ALSO DON QUIXOTE'S ILL SUCCESS IN THE BRAYING ADVENTURE, WHICH DID NOT END SO HAPPILY AS HE DESIRED AND EXPECTED.

CID HAMET, the author of this celebrated history, begins this chapter with this asseveration: "I swear as a true Catholic," which the translator illustrates and explains in this manner: That historian's swearing like a true Catholic, though he was a Mahometan Moor, ought to be received in no other sense than that, as a true Catholic, when he affirms anything with an oath, does or ought to swear truth, so would he relate the truth as impartially as a Christian would do if he had taken such an oath, in what he designed to write of Don Quixote; especially as to the account that is to be given us of the person who was known by the name of Master Peter, and the fortune-telling ape, whose answers occasioned such a noise, and created such an amazement all over the country. He says, then, that any one who has read the foregoing part of this history cannot but remember one Gines de Passamonte, whom Don Quixote had rescued with several other galley-slaves in Sierra Morena—a piece of service for which the knight was not over-burdened with thanks, and which that ungrateful pack of rogues repaid with a treatment altogether unworthy such a deliverance. This Gines de Passamonte—or, as Don Quixote called him, Ginesillo de Parapilla—was the very man that stole

Sancho's ass: the manner of which robbery, and the time when it was committed, being not inserted in the first part, has been the reason that some people have laid that which was caused by the printer's neglect to the inadvertency of the author. But it is beyond all question that Gines stole the ass while Sancho slept on his back, making use of the same trick and artifice which Brunelo practised when he carried off Sacrepante's horse from under his legs, at the siege of Albraca. However, Sancho got possession again, as has been told you before.

Gines, it seems, being obnoxious to the law, was apprehensive of the strict search that was made after him in order to bring him to justice for his repeated villanies, which were so great and numerous that he himself had wrote a large book of them; and therefore he thought it advisable to make the best of his way into the kingdom of Arragon, and having clapped a plaister over his left eye, resolved in that disguise to set up a puppet-show, and stroll with it about the country; for you must know he had not his fellow at anything that could be done by sleight of hand. Now it happened that in his way he fell into the company of some Christian slaves who came from Barbary, and struck a bargain with them for this ape, whom he taught to leap on his shoulder at a certain sign, and to make as if he whispered something in his ear. Having brought his ape to this, before he entered into any town he informed himself, in the adjacent parts, as well as he could, of what particular accidents had happened to this or that person; and, having a very retentive memory, the first thing he did was to give them a sight of his show, that represented sometimes one story and sometimes another, which were generally well known and taking among the vulgar. The next thing he had to do was to commend the wonderful qualities of his ape, and tell the company that the animal had the gift of revealing things past and present; but that in things to come he was altogether uninstructed. He asked two reals for every answer, though now and then he lowered his price as he felt the pulse of his customers. Sometimes when he came to the houses of people of whose concerns he had some account, and who would ask the ape no questions because they did not care to part with their money, he would notwithstanding be making signs to his ape, and tell them the animal had acquainted him with this or that story, according to the information he had before; and by that means he got a great credit among the common people, and drew a mighty crowd after him. At other times, though he knew nothing of the person, the subtilty of his wit supplied his want of knowledge, and brought him handsomely off; and nobody being so inquisitive or pressing as to make him declare by what means his ape attained to this gift of divination, he imposed on every one's understanding, and got almost what money he pleased.

He was no sooner come to the inn, but he knew Don Quixote, Sancho, and the rest of the company. But he had like to have paid dear for his knowledge, had the knight's sword fallen but a little lower when he made King Marsilius's head fly, and routed all his Moorish horse, as the reader may have observed in the foregoing chapter. And this may suffice in relation to Master Peter and his ape.

Now let us overtake our champion of La Mancha. After he had left the inn he resolved to take a sight of the river Ebro and the country about it, before he went to Saragosa, since he was not straitened for time, but might do that and yet arrive soon enough to make one at the jousts and tournaments at that city. Two days he travelled without meeting with anything worth his notice or the reader's, when on the third, as he was riding up a hill, he heard a great noise of drums, trumpets, and guns. At first he thought some regiment of soldiers was on its march that way, which made him spur up Rozinante to the brow of the hill, that he might see them pass by; and then he saw in a bottom above two hundred men, as near as he could guess, armed with various weapons, as lances, cross-bows, partisans, halberts, pikes, some few firelocks, and a great many targets. Thereupon he descended into the vale, and made his approaches towards the battalion so near as to be able to distinguish their banners, judge of their colours, and observe their devices; more especially one that was to be seen on a standard of white satin, on which was represented to the life a little jackass, much like a Sardinian ass-colt, holding up his head, stretching out his neck, and thrusting out his tongue, in the very posture of an ass that is braying, with this distich written in fair characters about it:—

"'Twas something more than nothing which, one day,
Made one and t'other worthy bailiff bray."

Don Quixote drew this inference from the motto, that those were the inhabitants of the braying town, and he acquainted Sancho with what he had observed, giving him also to understand that the man who had told them the story of the two braying aldermen was apparently in the wrong, since, according to the verses on the standard, they were two bailiffs and not two aldermen.

"It matters not one rush what you call them," quoth Sancho; "for those very aldermen that brayed might in time come to be made bailiffs of the town, and so both those titles might have been given them well enough. But what is it to you or me, or the story, whether the two brayers were aldermen or bailiffs, so they but brayed as we are told? As if a bailiff were not as likely to bray as an alderman!"

In short, both master and man plainly understood that the men who were thus up in arms were those that were jeered for braying, got together to fight the people of another town, who had indeed abused them more than was the part of good neighbours; thereupon Don Quixote advanced towards them, to Sancho's great grief, who had no manner of liking to such kind of adventures. The multitude soon got about the knight, taking him for some champion, who was come to their assistance. But Don Quixote, lifting up his vizor, with a graceful deportment rode up to the standard, and there all the chief leaders of the army got together about him, in order to take a survey of his person, no less amazed at this strange appearance than the rest. Don Quixote seeing them look so earnestly on him, and no man offer so much as a word or question, took occasion from their silence to break his own; and, raising his voice, "Good gentlemen," cried he, "I beseech you, with all the endearments imaginable, to give no interruption to the discourse I am now delivering to you, unless you find it distasteful or tedious; which if I am unhappy enough to occasion, at the least hint you shall give me, I will clap a seal on my lips, and a padlock on my tongue."

They all cried that he might speak what he pleased, and they would hear him with all their hearts. Having this licence, Don Quixote proceeded.

"Gentlemen," said he, "I am a knight-errant: arms are my exercise; and my profession is to show favour to those that are in necessity of favour, and to give assistance to those that are in distress. I have for some time been no stranger to the cause of your uneasiness, which excites you to take arms to be revenged on your insulting neighbours; and having often busied my intellectuals in making reflections on the motives which have brought you together, I have drawn this inference from it, that according to the laws of arms, you really injure yourselves, in thinking yourselves affronted; for no particular person can give an affront to a whole town and society of men, except it be by accusing them all of high-treason in general, for want of knowing on which of them to fix some treasonable action, of which he supposes some of them to be guilty. We have an instance of this nature in Don Diego Ordonnez de Lara, who sent a challenge to all the inhabitants of Zamora, not knowing that Vellido de Olfos had assassinated the king his master in that town, without any accomplices; and so, accusing and defying them all, the defence and revenge belonged to them all in general; though it must be owned that Don Diego was somewhat unreasonable in his defiance, and strained the point too far: for it was very little to the purpose to defy the dead, the waters, the bread, those that were yet unborn, with many other trifling matters mentioned in the challenge. But let that pass; for when once the choler boils over, the tongue grows unruly, and knows no moderation. Taking it for granted, then, that no particular person can affront a whole kingdom, province, city, commonwealth, or body politic, it is but just to conclude that it is needless to revenge such a pretended affront; since such an abuse is no sufficient provocation, and indeed, positively no affront. It would be a pretty piece of wisdom, truly, should those out of the town of Reloxa sally out every day on those who spend their ill-natured breaths, miscalling them everywhere. It would be a fine business indeed, if the inhabitants of those several famous towns that are nick-named by our rabble, and called the one cheesemongers, the other costermongers, these fishmongers, and those soap-boilers, should know no better than to think themselves dishonoured, and in revenge be always drawing out their swords at the least word, for every idle, insignificant quarrel. No, no, Heaven forbid! men of sagacity and wisdom, and well-governed commonwealths, are never induced to take up arms, nor endanger their persons and estates, but on the four following occasions:—In the first place, to defend the holy Catholic faith. Secondly, for the security of their lives, which they are commanded to preserve by the laws of God and nature. Thirdly, the preservation of their good name, the reputation of their family, and the conservation of their estates.

Fourthly, the service due to their prince in a just war; and if we please, we may add a fifth, which indeed may be referred to the second, the defence of our country. To these five capital causes may be subjoined several others, which may induce men to vindicate themselves, and have recourse even to the way of arms. But to take them up for mere trifles, and such occasions as rather challenge our mirth and contemptuous laughter than revenge, shows the person who is guilty of such proceedings to labour under a scarcity of sense. Besides, to seek after an unjust revenge (and indeed no human revenge can be just), is directly against the holy law we profess, which commands us to forgive our enemies, and to do good to those that hate us—an injunction which, though it seems difficult in the implicit obedience we should pay to it, yet is only so to those who have less of heaven than of the world, and more of the flesh than of the spirit. For the Redeemer of mankind, whose words never could deceive, said that his yoke was easy, and his burden light; and according to that he could prescribe nothing to our practice which was impossible to be done. Therefore, gentlemen, since reason and religion recommend love and peace to you, I hope you will not render yourselves obnoxious to all laws, both human and divine, by a breach of the public tranquillity."

"I am much mistaken," quoth Sancho to himself, "if this master of mine was not bred a parson; if not, he is as like one as one egg is like another."

Don Quixote paused a while, to take breath; and, perceiving his auditory still willing to give him attention, had proceeded in his harangue, had not Sancho's good opinion of his parts made him lay hold on this opportunity to talk in his turn.

"Gentlemen," quoth he, "my master, Don Quixote de la Mancha, once called the Knight of the Woful Figure, and now the Knight of the Lions, is a very judicious gentleman, and talks Latin and his own mother-tongue as well as any of your 'varsity doctors. Whatever discourse he takes in hand, he speaks ye to the purpose, and like a man of mettle; he has ye all the laws and rules of that same thing you call duel and punctilio of honour, at his fingers' end; so that you have no more to do but to do as he says, and if in taking his counsel you ever tread awry, let the blame be laid on my shoulders. And indeed, as you have already been told, it is a very silly fancy to be ashamed to hear one bray; for I remember when I was a boy, I could bray as often as I listed, and nobody went about to hinder me; and I could do it so rarely, and to the life, without vanity be it spoken that all the asses in our town would fall a-braying when they heard me bray; yet for all this I was an honest body's child, and came of good parentage, do ye see. It is true, indeed, four of the best young men in our parish envied me for this great ability of mine; but I cared not a rush for their spite. Now, that you may not think I tell you a lie, do but hear me and then judge; for this rare art is like swimming, which, when once learned, is never to be forgotten."

This said, he clapped both the palms of his hands to his nose, and fell a-braying so obstreperously, that it made the neighbouring valleys ring again. But while he was thus braying, one of those that stood next to him, believing he did it to mock them, gave

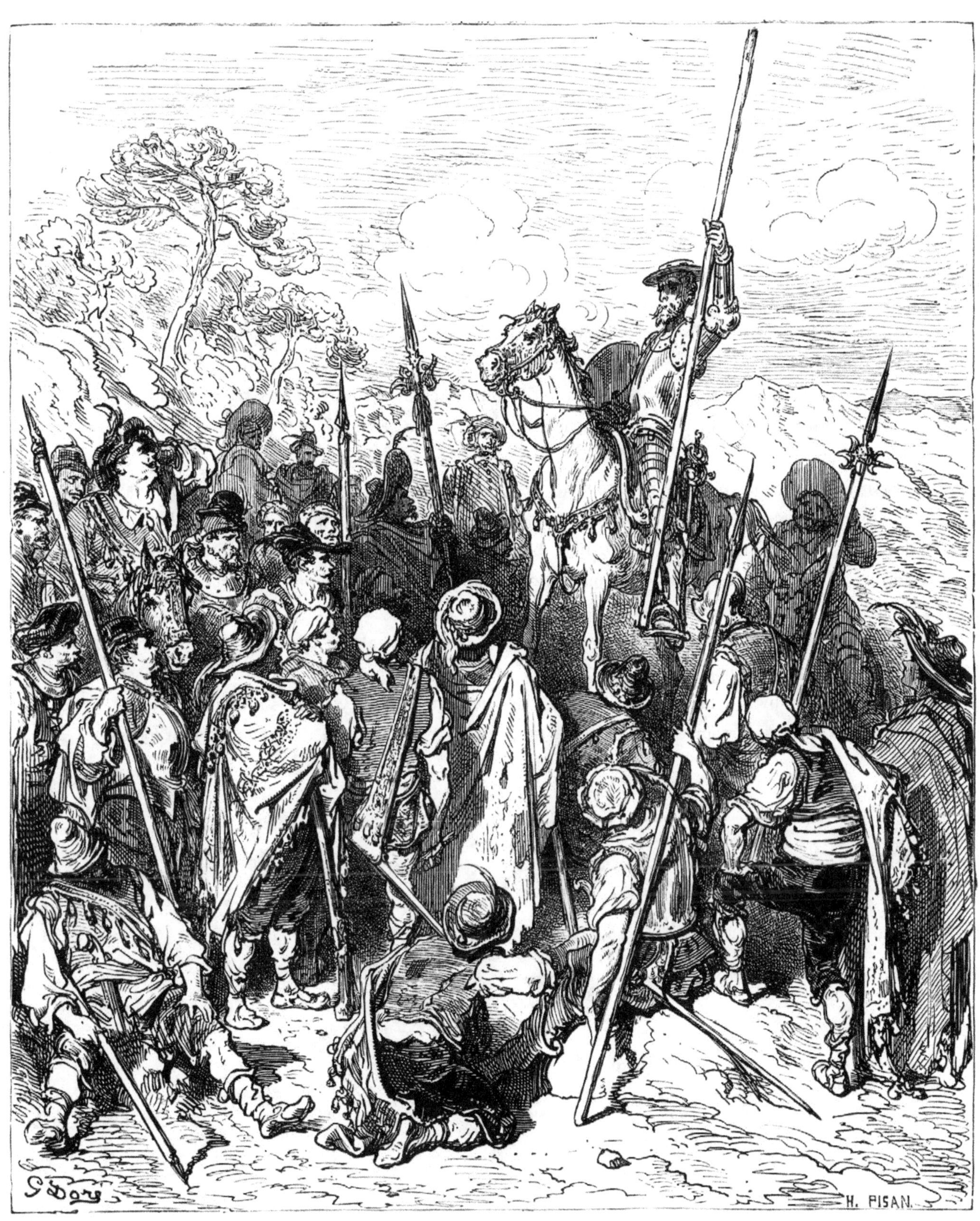

"According to the laws of arms, you really injure yourselves, in thinking yourselves affronted."

him such a hearty blow with a quarter-staff on his back, that down he brought him to the ground.

Don Quixote, seeing what a rough entertainment had been given to his squire, moved with his lance in a threatening posture towards the man that had used poor Sancho thus; but the crowd thrust themselves in such a manner between them, that the knight found it impracticable to pursue the revenge he designed. At the same time, finding that a shower of stones began to rain about his ears, and a great number of cross-bows and muskets were getting ready for his reception, he turned Rozinante's reins, and galloped from them as fast as four legs would carry him, sending up his hearty prayers to Heaven to deliver him from this danger; and being under grievous apprehension at every step, that he should be shot through the back, and have the bullet come out at his breast, he still went fetching his breath, to try if it did any ways fail him. But the country battalion were satisfied with seeing him fly, and did not offer to shoot at him.

As for Sancho, he was set upon his ass before he had well recovered his senses, which the blow had taken from him, and then they suffered him to move off; not that the poor fellow had strength enough to guide him, but Dapple naturally followed Rozinante of his own accord, not being able to be a moment from him. The Don being at a good distance from the armed multitude, faced about, and seeing Sancho pacing after him without any troublesome attendants, stayed for his coming up. As for the rabble, they kept their posts till it grew dark, and their enemies having not taken the field to give them battle, they marched home, so over-joyed to have shown their courage without danger, that, had they been so well bred as to have known the ancient custom of the Greeks, they would have erected a trophy in that place.

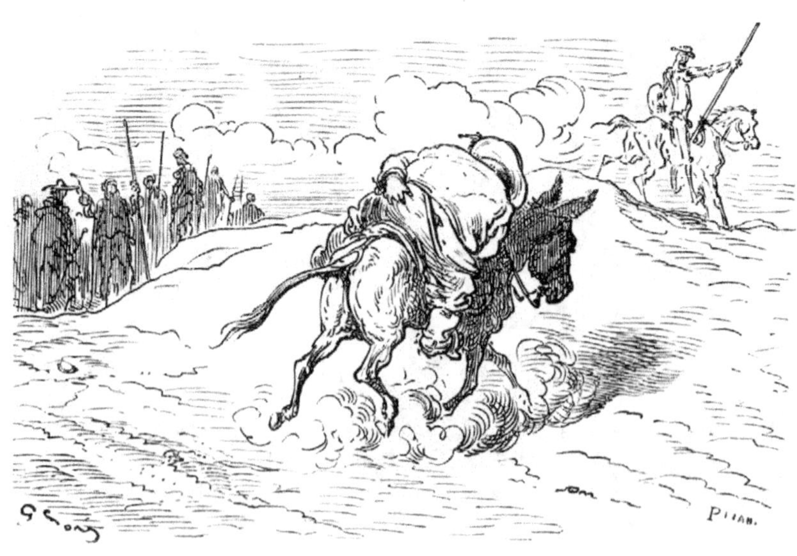

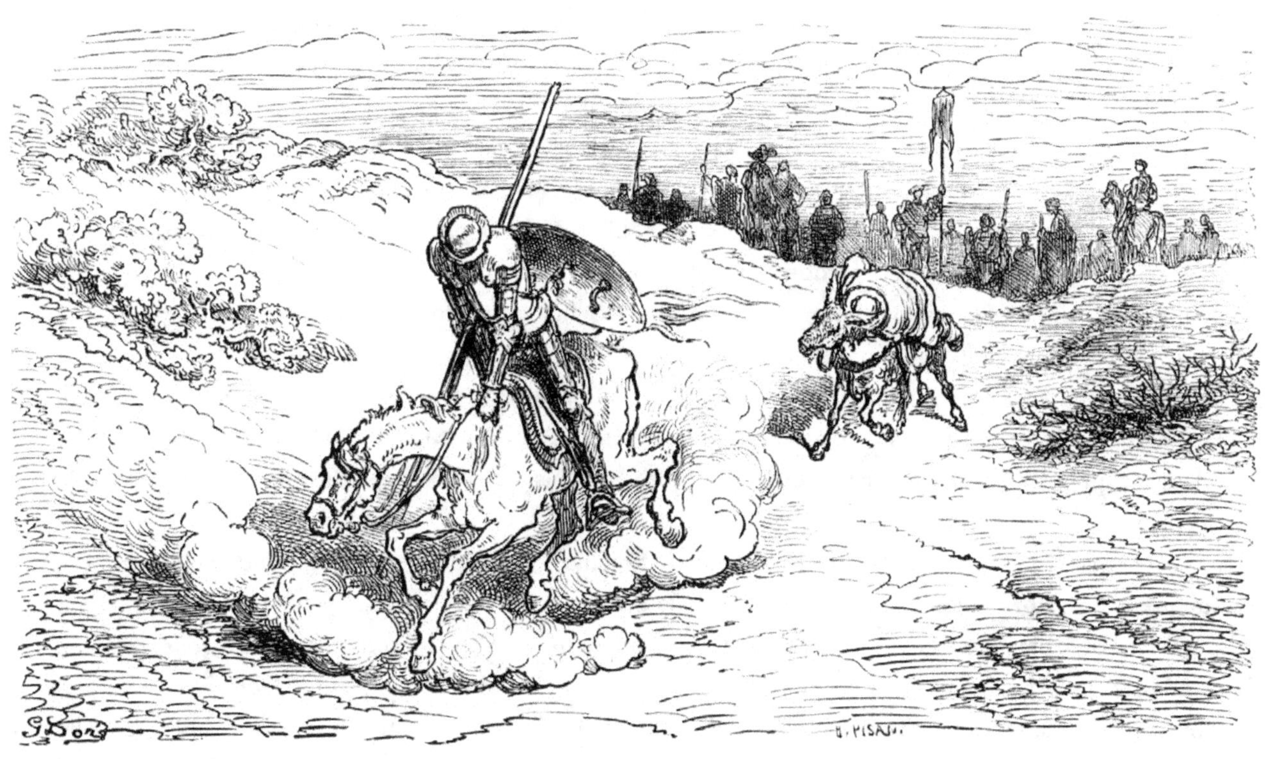

CHAPTER XXVIII.

OF SOME THINGS WHICH BENENGELI TELLS US HE THAT READS SHALL KNOW, IF HE READS THEM WITH ATTENTION.

WHEN the valiant man flies, he must have discovered some foul play, and it is the part of prudent persons to reserve themselves for more favourable opportunities. This truth is verified in Don Quixote, who, rather than expose himself to the fury of an incensed and ill-designing multitude, betook himself to flight, without any thoughts of Sancho, till he found himself beyond the reach of those dangers in which he had left his trusty squire involved. Sancho came after him, as we have told you before, laid across his ass, and having recovered his senses, overtook him at last, and let himself drop from his pack-saddle at Rozinante's feet, all battered and bruised, and in a sorrowful condition. Don Quixote presently dismounted to examine his wounds, and finding no bones broken, but his skin whole from head to feet, "You must bray," cried he, angrily, "you must bray, must you! It is a piece of excellent discretion to talk of halters in the house of a man whose father was hanged. What counterpart could you expect to your music, blockhead, but a thorough-bass of bastinadoes? Thank Providence, sirrah! that as they gave you a dry benediction with a quarter-staff, they did not cross you with a cutlass."

"I ha'nt breath to answer you at present," quoth Sancho, "but my back and shoulders speak enough for me. Pray let us make the best of our way from this dreadful place, and whene'er I bray again may I get such another blow. Yet I cannot help saying that your knights-errant can betake themselves to their heels upon occasion, and leave their trusty squires to be beaten like stock-fish in the midst of their enemies."

"A retreat is not to be accounted a flight," replied Don Quixote; "for know, Sancho, that courage which has not wisdom for its guide falls under the name of temerity; and the rash man's successful actions are rather owing to his good fortune than to his bravery. I own I did retire, but I deny that I fled; and in such a retreat I did but imitate many valiant men, who, not to hazard their persons indiscreetly, reserved themselves for a more fortunate hour. Histories are full of examples of this nature, which I do not care to relate at present, because they would be more tedious to me than they could be profitable to thee."

By this time Don Quixote had helped Sancho to bestride his ass, and being himself mounted on Rozinante, they paced softly along, and got into a grove of poplar-trees about a quarter of a league from the place where they mounted. Yet as softly as they rode, Sancho could not help now and then heaving up deep sighs and lamentable groans. Don Quixote asked him why he made such a heavy moan. Sancho told him that from his head to his feet he felt such grievous pains that he was ready to sink. "Without doubt," said Don Quixote, "the intenseness of thy torments is by reason the staff with which thou wert struck was broad and long, and so having fallen on certain parts of thy back, caused a contusion there, and affects them all with pain; and had it been of a greater magnitude, thy grievances had been so much the greater."

"Truly," quoth Sancho, "you have cleared that in very pithy words, of which nobody made any doubt. Bless me! was the cause of my ailing so hard to be guessed, that you must tell me that so much of me was sore as was hit by the weapon? Should my ankle-bone ache, and you scratch your head till you had found out the cause of it, I would think that something; but for you to tell me that place is sore where I was bruised, every fool could do as much. Faith and troth, sir master of mine, I grow wiser and wiser every day; I find you are like all the world, that lay to heart nobody's harms but their own. I find whereabouts we are, and what I am likely to get by you; for even as you left me now in the lurch, to be well belaboured and rib-roasted, and the other day to dance the caper-galliard in the blanket you wot of, so I must expect a hundred and a hundred more of these good vails in your service; and, as the mischief has now lighted on my shoulders, next bout I look for it to fly at my eyes. A plague of my jolter-head! I have been a fool and sot all along, and am never like to be wiser while I live. Would it not be better for me to trudge home to my wife and children, and look after my house with that little wit that Heaven has given me, without galloping after your tail high and low, through confounded cross-roads and bye-ways, and wicked and crooked paths that the ungodly themselves cannot find out? And then most commonly to have nothing to moisten one's weasand that is fitting for a Christian to drink, nothing but mere element and dog's porridge; and nothing to stuff one's puddings that is worthy of a Catholic stomach! Then, after a man has tired himself off his legs, when he would be glad of a good bed, to have a master cry, 'Here, are you sleepy? lie down, Mr. Squire, your bed is made; take six foot of good hard ground and measure your corpse there; and if that won't serve you, take as much more, and welcome. You are at rack and manger; spare not, I beseech your dogship; there is room enough.' I should like to lay hold of that unlucky son of mischief that first set people a-madding after this whim of knight-errantry, or at least the first ninny-hammer that had so little forecast as to turn squire to such a parcel of madmen as were your knights-errant——in the days of yore, I mean; I am better bred than to speak ill of those in our time; no, I honour them, since your worship has taken up this blessed calling; for you have a long sight, so that no one could out-reach you; you can see farther into a mill-stone than any."

"I durst lay a wager," said Don Quixote, "that now thou art suffered to prate without interruption, thou feelest no manner of pain in thy whole body. Pr'ythee talk on, my child; say anything that comes uppermost to thy mouth, or is burdensome to thy brain; so it but alleviates thy pain, thy impertinences will rather please than offend me; and if thou hast such a longing desire to be at home with thy wife and children, Heaven forbid I should be against it. Thou hast money of mine in thy hands; see how long it is since we sallied out last from home, and cast up the wages by the month, and pay thyself."

"An' it like your worship," quoth Sancho, "when I served my master Carrasco, father to the bachelor, your worship's acquaintance, I had two ducats a month, besides my victuals: I don't know what you'll give me; though I am sure there is more trouble in being squire to a knight-errant than in being servant to a farmer; for truly, we that go to plough and cart in a farmer's service, though we moil and sweat so a-days as not to have a dry thread to our backs, let the worst come to the worst, are sure of a bellyful at night out of the pot, and to snore in a bed. But I don't know when I have had a good meal's meat, or a good night's rest, in all your service, unless it were that short time when we were at Don Diego's house, and when I made a feast on the savoury skimming of Camacho's cauldron, and ate, drank, and lay at Mr. Basil's. All the rest of my time I have had my lodging on the cold ground, and in the open fields, subject to the inclemency of the sky, as you call it; living on the rinds of cheese, and crusts of mouldy bread; drinking sometimes ditch water, sometimes spring, as we chanced to light upon it in our way."

"Well," said Don Quixote, "I grant all this, Sancho; then how much more dost thou expect from me than thou hadst from thy master Carrasco?"

"Why, truly," quoth Sancho, "if your worship will pay me twelvepence a month more than Thomas Carrasco gave me, I shall think it very fair, and tolerable wages; but then, instead of the island which you know you promised me, I think you cannot in conscience

K K

give me less than six-and-thirty pence a month more, which will make in all thirty reals, neither more nor less."

"Very well," said Don Quixote, "let us see then; it is now twenty-five days since we set out from home—reckon what this comes to, according to the wages thou hast allowed thyself, and be thy own paymaster."

"Oh, dear!" quoth Sancho, "we are quite out in our account; for as to the governor of an island's place, which you promised to help me to, we ought to reckon from the time you made the promise to this very day."

"Well, and pray how long is it?" asked Don Quixote.

"If I remember rightly," quoth Sancho, "it is about some twenty years ago, two or three days more or less."

With that Don Quixote, hitting himself a good clap on the forehead, fell a-laughing heartily. "Why," cried he, "we have hardly been out two months from the very beginning of our first expedition, and in all the time we were in Sierra Morena, and our whole progress; and hast thou the impudence to affirm it is twenty years since I promised the grant of the island? I am now convinced thou hast a mind to make all the money which thou hast of mine in thy keeping go for the payment of thy wages. If this be thy meaning, well and good; e'en take it, and much good may it do thee; for, rather than be troubled any longer with such a varlet, I would contentedly see myself without a penny. But tell me, thou perverter of the laws of chivalry that relate to squires, where didst thou ever see or read that any squire to a knight-errant stood capitulating with his master as thou hast done with me, for so much, or so much a month? Launch, unconscionable wretch, thou cut-throat scoundrel! launch, launch, thou base spirit of Mammon, into the vast ocean of their histories; and if thou canst show me a precedent of any squire who ever dared to say, or but to think, as much as thou hast presumed to tell me, then will I give thee leave to affix it on my forehead, and hit me four fillips on the nose. Away then, pack off with thy ass this moment, and get thee home, for thou shalt never stay in my service any longer. Oh, how much bread, how many promises, have I now ill bestowed on thee! Vile, grovelling wretch, that hast more of the beast than of the man! When I was just going to prefer thee to such a post, that in spite of thy wife thou hadst been called my lord, thou sneakest away from me. Thou art leaving me, when I had fully resolved, without any more delay, to make thee lord of the best island in the world, sordid clod! Well mightest thou say indeed, that honey is not for the chaps of an ass. Thou art indeed a very ass; an ass thou wilt live, and an ass thou wilt die; for I dare say thou wilt never have sense enough while thou livest to know thou art a brute."

While Don Quixote thus upbraided and railed at Sancho, the poor fellow, all dismayed, and touched to the quick, beheld him with a wistful look; and the tears standing in his eyes for grief, "Good sweet sir," cried he, with a doleful and whining voice, "I confess I want nothing but a tail to be a perfect ass; if your worship will be pleased but to put me on one,

I shall deem it well placed, and be your most faithful ass all the days of my life: but forgive me, I beseech you, and take pity on my youth. Consider, I have but a dull headpiece of my own; and if my tongue runs at random sometimes, it is because I am more fool than knave, sir. 'Who errs and mends, to Heaven himself commends.'"

"I should wonder much," said Don Quixote, "if thou shouldest not interlard thy discourse with some pretty proverb. Well, I will give thee my pardon for this once, provided thou correct those imperfections that offend me, and showest thyself of a less craving temper. Take heart, then, and let the hopes which thou mayest entertain of the performance of my promise raise in thee a nobler spirit. The time will come; do not think it impossible because delayed."

Sancho promised to do his best, though he could not rely on his own strength.

Matters being thus amicably adjusted, they went into the grove, where the Don laid himself at the foot of an elm, and his squire at the foot of a beech; for every one of those trees, and such others, has always a foot, though never a hand. Sancho had but an ill night's rest of it, for his bruises made his bones more than ordinarily sensible of the cold. As for Don Quixote, he entertained himself with his usual imaginations. However, they both slept, and by break of day continued their journey towards the river Ebro, where they met—what shall be told in the next chapter.

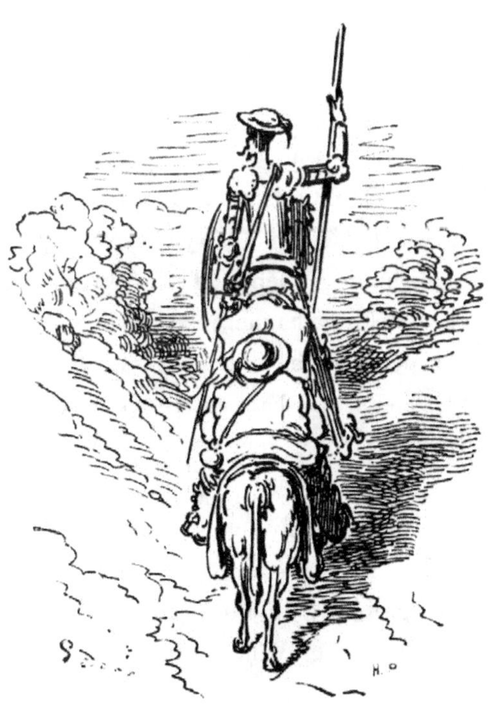

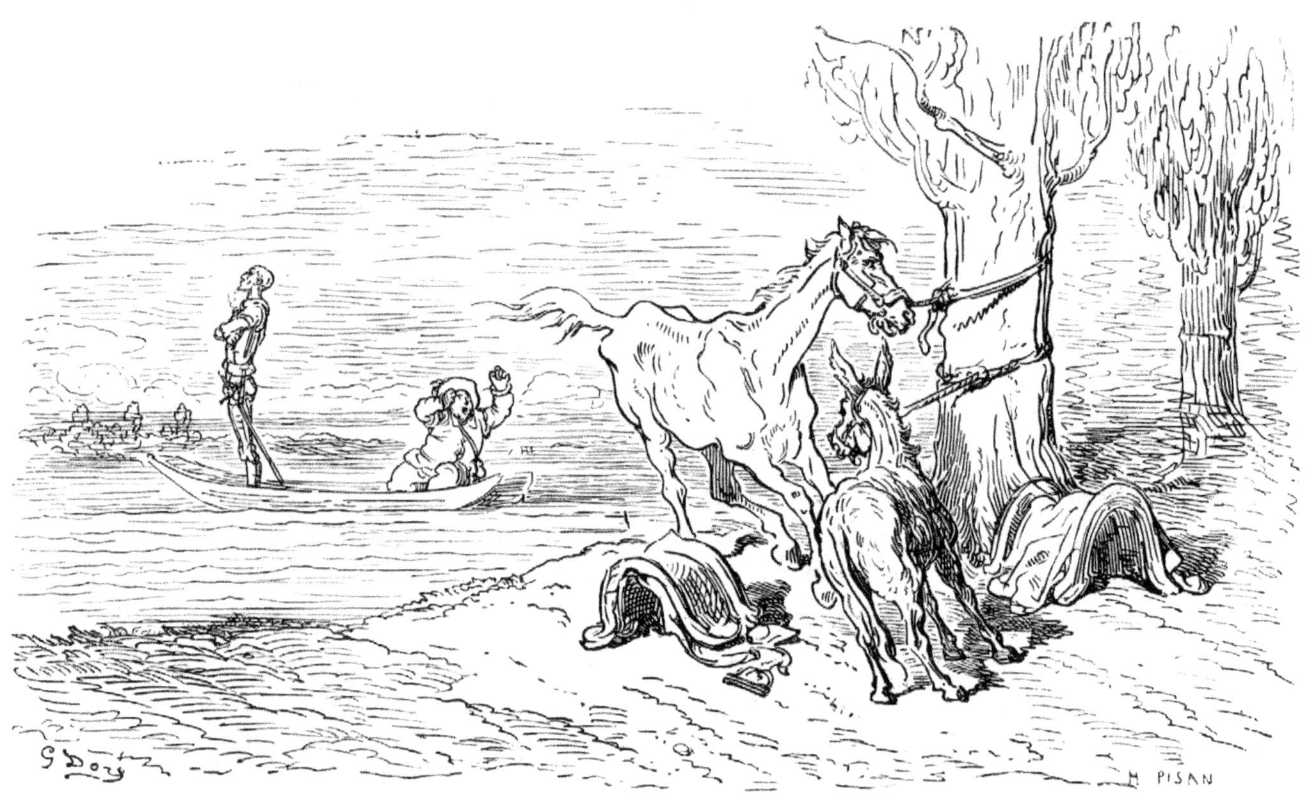

CHAPTER XXIX.

THE FAMOUS ADVENTURE OF THE ENCHANTED BARQUE.

FAIR and softly, step by step, Don Quixote and his squire got, in two days' time, to the banks of the river Ebro, which yielded a very entertaining prospect to the knight. The verdure of its banks, and the abounding plenty of the water, which, clear like liquid crystal, flowed gently along within the spacious channel, awaked a thousand amorous chimeras in his roving imagination, and more especially the thoughts of what he had seen in the cave of Montesinos; for though Master Peter's ape had assured him that it was partly false as well as partly true, he was rather inclined to believe it all true; quite contrary to Sancho, who thought it every tittle false.

While the knight went on thus agreeably amused, he spied a little boat without any oars or tackle, moored by the river-side to the stump of a tree; thereupon looking round about him, and discovering nobody, he presently alighted, and ordered Sancho to do the like, and tie their beasts fast to some of the elms or willows thereabouts. Sancho asked him what was the meaning of all this.

"Thou art to know," answered Don Quixote, "that most certain this boat lies here for no other reason but to invite me to embark in it for the relief of some knight, or other person of high degree, that is in great distress; for thus, according to the method of enchantments in the books of chivalry, when any knight whom they protect happens to be involved in some very great danger, from which none but some other valorous knight can set him free, then, though they may be two or three thousand leagues at least distant from each other, up the magician snatches the auxiliary champion in a cloud, or else provides him a boat, and in the twinkling of an eye, in either vehicle, through the airy fluid or the liquid plain, he wafts him to the place where his assistance is wanted. Just to the same intent does this very barque lie here; it is as clear as the day; and, therefore, before it be too late, Sancho, tie up Rozinante and Dapple, let us commit ourselves to the guidance of Providence; for embark I will, though bare-footed friars should beg me to desist."

"Well, well," quoth Sancho, "if I must, I must. Since you will every step be running into these—I do not know how to call them—these confounded vagaries, I have no more to do but to make a leg, and submit my neck to the collar; for, as the saying is, 'Do as thy master bid thee, though it be to sit down at his table.' But for all that, discharge my conscience I must, and tell you plainly, that blind as I am, I can see with half an eye that it is no enchanted barque, but some fisherman's boat; for there are many in this river, whose waters afford the best shads in the world."

This caution did Sancho give his master while he was tying the beasts to a tree, and going to leave them to the protection of enchanters, full sore against his will. Don Quixote bid him not be concerned at leaving them there, for the sage who was to carry them through in a journey of such an extent and longitude would be sure to take care of the animals.

"Nay, nay, as for that matter," quoth Sancho, "I do not understand your longitude; I never heard such a cramp word in my born days."

"Longitude," said Don Quixote, "is the same as length. I do not wonder that thou dost not understand the word, for thou art not obliged to understand Latin. Yet you shall have some forward coxcombs pretend to be knowing, when they are ignorant."

"Now the beasts are fast, sir," quoth Sancho; "what is next to be done?"

"Why now," answered Don Quixote, "let us recommend ourselves to Providence and weigh anchor, or, to speak plainly, embark and cut the cable." With that, leaping in, and Sancho following, he cut the rope, and so by degrees the stream carried the boat from the shore.

Now, when Sancho saw himself towards the middle of the river, he began to quake for fear; but nothing grieved his heart so much as to hear Dapple bray, and to see Rozinante struggle to get loose. "Sir," quoth he, "hark how my poor Dapple brays, to bemoan our leaving of him; and see how poor Rozinante tugs hard to break his bridle, and is even wild to throw himself after us. Alack and alack! my poor dear friends, peace be with you where you are, and when this mad freak, the cause of our doleful parting, is ended in repentance, may we be brought back to your sweet company again!"

This said, he fell a-blubbering, and set up such a howl, that Don Quixote had no patience with him, but looking angrily on him, "What dost fear," cried he, "thou great white-livered calf? What dost thou cry for? Who pursues thee? Who hurts thee, thou dastardly craven, thou cowardly mouse, thou soul of a milk-sop, thou heart of butter? Dost want for anything, base, unsatisfied wretch? What wouldst thou say, wert thou to climb bare-footed the rugged Riphean mountains? thou that sittest here in state like an archduke, plenty and delight on each side of thee, while thou glidest gently down the calm current of this delightful river, which will soon convey us into the main ocean. We have already flowed down some seven or eight hundred leagues. Had I but an astrolabe here to take the altitude of the pole, I could easily tell thee how far we have proceeded to an inch; though either I know but little, or we have just passed, or shall presently pass, the equinoctial line, that divides and cuts the two opposite poles at equal distances."

"And when we come to this same line you speak of," quoth Sancho, "how far have we gone then?"

"A mighty way," answered Don Quixote. "When we come under the line I spoke of, we shall have measured the other half of the terraqueous globe, which, according to the system and computation of Ptolemy, who was the greatest cosmographer in the world, contains three hundred and sixty degrees."

"Bless me!" quoth Sancho, "you have brought me now a notable fellow to be your voucher, goodman Tollme, with his amputation and cistern, and the rest of your gibberish."

Don Quixote smiled at Sancho's blunders, and going on, "The Spaniards," said he, "and all those that embark at Cadiz for the East Indies, to know whether they have passed the equinoctial line, according to an observation that has been often experienced, need do no more than look whether there be any vermin left alive among the ship's crew; for if they have passed it, not one is to be found in the ship, though they would give his weight in gold for him. Look, therefore, Sancho, and if thou findest any such still creeping about thee, then we have not yet passed the line; but if thou dost not, then we have surely passed it."

"Very little do I believe of all this," quoth Sancho. "However, I will do as you bid me. But hark you me, sir, now I think on it again, where is the need of trying these quirks? do not I see with my two eyes that we are not five rods' length from the shore? Look you, there stands Rozinante and Dapple upon the very spot where we left them; and now I look closely into the matter, I will take my corporal oath that we move no faster than a snail can gallop, or an ant can trot."

"No more words," said Don Quixote, "but make the experiment as I bid you, and let the rest alone. Thou dost not know what belongs to colures, lines, parallels, zodiacs, ecliptics, poles, solstices, equinoctials, planets, signs, points, and measures, of which the spheres celestial and terrestrial are composed; for didst thou know all these things, or some of them at least, thou mightest plainly perceive what parallels we have cut, what signs we have passed, and what constellations we have left, and are now leaving behind us. Therefore I would wish thee once again to search thyself; for I cannot believe but thou art as clear from vermin as a sheet of white paper."

Thereupon Sancho, advancing his hand very gingerly towards the left side of his neck, after he had groped awhile, lifted up his head, and, staring in his master's face, "Look you, sir," quoth he, pulling out something, "either your rule is not worth this, or we are many a fair league from the place you spoke of."

"How!" answered Don Quixote; "hast thou found something then, Sancho?"

"Ay, marry have I," quoth Sancho, "and more things than one too." And so saying, he shook and snapped his fingers, and then washed his whole hand in the river, down whose stream the boat drove gently along, without being moved by any secret influence or hidden enchantment, but only by the help of the current, hitherto calm and smooth.

By this time they descried two great water-mills in the middle of the river, which Don Quixote no sooner spied, but, calling to his squire, "Look, look, my Sancho!" cried he, "seest thou yon city or castle there? this is the place where some knight lies in distress, or some queen or princess is detained, for whose succour I am conveyed hither."

"Whatever do you mean with your city or castle?" cried Sancho. "Bless me! sir, do not you see as plain as the nose on your face, they are nothing but water-mills in the midst of the river, to grind corn?"

"Peace, Sancho," replied Don Quixote; "they look like water-mills, I grant you, but they are no such things. How often have I not told thee already do these magicians change and overturn everything as they please? not that they can change their very being, but they disguise and alter the appearances of them; of which we have an instance in the unhappy transformation of Dulcinea, the only refuge of my hope."

The boat being now got into the very strength of the stream, began to move less slowly than it did before. The people in the mills, perceiving the boat to come adrift full upon the mill-wheels, came running out with their long poles to stop it; and, as their faces and clothes were powdered all over with meal-dust, they made a very odd appearance. "So ho! there," cried they as loud as they could bawl; "what is in the fellows? are ye mad in the boat there? Hold! you will be drowned, or ground to pieces by the mill-wheels."

Don Quixote, having cast his eyes upon the millers, "Did I not tell thee, Sancho," said he, "that we should arrive where I must exert the strength of my arm? Look what hang-dogs, what horrid wretches, come forth to make head against me! how many hobgoblins oppose my passage! do but see what deformed physiognomies they have! mere bugbears! But I shall make ye know, scoundrels, how insignificant all your efforts must prove." Then, standing up in the boat, he began to threaten the millers in a haughty tone. "Ye paltry slaves," cried he, "base and ill-advised scum of the world, release instantly the captive person who is injuriously detained and oppressed within your castle or prison, be they of high or low degree; for I am Don Quixote de la Mancha, otherwise called the Knight of the Lions. for whom the happy achievement of this adventure is reserved by the decree of Heaven." This said, he unsheathed his sword, and began to fence with the air, as if he had been already engaging the millers; who, hearing, but not understanding, his mad words, stood ready with their poles to stop the boat, which was now near the mill-dam, and just entering the rapid stream and narrow channel of the wheels.

In the meantime Sancho was devoutly fallen on his knees, praying Heaven for a happy deliverance out of this mighty plunge but this one time. And indeed his prayers met with pretty good success; for the millers so bestirred themselves with their poles that they stopped the boat, yet not so cleverly but they overset it, tipping Don Quixote and Sancho over into the river. It was well for the knight that he could swim like a duck; and yet the weight of his armour sank him twice to the bottom; and had it not been for the millers who jumped into the water, and made a shift to pull out both the master and the man, in a manner craning them up, there had been an end of them both.

When they were both hauled ashore, more over-drenched than thirsty, Sancho betook himself to his knees again, and, with uplifted hands and eyes, made a long and hearty prayer, that Heaven might keep him from this time forwards clear of his master's rash adventures.

And now came the fishermen who owned the boat, and, finding it broken to pieces, fell upon Sancho, and began to strip him, demanding satisfaction both of him and his master for the loss of their barque. The knight, with a great deal of gravity and unconcern, as if he had done no manner of harm, told both the millers and the fishermen that he was ready to pay for the boat, provided they would fairly surrender the persons that were detained unjustly in their castle.

"What persons, or what castle, you mad oaf?" said one of the millers. "Marry, would you carry away the folk that come to grind their corn at our mills?"

"Well," said Don Quixote to himself, "man had as good preach to a stone wall as to expect to persuade with entreaties such dregs of human kind to do a good and generous action. Two sage enchanters certainly clash in this adventure, and the one thwarts the other. One provided me a barque, the other overwhelmed me in it. Heaven send us better times! There is nothing but plotting and counter-plotting, undermining and counter-mining in this world. Well, I can do no more." Then raising his voice, and casting a fixed eye on the water-mills, "My dear friends," cried he, "whoever you are that are immured in this prison, pardon me, I beseech ye; for so my ill fate and yours ordains, that I cannot free you from your confinement: the adventure is reserved for some other knight."

This said, he came to an agreement with the fishermen, and ordered Sancho to pay them fifty reals for the boat. Sancho pulled out the money with a very ill will, and parted with it with a worse, muttering between his teeth that two voyages like that would sink their whole stock.

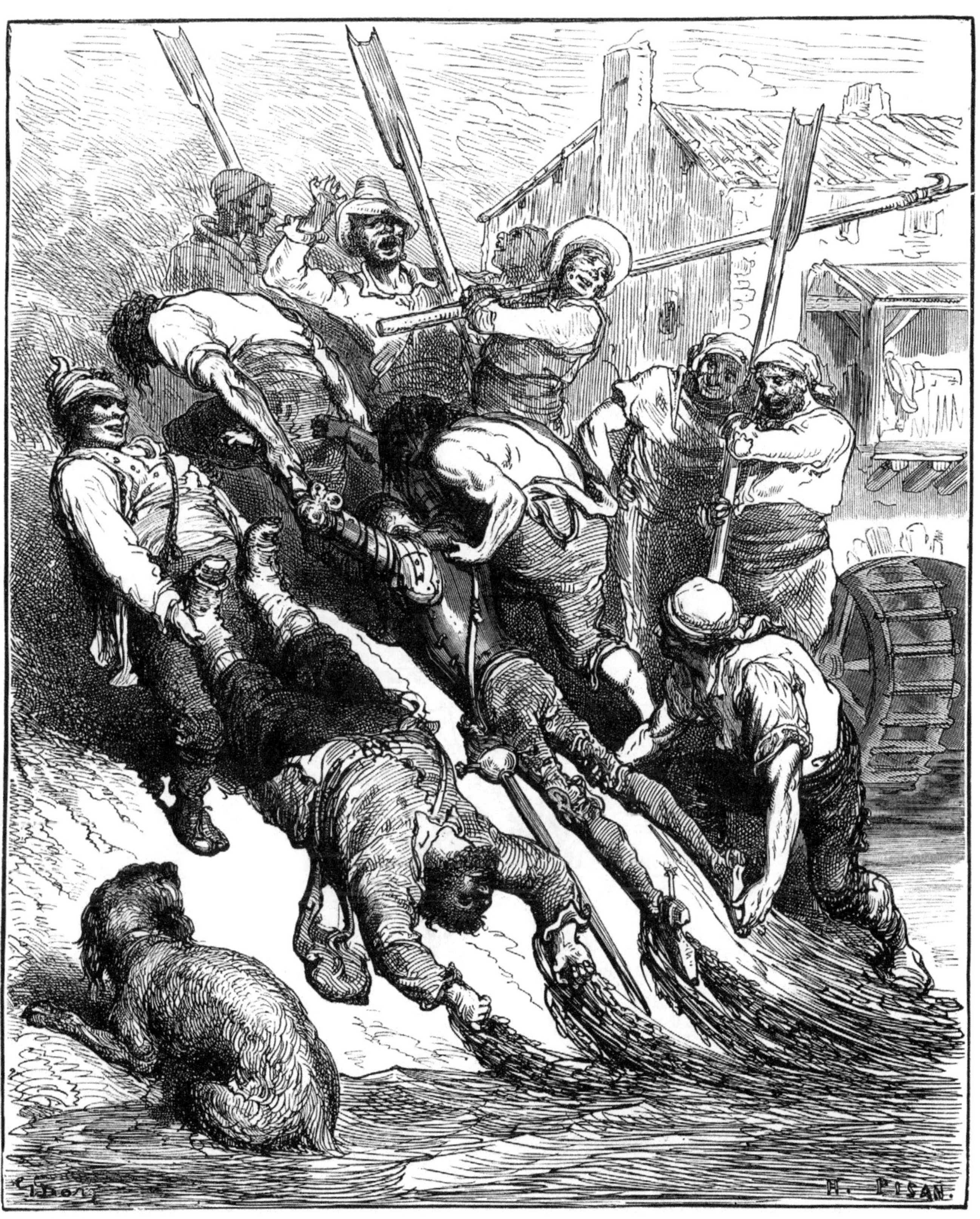

"They were both hauled ashore, more over-drenched than thirsty."

The fishermen and the millers could not forbear wondering at two such figures of human offspring, who neither spoke nor acted like the rest of mankind; for they could not so much as guess what Don Quixote meant by all his extravagant speeches. So, taking them for madmen, they left them, and went, the millers to their mills, and the fishermen to their huts. Don Quixote and Sancho returned to their beasts like a couple of as senseless animals, and thus ended the adventure of the enchanted barque.

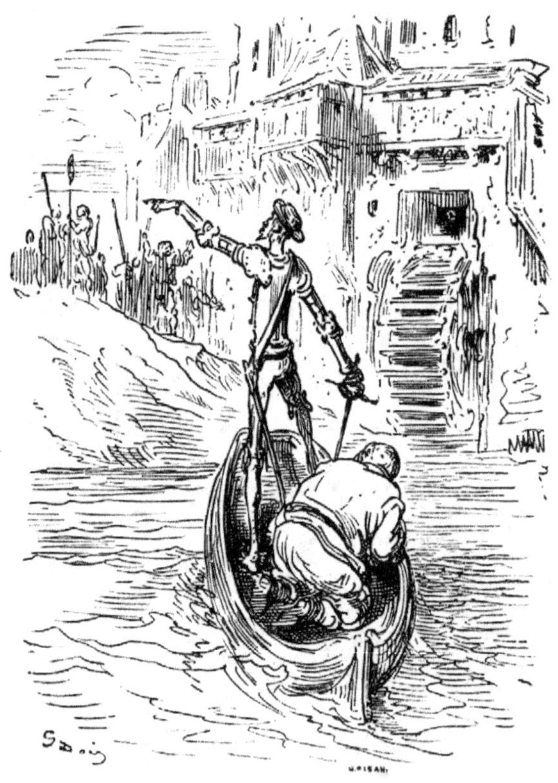

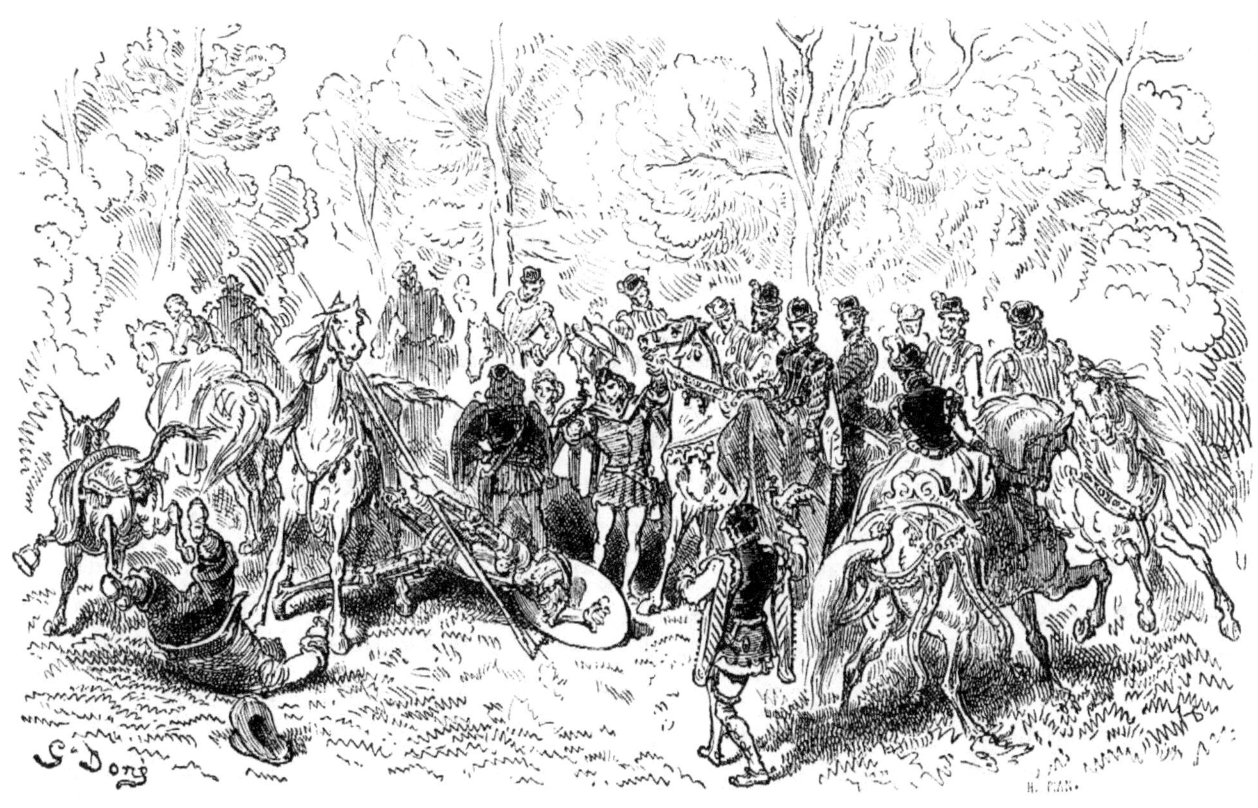

CHAPTER XXX.

WHAT HAPPENED TO DON QUIXOTE WITH THE FAIR HUNTRESS.

WITH wet bodies and melancholy minds, the knight and squire went back to Rozinante and Dapple; though Sancho was the more cast down, and out of sorts of the two; for it grieved him to the very soul to see the money dwindle, being as chary of that as of his heart's blood, or the apples of his eyes. To be short, to horse they went, without speaking one word to each other, and left the famous river; Don Quixote buried in his amorous thoughts, and Sancho in those of his preferment.

It happened that the next day about sunset, as they were coming out of a wood, Don Quixote cast his eyes round a verdant meadow, and at the farther end of it descried a company, whom, upon a nearer view, he judged to be persons of quality, that were taking the diversion of hawking. Approaching nearer yet, he observed among them a very fine lady upon a white pacing mare, in green trappings, and a saddle-cloth of silver. The lady herself was dressed in green, so rich and so gay, that nothing could be finer. She rode with a goshawk on her left fist, by which Don Quixote judged her to be of quality, and mistress of the train that attended; as indeed she was. Thereupon calling to his squire, "Son Sancho," cried he, "run and tell that lady on the palfrey that I, the Knight of the Lions, humbly salute her highness; and that if she pleases to give me leave, I should be proud to have the honour of waiting on her, and kissing her fair hands. But take special care, Sancho, how thou deliverest thy message, and be sure do not lard my compliments with any of thy proverbs."

"Why this to me?" quoth Sancho. "Marry, you need not talk of larding, as if I had never went ambassador before to a high and mighty dame."

"I do not know that ever thou didst," replied Don Quixote, "at least on my account, unless it were when I sent thee to Dulcinea."

"It may be so," quoth Sancho; "but a good paymaster needs no surety; and where there is plenty, the guests cannot be empty. That is to say, I need none of your telling nor tutoring about that matter; for, as silly as I look, I know something of everything."

"Well, well, go," said Don Quixote; "and Heaven inspire and guide thee."

Sancho put on, forcing Dapple from his old pace to a gallop; and, approaching the fair huntress, he alighted, and, falling on his knees, "Fair lady," quoth he, "that knight yonder, called the Knight of the Lions, is my master; I am his squire, Sancho Panza by name. This same Knight of the Lions, who but the other day was called the Knight of the Woful Figure, has sent me to tell you, that so please your worship's grace to give him leave, with your good liking, to do as he has a mind, which, as he says, and as I believe, is only to serve your high-flown beauty, and be your eternal vassal, you may chance to do a thing that would be for your own good, and he would take it for a hugeous kindness at your hands."

"Indeed, honest squire," said the lady, "you have acquitted yourself of your charge with all the graceful circumstances which such an embassy requires. Rise, pray rise, for it is by no means fit the squire to so great a knight as the Knight of the Woful Figure, to whose name and merit we are no strangers, should remain on his knees. Rise then, and desire your master by all means to honour us with his company, that my lord duke and I may pay him our respects at a house we have hard by."

Sancho got up, no less amazed at the lady's beauty than at her affability, but much more because she told him they were no strangers to the Knight of the Woful Figure.

"Pray," said the duchess, whose particular title we do not yet know, "is not this master of your's the person whose history came out in print by the name of 'The Renowned Don Quixote de la Mancha,' the mistress of whose affections is a certain lady called Dulcinea del Toboso?"

"The very same, an 't please your worship," said Sancho; "and that squire of his that is or should be in the book, Sancho Panza by name, is my own self, if I was not changed in my cradle; I mean changed in the press."

"I am mighty glad to hear all this," said the duchess. "Go then, friend Panza, and tell your master that I congratulate him upon his arrival in our territories, to which he is welcome, and assure him from me, that this is the most agreeable news I could possibly have heard."

Sancho, overjoyed with this gracious answer, returned to his master, to whom he repeated all that the great lady had said to him, praising, in his clownish phrase, her beauty and courtesy.

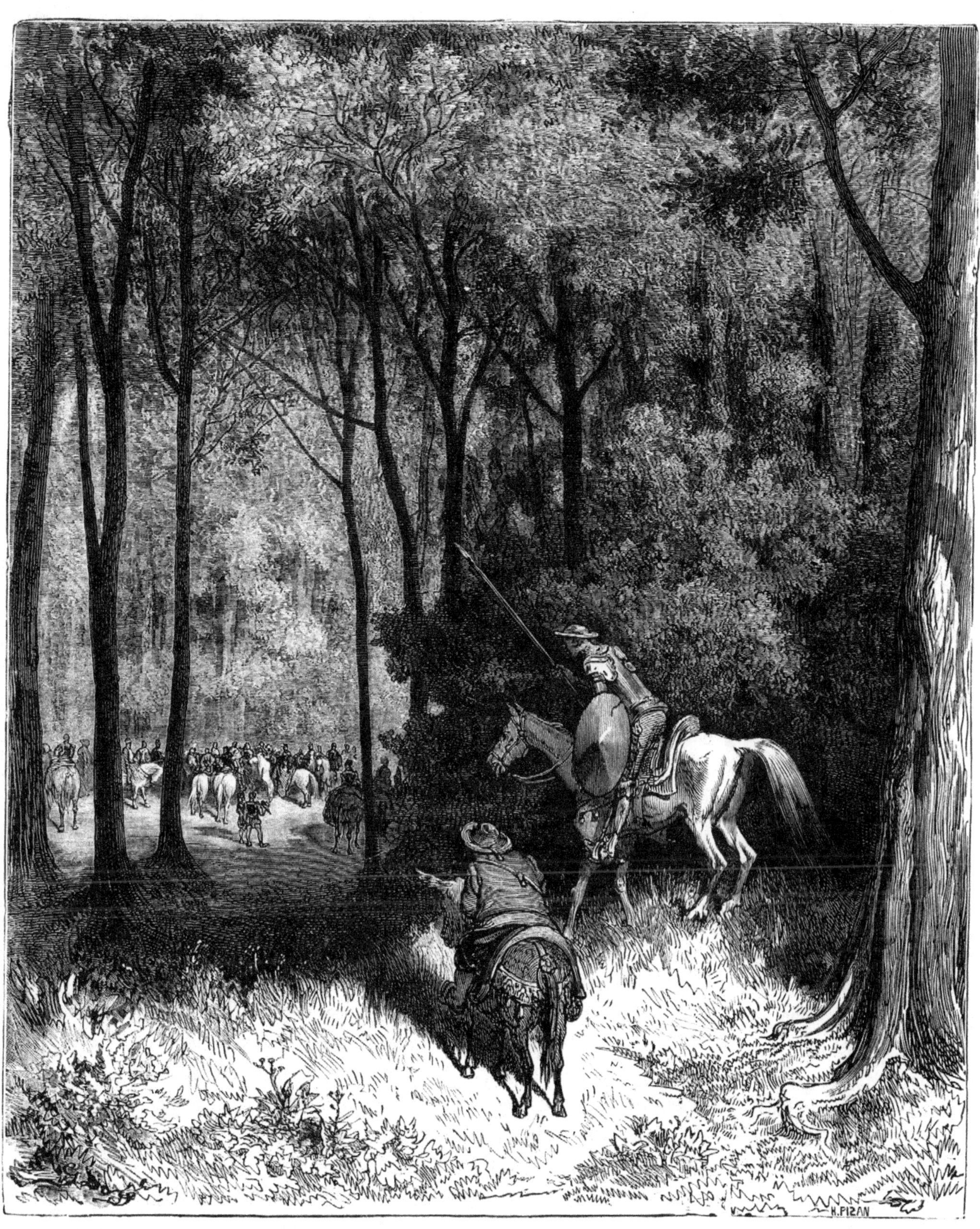

"Don Quixote descried a company, whom, upon a nearer view, he judged to be persons of quality."

Don Quixote, pleased with this good beginning, seated himself handsomely in the saddle, fixed his toes in his stirrups, set the beaver of his helmet as he thought best became his face, roused up Rozinante's mettle, and with a graceful assurance moved forwards to kiss the duchess's hand.

And now Don Quixote drew nigh with his vizor up; and Sancho seeing him offer to alight, made all the haste he could to be ready to hold his stirrup: but as ill-luck would have it, as he was throwing his leg over his pack-saddle to get off, he entangled his foot so strangely in the rope that served him instead of a stirrup, that not being able to get it out, he hung by the heel with his nose to the ground. On the other side, Don Quixote, who was used to have his stirrup held when he dismounted, thinking Sancho had hold of it already, lifted up his right leg over the saddle to alight; but as it happened to be ill-girt, down he brought it with himself to the ground, confounded with shame, and muttering between his teeth many a hearty curse against Sancho, who was all the while with his foot in the stocks. The duke seeing them in that condition, ordered some of his people to help them; and they raised Don Quixote, who was in no very good case with his fall; however, limping as well as he could, he went to pay his duty to the lady, and would have fallen on his knees at her horse's feet: but the duke alighting, would by no means permit it; and embracing Don Quixote, "I am sorry," said he, "Sir Knight of the Woful Figure, that such a mischance should happen to you at your first appearance in my territories, but the negligence of squires is often the cause of worse accidents."

"Most generous prince!" said Don Quixote, "I can think nothing bad that could befall me here, since I have had the happiness of seeing your grace: for though I had fallen low as the very centre, the glory of this interview would raise me up again. My squire indeed—a vengeance seize him for it!—is much more apt to give his saucy, idle tongue liberty, than to gird a saddle well; but prostrate or erect, on horseback or on foot, in any posture I shall always be at your grace's command, and no less at her grace's, your worthy consort's service. Worthy did I say? yes, she is worthy to be called the Queen of Beauty and Sovereign Lady of all Courtesy."

"Pardon me there," said the duke, "noble Don Quixote de la Mancha; where the peerless Dulcinea is remembered, the praise of all other beauties ought to be forgot."

Sancho was now got clear of the noose, and standing near the duchess, "An 't please your worship's highness," quoth he, before his master could answer, "it cannot be denied, nay, I dare vouch it in any ground in Spain, that my Lady Dulcinea del Toboso is very handsome and fair: but, where we least think, there starts the hare. I have heard your great scholards say, that she you call Dame Nature is like a potter, and he that makes one handsome pipkin may make two or three hundred. And so, do ye see, you may understand by this, that my lady duchess here does not a jot come short of my Lady Dulcinea."

Don Quixote, upon this, addressing himself to the duchess, "Your grace must know," said he, "that no knight-errant ever had such an eternal babbler, such a bundle of conceit for a squire, as I have; and if I have the honour to continue for some time in your service, your grace will find it true."

"I am glad," answered the duchess, "that honest Sancho has his conceits, it is a shrewd sign he is wise; for merry conceits, you know, sir, are not the offspring of a dull brain, and therefore if Sancho be jovial and jocose, I will warrant him also a man of sense."

"And a prater, madam," added Don Quixote.

"So much the better," said the duke; "for a man that talks well can never talk too much. But not to lose our time here, come on, Sir Knight of the Woful Figure——

"Knight of the Lions, your highness should say," quoth Sancho: "the Woful Figure is out of date, and so pray let the lions come in play."

"Well then," said the duke, "I entreat the Knight of the Lions to vouchsafe us his presence at a castle I have hard by, where he shall find such entertainment as is justly due to so eminent a personage, such honours as the duchess and myself are wont to pay all knights-errant that travel this way."

Sancho having by this got Rozinante ready, and girdled the saddle tight, Don Quixote mounted his steed, and the duke a stately horse of his own; and the duchess riding between them both, they moved towards the castle: she desiring that Sancho might always attend near her, for she was extremely taken with his notable sayings.

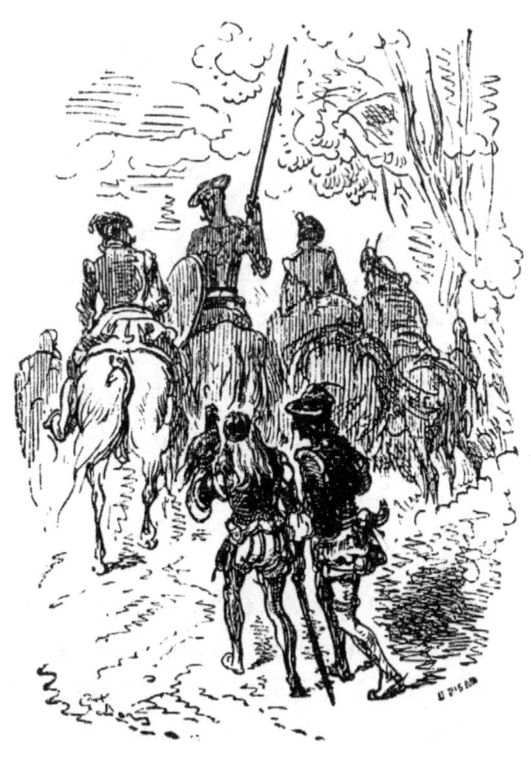

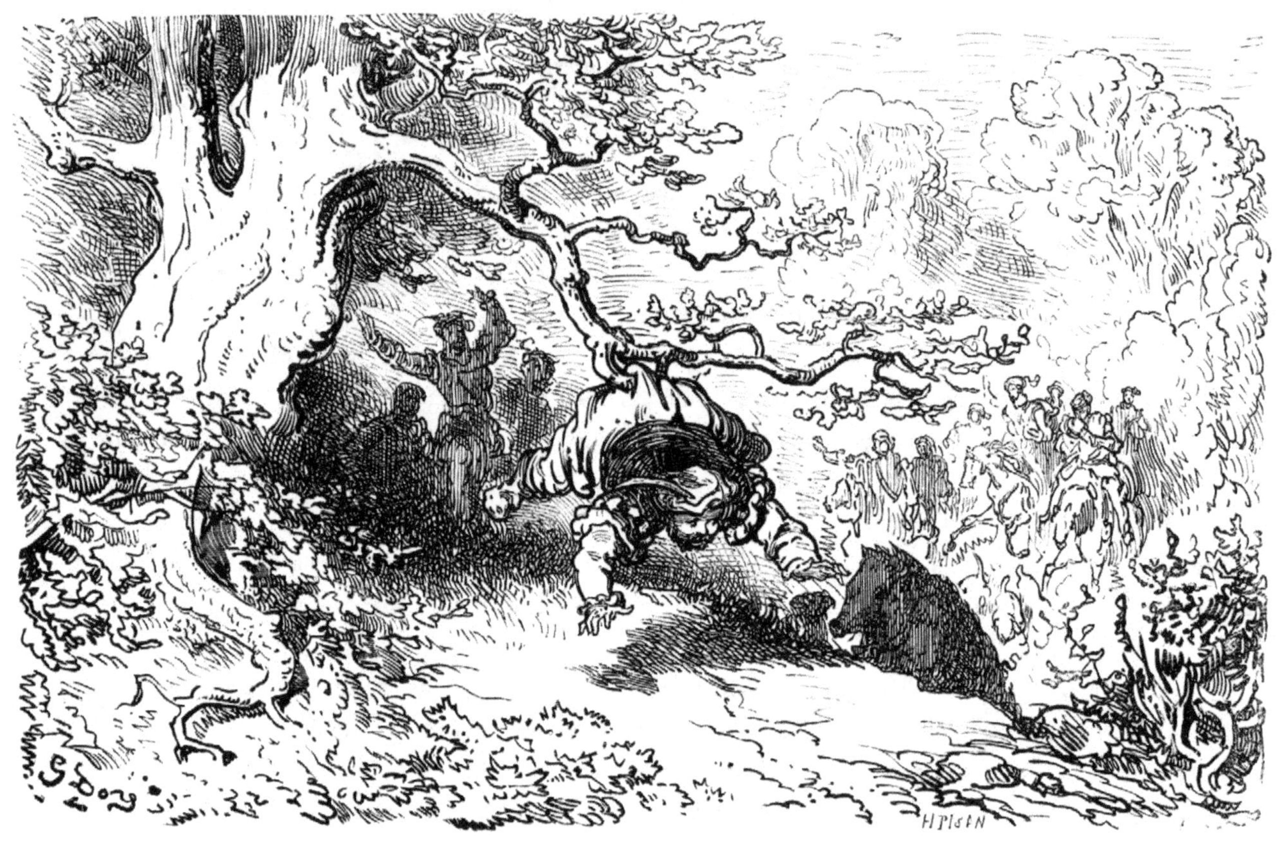

CHAPTER XXXI.

WHICH TREATS OF MANY AND GREAT MATTERS.

SANCHO was overjoyed to find himself so much in the duchess's favour, flattering himself that he should fare no worse at her castle than he had done at Don Diego's and Basil's houses; for he was ever a cordial friend to a plentiful way of living, and therefore never failed to take such opportunities by the foretop wherever he met them. Now the history tells us, that before they got to the castle, the duke rode away from them, to instruct his servants how to behave themselves toward Don Quixote; so that no sooner did the knight come near the gates, but he was met by two of the duke's lacqueys or grooms in long vests like night-gowns, of fine crimson satin. These suddenly took him in their arms, and lifting him from his horse without any further ceremony, "Go, great and mighty sir," said they, "and help my lady duchess down."

Thereupon Don Quixote went and offered to do it; and many compliments, and much ceremony passed on both sides: but in conclusion, the duchess's earnestness prevailed; for she would not alight from her palfrey but in the arms of her husband, excusing herself from incommoding so great a knight with so insignificant a burden. With that the duke took her down.

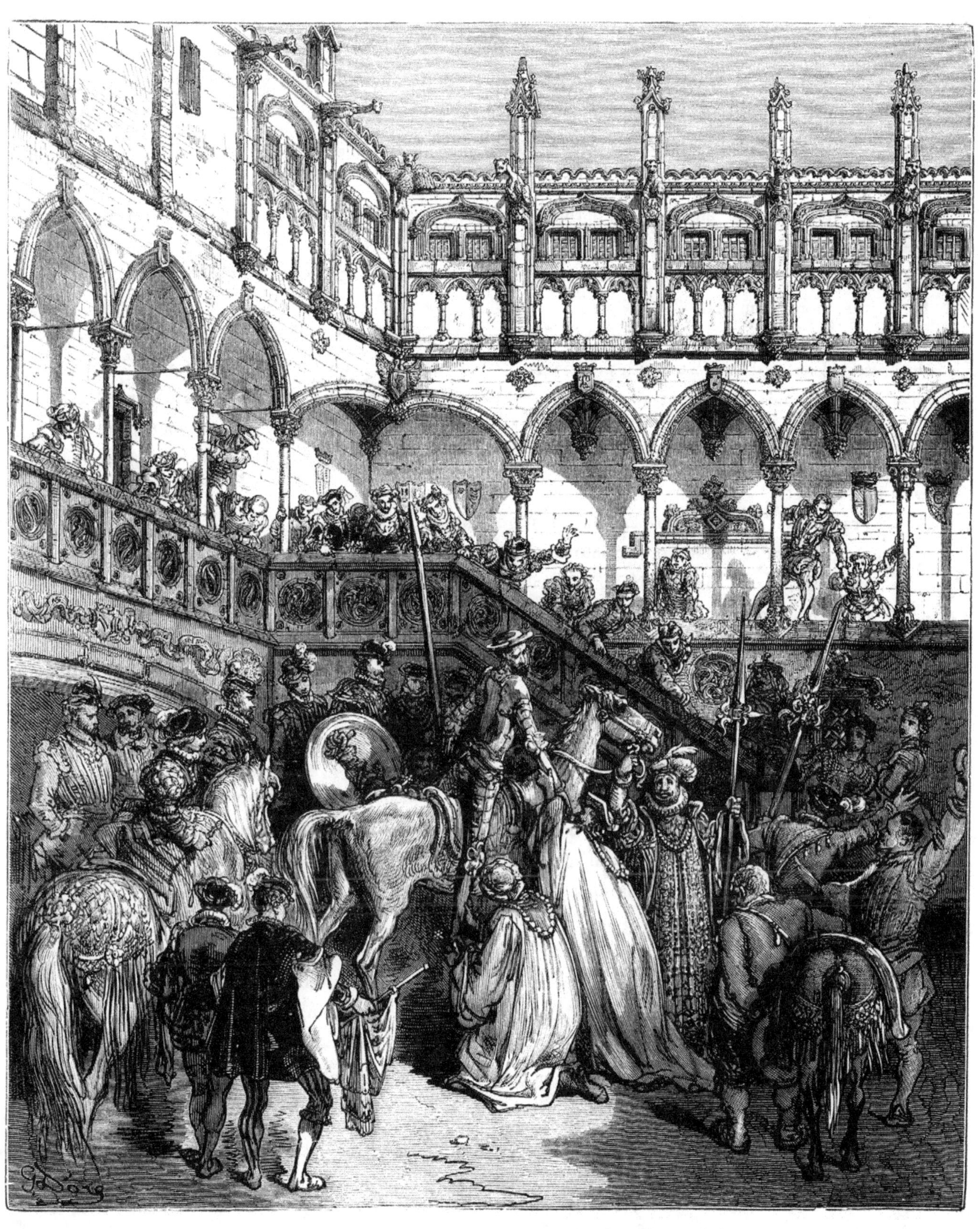

" 'Go, great and mighty sir,' said they, 'and help my lady duchess down.' "

L L

And now, being entered into a large court-yard, there came two beautiful damsels, who threw a long mantle of fine scarlet over Don Quixote's shoulders. In an instant, all the galleries about the court-yard were crowded with men and women, the domestics of the duke, who cried out, "Welcome, welcome, the flower and cream of knight-errantry!"

Then most, if not all of them, sprinkled whole bottles of sweet water upon Don Quixote, the duke, and the duchess: all which agreeably surprised the Don, and this was indeed the first day he knew and firmly believed himself to be a real knight-errant, and that his knighthood was more than fancy.

Sancho was so transported, that he even forsook his beloved Dapple, to keep close to the duchess, and entered the castle with the company; but his conscience flying in his face for leaving that dear companion, he went to a reverend old waiting-woman, of the duchess's retinue, and whispering her in the ear, "Mrs. Gonsalez, or Mrs. —— pray, forsooth, may I crave your name?"

"Donna Rodriguez de Grijalva is my name," said the old duenna; "what is your business with me, friend?"

"Pray now, mistress, do so much as go out at the castle gate, where you will find a dapple ass of mine; see him put into the stable, or else put him in yourself; for, poor thing! it is main fearful and timorsome, and cannot abide to be alone in a strange place."

"If the master," said she, pettishly, "has no more manners than the man, we shall have a fine time on 't. Get you gone, you saucy jack. I would have you to know that gentlewomen like me are not used to such drudgeries."

"Don't take pepper in your nose at it," replied Sancho; "as good as you have done it. I have heard my master say (and he knows all the histories in the world), that when Sir Lancelot came out of Britain, damsels looked after him, and waiting-women after his horse."

"Hark you, friend," quoth the waiting-woman; "if you be a buffoon, keep your stuff for those chapmen that will bid you fairer. I would not give a fig for all the jests in your budget."

"Well enough yet," quoth Sancho; "and a fig for you too, an' you go to that. Adad! should I take thee for a fig, I might be sure of a ripe one! Your fig is rotten ripe, forsooth; say no more: if sixty is the game, you are a peep out."

"You rascal," cried the waiting-woman, in a chafe, "whether I am old or no, Heaven best knows; I shall not stand to give an account to such a ragamuffin as thou!"

She spoke this so loud that the duchess overheard her, and, seeing the woman so altered, and as red as fire, asked what was the matter.

"Why, madam," said the waiting-woman, "here is a fellow would have me put his ass in the stable, telling me an idle story of ladies that looked after one Lancelot, and waiting-women after his horse; and, because I won't be his ostler, he very civilly calls me old."

"Old!" said the duchess; "that is an affront no woman can well bear. You are mistaken, honest Sancho, Rodriguez is very young; and the long veil she wears is more for authority and fashion-sake than upon account of her years."

"May there be never a good one in all those I have to live, quoth Sancho, "if I meant her any harm; only I have such a natural love for my ass, an 't like your worship, that I thought I could not recommend the poor tit to a more charitable body than this same Madam Rodriguez."

"Sancho," said Don Quixote, with a sour look, "does this talk befit this place? Do you know where you are?"

"Sir," quoth Sancho, "every man must tell his wants, be he where he will. Here I bethought myself of Dapple, and here I spoke of him. Had I called him to mind in the stable, I would have spoken of him there."

"Sancho has reason on his side," said the duke, "and nobody ought to chide him for it. Dapple shall have as much provender as he can eat, and be used as well as Sancho himself."

These small jars being over, which yielded diversion to all the company except Don Quixote, he was led up a stately staircase, and then into a noble hall, sumptuously hung with rich gold brocade. There his armour was taken off by six young damsels, all of them fully instructed by the duke and duchess how to behave themselves so towards Don Quixote, that he might look on his entertainment as conformable to those which the famous knights-errant received of old.

When he was unarmed he appeared in his close breeches and chamois doublet, raw-boned and meagre, tall and lanky, with a pair of lantern jaws, that met in the middle of his mouth; in short, he made so very odd a figure, that, notwithstanding the strict injunction the duke had laid on the young females who waited on him to stifle their laughter, they were hardly able to contain. They desired he would dress in the clothes they brought him; and, retiring to an adjacent chamber, he locked himself up with the squire, and then he began to take him to task.

"Now," said he, "modern buffoon and jolter-head of old, what canst thou say for thyself? Where learned you to abuse such a venerable gentlewoman, one so worthy of respect, as Donna Rodriguez? Was that a proper time to think of your Dapple? or can you think persons of quality, who nobly entertain the masters, forget to provide for their beasts? For Heaven's sake, Sancho, mend thy behaviour, and do not betray thy home-spun breeding, lest thou be thought a scandal to thy master. Dost not thou know, saucy rustic, that the world often makes an estimate of the master's discretion by that of his servant, and that one of the most considerable advantages the great have over their inferiors is to have servants as good as themselves? Art thou not sensible, pitiful fellow as thou art, the more unhappy I, that if they find thee a gross clown, or a mad buffoon, they will take me for some hedge-knight, or a paltry shifting rook? Pr'ythee, therefore, dear Sancho, shun these inconveniences; for he that aims too much at jests and drolling is apt to trip and tumble, and is at last despised as an insipid, ridiculous buffoon. Then curb thy tongue, think well, and ponder thy words before they get loose; we are come to a place whence, by the assistance of Heaven, and the force of this arm, we may depart better five to one in fortune and reputation."

Sancho promised to behave himself better for the future, and to sew up his mouth, or bite out his tongue, rather than speak one word which was not duly considered, and to the purpose, so that his master need not fear any one should find out what they were.

Don Quixote then dressed himself, put on his belt and sword, threw his scarlet cloak over his shoulders, and clapped on a monteer cap of green velvet, which had been left him by the damsels. Thus accoutred, he entered the state-room, where he found the damsels ranged in two rows, and immediately twelve pages came to conduct him to supper, letting him know that the duke and duchess expected him. Accordingly they led him in great pomp, some walking before and some behind, into another room, where a table was magnificently set out for four people.

As soon as he approached, the duke and the duchess came as far as the door to receive him, and with them a grave clergyman, one of those that assume to govern great men's houses, and who, not being nobly born themselves, do not know how to instruct those that are, but would have the liberality of the great measured by the narrowness of their own souls, making those whom they govern stingy, when they pretend to teach them frugality.

After a thousand courtly compliments on all sides, Don Quixote at last approached the table, between the duke and the duchess; and here arose a fresh contest; for the knight, being offered the upper end of the table, thought himself obliged to decline it. However, he could not withstand the duke's pressing importunities, but was forced at last to comply. The parson sat right against him, and the duke and the duchess on each side.

Sancho stood by all the while, gaping with wonder to see the honour done his master; and, observing how many ceremonies passed, and what entreaties the duke used to prevail with him to sit at the upper end of the table, "With your worship's leave," quoth he, "I will tell you what happened once in our town in reference to this stir and ado that you have had now about places."

The words were scarce out of his mouth, when Don Quixote began to tremble, as having reason to believe he was going to tell some impertinent thing or other.

Sancho had his eyes upon him, and, presently understanding his motions, "Sir," quoth he, "don't fear; I won't be unmannerly, I warrant you. I will speak nothing but what shall be pat to the purpose; I han't so soon forgot the lesson you gave me about talking sense or nonsense, little or much."

"I don't know what thou meanest," said Don Quixote; "say what thou wilt, so thou do it quickly."

"Well," quoth Sancho, turning to the duke, "what I am going to tell you is every tittle true. Should I trip never so little in my story, my master is here to take me up."

"Pr'ythee," said Don Quixote, "take heed what thou sayest."

"Nay, nay," quoth Sancho, "let me alone for that: I have heeded it and re-heeded it over and over, and that you shall see, I warrant you."

"Truly, my lord," said Don Quixote, "it were convenient that your grace should order this fellow to be turned out of the room, for he will plague you with a thousand impertinences."

"Oh! as for that, you must excuse us," said the duchess; "Sancho must not stir a step from me; I'll engage for him, he shall say nothing but what is very proper."

"Many and many years," quoth Sancho, "may your holiness live, madam duchess, for your good opinion of me, though it is more your goodness than my desert. Now then for my tale.

"Once upon a time a gentleman in our town, of a good estate and family, for he was of the blood of the Alamos of Medina del Campo, and married one Donna Mencia de Quinones, who was the daughter of Don Alonzo de Maranon, a Knight of the Order of St. Jago, the very same that was drowned in the Herradura, about whom that quarrel happened formerly in our town, in which I heard say that my master, Don Quixote, was embroiled, and little Tom, the madcap, who was the son of old Balvastro the farrier, happened to be sorely hurt. Is not all this true now, master?"

"Thou producest so many witnesses, Sancho," said Don Quixote, "and mentionest so many circumstances, that I must needs own I believe what thou sayest to be true. But go on, and shorten thy story; for I'm afraid thou wilt not have done these two days."

"Pray, don't let him shorten it," said the duchess; "let him go on his own way, though he were not to make an end of it these six days: I shall hear him with pleasure, and think the time as pleasantly employed as any I ever passed in my life."

"I say then, my masters," quoth Sancho, "that this same gentleman I told you of at first, and I know him as well as I know my right hand from my left, for it is not a bow-shot from my house to his; this gentleman invited a husbandman to dine with him, who was a poor man, but main honest——"

"On, friend," said the chaplain; "at the rate you proceed you won't have made an end before you come to your grave."

"I shall stop short of half way," quoth Sancho, "and if it be Heaven's blessed will: a little more of your Christian patience, good doctor! Now this same husbandman, as I said before, coming to this same gentleman's house, who had given him the invitation—Heaven rest his soul, poor heart! for he is now dead and gone; and more than that, they say he died the death of an angel. For my part, I was not by him when he died, for I was gone to harvest-work at that very time, to a place called Temblique."

"Pr'ythee, honest friend," said the clergyman, "leave your harvest-work, and come back quickly from Temblique, without staying to bury the gentleman, unless you have a mind to occasion more funerals; therefore, pray, make an end of your story."

"You must know then," quoth Sancho, "that as they two were ready to sit down at table—I mean the husbandman and the gentleman. Methinks I see them now before my eyes plainer than ever I did in my born days."

The duke and the duchess were infinitely pleased to find how Sancho spun out his story, and how the clergyman fretted at his prolixity, and Don Quixote spent himself with anger.

"Well," quoth Sancho, "to go on with my story, when they were going to sit down, the husbandman would not sit till the gentleman had taken his place; but the gentleman made him a sign to put himself at the upper end.

"'By no means, sir,' quoth the husbandman.

"'Sit down,' said the other.

"'Good your worship,' quoth the husbandman.

"'Sit where I bid thee,' said the gentleman.

"Still the other excused himself, and would not; and the gentleman told him he should, as meaning to be master in his own house. But the over-mannerly looby, fancying he should be very well-bred and civil in it, scraped, and cringed, and refused, till at last the gentleman, in a great passion, e'en took him by the shoulders, and forced him into the chair.

"'Sit there, clodpate,' cried he, 'for, let me sit wherever I will, that still will be the upper end, and the place of worship to thee.'

"And now you have my tale, and I think I have spoken nothing but what is to the purpose."

Don Quixote's face was in a thousand colours, that speckled its natural brown, so that the duke and duchess were obliged to check their mirth when they perceived Sancho's roguery, that Don Quixote might not be put too much out of countenance. And therefore to turn the discourse, that Sancho might not run into other fooleries, the duchess asked Don Quixote what news he had of the Lady Dulcinea, and how long it was since he had sent her any giants or robbers for a present, not doubting but that he had lately subdued many such.

"Alas! madam," answered he, "my misfortunes have had a beginning, but, I fear, will never have an end. I have vanquished giants, elves, and cut-throats, and sent them to the mistress of my soul, but where shall they find her? She is enchanted, madam, and transformed to the ugliest piece of rusticity that can be imagined."

"I don't know, sir," quoth Sancho; "when I saw her last she seemed to be the finest creature in the 'varsal world; thus far, at least, I can safely vouch for her upon my own knowledge, that for activity of body and leaping, the best tumbler of them all does not go beyond her. Upon my honest word, madam duchess, she will vault from the ground upon her ass like a cat."

"Have you seen her enchanted?" said the duke.

"Seen her!" quoth Sancho; "who was the first that hit upon this trick of her enchantment, think you, but I? She is as much enchanted as my father."

The clergyman, hearing them talk of giants, elves, and enchantments, began to suspect this was Don Quixote de la Mancha, whose history the duke so often used to read, though he had several times reprehended him for it, telling him it was a folly to read such. Being confirmed in his suspicion he addressed himself very angrily to the duke.

"My lord," said he, "your grace will have a large account to give one day for soothing this poor man's follies. I suppose this same Don Quixote, or Don Quite Sot, or whatever you are pleased to call him, cannot be quite so besotted as you endeavour to make him, by giving him sush opportunities to run on in his fantastical humours." Then, directing his discourse to Don Quixote, "Hark ye," said he, "Goodman Addlepate, who has put it into your crown that you are a knight-errant, that you vanquish giants and robbers? Go, go, get you home again, look after your children, if you have any, and what honest business you have to do, and leave wandering about the world, building castles in the air, and making yourself a laughing-stock to all that know you, or know you not. Where have you found, in the name of mischief, that there ever has been, or are now, any such things as knights-errant? Where will you meet with giants in Spain, or monsters in La Mancha? Where shall one find your enchanted Dulcineas, and all those legions of whimsies and chimeras that are talked of in your account, but in your own empty skull?"

Don Quixote gave this reverend person a hearing with great patience. But at last, seeing him silent, without minding his respect to the duke and duchess, up he started with indignation and fury in his looks, and said—— But his answer deserves a chapter by itself.

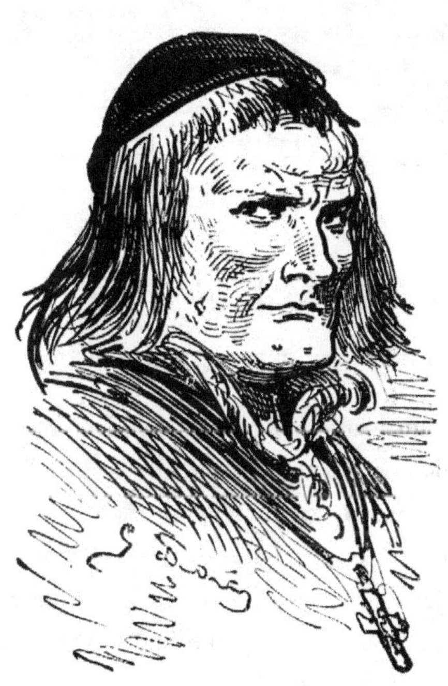

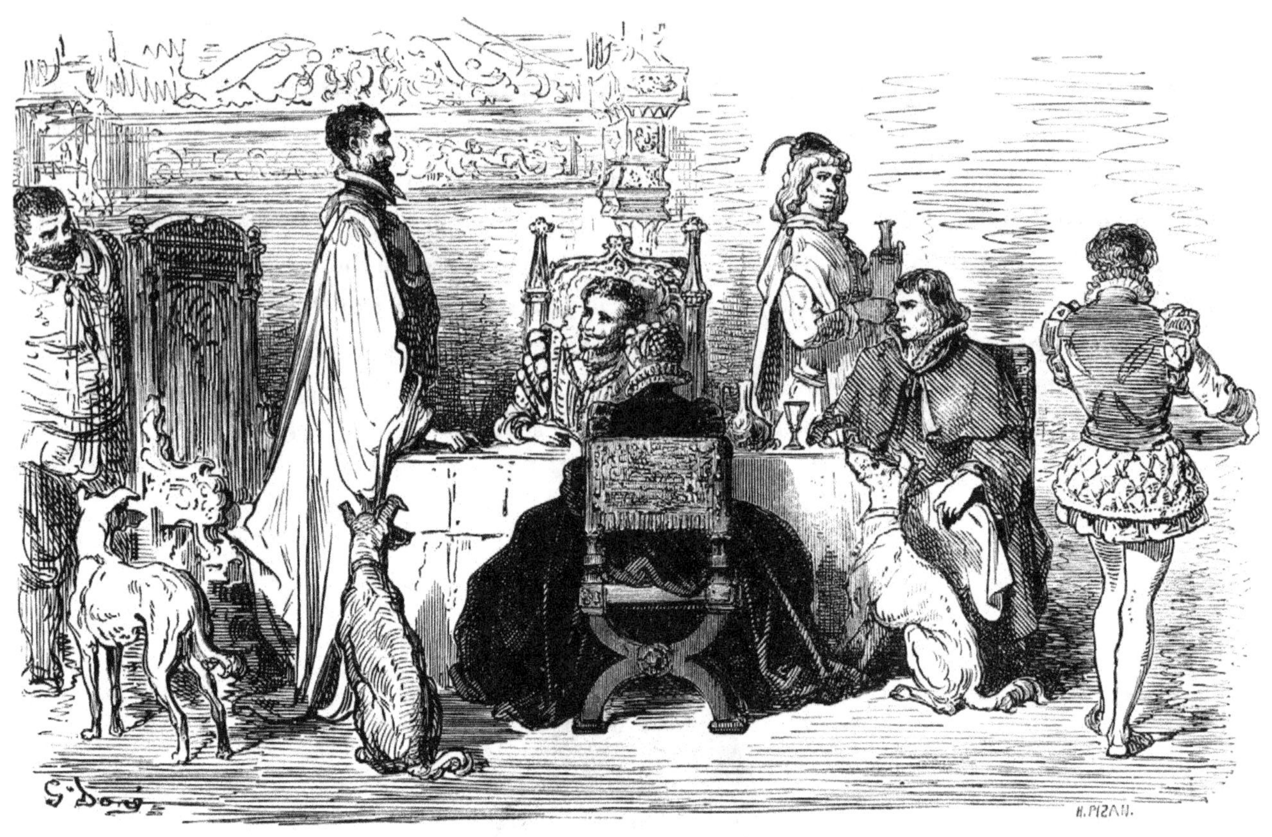

CHAPTER XXXII.

DON QUIXOTE'S ANSWER TO HIS REPROVER, WITH OTHER GRAVE AND MERRY ACCIDENTS.

DON QUIXOTE being thus suddenly got up, shaking from head to foot for madness, as if he had quicksilver in his bones, cast an angry look on his indiscreet censor, and, with an eager delivery, sputtering and stammering with choler—

"This place," cried he, "the presence of these noble persons, and the respect I have always had for your function, check my just resentment, and tie up my hands from taking the satisfaction of a gentleman. For these reasons, and since every one knows that you gown-men, as well as women, use no other weapons but your tongues, I will fairly engage you upon equal terms, and combat you with your own weapon. I should rather have expected sober admonitions from a man of your cloth, than infamous reproaches. Charitable and wholesome correction ought to be managed at another rate, and with more moderation. The least that can be said of this reproof which you have given me here so bitterly, and in public, is, that it has exceeded the bounds of Christian correction, and a gentle one had been much more becoming. Is it fit that, without any insight into the offence which you reprove, you should, without any more ado, call the offender fool, sot, and addlepate? Pray, sir, what foolish action have you seen me do, that should provoke you to give me such ill language, and bid me so magisterially go home to look after my wife and children, before you know whether I have any? Don't you think those deserve as severe a censure, who screw themselves into other men's houses, and pretend to rule the master? A fine world it is truly, when a poor pedant, who has seen no more of it than lies within twenty or thirty leagues about him, shall take upon him to prescribe laws to knight-errantry, and judge of those who profess it! You, forsooth, esteem it an idle undertaking, and time lost, to wander through the world, though scorning its pleasures, and sharing the hardships and toils of it, by which the virtuous aspire to the high seat of immortality. If persons of honour, knights, lords, gentlemen, or men of any birth, should take me for a fool or a coxcomb, I should think it an irreparable affront. But for mere scholars, that never trod the paths of chivalry, to think me mad, I despise and laugh at it. I am a knight, and a knight will I die, if so it please Omnipotence. Some choose the high road of haughty ambition; others the low ways of base, servile flattery; a third sort take the crooked path of deceitful hypocrisy; and a few, very few, that of true religion. I, for my own part, guided by my stars, follow the narrow track of knight-errantry; and, for the exercise of it, I despise riches, but not honour. I have redressed grievances, and righted the injured, chastised the insolent, vanquished giants, and trod elves and hobgoblins under my feet. I am in love, but no more than the profession of knight-errantry obliges me to be; my intentions are all directed to virtuous ends, and to do no man wrong, but good to all the world. And now let your graces judge whether a person who makes it his only study to practice all this deserves to be upbraided for a fool."

"Well said, i' faith!" quoth Sancho; "say no more for yourself, my good lord and master; stop when you are well; for there is not the least matter to be added more on your side, either in word, thought, or deed. Besides, since Mr. Parson has had the face to say, point-blank, as one may say, that there neither are, nor ever were, any knights-errant in the world, no marvel he does not know what he says."

"What!" said the clergyman, "I warrant you are that Sancho Panza to whom they say your master has promised an island?"

"Ay, marry am I," answered Sancho; "and I am he that deserves it as well as another body; and I am one of those of whom they say, 'Keep with good men, and thou shalt be one of them;' and of those of whom it is said again, 'Not with whom thou wert bred, but with whom thou hast fed;' as also, 'Lean against a good tree, and it will shelter thee.' I have leaned and stuck close to my good master, and kept him company this many a month; and now he and I are all one; and I must be as he is, an it be Heaven's blessed will; and so he live, and I live, he will not want kingdoms to rule, nor shall I want islands to govern."

"That thou shalt not, honest Sancho," said the duke; "for I, on the great Don Quixote's account, will now give thee the government of an odd one of my own of no small consequence."

"Down, down on thy knees, Sancho," cried Don Quixote, "and kiss his grace's feet for this favour."

Sancho did accordingly; but when the clergyman saw it, he got up in a great heat

"By the habit which I wear," cried he, "I can scarce forbear telling your grace that you are as mad as these sinful wretches. Well may they be mad, when such wise men as you humour and authorise their frenzy. You may keep them here, and stay with them yourself, if your grace pleases; but for my part, I will leave you and go home, to save myself the labour of reprehending what I cannot mend."

With that, leaving the rest of his dinner behind him, away he flung, the duke and the duchess not being able to pacify him; though, indeed, the duke could not say much to him, for laughing at his impertinent passion.

When he had done laughing, "Sir Knight of the Lions," said he, "you have answered so well for yourself and your profession, that you need no farther satisfaction of the angry clergyman; especially if you consider that it was not in his power to fix an affront on a person of your character."

"Very true, my lord," said Don Quixote; "and the reason is, because he that cannot receive an affront consequently can give none. Women, children, and churchmen, as they cannot vindicate themselves when they are injured, so neither are they capable of receiving an affront; for there is this difference betwixt an affront and injury, as your grace very well knows: an affront must come from a person that is both able to give it and maintain it when he has given it. An injury may be done by any sort of people whatsoever: for example, a man walking in the street about his business, is set upon by ten armed men, who cudgel him. He draws his sword to revenge the injury, but the assailants overpowering him, he cannot have the satisfaction he desired. This man is injured, but not affronted. But to confirm it by another instance: suppose a man comes behind another's back, hits him a box on the ear, and then runs away; the other follows him, but can't overtake him. He that has received the blow has received an injury, it is true, but not an affront; because to make it an affront, it should have been justified. But if he that gave it, though he did it basely, stands his ground, and faces his adversary, then he that received is both injured and affronted—injured, because he was struck in a cowardly manner; affronted, because he that struck him stood his ground to maintain what he had done. Therefore, according to the settled laws of duelling, I may be injured, but am not affronted. Children can have no resentment, and women can't fly, nor are they obliged to stand it out; and it is the same thing with the clergy, for they carry no arms, either offensive or defensive. Therefore, though they are naturally bound by the laws of self-preservation to defend themselves, yet are they not obliged to offend others. Upon second thoughts, then, though I said just now I was injured, I think now I am not; for he that can receive no affront can give none. Therefore I ought not to have any resentment for what that good man said; neither, indeed, have I any. I only wish he would have stayed a little longer, that I might have convinced him of his error in believing there were never any knights-errant in the world. Had Amadis, or any one of his innumerable race, but heard him say anything like this, I can assure his reverence it would have gone hard with him."

"I will be sworn it would," quoth Sancho; "they would have undone him as you would undo an oyster, and have cleft him from head to foot, as one would slice a pomegranate, or a ripe melon, take my word for it. They were a parcel of tough blades, and would not have swallowed such a pill. I verily believe, had Rinaldo of Montalban but heard the poor toad talk at this rate, he would have laid him on such a blow over the mouth with his shoulder-o'-mutton fist, as would have secured him from prating these three years. Ay, ay, if he had fallen into their clutches, see how he would have got out again!"

The duchess was ready to die with laughing at Sancho, whom she thought a more pleasant fool and a greater madman than his master; and she was not the only person at that time of this opinion. In short, Don Quixote being pacified, they made an end of dinner, and then, while some of the servants were taking away, there came in four damsels, one carrying a silver basin, another a ewer of the same metal; a third, two very fine towels over her arm, and the fourth, with her sleeves tucked above her elbows, held in her lily-white hand (for exceeding white it was) a large wash-ball of Naples soap. Presently she that held the basin went very civilly, and clapped it under Don Quixote's chin, while he, wondering at this extraordinary ceremony, yet fancying it was the custom of the country to wash the face instead of the hands, thrust out his long chin, without speaking a word, and then the ewer began to rain on his face, and the damsel that brought the wash-ball fell to work, and lathered his beard so effectually that the suds, like huge flakes of snow, flew all over the passive knight's face, insomuch that he was forced to shut his eyes.

The duke and the duchess, who knew nothing of the matter, stood wondering where this extraordinary scouring would end. The female barber, having thus laid the knight's face a-soaking a handful high in suds, pretended she wanted water, and sent another with the ewer for more, telling her the gentleman would stay for it. She went and left him in one of the most odd, ridiculous figures that can be imagined. There he sat exposed to all the company, with half a yard of neck stretched out his bristly beard and chaps all in a white foam, which did not at all mend his walnut complexion; insomuch that it is not a little strange how those that had so comical a spectacle before them could forbear laughing. The four malicious damsels who had a hand in the plot did not dare to look up, nor let their eyes meet those of their master or mistress, who stood strangely divided between anger and mirth, not knowing what to do in the case—whether they should punish the girls for their boldness, or reward them for the diversion they caused in seeing the knight in that posture.

At last the maid came back with the water, and the other having rinsed off the soap, she that held the linen gently wiped and dried the knight's beard and face; after which all four, dropping a low curtsey, were going out of the room. But the duke, that Don Quixote might not smell the jest, called to the damsel that carried the basin, and ordered her to come and wash him too, but be sure she had water enough. The wench, being sharp and cunning, came and put the basin under the duke's chin, as she had done to Don Quixote, but with a quicker dispatch; and, having dried him clean, they all made their honours, and went off.

Sancho took great notice of all the ceremonies at this washing.

"'S life!" quoth he, "I would fain know whether 'tis not the custom of this country to scrub the squire's beard as well as the knight's; for, o' my conscience, mine wants it not a little. Nay, if they would run it over with a razor too, so much the better."

"What art thou talking to thyself, Sancho?" said the duchess.

"Why, an 't like your grace's worship," quoth Sancho, "I am only saying that I have been told how, in other great houses, when the cloth is taken away, they use to give folks water to wash their hands, and not suds to scour their beards. I see now it is good to live and learn. There's a saying, indeed, 'He that lives long suffers much.' But I have a huge fancy, that to suffer one of these same scourings is rather a pleasure than a pain."

"Well, Sancho," said the duchess, "trouble thyself no farther."

"My beard is all I want to have scrubbed at present," quoth Sancho.

"Here, steward," said the duchess, "see that Sancho has what he has a mind to, and be sure do just as he would have you."

The steward told her grace that Signior Sancho should want for nothing; and so he took Sancho along with him to dinner.

Meanwhile Don Quixote stayed with the duke and duchess, talking of several matters, but all relating to arms and knight-errantry. The duchess then took an opportunity to desire the knight to give a particular description of the Lady Dulcinea del Toboso's beauty and accomplishments, not doubting but his good memory would enable him to do it well; adding withal, that according to the voice of fame, she must needs be the finest creature in the whole world, and consequently in all La Mancha.

With that, Don Quixote, fetching a deep sigh, "Madam," said he, "could I take out my heart, and expose it to your grace's view in a dish on this table, I might save my tongue the labour of attempting that which it cannot express, and you can scarce believe; for there your grace would see her beauty painted to the life. But why should I undertake to delineate and copy one by one each several perfection of the peerless Dulcinea? That burden must be sustained by stronger shoulders than mine: that task were worthy of the pencils of Parrhasius, Timantes, and Apelles, or the graving tools of Lysippus. The hands of the best painters and statuaries should indeed be employed to give in speaking paint, in marble and Corinthian brass, an exact copy of her beauties, while Ciceronian and Demosthenian eloquence laboured to reach the praise of her endowments."

"Pray, sir," asked the duchess, "what do you mean by that word Demosthenian?"

"Demosthenian eloquence, madam," said Don Quixote, "is as much as to say, the eloquence of Demosthenes, and the Ciceronian that of Cicero, the two greatest orators that ever were in the world."

"It is true," said the duke; "and you but showed your ignorance, my dear, in asking such a question. Yet the noble Don Quixote would highly oblige us, if he would but be pleased to attempt her picture now; for even in a rude draught of her lineaments, I question not but she will appear so charming, as to deserve the envy of the brightest of her sex."

"Ah! my lord," said Don Quixote, "it would be so indeed, if the misfortune which not long since befell her had not in a manner razed her idea out of the seat of my memory; and as it is, I ought rather to bewail her change than describe her person; for your grace must know that as I lately went to kiss her hands, and obtain her benediction and leave for my intended absence in quest of new adventures, I found her quite another creature than I expected. I found her enchanted, transformed from a princess to a country wench, from beauty to ugliness, from courtliness to rusticity, from light to darkness; in short, from Dulcinea del Toboso to a peasantess of Sayago."

"Bless us!" cried the duke with a loud voice, "what villain has done the world such an injury? Who has robbed it not only of the beauty that was its ornament, but of those charming graces that were its delight, and that virtue which was its living honour?"

"Who should it be," replied Don Quixote, "but one of those deceitful enchanters, one of those numerous envious fiends that without cessation persecute me; that wicked brood of evil, brought into the world to eclipse the glory of good and valiant men, and blemish their exploits, while they labour to exalt and magnify the actions of the bad? These magicians have before persecuted me, and persecute me now, and will continue till they have sunk me and my lofty deeds of chivalry into the profound abyss of oblivion. Yes, yes, they choose to wound me in that part which they are aware is most sensible, well knowing that to deprive a knight-errant of his lady is to rob him of those eyes with which he sees, of the sun that enlightens him, and the food that sustains him. For, as I have often said, a knight-errant without a lady is like a tree without leaves, a building without mortar, or a shadow without a body that causes it."

"I grant all this," said the duchess; "yet if we may believe the history of your life, which was lately published with universal applause, it seems to imply, to the best of my remembrance, that you never saw the Lady Dulcinea, and that there is no such lady in the world; but rather that she is a mere notional creature, engendered and brought forth by the strength and heat of your fancy, and there endowed with all the charms and good qualifications which you are pleased to ascribe to her."

"Much may be said upon this point," said Don Quixote; "Heaven knows whether there be a Dulcinea in the world or not, and whether she be a notional creature or not. These are mysteries not to be so narrowly inquired into. I do indeed make her the object of my contemplations, and, as I ought, look on her as a lady endowed with all those qualifications that may raise the character of a person to universal fame. She is to me beautiful without blemish, reserved without pride, amorous with modesty, agreeable for her courteous temper and her education, and, in short, of an illustrious parentage. For beauty displays its lustre to a higher degree of perfection when joined with noble blood, than it can in those that are meanly descended."

"The observation is just," said the duke; "but give me leave, sir, to propose to you a doubt, which the reading of that history has started in my mind. It is, that allowing there be a Dulcinea at Toboso, or elsewhere, and as beautiful as you describe her, yet I do not find she can any way equal in greatness of birth the Orianas, the Alastrajareas, the Madasimas, and a thousand others, of whom we read in those histories, with which you have been so conversant."

"To this," said Don Quixote, "I answer, that Dulcinea is the daughter of her own actions, and that virtue ennobles the blood. A virtuous man of mean condition is more to be esteemed than a vicious person of quality. Besides, Dulcinea is possessed of endowments that may entitle her to crowns and sceptres, since beauty alone has raised many of her sex to a throne. Where merit has no limits, hope may well have no bounds; and to be fair and virtuous is so extensive an advantage, that it gives, though not a formal, at least a virtual claim to larger fortunes."

"I must own, sir," said the duchess, "that in all your discourse you, as we say, proceed with the plummet of reason, and fathom all the depths of controversy. Therefore, I submit, and from this time I am resolved to believe, and will make all my domestics, nay, my husband, too, if there be occasion, believe and maintain, that there is a Dulcinea del Toboso extant, and living at this day; that she is beautiful and of good extraction; and to sum up all in a word, altogether deserving the services of so great a knight as the noble Don Quixote, which I think is the highest commendation I can bestow on her. But yet I must confess, there is still one scruple that makes me uneasy, and causes me to have an ill opinion of Sancho. It is, that the history tells us, that when Sancho Panza carried your letter to the Lady Dulcinea, he found her winnowing a sack of corn, by the same token that it was the worst sort of wheat, which makes me much doubt her quality."

"Your grace must know," answered Don Quixote, "that almost everything that relates to me is managed quite contrary to what the affairs of other knights-errant used to be. Whether it be the unfathomable will of Destiny, or the implacable malice of some envious enchanter orders it so, or no, I cannot well tell. For it is beyond all doubt, that most of us knights-errant still have had something peculiar in our fates. One has had the privilege to be above the power of enchantments, another invulnerable, as the famous Orlando, one of the twelve peers of France, whose flesh, they tell us, was impenetrable everywhere but in the sole of his left foot, and even there, too, he could be wounded with no other weapon than the point of a great pin; so that when Bernardo del Carpio deprived him of life at Roncesvalles, finding he could not wound him with his sword, he lifted him from the ground, and squeezed him to death in his arms; remembering how Hercules killed Antæus, that cruel giant, who was said to be the son of the Earth. Hence I infer, that probably I may be secured in the same manner, under the protection of some particular advantage, though it is not that of being invulnerable; for I have often found by experience that my flesh is tender and not impenetrable. Nor does any private prerogative free me from the power of enchantment; for I have found myself clapped into a cage, where all the world could not have locked me up, but the force of necromantic incantations. But since I got free again, I believe that even the force of magic will never be able to confine me thus another time. So that these magicians, finding they cannot work their wicked ends directly on me, revenge themselves by persecuting Dulcinea, for whom I live.

"I believe, when my squire went to her, they transformed her into a country dowdy, busied in the base employment of winnowing wheat. But I do aver that it was neither rye nor wheat, but Oriental pearl: and to prove this, I must acquaint your graces, that passing the other day by Toboso, I could not so much as find Dulcinea's palace; whereas my squire went the next day, and saw her in all her native charms, the most beautiful creature in the world; yet when I met her presently after, she appeared to me in the shape of an ugly, coarse, country mawkin, boorish, and ill-bred, though she really is discretion itself. And therefore, because I myself cannot be enchanted, the unfortunate lady must be thus enchanted, misused, disfigured, chopped and changed. Thus my enemies, wreaking their malice on her, have revenged themselves on me, which makes me abandon myself to sorrow, till she be restored to her former perfections.

"I have been the more large in this particular, that nobody might insist on what Sancho said of her sifting of corn; for if she appeared changed to me, what wonder is it if she seemed so to him? In short, Dulcinea is both illustrious and well-born, being descended of the most ancient and best families in Toboso; and now that town will be no less famous in after ages than Troy for Helen, or Spain for Cava, though on a more honourable account.

"As for Sancho Panza, I assure your grace he is one of the most pleasant squires that ever waited on a knight-errant. Sometimes he comes out with such sharp simplicities, that one is puzzled to judge whether he be more knave or fool. He doubts of everything, yet believes everything; and when one would think he had entangled himself in a piece of downright folly, beyond recovery, he brings himself off of a sudden so cleverly, that he is applauded to the skies. In short, I would not change him for the best squire that wears a head, though I might have a city to boot, and therefore I do not know whether I had best let him go to the government which your grace has been pleased to promise him; though, I must confess, his talents seem to lie pretty much that way: for, give never so little a whet to his understanding, he will manage his government as well as the king does his customs. Then experience convinces us that neither learning nor any other abilities are very material to a governor. Have we not a hundred of them that can scarce read a letter, and yet they govern as sharp as so many hawks? Their main business is only to mean well, and to be resolved to do their best; for they cannot want able counsellors to instruct them. Thus those governors who are men of the sword, and no scholars, have their assessors on the bench to direct them. My counsel to Sancho shall be, that he neither take bribes nor lose his privileges, with some other little instructions, which I have in my head for him, and which at a proper time I will communicate, both for his private advantage and the public good of the island he is to govern."

So far had the duke, the duchess, and Don Quixote been discoursing together, when they heard a great noise in the house, and by-and-by Sancho came running unexpectedly into the room where they sat, in a terrible fright, with a dish-clout before him instead of a bib. The scullions and other greasy rabble of the kitchen were after him, one of them pursuing him with a little kneading-trough full of dish-water, which he endeavoured to put under his chin, while another stood ready to have washed the poor squire with it.

"How now, fellow?" said the duchess; "what is the matter here? What would you do with this good man? Don't you consider he is a governor elect?"

"Madam," quoth the barber-scullion, "the gentleman won't let us wash him according to custom, as my lord duke and his master were."

"Yes, marry but I will," quoth Sancho, in a mighty huff, "but then it shall be with cleaner suds, cleaner towels, and not quite so slovenly paws; for there is no such difference between my master and me neither, that he must be washed with pure water, and I with any dirty suds: so far the customs of great men's houses are good as they give no offence; but this same washing in a puddle is worse penance than a friar's flogging. My beard is clean enough, and wants no such refreshing. Stand clear, you had best; for the first that comes to wash me, or touch a hair of my head (my beard I would say), I will take him such a dowse o' the ear, he shall feel it a twelvemonth after: for these kind of ceremonies and soapings, do ye see, look more like flouts and jeers than like a civil welcome to strangers."

The duchess was like to have burst her sides with laughing, to see Sancho's fury, and hear how he argued for himself. But Don Quixote did not very well like to see him with such a nasty dish-clout about his neck, and made the sport of the kitchen pensioners. Therefore, after he had made a deep bow to the duke, as it were desiring leave to speak, looking on the scullions—"Hark ye, gentlemen," cried he, very gravely, "pray let the young man alone, and get you gone as you came, if you think fit. My squire is as cleanly as another man; that trough won't do; you had better have brought him a dram-cup. Away; be advised by me, and leave him: for neither he nor I can abide such slovenly jestings."

"No, no," quoth Sancho, taking the words out of his master's mouth; "let them stay, and go on with their show. I'll pay my barbers, I'll warrant ye. They had as good take a lion by the beard as meddle with mine. Let them bring a comb hither, or what they will, and currycomb it; and if they find anything there that should not be there, I will give them leave to cut and mince me as small as a horse."

"Sancho is in the right," said the duchess, still laughing, "and will be in the right, in all he says; he is as clean and neat as can be, and needs none of your scouring. But you are a pack of unmannerly varlets, and, like saucy rascals as you are, cannot help showing your spite to the squires of knights-errant."

The greasy regiment, and even the steward who was with them, thought verily the duchess had been in earnest. So they took the cloth from Sancho's neck, and sneaked off quite out of countenance. Sancho, seeing himself delivered from his apprehension of this danger, ran and threw himself on his knees before the duchess. "Heaven bless your worship's grace," quoth he, "Madam Duchess. Great persons are able to do great kindnesses. For my part, I don't know how to make your worship amends for this you have done me now. I can only wish I might see myself an armed knight-errant for your sake, that I might spend all the days of my life in the service of so high a lady. I am a poor countryman,—my name is Sancho Panza,—children I have, and serve as a squire. If in any of these matters I can do you any good, you need but speak; I will be nimbler in doing than your worship shall be in ordering."

"It is evident, Sancho," said the duchess, "that you have learned civility in the school of courtesy itself, and have been bred up under the wings of Don Quixote, who is the very cream of compliment, and the flower of ceremonies. All happiness attend such a knight and such a squire; the one the north star of chivalry-errant, the other the bright luminary of squire-like fidelity. Rise, my friend Sancho, and assure yourself that, for the recompense of your civilities, I will persuade my lord duke to put you in possession of the government he promised you as soon as he can."

After this, Don Quixote went to take his afternoon's sleep; but the duchess desired Sancho, if he were not very sleepy, he would pass the afternoon with her and her women in a cool room. Sancho told her grace that indeed he did use to take a good sound nap, some four or five hours long, in a summer's afternoon; but to do her good honour a kindness, he would break an old custom for once, and do his best to hold up that day, and wait on her worship. The duke, on his side, gave fresh orders that Don Quixote should be entertained exactly like a knight-errant, without deviating the least step from the road of chivalry, such as is observable in books of that kind.

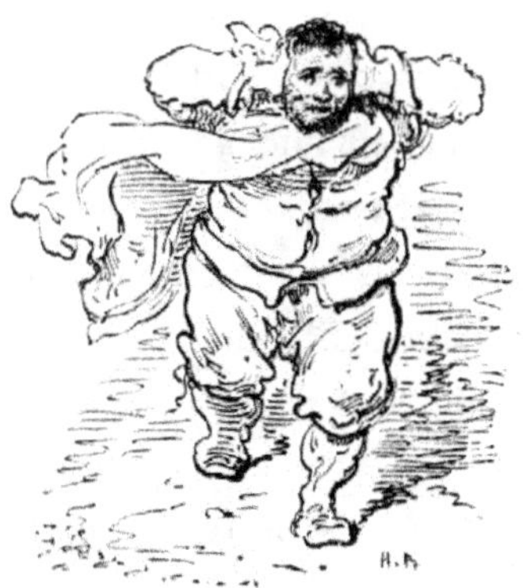

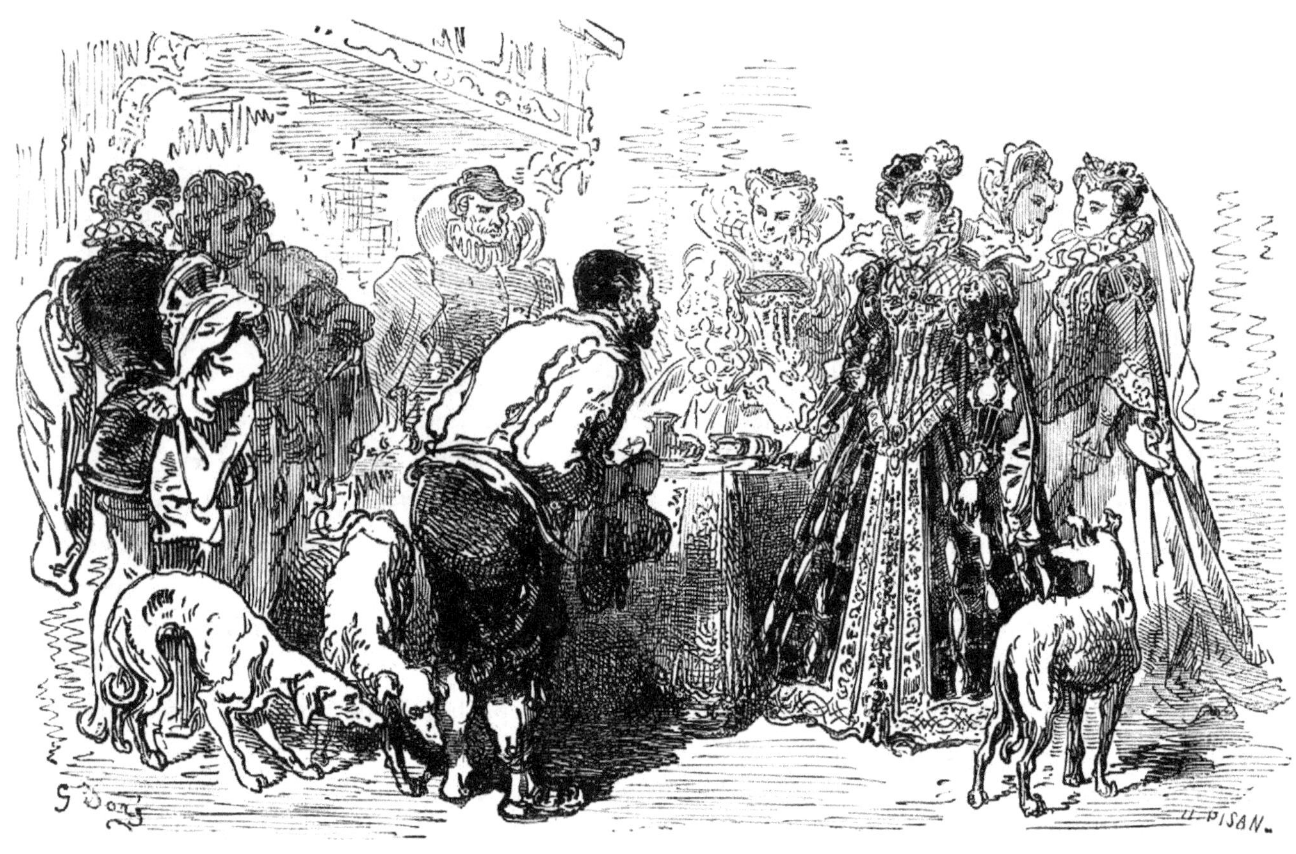

CHAPTER XXXIII.

THE SAVOURY CONFERENCE WHICH THE DUCHESS AND HER WOMEN HELD WITH SANCHO PANZA, WORTH YOUR READING AND OBSERVATION.

THE story afterwards informs us that Sancho slept not a wink all that afternoon, but waited on the duchess as he had promised. Being mightily taken with his comical discourse, she ordered him to take a low chair, and sit by her; but Sancho, who knew better things, absolutely declined it, till she pressed him again to sit, as he was a governor, and speak as he was a squire; in both which capacities he deserved the very seat of Cid Ruy Diaz, the famous champion. Sancho shrugged up his shoulders, and obeyed, and all the duchess's women standing round about her to give her silent attention, she began the conference.

"Now that we are in private," said she, "and nobody to overhear us, I would desire you, my lord governor, to resolve me of some doubts in the printed history of the great Don Quixote, which puzzle me very much. First, I find that the good Sancho had never seen Dulcinea—the Lady Dulcinea del Toboso, I should have said—nor carried her his master's letter, as having left the table-book behind him in Sierra Morena; how then durst he feign an answer, and pretend he found her winnowing wheat? a fiction and banter so injurious to the reputation of the peerless Dulcinea, and so great a blemish on the character of a faithful squire!"

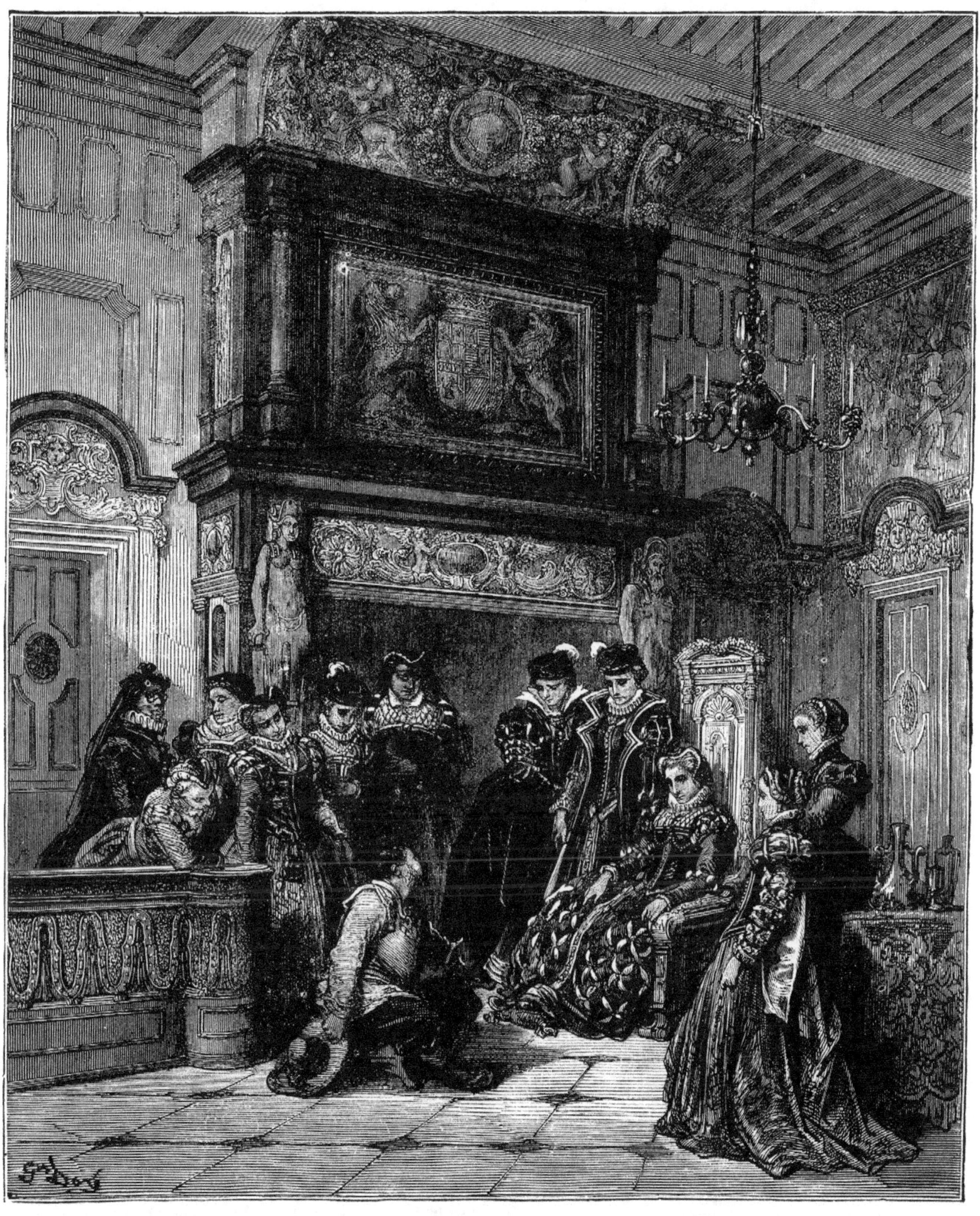

"At the duchess's request, he related the whole passage of the late pretended enchantment very faithfully."

Here Sancho got up without speaking a word, laid his finger on his lips, and, with his body bent, crept cautiously round the room, lifting up the hangings, and peeping in every hole and corner. At last, finding the coast clear, he returned to his seat. "Now," quoth he, "Madam Duchess, since I find there is nobody here but ourselves, you shall e'en hear, without fear or favour, the truth of the story, and what else you will ask of me, but not a word of the pudding. First and foremost I must tell you, I look on my master, Don Quixote, to be no better than a downright madman, though sometimes he will stumble on a parcel of sayings so quaint, and so tightly put together, that nobody could mend them; but in the main I can't beat it out of my noddle but that he is as mad as a March hare. Now, because I am pretty confident of knowing his blind side, whatever crotchets come into my crown, though without either head or tail, yet can I make them pass upon him for gospel. Such was the answer to his letter, and another sham that I put upon him but the other day, and is not in print yet, touching my Lady Dulcinea's enchantment; for you must know, between you and I, she is no more enchanted than the man in the moon."

With that, at the duchess's request, he related the whole passage of the late pretended enchantment very faithfully, to the great diversion of the hearers.

"But, sir," said the duchess, "I have another scruple in this affair no less unaccountable than the former; for I think I hear something whisper me in the ear, and say, If Don Quixote de la Mancha be such a shallow-brains, why does Sancho Panza, who knows him to be so, wait upon this madman, and rely thus upon his vain, extravagant promises? I can only infer from this, that the man is more a fool than the master; and if so, will not Madam Duchess be thought as mad as either of them, to bestow the government of an island, or the command of others, on one who can't govern himself?"

"By our Lady," quoth Sancho, "your scruple comes in pudding time! But I need not whisper in your ear; it may e'en speak plain, and as loud as it will. I am a fool, that is certain; for if I had been wise, I had left my master many a fair day since; but it was my luck, and my vile errantry, and that is all can be said on 't. I must follow him through thick and thin. We are both towns-born children; I have eaten his bread—I love him well, and there is no love lost between us. He pays me very well, he has given me three colts, and I am so very true and trusty to him, that nothing but death can part us. And if your high and mightiness does not think fit to let me have this same government, why, so be it; with less was I born, and with less shall I die; it may be for the good of my conscience to go without it. I am a fool, it is true, but yet I understand the meaning of the saying, 'The emmet had wings to do her hurt;' and Sancho the squire may sooner get to heaven than Sancho the governor. There is as good bread baked here as in France, and Joan is as good as my lady in the dark. 'In the night all cats are grey.' 'Unhappy he is that wants his breakfast at two in the afternoon.' 'It is always good fasting after a good breakfast.' There is no man has a stomach a yard bigger than another; but let it be never so big, there will be hay and straw enough to fill it. A bellyful is a bellyful. 'The sparrow speeds as well as the sparrow-hawk.' 'Good serge is fine, but coarse cloth is warm; and four yards of the one are as long as four yards of the other.' When the hour is come we must all be packed off: the prince and the peasant go the same way at last; the road is no fairer for the one than the other. The Pope's body takes up no more room than the sexton's, though one be taller; for when they come to the pit all are alike, or made so in spite of our teeth; and so good night, or good morrow, which you please. And let me tell you again, if you don't think fit to give me an island because I am a fool, I will be so wise as not to care whether you do or no. It is an old saying, 'The devil lurks behind the cross.' 'All is not gold that glisters.' From the tail of the plough Bamba was made King of Spain; and from his silks and riches was Rodrigo cast to be devoured by the snakes, if the old ballads say true, and sure they are too old to tell a lie."

"That they are indeed," said Donna Rodriguez, the old waiting woman, who listened among the rest; "for I remember one of the ballads tells us how Don Rodrigo was shut up alive in a tomb full of toads, snakes, and lizards; and how, after two days, he was heard to cry out of the tomb in a low and doleful voice, 'Now they eat me, now they gnaw me, in the part where I sinned most.' And according to this the gentleman is in the right in saying he had rather be a poor labourer than a king to be gnawed to death by vermin."

Sancho's proverbial aphorisms, and the simple waiting woman's comment upon the text, were no small diversion to the duchess. "You know," said she, "honest Sancho, that the promise of a gentleman or knight must be as precious and sacred to him as his life; I make no question then but that my lord duke, who is also a knight, though not of your master's order, will infallibly keep his word with you in respect of your government. Take courage then, Sancho, for when you least dream on 't, in spite of all the envy and malice of the world, you will suddenly see yourself in full possession of your government, and seated in your chair of state in your rich robes, with all your marks and ornaments of power about you. But be sure to administer true justice to your vassals, who, by their loyalty and discretion, will merit no less at your hands."

"As for the governing part," quoth Sancho, "let me alone: I was ever charitable and good to the poor, and scorn to take the bread out of another man's mouth. On the other side, by our Lady, they shall play me no foul play. I am an old cur at a crust, and can sleep dog-sleep when I list. I can look sharp as well as another, and let me alone to keep the cobwebs out of my eyes. I know where the shoe wrings me. I will know who and who is together. 'Honesty is the best policy:' I will stick to that. The good shall have my hand and heart, but the bad neither foot nor fellowship. And in my mind, the main thing in this point of governing is to make a good beginning. I will lay my life, that as simple as Sancho sits here, in a fortnight's time he will manage ye this same island as rightly as a sheaf of barley."

"You say well, Sancho," said the duchess, "for time ripens all things. No man is born wise. Bishops are made of men, and not of stones. But to return once more to the Lady Dulcinea; I am more than half persuaded that Sancho's design of putting the trick upon his master was turned into a greater cheat upon himself. For I am well assured that the creature whom you fancy to be a country wench, and took so much pains to persuade your master was Dulcinea del Toboso, was really the same Dulcinea del Toboso, and really enchanted, as Don Quixote thought; and the magicians that persecute your master first invented that story, and put it into your head. For you must know that we have our enchanters here, that have a kindness for us, and give us an account of what happens in the world faithfully and impartially, without any tricks or equivocations. And take my word for it, the jumping country wench was, and is still, Dulcinea del Toboso, who is as certainly enchanted as the mother that bore her; and when we least expect it, we shall see her again in her true shape, and in all her native lustre; and then Sancho will find it was he himself was bubbled."

"Troth, madam," quoth Sancho, "all this might well be: and now I am apt to believe what my master tells me of the cave of Montesinos; where, as he says, he saw my Lady Dulcinea del Toboso in the selfsame garb, and as handsome as I told him I had seen her when it came into my noddle to tell him she was enchanted. Ay, my lady, it must be quite contrary to what I weened, as your worship's grace well observes; for, bless us! who could possibly imagine that such a numskull as I should have it in him to devise so cunning a trick of a sudden? Besides, who can think that my master is such a goose as to believe so unlikely a matter upon the single vouching of such a dunderhead fellow as I? But for all that, my good lady, I hope you know better things than to think me a knave; a lack a day! it can't be expected that such an ignoramus as I am should be able to divine into the tricks and wiles of wicked magicians. I invented that flam only, because my master would never leave teasing me; but I had no mind to abuse him, not I; and if it fell out otherwise than I mean, who can help it? Heaven knows my heart."

"That is honestly said," answered the duchess; "but pray tell me, Sancho, what was it you were speaking of the cave of Montesinos? I have a great mind to know the story."

Thereupon Sancho having related the whole matter to the duchess, "Look you," said she, "this exactly makes out what I said to you just now; for since the great Don Quixote affirms he saw there the same country wench that Sancho met coming from Toboso, it is past all doubt it was Dulcinea; and this shows the enchanters are a subtle sort of people, that will know everything, and give a quick and sure information."

"Well," quoth Sancho, "if my Lady Dulcinea del Toboso be enchanted, it is the worse for her. What have I to do to quarrel with all my master's enemies? They can't be few for aught I see, and they are plaguy fellows to deal withal. Thus much I dare say, she I saw was a country wench; a country wench I took her to be, and a country wench I left her. Now if that same dowdy was Dulcinea in good earnest, how can I help it? I ought not to be called to an account for it. No, let the saddle be set upon the right horse, or we shall ne'er have done. Sancho told me this, cries one; Sancho told me that, cries t'other: Sancho o' this side, Sancho o' that side; Sancho did this, and Sancho did that; as if Sancho were I don't know who, and not the same Sancho that goes already far and near through the world in books, as Samson Carrasco tells me, and he is no less than a bachelor of arts at Salamanca 'varsity; and such folks as he can't tell a lie, unless they be so disposed, or it stands them in good stead. So let nobody meddle or make, nor offer to pick a quarrel with me about the matter, since I am a man of reputation; and as my master says, 'a good name is better than riches.' Clap me but into this same government once, and you shall see wonders. He that has been a good servant will make a good master; a trusty squire will make a rare governor, I will warrant you."

"Sancho speaks like an oracle," said the duchess; "everything he says is a sentence like those of Cato, or at least the very marrow of Michael Verino: *Florentibus occidit annis*—that is, he died in his spring. In short, to speak after his way, 'under a bad cloak look for a good drinker.'"

"Faith and troth, Madam Duchess," quoth Sancho, "I never drank out of malice in my born days; for thirst perhaps I may; for I have not a bit of hypocrisy in me. I drink when I have occasion, and sometimes when I have no occasion; I am no proud man, d'ye see, and when the liquor is offered me I whip it off, that they may not take me for a churl or a sneaksby, or think I don't understand myself nor good manners; for when a friend or a good fellow drinks and puts the glass to one, who can be so hard-hearted as to refuse to pledge him, when it costs nothing but to open one's mouth? However, I commonly look before I leap, and take no more than needs must. And truly there's no fear that we poor squires to knights-errant should be great trespassers that way. Alack a day! mere element must be our daily beverage—ditch-water, for want of better—in woods and deserts, on rocks and mountains, without lighting on the blessing of one merciful drop of wine, though you would give one of your eyes for a single gulp."

"I believe it, Sancho," said the duchess; "but now it grows late, and therefore go and take some rest; after that we'll have a longer conversation, and will take measures about *clapping* you suddenly into this same government, as you are pleased to word it."

Sancho kissed the duchess's hand once more, and begged her worship's grace that special care might be taken of his Dapple, for that he was the light of his eyes.

"What is that Dapple?" asked the duchess.

"My beast, an 't like your honour," answered Sancho; "my ass I would say, saving your presence; but because I won't call him ass, which is so common a name among men, I call him Dapple. It is the very same beast I would have given charge of to that same gentle-woman when I came first to this castle; but her temper was up presently, and she flew out as if I had called her ugly face, old witch, and what not. However, I'll be judged by any one whether such like sober grave bodies as she and other duennas are be not fitter to look after asses than to sit with a prim countenance to grace a fine state room. Passion of my heart! what a deadly grudge a certain gentleman of our town, that shall be nameless, had to these creatures! I mean, these old waiting gentlewomen."

"Some filthy clown, I dare engage," said Donna Rodriguez, the duenna; "had he been a gentleman, or a person of good breeding, he would have praised them up to the skies."

"Well," said the duchess, "let us have no more of that; let Donna Rodriguez hold her tongue, and Signior Sancho Panza go to his repose, and leave me to take care of his Dapple's good entertainment; for since I find him to be one of Sancho's movables, I will place him in my esteem above the apple of my eye."

"Place him in the stable, my good lady," replied Sancho; "that is as much as he deserves; neither he nor I are worthy of being placed a minute of an hour where you said. Bless me! I'd sooner be stuck with a butcher's knife, than you should be served so; I am better bred than that comes to; for though my lord and master has taught me that in point of behaviour one ought rather to over-do than under-do, yet when the case lies about an ass and the ball of one's eye, it is best to think twice, and go warily about the matter."

"Well," said the duchess, "your ass may go with you to the government, and there you may feed him, and pamper him, and make as much of him as you please."

"Ah! my lady," quoth Sancho, "don't let your worship think this will be such a strange matter neither. I have seen more asses than one go to a government before now; and if mine goes too, it will be no new thing, I trow"

Sancho's words again set the duchess a-laughing; and so sending him to take his rest, she went to the duke, and gave him an account of the pleasant discourse between her and the squire. After this they resolved to have some notable contrivance to make sport with Don Quixote, and of such a romantic cast as should humour his knight-errantry. And so successful they were in their management of that interlude, that it may well be thought one of the best adventures in this famous history.

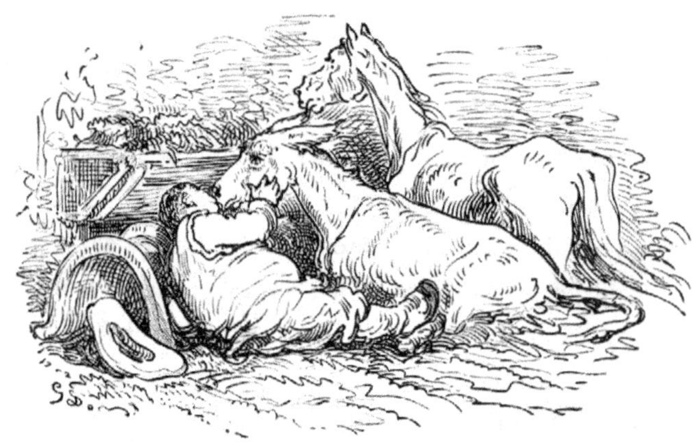

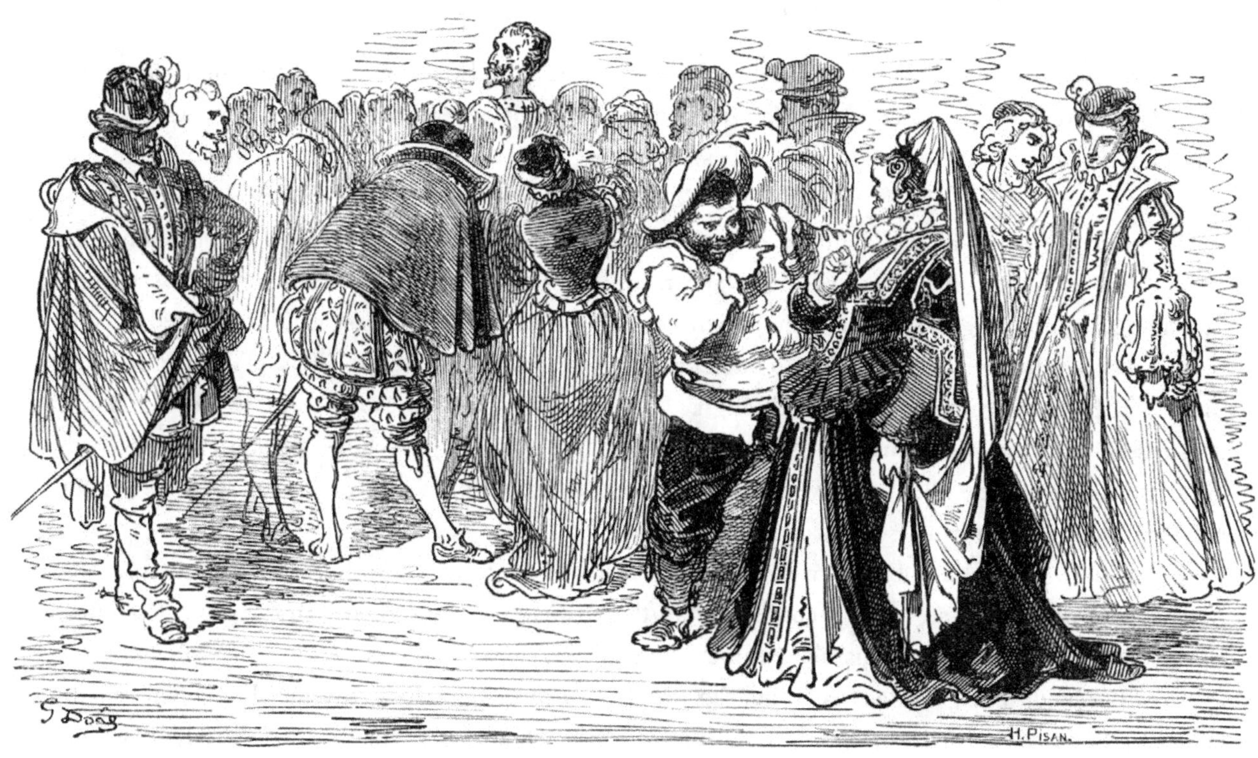

CHAPTER XXXIV.

CONTAINING WAYS AND MEANS FOR DISENCHANTING THE PEERLESS DULCINEA DEL TOBOSO, BEING ONE OF THE MOST FAMOUS ADVENTURES IN THE WHOLE BOOK.

THE duke and duchess were extremely diverted with the humours of their guests. Resolving, therefore, to improve their sport, by carrying on some pleasant design, that might bear the appearance of an adventure, they took the hint from Don Quixote's account of the cave of Montesinos, as a subject from which they might raise an extraordinary entertainment; the rather, since, to the duchess's amazement, Sancho's simplicity was so great, as to believe that Dulcinea del Toboso was really enchanted, though he himself had been the first contriver of the story, and her only enchanter.

Accordingly, having given directions to their servants that nothing might be wanting, and proposed a day for hunting the wild boar, in five or six days they were ready to set out, with a train of huntsmen and other attendants not unbecoming the greatest prince. They presented Don Quixote with a hunting suit, but he refused it, alleging it superfluous, since he was, in a short time, to return to the hard exercise of arms, and could carry no sumpters nor wardrobes along with him: but Sancho readily accepted one of fine green cloth, with design to sell it the first opportunity.

The day prefixed being come, Don Quixote armed, and Sancho equipped himself in his new suit, and mounting his ass, which he would not quit for a good horse that was offered him, he crowded in among the train of sportsmen. The duchess also, in a dress both odd and gay, made one of the company. The knight, who was courtesy itself, very gallantly would needs hold the reins of her palfrey, though the duke seemed very unwilling to let him. In short, they came to the scene of their sport, which was in a wood between two very high mountains, where, alighting, and taking their several stands, the duchess, with a pointed javelin in her hand, attended by the duke and Don Quixote, took her stand in a place where they knew the boars were used to pass through. The hunters posted themselves in several lanes and paths, as they most conveniently could; but as for Sancho, he chose to stay behind them all with his Dapple, whom he would by no means leave for a moment, for fear the poor creature should meet with some sad accident.

And now the chase began with full cry, the dogs opened, the horns sounded, and the huntsmen hallooed in so loud a concert, that there was no hearing one another. Soon after, a hideous boar, of a monstrous size, came on, gnashing his teeth and tusks, and foaming at the mouth; and, being baited hard by the dogs, and followed close by the huntsmen, made furiously towards the pass which Don Quixote had taken; whereupon the knight, grasping his shield and drawing his sword, moved forward to receive the raging beast. The duke joined him with a boar-spear, and the duchess would have been foremost, had not the duke prevented her. Sancho alone, seeing the furious animal, resolved to shift for one, and leaving Dapple, away he scudded, as fast as his legs would carry him, towards a high oak, to the top of which he endeavoured to clamber; but, as he was getting up, one of the boughs unluckily broke, and down he was tumbling, when a snag or stump of another bough caught hold of his new coat, and stopped his fall, slinging him in the air by the middle, so that he could neither get up nor down. His fine green coat was torn, and he fancied every moment the wild boar was running that way, with foaming chaps, and dreadful tusks, to tear him to pieces; which so disturbed him, that he roared and bellowed for help, as if some wild beast had been devouring him in good earnest.

At last the tusky boar was laid at his length, with a number of pointed spears fixed in him; and Dox Quixote, being alarmed by Sancho's noise, which he could distinguish easily, looked about, and discovered him swinging from the tree with his head downwards, and close by him poor Dapple, who, like a true friend, never forsook him in his adversity; for Cid Hamet observes, that they were such true and inseparable friends, that Sancho was seldom seen without Dapple, or Dapple without Sancho. Don Quixote went and took down his squire, who, as soon as he was at liberty, began to examine the damage his fine hunting suit had received, which grieved him to the soul; for he prized it as much as if it had made him heir to an estate.

Meanwhile, the boar being laid across a large mule, and covered with branches of rose-mary and myrtle, was carried in triumph, by the victorious huntsmen, to a large field-tent, pitched in the middle of the wood, where an excellent entertainment was provided, suitable to the magnificence of the founder.

Sancho drew near the duchess, and showing her his torn coat, "Had we been hunting the hare now, or catching of sparrows," quoth he, "my coat might have slept in a whole skin. For my part, I wonder what pleasure there can be in beating the bushes for a beast which, if it does but come at you, will run its plaguy tusks in your side, and be the death of you. I have not forgotten an old song to this purpose:—

"'May Fabila's sad fate be thine,
And make thee food for bears or swine.'"

"That Fabila," said Don Quixote, "was a king of the Goths, who going a-hunting once, was devoured by a bear."

"That is it, I say," quoth Sancho; "and, therefore, why should kings and other great folks run themselves into harm's way, when they may have sport enough without it? Mercy on me! what pleasure can you find, any of you all, in killing a poor beast that never meant any harm?"

"You are mistaken, Sancho," said the duke; "hunting wild beasts is the most proper exercise for knights and princes; for in the chase of a stout, noble beast may be represented the whole art of war—stratagems, policy, and ambuscades—with all other devices usually practised to overcome an enemy with safety. Here we are exposed to the extremities of heat and cold; ease and laziness can have no room in this diversion; by this we are inured to toil and hardship, our limbs are strengthened, our joints made supple, and our whole body hale and active. In short, it is an exercise that may be beneficial to many, and can be prejudicial to none; and the most enticing property is its rarity, being placed above the reach of the vulgar, who may indeed enjoy the diversion of other sorts of game, but not this nobler kind, nor that of hawking, a sport also reserved for kings and persons of quality. Therefore, Sancho, let me advise you to alter your opinion, when you become a governor; for then you will find the great advantage of these sports and diversions."

"You are out far wide, sir," quoth Sancho; "it were better that a governor had his legs broken, and be laid up at home, than to be gadding abroad at this rate. It would be a pretty business, forsooth, when poor people come, weary and tired, to wait on the governor about business, that he should be rambling about the woods for his pleasure! There would be a sweet government truly! Good faith, sir, I think these sports and pastimes are fitter for those that have nothing to do than for governors. No; I intend my recreation shall be a game at whist at Christmas, and ninepins on holidays; but, for your hunting, as you call it, it goes mightily against my calling and conscience."

"I wish, with all my heart," said the duke, "that you may prove as good as you promise; but saying and doing are different things."

"Well, well," quoth Sancho, "be it how it will, I say that an honest man's word is as good as his bond. 'Heaven's help is better than early rising.' It is the belly makes the feet amble, and not the feet the belly. My meaning is, that, with Heaven's help, and my honest endeavours, I shall govern better than any goshawk. Do but put your finger in my mouth, and try if I cannot bite."

"A curse on thee, and thy impertinent proverbs," said Don Quixote: "shall I never get thee to talk sense, without a string of that disagreeable stuff? I beseech your graces, do not countenance this eternal dunce, or he will tease your very souls with a thousand unseasonable and insignificant old saws, for which I wish his mouth stitched up, and myself a mischief if I hear him."

"Oh, sir," said the duchess, "Sancho's proverbs will always please for their sententious brevity, though they were as numerous as a printed collection; and, I assure you, I relish them more than I would do others, that might be better and more to the purpose."

After this, and such like diverting talk, they left the tent, and walked into the wood, to see whether any game had fallen into their nets. Now, while they were thus intent upon their sport, the night drew on apace, and more cloudy and overcast than was usual at that time of the year, which was about mid-summer, but it happened very critically for the better carrying on the intended contrivance. A little while after the close of the evening, when it grew quite dark, in a moment the wood seemed all on fire, and blazed in every quarter. This was attended with an alarming sound of trumpets, and other warlike instruments, answering one another from all sides, as if several parties of horse had been hastily marching through the wood. Then presently was heard a confused noise of Moorish cries, such as are used in joining battle; which, together with the rattling of the drums, the loud sound of the trumpets, and other instruments of war, made such a hideous and dreadful concert in the air, that the duke was amazed, the duchess astonished, Don Quixote surprised, and Sancho shook like a leaf; and even those that knew the occasion of all this were affrighted.

This consternation caused a general silence; and, by-and-by, one riding post, equipped very strangely, passed by the company, winding a huge hollow horn, that made a horrible hoarse noise. "Hark you, post," said the duke, "whither so fast? what are you? and what parties of soldiers are those that march across the wood?"

"I am one," cried the post, in a horrible tone, "who go in quest of Don Quixote de la Mancha; and those that are coming this way are six bands of necromancers, that conduct the peerless Dulcinea del Toboso, enchanted in a triumphant chariot. She is attended by that gallant French knight, Montesinos, who comes to give information how she may be freed from enchantment."

"Wert thou as much a deceiver," said the duke, "as thy shape speaks thee to be, thou wouldst have known this knight here before thee to be that Don Quixote de la Mancha whom thou seekest."

"Before Heaven, and on my conscience," replied the man, "I never thought on it; for I have so many things in my head, that it almost distracts me; I had quite and clean forgotten my errand."

"Surely," quoth Sancho, "this man must be a very honest fellow, and a good Christian; for he swears as devoutly by Heaven and his conscience as I should do; and now I am apt to believe there be some good people where we least expect them."

At the same time, the man, directing himself to Don Quixote, without dismounting, "To thee, O Knight of the Lions," cried he (and I wish thee fast in their claws), "to thee am I sent by the valiant but unfortunate Montesinos, to bid thee attend his coming in this very place, whither he brings one whom they call Dulcinea del Toboso, in order to give thee instructions touching her disenchantment. Now I have delivered my message, I must fly, and those that are like me be with thee, and angels guard the rest."

This said, he winded his monstrous horn, and, without staying for an answer, disappeared.

This increased the general consternation, but most of all surprised Don Quixote and Sancho; the latter to find that, in spite of truth, they still would have Dulcinea to be enchanted, and the knight to think that the adventures of the cave of Montesinos were turned to reality. While he stood pondering these things in his thoughts, "Well, sir," said the duke to him, "what do you intend to do? will you stay?"

"Stay!" cried Don Quixote, "shall I not? I will stay here, intrepid and courageous, though all the powers enclose me round."

"So you may, if you will," quoth Sancho; "but, if any more men or horns come hither, they shall as soon find me in Flanders as here."

Now the night grew darker and darker, and several shooting lights were seen glancing up and down the wood, like meteors or glaring exhalations from the earth. Then was heard a horrid noise, like the creaking of the ungreased wheels of heavy wagons, from which piercing and ungrateful sound bears and wolves themselves are said to fly. This odious jarring was presently seconded by a greater, which seemed to be the dreadful din and shocks of four several engagements, in each quarter of the wood, with all the sounds and hurry of so many joined battles. On one side were heard several peals of cannon; on the other, the discharging of numerous volleys of small shot; here the shouts of the engaging parties that seemed to be near at hand; there, cries of the Moors, that seemed at a great distance. In short, the strange, confused intermixture of drums, trumpets, cornets, horns, the thundering of the cannon, the rattling of the small shot, the creaking of the wheels, and the cries of the combatants, made the most dismal noise imaginable, and tried Don Quixote's courage to the uttermost. But poor Sancho was annihilated, and fell into a swoon upon the duchess's skirts, who, taking care of him, and ordering some water to be sprinkled on his face, at last recovered him, just as the foremost of the creaking carriages came up, drawn by four heavy oxen, covered with mourning, and carrying a large lighted torch upon each horn. On the top of the cart or wagon was an exalted seat, on which sat a venerable old man, with a beard as white as snow, and so long that it reached down to his girdle. He was clad in a long gown of black buckram, as were also two that drove the wagons, both so very monstrous and ugly, that Sancho, having seen them once, was forced to shut his eyes, and would not venture upon a second look.

The cart, which was stuck full of lights within, being approached to the standing, the reverend old man stood up, and cried with a loud voice, "I am the Sage Lirgander;" and the cart passed on without one word more being spoken.

Then followed another cart, with another grave old man, who making the cart stop at a convenient distance, rose up from his high seat, and, in as deep a tone as the first, cried, "I am the Sage Alquife, great friend to Urganda the Unknown:" and so went forward.

He was succeeded by a third cart, that moved in the same solemn pace, and bore a person not so ancient as the rest, but a robust and sturdy, sour-looking, ill-favoured fellow, who rose up from his throne, like the rest, and with a more hollow and diabolical voice, cried out, "I am Archelaus the Enchanter, the mortal enemy of Amadis de Gaul, and all his race:" this said, he passed by like the other carts, which, taking a short turn, made a halt, and the grating noise of the wheels ceasing, an excellent concert of sweet music was heard, which mightily comforted poor Sancho, and passing with him for a good omen, "My lady," quoth he to the duchess, from whom he would not budge an inch, "there can be no mischief sure where there is music."

"We shall know presently what this will come to," said Don Quixote; and he said right, for you will find it in the next chapter.

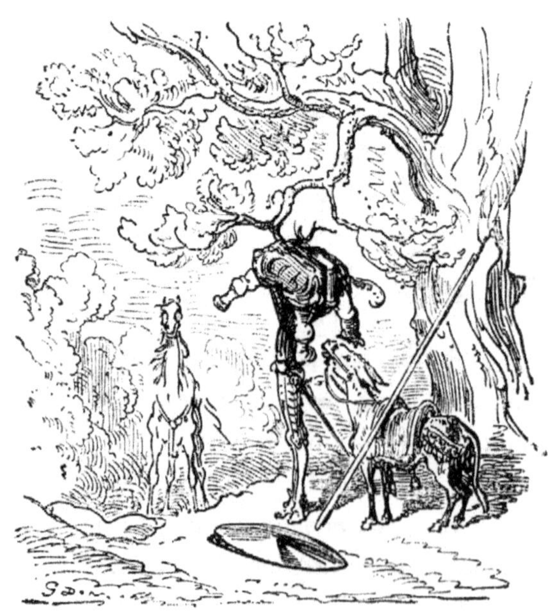

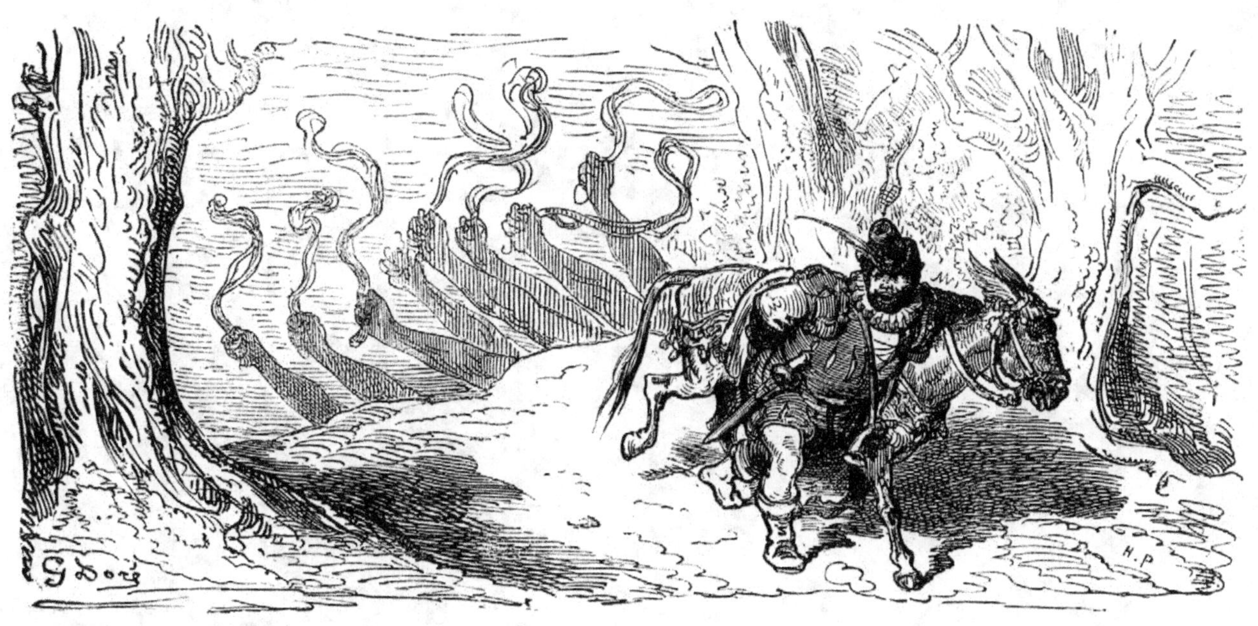

CHAPTER XXXV.

WHEREIN IS CONTAINED THE INFORMATION GIVEN TO DON QUIXOTE HOW TO DISENCHANT DULCINEA, WITH OTHER WONDERFUL PASSAGES.

WHEN the pleasant music drew near, there appeared a stately triumphal chariot, drawn by six dun mules, covered with white, upon each of which sat a penitent, clad also in white, and holding a great lighted torch in his hand. The carriage was twice or thrice longer than any of the former, twelve other penitents being placed at the top and sides, all in white, and bearing likewise each a lighted torch, which made a dazzling and surprising appearance. There was a high throne erected at the farther end, on which sat a nymph arrayed in cloth of silver, with many golden spangles glittering all about her, which made her dress, though not rich, appear very glorious. Her face was covered with transparent gauze, through the flowing folds of which might be descried a most beautiful face; and, by the great light which the torches gave, it was easy to discern that, as she was not less than seventeen years of age, neither could she be thought above twenty. Close by her was a figure, clad in a long gown, like that of a magistrate, reaching down to its feet, and its head covered with a black veil. When they came directly opposite to the company, the shawms or hautboys that played before immediately ceased, and the Spanish harps and lutes, that were in the chariot, did the like; then the figure in the gown stood up, and, opening its garments, and throwing away its mourning veil, discovered a bare and frightful skeleton, that represented the deformed figure of Death, which startled Don Quixote, made Sancho's bones rattle in his skin for fear, and caused the duke and the

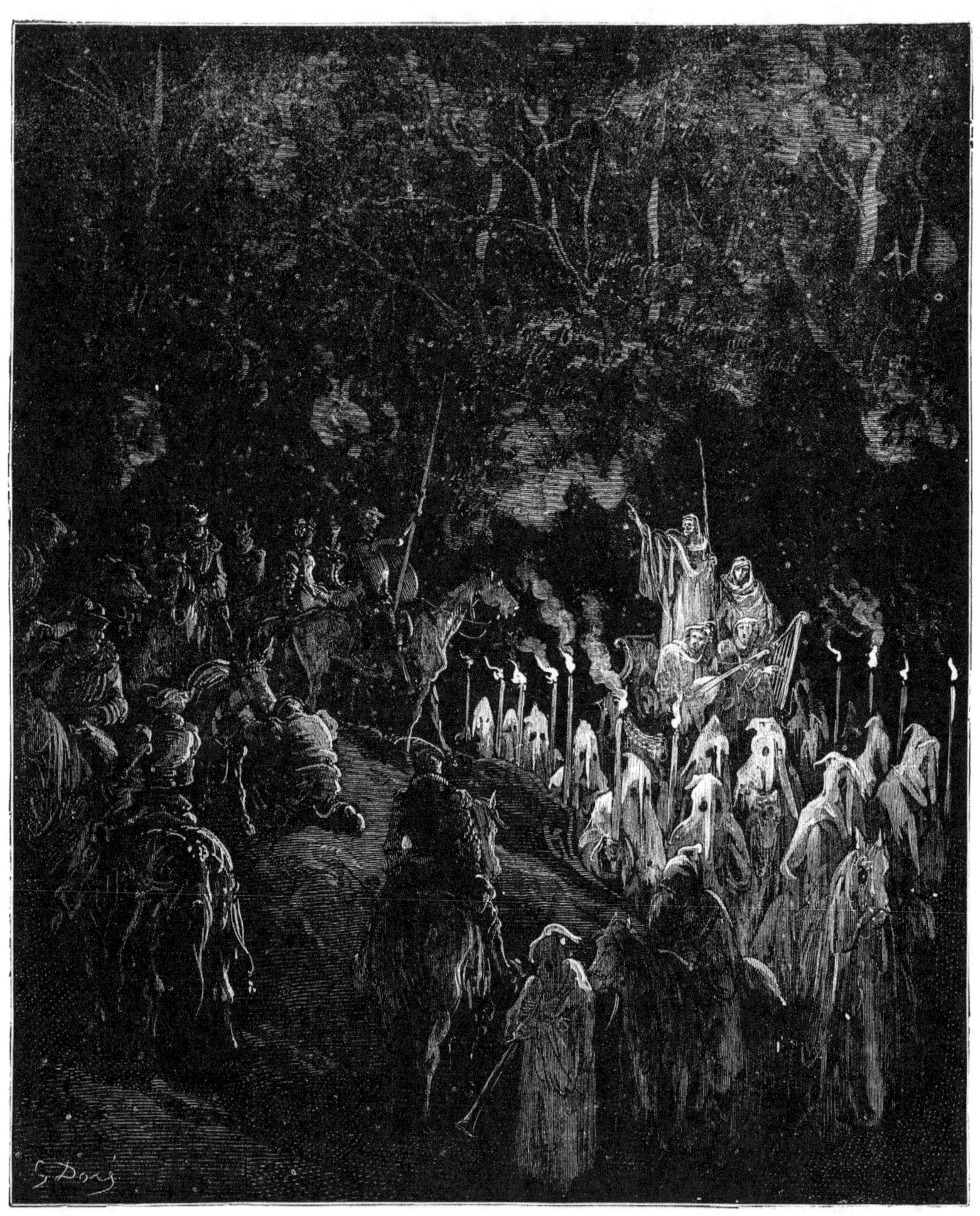

"The figure in the gown stood up."

duchess to seem more than commonly disturbed. This living Death being thus got up, in a dull, heavy, sleeping tone, as if its tongue had not been well awake, began in this manner :—

MERLIN'S SPEECH.

Behold old Merlin, in romantic writ
Miscall'd the spurious progeny of hell ;
A falsehood current with the stamp of age ;
I reign the prince of Zoroastic science,
That oft evokes and rates the rigid powers :
Archive of Fate's dread records in the skies,
Coëvous with the chivalry of yore ;
All brave knights-errant still I've deem'd my charge,
Heirs of my love, and fav'rites of my charms.
While other magic seers, averse from good,
Are dire and baleful like the seat of woe,
My nobler soul, where power and pity join,
Diffuses blessings, as they scatter plagues.
Deep in the nether world, the dreary caves,
Where my retreated soul, in silent state,
Forms mystic figures and tremendous spells,
I heard the peerless Dulcinea's moans.
Apprised of her distress, her frightful change,
From princely state, and beauty near divine,
To the vile semblance of a rustic wench,
The dire misdeed of necromantic hate,
I sympathised, and awfully revolved
Twice fifty thousand scrolls, occult and loath'd,
Some of my art, hell's black philosophy ;
Then closed my soul within this bony trunk,
This ghastly form, the ruins of a man ;
And rise in pity to reveal a cure
To woes so great, and break the cursed spell.
Oh, glory, thou, of all that e'er could grace
A coat of steel, and fence of adamant !
Light, lantern, path, and polar star and guide
To all who dare dismiss ignoble sleep,
And downy ease, for exercise of arms,
For toils continual, perils, wounds and blood !
Knight of unfathom'd worth, abyss of praise,
Who blend'st in one the prudent and the brave :
To thee, great Quixote, I this truth declare ;
That, to restore her to her state and form,
Toboso's pride, the peerless Dulcinea,
'Tis Fate's decree, that Sancho, thy good squire,
On his bare brawny quarters should bestow
Three thousand lashes, and eke three hundred more,
Each to afflict and sting, and gall him sore ;
So shall relent the authors of her woes,
Whose awful will I for her ease disclose.

"Bless me!" quoth Sancho; "three thousand lashes! I will not give myself three; I will as soon give myself three stabs in the stomach. Passion of my heart! Mr. Merlin, if you have no better way for disenchanting the Lady Dulcinea, she may even lie bewitched to her dying day for me."

"How now, opprobrious rascal!" cried Don Quixote. "Sirrah, I will take you and tie your dogship to a tree, and there I will not only give you three thousand three hundred lashes, but six thousand six hundred, ye varlet! and so smartly, that you shall feel them still, though you rub your body three thousand times, scoundrel!"

"Hold, hold!" cried Merlin, hearing this, "this must not be; the stripes inflicted on honest Sancho must be voluntary, and only laid on when he thinks most convenient. No set time is fixed for the task; and if he has a mind to have abated one half of this atonement, it is allowed, provided the remaining stripes be struck by a strange hand, and heavily laid on."

"Hold you there," quoth Sancho; "neither a strange hand nor my own, heavy or light, shall touch me. Let my master Don Quixote whip himself; as for any whipping of me, I refuse it flat and plain."

No sooner had Sancho thus spoken his mind, than the nymph that sat by Merlin's ghost in the glittering apparel, rising, and lifting up her thin veil, discovered a very beautiful face; and with a masculine grace, and no very agreeable voice, addressing Sancho, "Oh, thou

N N

disastrous squire," said she; "thou lump, with no more soul than a broken pitcher, heart of cork, and bowels of flint! Hadst thou been commanded, base sheep-stealer! to have thrown thyself headlong from the top of a high tower to the ground; hadst thou been desired, enemy of mankind! to have swallowed a dozen of toads, two dozen of lizards, and three dozen of snakes; or hadst thou been requested to have butchered thy wife and children, I should not wonder that it had turned thy squeamish stomach; but to make such a hesitation at three thousand three hundred stripes, which every puny schoolboy makes nothing of receiving every month, it is amazing, nay, astonishing to the tender and commiserating feelings of all that hear thee, and will be a blot in thy escutcheon to all futurity. Look up, thou wretched and marble-hearted animal! look up, and fix thy huge, lowering goggle-eyes upon the bright luminaries of my sight. Behold these briny torrents, which, streaming down, furrow the flowery meadows of my cheeks. Relent, base and inexorable monster—relent; let thy savage breast confess at last a sense of my distress, and, moved with the tenderness of my youth, that consumes and withers in this vile transformation, crack this sordid shell of rusticity that envelopes my blooming charms. In vain has the goodness of Merlin permitted me to re-assume a while my native shape, since neither that nor the tears of beauty in affliction, which are said to reduce obdurate rocks to the softness of cotton, and tigers to the tenderness of lambs, are sufficient to melt thy haggard breast. Scourge, scourge that brawny hide of thine, stubborn and unrelenting brute—that coarse enclosure of thy coarser soul; and rouse up thus thyself from that base sloth that makes thee live only to eat and pamper thy lazy flesh, indulging still thy voracious appetite. But if my entreaties and tears cannot work thee into a reasonable compliance, if I am not yet sufficiently wretched to move thy pity, at least let the anguish of that miserable knight, thy tender master, mollify thy heart."

"What is your answer now, Sancho?" said the duchess.

"I say, as I said before," quoth Sancho, "as for the flogging, I pronounce it flat and plain."

"Renounce, you mean," said the duke.

"Good, your worship," quoth Sancho; "this is no time for me to mind niceties and spelling of letters: I have other fish to fry. This plaguy whipping-bout makes me quite distracted. I do not know what to say or do; but I would fain know of my Lady Dulcinea del Toboso where she picked up this kind of breeding, to beg thus like a sturdy beggar! Here she comes, to desire me to lash myself as raw as a piece of beef, and the best word she can give is, 'soul of a broken pitcher,' 'monster,' 'brute,' 'sheep-stealer,' with a ribble-rabble of saucy nick-names, that any one would object to bear. Do you think, mistress of mine, that my skin is made of brass? Or shall I get anything by your disenchantment? Beshrew her heart! where is the fine present she has brought along with her to soften me? A basket of fine linen, holland shirts, caps, and socks (though I wear none), had been somewhat like; but to fall upon me and bespatter me thus with dirty names, do you think that will do? No, in faith. Remember the old sayings, 'A golden load makes the burden light;' 'Gifts will enter stone walls.' Nay, my master too, who one would think should tell me a fine story, and coax me up with dainty sugar-plum words, talks of tying me to a tree, forsooth, and of doubling the whipping! Methinks those troublesome people should know who they prate to. It is not only a squire-errant they would have to whip himself, but a governor! and there is no more to do, think they, but up and ride. Let them even learn manners. There is a time for some things, and a time for all things; a time for great things, and a time for small things. Am I now in a humour to hear petitions, do you think? Just when my heart is ready to burst for having torn my new coat, they would have me tear my own flesh too."

"Upon my honour, Sancho," said the duke, "if you do not relent, you shall have no government. It would be a fine thing, indeed, that I should send among my islanders a merciless, hard-hearted tyrant, whom neither the tears of distressed damsels nor the admonitions of wise, ancient, and powerful enchanters can move to compassion. In short, sir, no stripes, no government."

"But," quoth Sancho, "may not I have a day or two to consider on it?"

"Not a minute," cried Merlin; "you must declare now, and in this very place, what you resolve to do, for Dulcinea must be again transformed into a country wench, and carried back immediately to the cave of Montesinos, there to remain till the number of stripes be made out."

"Come, come, honest Sancho," said the duchess, "pluck up a good courage, and show your gratitude to your master, whose bread you have eaten, and to whose generous nature and high feats of chivalry we are all so much obliged."

"Hark you, Mr. Merlin," quoth Sancho, without giving the duchess an answer; "pray, will you tell me one thing? How comes it about that this same man that came before you brought my master word from Signior Montesinos that he would be here, and give him directions about this disenchantment, and yet we hear no news of Montesinos all this while?"

"Pshaw!" answered Merlin, "the fellow is an ass and a lying rascal; he came from me, and not from Montesinos; for he, poor man! is still in his cave, expecting the dissolution of the spell that confines him there yet. But if he owes you any money, or you have any business with him, he shall be forthcoming when and where you please. Now, pray make an end, and undergo this small penance; it will do you a world of good, as a healthy exercise; for you are of a very sanguine complexion, Sancho, and losing a little blood will do you no harm."

"Well," quoth Sancho, "there is like to be no want of physicians in this world, I find; the very conjurors set up for doctors too. Then, since everybody says as much (though I can hardly believe it), I am content to give myself the three thousand three hundred stripes, upon condition that I may be paying them off as long as I please; observe that: though I will be out of debt as soon as I can, that the world may not be without the pretty face of the Lady Dulcinea del Toboso, which, I must own, I could never have believed to have been so handsome. Mr. Merlin (because he knows all things) shall be obliged to reckon the lashes, and take care I do not give myself one more than the tale."

"There is no fear of that," said Merlin; "for at the very last lash the Lady Dulcinea will be disenchanted, come straight to you, make you a curtsey, and give you thanks. Heaven forbid I should wrong any man of the least hair of his head."

"Well," quoth Sancho, "what must be, must be; I yield to my hard luck, and on the aforesaid terms take up with my penance."

Scarcely had Sancho spoken, when the music struck up again, and a congratulatory volley of small shot was immediately discharged. Don Quixote fell on Sancho's neck, hugging and kissing him a thousand times. The duke, the duchess, and the whole company seemed mightily pleased. The chariot moved on, and as it passed by the fair Dulcinea made the duke and duchess a bow, and Sancho a low curtsey.

And now the morn began to spread her smiling looks in the eastern quarter of the skies, and the flowers of the field to disclose their bloomy folds, and raise their fragrant heads. The brooks, now cool and clear, in gentle murmurs, played with the grey pebbles, and flowed along to pay their liquid crystal tribute to the expecting rivers. The sky was clear, the air serene, swept clean by brushing winds for the reception of the shining light, and everything, not only jointly, but in its separate gaiety, welcomed the fair Aurora, and, like her, foretold a fairer day. The duke and duchess, well pleased with the management and success of the hunting, and the counterfeit adventure, returned to the castle, resolving to make a second essay of the same nature, having received as much pleasure from the first as any reality could have produced.

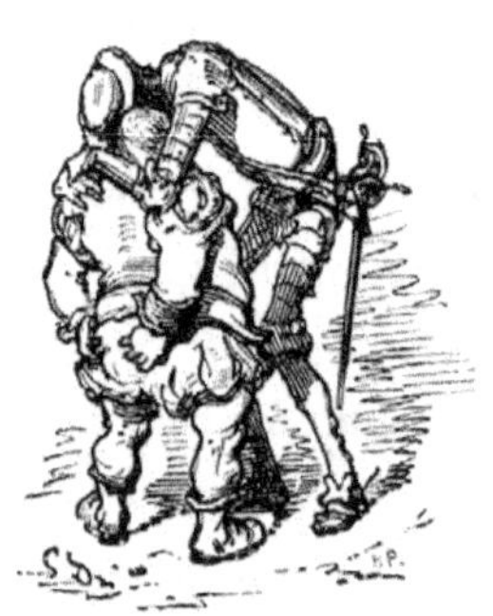

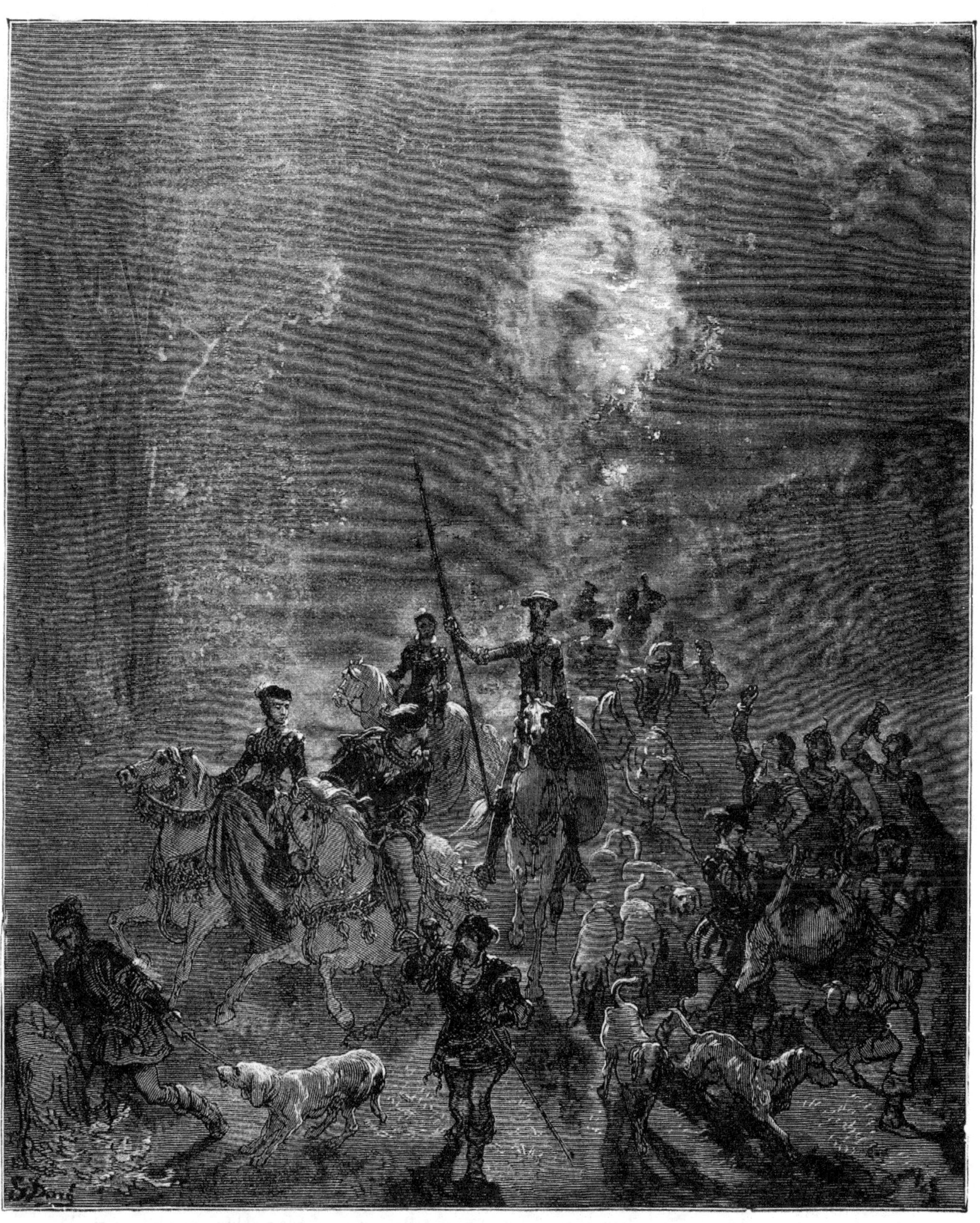

"The morn began to spread her smiling looks in the eastern quarter of the skies"

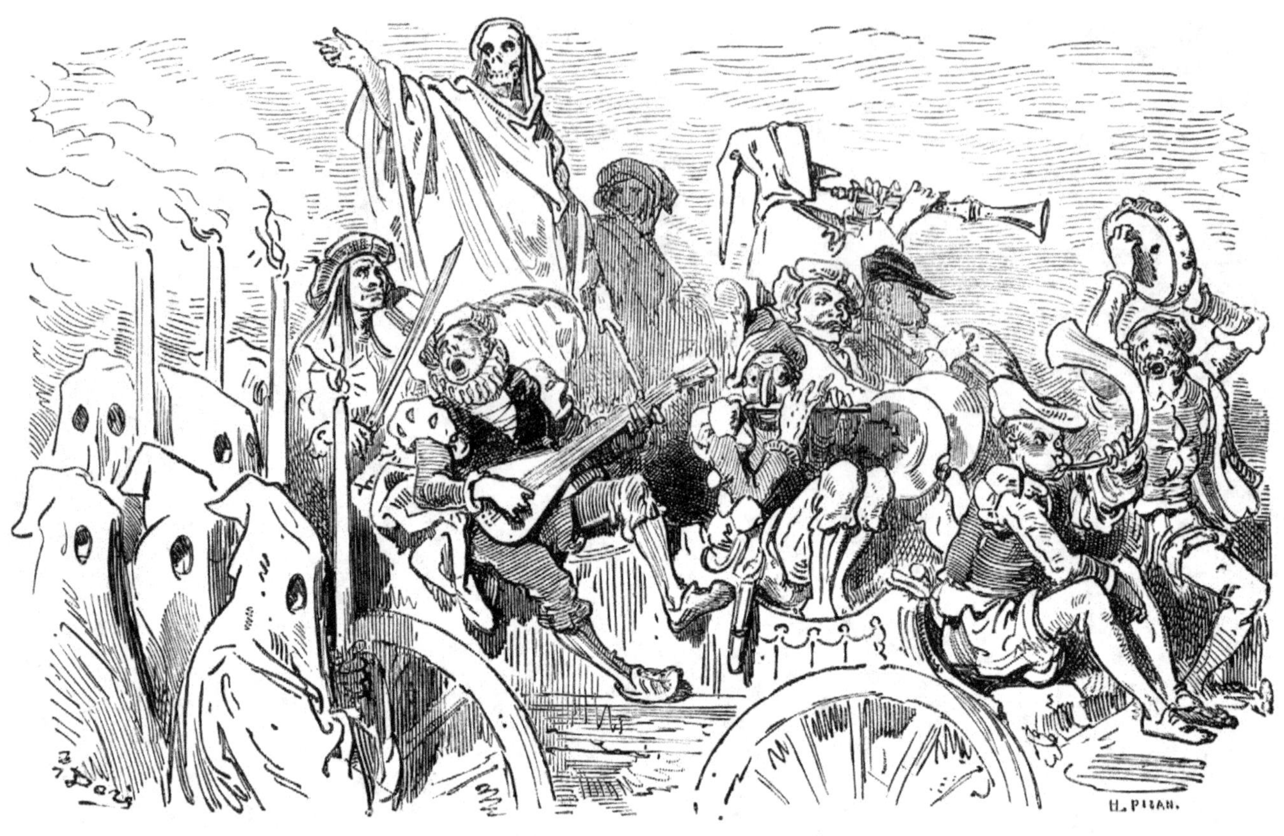

CHAPTER XXXVI.

THE STRANGE AND NEVER THOUGHT-OF ADVENTURE OF THE DISCONSOLATE MATRON, ALIAS THE COUNTESS TRIFALDI, WITH SANCHO PANZA'S LETTER TO HIS WIFE, TERESA PANZA.

THE whole contrivance of the late adventure was plotted by the duke's steward, a man of wit, and a facetious and quick fancy. He made the verses, acted Merlin himself, and instructed a page to personate Dulcinea. And now, by his master's appointment, he prepared another scene of mirth, as pleasant and as artful and surprising as can be imagined.

The next day the duchess asked Sancho whether he had begun his penitential task, to disenchant Dulcinea.

"Ay, marry have I," quoth Sancho, "for I have already lent myself five lashes on the back."

"With what, friend?" asked the duchess.

"With the palm of my hand," answered Sancho.

"Your hand!" said the duchess; "those are rather claps than lashes, Sancho; I doubt Father Merlin will not be satisfied at so easy a rate; for the liberty of so great a lady is not to be purchased at so mean a price. No, you should lash yourself with something that may make you smart: a good friar's scourge, a cat-of-nine-tails, or penitent's whip, would do well;

for letters written in blood stand good; but works of charity faintly and coldly done, lose their merit and signify nothing."

"Then, madam," quoth he, "will your worship's grace do so much as help me to a convenient rod, such as you shall think best; though it must not be too smarting, neither; for faith, though I am a clown, my flesh is as soft as any one's in the land, no disparagement to anybody, either."

"Well, well, Sancho," said she, "it shall be my care to provide you a whip that shall suit your soft constitution, as if they were twins."

"But now, my dear madam," quoth he, "you must know I have written a letter to my wife, Teresa Panza, to give her to understand how things are with me. I have it in my bosom, and it is just ready to send away; it wants nothing but the direction on the outside. Now I would have your wisdom to read it, and see if it be not written like a governor; I mean, in such a style as governors should write."

"And who penned it?" asked the duchess.

"What a question that is now!" quoth Sancho. "Who should pen it but myself, sinner as I am?"

"And did you write it too?" said the duchess.

"Not I," quoth Sancho; "for I can neither write nor read, though I can make my mark."

"Let me see the letter," said the duchess; "for I dare say your wit is set out in it to some purpose."

Sancho pulled the letter out of his bosom unsealed, and the duchess having taken it, read what follows.

"*Sancho Panza to his Wife, Teresa Panza.*

"If I am well lashed, yet I am whipped into a government: if I have got a good government, it cost me many a good lash. Thou must know, my Teresa, that I am resolved thou shalt ride in a coach; for now, any other way of going is to me but creeping on all-fours, like a kitten. Thou art now a governor's wife; guess whether any one will dare to tread on thy heels. I have sent thee a green hunting-suit which my lady duchess gave me. Pray see and get it turned into a petticoat and jacket for our daughter. The folks in this country are very ready to talk little good of my master, Don Quixote. They say he is a mad-wise-man, and a pleasant madman, and that I am not a jot behind-hand with him. We have been in the cave of Montesinos, and Merlin the wizard has pitched on me to disenchant Dulcinea del Toboso, the same who among you is called Aldonza Lorenzo. When I have given myself three thousand three hundred lashes, lacking five, she will be as disenchanted as the mother that bore her. But not a word of the pudding; for if you tell your case among a parcel of tattling gossips, you will never have done; one will cry it is white, and others it is black. I am to go to my government very suddenly, whither I go with a huge mind to make money, as I am told all new governors do. I will first see how matters go, and then send thee word whether thou hadst best come or no. Dapple is well, and gives his humble service to you. I will not part with him, though I were to be made the Great Turk. My lady duchess kisses thy hands a thousand times over; pray return her two thousand for her one: for there is nothing cheaper than fair words, as my master says. Heaven has not been pleased to make me light on another cloak-bag, with a hundred pieces of gold in it, like those you wot of. But all in good time: do not let that vex thee, my jug; the government will make it up, I will warrant thee. Though after all, one thing sticks plaguily in my gizzard: they tell me, that when once I have tasted of it, I shall be ready to eat my very fingers after it, so savoury is the sauce. Should it fall out so, I should make but an ill hand of it; and yet your maimed, crippled alms-folks pick up a pretty livelihood, and make their begging as good as a prebend. So that, one way or other, old girl, matters will go swimmingly, and thou wilt be rich and happy. Heaven make thee so, as well as it may; and keep me for thy sake. From this castle, the 20th of June, 1614.—Thy husband the Governor, "SANCHO PANZA."

"Methinks, Mr. Governor," said the duchess, having read the letter, "you are out in two particulars; first, when you intimate that this government was bestowed on you for the stripes you are to give yourself; whereas you may remember it was allotted you before this disenchantment was dreamed of. The second branch that you failed in is the discovery of your avarice, which is the most detestable quality in governors; because their self-interest is always indulged at the expense of justice. You know the saying, 'Covetousness breaks the sack,' and that vice always prompts a governor to fleece and oppress the subject."

"Truly, my good lady," quoth Sancho, "I meant no harm: I did not well think of what I wrote; and if your grace's worship does not like this letter, I will tear it and have another: but remember the old saying, 'Seldom comes a better.' I shall make but sad work of it, if I must pump my brains for it."

"No, no," said the duchess; "this will do well enough, and I must have the duke see it."

They went into the garden, where they were to dine that day, and there she showed the duke the learned epistle, which he read over with a great deal of pleasure.

After dinner Sancho was entertaining the company very pleasantly, with some of his savoury discourse, when suddenly they were surprised with the mournful sound of a fife, which played in concert with a hoarse, unbraced drum. All the company seemed amazed and discomposed at the unpleasing noise; but Don Quixote especially was so alarmed with this solemn martial harmony, that he could not compose his thoughts. Sancho's fear undoubtedly wrought the usual effects, and carried him to crouch by the duchess.

During this consternation, two men, in deep mourning-cloaks trailing on the ground, entered the garden, each of them beating a large drum, covered also with black, and with these a third playing on a fife, in mourning like the rest. They ushered in a person of gigantic stature, to which the long black garb in which he was wrapped up was no small addition. It had a train of a prodigious length, and over the cassock was girt a broad black belt, which slung a scimitar of a mighty size. His face was covered with a thin black veil, through which might be discerned a beard of a vast length, as white as snow. The solemnity of his pace kept exact time to the gravity of the music: in short, his stature, his motion, his black hue, and his attendance were every way surprising and astonishing. With this state and formality he approached, and fell on his knees at a convenient distance before the duke; who not suffering him to speak till he arose, the monstrous spectre erected his bulk, and throwing off his veil, discovered the most terrible, hugeous, white, broad, prominent, bushy beard that ever mortal eyes were frighted at. Then fixing his eyes on the duke, and with a deep, sonorous voice, roaring out from the ample cavern of his spreading lungs—

"Most high and potent lord," cried he, "my name is Trifaldin with the white beard, squire to the Countess Trifaldi, otherwise called the Disconsolate Matron, from whom I am ambassador to your grace, begging admittance for her ladyship to come and relate, before your magnificence, the unhappy and wonderful circumstances of her misfortune. But first, she desires to be informed whether the valorous and invincible knight, Don Quixote de la Mancha, resides at this time in your castle; for it is in quest of him that my lady has travelled without coach or palfrey, hungry and thirsty; and, in short, without breaking her fast, from the kingdom of Candaya, all the way to these your grace's territories—a thing incredibly miraculous, if not wrought by enchantment. She is now without the gate of this castle, waiting only for your grace's permission to enter."

This said, the squire coughed, and with both his hands stroked his unwieldy beard from the top to the bottom, and with a formal gravity waited the duke's answer.

"Worthy Squire Trifaldin with the white beard," said the duke, "long since have we heard of the misfortunes of the Countess Trifaldi, whom enchanters have occasioned to be called the Disconsolate Matron; and therefore, most stupendous squire, you may tell her that she may make her entry; and that the valiant Don Quixote de la Mancha is here present, on whose generous assistance she may safely rely for redress. Inform her also from me, that if she has occasion for my aid, she may depend on my readiness to do her service, being obliged, as I am a knight, to be aiding and assisting, to the utmost of my power, to all persons of her sex in distress, especially widowed matrons, like her ladyship."

Trifaldin, hearing this, made his obeisance with the knee, and, beckoning to the fife and drums to observe his motion, they all marched out in the same solemn procession as they entered, and left all the beholders in a deep admiration of his proportion and deportment.

Then the duke, turning to Don Quixote, "Behold, Sir Knight," said he, "how the light and the glory of virtue dart their beams through the clouds of malice and ignorance, and shine to the remotest parts of the earth. It is hardly six days since you have vouchsafed to honour this castle with your presence, and already the afflicted and distressed flock hither from the uttermost regions, not in coaches, or on dromedaries. but on foot, and without eating by the way; such is their confidence in the strength of that arm, the fame of whose great exploits flies and spreads everywhere, and makes the whole world acquainted with your valour."

"What would I give, my lord," said Don Quixote, "that the same holy pedant were here now, who, the other day at your table, would have run down knight-errantry at such a rate, that the testimony of his own eyes might convince him of the absurdity of his error, and let him see that the comfortless and afflicted do not, in enormous misfortunes, and uncommon adversity, repair for redress to the doors of droning churchmen, or your little parish priests of villages; nor to the fireside of your country gentleman, who never travels beyond his landmark; nor to the lolling lazy courtier, who rather hearkens after news which he may relate than endeavours to perform such deeds as may deserve to be recorded and related! No, the protection of damsels, the comfort of widows, the redress of the injured, and the support of the distressed, are nowhere so perfectly to be expected as from the generous professors of knight-errantry. Therefore I thank Heaven a thousand times for having qualified me to answer the necessities of the miserable by such a function. As for the hardships and accidents that may attend me, I look upon them as no discouragements, since proceeding from so noble a cause. Then let this matron be admitted to make known her request, and I will refer her for redress to the force of my arm, and the intrepid resolution of my courageous soul."

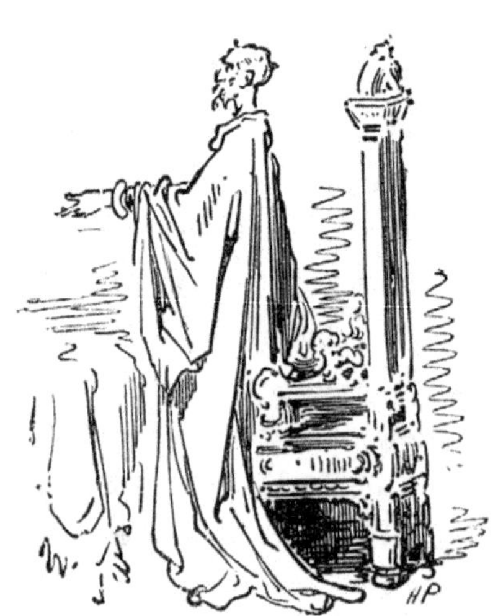

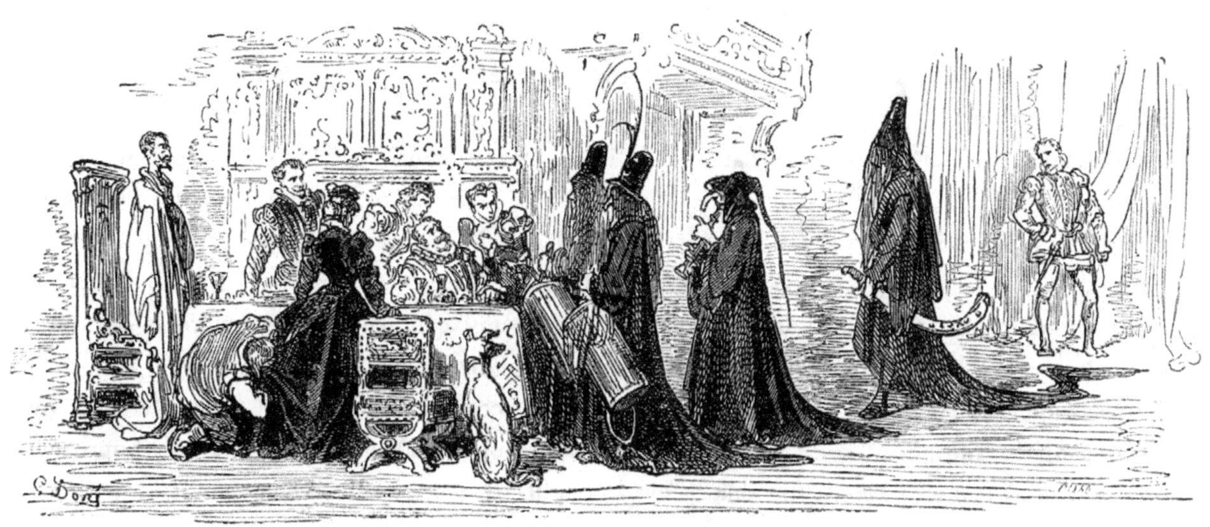

CHAPTER XXXVII.

THE FAMOUS ADVENTURE OF THE DISCONSOLATE MATRON CONTINUED.

THE duke and duchess were mightily pleased to find Don Quixote wrought up to a resolution so agreeable to their design. But Sancho, who made his observations, was not so well satisfied. "I am in a bodily fear," quoth he, "that this same Mistress Waiting-woman will be a balk to my preferment. I remember I once knew a Toledo apothecary, that talked like a canary bird, and used to say, 'Wherever come old waiting-women, good luck can happen there to no man.' Bless me! he knew them too well, and therefore valued them accordingly. He could have eaten them all with a grain of salt. Since, then, the best of them are so plaguy troublesome and impertinent, what will those be that are in doleful dumps, like this same Countess Threefolds, three skirts, or three tails, what do you call her?"

"Hold your tongue, Sancho," said Don Quixote. "This matron, that comes so far in search of me, lives too remote to lie under the lash of the apothecary's satire. Besides, you are to remember she is a countess; and when ladies of that quality become governantes, or waiting-women, it is only to queens or empresses; and in their own houses they are as absolute ladies as any others, and attended by other waiting-women."

"Ay, ay," cried Donna Rodriguez, who was present, "there are some that serve my lady duchess here in that capacity, that might have been countesses too, had they had better luck. But we are not all born to be rich, though we are all born to be honest. When all is said, whoever will offer to meddle with waiting-women will get little by it. 'Many go out for wool, and come home shorn themselves.' These squires, forsooth, can find no other pastime than to abuse us, and tell idle stories of us, unburying our bones, and burying our reputation. But their tongues are no slander; and I can tell those silly rake-shames, that, in spite of their flouts, we shall keep the upper hand of them, and live in the world in the better sort of houses. though we starve for it."

"I fancy," said the duchess, "that honest Rodriguez is much in the right: but we must now choose a fitter time for this dispute, to confound the ill opinion of that wicked apothecary, and to root out that which the great Sancho Panza has fixed in his breast."

"For my part," quoth Sancho, "I will not dispute with her; for since the thoughts of being a governor have steamed up into my brains, all my concern for the squire is vanished into smoke; and I care not a wild fig for all the waiting-women in the world."

This subject would have engaged them longer in discourse, had they not been cut short by the sound of the fife and drums that gave them notice of the Disconsolate Matron's approach. Thereupon the duchess asked the duke how it might be proper to receive her, and how far ceremony was due to her quality as a countess.

"Look you," quoth Sancho, striking in before the duke could answer, "I would advise you to meet her countess-ship half-way; but for the waiting-womanship, do not stir a step."

"Who bids you trouble yourself?" said Don Quixote.

"Who bid me?" answered Sancho; "why, I myself did. Have not I been squire to your worship, and thus served a 'prenticeship to good manners? And have not I had the Flower of Courtesy for my master, who has often told me a man may as well lose at one-and-thirty with a card too much, as a card too little? Good wits jump; 'a word to the wise is enough.'"

"Sancho says well," said the duke; "to decide the matter, we will first see what kind of a countess she is, and behave ourselves accordingly."

Now the fife and the drums entered as before. But here the author ends this short chapter, and begins another, prosecuting the same adventure, which is one of the most notable in the history.

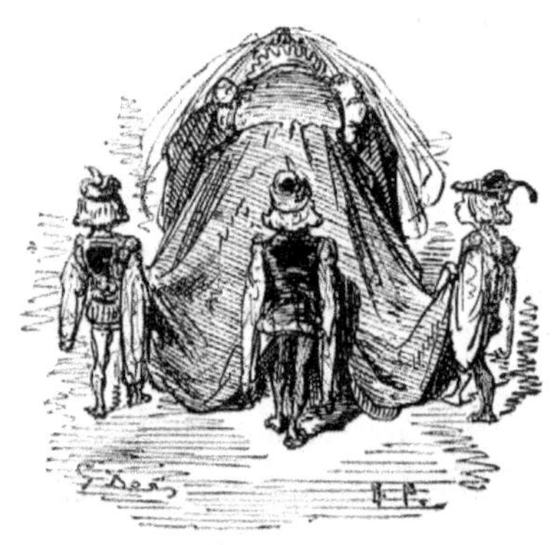

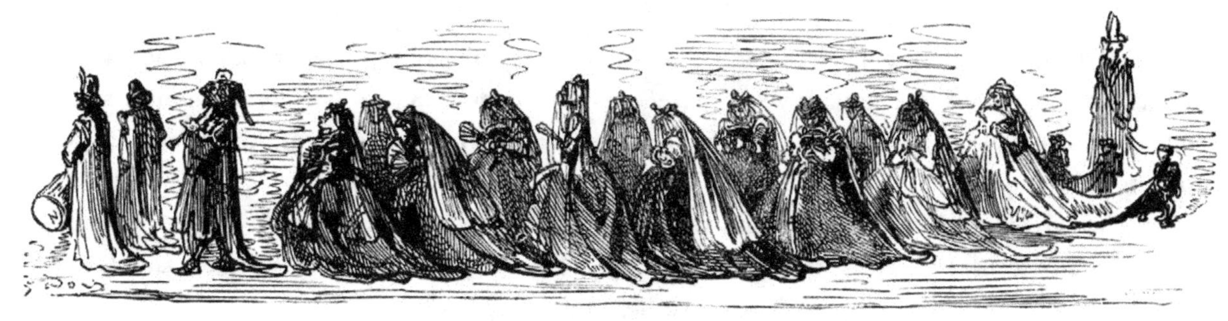

CHAPTER XXXVIII.

THE ACCOUNT WHICH THE DISCONSOLATE MATRON GIVES OF HER MISFORTUNE.

THE doleful drums and fife were followed by twelve elderly waiting-women, that entered the garden ranked in pairs, all clad in large mourning habits, that seemed to be of milled serge, over which they wore veils of white calico, so long, that nothing could be seen of their black dress but the very bottom. After them came the Countess Trifaldi, handed by her squire, Trifaldin with the white beard. The lady was dressed in a suit of the finest baize, which, had it been napped, would have had tufts as big as Rounceval pease. Her train, or tail, which you will, was mathematically divided into three equal skirts, or angles, and borne up by three pages in mourning; and from this pleasant triangular figure of her train, as every one conjectured, was she called Trifaldi, as one should say, the Countess of Three-Folds, or Three-Skirts. Benengeli is of the same opinion, though he affirms that her true title was the Countess of Lobuna, or of Wolf-Land, from the abundance of wolves bred in her country; and, had they been foxes, she had, by the same rule, been called the Countess of Zorruna, or of Fox-Land; it being a custom, in those nations, for great persons to take their denominations from the commodity with which their country most abounds. However, this countess chose to borrow her title from this new fashion of her own invention, and leaving her name of Lobuna, took that of Trifaldi.

Her twelve female attendants approached with her in a procession pace, with black veils over their faces; not transparent, like that of Trifaldin, but thick enough to hinder altogether the sight of their countenances. As soon as the whole train of waiting-women was come in, the duke, the duchess, and Don Quixote stood up, and so did all those who were with them. Then the twelve women, ranging themselves in two rows, made a lane for the countess to march up between them, which she did, still led by Trifaldin, her squire. The duke, the duchess, and Don Quixote advancing about a dozen paces to meet her, she fell on her knees, and, with a voice rather hoarse and rough than clear and delicate, "May it please your highnesses," said she, "to spare yourselves the trouble of receiving with so much ceremony and compliment a man (a woman, I would say) who is your devoted servant. Alas! the sense of my misfortunes has so troubled my intellectuals, that my responses cannot be supposed able to answer the critical opinion of your presence. My understanding has forsaken me, and is gone a wool-gathering; and sure it is far remote, for the more I seek it, the more unlikely I am to find it again."

"The greatest claim, madam," answered the duke, "that we can lay to sense is a due respect and decent deference to the worthiness of your person, which, without any further view, sufficiently bespeaks your merit and excellent qualifications."

Then, begging the honour of her hand, he led her up and placed her in a chair by his duchess, who received her with all the ceremony suitable to the occasion.

Don Quixote said nothing all this while, and Sancho was sneaking about, and peeping under the veils of the lady's women, but to no purpose, for they kept themselves very close and silent, until she at last thus began: "Confident I am, thrice potent lord, thrice beautiful lady, and thrice intelligent auditors, that my most unfortunate miserableness shall find, in your most generous and compassionate bowels, a most misericordial sanctuary; my miserableness, which is such as would liquefy marble, malleate steel, and mollify adamantine rocks. But, before the rehearsal of my ineffable misfortunes enter, I will not say your ears, but the public mart of your hearing faculties, I earnestly request that I may have cognisance whether the cabal, choir, or conclave of this most illustrissimous appearance be not adorned with the presence of the adjutoriferous Don Quixote de la Manchissima, and his squirissimous Panza."

"Panza is at your elbowissimus," quoth Sancho, before anybody else could answer, "and Don Quixotissimo likewise; therefore, most dolorous medem, you may tell out your teale, for we are all ready to be your ladyship's servitorissimus, to the best of our capacities, and so forth."

Don Quixote then advanced, and addressing the countess, "If your misfortunes, embarrassed lady," said he, "may hope any redress from the power and assistance of knight-errantry, I offer you my force and courage; and, such as they are, I dedicate them to your service. I am Don Quixote de la Mancha, whose profession is a sufficient obligation to succour the distressed, without the formality of preambles, or the elegance of oratory, to circumvent my favour. Therefore, pray, madam, let us know by a succinct and plain account of your calamities, what remedies should be applied; and, if your griefs are such as do not admit of a cure, assure yourself at least that we will comfort you in your afflictions, by sympathising in your sorrow."

The lady, hearing this, threw herself at Don Quixote's feet, in spite of his kind endeavours to the contrary; and, striving to embrace them, "Most invincible knight," said she, "I prostrate myself at these feet, the foundations and pillars of chivalry-errant, the supporters of my drooping spirits, whose indefatigable steps alone can hasten my relief, and the cure of my afflictions. Oh, valorous knight-errant, whose real achievements eclipse and obscure the fabulous legend of the Amadises, Esplandians, and Belianises!" Then, turning from Don Quixote, she laid hold on Sancho, and squeezing his hands very hard, "And thou, the most loyal squire that ever attended on the magnanimity of knight-errantry, whose goodness is more extensive than the beard of my usher Trifaldin! how happily have thy stars placed thee under the discipline of the whole martial college of chivalry professors, centred and epitomised in the single Don Quixote! I conjure thee, by thy love of goodness, and thy unspotted loyalty to so great a master, to employ thy moving and interceding eloquence in my behalf, that eftsoons his favour may shine upon this humble and most disconsolate countess."

"Look you, Madam Countess," quoth Sancho, "as for measuring my goodness by your squire's beard, that is neither here nor there; so that my soul go to heaven when I depart this life, I do not matter the rest; for, as for the beards of this world, it is not what I stand upon, so that, without all this pawing and wheedling, I will put in a word or two for you to my master. I know he loves me; and, besides, at this time, he stands in need of me about a certain business, and he shall do what he can for you. But, pray, discharge your burthened mind; unload, and let us see what griefs you bring, and then leave us to take care of the rest."

The duke and duchess were ready to burst with laughing, to find the adventure run in this pleasant strain; and they admired, at the same time, the rare cunning and management of Trifaldi, who, resuming her seat, thus began her story: "The famous kingdom of Candaya, situate between the Great Taprobana and the South Sea, about two leagues beyond Cape Comorin, had for its queen the Lady Donna Maguntia, whose husband, King Archipielo dying, left the Princess Antonomasia, their only child, heiress to the crown. This princess was educated and brought up under my care and direction, I being the eldest and first lady of the bed-chamber to the queen, her mother. In process of time, the young princess arrived at the age of fourteen years, and appeared so perfectly beautiful, that it was not in the power of Nature to give any addition to her charms; what is yet more, her mind was no less adorned than her body. Wisdom itself was but a fool to her. She was no less discreet than fair, and the fairest creature in the world: and so she is still, unless the fatal knife, or unrelenting shears, of the envious and inflexible sisters have cut her thread of life. But sure the heavens would not permit such an injury to be done to the earth, as the lopping off the loveliest branch that ever adorned the garden of the world.

"Her beauty, which my unpolished tongue can never sufficiently praise, attracting all eyes, soon got her a world of adorers, many of them princes, who were her neighbours, and more distant foreigners; among the rest, a private knight, who resided at court, and was so audacious as to raise his thoughts to that heaven of beauty. This young gentleman was indeed master of all gallantries that the air of his courtly education could inspire; and so, confiding in his youth, his handsome mien, his agreeable air and dress, his graceful carriage, and the charms of his easy wit, and other qualifications, he followed the impulse of his inordinate and most presumptuous passion. I must needs say that he was an extraordinary person; he played to a miracle on the guitar, and made it speak not only to the ears, but to the very soul. He danced to admiration, and had such a rare knack at making bird-cages, that he might have got an estate by that very art; and, to sum up all his accomplishments, he was a poet. So many endowments were sufficient to have moved a mountain, and much more the heart of a young, tender virgin. But all his fine arts and soothing behaviour had proved ineffectual against my beautiful charge, if the cunning rogue had not first conquered me. The wily villain endeavoured to bribe the keeper, so to secure the keys of the fortress. In short, he so plied me with pleasing trifles, and so insinuated himself into my soul, that, at last, he perfectly bewitched me, and made me give way, before I was aware, to what I should never have permitted. But that which first wrought me to his purpose was a copy of verses he sung one night under my window, which, if I remember right, began thus :—

A SONG.

A secret fire consumes my heart;
  And, to augment my raging pain,
The charming foe that rais'd the smart,
  Denies me freedom to complain.
But sure 'tis just we should conceal
The bliss and woe in love we feel:
  For, oh! what human tongue can tell
  The joys of heaven, or pains of hell?

"The words were to me so many pearls of eloquence, and his voice sweeter to my ears than sugar to the taste. The reflection on the misfortune which these verses brought on me has often made me applaud Plato's design of banishing all poets from a good commonwealth. For, instead of composing lamentable verses, like those of the Marquis of Mantua, that make the women and children cry by the fireside, they try their utmost skill on such soft strokes as enter the soul, and wound it, like that thunder which hurts and consumes all within, yet leaves the garment sound. Another time he entertained me with the following song:—

A SONG.

Death, put on some kind disguise,
And at once my heart surprise
For 'tis such a curse to live,
  And so great a bliss to die,
Shouldst thou any warning give,
  I'd relapse to life for joy

"Many other verses of this kind he plied me with, which charmed when read, but transported when sung. For you must know that, when our eminent poets debase themselves to the writing a sort of composure called love-madrigals and roundelays, now much in vogue in Candaya, those verses are no sooner heard than they presently produce a dancing of souls, tickling of fancies, emotion of spirits; and, in short, a pleasing distemper in the whole body, as if quicksilver shook it in every part.

"So that, once more, I pronounce those poets very dangerous, and fit to be banished to the Isles of Lizards; though, truly, I must confess, the fault is rather chargeable on those foolish people that commend, and the silly wenches that believe them. For, had I been as cautious as my place required, his amorous serenades could never have moved me; nor would I have believed his poetical cant, such as, 'I dying live,' 'I burn in ice,' 'I shiver in flames,' 'I hope in despair,' 'I go, yet stay;' with a thousand such contradictions, which make up the greatest part of those kind of compositions. As ridiculous are their promises of the Phœnix of Arabia, Ariadne's crown, the coursers of the sun, the pearls of the southern ocean, the gold of Tagus, the balsam of Panchaya, and Heaven knows what!

"But whither, woe 's me! whither do I wander, miserable woman? What madness prompts me to accuse the faults of others, having so long a score of my own to answer for? Alas! not his verses, but my own inclination; not his music, but my own levity; not his wit, but my own folly, opened a passage, and levelled the way for Don Clavijo (for that was the name of the knight). In short, I procured him admittance; and, by my connivance, he very often met Antonomasia, who, poor lady! was rather deluded by me than by him. But, wicked as I was, it was upon the honourable score of marriage; for, had he not been engaged to be her husband, he should not have touched the very shadow of her shoe-string. The intrigue was kept very close for some time, by my cautious management; but, at last, consulting upon the matter, we found there was but one way; Don Clavijo should demand the young lady in marriage before the curate, by virtue of a promise under her hand, which I dictated for the purpose, and so binding, that all the strength of Samson himself could not have broken the tie. The business was put in execution, the note was produced before the priest, who, examining the lady, and finding her confession to agree with the tenor of the contract, put her in custody of a very honest sergeant."

"Bless us!" quoth Sancho, "sergeants too, and poets, and songs, and verses, in your country! o' my conscience, I think the world is the same all the world over. But go on, Madam Trifaldi, I beseech you, for it is late, and I am upon thorns till I know the end of this story."

"I will," answered the countess.

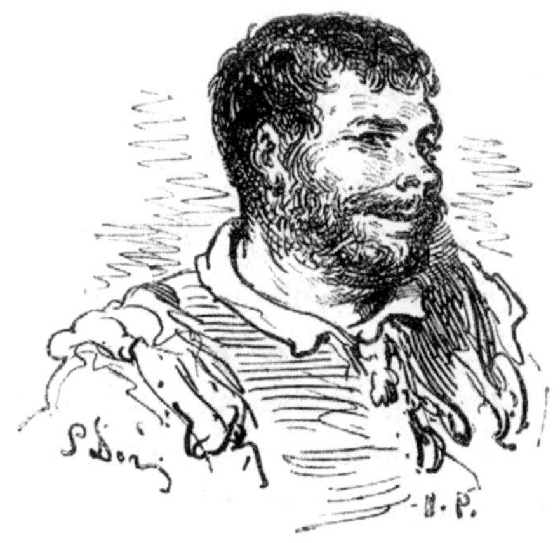

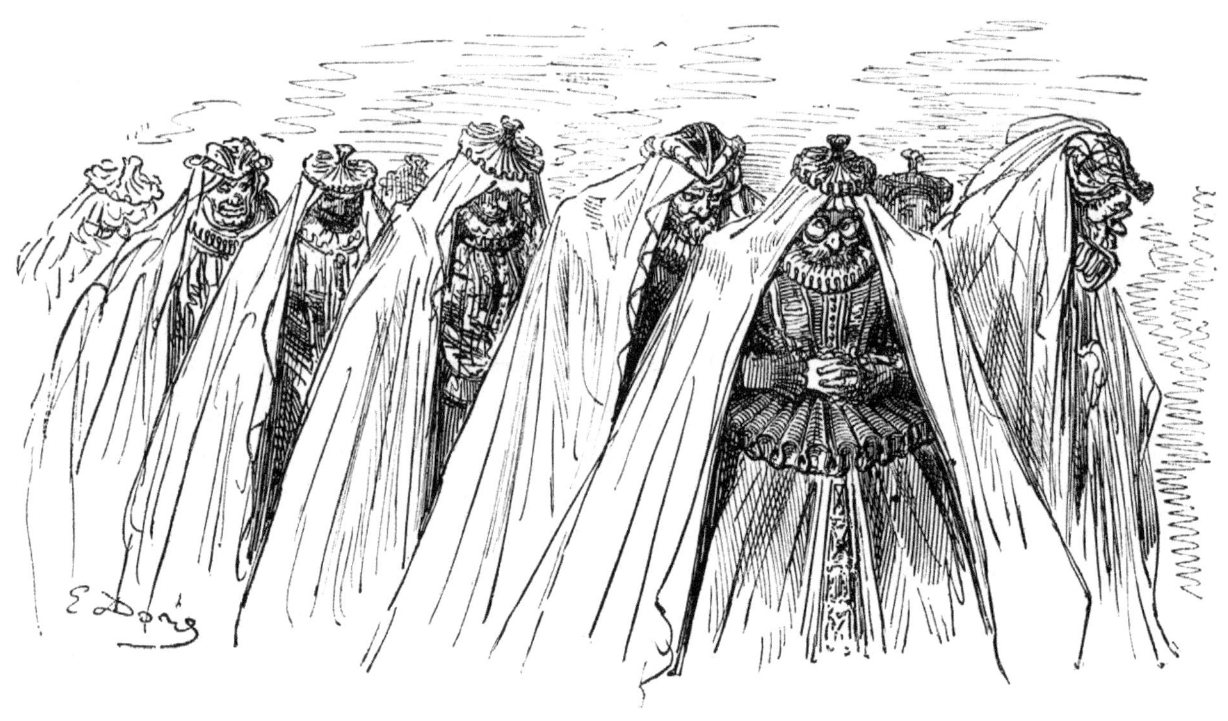

CHAPTER XXXIX.

WHERE TRIFALDI CONTINUES HER STUPENDOUS AND MEMORABLE STORY.

IF every word that Sancho spoke gave the duchess new pleasure, everything he said put Don Quixote to as much pain; so that he commanded him silence, and gave the matron opportunity to go on. "In short," said she, "the business was debated a good while; and, after many questions and answers, the princess firmly persisting in her first declaration, judgment was given in favour of Don Clavijo, which Queen Maguntia, her mother, took so to heart that we buried her about three days after."

"Then, without doubt, she died," quoth Sancho.

"That is a clear case," replied Trifaldin; "for, in Candaya, they do not use to bury the living, but the dead."

"But, with your good leave, Mr. Squire," answered Sancho, "people that were in a swoon have been buried alive before now; and methinks Queen Maguntia should only have swooned away, and not have been in such haste to have died in good earnest; for, 'while there is life there is hope,' and there is a remedy for all things but death. I do not find the young lady was so much out of the way neither, that the mother should lay it so grievously to heart. Indeed, had she married a footman, or some other servant in the family, as I am told many others have done, it had been a very bad business, and past curing; but, for the queen to make such a heavy outcry, when her daughter married such a fine-bred young knight, faith and troth, I think the business had better have been made up. It was a slip, but not such a heinous one as some would think; for, as my master here says, and he will not let me tell a lie, as of scholars they make bishops, so of your knights (chiefly if they be errant) one may easily make kings and emperors."

"That is most certain," said Don Quixote. "Turn a knight-errant loose into the wide world, with two-penny worth of good fortune, and he is *in potentia propinqua* (*proxima*, I would say) the greatest emperor in the world. But let the lady proceed, for hitherto her story has been very pleasant, and I doubt the most bitter part of it is still untold."

"The most bitter, truly, sir," answered she; "and so bitter, that wormwood and every bitter herb, compared to it, are as sweet as honey.

"The queen being really dead," continued she, "and not in a trance, we buried her; and, scarce had we done her the last offices, and taken our last leave, when (*quis talia fando temperet a lachrymis?* who can relate such woes, and not be drowned in tears?) the giant Malambruno, cousin-german to the deceased queen, who, besides his native cruelty, was also a magician, appeared upon her grave, mounted on a wooden horse, and, by his dreadful, angry looks, showed he came thither to revenge the death of his relation, by punishing Don Clavijo for his presumption, and Antonomasia for her oversight. Accordingly, he immediately enchanted them both upon the very tomb; transforming her into a brazen female monkey, and the young knight into a hideous crocodile, of an unknown metal; and, between them both, he set an inscription, in the Syriac tongue, which we have got since translated into the Candayan, and then into Spanish, to this effect:

"'These two presumptuous lovers shall never recover their natural shapes, till the valorous Knight of La Mancha enter into a single combat with me; for, by the irrevocable decrees of fate, this unheard-of adventure is reserved for his unheard-of courage.'

"This done, he drew a broad scimitar, of a monstrous size, and, catching me fast by the hair, made an offer to cut my throat, or to whip off my head. I was frighted almost to death, my hair stood on end, and my tongue clave to the roof of my mouth. However, recovering myself as well as I could, trembling and weeping, I begged mercy in such a moving accent, and in such tender, melting words, that, at last, my entreaties prevailed on him to stop the cruel execution. In short, he ordered all the waiting-women at court to be brought before him, the same that you see here at present; and, after he had aggravated our breach of trust, and railed against the deceitful practices, and what else he could urge in scandal of our profession, reviling us for the fact of which I alone stood guilty—'I will not punish you with instant death,' said he, 'but inflict a punishment which shall be a lasting and eternal mortification.'

"Now, in the very instant of his denouncing our sentence, we felt the pores of our faces to open, and all about them perceived an itching pain, like the pricking of pins and needles. Thereupon clapping our hands to our faces, we found them as you shall see them immediately."

Saying this, the Disconsolate Matron, and her attendants, throwing off their veils, exposed their faces, all rough with bristly beards, some red, some black, some white, and others motley. The duke and duchess wondered, Don Quixote and Sancho were astonished, and the standers by were thunder-struck.

"Thus," said the countess, proceeding, "has that wicked and evil-minded Malambruno served us, and planted these rough and horrid bristles on our faces, otherwise most delicately smooth. Oh! that he had chopped off our heads with his monstrous scimitar, rather than to have disgraced our faces with these brushes upon them! For, gentlemen, if you rightly and truly consider it, what I have to say should be attended with a flood of tears; but such rivers and oceans have fallen from me already upon this doleful subject, that my eyes are as dry as chaff; and, therefore, pray let me speak without tears at this time. Where, alas! shall a waiting-woman dare to show her head with such a furze-bush upon her chin? What charitable person will entertain her? What relations will own her? At the best, we can scarcely make our faces passable, though we torture them with a thousand slops and washes; and, even thus, we have much ado to get the men to care for us. What will become of her, then, that wears a thicket upon her face? Oh, ladies and companions of my misery! in an ill hour were we begotten, and in a worse came we into the world!"

With these words the Disconsolate Matron seemed to faint away.

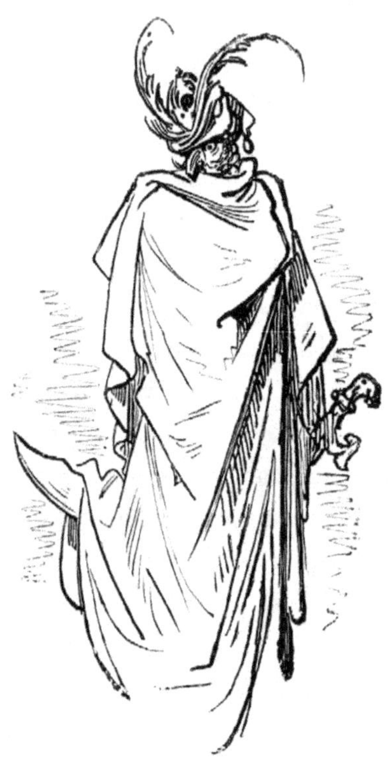

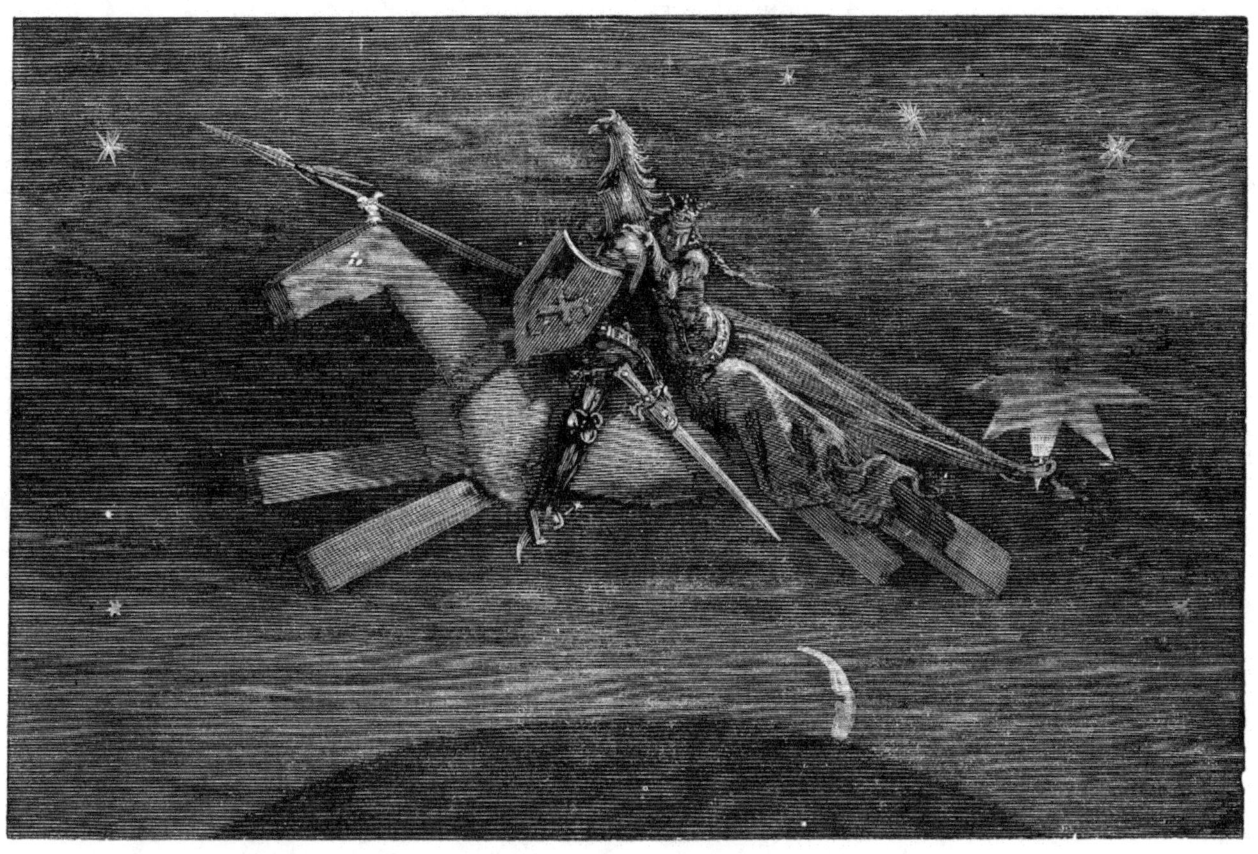

CHAPTER XL.

OF SOME THINGS THAT RELATE TO THIS ADVENTURE, AND APPERTAIN TO THIS MEMORABLE STORY.

ALL persons that love to read histories of the nature of this, must certainly be very much obliged to Cid Hamet, the original author, who has taken such care in delivering every minute particular distinctly entire, without concealing the least circumstance that might heighten the humour, or, if omitted, have obscured the light and the truth of the story. He draws lively pictures of the thoughts, discovers the imaginations, satisfies curiosity in secrets, clears doubts, resolves arguments; and, in short, makes manifest the least atoms of the most inquisitive desire. Oh, most famous author! oh, fortunate Don Quixote! oh, renowned Dulcinea! oh, facetious Sancho! jointly and severally may you live, and continue to the latest posterity, for the general delight and recreation of mankind. But the story goes on.

"Now, on my honest word," quoth Sancho, when he saw the matron in a swoon, "and by the blood of all the Panzas, my forefathers, I never heard nor saw the like, neither did my master ever tell me, or so much as conceive in that working headpiece of his, such an adventure as this. Now, all the spirits (and I would not curse anybody) run away with thee, thou giant Malambruno! Couldst thou find no other punishment for these poor sinners, but by clapping scrubbing-brushes about their muzzles? Had it not been much better to slit their nostrils half way up their noses, though they had snuffled for it a little, than to have planted these quick-set hedges over their chaps? I will lay any man a wager now, the poor creatures have not money enough to pay for their shaving."

"It is but too true, sir," said one of them, "we have not wherewithal to pay for taking our beards off; so that some of us, to save charges, are forced to lay on plaisters of pitch that pull away roots and all, and leave our chins as smooth as the bottom of a stone-mortar. There is indeed a sort of women in Candaya, that go about from house to house to take off the down or hairs that grow about the face, trim the eye-brows, and do twenty other little private jobs for the women; but we here, who are my lady's duennas, would never have anything to do with them, for they have got ill names; so, if my Lord Don Quixote do not relieve us, our beards will stick by us as long as we live."

"I will have mine plucked off hair by hair among the Moors," answered Don Quixote, "rather than not free you from yours."

"Ah, valorous knight!" cried the Countess Trifaldi, recovering that moment from her fit, "the sweet sound of your promise reached my hearing in the very midst of my trance, and has perfectly restored my senses. I beseech you therefore once again, most illustrious sir, and invincible knight-errant, that your gracious promise may soon have the wished-for effect."

"I will be guilty of no neglect, madam," answered Don Quixote. "Point out the way, and you shall soon be convinced of my readiness to serve you."

"You must know then, sir," said the Disconsolate Lady, "from this place to the kingdom of Candaya, by computation, we reckon about five thousand leagues, two or three more or less: but if you ride through the air in a direct line, it is not above three thousand two hundred and twenty-seven. You are likewise to understand, that Malambruno told me that when fortune should make me find out the knight who is to dissolve our enchantment, he would send him a famous steed, much easier, and less resty and full of tricks, than those jades that are commonly let out to hire, as being the same wooden horse that carried the valorous Peter of Provence and the fair Magalona, when he stole her away. It is managed by a wooden peg in its forehead, instead of a bridle, and flies so swiftly through the air as if all the spirits of evil were switching him, or blowing fire in his tail. This courser tradition delivers to have been the handiwork of the sage Merlin, who never lent him to any but particular friends, or when he was paid sauce for him. Among others, his friend Peter of Provence borrowed him, and by the help of his wonderful speed stole away the fair Magalona, as I said, setting her behind on the crupper (for you must know he carries double), and so towering up in the air, he left the people that stood near the place whence he started gaping, staring, and amazed.

"Since that journey we have heard of nobody that has backed him; but this we know, that Malambruno, since that, got him by his art, and has used, ever since, to post about to all parts of the world. He is here to-day, and to-morrow in France, and the next day in America. And one of the best properties of the horse is, that he costs not a farthing in keeping, for he neither eats nor sleeps, neither needs he any shoeing; besides, without having wings, he ambles so very easy through the air, that you may carry in your hand a cup full of water a thousand leagues, and not spill a drop; so that the fair Magalona loved mightily to ride him."

"Nay," quoth Sancho, "as for an easy pacer, commend me to Dapple. Indeed, he is none of your highflyers, he cannot gallop in the air; but, on the king's highway, he shall pace you with the best ambler that ever went on four legs."

This set the whole company a-laughing; but then the Disconsolate Lady going on, "This horse," said she, "will certainly be here within half an hour after it is dark, if Malambruno designs to put an end to our misfortunes, for that was the sign by which I should discover my deliverer."

"And pray, forsooth," quoth Sancho, "how many will this same horse carry upon occasion?"

"Two," answered she; "one on the saddle, and the other behind on the crupper, and those two are commonly the knight and the squire, if some stolen damsel be not to be one."

"Good disconsolate madam," quoth Sancho, "I would fain know the name of this nag."

"The horse's name," answered she, "is neither Pegasus, like Bellerophon's; nor Bucephalus, like Alexander's; nor Brilladoro, like Orlando's; nor Bayard, like Rinaldo's; nor Frontin, like Rogero's; nor Bootes, nor Pyrithous, like the horses of the Sun; neither is he called Orelia, like the horse which Roderigo, the last King of Spain of the Gothic race, bestrode that unfortunate day when he lost the battle, the kingdom, and his life."

"I will lay you a wager," quoth Sancho, "since the horse goes by none of those famous names, he does not go by that of Rozinante neither, which is my master's horse, and another guess-beast than you have reckoned up."

"It is very right," answered the bearded lady; "however, he has a very proper and significant name, for he is called Clavileno, or Wooden Peg the Swift, from the wooden peg in his forehead; so that, from the significancy of name at least, he may be compared with Rozinante."

"I find no fault with his name," quoth Sancho; "but what kind of bridle or halter do you manage him with?"

"I told you already," replied she, "that he is guided by the peg, which, being turned this way or that way, he moves accordingly, either mounting aloft in the air, or almost brushing and sweeping the ground, or else flying in the middle region, the way which ought indeed most to be chosen in all affairs of life."

"I should be glad to see this notable tit," quoth Sancho; "but do not desire to get on his back, either before or behind. No, by my holy dame, you may as well expect pears from an elm. It were a pretty jest, I trow, for me that can hardly sit my own Dapple, with a pack-saddle as soft as silk, to suffer myself to be horsed upon a hard wooden thing, without either cushion or pillow under my seat. Before George! I will not gall myself to take off the best lady's beard in the land. Let them that have beards wear them still, or get them whipped off as they think best; I will not take such a long jaunt with my master, not I. There is no need of me in this shaving of beards, as there was in Dulcinea's business."

"Upon my word, dear sir, but there is," replied Trifaldi; "and so much, that without you nothing can be done."

"God save the king!" cried Sancho; "what have we squires to do with our master's adventures? We must bear the trouble, forsooth, and they run away with the credit! Bless me! it were something would those that write their stories but give the squires their due shares in their books; as thus, 'Such a knight ended such an adventure; but it was with the help of such a one, his squire, without which he certainly could never have done it.' But they shall barely tell you in their histories, 'Sir Paralipomenon, Knight of the Three Stars, ended the adventure of the six hobgoblins,' and not a word all the while of his squire's person, as if there were no such man, though he was by all the while. In short, good people, I do not like it; and, once more, I say, my master may even go by himself for Sancho, and joy betide him. I will stay and keep Madam Duchess company here; and mayhap, by that time he comes back, he will find his Lady Dulcinea's business pretty forward, for I mean to give myself a whipping, till I brush off the very hair, at idle times, that is, when I have nothing else to do."

"Nevertheless, honest Sancho," said the duchess, "if your company be necessary in this adventure, you must go, for all good people will make it their business to entreat you; and it would look very ill, that, through your vain fears, these poor gentlewomen should remain thus with rough and bristly faces."

"God save the king, I cry again," said Sancho; "were it a piece of charity for the relief of some good, sober gentlewoman, or poor, innocent hospital-girls, something might be said; but to gall my sides, and venture my neck, to unbeard a pack of idling, trolloping chamber-jades, with a murrain! Not I, let them go elsewhere for a shaver. I wish I might see the whole tribe of them wear beards, from the highest to the lowest, from the proudest to the primest, all hairy like so many she-goats."

"You are very angry with the waiting-women, Sancho," said the duchess; "that apothecary has inspired you with this bitter spirit. But you are to blame, friend, for I will assure you there are some in my family that may serve for patterns of discretion to all those of their function; and Donna Rodriguez here will let me say no less."

"Ay, ay, madam," said Donna Rodriguez, "your grace may say what you please. This is a censorious world we live in, but Heaven knows all; and whether good or bad, bearded or unbearded, we waiting-gentlewomen had mothers as well as the rest of our sex; and since

Providence has made us as we are, and placed us in the world, it knows wherefore; and so we trust in its mercy, and nobody's beard."

"Enough, Donna Rodriguez," said Don Quixote. "As for you, Lady Trifaldi, and other distressed matrons, I hope that Heaven will speedily look with a pitying eye on your sorrows, and that Sancho will do as I shall desire. I only wish Clavileno would once come, that I may encounter Malambruno; for I am sure no razor should be more expeditious in shaving your ladyship's beard, than my sword to shave that giant's head from his shoulders. Heaven may a while permit the wicked, but not for ever."

"Ah! most valorous champion," said the Disconsolate Matron, "may all the stars in the celestial regions shed their most propitious influence on your generous valour, which thus supports the cause of our unfortunate office, so exposed to the poisonous rancour of apothecaries, and so reviled by saucy grooms and squires. Now, an ill-luck attend the low-spirited being who, in the flower of her youth, will not rather choose to turn nun than waiting-woman! Poor, forlorn, contemned creatures as we are, though descended, in a direct line from father to son, from Hector of Troy himself; yet would not our ladies find a more civil way to speak to us than thee and thou, though it were to gain them a kingdom. Oh, giant Malambruno! thou who, though an enchanter, art always most faithful to thy word, send us the peerless Clavileno, that our misfortunes may have an end; for if the weather grows hotter than it is, and these shaggy beards still sprout about our faces, what a sad pickle will they be in!"

The Disconsolate Lady uttered these lamentations in so pathetic a manner, that the tears of all the spectators waited on her complaints; and even Sancho himself began to water his plants, and condescended at last to share in the adventure, and attend his master to the very fag-end of the world, so he might contribute to the clearing away the weeds that overspread those venerable faces.

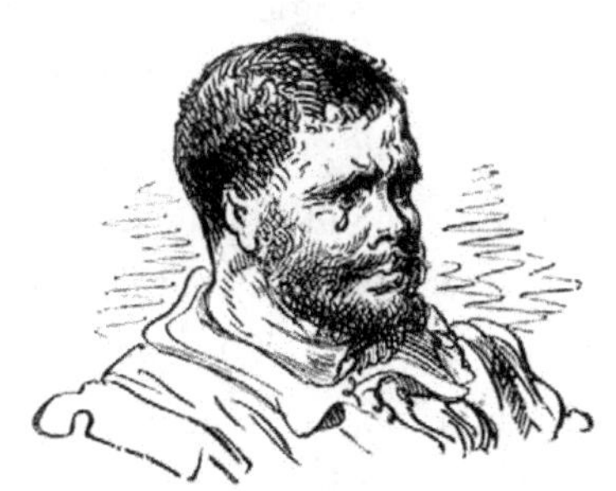

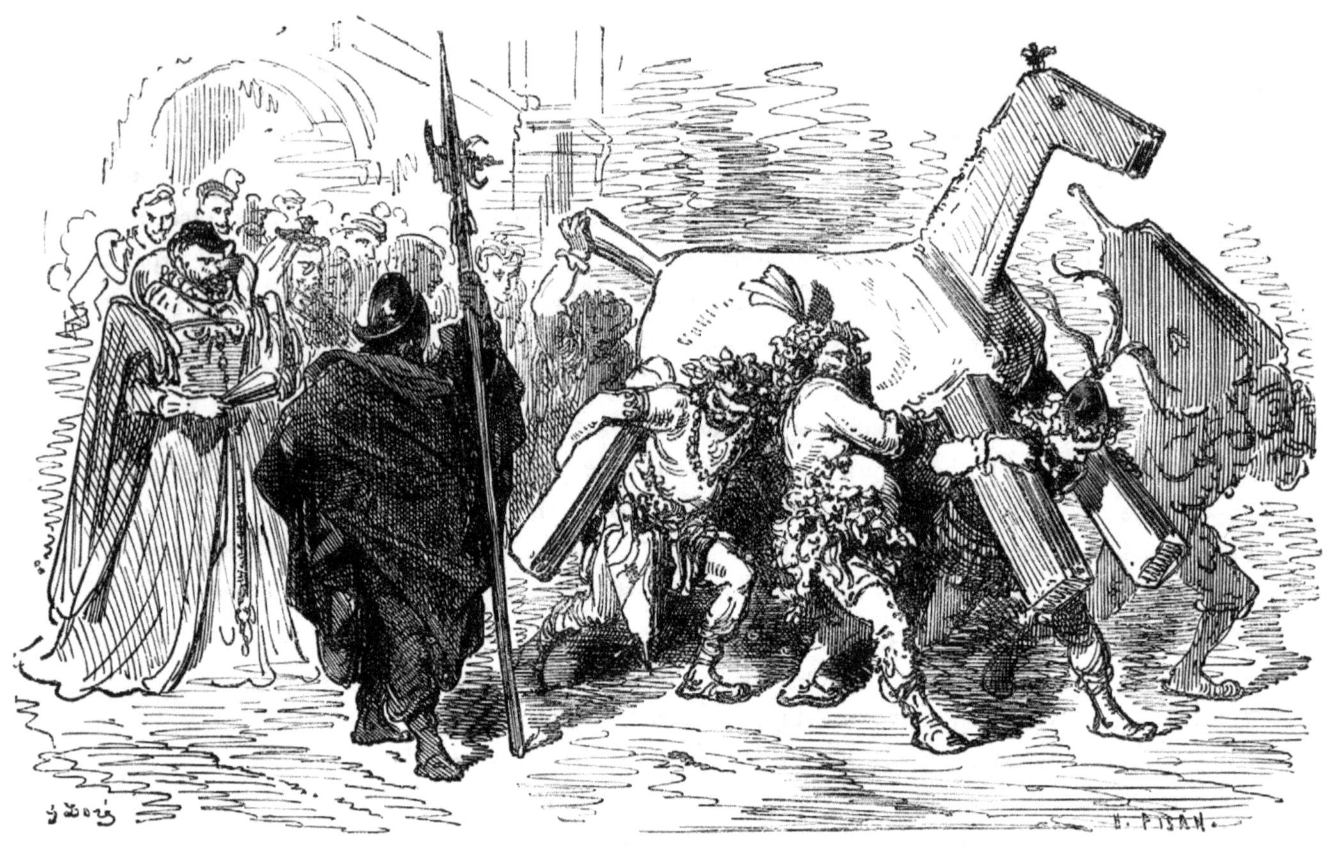

CHAPTER XLI.

OF CLAVILENO'S (ALIAS WOODEN PEG'S) ARRIVAL, WITH THE CONCLUSION OF THIS TEDIOUS ADVENTURE.

THESE discourses brought on the night, and with it the appointed time for the famous Clavileno's arrival. Don Quixote, very impatient at his delay, began to fear that either he was not the knight for whom this adventure was reserved or else that the giant Malambruno had not courage to enter into a single combat with him. But, unexpectedly, who should enter the garden but four savages, covered with green ivy, bearing on their shoulders a large wooden horse, which they sat on his legs before the company; and then one of them cried out, "Now let him that has courage mount this engine."

"I am not he," quoth Sancho, "for I have no courage, nor am I a knight."

"And let him take his squire behind him, if he has one," continued the savage; "with this assurance from the valorous Malambruno, that no foul play shall be offered, nor will he use anything but his sword to offend him. It is but only turning the peg before him, and the horse will transport him through the air to the place where Malambruno attends their coming. But let them blindfold their eyes, lest the dazzling and stupendous height of their career should make them giddy; and let the neighing of the horse inform them that they are arrived at their journey's end."

Thus having made his speech, the savage turned about with his companions, and, leaving Clavileno, they marched out handsomely the same way they came in.

The Disconsolate Matron, seeing the horse, almost with tears addressed Don Quixote. "Valorous knight," cried she, "Malambruno is a man of his word; the horse is here, our beards bud on; therefore I and every one of us conjure you, by all the hairs on our chins, to hasten our deliverance, since there needs no more but that you and your squire get up, and give a happy beginning to your intended journey."

"Madam," answered Don Quixote, "I will do it with all my heart; I will not so much as stay for a cushion, or to put on my spurs, but mount instantly; such is my impatience to disbeard your ladyship's face, and restore you to all your former gracefulness."

"That is more than I should do," quoth Sancho; "I am not in such plaguy haste, not I; and if the quick-set hedges on their snouts cannot be lopped off without my riding on that hard crupper, let my master furnish himself with another squire, and these gentlewomen get some other barber. I am no witch, sure, to ride through the air at this rate on a broom-stick! What will my islanders say, think ye, when they hear their governor is flying like a paper kite? Besides, it is three or four thousand leagues from hence to Candaya; and what if the horse should tire upon the road, or the giant grow humorsome? what would become of us then? No, no, I know better things. What says the old proverb? 'Delays breed danger;' and, 'When a cow is given thee, run and halter her.' I am the gentlewoman's humble servant, but they and their beards must excuse me, faith! St. Peter is well at Rome, that is to say, here I am much made of, and, by the master of the house's good will, I hope to see myself a governor."

"Friend Sancho," said the duke, "as for your island, it neither floats nor stirs, so there is no fear it should run away before you come back; the foundations of it are fixed and rooted in the profound abyss of the earth. Now, because you must needs think I cannot but know that there is no kind of office of any value that is not purchased with some sort of bribe, or gratification of one kind or other, all that I expect for advancing you to this government is only that you wait on your master in this expedition, that there may be an end of this memorable adventure. And I here engage my honour, that whether you return on Clavileno with all the speed his swiftness promises, or that it should be your ill fortune to be obliged to foot it back like a pilgrim, begging from inn to inn, and door to door, still, whenever you come you will find your island where you left it, and your islanders as glad to receive you for their governor as ever. And for my own part, Signior Sancho, you would very much wrong my friendship, should you in the least doubt my readiness to serve you."

"Good your worship, say no more," cried Sancho; "I am but a poor squire, and your goodness is too great a load for my shoulders. But hang baseness; mount, master, and blindfold me, somebody; wish me a good voyage, and pray for me. But hark ye, good folks, when I am got up, and fly in the skies, may not I say my prayers, and call on the angels myself to help me, trow?"

"Yes, yes," answered Trifaldi; "for Malambruno, though an enchanter, is nevertheless a Christian, and does all things with a great deal of sagacity, having nothing to do with those he should not meddle with."

"Come on, then," quoth Sancho.

"Thy fear, Sancho," said Don Quixote, "might, by a superstitious mind, be thought ominous. Since the adventure of the fulling-mills, I have not seen thee possessed with such a panic terror. But hark ye, begging this noble company's leave, I must have a word with you in private."

Then withdrawing into a distant part of the garden among some trees, "My dear Sancho," said he, "thou seest we are going to take a long journey; thou art no less sensible of the uncertainty of our return, and Heaven alone can tell what leisure or conveniency we may have in all that time. Let me therefore beg thee to slip aside to thy chamber, as if it were to get thyself ready for our journey, and there presently dispatch me only some five hundred lashes, on account of the three thousand three hundred thou standest engaged for; it will soon be done, and a business well begun, you know, is half ended."

"Stark mad, before George!" cried Sancho. "I wonder you are not ashamed, sir. I am just going to ride the wooden horse, and you would have me flay myself! Come, come, sir, let us do one thing after another; let us get off these women's whiskers, and then I will feague it away for Dulcinea. I have no more to say on the matter at present."

"Well, honest Sancho," replied Don Quixote, "I will take thy word for once, and I hope thou wilt make it good; for I believe thou art more fool than knave."

"I am what I am," quoth Sancho; "but whatever I be I will keep my word, never fear it."

Upon this they returned to the company; and, just as they were going to mount, "Blind thy eyes, Sancho," said Don Quixote, "and get up. Sure he that sends so far for us can have no design to deceive us; since it would never be to his credit to delude those that rely on his word of honour; and, though the success should not be answerable to our desires, still the glory of so brave an attempt will be ours, and it is not in the power of malice to eclipse it."

"To horse, then, sir," cried Sancho, "to horse. The tears of these poor bearded gentle-women have melted my heart, and methinks I feel the bristles sticking in it. I shall not eat a bit to do me good, till I see them have as pretty dimpled smooth chins, and soft lips, as they had before. Mount, then, I say, and blindfold yourself first; for, if I must ride behind, it is a plain case you must get up before me."

"That is right," said Don Quixote; and, with that, pulling a handkerchief out of his pocket, he gave it to the Disconsolate Matron to hoodwink him close. She did so; but, presently after, uncovering himself, "If I remember right," said he, "we read in Virgil of the

Trojan Palladium, that wooden horse which the Greeks offered Pallas, full of armed knights, who afterwards proved the total ruin of that famous city. It were prudent, therefore, before we get up, to probe this steed, and see what he has inside."

"You need not," said the Countess Trifaldi; "I dare engage there is no ground for any such surmise; for Malambruno is a man of honour, and would not so much as countenance any base or treacherous practice; and whatever accident befalls you I dare answer for."

Upon this Don Quixote mounted, without any reply, imagining that what he might further urge concerning his security would be a reflection on his valour. He then began to try the pin, which was easily turned; and as he sat, with his long legs stretched at length for want of stirrups, he looked like one of those antique figures in a Roman triumph, woven in some old piece of arras.

Sancho, very leisurely and unwillingly, was made to climb up behind him; and, fixing himself, as well as he could, on the crupper, felt it somewhat hard and uneasy. With that, looking on the duke, "Good, my lord," quoth he, "will you lend me something to clap under me; some pillow from the page's bed, or the duchess's cushion of state, or anything? for this horse's crupper is so confounded hard, I fancy it is rather marble than wood."

"It is needless," said the countess; "for Clavileno will bear no kind of furniture upon him; so that, for your greater ease, you had best sit sideways, like a woman."

Sancho took her advice; and then, after he had taken his leave of the company, they bound a cloth over his eyes; but, presently after, uncovering his face, with a pitiful look on all the spectators, "Good, tender-hearted Christians," cried he, with tears in his eyes, "bestow a few Pater Nosters and Ave Marias on a poor departing brother, and pray for my soul, as you expect the like charity yourselves in such a condition!"

"What! you rascal," said Don Quixote, "do you think yourself at the gallows, and at the point of death, that you hold forth in such a lamentable strain? Dastardly wretch! dost thou not know that the fair Magalona once sat in thy place, and alighted from thence, not into the grave, thou chicken-hearted varlet, but into the throne of France, if there is any truth in history? And do not I sit by thee, that I may vie with the valorous Peter of Provence, and press the seat that was once pressed by him? Come, blindfold thy eyes, poor spiritless animal! and let me not know thee betray the least symptom of fear."

"Well," quoth Sancho, "hoodwink me then among you: but it is no marvel one should be afraid, when you will not let one say his prayers, nor be prayed for, though, for aught I know, we may have a legion of imps about our ears, to clap us up in some strange place presently."

Now, both being hoodwinked, and Don Quixote perceiving everything ready for their setting out, began to turn the pin; and, no sooner had he set his hand to it, than the waiting-women and all the company set up their throats, calling out, "Speed you, speed you well, valorous knight! Heaven be your guide, undaunted squire! Now, now, you fly aloft! See how they cut the air more swiftly than an arrow! Now they mount, and tower, and soar, while the gazing world wonders at their course. Sit fast, sit fast, courageous Sancho! you do not sit steady; have a care of falling; for, should you now drop from that amazing height, your fall would be greater than the aspiring youth's that misguided the chariot of the Sun."

All this Sancho heard, and, girting his arms fast about his master's waist, "Sir," quoth he, "why do they say we are so high, since we can hear their voices? Truly, I hear them so plainly, that one would think they were close by us."

"Never mind that," answered Don Quixote; "for in these extraordinary kinds of flight we must suppose our hearing and seeing will be extraordinary also. But do not hold me so hard, for you will make me tumble off. What makes thee tremble so? I am sure I never rode easier in all my life; our horse goes as if he did not move at all. Come, then, take courage; we make swinging way, and have a fair and merry gale."

"I think so, too," quoth Sancho; "for I feel the wind puff as briskly upon me here as if I do not know how many pairs of bellows were blowing wind on me."

Sancho was not altogether in the wrong; for two or three pairs of bellows were indeed levelled at him then, which gave air very plentifully; so well had the plot of this adventure been laid by the duke, the duchess, and their steward.

Don Quixote at last feeling the wind, "Sure," said he, "we must be risen to the middle region of the air, where the winds, hail, snow, thunder, lightning, and other meteors are produced; so that, if we mount at this rate, we shall be in the region of fire presently; and what is worse, I do not know how to manage this pin, so as to avoid being scorched and roasted alive."

At the same time some flax, with other combustible matter, which had been got ready, was clapped at the end of a long stick, and set on fire at a small distance from their noses; and the heat and smoke affecting the knight and the squire, "May I be hanged," quoth Sancho, "if we be not come to this fire-place you talk of, or very near it, for the half of my beard is singed already. I have a huge mind to peep out, and see whereabouts we are."

"By no means," answered Don Quixote. "I remember the strange but true story of Dr. Torralva, who was carried to Rome, hoodwinked and bestriding a reed, in twelve hours' time. There he saw the dreadful tumult, assault, and death of the Constable of Bourbon; and the next morning he found himself at Madrid, where he related the whole story. Among other things, he said, as he went through the air, he was bid to open his eyes, which he did, and then he found himself so near the moon, that he could touch it with his finger; but durst not look towards the earth, lest the distance should make his brains turn round. So, Sancho, we must not unveil our eyes, but rather wholly trust to the care and providence of him that has charge of us, and fear nothing, for we only mount high to come souse down, like a hawk, upon the kingdom of Candaya, which we shall reach presently; for, though it appears to us not half an hour since we left the garden, we have, nevertheless, travelled over a vast tract of air."

"I know nothing of the matter," replied Sancho; "but of this I am very certain that if your Madam Magulane, or Magalona (what do you call her ?), could sit this wooden crupper without a good cushion, she must have had a harder skin than mine."

This dialogue was certainly very pleasant all this while to the duke and duchess, and the rest of the company; and now, at last, resolving to put an end to this extraordinary adventure, which had so long entertained them successfully, they ordered one of their servants to give fire to Clavileno's tail; and the horse being stuffed full of squibs, crackers, and other fireworks, burst presently into pieces, with a mighty noise, throwing the knight one way, and the squire another, both sufficiently singed. By this time the Disconsolate Matron and bearded regiment were vanished out of the garden, and all the rest, counterfeiting a trance, lay flat upon the ground. Don Quixote and Sancho, sorely bruised, made shift to get up, and, looking about, were amazed to find themselves in the same garden whence they took horse, and see such a number of people lie dead, as they thought, on the ground. But their wonder was diverted by the appearance of a large lance stuck in the ground, and a scroll of white parchment fastened to it by two green silken strings, with the following inscription upon it in golden characters :—

"The renowned knight, Don Quixote de la Mancha, achieved the adventure of the Countess Trifaldi, otherwise called the Disconsolate Matron, and her companions in distress, by barely attempting it. Malambruno is fully satisfied. The waiting-gentlewomen have lost their beards. King Clavijo and Queen Antonomasia have resumed their pristine shapes; and, when the squire's penance shall be finished, the white dove shall escape the pounces of the hawks that pursue her. This is pre-ordained by the Sage Merlin, the prince of enchanters."

Don Quixote having read this oracle, and construing it to refer to Dulcinea's disenchantment, rendered thanks to Heaven for so great a deliverance; and approaching the duke and duchess, who seemed as yet in a swoon, he took the duke by the hand: "Courage, courage! noble sir," cried he; "there is no danger; the adventure is finished without bloodshed, as you may read it registered in that record."

The duke, yawning and stretching as if he had been waked out of a sound sleep, recovered himself by degrees, as did the duchess and the rest of the company. The duke, rubbing his eyes, made a shift to read the scroll; then, embracing Don Quixote, he extolled his valour to the skies, assuring him he was the bravest knight the earth had ever possessed. As for Sancho, he was looking up and down the garden for the Disconsolate Matron, to see what sort of a face she had got, now her furze-bush was off. But he was informed that as Clavileno came down flaming in the air, the countess, with her women, vanished immediately, but not one of them chin-bristled, nor so much as a hair upon their faces.

Then the duchess asked Sancho how he had fared in his long voyage.

"Why truly, madam," answered he, "I have seen wonders; for you must know that, though my master would not suffer me to pull the cloth from my eyes, yet as I have a kind of itch to know everything, and a spice of the spirit of contradiction, still hankering after what is forbidden me, so when, as my master told me, we were flying through the region of fire, I pushed my handkerchief a little above my nose, and looked down, and what do you think I saw? I spied the earth a hugeous way afar off below me (Heaven bless us!), no bigger than a mustard-seed; and the men walking to and fro upon it, not much larger than hazel-nuts. Judge now if we were not got up woundy high!"

"Have a care what you say, my friend," said the duchess; "for if the men were bigger than hazel-nuts, and the earth no bigger than a mustard-seed, one man must be bigger than the whole earth, and cover it so that you could not see it."

"Like enough," answered Sancho; "but for all that, do you see, I saw it with a kind of a side-look upon one part of it, or so."

"Look you, Sancho," replied the duchess, "that will not bear; for nothing can be wholly seen by any part of it."

"Well, well, madam," quoth Sancho, "I do not understand your parts and wholes: I saw it, and there is an end of the story. Only you must think, that as we flew by enchantment, so we saw by enchantment; and thus I might see the earth, and all the men, which way soever I looked. I will warrant you will not believe me neither when I tell you that, when I thrust up the kerchief above my brows, I saw myself so near heaven, that between the top of my cap and the main sky, there was not a span and a half. And, Heaven bless us! forsooth, what a hugeous great place it is! and we happened to travel that road where the seven she goat stars were; and, faith and troth! I had such a mind to play with them (having been once a goat-herd myself), that I fancy I would have cried myself to death, had I not done it. So, soon as I spied them, what does me but sneaks down very soberly from behind my master, without telling any living soul, and played and leaped about for three-quarters of an hour, by the clock, with the pretty nanny-goats, who are as sweet and fine as so many marigolds; and honest Wooden Peg stirred not one step all the while."

"And while Sancho employed himself with the goats," asked the duke, "how was Don Quixote employed?"

"Truly," answered the knight, "I am sensible all things were altered from their natural course; therefore what Sancho says seems the less strange to me. But, for my own part, I neither saw heaven nor hell, sea nor shore. I perceived, indeed, we passed through the middle region of the air, and were pretty near that of fire, but that we came so near heaven as Sancho says is altogether incredible; because we then must have passed quite through the fiery region, which lies between the sphere of the moon and the upper region of the air. Now it was impossible for us to reach that part where are the Pleiades, or the Seven Goats, as Sancho calls them, without being consumed in the elemental fire; and, therefore, since we escaped those flames, certainly we did not soar so high, and Sancho either lies or dreams."

"I neither lie nor dream," replied Sancho. "Indeed, I can tell you the marks and colour of every goat among them: if you do not believe me, do but ask and try me."

"Well," said the duchess, "pr'ythee tell me, Sancho."

"Look you," answered Sancho, "there were two of them green, two carnation, two blue, and one party-coloured."

"Truly," said the duke, "that is a new kind of goats you have found out, Sancho; we have none of those colours upon earth."

"Sure, sir," replied Sancho, "you will make some sort of difference between heavenly she goats and the goats of this world?"

"But, Sancho," said the duke, "among these she goats did you never see a he? not one horned beast of the masculine gender?"

"Not one, sir; I saw no other horned thing but the moon; and I have been told that neither he goats nor any other cornuted tups are suffered to lift their horns beyond those of the moon."

They did not ask Sancho any more questions about his airy voyage; for, in the humour he was in, they judged he would not stick to ramble all over the heavens, and tell them news of whatever was doing there, though he had not stirred out of the garden all the while.

"Sancho," said Don Quixote, whispering him in the ear, "since thou wouldst have us believe what thou hast seen in heaven, I desire thee to believe what I saw in the cave of Montesinos. Not a word more."

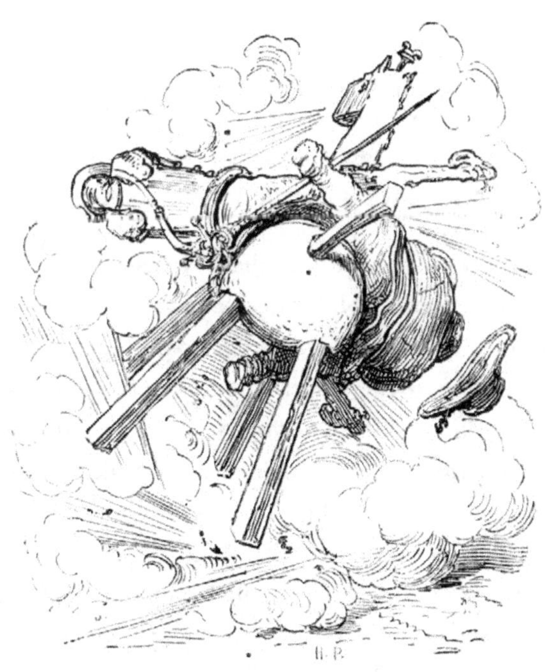

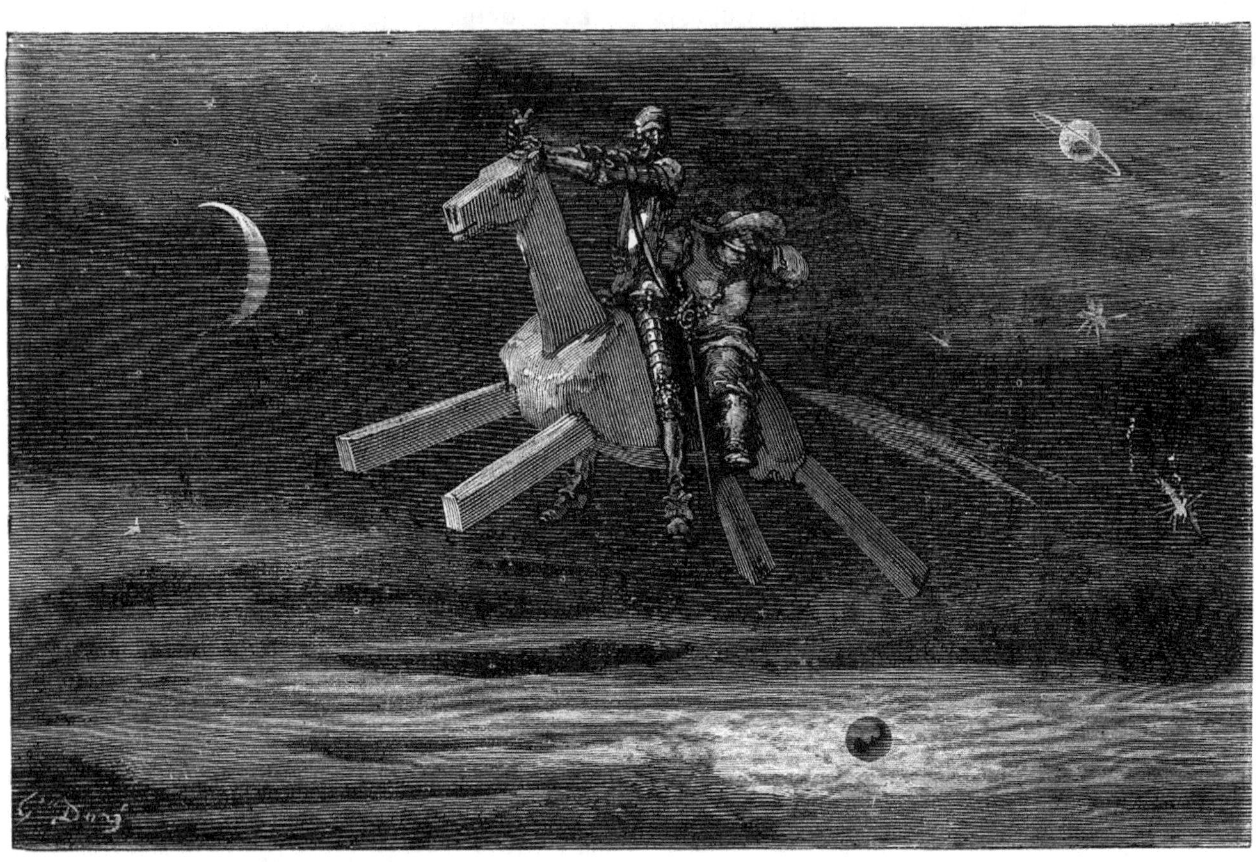

CHAPTER XLII.

THE INSTRUCTIONS WHICH DON QUIXOTE GAVE SANCHO PANZA BEFORE HE WENT TO THE GOVERNMENT OF HIS ISLAND, WITH OTHER MATTERS OF MOMENT.

THE satisfaction which the duke and duchess received by the happy success of the adventure of the Disconsolate Matron, encouraged them to carry on some other pleasant project, since they could, with so much ease, impose upon the credulity of Don Quixote and his squire. Having therefore giving instructions to their servants and vassals how to behave themselves towards Sancho in his government, the day after the scene of the wooden horse, the duke bid Sancho prepare, and be in readiness to take possession of his government; for now his islanders wished as heartily for him as they did for rain in a dry summer. Sancho made a humble bow, and looking demurely on the duke, "Sir," quoth he, "since I came down from heaven, whence I saw the earth so very small, I am not half so hot as I was for being a governor. For what greatness can there be in being at the head of a puny dominion, that is but a little nook of a tiny mustard-seed? and what dignity and power can a man be reckoned to have in governing half-a-dozen men no bigger than hazel-nuts? For I could not think there were any more in the whole world. No, if your grace would throw away upon me never so little a corner in heaven, though it were but half a league or so, I would take it with better will than I would the largest island on earth."

"Friend Sancho," answered the duke, "I cannot dispose of an inch of heaven; for that is the province of God alone: but what I am able to bestow I give you; that is, an island, tight and clever, round and well-proportioned, fertile and plentiful to such a degree, that if you have but the art and understanding to manage things right, you may hoard there both of the treasures of this world and the next."

"Well, then," quoth Sancho, "let me have this island, and I will do my best to be such a governor, that, in spite of rogues, I shall not want a small nook in heaven one day or other. It is not out of covetousness neither, that I would leave my little cot, and set up for somebody, but merely to know what kind of thing it is to be a governor."

"Oh, Sancho!" said the duke; "when once you have had a taste of it, you will never leave licking your fingers, it is so sweet and bewitching a thing to command and be obeyed. I am confident, when your master comes to be an emperor (as he cannot fail to be, according to the course of his affairs), he will never, by any consideration, be persuaded to abdicate; his only grief will be that he was one no sooner."

"Troth, sir," replied Sancho, "I am of your mind; it is a dainty thing to command, though it were but a flock of sheep."

"Oh, Sancho!" cried the duke, "let me live and die with thee: for thou hast an insight into everything. I hope thou wilt prove as good a governor as thy wisdom bespeaks thee. But no more at this time; to-morrow, without further delay, you set forward to your island, and shall be furnished this afternoon with equipage and dress answerable to your post, and all other necessaries for your journey."

"Let them dress me as they will," quoth Sancho, "I shall be the same Sancho Panza still."

"That is true," said the duke, "yet every man ought to wear clothes suitable to his place and dignity; for a lawyer should not go dressed like a soldier, nor a soldier like a priest. As for you, Sancho, you are to wear the habit both of a captain and a civil magistrate; so your dress shall be a compound of those two; for in the government that I bestow on you, arms are as necessary as learning, and a man of letters as requisite as a swordsman."

"Nay, as for letters," quoth Sancho, "I cannot say much for myself: for as yet I scarce know my A, B, C; but yet, if I can but remember my Christ's-cross, it is enough to make me a good governor. As for my arms, I will not quit my weapon as long as I can stand, and so Heaven be our guard!"

"Sancho cannot do amiss," said the duke, "while he remembers these things."

By this time Don Quixote arrived, and hearing how suddenly Sancho was to go to his government, with the duke's permission, he took him aside to give him some good instructions for his conduct in the discharge of his office.

Being entered Don Quixote's chamber, and the door shut, he almost forcibly obliged Sancho to sit by him; and then, with a grave and deliberate voice, he thus began:—

"I give Heaven infinite thanks, friend Sancho, that, before I have the happiness of being put in possession of my hopes, I can see thine already crowned; fortune hastening to meet thee with thy wishes. I, who had assigned the reward of thy services upon my happy success, am yet but on the way to preferment; and thou, beyond all reasonable expectation, art arrived at the aim and end of thy desires. Some are assiduous, solicitous, importunate, rise early, bribe, entreat, press, will take no denial, obstinately persist in their suit, and yet at last never obtain it. Another comes on, and, by a lucky hit or chance, bears away the prize, and jumps into the preferment which so many had pursued in vain; which verifies the saying,

'The happy have their days, and those they choose;
The unhappy have but hours, and those they lose.'

Thou, who seemest to me a very blockhead, without sitting up late, or rising early, or any manner of fatigue or trouble, only the air of knight-errantry being breathed on thee, art advanced to the government of an island in a trice, as if it were a thing of no moment, a very trifle. I speak this, my dear Sancho, not to upbraid thee, nor out of envy, but only to let thee know thou art not to attribute all this success to thy own merit, while it is entirely owing to the kind heavenly Disposer of human affairs, to whom thy thanks ought to be returned. But, next to Heaven, thou art to ascribe thy happiness to the greatness of the profession of knight-errantry, which includes within itself such stores of honour and preferment.

"Being convinced of what I have already said, be yet attentive, oh, my son, to what I, thy Cato, have further to say: listen, I say, to my admonitions, and I will be thy north star, and thy pilot to steer and bring thee safe into the port of honour, out of the tempestuous ocean, into which thou art just going to launch; for offices and great employments are no better than profound gulphs of confusion.

"First of all, oh, my son, fear God: for the fear of God is the beginning of wisdom, and wisdom will never let thee go astray.

"Secondly, consider what thou wert, and make it thy business to know thyself, which is the most difficult lesson in the world. Yet from this lesson thou wilt learn to avoid the frog's foolish ambition of swelling to rival the bigness of the ox; else the consideration of your having been a hog-driver will be, to the wheel of your fortune, like the peacock's ugly feet."

"True," quoth Sancho, "but I was then but a little boy; for when I grew up to be somewhat bigger, I drove geese, and not hogs; but methinks that is nothing to the purpose, for all governors cannot come from kings and princes."

"Very true," pursued Don Quixote; "therefore those who want a noble descent must allay the severity of their office with mildness and civility, which, directed by wisdom, may secure them from the murmurs and malice from which no state or condition is exempt.

"Be well pleased with the meanness of thy family, Sancho, nor think it a disgrace to own thyself derived from labouring men; for, if thou art not ashamed of thyself, nobody else will strive to make thee so. Endeavour rather to be esteemed humble and virtuous, than proud and vicious. The number is almost infinite of those who, from low and vulgar births, have been raised to the highest dignities, to the Papal chair, and the imperial throne; and this I could prove by examples enough to tire thy patience.

"Make virtue the medium of all thy actions, and thou wilt have no cause to envy those whose birth gives them the titles of great men and princes; for nobility is inherited, but virtue acquired: and virtue is worth more in itself than nobleness of birth.

"If any of thy poor relations come to see thee, never reject nor affront them; but, on the contrary, receive and entertain them with marks of favour; in this thou wilt display a generosity of nature, and please Heaven, that would have nobody to despise what it has made.

"If thou sendest for thy wife, as it is not fit a man in thy station should be long without his wife, and she ought to partake of her husband's good fortune, teach her, instruct her, polish her the best thou canst, till her native rusticity is refined to a handsomer behaviour; for often an ill-bred wife throws down all that a good and discreet husband can build up.

"Shouldst thou come to be a widower (which is not impossible), and thy post recommend thee to a bride of a higher degree, take not one that shall, like a fishing-rod, only serve to catch bribes. For, take it from me, the judge must, at the general and last court of judicature, give a strict account of the discharge of his duty, and must pay severely at his dying day for what he has suffered his wife to take.

"Let never obstinate self-conceit be thy guide; it is the vice of the ignorant, who vainly presume on their understanding.

"Let the tears of the poor find more compassion, though not more justice, than the informations of the rich.

"Be equally solicitous to find out the truth, where the offers and presents of the rich, and the sobs and importunities of the poor, are in the way.

"Wherever equity should or may take place, let not the extent or rigour of the law bear too much on the delinquent; for it is not a better character in a judge to be rigorous, than to be indulgent.

"When the severity of the law is to be softened, let pity, not bribes, be the motive.

"If thy enemy have a cause before thee, turn away thy eyes from thy prejudices, and fix them on the matter of fact.

"In another man's cause be not blinded by thy own passions, for those errors are almost without remedy; or their cure will prove expensive to thy wealth and reputation.

"When a beautiful woman comes before thee, turn away thy eyes from her tears, and thy ears from her lamentations; and take time to consider sedately her petition, if thou wouldst not have thy reason and honesty lost in her sighs and tears.

"Revile not with words those whom their crimes oblige thee to punish in deed: for the punishment is enough to the wretches, without the addition of ill language.

"In the trial of criminals, consider as much as thou canst, without prejudice to the plaintiff, how defenceless and open the miserable are to the temptations of our corrupt and depraved nature, and so far show thyself full of pity and clemency; for though God's attributes are equal, yet his mercy is more attractive and pleasing in our eyes than his justice.

"If thou observest these rules, Sancho, thy days shall be long, thy fame eternal, thy recompense full, and thy felicity unspeakable. Thou shalt marry thy children and grandchildren to thy heart's desire; they shall want no titles. Beloved of all men, thy life shall be peaceable, thy death in a good and venerable old age, and the offspring of thy grandchildren, with their soft, youthful hands, shall close thy eyes.

"The precepts I have hitherto given thee regard the good and ornament of thy mind; now give attention to those directions that relate to the adorning of thy body."

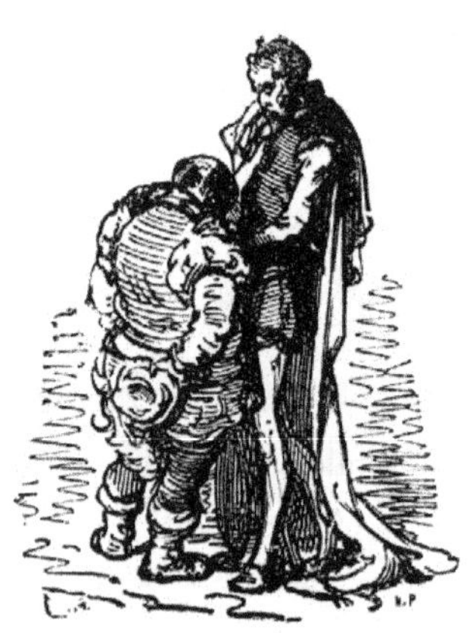

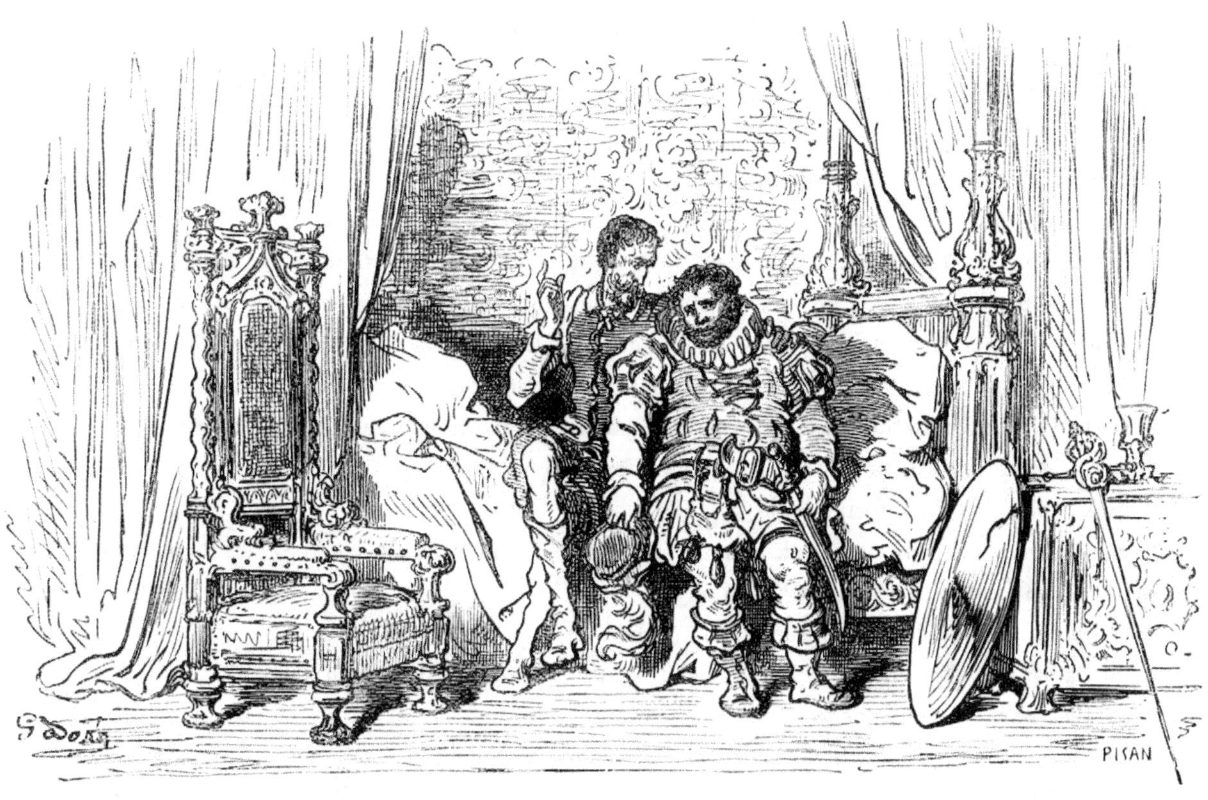

CHAPTER XLIII.

THE SECOND PART OF DON QUIXOTE'S ADVICE TO SANCHO PANZA.

WHO would not have taken Don Quixote for a man of extraordinary wisdom, and as excellent morals, having heard him documentise his squire in this manner? only, as we have often observed in this history, the least talk of knight-errantry spoiled all, and made his understanding muddy; but in everything else his judgment was very clear, and his apprehension very nice, so that every moment his actions used to discredit his judgment, and his judgment his actions. But in these economical precepts which he gave Sancho, he showed himself master of a pleasant fancy, and mingled his judgment and extravagance in equal proportions. Sancho lent him a great deal of attention, in hopes to register all those good counsels in his mind, and put them in practice; not doubting but by their means he should acquit himself of his duty like a man of honour.

"As to the government of thy person and family," pursued Don Quixote, "my first injunction is cleanliness. Pair thy nails, nor let them grow as some do, whose folly persuades them that long nails add to the beauty of the hand; till they look more like kestrils' claws than a man's nails. It is foul and unsightly.

"Keep thy clothes tight about thee; for a slovenly looseness is an argument of a careless mind; unless such a negligence, like that of Julius Cæsar, be affected for some cunning design.

"Prudently examine what thy income may amount to in a year: and if sufficient to afford thy servants liveries, let them be decent and lasting, rather than gaudy and for show; and for the overplus of thy good husbandry, bestow it on the poor: that is, if thou canst keep six footmen, keep but three; and let what would maintain three more be laid out in charitable uses. By that means thou wilt have attendants in heaven, as well as on earth, which our vain-glorious great ones, who are strangers to this practice, are not likely to have.

"Lest thy breath betray thy peasantry, defile it not with onions and garlic.

"Walk with gravity, and speak with deliberation, and yet not as if thou didst hearken to thy own words; for all affectation is a fault.

"Eat little at thy dinner, and less at supper; for the stomach is the storehouse, whence health is to be imparted to the whole body.

"Drink moderately; for drunkenness neither keeps a secret nor observes a promise.

"Be careful not to chew on both sides; that is, fill not thy mouth too full.

"In the next place, Sancho," said the knight, "do not overlard your common discourse with that glut of proverbs which you mix in it continually; for though proverbs are properly concise and pithy sentences, yet as thou bringest them in, in such a huddle, by the head and shoulders, thou makest them look like so many absurdities."

"Alas! sir," quoth Sancho, "this is a disease that Heaven alone can cure; for I have more proverbs than will fill a book; and when I talk, they crowd so thick and fast to my mouth, that they quarrel which shall get out first; so that my tongue is forced to let them out as fast, first come first served, though nothing to my purpose. But henceforwards I will set a watch on my mouth, and let none fly out but such as shall befit the gravity of my place. For 'in a rich man's house, the cloth is soon laid:' 'Where there is plenty, the guests cannot be empty.' 'A blot's no blot till it is hit.' 'He is safe who stands under the bells.' 'You cannot eat your cake and have your cake:' and 'Store's no sore.'"

"Go on, go on, friend," said Don Quixote; "thread, tack, stitch on, heap proverb upon proverb; out with them, man; there is nobody coming. My mother whips me, and I whip the gig. I warn thee to forbear foisting in a rope of proverbs everywhere, and thou blunderest out a whole litany of old saws, as much to the purpose as the last year's snow! Observe me, Sancho, I condemn not the use of proverbs: but it is most certain that such a confusion and hodge-podge of them as thou throwest out and draggest in by the hair together, makes conversation fulsome and poor.

"When thou dost ride, cast not thy body all on the crupper, nor hold thy legs stiff down, and straddling from the horse's belly; nor yet so loose, as if thou wert still on Dapple; for the air and gracefulness of sitting a horse distinguishes sometimes a gentleman from a groom. Sleep with moderation; for he that rises not with the sun loses so much day. And remember this, Sancho, that diligence is the mother of good fortune: sloth, on the contrary, never effected anything that sprung from a good and reasonable desire.

"The advice which I shall conclude with I would have thee to be sure to fix in thy memory, though it relate not to the adorning of thy person; for, I am persuaded, it will redound as much to thy advantage as any I have yet given thee. And this is it:—

"Never undertake to dispute nor decide any controversies concerning the pre-eminence of families; since, in the comparison, one must be better than the other: for he that is lessened by thee will hate thee, and the other whom thou preferrest will not think himself obliged to thee.

"As for thy dress, wear close breeches and hose, a long coat, and a cloak a little longer. I do not advise thee to wear wide-knee'd breeches, or trunk hose, for they become neither swordsmen nor men of business.

"This is all the advice, friend Sancho, I have to give thee at present. If thou takest care to let me hear from thee hereafter, I shall give thee more, according as thy occasions and emergencies require."

"Sir," said Sancho, "I see very well that all you have told me is mighty good, wholesome, and to the purpose; but what am I the better if I cannot keep it in my head? I grant you, I shall not easily forget that about pairing my nails, and marrying again, if I should have the luck to bury my wife. But for all that other gallimaufry, and heap of stuff, I can no more remember one syllable of it than the shapes of last year's clouds. Therefore, let me have it in black and white, I beseech you. It is true, I can neither write nor read, but I will give it to my father-confessor, that he may beat and hammer it into my noddle, as occasion serves."

"O Heaven!" cried Don Quixote, "how scandalous it looks in a governor not to be able to write or read! I must needs tell thee, Sancho, that for a man to be so illiterate, or to be left-handed, implies that either his parents were very poor and mean, or that he was of so perverse a nature he could not receive the impressions of learning, nor anything that is good. Poor soul, I pity thee! this is indeed a very great defect. I would have thee at least learn to write thy name."

"Oh! as for that," quoth Sancho, "I can do well enough: I can set my name; for when I served several offices in our parish, I learned to scrawl a sort of letters, such as they mark bundles of stuff with, which they told me spelt my name. Besides, I can pretend my right hand is lame, and so another shall sign for me; for there is a remedy for all things but death. And since I have the power, I will do what I list; for, as the saying is, 'He whose father is judge, goes safe to his trial.' And, as I am a governor, I hope I am somewhat higher than a judge. 'New lords, new laws.' Ay, ay, let them come as they will, and play at bo-peep. Let them backbite me to my face, I will bite-back the biters. Let them come for wool, and I will send them home shorn. 'Whom God loves, his house happy proves.'

'The rich man's follies pass for wise sayings in this world.' So I, being rich, do you see, and a governor, and too free-hearted into the bargain, as I intend to be, I shall have no faults at all."

"If thou dost not discharge the part of a good governor," replied Don Quixote, "thine will be the fault, though the shame and discredit will be mine. However, this is my comfort, I have done my duty in giving thee the best and most wholesome advice I could: and so Heaven prosper and direct thee in thy government, and disappoint my fears for thy turning all things upside down in that poor island."

"Look you, sir," quoth Sancho; "if you think me not fit for this government, I will think no more on it. I hope I can live plain Sancho still, upon a luncheon of bread, and a clove of garlic, as contented as Governor Sancho upon capons and partridges. Death and sleep make us all alike, rich and poor, high and low. Do but call to mind what first put this whim of government into my noddle: you will find it was your own self; for, as for me, I know no more what belongs to islands and governors than a blind buzzard."

"These last words of thine, Sancho," said Don Quixote, "in my opinion, prove thee worthy to govern a thousand islands. Thou hast naturally a good disposition, without which all knowledge is insufficient. Recommend thyself to Divine Providence, and be sure never to depart from uprightness of intention; I mean, have still a firm purpose and design to be thoroughly informed in all the business that shall come before thee, and act upon just grounds, for Heaven always favours good desires. And so let us go to dinner, for I believe now the duke and duchess expect us."

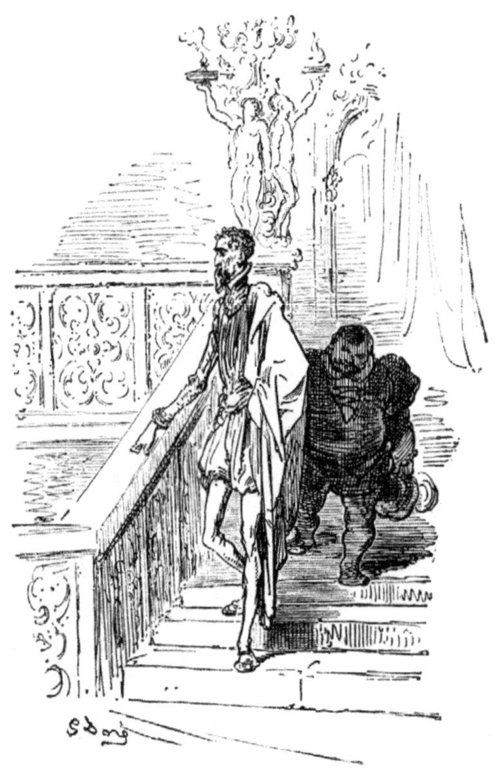

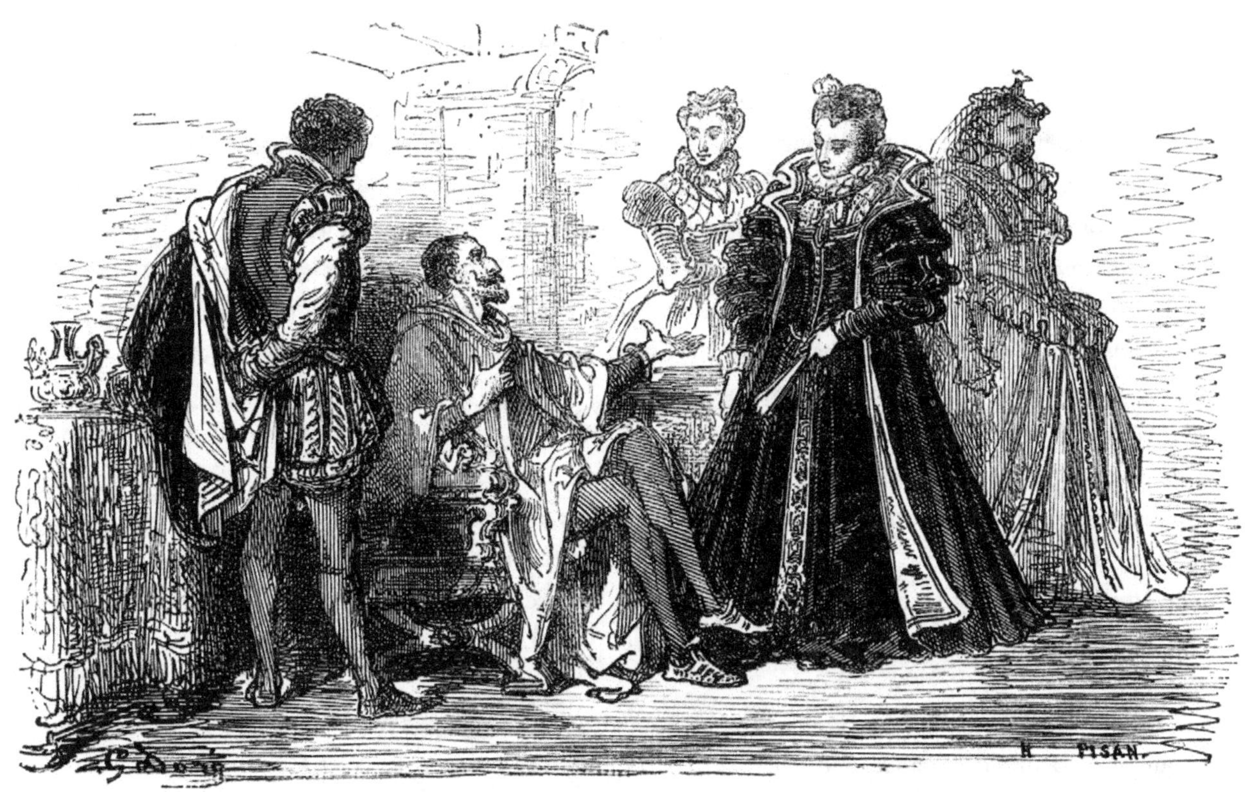

CHAPTER XLIV.

HOW SANCHO PANZA WAS CARRIED TO HIS GOVERNMENT, AND OF THE STRANGE ADVENTURE THAT BEFELL DON QUIXOTE IN THE CASTLE.

WE have it from the traditional account of this history, that there is a manifest difference between the translation and the Arabic in the beginning of this chapter; Cid Hamet having, in the original, taken an occasion of criticising on himself, for undertaking so dry and limited a subject, which must confine him to the bare history of Don Quixote and Sancho, and debar him the liberty of launching into episodes and digressions, that might be of more weight and entertainment. To have his fancy, his hand, and pen bound up to a single design, and his sentiments confined to the mouths of so few persons, he urged as an insupportable toil, and of small credit to the undertaker; so that, to avoid this inconveniency, he has introduced into the first part some novels, as that of "The Captive," which were in a manner distinct from the design, though the rest of the stories which he brought in there fall naturally enough in with Don Quixote's affairs, and seem of necessity to claim a place in the work. It was his opinion, likewise, as he told us, that the adventures of Don Quixote requiring so great a share of the reader's attention, his novels must expect but an indifferent reception, or, at most, but a cursory view, not sufficient to discover their artificial contexture; which must have been very obvious had they been published by themselves, without the interludes of Don Quixote's madness, or Sancho's impertinence. He has, therefore, in this Second Part, avoided all distinct and independent stories, introducing only such as have the appearance of episodes, yet flow naturally from the design of the story, and these but seldom, and with as much brevity as they can be expressed. Therefore, since he has tied himself up to such narrow bounds, and confined his understanding and parts, otherwise capable of the most copious subjects, to the pure matter of this present undertaking, he begs it may add a value to his work, and that he may be commended, not so much for what he has written as for what he has forborne to write. And then he proceeds in his history as follows :—

After dinner Don Quixote gave Sancho, in writing, the copy of his verbal instructions, ordering him to get somebody to read them to him. But the squire had no sooner got them, than he dropped the paper, which fell into the duke's hands, who communicating the same to the duchess, they found a fresh occasion of admiring the mixture of Don Quixote's good sense and extravagance ; and so, carrying on the humour, they sent Sancho that afternoon, with a suitable equipage, to the place he was to govern, which, wherever it lay, was to be an island to him.

It happened that the management of this affair was committed to a steward of the duke's, a man of a facetious humour, and who had not only wit to start a pleasant design, but discretion to carry it on—two qualifications which make an agreeable consort when they meet, nothing being truly agreeable without good sense. He had already personated the Countess Trifaldi very successfully; and, with his master's instructions in relation to his behaviour towards Sancho, could not but discharge his trust to a wonder. Now it fell out that Sancho no sooner cast his eyes on the steward, than he fancied he saw the very face of Trifaldi ; and turning to his master, "I shall wonder, sir," quoth he, "if you don't own that this same steward of the duke's here has the very phiz of my Lady Trifaldi."

Don Quixote looked very earnestly on the steward, and having perused him from top to toe, "Sancho," said he, "thou needest not give thyself any trouble to confirm this matter; I see their faces are the very same. Yet, for all that, the steward and the Disconsolate Lady cannot be the same person, for that would imply a very great contradiction, and might involve us in more abstruse and difficult doubts than we have conveniency now to discuss or examine. Believe me, friend, our devotion cannot be too earnest, that we may be delivered from the power of these enchantments."

"Indeed, sir," quoth Sancho, "you may think I am in jest, but I heard him open just now, and I thought the very voice of Madam Trifaldi sounded in my ears. But mum is the word; I say nothing, though I shall watch his ways, to find out whether I am right or wrong in my suspicion."

"Well, do so," said Don Quixote, "and fail not to acquaint me with all the discoveries thou canst make in this affair, and other occurrences in thy government."

At last Sancho set out with a numerous train. He was dressed like a man of the long

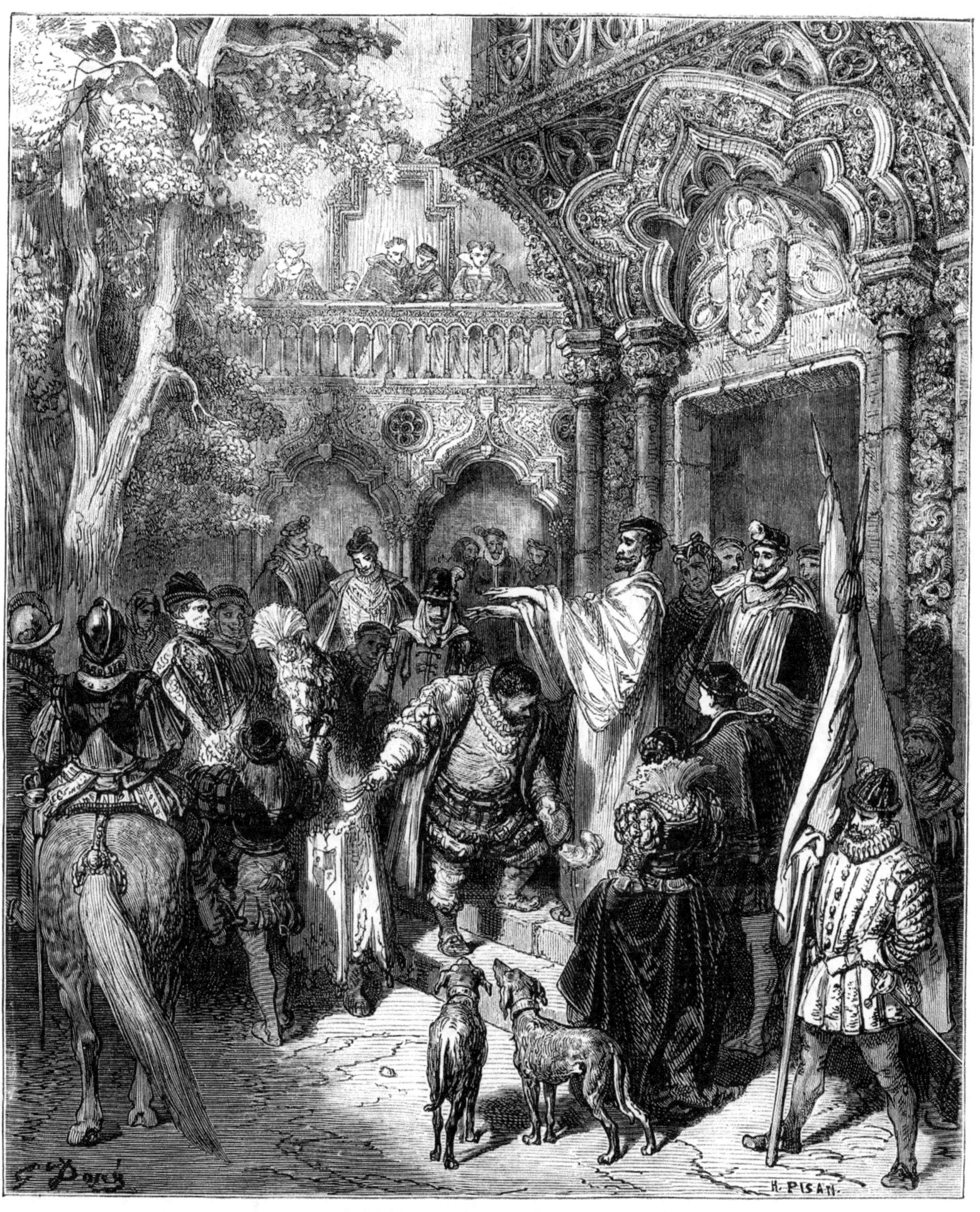

"He kissed the duke and duchess's hand at parting, and received his master's benediction."

robe, and wore over his other clothes a white sad-coloured coat or gown, of watered camlet, and a cap of the same stuff. He was mounted on a mule, and behind him, by the duke's order, was led his Dapple, bridled and saddled like a horse of state, in gaudy trappings of silk; which so delighted Sancho, that every now and then he turned his head about to look upon him, and thought himself so happy, that now he would not have changed fortunes with the Emperor of Germany. He kissed the duke and duchess's hands at parting, and received his master's benediction, while the Don wept, and Sancho blubbered abundantly.

Now, reader, let the noble governor depart in peace, and speed him well. His administration in his government may perhaps make you laugh to some purpose, when it comes in play. But, in the meantime, let us observe the fortune of his master the same night; for though it do not make you laugh outright, it may chance to make you draw in your lips, and show your teeth like a monkey; for it is the property of his adventures to create always either surprise or merriment.

It is reported, then, that immediately upon Sancho's departure, Don Quixote found the want of his presence; and, had it been in his power, he would have revoked his authority, and deprived him of his commission. The duchess, perceiving his disquiet, and desiring to understand the cause of his melancholy, told him that if it was Sancho's absence made him uneasy, she had squires enough, and damsels in her house, that should supply his place in any service he would be pleased to command them. "It is true, madam," answered Don Quixote, "I am somewhat concerned for the absence of Sancho; but there is a more material cause of my present uneasiness, and I must beg to be excused if, among the many obligations your grace is pleased to confer on me, I decline all but the good intention that has offered them. All I have further to crave is your grace's permission to be alone in my apartment, and to be my own servant."

"Enough, enough, noble sir," said the duchess; "I will give orders that not so much as the buzzing of a fly shall disturb you. May the great Dulcinea del Toboso live a thousand ages, and her fame be diffused all over the habitable globe, since she has merited the love of so valorous and loyal a knight; and may indulgent Heaven incline the heart of our governor, Sancho Panza, to put a speedy end to his discipline, that the beauties of so great a lady may be restored to the view of the admiring world!"

"Madam," returned Don Quixote, "your grace has spoken like yourself; so excellent a lady could utter nothing but what denotes the goodness and generosity of her mind. And certainly, it will be Dulcinea's peculiar happiness to have been praised by you, for it will raise her character more to have had your grace for her panegyrist, than if the best orators in the world had laboured to set it forth."

"Sir," said the duchess, waiving this discourse, "it is supper-time, and my lord expects us. Come, then, let us to supper, that you may go to bed betimes, for you must needs be weary still with the long journey you took to Candaya yesterday."

"Indeed, madam," answered Don Quixote, "I feel no manner of weariness; for I can safely swear to your grace, that I never rode an easier beast, nor a better goer, than Clavileno. For my part, I cannot imagine what could induce Malambruno to part with so swift and gentle a horse, and to burn him too, in such a manner."

"It is to be supposed," said the duchess, "that being sorry for the harm he had done, not only to the Countess Trifaldi and her attendants, but to many others, and repenting of the bad deeds which, as a wizard and a necromancer, he doubtless had committed, he had a mind to destroy all the instruments of his wicked profession, and accordingly he burned Clavileno as the chief of them, that engine having served him to rove all over the world; or perhaps he did not think any man worthy of bestriding him after the great Don Quixote, and so, with his destruction, and the inscription which he has caused to be set up, he has eternised your valour."

Don Quixote returned his thanks to the duchess, and after supper retired to his chamber. He shut the door of his chamber after him, and undressed himself by the light of two wax candles. But, oh! the misfortune that befell him, unworthy of such a person. As he was straining to put off his hose, there fell about four-and-twenty stitches of one of his stockings, which made it look like a lattice window. The good knight was extremely afflicted, and would have given an ounce of silver for a drachm of green silk; green silk, I say, because his stockings were green.

Here Benengeli could not forbear exclaiming, "Oh, poverty! poverty! what could induce that great Cordova poet to call thee a holy, thankless gift! Even I, that am a Moor, have learned by the converse I have had with Christians, that holiness consists in charity, in humility, in faith, in obedience, and in poverty. But sure, he who can be contented when poor, had need to be strengthened by God's peculiar grace, unless the poverty which is included among these virtues be only that poorness in spirit which teaches us to use the things of this world as if we had them not. But thou, second poverty, fatal indigence, of which I am now speaking, why dost thou intrude upon gentlemen, and affect well-born souls more than other people? Why dost thou reduce them to cobble their shoes, and wear some silk, some hair, and some glass buttons on the same tattered waistcoat, as if it were only to betray variety of wretchedness? Why must their ruffs be of such a dismal hue, in rags, dirty, rumpled, and ill-starched? (and by this you may see how ancient is the use of starch and ruffs). How miserable is a poor gentleman, who, to keep up his honour, starves his person, fares sorrily, or fasts unseen, within his solitary, narrow apartment; then putting the best face he can upon the matter, comes out picking his teeth, though it is but an honourable hypocrisy, and though he has eaten nothing that requires that nice exercise! Unhappy he, whose honour is in continual alarm, who thinks that, at a mile's distance, every one discovers the patch in his shoe, the sweat of his forehead soaked through his old rusty hat, the bareness of his clothes, and the very hunger of his famished stomach!"

All these melancholy reflections were renewed in Don Quixote's mind by the rent in his stocking. However, for his consolation, he bethought himself that Sancho had left him a pair of light boots, which he designed to put on the next day.

In short, to bed he went, with a pensive, heavy mind; the thought of Sancho's absence, and the irreparable damage that his stocking had received, made him uneasy; he would have darned it, though it had been with silk of another colour, one of the greatest tokens of want a poor gentleman can show during the course of his tedious misery. At last he put out the lights, but it was sultry hot, and he could not compose himself to rest. Getting up, therefore, he opened a little shutter of a barred window, that looked into a fine garden, and was presently sensible that some people were walking and talking there. He listened, and as they raised their voices, he easily overheard their discourse.

"No more, dear Emerenia," said one to the other. "Do not press me to sing; you know that from the first moment this stranger came to the castle, and my unhappy eyes gazed on him, I have been too conversant with tears and sorrow to sing or relish songs. Alas! all music jars when the soul is out of tune. Besides, you know the least thing wakens my lady, and I would not for the world she should find us here. But, grant she might not wake, what will my singing signify, if this new Æneas, who is come to our habitation to make me wretched, should be asleep, and not hear the sound of my complaint?"

"Pray, my dear Altisidora," said the other, "do not make yourself uneasy with those thoughts; for, without doubt, the duchess is fast asleep, and everybody in the house but we and the lord of thy desires. He is certainly awake; I heard him open his window just now; then sing, my poor grieving creature, sing and join the melting music of the lute to the soft accents of thy voice. If my lady happen to hear us, we will pretend we came out for a little air. The heat within doors will be our excuse."

"Alas! my dear," replied Altisidora, "it is not that frightens me most: I would not have my song betray my thoughts, for those that do not know the mighty force of love will be apt to take me for a light and indiscreet creature; but yet, since it must be so, I will venture: better shame on the face, than sorrow in the heart."

This said, she began to touch her lute so sweetly, that Don Quixote was ravished. At the same time, an infinite number of adventures of this nature, such as he had read of in his idle books of knight-errantry; windows, grates, gardens, serenades, amorous meetings, parleys, and fopperies, all crowded into his imagination, and he presently fancied that one of the duchess's damsels was fallen in love with him, and struggled with her modesty to conceal her passion. He began to be apprehensive of the danger to which his fidelity was exposed, but yet firmly determined to withstand the powerful allurement; and so, recommending himself, with a great deal of fervency, to his Lady Dulcinea del Toboso, he resolved to hear the music; and, to let the serenading ladies know he was awake, he feigned a kind of sneeze, which did not a little please them, for it was the only thing they wanted, to be assured their jest was

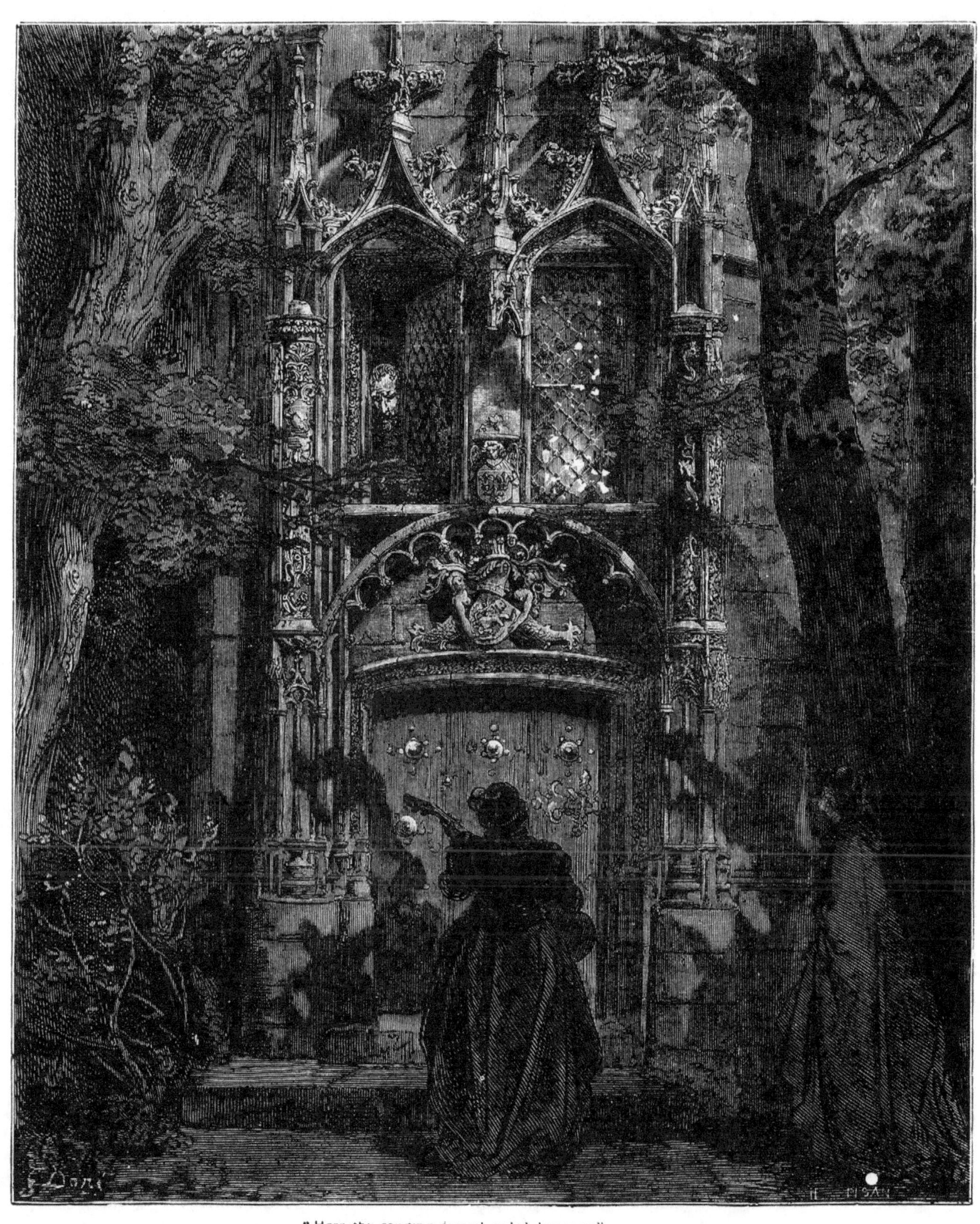

"Here the courting damsel ended her song."

not lost. With that, Altisidora, having tuned her lute afresh, after a flourish, began the following song :—

THE MOCK SERENADE.

Wake, Sir Knight, now love's invading,
Sleep in holland sheets no more ;
When a nymph is serenading,
'Tis an arrant shame to snore.

Hear a damsel, tall and tender,
Mourning in most rueful guise,
With heart almost burn'd to cinder,
By the sunbeams of thy eyes.

To free damsels from disaster
Is, they say, your daily care ;
Can you, then, deny a plaister
To a wounded virgin here?

Tell me, doughty youth, who cursed thee
With such humours and ill-luck?
Was 't some sullen bear dry-nursed thee,
Or she-dragon gave thee suck?

Dulcinea, that virago,
Well may brag of such a kid ;
Now her name is up, and may go
From Toledo to Madrid.

Would she but her prize surrender,
(Judge how on thy face I dote!)
In exchange I'd gladly send her
My best gown and petticoat.

Happy I, would fortune doom thee
But to have me near thy bed,
Stroke thee, pat thee, curry-comb thee,
And hunt o'er thy solid head!

But I ask too much sincerely,
And I doubt I ne'er must do 't ;
I'd but kiss thy toe, and fairly
Get the length thus of thy foot.

How I'd rig thee, and what riches
Should be heap'd upon thy bones ;
Caps and socks, and cloaks and breeches,
Matchless pearls, and precious stones.

Do not from above, like Nero,
See me burn, and slight my woe!
But, to quench my fires, my hero,
Cast a pitying eye below.

I'm a virgin-pullet, truly,
One more tender ne'er was seen,
A mere chicken, fledg'd but newly ;
Hang me if I'm yet fifteen.

Wind and limb, all's tight about me,
My hair dangles to my feet ;
I am straight, too ; if you doubt me,
Trust your eyes, come down and see 't.

I've a bob-nose has no fellow,
And a sparrow's mouth as rare ;
Teeth like topazes, all yellow,
Yet I'm deem'd a beauty here.

You know what a rare musician
(If you'd hearken) courts your choice ;
I can say my disposition
Is as taking as my voice.

These, and such like charms, I've plenty;
I'm a damsel of this place ;
Let Altisidora tempt ye,
Or she's in a woful case.

Here the courting damsel ended her song, and the courted knight began his expostulation. "Why," said he, with a sigh heaved from the bottom of his heart, "why must I be so unhappy a knight, that no damsel can gaze on me without falling in love? Why must the peerless Dulcinea del Toboso be so unfortunate as not to be permitted the single enjoyment of my transcendant fidelity? Queens, why do you envy her? Empresses, why do you persecute her? Damsels of fifteen, why do you attempt to deprive her of her right? Leave, oh, leave the unfortunate fair! Let her triumph, glory, and rejoice in the quiet possession of the heart which love has allotted her, and the absolute sway which she bears over my yielding soul. Away, unwelcome crowd of loving impertinents; Dulcinea alone can soften my manly temper, and mould me as she pleases. For her I am all sweetness; for you I am bitterness itself. There is to me no beauty, no prudence, no modesty, no gaiety, no nobility among your sex, but in Dulcinea alone. All other women seem to be deformed, silly, wanton, and base born, when compared with her. Nature brought me forth only that I should be devoted to her service. Let Altisidora weep or sing, let the lady despair on whose account I have received so many blows in the disastrous castle of the enchanted Moor, still I am Dulcinea's, and hers alone, dead or alive; dutiful, unspotted, and unchanged, in spite of all the necromantic powers in the world." This said, he hastily clapped down the window, and flung himself into his bed with as high an indignation as if he had received some great affront. There let us leave him a while, in regard the great Sancho Panza calls upon us to see him commence his famous government.

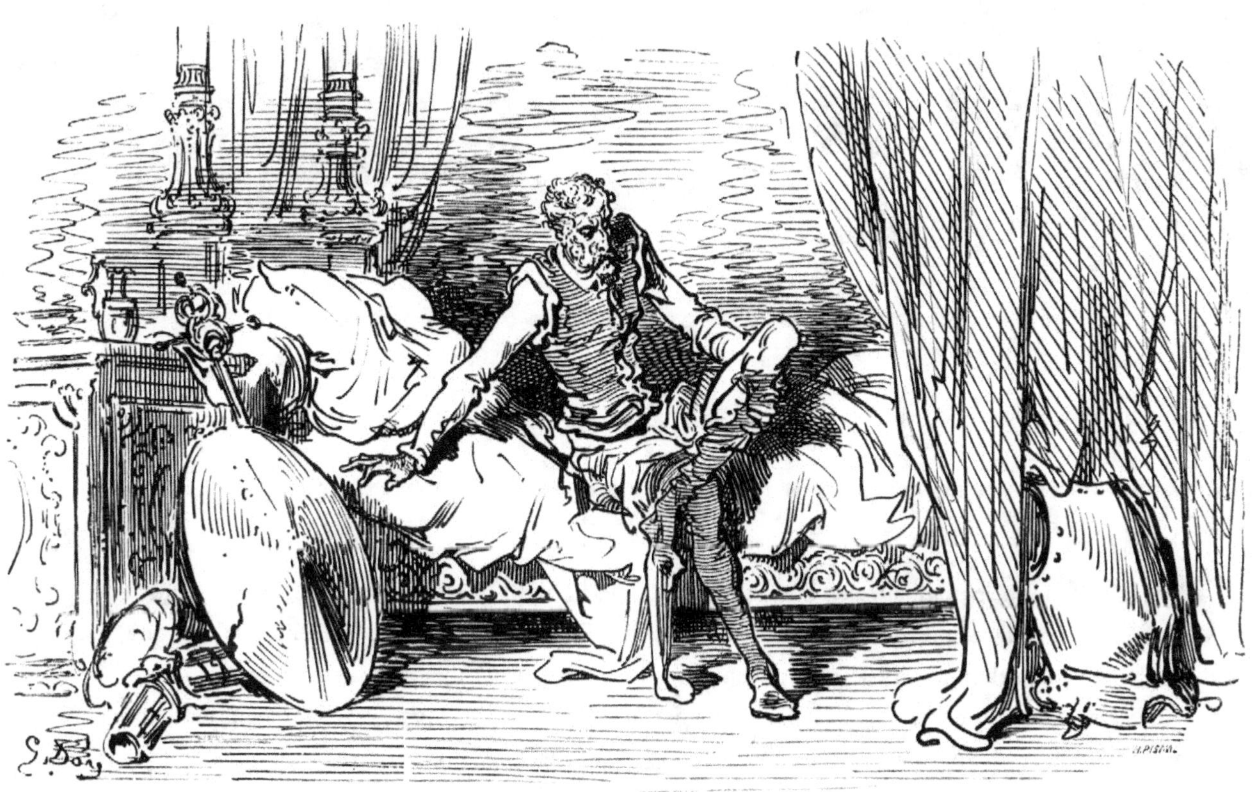

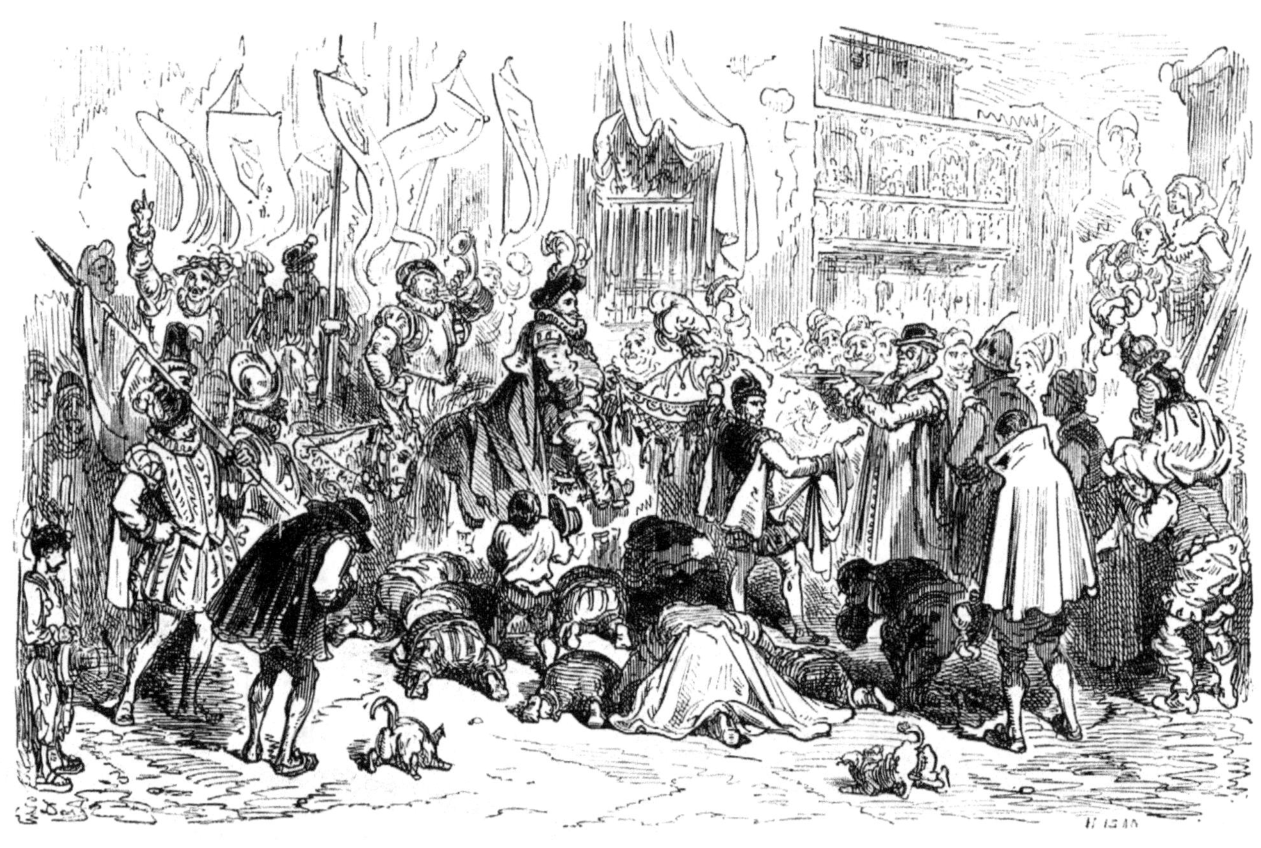

CHAPTER XLV.

HOW THE GREAT SANCHO PANZA TOOK POSSESSION OF HIS ISLAND, AND IN WHAT MANNER HE BEGAN TO GOVERN.

OH, thou perpetual surveyor of the antipodes, bright luminary of the world, and eye of heaven! sweet fermenter of liquids! here Timbrius called, there Phœbus; in one place an archer, in another a physician; parent of poesy and inventor of music; perpetual mover of the universe, who, though thou seemest sometimes to set, art always rising! oh, sun, on thee I call for help! Inspire me, I beseech thee! Warm and illumine my gloomy imagination, that my narration may keep pace with the great Sancho Panza's actions through his government; for without thy powerful influence, I feel myself benumbed, dispirited, and confused.

Now I proceed.

Sancho, with all his attendants, came to a town that had about a thousand inhabitants, and was one of the best where the duke had any power. They gave him to understand that the name of the place was the island of Barataria, either because the town was called Barataria, or because the government cost him so cheap. As soon as he came to the gates (for it was walled) the chief officers and inhabitants, in their formalities, came out to receive him,

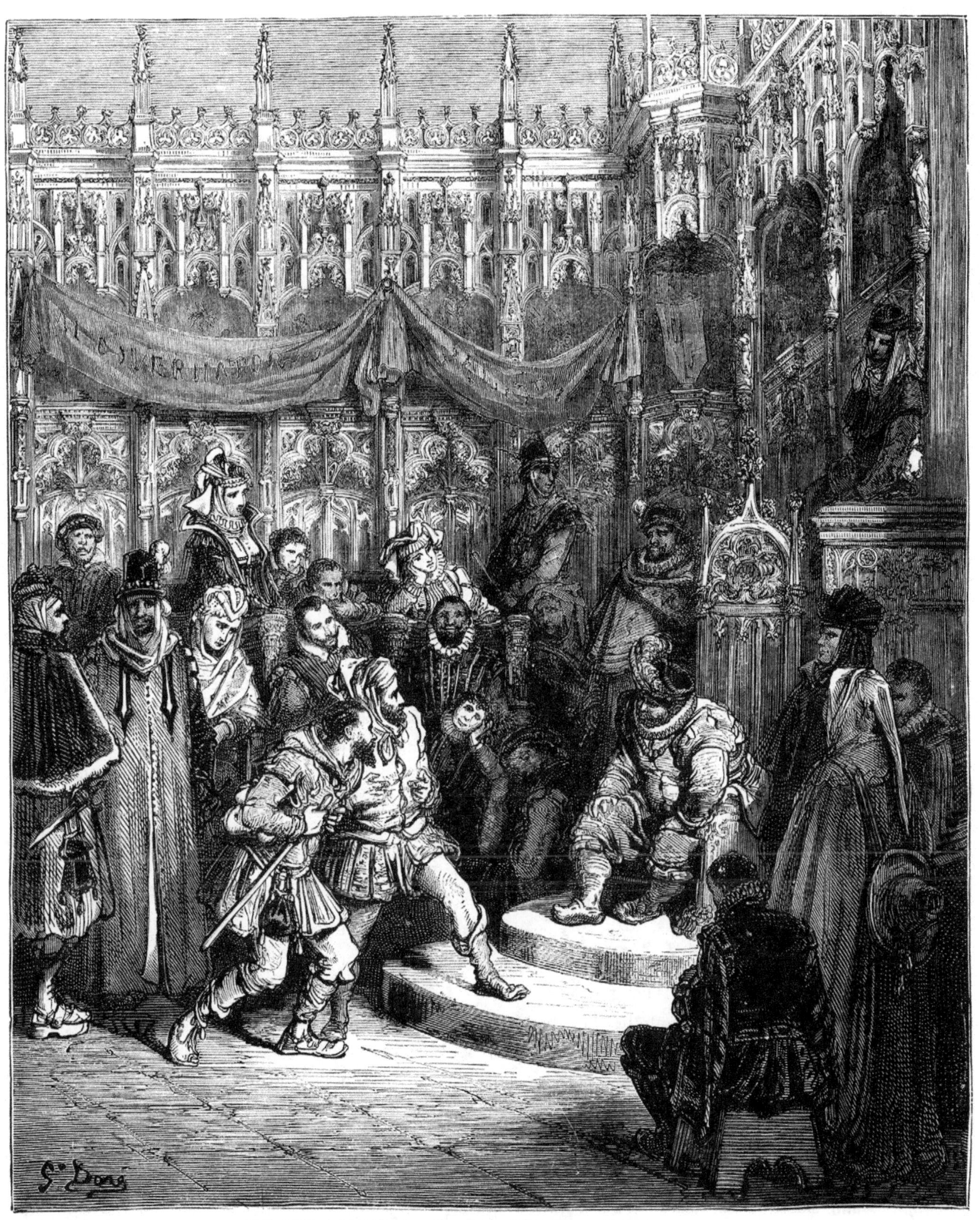

THE LORD GOVERNOR SANCHO PANZA ADMINISTERING JUSTICE.

the bells rung, and all the people gave demonstrations of their joy. The new governor was then carried in pomp to the great church, to give Heaven thanks; and, after some ridiculous ceremonies, they delivered him the keys of the gates, and received him as perpetual governor of the island of Barataria. In the meantime, the garb, the port, the huge beard, and the short and thick shape of the new governor, made every one who knew nothing of the jest wonder; and even those who were privy to the plot, who were many, were not a little surprised.

In short, from the church they carried him to the court of justice; where, when they had placed him in his seat, "My lord governor," said the duke's steward, "it is an ancient custom here, that he who takes possession of this famous island must answer to some intricate question; and, by the return he makes, the people feel the pulse of his understanding, and, by an estimate of his abilities, judge whether they ought to rejoice or to be sorry for his coming."

All the while the steward was speaking, Sancho was staring on an inscription in large characters on the wall over against his seat; and, as he could not read, he asked what was the meaning of that which he saw painted there upon the wall.

"Sir," said they, "it is an account of the day when your lordship took possession of this island; and the inscription runs thus: 'This day, being such a day of this month, in such a year, the Lord Don Sancho Panza took possession of this island, which may he long enjoy.'"

"And who is he," asked Sancho, "whom they call Don Sancho Panza?"

"Your lordship," answered the steward; "for we know of no other Panza in this island."

"Well, friend," said Sancho, "pray take notice that Don does not belong to me, nor was it borne by any of my family before me. Plain Sancho Panza is my name; my father was called Sancho, my grandfather Sancho, and all of us have been Panzas, without any Don or Donna added to our name. Now do I already guess your Dons are as thick as stones in this island. But it is enough that Heaven knows my meaning. If my government happens to last but four days to an end, it shall go hard but I will clear the island of those swarms of Dons that must needs be as troublesome as so many flesh-flies. Come, now for your question, good Mr. Steward, and I will answer it as well as I can, whether the town be sorry or pleased."

At the same instant two men came into the court, the one dressed like a country fellow, the other like a tailor, with a pair of shears in his hand. "If it please you, my lord," cried the tailor, "I and this farmer here are come before your worship. This honest man came to my shop yesterday, for, saving your presence, I am a tailor; so, my lord, he showed me a piece of cloth. 'Sir,' quoth he, 'is there enough of this to make a cap?' Whereupon I measured the stuff, and answered him, 'Yes, if it like your worship.' Now, as I imagined, do you see, he could not but imagine (and perhaps he imagined right enough) that I had a mind to cabbage some of his cloth, judging hard of us honest tailors. 'Pr'ythee,' quoth he, 'look there be not enough for two caps.' Now I smelt him out, and told him there was. Whereupon the old knave (if it like your worship), going on to the same tune, bid me look again, and see whether it would not make three; and at last, if it would not make five. I was resolved to humour my customer, and said it might; so we struck a bargain. Just now the man is come for his caps, which I gave him, but when I asked him for my money, he will have me give him his cloth again, or pay him for it."

"Is this true, honest man?" said Sancho to the farmer.

"Yes, if it please you," answered the fellow; "but pray, let him show the five caps."

"With all my heart," cried the tailor; and with that, pulling his hand from under his cloak, he held up five little tiny caps, hanging upon his four fingers and thumb, as upon so many pins. "There," quoth he, "you see the five caps this good gaffer asks for; and may I never whip a stitch more if I have wronged him of the least snip of his cloth."

The sight of the caps, and the oddness of the cause, set the whole court a-laughing. Only Sancho sat gravely considering a while, and then, "Methinks," said he, "this suit here needs not be long depending, but may be decided without any more ado, with a great deal of equity; and therefore the judgment of the court is, that the tailor shall lose his making, and the countryman his cloth, and that the caps be given to the poor prisoners, and so let there be an end of the business."

If this sentence provoked the laughter of the whole court, the next no less raised their admiration. For after the governor's order was executed, two old men appeared before him, one of them with a large cane in his hand, which he used as a staff. "My lord," said the other, who had none, "some time ago I lent this man ten gold crowns to do him a kindness, which money he was to repay me on demand. I did not ask him for it again in a good while, lest it should prove a greater inconveniency to him to repay me than he laboured under when he borrowed it. However, perceiving that he took no care to pay me, I have asked him for my due; nay, I have been forced to dun him hard for it. But still he did not only refuse to pay me again, but denied he owed me anything, and said, that if I lent him so much money, he certainly returned it. Now, because I have no witnesses of the loan, nor he of the pretended payment, I beseech your lordship to put him to his oath, and if he will swear he has paid me, I will freely forgive him before God and the world."

"What say you to this, old gentleman with the staff?" asked Sancho.

"Sir," answered the old man, "I own he lent me the gold; and since he requires my oath, I beg you will be pleased to hold down your rod of justice, that I may swear upon it how I have honestly and truly returned him his money."

Thereupon the governor held down his rod, and in the meantime the defendant gave his cane to the plaintiff to hold, as if it hindered him, while he was to make a cross and swear over the judge's rod. This done, he declared that it was true the other had lent him ten crowns, but that he had really returned him the same sum into his own hands; and that because he supposed the plaintiff had forgotten it, he was continually asking him for it. The great governor hearing this, asked the creditor what he had to reply. He made answer, that since his adversary had sworn it, he was satisfied, for he believed him to be a better Christian than offer to forswear himself, and that perhaps he had forgotten he had been repaid. Then the defendant took his cane again, and having made a low obeisance to the judge, was immediately leaving the court, which, when Sancho perceived, reflecting on the passage of the cane, and admiring the creditor's patience, after he had studied a while with his head leaning over his stomach, and his fore-finger on his nose, on a sudden he ordered the old man with the staff to be called back. When he was returned, "Honest man," said Sancho, "let me see that cane a little, I have a use for it."

"With all my heart," answered the other; "sir, here it is."

And with that he gave it him. Sancho took it, and giving it to the other old man, "There," said he, "go your ways, and Heaven be with you, for now you are paid."

"How so, my lord?" cried the old man; "do you judge this cane to be worth ten gold crowns?"

"Certainly," said the governor, "or else I am the greatest dunce in the world. And now you shall see whether I have not a head-piece fit to govern a whole kingdom upon a shift."

This said, he ordered the cane to be broken in open court, which was no sooner done, than out dropped the ten crowns. All the spectators were amazed, and began to look on their governor as a second Solomon. They asked him how he could conjecture that the ten crowns were in the cane. He told them that, having observed how the defendant gave it to the plaintiff to hold while he took his oath, and then swore he had truly returned him the money into his own hands, after which he took his cane again from the plaintiff; this considered, it came into his head that the money was lodged within the reed; from whence may be learned, that though sometimes those that govern are destitute of sense, yet it often pleases God to direct them in their judgment. Besides, he had heard the curate of his parish tell of such another business, and he had so special a memory, that were it not that he was so unlucky as to forget all he had a mind to remember, there could not have been a better in the whole island. At last the two old men went away, the one to his satisfaction, the other with much shame and disgrace; and the beholders were astonished; insomuch, that the person who was commissioned to register Sancho's words and actions, and observe his behaviour, was not able to determine whether he should not give him the character of a wise man, instead of that of a fool, which he had been thought to deserve.

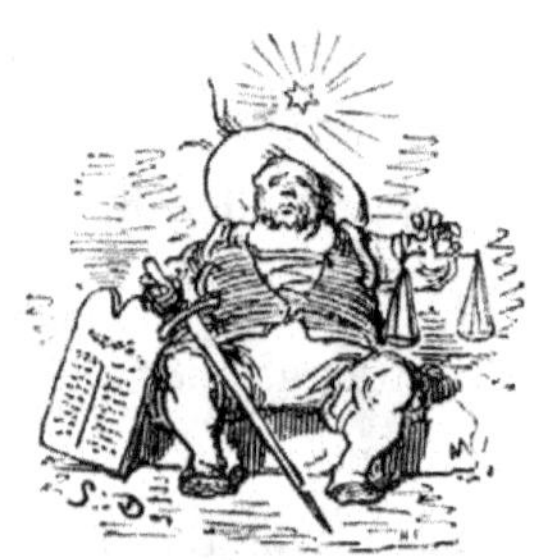

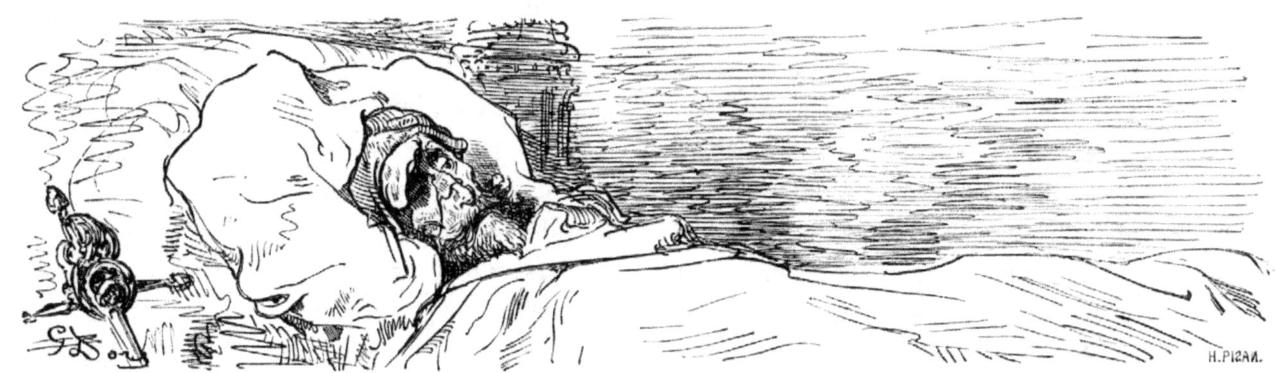

CHAPTER XLVI.

OF THE DREADFUL ALARM GIVEN TO DON QUIXOTE BY THE BELLS AND CATS, DURING THE COURSE OF ALTISIDORA'S AMOUR.

WE left the great Don Quixote profoundly buried in the thoughts into which the enamoured Altisidora's serenade had plunged him. He threw himself into his bed, but the cares and anxieties which he brought thither with him, like so many insects, allowed him no repose, and the misfortune of his torn stocking added to his affliction. But as time is swift, and no bolts nor chains can bar his rapid progress, posting away on the wings of the hours, the morning came on apace. At the return of light, Don Quixote, more early than the sun, forsook his downy bed, put on his chamois apparel, and, drawing on his walking boots, concealed in one of them the disaster of his hose. He threw his scarlet cloak over his shoulder, and clapped on his valiant head his cap of green velvet edged with silver lace. Over his right shoulder he hung his belt, the sustainer of his trusty executing sword. Round his wrist he wore the rosary, which he always carried about him; and thus accoutred, with a great deal of state and majesty, he moved towards the ante-chamber, where the duke and duchess were ready dressed, and, in a manner, expecting his coming. As he went through a gallery, he met Altisidora and her companion, who waited for him in the passage; and no sooner did Altisidora espy him, than she dissembled a swooning fit, and immediately dropped into the arms of her friend, who presently began to unlace her dress; which Don Quixote perceiving, he approached, and, turning to the damsel, "I know the meaning of all this," said he, "and whence these accidents proceed."

"You know more than I do," answered the assisting damsel; "but this I am sure of, that hitherto there is not a damsel in this house that has enjoyed her health better than Altisidora. I never knew her make the least complaint before. A vengeance seize all the knights-errant in the world, if they are all so ungrateful. Pray, my Lord Don Quixote, retire, for this poor young creature will not come to herself while you are by."

"Madam," answered the knight, "I beg that a lute may be left in my chamber this evening, that I may assuage this lady's grief as well as I can; for in the beginning of an amour, a speedy and free discovery of our aversion or pre-engagement is the most effectual cure."

This said, he left them, that he might not be found alone with them by those that might happen to go by. He was scarce gone when Altisidora's counterfeited fit was over; and, turning to her companion, "By all means," said she, "let him have a lute; for without doubt the knight has a mind to give us some music, and we shall have sport enough."

Then they went and acquainted the duchess with their proceeding, and Don Quixote's desiring a lute; whereupon, being overjoyed at the occasion, she plotted with the duke and her woman a new contrivance, to have a little harmless sport with the Don. After this they awaited, with a pleasing impatience, the return of night, which stole upon them as fast as had done the day, which the duke and duchess passed in agreeable converse with Don Quixote. The same day she dispatched a trusty page of hers, who had personated Dulcinea in the wood, to Teresa Panza, with her husband's letter, and the bundle of clothes which he had left behind him, charging him to bring her back a faithful account of every particular between them.

At last, it being eleven o'clock at night, Don Quixote retired to his apartment, and finding a lute there, he tuned it, opened the window, and perceiving there was somebody walking in the garden, he ran over the strings of the instrument; and having tuned it again as nicely as he could, he coughed and cleared his throat, and then, with a voice somewhat hoarse, yet not unmusical, he sung the following song, which he had composed himself that very day:—

THE ADVICE.

Love, a strong designing foe,
  Careless hearts with ease deceives;
Can thy breast resist his blow,
  Which your sloth unguarded leaves?

If you're idle, you're destroy'd,
  All his art on you he tries;
But be watchful and employ'd,
  Straight the baffled tempter flies.

Maids for modest grace admired,
  If they would their fortunes raise,
Must in silence live retired;
  'Tis their virtue speaks their praise.

Prudent men in this agree,
  Whether arms or courts they use;
They may trifle with the free,
  But for wives the virtuous choose.

Wanton loves, which, in their way,
  Roving travellers put on,
In the morn are fresh and gay,
  In the evening cold and gone.

Loves, that come with eager haste,
  Still with equal haste depart;
For an image ill imprest
  Soon is vanish'd from the heart.

On a picture fair and true
  Who would paint another face?
Sure no beauty can subdue,
  While a greater holds the place.

The divine Tobosan fair,
  Dulcinea, claims me whole;
Nothing can her image tear;
  'Tis one substance with my soul.

Then let fortune smile or frown,
  Nothing shall my faith remove;
Constant truth, the lover's crown,
  Can work miracles in love.

No sooner had Don Quixote made an end of his song, to which the duke duchess, Altisidora,

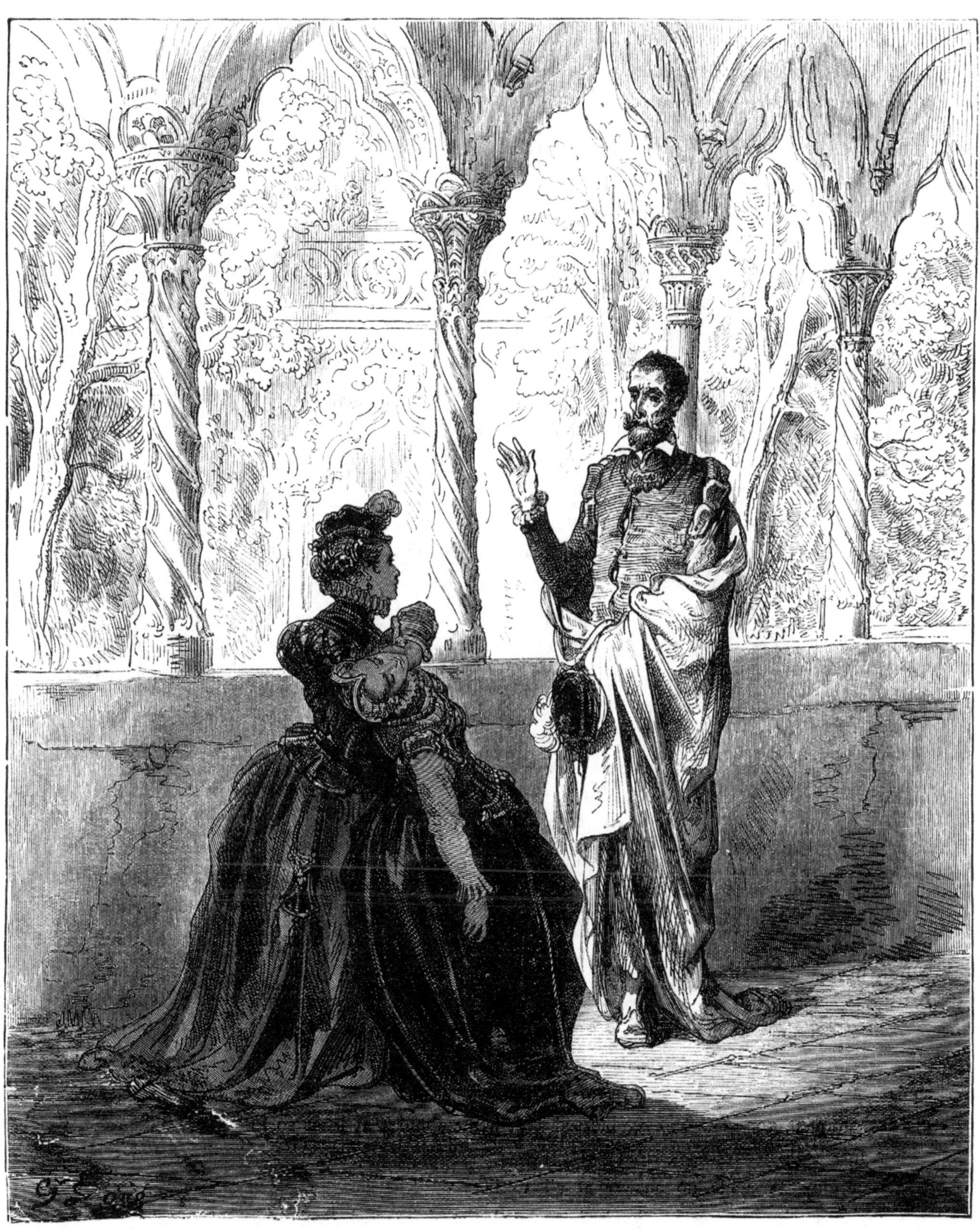

"Pray, my Lo.d Don Quixote, retire, for this poor young creature will not come to herself while you are by."

and almost all the people in the castle, listened all the while, than on a sudden, from an open gallery that was directly over the knight's window, they let down a rope, with at least a hundred little tinkling bells hanging about it. After that came down a great number of cats, poured out of a huge sack, all of them with smaller bells tied to their tails. The jangling of the bells, and the squalling of the cats, made such a dismal noise, that the very contrivers of the jest themselves were scared for a time, and Don Quixote was strangely surprised, and quite dismayed. At the same time, as ill luck would have it, two or three frighted cats leaped in through the bars of his chamber window, and, running up and down the room like so many evil spirits, one would have thought a whole legion of them had been flying about the chamber. They put out the candles that stood lighted there, and endeavoured to get out. Meanwhile the rope, with the bigger bells about it, was pulled up and down, and those who knew nothing of the contrivance were greatly surprised. At last, Don Quixote, recovering from his astonishment, drew his sword, and fenced and laid about him at the window, crying aloud, "Avaunt, ye wicked enchanters! hence, scoundrels! for I am Don Quixote de la Mancha, and all your devices cannot work their ends against me." And then, running after the cats that frisked about the room, he began to thrust and cut at them furiously, while they strove to get out. At last they made their escape at the window, all but one of them, who, finding himself hard put to it, flew in his face, and laying hold on his nose with his claws and teeth, put him to such pain, that the Don began to roar out as loud as he could. Thereupon the duke and the duchess, imagining the cause of his outcry, ran to his assistance immediately; and, having opened the door of his chamber with a master key, found the poor knight struggling hard with the cat, that would not quit its hold. By the light of the candles which they had with them, they saw the unequal combat. The duke offered to interpose, and take off the animal, but Don Quixote would not permit him. "Let nobody take him off," cried he; "let me alone hand to hand with this fiend, this sorcerer, this necromancer! I'll make him know what it is to deal with Don Quixote de la Mancha." But the cat not minding his threats, growled on, and still held fast, till at length the duke got its claws unhooked from the knight's flesh, and flung the beast out at the window. Don Quixote's face was hideously scratched, and his nose in no very good condition. Yet nothing vexed him so much as that they had rescued out of his hands that villainous necromancer. Immediately some ointment was sent for, and Altisidora herself, with her own lily-white hands, applied some plaisters to his sores, and whispering in his ear, as she was dressing him, "Cruel, hard-hearted knight!" said she, "all these disasters are befallen thee as a just punishment for thy obdurate stubbornness and disdain. May thy squire Sancho forget to whip himself, that thy darling Dulcinea may never be delivered from her enchantment, nor thou be ever blessed with her embraces, at least so long as I, thy neglected adorer, live."

Don Quixote made no answer at all to this, only he heaved a profound sigh, and then went to take his repose, after he had returned the duke and duchess thanks, not so much for their assistance against that rascally crew of caterwauling and jangling enchanters, for he defied them all, but for their kindness and good intent. Then the duke and duchess left him, not a little troubled at the miscarriage of their jest, which they did not think would have proved so fatal to the knight, as to oblige him, as it did, to keep his chamber five days, during which time there happened to him another adventure, more pleasant than the last, which, however, cannot be now related, for the historian must return to Sancho Panza, who was very busy and no less pleasant in his government.

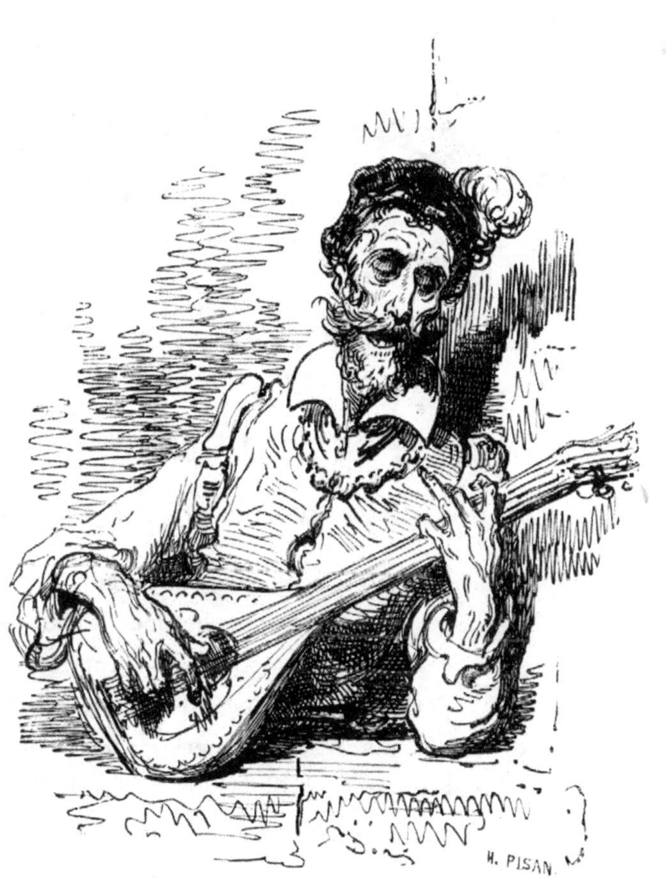

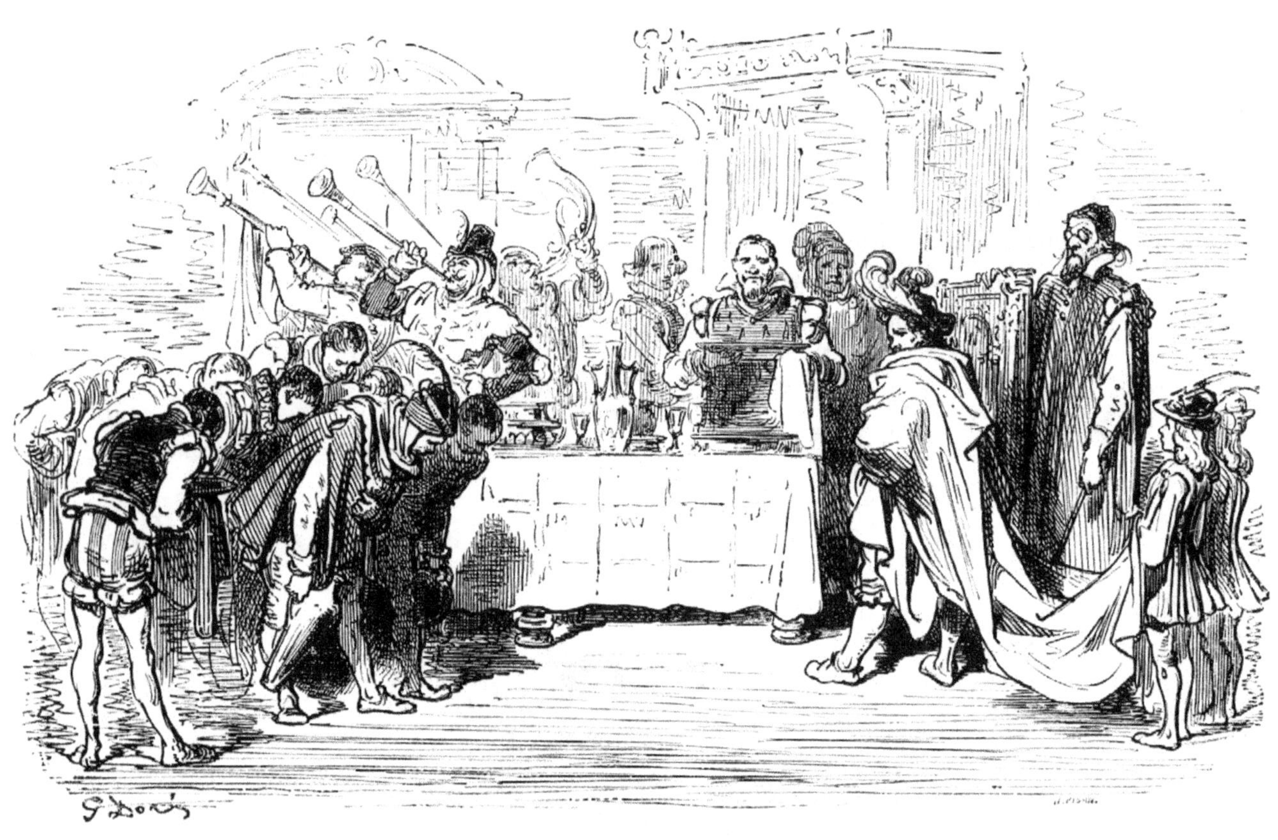

CHAPTER XLVII.

A FURTHER ACCOUNT OF SANCHO PANZA'S BEHAVIOUR IN HIS GOVERNMENT.

THE history informs us that Sancho was conducted from the court of justice to a sumptuous palace, where, in a spacious room, he found the cloth laid, and a most neat and magnificent entertainment prepared. As soon as he entered, the wind-music played and four pages waited on him, in order to the washing his hands, which he did with a great deal of gravity. And now the instruments ceasing, Sancho sat down at the upper end of the table, for there was no seat but there, and the cloth was only laid for one. A certain personage, who afterwards appeared to be a physician, came and stood at his elbow, with a whalebone wand in his hand. Then they took off a curious white cloth that lay over the dishes on the table, and discovered great variety of fruit, and other eatables. One that looked like a student said grace; a page put a laced bib under Sancho's chin, and another, who did the office of server, set a dish of fruit before him. But he had hardly put one bit into his mouth, before the physician touched the dish with his wand, and then it was taken away by a page in an instant. Immediately another, with meat, was clapped in the place, but Sancho no sooner offered to taste it than the doctor, with the wand, conjured it away as fast as the

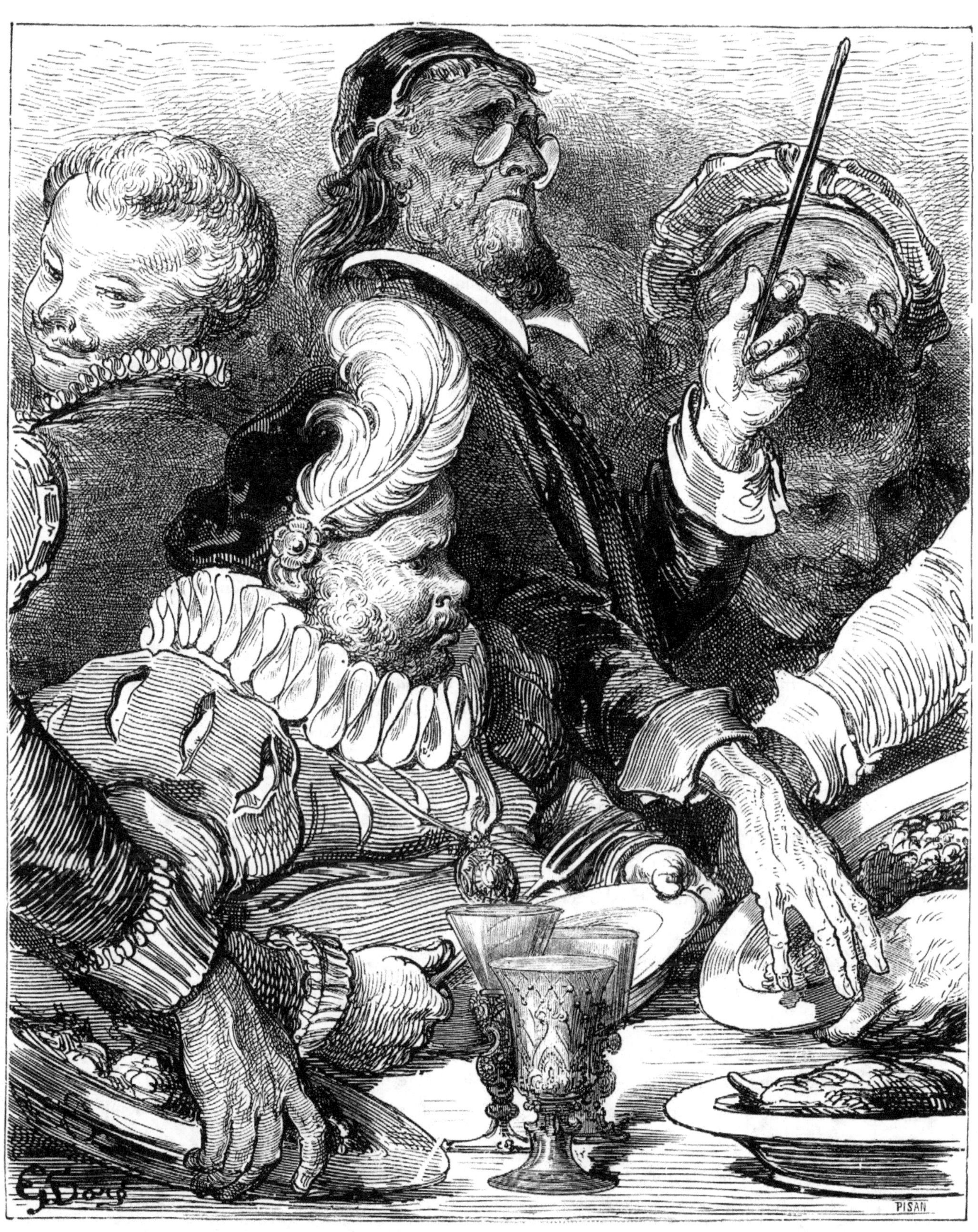

"'*Absit!*' cried the doctor."

fruit. Sancho was amazed at this sudden removal, and looking about him on the company, asked them, whether they used to tantalise people at that rate, feeding their eyes and starving their bellies.

"My lord governor," answered the physician, "you are to eat here no otherwise than according to the use and custom of other islands where there are governors. I am a doctor of physic, my lord, and have a salary allowed me in this island for taking charge of the governor's health, and I am more careful of it than of my own, studying night and day his constitution, that I may know what to prescribe when he falls sick. Now, the chief thing I do is to attend him always at his meals, to let him eat what I think convenient for him, and to prevent his eating what I imagine to be prejudicial to his health, and offensive to his stomach. Therefore I now ordered the fruit to be taken away, because it is too cold and moist; and the other dish, because it is as much too hot, and over-seasoned with spices, which are apt to increase thirst; and he that drinks much destroys and consumes the radical moisture, which is the fuel of life.

"So, then," quoth Sancho, "this dish of roasted partridges can do me no manner of harm."

"Hold," said the physician, "the lord governor shall not eat of them while I live to prevent it."

"Why so?" cried Sancho. "Because," answered the doctor, "our great master, Hippocrates, the north star and luminary of physic, says, in one of his aphorisms. *Omnis saturatio mala, perdicis autem pessima;* that is, 'All repletion is bad, but that of partridges is worst of all.'"

"If it be so," said Sancho, "let Mr. Doctor see which of all these dishes on the table will do me the most good and least harm, and let me eat my bellyful of that, without having it whisked away with his wand. For, by my hopes and the pleasures of government, as I live, I am ready to die with hunger; and not to allow me to eat any victuals (let Mr. Doctor say what he will) is the way to shorten my life, and not to lengthen it."

"Very true, my lord," replied the physician; "however, I am of opinion you ought not to eat of these rabbits, as being a hairy, furry sort of food; nor would I have you taste that veal. Indeed, if it were neither roasted nor pickled, something might be said; but, as it is, it must not be."

"Well, then," said Sancho, "what think you of that huge dish yonder, that smokes so? I take it to be an *olla podrida;* and that being a hodge-podge of so many sorts of victuals, sure I cannot but light upon something there that will nick me, and be both wholesome and toothsome."

"*Absit!*" cried the doctor; "far be such an ill thought from us. No diet in the world yields worse nutriment than those mish-mashes do. No, leave that luxurious compound to your rich monks and prebendaries, your masters of colleges and lusty feeders at country weddings;

but let them not encumber the tables of governors, where nothing but delicate, unmixed viands, in their prime, ought to make their appearance. The reason is, that simple medicines are generally allowed to be better than compounds; for in a composition there may happen a mistake, by the unequal proportion of the ingredients; but simples are not subject to that accident. Therefore, what I would advise at present, as a fit diet for the governor, for the preservation and support of his health, is a hundred of small wafers, and a few thin slices of marmalade, to strengthen his stomach, and help digestion." Sancho, hearing this, leaned back upon his chair, and, looking earnestly in the doctor's face, very seriously asked him what his name was, and where he had studied? "My lord," answered he, "I am called Dr. Pedro Rezio de Aguero. The name of the place where I was born is Tirteafuera, and lies between Caraquel and Almodabar del Campo, on the right hand; and I took my degree of doctor in the University of Ossuna."

"Hark you," said Sancho, in a mighty chafe, "Mr. Doctor Pedro Rezio de Aguero, born at Tirteafuera, that lies between Caraquel and Almodabar del Campo, on the right hand, and who took your degrees of doctor at the University of Ossuna, and so forth, take yourself away! Avoid the room this moment, or, by the sun's light, I'll get me a good cudgel, and, beginning with your carcase, will so belabour and rib-roast all the physic-mongers in the island, that I will not leave therein one of the tribe of those, I mean, that are ignorant quacks; for, as for learned and wise physicians, I will make much of them, and honour them like so many angels. Once more, Pedro Rezio, I say, get out of my presence. Avaunt! or I will take the chair I sit upon, and comb your head with it to some purpose, and let me be called to an account about it when I give up my office; I do not care, I will clear myself by saying I did the world good service in ridding it of a bad physician, the plague of a commonwealth. Bless me! let me eat, or let them take their government again; for an office that will not afford a man his victuals is not worth two horse-beans." The physician was terrified, seeing the governor in such a heat, and would that moment have slunk out of the room, had not the sound of a post-horn in the street been heard; whereupon the steward, immediately looking out of the window, turned back, and said there was an express come from the duke, doubtless with some despatch of importance.

Presently the messenger entered sweating, with haste and concern in his looks, and, pulling a packet out of his bosom, delivered it to the governor. Sancho gave it to the steward, and ordered him to read the direction, which was this: "To Don Sancho Panza, governor of the island of Barataria, to be delivered into his own hands, or those of his secretary."

"Who is my secretary?" cried Sancho.

"It is I, my lord," answered one that was standing by; "for I can read and write, and am a Biscayner."

"That last qualification is enough to make thee set up for secretary to the emperor himself," said Sancho. "Open the letter, then, and see what it says." The new secretary did

R R

so, and, having perused the despatch by himself, told the governor that it was a business that was to be told only in private. Sancho ordered every one to leave the room, except the steward and the carver, and then the secretary read what follows :—

"I have received information, my Lord Don Sancho Panza, that some of our enemies intend to attack your island with great fury, one of these nights. You ought, therefore, to be watchful, and stand upon your guard, that you may not be found unprovided. I have also had intelligence from faithful spies, that there are four men got into the town in disguise, to murder you, your abilities being regarded as a great obstacle to the enemy's designs. Look about you, take heed how you admit strangers to speak with you, and eat nothing that is laid before you. I will take care to send you assistance, if you stand in need of it. And, in everything, I rely on your prudence. From our castle, the 16th of August, at four in the morning.—Your friend, THE DUKE."

Sancho was astonished at the news, and those that were with him were no less concerned. But, at last, turning to the steward, "I will tell you," said he, "what is first to be done in this case, and that with all speed. Clap me that same Doctor Rezio in a dungeon, for, if anybody has a mind to kill me, it must be he, and that with a lingering death, the worst of deaths—hunger-starving."

"However," said the carver, "I am of opinion your honour ought not to eat any of the things that stand here before you, for they were sent in by some of the convents; and it is a common saying, 'The devil lurks behind the cross.'"

"Which nobody can deny," quoth Sancho; "and, therefore, let me have for the present but a luncheon of bread and some four pound of raisins; there can be no poison in that; for, in short, I cannot live without eating; and, if we must be in readiness against these battles, we had need be well victualled, for it is the belly keeps up the heart, and not the heart the belly. Meanwhile, secretary, do you send my lord duke an answer, and tell him his order shall be fulfilled in every part, without fail. Remember me kindly to my lady duchess, and beg of her not to forget to send one on purpose, with my letter and bundle, to Teresa Panza, my wife, which I shall take as a special favour, and I will be mindful to serve her to the best of my power. And when your hand is in, you may crowd in my service to my master, Don Quixote de la Mancha, that he may see I am neither forgetful nor ungrateful. The rest I leave to you; put in what you will, and do your part like a good secretary and a staunch Biscayner. Now, take away here, and bring me something to eat, and then you shall see that I am able to deal with all the spies, wizards, and cut-throat dogs that dare to meddle with me and my island."

At that time, a page entering the room, "My lord," said he, "there is a countryman without desires to speak with your lordship about business of great consequence."

"It is a strange thing," cried Sancho, "that one must still be plagued with these men of business! Is it possible they should be such sots, as not to understand that this is not a time for business? Do they fancy that we governors and distributors of justice are made of iron and marble, and have no need of rest and refreshment, like other creatures of flesh and blood? Well, before Heaven, and on my conscience, if my government does but last, as I shrewdly guess it will not, I will get some of these men of business laid by the heels. Well, for once, let the fellow come in; but, first, take heed he be not one of the spies or ruffian rogues that would murder me."

"As for that," said the page, "I dare say he had no hand in the plot. Poor soul! he looks as if he could not help it. There is no more harm in him, seemingly, than in a piece of good bread."

"There is no need to fear," said the steward, "since we are all here by you."

"But, hark you," quoth Sancho, "now Doctor Rezio is gone, might not I eat something that has some substance in it, though it were but a crust and an onion?"

"At night," answered the carver, "your honour shall have no cause to complain; supper shall make amends for the want of your dinner."

"Heaven grant it may!" said Sancho.

Now the countryman came in, and by his looks seemed to be a good, harmless, silly soul. As soon as he entered the room, "Which is my lord governor?" quoth he.

"Who but he that sits in the chair?" answered the secretary.

"I humble myself to his worship's presence," quoth the fellow; and with that, falling on his knees, begged to kiss his hand, which Sancho refused, but bid him rise, and tell him what he had to say. The countryman then got up: "My lord," quoth he, "I am a husbandman of Miguel Turra, a town some two leagues from Ciudad-Real."

"Here is another Tirteafuera," quoth Sancho. "Well, go on, friend; I know the place full well: it is not far from our town."

"If it please you," said the countryman, "my business is this: I was married, by Heaven's mercy, in the face of our holy mother, the Roman Catholic Church, and I have two boys that take their learning at the college; the youngest studies to become a bachelor, and the eldest to be a master of arts. I am a widower, because my wife is dead; she died, if it please you, or, to speak more truly, she was killed, as a body may say, by a doctor, who gave her a wrong medicine."

"So, then," quoth Sancho, "had not your wife died, or had they not made her die, you had not been a widower."

"Very true," answered the man.

"We are much the nearer," cried Sancho; "go on, honest friend, and pr'ythee dispatch, for it is rather time to take an afternoon's nap, than to talk of business."

"Now, sir, I must tell you," continued the farmer, "that that son of mine, the bachelor of arts that is to be, fell in love with a maiden of our town, Clara Perlerino by name, the daughter of Andrew Perlerino, a mighty rich farmer; and Perlerino is not the right name neither, but, because the whole generation of them is troubled with the palsy, they used to be called, from the name of that ailing, Perlaticos, but now they go by that of Perlerino; and, truly, it fits the young woman rarely, for she is a precious pearl for beauty, especially if you stand on her right side, and view her—she looks like a flower in the fields. On the left, indeed, she does not look altogether so well, for there she wants an eye, which she lost by the small pox, that has digged many pits somewhat deep all over her face; but those that wish her well say that is nothing, and that those pits are so many graves to bury lovers' hearts in. She is so cleanly, that, because she will not have her nose drop upon her lips, she carries it cocked up; and her nostrils are turned up on each side, as if they shunned her mouth, that is somewhat of the widest; but, for all that, she looks exceedingly well; and, were it not for some ten or dozen of her butter-teeth and grinders which she wants, she might set up for one of the cleverest lasses in the country. As for her lips, I do not know what to say of them, for they are so thin and so slender, that, were it the fashion to wind lips as they do silk, one might make a skein of hers; besides, they are not of the ordinary hue of common lips; no, they are of the most wonderful colour that ever was seen, as being speckled with blue, green, and orange tawny. I hope my lord governor will pardon me for dwelling thus on the picture and several rare features of her that is one day to be my daughter, seeing it is merely out of my hearty love and affection for the girl."

"Pr'ythee, paint on as long as thou wilt," said Sancho; "I am mightily taken with this kind of painting."

"Could I set before your eyes her pretty carriage and her shape," quoth the fellow, "you would admire. But that is not to be done, for she is so crooked and crumpled up together, that her knees and her chin meet; and yet any one may perceive that, if she could but stand upright, her head would touch the very ceiling; and she would have given her hand to my son the bachelor, in the way of matrimony, before now, but that she is not able to stretch it forth, the sinews being quite shrunk up. However, the broad, long-guttered nails add no small grace to it, and may let you know what a well-made hand she has."

"So far, so good," said Sancho; "but let us suppose you have drawn her from head to foot; what is it you would be at now? Come to the point, friend, without so many windings and turnings, and going round about the bush."

"Sir," said the farmer, "I would desire your honour to do me the kindness to give me a letter of accommodation to the father of my daughter-in-law, beseeching him to be pleased to let the marriage be fulfilled, seeing we are not unlike neither in estate nor bodily concerns; for, to tell you the truth, my lord governor, my son is bewitched, and there is not a day passes over his head but the foul fiends torment him three or four times; and, having once had the ill-luck to fall into the fire, the skin of his face is shrivelled up like a piece of parchment, and his eyes are somewhat sore, and full of rheum. But, when all is said, he has the temper of an angel."

"Have you anything else to ask, honest man?" said Sancho.

"Only one thing more," quoth the farmer; "but I am somewhat afraid to speak it; yet I cannot find in my heart to let it rot within me; and therefore, fall back fall edge, I must out with it. I would desire your worship to bestow on me some three hundred or six hundred ducats towards my bachelor's portion, only to help him to begin the world, and furnish him a house; for, in short, they would live by themselves, without being subject to the impertinencies of a father-in-law."

"Well," said Sancho, "see if you would have anything else; if you would, do not let fear or bashfulness be your hindrance: out with it, man."

"No, truly," quoth the farmer; and he had scarcely spoken the words, when the governor, starting up, and laying hold of the chair he sat on, "You brazen-faced, silly, impudent country booby," cried he, "get out of my presence this moment, or, by the blood of the Panzas, I will crack your jolter-head with this chair! What care I for Miguel Turra, or all the generation of the Perlerinos? Avoid the room, I say, or, by the life of the duke, I'll be as good as my word, and ding out thy cuckoo brains. It is not a day and a half that I have been governor, and thou wouldst have me have six hundred ducats already, dunderheaded sot!"

The steward made signs to the farmer to withdraw, and he went out accordingly, hanging down his head, and, to all appearance, very much afraid lest the governor should make good his angry threats; for the cunning knave knew very well how to act his part. But let us leave Sancho in his angry mood, and let there be peace and quietness, while we return to Don Quixote, whom we left with his face covered over with plaisters, the scratches which he had got when the cat so clapper-clawed him having obliged him to no less than eight days' retirement; during which time there happened that to him which Cid Hamet promises to relate with the same punctuality and veracity with which he delivers the particulars of this history, how trivial soever they may be.

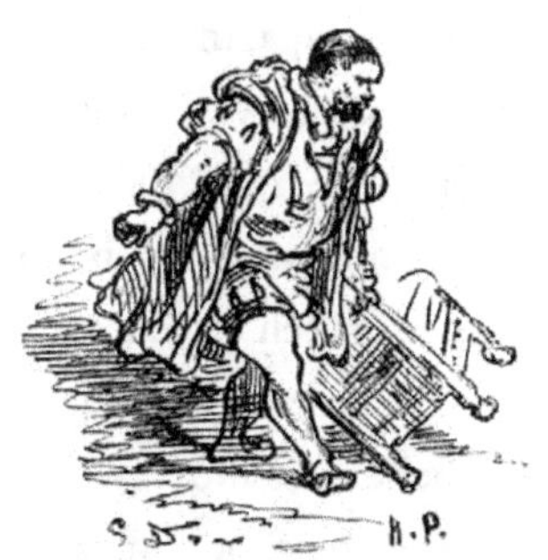

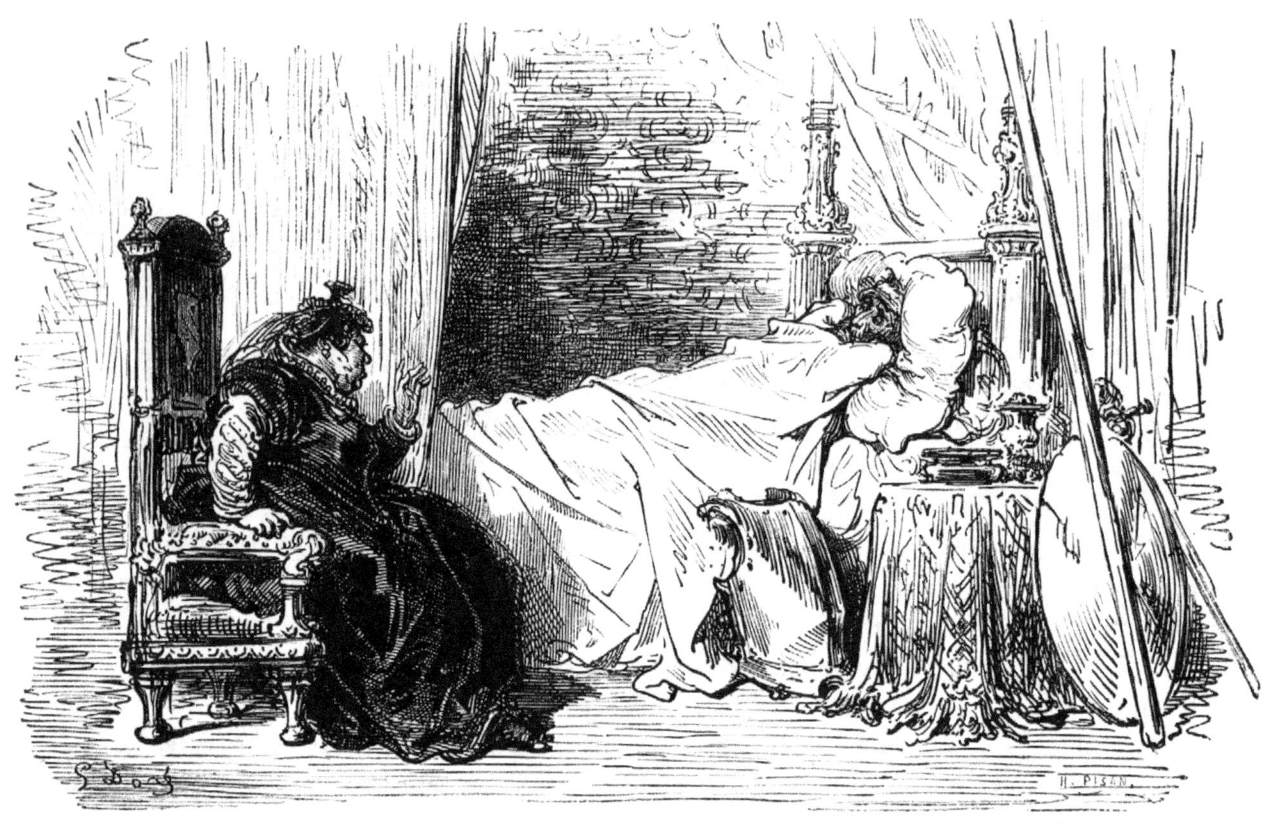

CHAPTER XLVIII.

WHAT HAPPENED TO DON QUIXOTE WITH DONNA RODRIGUEZ, THE DUCHESS'S WOMAN; AS ALSO OTHER PASSAGES WORTHY TO BE RECORDED AND HAD IN ETERNAL REMEMBRANCE.

DON QUIXOTE, thus unhappily hurt, was extremely sullen and melancholy, his face wrapped up and marked, not by the hand of a superior being, but the paws of a cat, a misfortune incident to knight-errantry. He was six days without appearing in public; and one night, when he was thus confined to his apartment, as he lay awake reflecting on his misfortunes and Altisidora's importunities, he perceived somebody was opening his chamber-door with a key. Up he got in the bed, wrapped from head to foot in a yellow satin quilt, with a woollen cap on his head, his face and his moustachios bound up, his face to heal his scratches, and his moustachios to keep them down; in which posture he looked like the strangest apparition that can be imagined. He fixed his eyes towards the door, and when he expected to have seen the yielding and doleful Altisidora, he beheld a most reverend matron approaching in a white veil, so long that it covered her from head to foot. Betwixt her left-hand fingers she carried half a candle lighted, and held her right before her face, to keep the blaze of the taper from her eyes, which were hidden by a huge pair of spectacles. All the way she trod very softly, and moved at a very slow pace. Don Quixote watched her motions, and observing her garb

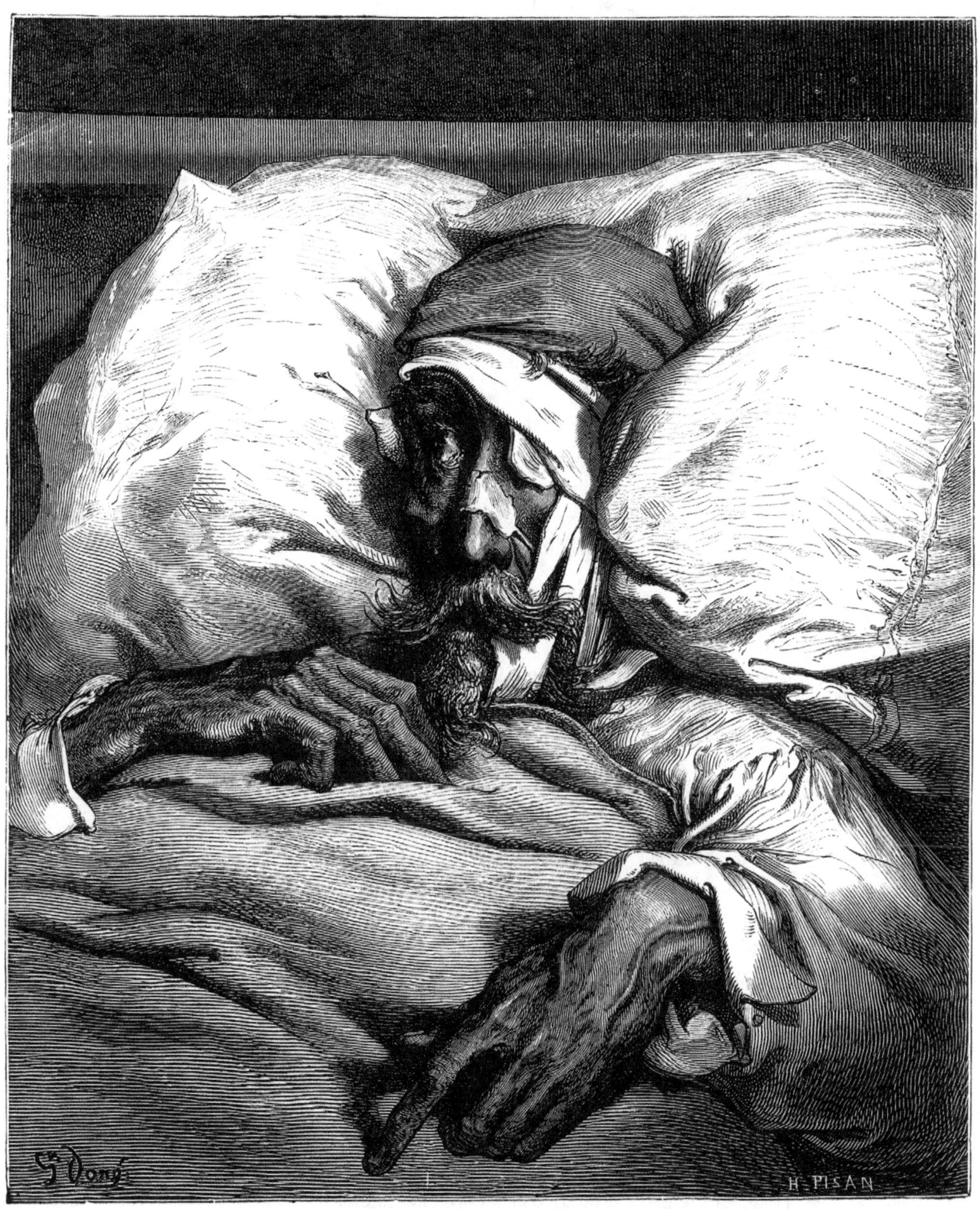

"Don Quixote, thus unhappily hurt, was extremely sullen and melancholy."

and silence, took her for some witch or enchantress that came in that dress to practise her wicked sorceries upon him, and began to make the sign of the cross as fast as he could. The vision advanced all the while, and being got to the middle of the chamber, lifted up its eyes, and saw Don Quixote thus making a thousand crosses on his breast. But if he was astonished at the sight of such a figure, she was no less affrighted at his; so that, as soon as she spied him thus wrapped up in yellow, so lank, bepatched, and muffled up, "Bless me!" cried she "What is this?"

With the sudden fright she dropped the candle, and now, being in the dark, as she was running out, the length of her dress made her stumble, and down she fell in the middle of the chamber. Don Quixote at the same time was in great anxiety. "Phantom," cried he, "or whatsoever thou art, I conjure thee to tell me who thou art, and what thou requirest of me. If thou art a soul in torment, tell me, and I will endeavour thy ease to the utmost of my power; for I am a catholic Christian, and love to do good to all mankind; for which reason I took upon me the order of knight-errantry, whose extensive duties engage me to relieve all in distress."

The poor old woman, hearing herself thus conjured, judged Don Quixote's fears by her own, and therefore, with a low and doleful voice, "My Lord Don Quixote," said she, "if you are he, I am neither a phantom nor a ghost, as I suppose you fancy, but Donna Rodriguez, my lady duchess's matron of honour, who come to you about a certain grievance, of the nature of those which you use to redress."

"Tell me, Donna Rodriguez," said Don Quixote, "are not you come to manage some love intrigue? If you are, take it from me, you will lose your labour. It is all in vain, thanks to the peerless beauty of my Lady Dulcinea del Toboso. In a word, madam, provided you come not on some such embassy, you may go light your candle and return, and we will talk of anything you please; but remember, I bar all dangerous insinuations, all amorous enticements."

"What!" cried the matron; "I find you do not know me, sir. But stay a little, I will go light my candle, and then I will tell you my misfortunes, for it is you that sets to right everything in the world."

This said, away she went, without stopping for an answer

Don Quixote waited for her a while quietly, but his working brain soon started a thousand chimeras concerning this new adventure, and he fancied he did ill in giving way, though but to a thought of endangering his faith to his mistress. So he started from the bed to lock the door and shut out Donna Rodriguez; but in that very moment she happened to come in with a wax candle lighted; at which time spying the knight near her, wrapped in his quilt, his face bound up, and a woollen cap on his head, she was frighted again, and started two or three steps back.

Here Cid Hamet (making a parenthesis) swears by Mahomet he would have given the

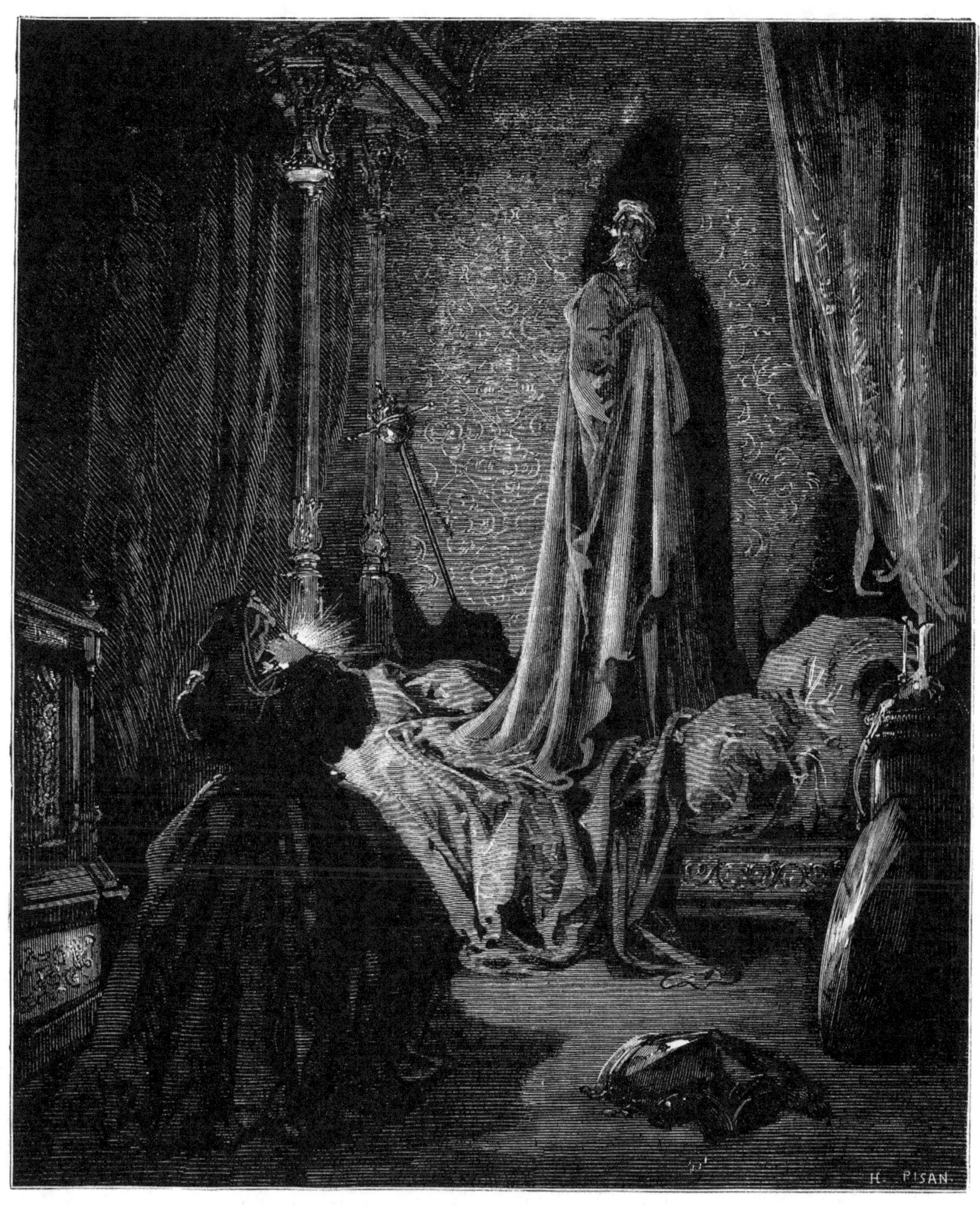

"'Bless me!' cried she, 'what is this?'"

best coat of two that he had, only to have seen the knight and the matron thus. To make short, Don Quixote went to bed again, and Donna Rodriguez sat down in a chair at some distance, without taking off her spectacles, or setting down the candle. Don Quixote crowded up together, and covered himself close, all but his face, and after they had both remained in silence, the first that broke it was the knight.

"Now, madam," said he, "you may freely unburden your heart, sure of attention to your complaints from chaste ears, and assistance in your distress from a compassionate heart."

"I believe as much," said the matron, "and promised myself no less charitable an answer from a person of so graceful and pleasing a presence. The case then is, noble sir, that though you see me sitting in this chair, in the middle of Arragon, in the habit of an insignificant, unhappy duenna, I am of Asturias de Oviedo, and one of the best families in that province. But my hard fortune, and the neglect of my parents, who fell to decay too soon, I cannot tell how, brought me to Madrid, where, because they could do no better, for fear of the worst, they placed me with a court lady, to be her chamber-maid. And, though I say it, for all manner of plain work I was never outdone by any one in all my life. My father and mother left me at service, and returned home, and some few years after they both died, and went to heaven, I hope; for they were very good and religious Catholics. Then was I left an orphan, and wholly reduced to the sorrowful condition of such court servants, wretched wages, and a slender allowance. About the same time the gentleman-usher fell in love with me before I dreamt of any such thing, Heaven knows. He was somewhat stricken in years, had a fine beard, was a personable man, and, what is more, as good a gentleman as the king, for he was of the mountains. We did not carry matters so close in our love but it came to my lady's ear; and so, to hinder people's tongues, without any more ado, she caused us to be married in the face of our holy mother, the Catholic Church. My husband (rest his soul!) died a while after of a fright; and had I but time to tell you how it happened, I dare say you would wonder." Here she began to weep piteously. "Good sir," cried she, "I must beg your pardon, for I cannot contain myself. As often as I think of my poor husband I cannot forbear shedding of tears. Bless me! how he looked, and with what stateliness he would ride, with my lady behind him, on a stout mule as black as jet; for coaches and chairs were not used then as they are now-a-days, but the ladies rode behind the gentlemen-ushers. And now my tongue is in, I cannot help telling you the whole story, that you may see what a fine, well-bred man my dear husband was, and how nice in every punctilio.

"One day, at Madrid, as he came into St. James's Street, which is somewhat narrow, with my lady behind him, he met a judge of the court, with two officers before him; whereupon as soon as he saw him, to show his respect, my husband turned about his mule, as if he designed to have waited on him. But my lady whispered him in the ear, 'What do you mean, blockhead?' said she; 'do not you know I am here?' The judge, on his side, was no less civil; and stopping his horse, 'Sir,' said he, 'pray keep your way; you must not wait on me; it becomes me rather to wait on my Lady Gasilda' (for that was my lady's name). However, my husband, with his hat in his hand, persisted in his civil intentions. But at last the lady, being very angry with him for it, took a great pin, or rather, as I am apt to believe, a bodkin, out of her case, and run it into his back; upon which, my husband suddenly starting and crying out, fell out of the saddle, and pulled down my lady after him. Immediately two of her footmen ran to help her, and the judge and his officers did the like. The gate of Guadalajara was presently in a hubbub (the idle people about the gate, I mean). In short, my lady returned home a-foot, and my husband went to a surgeon, complaining that he was pricked through the lungs. And now this civility of his was talked of everywhere, insomuch that the very boys in the streets would flock about him and cheer him; for which reason, and because he was somewhat short-sighted, my lady dismissed him her service, which he took so to heart, poor man! that it cost him his life soon after. Now was I left a poor, helpless widow, and with a daughter to keep, who still increased in beauty as she grew up, like the foam of the sea. At length, having the name of an excellent workwoman at my needle, my lady duchess, who was newly married to his grace, took me to live with her here in Arragon, and my daughter as well as myself. In time the girl grew up, and became the most accomplished creature in the world. She sings like a lark, dances like a fairy, trips like a wild buck, writes and reads like a schoolmaster, and casts accounts like a usurer. I say nothing of her neatness, but certainly the purest spring water that runs is not more cleanly; and then for her age, she is now, if I mistake not, just sixteen years, five months, and three days old. Now, who should happen to fall in love with this daughter of mine but a mighty rich farmer's son, that lives in one of my lord duke's villages not far off; and, indeed, I cannot tell how he managed matters, but he plied her so close, that, upon a promise of marriage, he wheedled her into a consent, and now refuses to make his word good. The duke is no stranger to the business, for I have made complaint to him about it many and many times, and begged of him to enjoin the young man to wed my daughter; but he turns his deaf ear to me, and cannot endure I should speak to him of it, because the young knave's father is rich, and lends the duke money, and is bound for him upon all occasions, so that he would by no means disoblige him.

"Therefore, sir, I apply myself to your worship, and beseech you to see my daughter righted, either by entreaties or by force, seeing everybody says you were sent into the world to redress grievances, and assist those in adversity. Be pleased to cast an eye of pity on my daughter's orphan state, her beauty, her youth, and all her other good parts; for, on my conscience, of all the damsels my lady has, there is not one can come up to her by a mile; no, not she that is cried up as the airiest and finest of them all, whom they call Altisidora: I am sure she is not to be named the same day; for, let me tell you, sir, 'all is not gold that glitters.' This same Altisidora, after all, is a hoity-toity, that has more vanity than beauty, and less modesty than confidence. Nay, my lady duchess, too—but I must say no more, for, as they say, walls have ears."

Scarce had Donna Rodriguez said these words, when at one bounce the chamber-door flew open, whereupon she was seized with such a terrible fright, that she let fall her candle, and the room remained as dark as a wolf's mouth, as the saying is, and presently the poor duenna felt somebody hold her by the throat, and squeeze her so hard, that it was not in her power to cry out; and another laid on her so unmercifully with a slipper, or some such thing, that it would have moved any one, but those that did it, to pity. Don Quixote was not without compassion, yet he did not think fit to stir from the bed, but lay snug and silent all the while, not knowing what the meaning of this bustle might be, fearing lest the tempest that poured on the matron might also light upon himself; and not without reason, for, indeed, after the mute executioners had well cured the old gentlewoman (who durst not cry out), they came to Don Quixote, and turning up the bed-clothes, pinched him so hard and so long, that, in his own defence, he could not forbear laying about him with his fists as well as he could, till at last, after the scuffle had lasted about half an hour, the invisible phantoms vanished.

Donna Rodriguez, lamenting her hard fortune, left the room without speaking a word to the knight. As for him, he remained where he was, sadly pinched and tired, and very moody and thoughtful, not knowing who this wicked enchanter should be that had used him in that manner. But we shall know that in its proper time. Now let us leave him, and return to Sancho Panza, who calls upon us, as the order of our history requires.

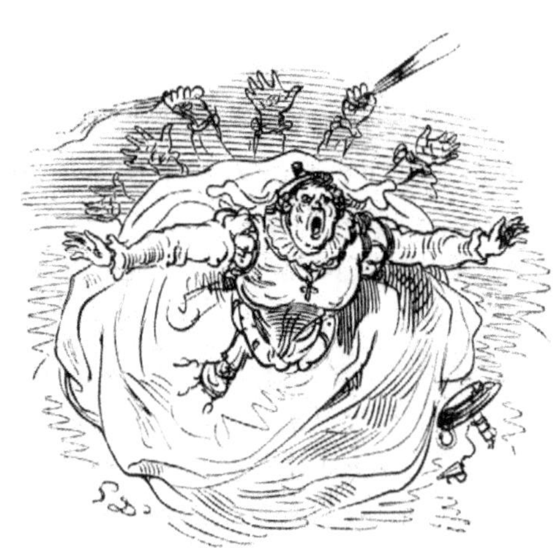

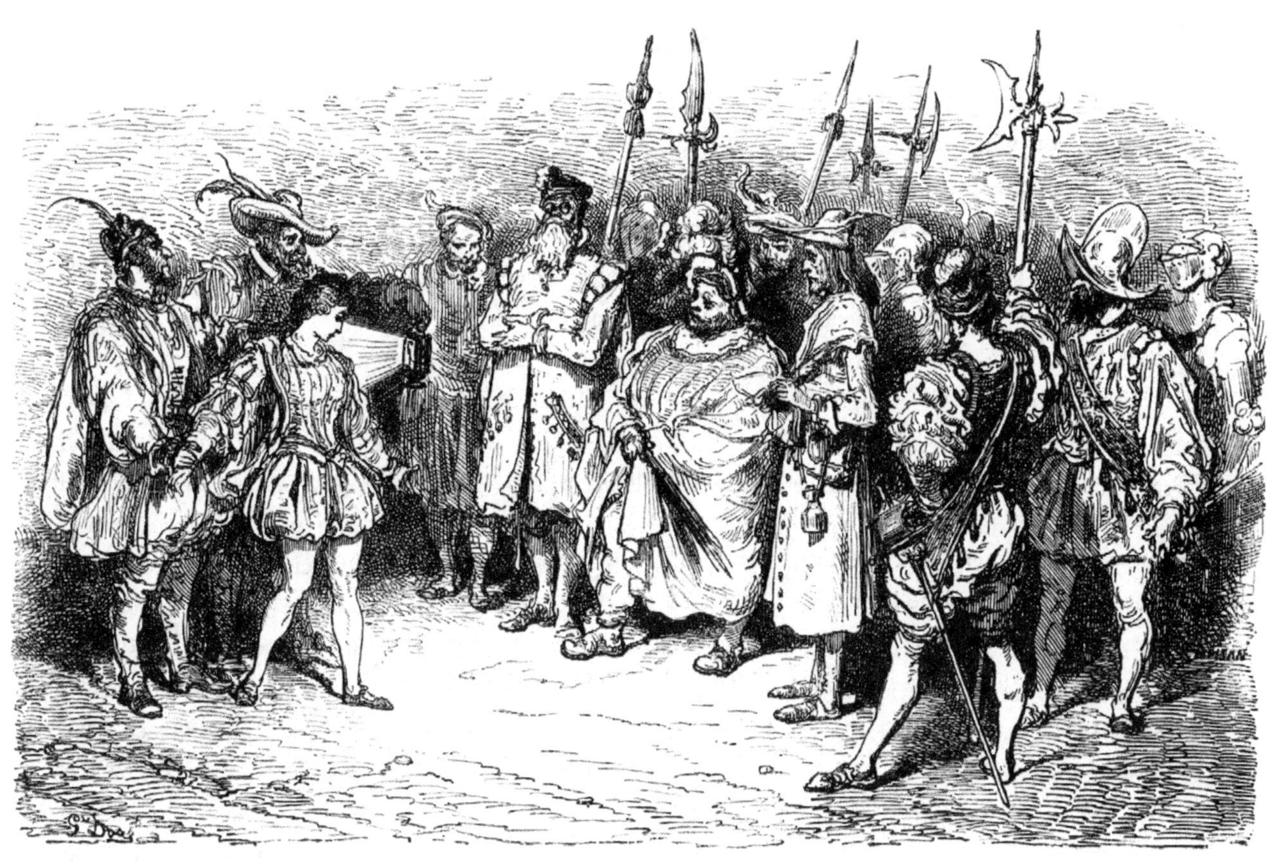

CHAPTER XLIX.

WHAT HAPPENED TO SANCHO PANZA AS HE WENT THE ROUNDS IN HIS ISLAND.

WE left our mighty governor much out of humour, and in a pelting chafe with that saucy knave of a countryman, who, according to the instructions he had received from the steward, and the steward from the duke, had bantered his worship with his impertinent description. Yet, as much a dunce and fool as he was, he made his party good against them all. At last, addressing himself to those about him, among whom was Dr. Pedro Rezio, who had ventured into the room again, after the consult about the duke's letter was over, "Now," said he, "do I find in good earnest that judges and governors must be made of brass, or ought to be made of brass, that they may be proof against the importunities of those that pretend business, who, at all hours, and at all seasons, would be heard and dispatched, without any regard to anybody but themselves, let what come of the rest, so their turn is served. Now, if a poor judge does not hear and dispatch them presently, either because he is otherwise busy and cannot, or because they do not come at a proper season, then do they grumble, and give him their blessing backwards, rake up the ashes of his forefathers, and would gnaw his very bones. But with your leave, good Mr. Busybody, with all your business, you are too hasty;

pray have a little patience, and wait a fit time to make your application. Do not come at dinner-time, or when a man is going to sleep, for we judges are flesh and blood, and must allow nature what she naturally requires; unless it be poor I, who am not to allow mine any food, thanks to my friend, Mr. Doctor Pedro Rezio Tirteafuera, here present, who is for starving me to death, and then swears it is for the preservation of my life. Heaven grant him such a life, I pray, for the good physicians deserve palms and laurels."

All that knew Sancho wondered to hear him talk so sensibly, and began to think that offices and places of trust inspired some men with understanding, as they stupefied and confounded others. However, Dr. Pedro Rezio Anguero de Tirteafuera promised him he should sup that night, though he trespassed against all the aphorisms of Hippocrates. This pacified the governor for the present, and made him wait with a mighty impatience for the evening and supper. To his thinking, the hour was so long a-coming, that he fancied time stood still; but yet at last the wished-for moment came, and they served him up some minced beef, with onions, and some calves' feet, somewhat stale. The hungry governor presently fell to with more eagerness and appetite than if they had given him Milan godwits, Roman pheasants, Sorrentum veal, Moron partridges, or Lavajos green geese. And after he had pretty well taken off the sharp edge of his stomach, turning to the physician, "Look you," quoth he, "Mr. Doctor, hereafter never trouble yourself to get me dainties or tit-bits to humour my stomach; that would but take it quite off the hinges, by reason it has been used to nothing but good beef, bacon, pork, goat's flesh, turnips, and onions; and if you ply me with your kick-shaws, your nice courtiers' fare, it will but make my stomach squeamish and untoward, and I should perfectly loath them one time or another. However, I shall not take it amiss if Master Sewer will now and then get me one of those *olla podridas*, and the stronger they are the better, where all sorts of good things are rotten stewed, and, as it were, lost in one another; and the more they are thus rotten, and like their name, the better the smack; and there you make a jumble of what you will, so it be eatable; and I shall remember him, and make him amends one of these days. But let nobody put tricks upon travellers, and make a fool of me; for either we are or we are not. Let us be merry and wise; when God sends his light, he sends it to all. I will govern this island fair and square, without underhand dealings or taking of bribes; but take notice, I will not bate an inch of my right, and therefore let every one carry an even hand, and mind their hits, or else I would have them to know there are rods in pickle for them. They that urge me too far shall rue for it; make yourself honey, and the flies will eat you."

"Indeed, my lord governor," said the steward, "your lordship is much in the right in all you have said; and I dare engage for the inhabitants of this island, that they will obey and observe your commands with diligence, love, and punctuality; for your gentle way of governing, in the beginning of your administration, does not give them the least opportunity to act or to design anything to your lordship's disadvantage."

"I believe as much," answered Sancho, "and they would be silly wretches, should they offer to do or think otherwise. Let me tell you too, it is my pleasure you take care of me and my Dapple, that we may both have our food as we ought, which is the most material business. Next, let us think of going the rounds, when it is time for me to do it; for I intend to clear this island of all filth and rubbish, of all rogues and vagrants, idle husks and sturdy beggars. For I would have you to know, my good friends, that your slothful, lazy, lewd people in a commonwealth are like drones in a beehive, that waste and devour the honey which the labouring bees gather. I design to encourage the husbandmen, preserve the privileges of the gentry, reward virtuous persons, and, above all things, reverence religion, and have regard to the honour of religious men. What think you of this, my good friends? Do I talk to the purpose, or do I talk idly?"

"You speak so well, my lord governor," answered the steward, "that I stand in admiration to hear a man so unlettered as you are (for I believe your lordship cannot read at all) utter so many notable things, and in every word a sentence, far from what they who have sent you hither, and they who are here present, ever expected from your understanding. But every day produces some new wonder; jests are turned into earnest, and those who designed to laugh at others happen to be laughed at themselves."

It being now night, and the governor having supped, with Dr. Rezio's leave, he prepared to walk the rounds, and set forward, attended by the steward, the secretary, the gentleman waiter, the historiographer, who was to register his acts, several serjeants, and other limbs of the law, so many in number, that they made a little battalion, in the middle of which the great Sancho marched, with his rod of justice in his hand, in a notable manner. They had not walked far in the town, before they heard the clashing of swords, which made them hasten to the place whence the noise came. Being come thither, they found only two men fighting, who gave over, perceiving the officers.

"What!" cried one of them at the same time, "do they suffer folks to be robbed in this town, in defiance of Heaven and the king? Do they let men be stripped in the middle of the street?"

"Hold, honest man," said Sancho; "have a little patience, and let me know the occasion of this fray, for I am the governor."

"My lord," said the other party, "I will tell you in a few words. Your lordship must know that this gentleman, just now, at a gaming ordinary over the way, won above a thousand reals, Heaven knows how. I stood by all the while, and gave judgment for him in more than one doubtful cast, though I could not well tell how to do it in conscience. He carried off his winnings, and when I expected he would have given me a crown gratuity, as it is a claim among gentlemen of my fashion, who frequent gaming ordinaries, from those that play high and win, for preventing quarrels, being at their backs and giving judgment right or wrong, nevertheless he went away without giving me anything. I ran after him, not very well pleased with his proceeding, yet very civilly desired him to consider I was his friend, that he knew me to be a gentleman, though fallen to decay, who had nothing to live upon, my friends having brought me up to no employment; and therefore I entreated him to be so kind as to give me eight reals; but the stingy soul, a greater thief than Cacus, and a worse sharper than Andradilla, would give me but sneaking four reals. And now, my lord, you may see how little shame and conscience there is in him. But in faith, had not your lordship come just in the nick, I would have made him disgorge his winnings, and taught him the difference between a rook and a jackdaw."

"What say you to this?" cried Sancho to the other.

The other made answer, that he could not deny what his antagonist had said, that he would give him but four reals, because he had given him money several times before; and they who expect benevolence should be mannerly, and be thankful for what is given them, without haggling with those that have won, unless they know them to be common cheats, and the money not won fairly; and that to show he was a fair gamester, and no sharper, as the other said, there needed no better proof than his refusal to give him anything, since the sharpers are always in fee with these bully-rooks, who know them, and wink at their cheats."

"That is true," said the steward. "Now, what would your lordship have us to do with these men?"

"I will tell you," said Sancho. "First, you that are the winner, whether by fair play or by foul, give your bully-back here a hundred reals immediately, and thirty more for the poor prisoners; and you that have nothing to live on, and were brought up to no employment, and go sharping up and down from place to place, pray take your hundred reals, and be sure by to-morrow to go out of this island, and not to set foot in it again these ten years and a day, unless you have a mind to make an end of your banishment in another world; for if I find you here, I will make you swing on a gibbet, with the help of the hangman. Away, and let nobody offer to reply, or I will lay him by the heels."

Thereupon the one disbursed, and the other received; the first went home, and the last went out of the island; and then the governor, going on, "Either I shall want of my will," said he, "or I will put down these disorderly gaming-houses."

"As for this house in question," said one of the officers, "I suppose it will be a hard matter to put it down, for it belongs to a person of quality, who loses a great deal more by play at the year's end than he gets by his cards You may show your authority against other gaming-houses of less note, that do more mischief, and harbour more dangerous people, than the houses of gentlemen and persons of quality, where your notorious sharpers dare not use their sleights of hand. And since gaming is a vice that is become a common practice, it is better to play in good gentlemen's houses than in those of under officers, where they shall draw you in a poor bubble, and after they have kept you playing all the night long, send you away stripped to the skin."

"Well, all in good time," said Sancho: "I know there is a great deal to be said on this."

At the same time one of the officers came, holding a youth, and having brought him before the governor, "If it please your worship," said he, "this young man was coming towards us, but as soon as he perceived it was the rounds, he sheered off, and set a-running as fast as his legs would carry him—a sign he is no better than he should be. I ran after him, but had not he happened to fall, I had never come up with him."

"What made you run away, friend?" said Sancho.

The youth replied, "I ran, my lord, to avoid answering the multitude of questions which officers of justice are so accustomed to ask."

"What trade are you of?" quoth Sancho.

"A weaver," answered the youth.

"And what do you weave?" quoth Sancho.

"Iron heads for spears, an it please your worship."

"You are pleasant with me, and value yourself upon being a jester," quoth Sancho. "Very well, sir; and whither were you going?"

"To take the air, sir," replied the lad.

"And, pray, where do people take the air in this island?" said Sancho.

"Where it blows," answered the youth.

"Good," quoth Sancho; "you answer to the purpose; you are a discreet young man. But now, make account that I am the air, and that I blow on you, and drive you to gaol. Here, lay hold of him, and take him to prison: I will make him sleep there to-night."

Quoth the youth, "Your honour can no more do that than you can make me king."

"Why cannot I make you sleep in prison?" demanded Sancho. "Have I not power to confine or release you, as I please?"

"Whatever power your worship may have, you have not enough to make me sleep in prison."

"Indeed!" replied Sancho. "Away with him immediately, that he may see his mistake with his own eyes; and, lest the gaoler should put his interested generosity in practice, if he suffer you to stir a step from the prison, I will sconce him in two thousand ducats."

"All this is only laughable," answered the youth; "for still I defy all the world to make me sleep this night in prison."

"Tell me, rascal," quoth Sancho, "hast thou any angel to rescue thee, by unloosing the fetters I intend to have riveted on thy limbs?"

"My lord governor," answered the youth, with an air of pleasantry, "let us consult reason a little, and come to the point. Supposing your worship were to order me to gaol, to load me with chains and fetters, to confine me in a dungeon, and impose heavy penalties upon the gaoler, if he permit me to stir out; and suppose these orders punctually obeyed; yet, for all that, if I have no mind to sleep, but to keep awake all night, without so much as shutting my eyelids, can your worship, with all your power, make me sleep whether I will or no?"

"No, certainly," said the secretary; "and the young man has proved his assertion."

"Granted," quoth Sancho, "provided he would forbear sleeping only to have his own will, and not out of pure contradiction to mine."

"Truly, my lord," said the youth, "I never thought of such a thing."

"Then, God be with you," quoth Sancho; "go, sleep at home, and I wish you a good night's rest, which I shall not attempt to disturb; but I would advise you in future to be less jocose with officers of justice, for you may meet with one that may lay the joke over your noddle."

The youth went his way, and the governor continuing his round, a couple of sergeants presently came with a person in custody, and said, "My lord governor, this here person, who seems to be a man, is not so, but a woman, and no ugly one either, in man's clothes." Two or three lanterns being immediately lifted up to her face, it was discovered by their light that it was indeed that of a female, seemingly about sixteen years of age, beautiful as a thousand pearls, with her hair tucked up under a net-work caul of green silk and gold. Having viewed her from head to foot, it appeared that she had flesh-coloured stockings, with garters of white taffeta, and tassels of gold and seed-pearl; breeches of green and gold tissue, a loose coat of the same, and a superb waistcoat of white and gold stuff. Her shoes were white, and such as are worn by men. She had no sword, but a very rich dagger; and on her fingers were many rings of great value. In a word, all who beheld her were struck with admiration, but nobody knew the lady, and even such of the inhabitants of the town who were present said they could not imagine who she could be. The persons who were in the secret of the jests put upon Sancho wondered the most, for this adventure was not of their contriving; and therefore they were in suspense, expecting the issue of so unforeseen an incident. Sancho, struck like the rest with the beauty of the damsel, asked her who she was, whither she was going, and what had moved her to dress herself in that manner. Fixing her eyes on the ground, she answered, with a modest bashfulness, "Sir, I cannot declare so publicly what it concerns me so much to conceal; of one thing, however, I must beg leave to assure your worship, that I am no thief, no criminal person, but an unhappy maiden whom the force of jealousy has tempted to break through the rules of female decorum."

The steward, hearing this, said to Sancho, "My lord governor, order all your attendants to go aside, that this lady may speak her mind with less concern."

The governor did so, and they all retired to a distance, the steward, the sewer, and the secretary excepted. The damsel then proceeded, saying, "I am the daughter, gentlemen, of Pedro Perez Mazorca, who farms the wool of this town, and comes frequently to my father's house."

"This will not pass, madam," said the steward; "for I know Pedro Perez well, and am sure he has no child, neither son nor daughter: besides, you say he is your father, and immediately add that he comes frequently to your father's house."

"I took notice of that," quoth Sancho.

"Indeed, gentlemen," answered the damsel, "I am in such confusion, that I know not what I say: but the truth is, I am the daughter of Diego de la Llana, whom you all know."

"This may do," answered the steward; "for with Diego de la Llana I am also acquainted, and know that he is a gentleman of rank and fortune, and has both a son and a daughter: but since he has been a widower, the face of this daughter has never been seen; for he keeps her so closely shut up, that he will not give the sun leave to shine upon her; and report says she is extremely handsome."

"That unfortunate daughter am I, and too true is what you state respecting my rigorous confinement," answered the damsel. "Whether fame lies, as to my beauty, you, gentlemen, can judge, since you have seen me:" and she began to weep bitterly; upon which the secretary said in a whisper to the sewer, "Something of importance must have happened to have induced so considerable a person as this young lady to leave her home in such a dress, and at so unseasonable an hour."

"No doubt," answered the sewer; "and the suspicion is confirmed by her tears."

Sancho comforted her as well as he could, and desired her to tell them the whole matter, without fear; assuring her they would all endeavour to serve her with sincerity.

"The case then is, gentlemen," she replied, "that my father has kept me locked up for the long space of ten years; such being the time that has elapsed since death deprived me of my mother. Mass is said in our house in a splendid chapel, and during the period I have mentioned I have seen nothing but the sun in the heavens by day, and the moon and stars by night. I am utterly unacquainted with the streets, squares, churches, and every inhabitant of the town, except my father, my brother, and Pedro Perez, the wool-farmer, whose visits to our house led me to say he was my father, to conceal the truth. Being debarred the privilege of going out, so much as to church, has for days and months greatly disquieted me. I wished to see the world, or at least the town in which I was born, and could not consider the wish as any breach of that decency which young ladies ought always to observe. When I heard of bull-feasts, of darting javelins on horseback, and of the representation of plays, I requested my brother, who is a year younger than myself, to tell me what those and several other things that I had never seen meant, which he used to do in the best manner he could; and the desire I had of seeing them was but the more inflamed. In a word, to shorten my story, I prayed and entreated him—oh, that I had never so prayed, never so entreated!" and again she was overcome with weeping.

"Proceed, madam," said the steward, "and make an end of your story, for your words and tears keep us in painful anxiety."

Accordingly, interrupted by occasional sobs and sighings, she thus continued: "My whole misfortune and unhappiness consists only in this—I requested my brother to dress me in his clothes, and take me out, some night, while my father should be asleep, to see the town. Importuned by my entreaties, he complied at last, and gave me this dress, disguising himself at the same time in a suit of mine, which fits as if it were made for him; and as he has not so much as one hair of a beard, he might be taken for a very beautiful young girl. It was not above an hour ago that we escaped from the house; and, guided by a footboy and our own unruly fancies, we had traversed the whole town, and were returning home, when, seeing a number of people approaching, my brother said to me, 'Sister, this must be the round; put wings to your feet, and fly after me, that they may not know us, for woe betide us if they should!' And he turned instantly back, and began, not to run, but to fly. In attempting to follow, I fell down from fright, before I had taken six steps; and the officer of justice coming up, I was seized, and brought before your honour, where my indiscreet longing has exposed me to shame before so many people."

"Then, in reality, madam," quoth Sancho, "no other mishap has befallen you; and it was not jealousy, as you told us at the beginning of your story, that led you from home?"

"Nothing else," replied the damsel, "has befallen me, nor is there any jealousy in the case; it was merely a desire of seeing the world, or rather the streets of this town, for my curiosity went no farther."

The appearance of the brother in the custody of two sergeants, who had pursued and overtaken him, as he fled from his sister, confirmed the truth of what she had said. The female dress of the young man consisted merely of a rich petticoat, and a blue damask mantle, with a splendid border; for he had no cap or ornament of any kind on his head, but his own beautiful hair, which was so fair and glossy that it seemed so many ringlets of the purest gold. The governor, the steward, and the sewer, taking him aside, out of the hearing of his sister, asked him how he came to be in that disguise: and, with no less bashfulness and concern, he told the same story as she had done, to the unspeakable joy of the enamoured sewer. But the governor said, "Really, young gentlefolks, this is a very childish frolic; and in relating it there needed not half so many sighs and tears: had you but said, 'Our names are so-and-so, and we stole out of our father's house by such and such a contrivance, only out of curiosity, and with no other design whatever,' the tale had been told as soon as begun, and all these takings-on, these moanings and groanings, might have been spared."

"Yes, sir," answered the damsel; "but the confusion I was in was so great, that it did not suffer me to demean myself as I ought."

"There is no harm done," answered Sancho: "we will see you safe to your father's house; perhaps he has not missed you. And henceforward be less childish, and not so eager to play the vagrant; for 'the modest maid, and a broken leg, should stay at home;' and 'the woman and the hen are lost by gadding;' and 'she who desires to see, desires no less to be seen.' And this is all I shall say upon the subject."

The youth thanked the governor for the intended favour of seeing them safe home, and they bent their course towards the house, which was not far off. When they arrived, the brother threw up a small stone to a grated window, and a servant-maid, who waited for them, immediately came down and opened the door, and the rovers went in, leaving every one in admiration at their genteel deportment and beauty, as well as at their singular desire of seeing the world by night, without stirring out of the town, which was imputed to their tender years.

The sewer's heart being pierced through and through, he purposed within himself to demand the young lady, the next day, of her father in marriage, taking it for granted that, being a servant of the duke, he could not be refused. Sancho, too, had similar thoughts of matching the young man with his daughter Sanchica, and determined to bring it about the first opportunity, presuming, from his quality of governor, that, look where he would for an alliance, he had only to ask and have. Thus ended that night's round, and, two days after, the great Sancho's government also terminated, by which all his designs and expectations were overturned and destroyed, as shall hereafter be shown.

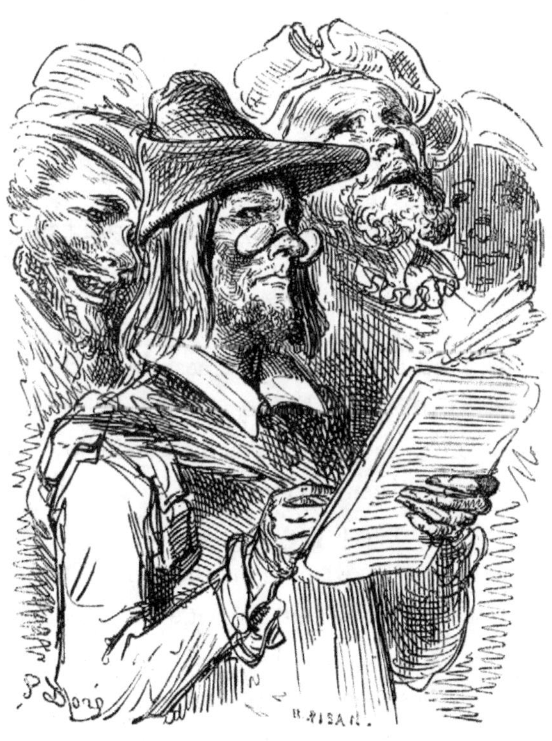

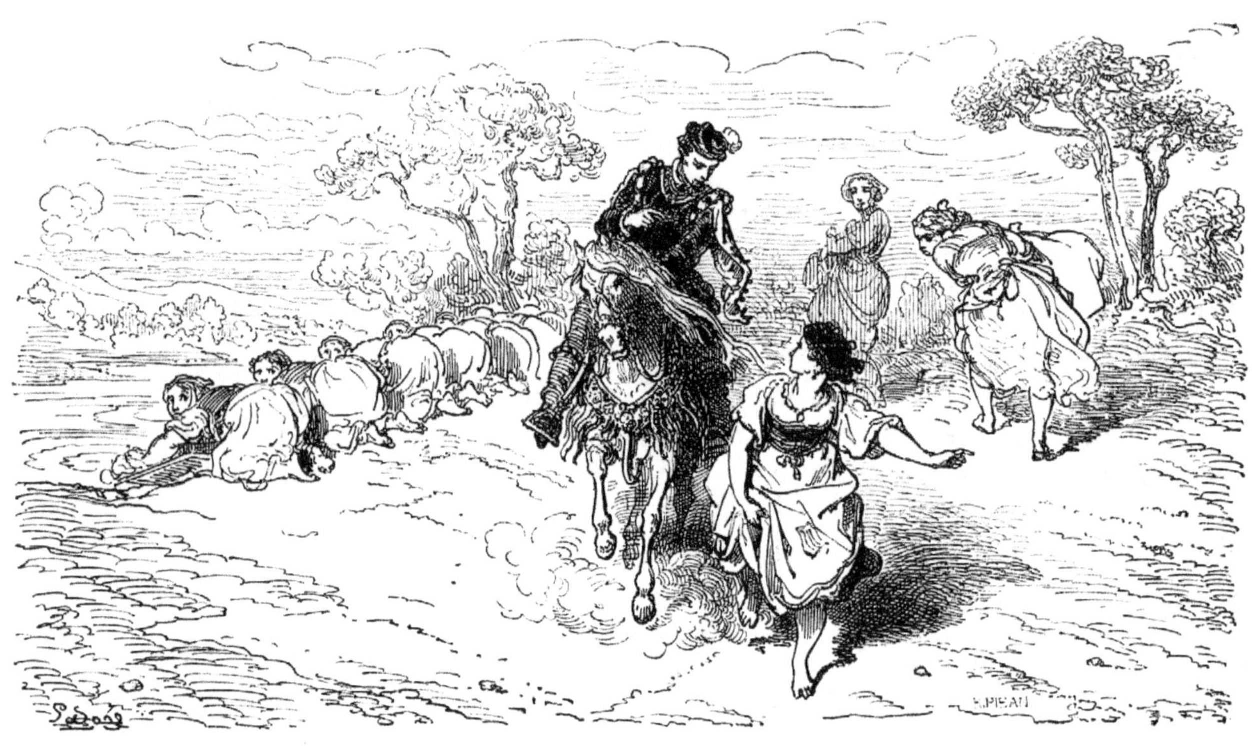

CHAPTER L.

IN WHICH IS DECLARED WHO WERE THE ENCHANTERS AND EXECUTIONERS THAT WHIPPED THE DUENNA, AND PINCHED AND SCRATCHED DON QUIXOTE; WITH THE SUCCESS OF THE PAGE WHO CARRIED THE LETTER TO TERESA PANZA, SANCHO'S WIFE.

CID HAMET, the most punctual and diligent searcher after the minutest circumstances, even to the very atoms of this true history, says that, when Donna Rodriguez quitted her chamber to go to Don Quixote's, another donna, her bedfellow, being awake, perceived it; and, as all duennas have the itch of listening after, prying into, and smelling out things, she followed her so softly, that good Rodriguez was not in the least aware of it; and, as soon as she saw her enter, that she might not be wanting in the general humour of her tribe, which is to be tale-bearers, away she tripped that instant to acquaint the duchess with the proceeding. The duchess acquainted the duke, and begged that she and Altisidora might be permitted to go and see what was the duenna's business with the knight. The duke consenting, they both gently, step by step, crept, as it were, and posted themselves close to the door of the chamber; so close indeed, that not a word that was said within escaped them: and when the duchess heard the duenna expose her failings, neither could she nor Altisidora bear it; and accordingly, brimful of choler, they burst into the room, and pinched Don Quixote, and whipped the duenna in the manner related above; for affronts levelled against the beauty and vanity of women awaken their wrath in an extraordinary manner, and inflame them with a desire of revenge that is scarcely governable.

The duchess recounted to the duke all that had passed, with which he was much diverted; and proceeding in her design of making farther sport with Don Quixote, she dispatched the page, who had acted the part of Dulcinea in the projected disenchantment of that lady, to Teresa Panza, with her husband's letter (for Sancho was so taken up with his government that he had quite forgotten it), and another from herself, together with a large string of rich corals by way of present.

Now the history informs us that the page was a very discreet and shrewd fellow, and, being extremely desirous of pleasing his lord and lady, he departed, in happy mood, for Sancho's village; and, being arrived near it, he inquired of some females whom he saw washing their linen in a brook, if they knew where one Teresa Panza lived.

The question was no sooner asked than a young wench, who was of the number, started up and said, "That Teresa Panza, sir, is my mother, and that Sancho my father, and that knight our master."

"Are they so?" quoth the page; "then bring me to your mother, young damsel, for I have a letter and a present for her from that same father of yours."

"That will I, with all my heart, sir," answered the girl, who seemed to be about fourteen years of age; and, leaving the linen she was washing to one of her companions, without putting anything on her head or her feet, with bare legs, and dishevelled hair, she ran skipping before the page's horse, saying, "Come along, sir, for our house stands just at the entrance of the village, and there you will find my mother in trouble enough, through not having heard for so long a time any news of my father."

"I bring her news," quoth the page, "that she may well thank God for."

In short, with jumping, running, and capering, the girl soon reached the village, and before she entered the house she called aloud at the door, "Come out, mother Teresa, come out! for here is a gentleman who brings letters and other things from my good father."

Hearing her daughter's voice, Teresa Panza made her appearance, having in her hand a distaff of tow which she had been spinning, dressed in a grey petticoat, so short that it looked as if it had been docked at the placket, and a grey bodice, her smock sleeves hanging slatternly about it. She was not old, though she seemed to have seen forty, and was strong, hale, sinewy, and hard as a hazel-nut. Seeing her daughter, and a page with her on horseback, she said, "What is the matter, girl? what gentleman is this?"

"It is a humble servant of my Lady Donna Teresa Panza," answered the page; and he flung himself from his horse, and, with great respect, went and kneeled before her, saying, "Be pleased, Signora Donna Teresa, to permit me to kiss your ladyship's hand, as the lawful and only wife of Signor Don Sancho Panza, sole governor of the island of Barataria."

"Ah! dear sir, forbear! do not do so," answered Teresa; "for I am no court dame, but a poor countrywoman, daughter of a ploughman, and wife of a squire-errant, and not of any governor whatever."

"Your ladyship," answered the page, "is the most worthy consort of an archworthy governor; and for proof of what I say, be pleased, madam, to receive this letter and this present." He then drew from his pocket a string of corals, every bead set in gold; and, putting it round her neck, he said, "This letter is from my lord governor, and another that I have, and these corals are from my lady duchess, who sends me to your ladyship, with her congratulations."

Teresa was perfectly amazed, and her daughter no less so, and the girl said, "May I die, if our master Don Quixote be not at the bottom of this good business, and has given my father, at last, the government or earldom he so often promised him."

"It is even so," answered the page; "and, for Signor Don Quixote's sake, my lord Sancho is now governor of the island of Barataria, as you will see by his letter."

"Pray, young gentleman," quoth Teresa, "be pleased to read it to me; for, though I can spin, I cannot read a tittle."

"Nor I neither," added Sanchica; "but stay a moment and I will call somebody that can, though it be the priest himself, or the bachelor, Samson Carrasco, who will come with all their hearts to hear news of my father."

"There is no need of calling anybody," quoth the page; "for, though I cannot spin, I can read, and you shall hear it immediately." Accordingly he read it; and then delivered that from the duchess, which was as follows:—

"Friend Teresa,—The good qualities, both as to talents and integrity, of your husband Sancho have moved and induced me to desire the duke, my spouse, to give him the government of one of the many islands under his jurisdiction; and I am informed he governs like any hawk, at which I and my lord duke are mightily pleased: and I give great thanks to Heaven that I have not been deceived in my recommendation. For, let me tell Madam Teresa, it is a difficult thing to find a good governor now-a-days, and God make me as good as Sancho governs well. I send you herewith, my dear lady governess, a string of corals set in gold: I wish they were of Oriental pearl; but 'who gives thee an egg has no mind to see thee dead.' The time will come when we shall be better acquainted, and converse together, and who knows what may happen? Commend me to Sanchica, your daughter, and tell her from me to get herself ready, for I mean to marry her toppingly when she least thinks of it. I am told the acorns of your town are very large; pray send me some two or three dozen of them, for I shall esteem them the more as coming from your hand: and write to me immediately, advising me of your health and welfare. If you want anything, you need but open your mouth and it shall be measured. So God have you in his holy keeping.

"Your loving friend,

From this place. "The Duchess."

"Ah!" quoth Teresa, on hearing the letter, "how good, how plain, how humble a lady! Let me be buried with such ladies as this, and not your gentlewomen of this town, who think, because they are quality-folks, the wind must not blow upon them; and they go to church with as much vanity as if they were very queens. One would think they took it for a disgrace to look upon a poor peasant woman; and see here how this good lady, though she be a duchess, calls me friend, and treats me as if I were her equal; and equal may I see her to the highest steeple in La Mancha. As to the acorns, sir, I will send her ladyship a whole peck, and such choice ones that people shall come far and near to see and admire them. And now, Sanchica, look to the entertainment of this gentleman, and make much of him; take care of his horse, and bring some new-laid eggs out of the stable, and slice some rashers of bacon, and let us treat him like any prince; for the good news he has brought us, and his own good looks, deserve no less; and, in the meanwhile, I will step with the news of our joy to my neighbours, and especially to our father the priest, and to Master Nicholas the barber, who are, and always have been, your father's great friends."

"Yes, mother, I will," answered Sanchica; "but, hark you, mother, I must have half that string of corals, for I do not take my lady duchess to be such a fool as to send it all to you."

"No, it is all for you, daughter," answered Teresa; "but let me wear it a few days about my neck, for methinks it cheers my very heart."

"Your heart will be still more cheered," quoth the page, "when you shall see the bundle I have in this portmanteau; it is a suit of superfine cloth, which the governor wore only one day at a hunting-match, and he has sent it all for the use of Signora Sanchica."

"May he live a thousand years!" answered Sanchica; "and the bearer neither more nor less, ay, and two thousand, if need be."

Teresa now sallied forth with the letters, and the beads about her neck, playing with her fingers upon the letters, as she went along, as if they had been a timbrel; and accidentally meeting the priest and Samson Carrasco, she began to dance, and say, "In faith we have no poor relations now; we have caught a government. Ay, ay, let the proudest gentlewoman of them all meddle with me, I will make her know her distance."

"How now, Teresa?" said the curate; "what mad fit is this? what papers are those in your hand?"

"No mad fit at all," answered Teresa; "but these are letters from duchesses and governors, and these beads about my neck are right coral, the Ave Marias I mean; and the Pater Nosters are of beaten gold: and I am a madam governess, I will assure you."

"Verily," said the curate, "there is no understanding you, Teresa; we do not know what you mean."

"There is what will clear the riddle," quoth Teresa; and with that she gave them the letters.

Thereupon, the curate having read them aloud, that Samson Carrasco might also be informed, they both stood and looked on one another, and were more at a loss than before.

The bachelor asked her who brought the letter. Teresa told them they might go home with her and see. It was a sweet, handsome young man, as fine as anything; and that he had brought her another present worth twice as much.

The curate took the string of beads from her neck, and viewed it several times over, and, finding that it was a thing of value, he could not conceive the meaning of all this. "By the habit that I wear," cried he, "I cannot tell what to think of this business. In the first place, I am convinced these beads are right coral, and gold; and, in the next, here is a duchess sends to beg a dozen or two of acorns."

"Crack that nut if you can," said Samson Carrasco. "But come, let us go and see the messenger, and probably he will clear our doubts."

Thereupon, going with Teresa, they found the page sifting a little corn for his horse, and Sanchica cutting a rasher of bacon, to be fried with eggs, for his dinner. They both liked the page's mien and his garb; and after the usual compliments, Samson desired him to tell them some news of Don Quixote and Sancho Panza; for though they had read a letter from the latter to his wife, and another from the duchess, they were no better than riddles to them, nor could they imagine how Sancho should come by a government, especially of an island, well knowing that all the islands in the Mediterranean, or the greatest part of them, were the king's.

"Gentlemen," answered the page, "it is a certain truth that Signor Sancho Panza is a governor, but whether it be of an island or not I do not pretend to determine; but this I can assure you, that he commands in a town that has above a thousand inhabitants. And as for my lady duchess's sending to a countrywoman for a few acorns, that is no such wonder, for she is so free from pride that I have known her send to borrow a comb of one of her neighbours. You must know our ladies of Arragon, though they are as noble as those of Castile, do not stand so much upon formalities and punctilios, neither do they take so much state upon them, but treat people with more familiarity."

While they were thus discoursing, in came Sanchica skipping, with her lap full of eggs, and turning to the page, "Pray, sir," said she, "tell me, does my father wear trunk-breeches now he is a governor?"

"Truly," said the page, "I never minded it, but without doubt he does."

"Oh, gemini!" cried the young wench, "what would I not give to see my father in his trunk-breeches! Is it not a strange thing that ever since I can remember myself I have wished to see my father in trunk-breeches?"

"You will see him as you would have him," said the page, "if your ladyship does but live. Indeed, if his government holds but two months, you will see him go with an umbrella over his head."

The curate and the bachelor plainly perceived that the page did but laugh at the mother and daughter; but yet the costly string of beads, and the hunting suit, which by this time Teresa had let them see, confounded them again.

"Good master curate," quoth she, "do so much as inquire whether any of our neighbours are going to Madrid or Toledo. I would have them buy me a hugeous farthingale of the newest and most courtly fashion, and the very finest that can be got for money; for, by my holidame, I mean to credit my husband's government as much as I can; and if they vex me, I will hie me to that same court, and ride in my coach, too, as well as the best of them; for she that is a governor's lady may very well afford to have one."

"Oh, rare mother!" cried Sanchica, "would it were to-night before to-morrow. Mayhap, when they saw me sitting in our coach by my lady mother, they would jeer and flout: 'Look, look!' would they say, 'yonder is goody Trollop, the plough-jobber's bairn! How she flaunts it, and goes on lolling in her coach like a little Pope Joan!' But what would I care? Let them trudge on in the dirt, while I ride by in my coach. Shame and ill luck go along with all your little backbiting scrubs! 'Let them laugh that win.' Am I not in the right, mother?"

"Ay, marry, art thou, child," quoth Teresa; "and, indeed, my good honey Sancho has often told me all these good things, and many more, would come to pass; and thou shalt see, daughter, I will never rest till I get to be a countess. There must be a beginning in all things, as I have heard it said by thy father, who is also the father of proverbs. 'When a cow is given thee, run and take her with a halter.' When they give thee a government, take it; when an earldom, catch it; and when they whistle to thee with a good gift, snap at it. 'That which is good to give is good to take,' girl. It were a pretty fancy, trow, to lie snoring a-bed, and when good luck knocks, not to rise and open the door."

"Ay," quoth Sanchica, "what is it to me, though they should say all they have a mind to say? When they see me so tearing fine, and so woundy great, let them spit their venom and say, 'Set a beggar on horseback,' and so forth."

"Who would not think," said the curate, hearing this, "but that the whole race of the Panzas came into the world with their heads stuffed with proverbs? I never knew one of the name but threw them out at all times, let the discourse be what it would."

"I think so, too," said the page, "for his honour, the governor, blunders them out at every turn; many times, indeed, wide from the purpose; however, always to the satisfaction of the company, and with high applause from my lord and lady."

"Then, sir, you assure us still," said Carrasco, "that Sancho is really a governor, and that a duchess sends these presents and letters upon his account; for though we see the things, and read the letters, we can scarce prevail with ourselves to believe it, but are apt to run into our friend Don Quixote's opinion, and look on all this as the effect of some enchantment; so that I could find in my heart to feel and try whether you are a visionary messenger or a creature of flesh and blood."

"For my part, gentlemen," answered the page, "all I can tell you is that I am really the messenger I appear to be; that the Lord Sancho Panza is actually a governor, and that the duke and the duchess, to whom I belong, are able to give and have given him that government, where, I am credibly informed, he behaves himself most worthily. Now, if there be any enchantment in the matter, I leave you to examine that; for I know no more."

"That may be," said the bachelor, "but yet *dubitat Augustinus.*"

"You may doubt if you please," replied the page, "but I have told you the truth, which will always prevail over falsehood and rise uppermost, as oil does above water. But if you will *operibus credere, et non verbis,* let one of you go along with me, and you shall see with your eyes what you will not believe by the help of your ears."

"I will go with all my heart," quoth Sanchica; "take me up behind ye, sir; I have a huge mind to see my father."

"The daughters of governors," said the page, "must not travel thus unattended, but in coaches or litters, and with a handsome train of servants."

"Bless me!" quoth Sanchica, "I can go a journey as well on an ass as in one of your coaches. I am none of your tender, squeamish things, not I."

"Peace, chicken!" quoth the mother; "thou dost not know what thou sayest; the gentleman is in the right: times are altered. When it was plain Sancho, it was plain Sanchica; but now he is a governor, thou art a lady: I cannot well tell whether I am right or no."

"My Lady Teresa says more than she is aware of," said the page. "But now," continued he, "give me a mouthful to eat as soon as you can, for I must go back this afternoon."

"Be pleased then, sir," said the curate, "to go with me and partake of a slender meal at my house, for my neighbour Teresa is more willing than able to entertain so good a guest."

The page excused himself a while, but at last complied, being persuaded it would be much for the better; and the curate, on his side, was glad of his company, to have an opportunity to inform himself at large about Don Quixote and his proceedings.

The bachelor proffered Teresa to write her answers to her letters, but as she looked upon him to be somewhat waggish, she would not permit him to be of her counsel; so she gave a roll and a couple of eggs to a young acolyte of the church, and he wrote two letters for her; one to her husband, and the other to the duchess, all of her own inditing.

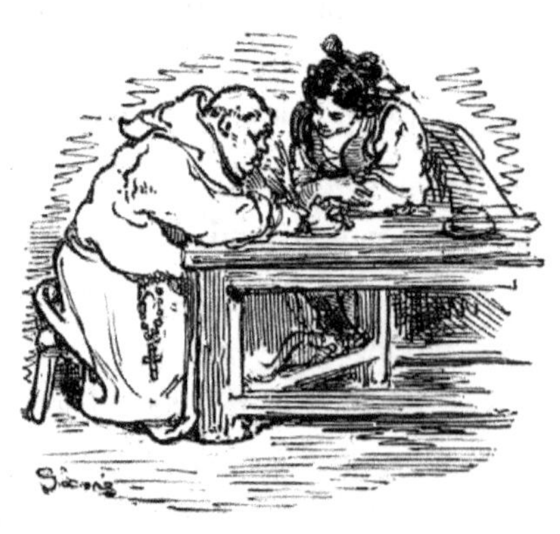

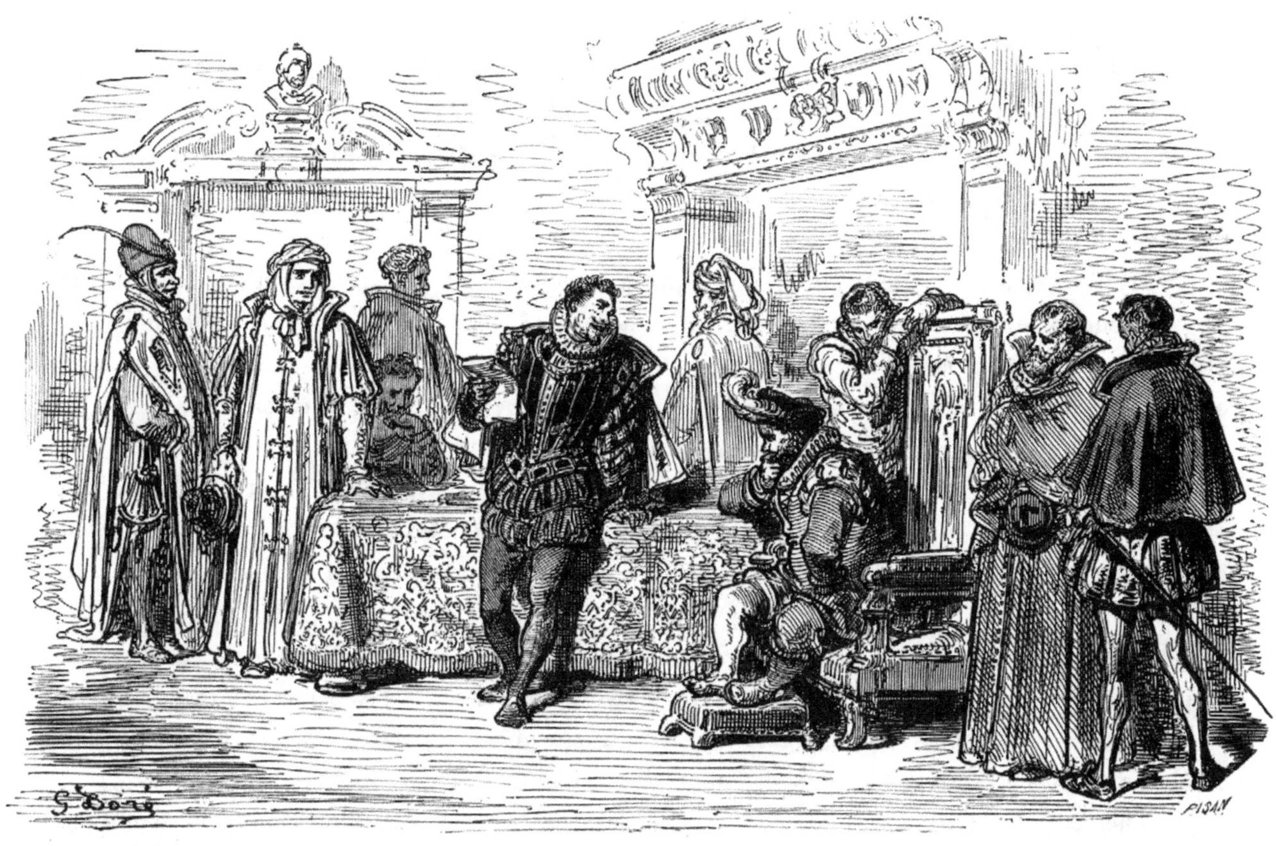

CHAPTER LI.

A CONTINUATION OF SANCHO PANZA'S GOVERNMENT, WITH OTHER PASSAGES, SUCH AS THEY ARE.

THE morning of that day arose which succeeded the governor's rounding night, the remainder of which the gentleman-waiter spent not in sleep, but in the pleasing thoughts of the lovely face and charming grace of the disguised virgin; on the other side the steward bestowed that time in writing to his lord and lady what Sancho did and said, wondering no less at his actions than at his expressions, both which displayed a strange intermixture of discretion and simplicity.

At last the lord governor was pleased to rise, and, by Dr. Pedro Rezio's order, they brought him for his breakfast a little conserve and a draught of fair water, which he would have exchanged with all his heart for a good luncheon of bread and a bunch of grapes; but seeing he could not help himself, he was forced to make the best of a bad market, and seem to be content, though full sore against his will and appetite; for the doctor made him believe that to eat but little, and that which was dainty, enlivened the spirits and sharpened the wit; and, consequently, such a sort of diet was most proper for persons in authority and weighty employments, wherein there is less need of the strength of the body than that of the mind. This sophistry served to famish Sancho, who, half-dead with hunger, cursed in his heart both the government and him that had given it him. However, hungry as he was, by the strength of his slender breakfast, he failed not to give audience that day; and the first that came before him was a stranger, who put the following case to him, the stewards and the rest of the attendants being present:—

"My lord," said he, "a large river divides in two parts one and the same lordship. I beg your honour to lend me your attention, for it is a case of great importance and some difficulty. Upon this river there is a bridge, at the one end of which there stands a gallows and a kind of court of justice, where four judges used to sit for the execution of a certain law made by the lord of the land and river, which runs thus:—

"'Whoever intends to pass from one end of this bridge to the other must first, upon his oath, declare whither he goes and what his business is. If he swear truth, he may go on; but if he swear false, he shall be hanged, and die without remission upon the gibbet at the end of the bridge.'

"After due promulgation of this law, many people, notwithstanding its severity, adventured to go over this bridge, and as it appeared they swore true, the judges permitted them to pass unmolested. It happened one day that a certain passenger being sworn, declared, that by the oath he had taken, he was come to die upon that gallows, and that was all his business.

"This put the judges to a nonplus; 'for,' said they, 'if we let this man pass freely he is forsworn, and, according to the letter of the law, he ought to die; if we hang him, he has sworn truth, seeing he swore he was to die on that gibbet; and then by the same law we should let him pass.'

"Now, your lordship's judgment is desired what the judges ought to do with this man; for they are still at a stand, not knowing what to determine in this case; and having been informed of your sharp wit and great capacity in resolving difficult questions, they sent me to beseech your lordship, in their names, to give your opinion in so intricate and knotty a case."

"To deal plainly with you," answered Sancho, "those worshipful judges that sent you hither might as well have spared themselves the trouble, for I am more inclined to dulness, I assure you, than sharpness; however, let me hear your question once more, that I may thoroughly understand it, and perhaps I may at last hit the nail upon the head." The man repeated the question again and again; and when he had done, "To my thinking," said Sancho, "this question may be presently answered, as thus: The man swore he came to die on the gibbet, and if he die there, he swore true, and, according to the law, he ought to be free and go over the bridge. On the other side, if you do not hang him, he swore false, and by the same law he ought to be hanged."

"It is as your lordship says," replied the stranger; "you have stated the case right."

"Why, then," said Sancho, "even let that part of the man that spoke true freely pass, and hang the other part of the man that swore false, and so the law will be fulfilled."

"But then, my lord," replied the stranger, "the man must be divided into two parts, which, if we do, he certainly dies, and the law, which must, every tittle of it, be observed, is not put in execution."

"Well, hark you me, honest man," said Sancho, "either I am a very dunce, or there is as much reason to put this same person you talk of to death, as to let him live and pass the bridge; for if the truth saves him, the lie condemns him. Now the case stands thus: I would have you tell those gentlemen that sent you to me, since there is as much reason to bring him off as to condemn him, that they even let him go free; for it is always more commendable to do good than hurt. And this I would give you under my own hand if I could write. Nor do I speak this of my own head; but I remember one precept, among many others, that my master, Don Quixote, gave me the night before I went to govern this island, which was, that when the scale of justice is even, or a case is doubtful, we should prefer mercy before rigour; and it has pleased God I should call it to mind so luckily at this juncture."

"For my part," said the steward, "this judgment seems to me so equitable that I do not believe Lycurgus himself, who gave the laws to the Lacedæmonians, could ever have decided the matter better than the great Sancho has done.

"And now, sir, sure there is enough done for this morning; be pleased to adjourn the court, and I will give order that your excellency may dine to your heart's content."

"Well said," cried Sancho; "that is all I want, and then a clear stage and no favour. Feed me well, and then ply me with cases and questions thick and threefold; you shall see me untwist them, and lay them open as clear as the sun."

The steward was as good as his word, believing it would be a burden to his conscience to famish so wise a governor: besides, he intended the next night to put in practice the last trick which he had commission to pass upon him.

Now Sancho having plentifully dined that day, in spite of all the aphorisms of Dr. Tirteafuera, when the cloth was removed, in came an express with a letter from Don Quixote to the governor. Sancho ordered the secretary to read it to himself, and if there was nothing in it for secret perusal, then to read it aloud.

The secretary having first run it over accordingly, "My lord," said he, "the letter may not only be publicly read, but deserves to be engraved in characters of gold; and thus it is."

Don Quixote de la Mancha to Sancho Panza, Governor of the Island of Barataria.

"When I expected to have had an account of thy carelessness and impertinences, friend Sancho, I was agreably disappointed with news of thy wise behaviour; for which I return particular thanks to Heaven, that can raise the lowest from their poverty, and turn the fool into a man of sense. I hear thou governest with all the discretion of a man; and that whilst thou approvest thyself one, thou retainest the humility of the meanest creature. But I desire thee to observe, Sancho, that it is many times very necessary and convenient to thwart the humility of the heart for the better support of the authority of a place. For the ornament of a person that is advanced to an eminent post must be answerable to its greatness, and not debased to the inclination of his former meanness. Let thy apparel be neat and handsome; even a stake well dressed does not look like a stake. I would not have thee wear foppish, gaudy things, nor affect the garb of a soldier in the circumstances of a magistrate; but let thy dress be suitable to thy degree, and always clean and decent.

"To gain the hearts of thy people, among other things, I have two chiefly to recommend: One is, to be affable, courteous, and fair to all the world. I have already told thee of that. And the other, to take care that plenty of provisions be never wanting, for nothing afflicts or urges more the spirits of the poor than scarcity and hunger.

"Do not put out many new orders; and if thou dost put out any, see that they be wholesome and good, and especially that they be strictly observed; for laws not well obeyed are no better than if they were not made, and only show that the prince who had the wisdom and authority to make them had not the resolution to see them executed; and laws that only threaten, and are not kept, become like the log that was given to the frogs to be their king, which they feared at first, but at last scorned and trampled on.

"Be a father to virtue, but a father-in-law to vice. Be not always severe, nor always merciful; choose a mean between these two extremes, for that middle point is the centre of discretion.

"Visit the prisons, the shambles, and the public markets, for the governor's presence is highly necessary in such places.

"Comfort the prisoners that hope to be quickly dispatched.

"Be a terror to the butchers, that they may be fair in their weights, and keep hucksters and fraudulent dealers in awe, for the same reason.

"Shouldst thou unhappily be inclined to be covetous, or a glutton, as I hope thou art not, avoid showing thyself guilty of those vices; for when the town, and those that come near thee, have discovered thy weakness, they will be sure to try thee on that side, and tempt thee to thy everlasting ruin.

"Read over and over, and seriously consider the admonitions and documents I gave thee in writing before thou wentest to thy government, and thou wilt find the benefit of it in all those difficulties and emergencies that so frequently attend the function of a governor.

"Write to thy lord and lady, and show thyself grateful; for ingratitude is the offspring of pride, and one of the worst corruptions of the mind: whereas he that is thankful to his benefactors gives a testimony that he will be so to God, who has done him so much good.

"My lady duchess dispatched a messenger on purpose to thy wife Teresa, with thy hunting suit and another present. We expect his return every moment.

"I have been somewhat out of order by a certain cat encounter I had lately, not much to the advantage of my nose; but all that is nothing, for if there are necromancers that misuse me, there are others ready to defend me.

"Send me word whether the steward that is with thee had any hand in the business of the Countess of Trifaldi, as thou wert once of opinion; and let me also have an account of whatever befalls thee, since the distance between us is so small. I have thoughts of leaving this idle life ere long, for I was not born for luxury and ease.

"A business has offered that I believe will make me lose the duke and duchess's favour; but, though I am heartily sorry for it, that does not alter my resolution; for, after all, I owe more to my profession than to complaisance, and, as the saying is, *Amicus Plato, sed magis amica veritas.* I send thee this scrap of Latin, flattering myself that since thou camest to be a governor thou mayest have learned something of that language. Farewell, and Heaven keep thee above the pity of the world.

"Thy friend,

"DON QUIXOTE DE LA MANCHA."

Sancho gave great attention to the letter, and it was highly applauded, both for sense and integrity, by everybody that heard it. After that, he rose from table, and, calling the secretary, went without any further delay and locked himself up with him in his chamber to write an answer to his master, Don Quixote. He ordered the scribe to set down word for word what he dictated, without adding or diminishing the least thing; which being strictly observed, this was the tenor of the letter:—

Sancho Panza to Don Quixote de la Mancha.

"I am so taken up with business that I have not time to scratch my head or pare my nails, which is the reason they are so long—God help me! I tell you this, dear master of mine, that you may not marvel why I have not yet let you know whether it goes well or ill with me in this same government, where I am more hunger-starved than when you and I wandered through woods and wildernesses.

"My lord duke wrote to me the other day, to inform me of some spies that were got into this island to kill me; but as yet I have discovered none but a certain doctor, hired by the islanders to kill all the governors that come near it. They call him Dr. Pedro Rezio de Anguero, and he was born at Tirteafuera. His name is enough to make me fear he will be the death of me. This same doctor says of himself that he does cure diseases when you have them; but when you have them not, he only pretends to keep them from coming. The physic he uses is fasting upon fasting, till he turns a body to a mere skeleton; as if to be wasted to skin and bones were not as bad as a fever. In short, he starves me to death; so that when I thought, as being a governor, to have my belly full of good hot victuals and cool liquor, and to refresh my body in Holland sheets, and on a soft feather bed, I am come to do penance like a hermit; and, as I do it unwillingly, I am afraid of what will come to me at last.

"All this while I have not yet so much as fingered the least penny of money, either for fees, bribes, or anything; and how it comes to be no better with me I cannot for my soul imagine, for I have heard, by the by, that the governors who come to this island are wont to have a very good gift, or, at least, a very round sum lent them by the town before they enter. And they say, too, that this is the usual custom, not only here, but in other places.

"Last night, in going my rounds, I met with a mighty handsome damsel in boy's clothes, and a brother of hers in woman's apparel. My gentleman-waiter fell in love with the girl, and intends to make her his wife, as he says. As for the youth, I have pitched on him to be my son-in-law. To-day we both design to discourse the father, one Diego de la Llana, who is a gentleman, and an old Christian, every inch of him.

"I visit the markets as you advised me, and yesterday found one of the hucksters selling hazel nuts. She pretended they were all new, but I found she had mixed a whole bushel of old, empty, rotten nuts among the same quantity of new. With that I judged them to be given to the hospital-boys, who knew how to pick the good from the bad, and gave sentence against her that she should not come into the market in fifteen days; and people said I did well. What I can tell you is, that, if you will believe the folks of this town, there is not a more rascally sort of people in the world than these market-women, for they are all a saucy, foul-mouthed, impudent rabble; and I judge them to be so by those I have seen in other places.

"I am mighty well pleased that my lady duchess has written to my wife, Teresa Panza, and sent her the token you mention. It shall go hard but I will requite her kindness one time or other. Pray give my service to her, and tell her from me she has not cast her gift in a broken sack, as something more than words shall show.

"If I might advise you, and had my wish, there should be no falling out between your worship and my lord and lady; for, if you quarrel with them, it is I must come by the worst for it. And, since you mind me of being grateful, it will not look well in you not to be so to those who have made so much of you at their castle.

"As for your cat affair, I can make nothing of it, only I fancy you are still haunted after the old rate. You will tell me more when we meet.

"I would fain have sent you a token, but I do not know what to send, unless it were some little pipes, which they make here very curiously, and fix most cleverly. But, if I stay in my place, it shall go hard but I will get something worth the sending to you, be it what it will.

"If my wife Teresa Panza writes to me, pray pay the postage, and send me the letter; for I mightily long to hear how it is with her and my house and children.

"So Heaven preserve you from ill-minded enchanters, and send me safe and sound out of this government, which I am much afraid of, as Dr. Pedro Rezio diets me.

"Your worship's servant,

"SANCHO PANZA, the Governor."

The secretary made up the letter, and immediately dispatched the express. Then those who carried on the plot against Sancho combined together, and consulted how to remove him from the government; and Sancho passed that afternoon in making several regulations for the better establishment of that which he imagined to be an island. He published an order against the higglers and forestallers of the markets, and another to encourage the bringers-in of wines from any part whatever, provided the owners declared of what growth they were, that they might be rated according to their value and goodness; and that they who should adulterate wine with water, or give it a wrong name, should be punished with death. He lowered the price of all kinds of apparel, and particularly that of shoes, as thinking it exorbitant. He regulated servants' wages that were unlimited before, and proportioned them to the merit of their service. He laid severe penalties upon all those that should sing or vend lewd and immoral songs and ballads, either in the open day or in the dusk of the evening; and also forbid all blind people the singing about miracles in rhymes, unless they produced authentic testimonies of their truth; for it appeared to him that most of those that were sung in such a manner were false, and a disparagement to the true.

He appointed a particular officer to inspect the poor, not to persecute, but to examine them, and know whether they were truly such; for, under pretence of counterfeit lameness and artificial sores, many impudently rob the true poor of charity, to spend it in riot and drunkenness.

In short, he made so many wholesome ordinances that to this day they are observed in that place, and called "The Constitutions of the great Governor, Sancho Panza."

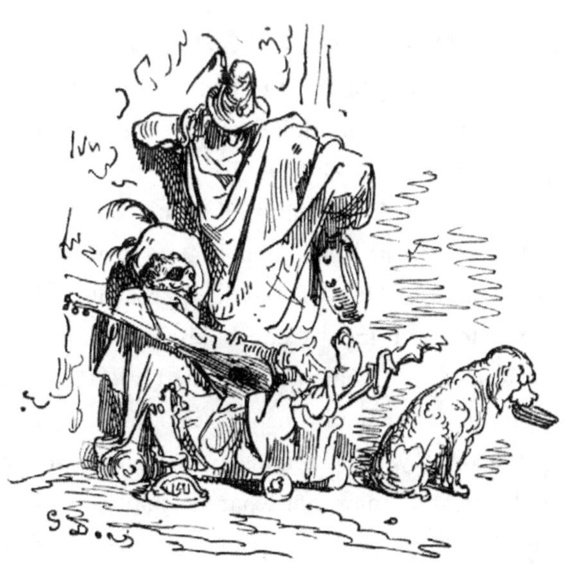

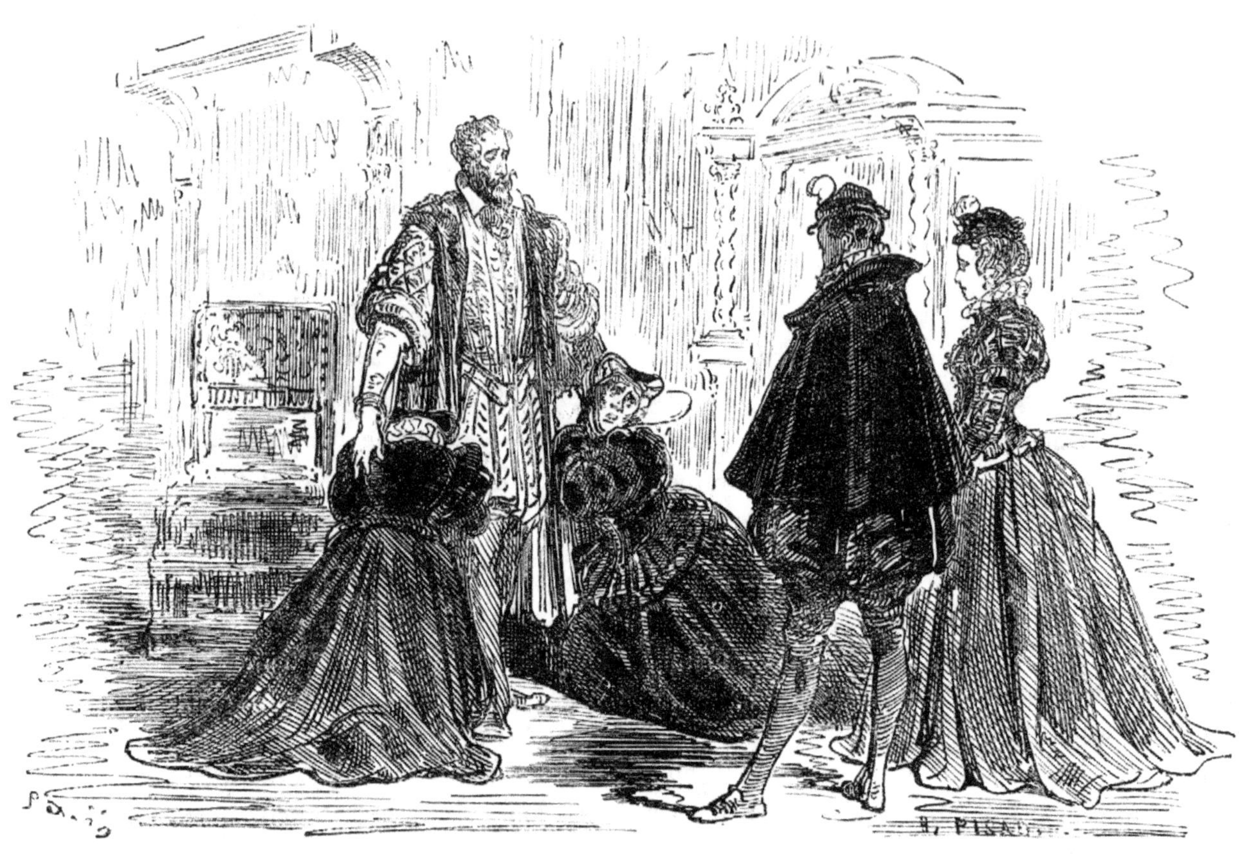

CHAPTER LII.

A RELATION OF THE ADVENTURES OF THE SECOND DISCONSOLATE OR DISTRESSED MATRON, OTHERWISE CALLED DONNA RODRIGUEZ.

CID HAMET relates that, Don Quixote's scratches being healed, he began to think the life he led in the castle not suitable to the order of knight-errantry which he professed; he resolved, therefore, to take leave of the duke and duchess, and set forwards for Saragosa, where, at the approaching tournament, he hoped to win the armour, the usual prize at the festivals of that kind. Accordingly, as he sat at table with the lord and lady of the castle, he began to acquaint them with his design, when behold two women entered the great hall, clad in deep mourning from head to foot. One of them, approaching Don Quixote, threw herself at his feet, where, lying prostrate, and in a manner kissing them, she fetched such deep and doleful sighs, and made such sorrowful lamentations, that all those who were by were not a little surprised. And, though the duke and duchess imagined it to be some new device of their servants against Don Quixote, yet, perceiving with what earnestness the woman sighed and lamented, they were in doubt and knew not what to think; till the compassionate champion, raising her from the ground, engaged her to lift up her veil and discover, what they least expected, the face of Donna Rodriguez, the duenna of the family; and the other mourner proved to be her daughter, whom the rich farmer's son had deluded. All those that knew them were in great admiration, especially the duke and duchess; for, though they knew her simplicity and indiscretion, they did not believe her so far gone in madness. At last the sorrowful matron, addressing herself to the duke and the duchess, "May it please your graces," said she, "to permit me to direct my discourse to this knight, for it concerns me to get out of an unlucky business into which the impudence of a treacherous villain has brought us." With that the duke gave her leave to say what she would; then, applying herself to Don Quixote, "It is not long," said she, "valorous knight, since I gave your worship an account how basely and treacherously a young graceless farmer had used my dear child, the poor, undone creature here present; and you then promised me to stand up for her and see her righted; and now I understand you are about to leave this castle in quest of the good adventures Heaven shall send you. And, therefore, before you are gone nobody knows whither, I have this boon to beg of your worship, that you would do so much as challenge this sturdy clown, and make him marry my daughter, according to his promise. For, as for my lord duke, it is a folly to think he will ever see me righted, for the reason I told you in private. And so Heaven preserve your worship, and still be our defence."

"Worthy matron," answered Don Quixote, with a great deal of gravity and solemn form, "moderate your tears, or, to speak more properly, dry them up, and spare your sighs, for I take upon me to see your daughter's wrongs redressed; though she had done much better had not her too great credulity made her trust the protestations of lovers, which generally are readily made, but most uneasily performed. Therefore, with my lord duke's permission, I will instantly depart to find out this ungracious wretch; and, as soon as he is found, I will challenge him, and kill him, if he persists in his obstinacy; for the chief end of my profession is to pardon the submissive and to chastise the stubborn, to relieve the miserable and destroy the cruel."

"Sir Knight," said the duke, "you need not give yourself the trouble of seeking the fellow of whom that good matron complains; nor need you ask me leave to challenge him; for I already engage that he shall meet you in person to answer it here in this castle, where safe lists shall be set up for you both, observing all the laws of arms that ought to be kept in affairs of this kind, and doing each party justice, as all princes ought to do that admit of single combats within their territories."

"Upon that assurance," said Don Quixote, "with your grace's leave, I, for this time, waive my punctilio of gentility, and, debasing myself to the meanness of the offender, qualify him to measure lances with me; and so, let him be absent or present, I challenge and defy him, as a villain that has deluded this poor creature; and he shall either perform his promise of making her his lawful wife, or die in the contest."

With that, pulling off his glove, he flung it down into the middle of the hall, and the duke took it up, declaring, as he already had done, that he accepted the challenge in the name of his vassal; fixing the time for combat to be six days after, and the place to be the castle court; the arms to be such as are usual among knights, as lance, shield, armour of proof, and all other pieces, without fraud, advantage, or enchantment, after search made by the judges of the field.

"But, in the first place," added the duke, "it is requisite that these persons commit the justice of their cause into the hands of their champion, for otherwise there will be nothing done, and the challenge is void, in course."

"I do," answered the matron.

"And so do I," added the daughter, all ashamed, blubbering, and in a crying tone.

The preliminaries being adjusted, and the duke having resolved with himself what to do in the matter, the mourning petitioners went away, and the duchess ordered they should no longer be looked on as her domestics, but as ladies-errants, that came to demand justice in her castle; and, accordingly, there was a peculiar apartment appointed for them, where they were served as strangers, to the amazement of the other servants, who could not imagine what would be the end of Donna Rodriguez and her forsaken daughter's ridiculous, confident undertaking.

Presently, after this, to complete their mirth, and, as it were, for the last course, in came the page that had carried the letters and the presents to Teresa Panza. The duke and duchess were overjoyed to see him returned, having a great desire to know the success of his journey. They inquired of him accordingly; but he told them that the account he had to give them could not well be delivered in public, nor in few words, and therefore begged their graces would be pleased to take it in private, and, in the meantime, entertain themselves with those letters. With that, taking out two, he delivered them to her grace. The superscription of the one was, "These for my Lady Duchess, of I do not know what place;" and the direction of the other thus, "To my Husband, Sancho Panza, Governor of the Island of Barataria, whom Heaven prosper as many or more years than me."

The duchess sat upon thorns till she had read her letter; so, having opened it, and ran it over to herself, finding there was nothing of secrecy in it, she read it out aloud, that the whole company might hear what follows:—

Teresa Panza's Letter to the Duchess.

"My Lady,—The letter your honour sent me pleased me hugeously; for, troth, it is what I heartily longed for. The string of coral is a good thing, and my husband's hunting-suit may come up to it. All our town takes it mightily kindly, and is very glad that your honour has made my spouse a governor, though nobody will believe it, especially our curate, Master Nicholas, the barber, and Samson Carrasco, the bachelor. But what care I whether they do or no? So it be true, as it is, let every one have their saying. Though (it is a folly to lie) I had not believed it neither, but for the coral and the suit; for everybody here takes my husband to be a dolt, and cannot, for the blood of them, imagine what he can be fit to govern, unless it be a herd of goats. Well, Heaven be his guide, and speed him as he sees best for his children! As for me, my dear lady, I am resolved, with your good liking, to make hay while the sun shines, and go to court, to loll it along in a coach, and make a world of my back-friends, that envy me already, stare their eyes out. And, therefore, good your honour, pray bid my husband send me store of money, for I believe it is dear living at court; one can have but little bread there for sixpence, and a pound of flesh is worth thirty maravedis, which would make one stand amazed. And if he is not for my coming, let him send me word in time, for my feet itch to be jogging; for my gossips and neighbours tell me that if I and my daughter go about the court as we should, spruce and fine, and at a tearing rate, my husband will be better known by me than I by him; for many cannot choose but ask, 'What ladies are these in the coach?' with that, one of my servants answers, 'The wife and daughter of Sancho Panza, governor of the island of Barataria;' and thus shall my husband be known, and I honoured, far and near; and so have at all; Rome has everything.

"You cannot think how I am troubled that we have gathered no acorns hereaway this year; however, I send your highness about half a peck, which I have culled one by one; I went to the mountains on purpose, and got the biggest I could find. I wish they had been as big as ostrich eggs.

"Pray let not your pomposity forget to write to me, and I will be sure to send you an answer, and let you know how I do, and send you all the news in our village, where I am waiting, and praying the Lord to preserve your highness, and not to forget me. My daughter Sanchica, and my son, kiss your worship's hands.

"She that wishes rather to see you than write to you.

"Your servant,

"TERESA PANZA."

This letter was very entertaining to all the company, especially to the duke and duchess, insomuch that her grace asked Don Quixote whether it would be amiss to open the governor's letter, which she imagined was a very good one. The knight told her that, to satisfy her curiosity, he would open it, which being done, he found what follows:—

Teresa Panza's Letter to her Husband, Sancho Panza.

"I received thy letter, dear honey Sancho, and I vow and swear to thee, as I am a Catholic Christian, I was within two fingers' breadth of running mad for joy. Look you, my chuck, when I heard thou wert made a governor, I was so transported, I had like to have fallen down dead with mere gladness; for thou knowest sudden joy is said to kill as soon as great sorrow. As for thy daughter Sanchica, she was not able to do anything for some days, for very pleasure. I had the suit thou sentest me before my eyes, and the lady duchess's corals about my neck, held the letter in my hands, and had him that brought them standing by me, and for all that I thought what I saw and felt was but a dream. For who could have thought a goatherd should ever come to be governor of islands? But what said my mother? 'Who a great deal would see, a great while must live.' I speak this because, if I live longer, I mean to see more; for I shall never be at rest till I see thee a farmer or receiver of the customs; for though they be officers that send many to ruin, for all that, they bring grist to the mill. My lady duchess will tell thee how I long to go to court. Pray, think of it, and let me know thy mind; for I mean to credit thee there by going in a coach.

"Neither the curate, the barber, the bachelor, nor the sexton will believe thou art a governor; but say it is all juggling or enchantment, as all thy master Don Quixote's concerns used to be; and Samson threatens to find thee out, and put this maggot of a government out of thy pate, and Don Quixote's madness out of his coxcomb. For my part, I do but laugh at them, and look upon my string of coral, and contrive how to fit up the suit thou sentest me into a gown for thy daughter.

"I sent my lady the duchess some acorns; I would they were beaten gold. I pr'ythee send me some strings of pearl, if they be in fashion in thy island.

"The news here is that Berrueca has married her daughter to a sorry painter that came hither pretending to paint anything. The township sent him to paint the king's arms over the town hall. He asked two ducats for the job, which they paid him: so he fell to work, and was eight days a-daubing, but could make nothing of it, and said he could not hit upon such kind of work, and so gave them their money again. Yet, for all this, he married with the name of a good workman. The truth is, he has left his pencil upon it, and taken the spade, and goes to the field like a gentleman. Pedro de Lobo's son has taken orders, and shaved his crown, meaning to be a priest. Minguilla, Mingo Salvato's granddaughter, heard of it, and sues him upon a promise of marriage. We have no olives this year, nor is there a drop of vinegar to be got for love or money. Sanchica makes bone-lace, and gets her three-halfpence a day clear, which she saves in a box with a slit, to go towards buying household stuff. But now she is a governor's daughter she has no need to work, for thou wilt give her a portion. The fountain in the market is dried up. A thunderbolt lately fell upon the pillory: there may they all light. I expect thy answer to this, and thy resolution concerning my going to court. So Heaven send thee long to live, longer than myself, or rather as long; for I would not willingly leave thee behind me in this world.

"Thy Wife,

"TERESA PANZA."

These letters were admired, and caused a great deal of laughter and diversion; and, to complete the mirth, at the same time the express returned that brought Sancho's answer to Don Quixote, which was likewise publicly read, and startled all the hearers, who took the governor for a fool. Afterwards the duchess withdrew to know of the page what he had to relate of Sancho's village; of which he gave her a full account, without omitting the least particular. He also brought her the acorns, and a cheese which Teresa had given him for a very good one, and better than those of Troncheon, which the duchess gratefully accepted. Now let us leave her, to tell the end of the government of great Sancho Panza, the flower and mirror of all island governors.

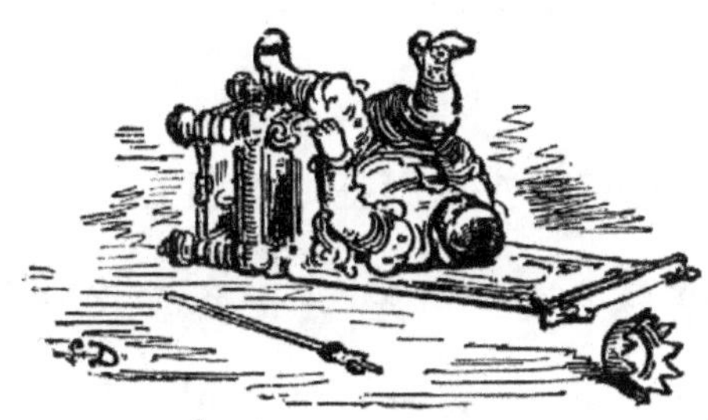

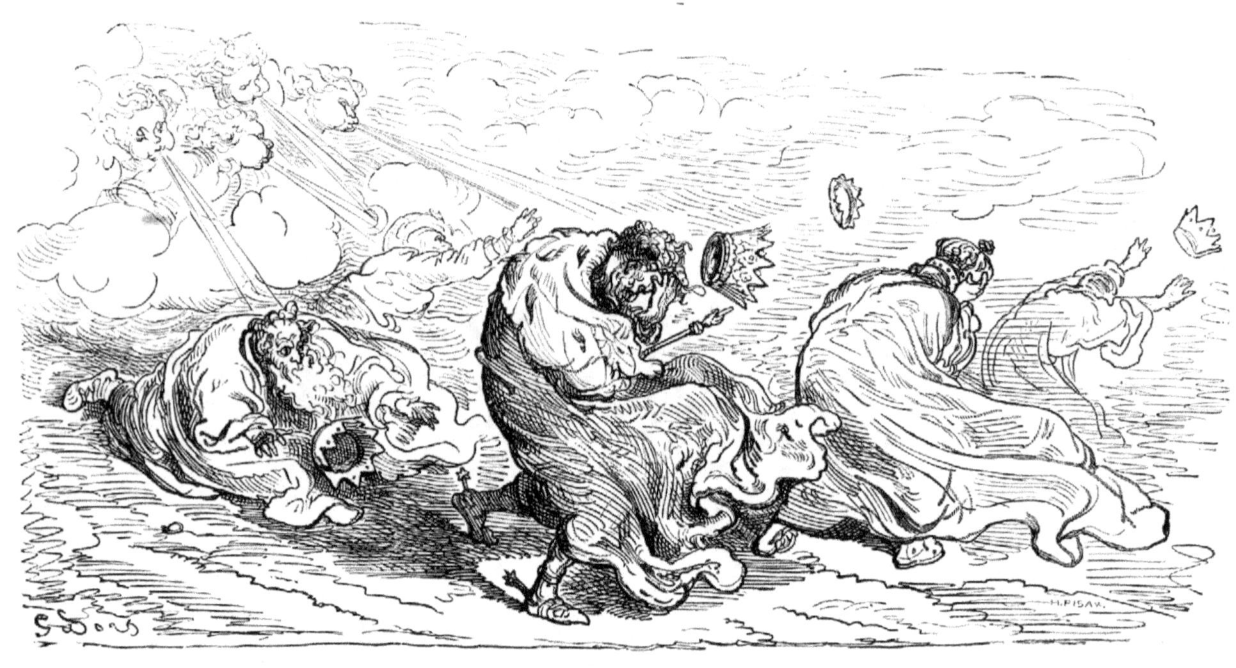

CHAPTER LIII.

THE TOILSOME END AND CONCLUSION OF SANCHO PANZA'S GOVERNMENT.

TO think the affairs of this life are always to remain in the same state is an erroneous fancy. The face of things rather seems continually to change and roll with circular motion; summer succeeds the spring, autumn the summer, winter the autumn, and then spring again. So time proceeds in this perpetual round; only the life of man is ever hastening to its end, swifter than time itself, without hopes to be renewed, unless in the next, that is unlimited and infinite. This says Cid Hamet, the Mahometan philosopher. For even by the light of Nature, and without that of faith, many have discovered the swiftness and instability of this present being, and the duration of the eternal life which is expected. But this moral reflection of our author is not here to be supposed as meant by him in its full extent; for he intended it only to show the uncertainty of Sancho's fortune, how soon it vanished like a dream, and how from his high preferment he returned to his former low station.

It was now but the seventh night, after so many days of his government, when the careful governor had betaken himself to his repose, sated not with bread and wine, but cloyed with hearing causes, pronouncing sentences, making statutes, and putting out orders and proclamations. Scarce was sleep, in spite of wakeful hunger, beginning to close his eyes, when of a sudden he heard a great noise of bells, and most dreadful outcries, as if the whole island had been sinking. Presently he started, and sat up in bed, and listened with great attention, to try if he could learn how far this uproar might concern him. But, while he was thus hearkening

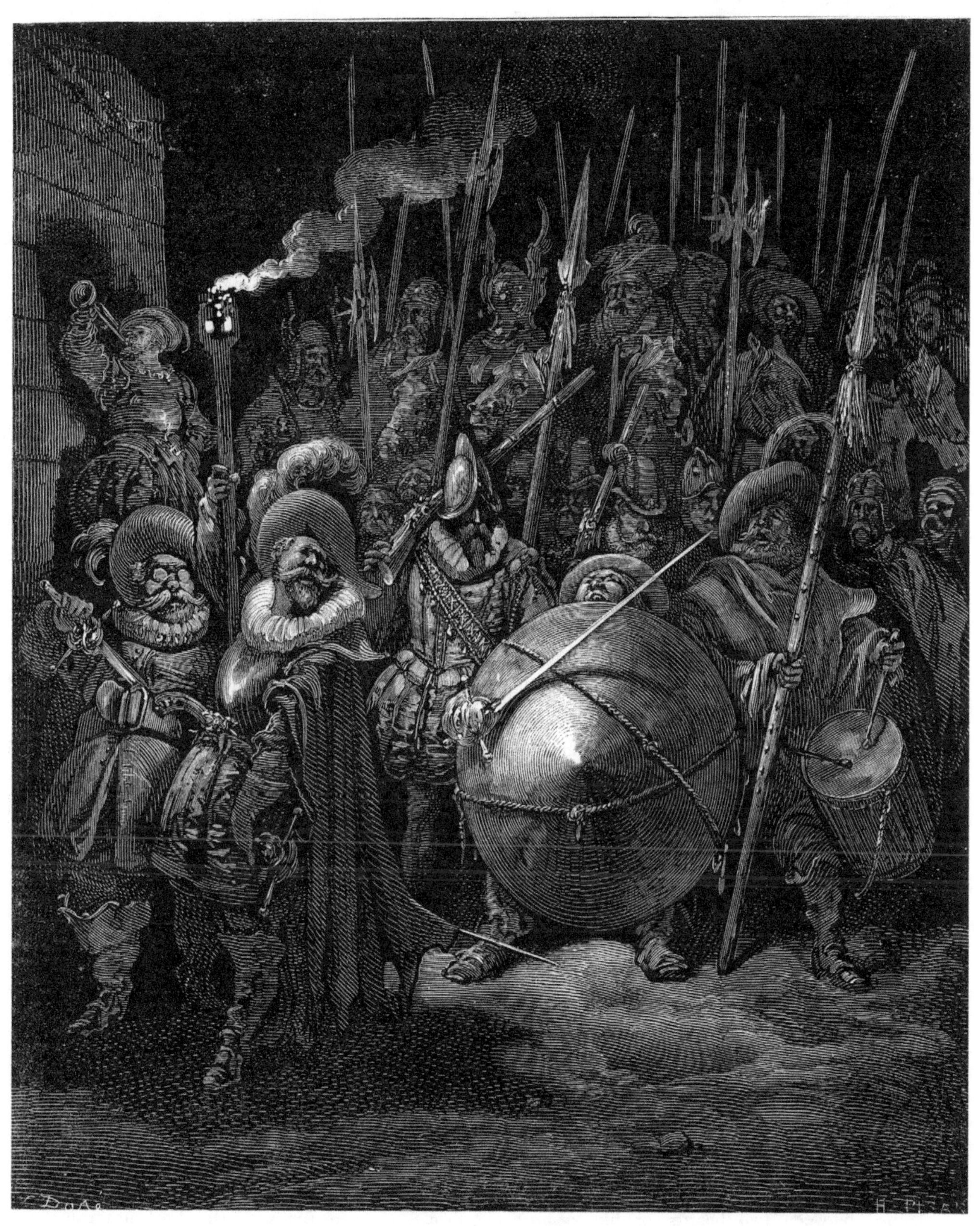

"'March!' quoth Sancho, 'How do you think I am able to do it?'"

in the dark, a great number of drums and trumpets were heard, and that sound being added to the noise of the bells and the cries, gave so dreadful an alarm that his fear and terror increased, and he was in a sad consternation. Up he leaped out of his bed, and put on his slippers, the ground being damp, and without anything else on but his shirt, ran and opened his chamber door, and saw about twenty men come running along the galleries with lighted links in one hand, and drawn swords in the other, all crying out, "Arm, my lord governor, arm! a world of enemies are got into the island, and we are undone, unless your valour and conduct relieve us." Thus bawling and running with great fury and disorder, they got to the door where Sancho stood quite scared out of his senses. "Arm, arm this moment, my lord!" cried one of them, "if you have not a mind to be lost with the whole island."

"What would you have me arm for?" quoth Sancho; "do I know anything of arms or fighting, think you? Why do you not rather send for Don Quixote, my master? he will dispatch your enemies in a trice. Alas! as I am a sinner to Heaven, I understand nothing of this hasty service."

"For shame, my lord governor!" said another. "What a faint-heartedness is this? See, we bring you here arms offensive and defensive! Arm yourself, and march to the market-place! Be our leader and captain, as you ought, and show yourself a governor!"

"Why, then, arm me, and good luck attend me," quoth Sancho.

With that they brought him two large shields which they had provided, and, without letting him put on his other clothes, clapped them over his shirt, and tied the one behind upon his back, and the other before upon his breast, having got his arms through some holes made on purpose. Now, the shields being fastened to his body as hard as cords could bind them, the poor governor was cased up and immured as straight as an arrow, without being able so much as to bend his knees, or stir a step. Then, having put a lance into his hand for him to lean upon, and keep himself up, they desired him to march, and lead them on, and put life into them all, telling him that they did not doubt of victory since they had him for their commander.

"March!" quoth Sancho, "how do you think I am able to do it, squeezed as I am? These boards stick so plaguy close to me, I cannot so much as bend the joints of my knees; you must even carry me in your arms, and lay me across or set me upright before some passage, and I will make good that spot of ground, either with this lance or my body."

"Fie, my lord governor!" said another; "it is more your fear than your armour that stiffens your legs, and hinders you from moving. Move, move, march on! it is high time; the enemy grows stronger, and the danger presses."

The poor governor, thus urged and upbraided, endeavoured to go forwards, but the first motion he made threw him to the ground at the full length, so heavily, that he gave over all his bones for broken; and there he lay, like a huge tortoise in his shell, or a flitch of bacon clapped between two boards, or like a boat overturned upon a flat with the keel upwards.

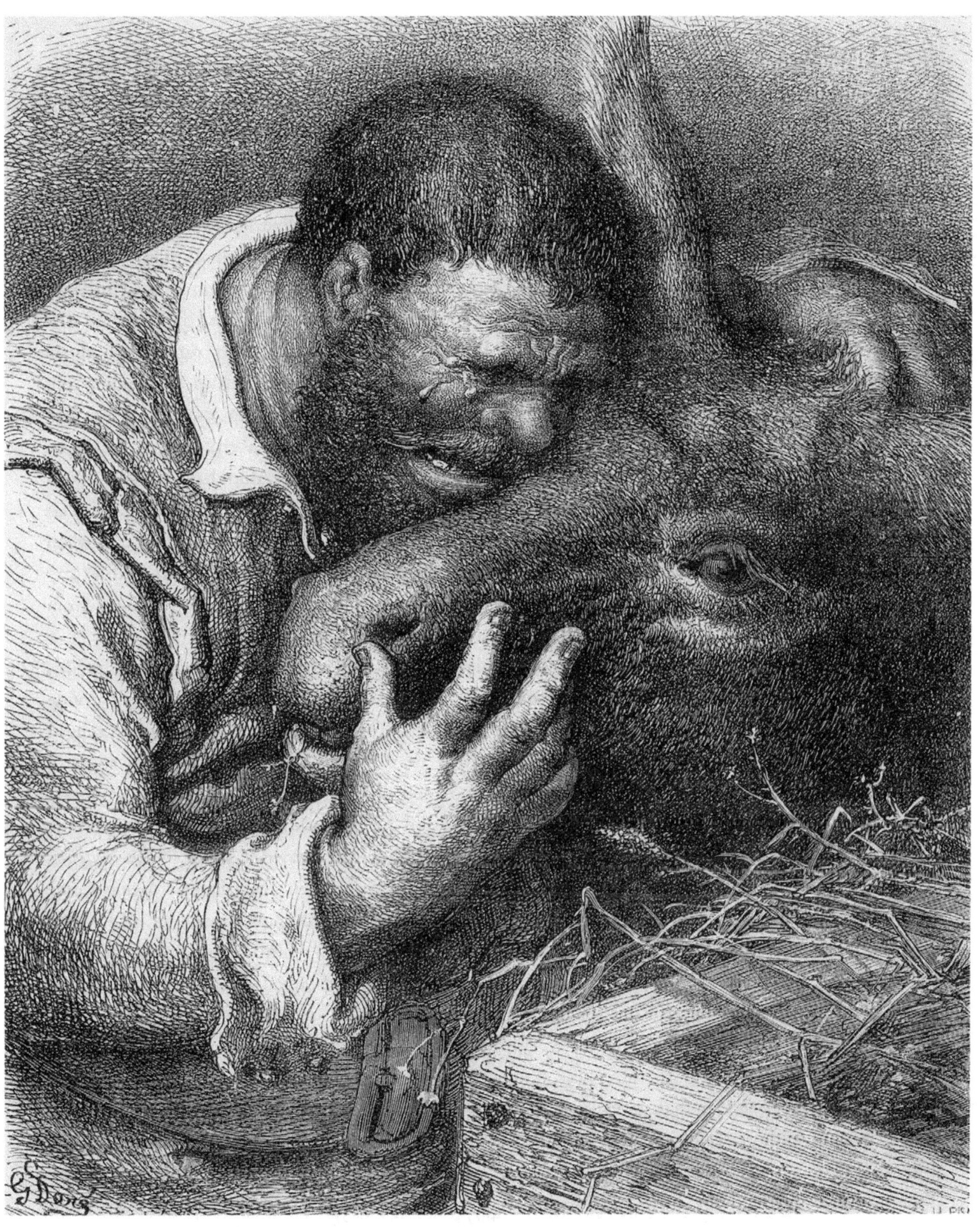

"'Come hither,' said he, 'my friend; thou faithful companion and fellow-sharer in my travels and miseries.'"

Nor had those drolling companions the least compassion upon him as he lay; quite contrary, having put out their lights, they made a terrible noise, and clattered with their swords, and trampled too and again upon the poor governor's body, and laid on furiously with their swords upon his shields, insomuch that, if he had not shrunk his head into them for shelter, he had been in a woful condition. Squeezed up in his narrow shell, he was in a grievous fright and a terrible sweat, praying from the bottom of his heart for deliverance from the cursed trade of governing islands. Some kicked him, some stumbled and fell upon him, and one among the rest jumped full upon him, and there stood for some time as on a watch-tower, like a general encouraging his soldiers and giving orders, crying out, "There, boys, there! the enemies charge most on that side; make good that breach, secure that gate, down with those scaling ladders, fetch fire-balls, more grenades, burning pitch, rosin, and kettles of scalding oil. Intrench yourselves, get beds, quilts, cushions, and barricade the streets;" in short, he called for all the instruments of death, and all the engines used for the defence of a city that is besieged and stormed. Sancho lay snug, though sadly bruised; and while he endured all quietly, "Oh, that it would please the Lord," quoth he to himself, "that this island were but taken, or that I were fairly dead, or out of this peck of troubles!" At last Heaven heard his prayers; and, when he least expected it, he heard them cry, "Victory! victory! the enemy is routed! Now, my lord governor, rise; come and enjoy the fruits of conquest, and divide the spoils taken from the enemy by the valour of your invincible arms."

"Help me up," cried poor Sancho, in a doleful tone; and when they had set him on his legs, "Let all the enemy I have routed," quoth he, "be nailed to my forehead. I will divide no spoils of enemies; but, if I have one friend here, I only beg he would give me a draught of wine to comfort me, and help to dry up the sweat that I am in, for I am all over water."

Thereupon they wiped him, gave him wine, and took off his shields. After that, as he sat upon his bed, what with his fright, and what with the toil he had endured, he fell into a swoon, insomuch that those who acted this scene began to repent they had carried it so far. But Sancho, recovering from his fit in a little time, they also recovered from their uneasiness. Being come to himself, he asked what o'clock it was. They answered it was now break of day. He said nothing, but without any word, began to put on his clothes. While this was doing, and he continued seriously silent, all the eyes of the company were fixed upon him, wondering what could be the meaning of his being in such haste to put on his clothes. At last he made an end of dressing himself, and, creeping along softly (for he was too much bruised to go along very fast), he got to the stable, followed by all the company, and, coming to Dapple, he embraced the quiet animal, gave him a loving kiss on the forehead, and, with tears in his eyes, "Come hither," said he, "my friend; thou faithful companion and fellow-sharer in my travels and miseries: when thee and I consorted together, and all my cares were but to mend thy furniture and feed thy little carcass, then happy were my days, my months, and years. But since I forsook thee, and clambered up the towers of ambition and pride, a thousand woes, a thousand torments, and four thousand tribulations have haunted and worried my soul." While he was talking thus, he fitted on his pack-saddle, nobody offering to say anything to him. This done, with a great deal of difficulty he mounted his ass, and then addressing himself to the steward, the secretary, the gentleman-waiter, and Doctor Pedro Rezio, and many others that stood by, "Make way, gentlemen," said he, "and let me return to my former liberty. Let me go, that I may seek my old course of life, and rise again from that death which buries me here alive. I was not born to be a governor, nor to defend islands nor cities from enemies that break in upon them. I know better what belongs to ploughing, delving, pruning, and planting of vineyards, than how to make laws, and defend countries and kingdoms. 'St. Peter is very well at Rome;' which is as much as to say, let every one stick to the calling he was born to. A spade does better in my hand than a governor's truncheon, and I had rather fill my belly with a mess of plain porridge, than lie at the mercy of a coxcombly physic-monger, that starves me to death. I had rather solace myself under the shade of an oak in summer, and wrap up my body in a double sheep-skin in the winter, at my liberty, than lay me down with the slavery of a government, in fine Holland sheets, and case my hide in furs and richest sables. Heaven be with you, gentlefolks, and pray tell my lord duke from me, that naked I was born, and naked I am at present. I have neither won nor lost, which is as much as to say, without a penny I came to this government, and without a penny I leave it—quite contrary to what other governors of islands used to do, when they leave them. Clear the way, then, I beseech you, and let me pass; I must get myself wrapped up all over in cerecloth, for I do not think I have a sound rib left, thanks to the enemies that have walked over me all night long."

"This must not be, my lord governor," said Dr. Rezio, "for I will give your honour a balsamic drink, that is a specific against falls, dislocations, contusions, and all manner of bruises, and that will presently restore you to your former health and strength; and then, for your diet, I promise to take a new course with you, and to let you eat abundantly of whatsoever you please."

"It is too late, Mr. Doctor," answered Sancho; "you should as soon make me turn Turk, as hinder me from going. No, no, these tricks shall not pass upon me again; you shall as soon make me fly to heaven without wings, as get me to stay here, or ever catch me nibbling at a government again, though it were served up to me in a covered dish. I am of the blood of the Panzas, and we are all wilful and positive. If once we cry odd, it shall be odd, in spite of all mankind, though it be even. Go to, then; let the emmet leave behind him, in this stable, those wings that lifted him up in the air, to be a prey to martlets and sparrows. Fair and softly. Let me now tread again on plain ground; though I may not wear pinked Cordovan leather pumps, I shall not want a pair of sandals to my feet. 'Every sheep to her mate.' 'Let not the cobbler go beyond his last;' and so, let me go, for it is late."

"My lord governor," said the steward, "though it grieves us to part with your honour, your sense and Christian behaviour engaging us to covet your company, yet we would not presume to stop you against your inclination; but you know that every governor, before he leaves the place he has governed, is bound to give an account of his administration. Be pleased, therefore, to do so for the ten days you have been among us, and then peace be with you."

"No man has power to call me to an account," replied Sancho, "unless it be my lord duke's appointment. Now, to him it is that I am going, and to him I will give a fair and square account. And, indeed, going away so bare as I do, there needs no greater signs that I have governed like an angel."

"In truth," said Dr. Rezio, "the great Sancho is in the right; and I am of opinion we ought to let him go, for certainly the duke will be very glad to see him."

Thereupon they all agreed to let him pass, offering first to attend him, and supply him with whatever he might want in his journey, either for entertainment or convenience. Sancho told them that all he desired was a little corn for his ass, and half a cheese and half a loaf for himself, having occasion for no other provisions in so short a journey. With that they all embraced him, and he embraced them all, not without tears in his eyes, leaving them in admiration of the good sense which he discovered, both in his discourse and unalterable resolution.

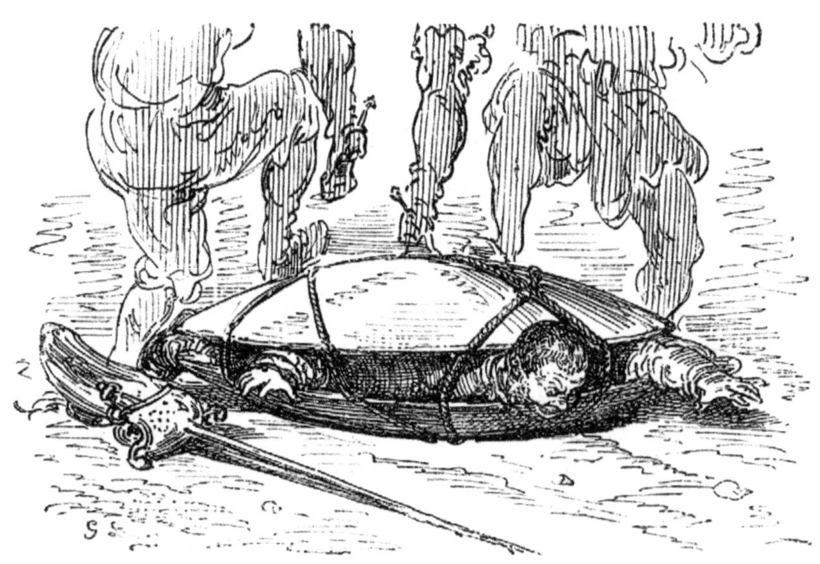

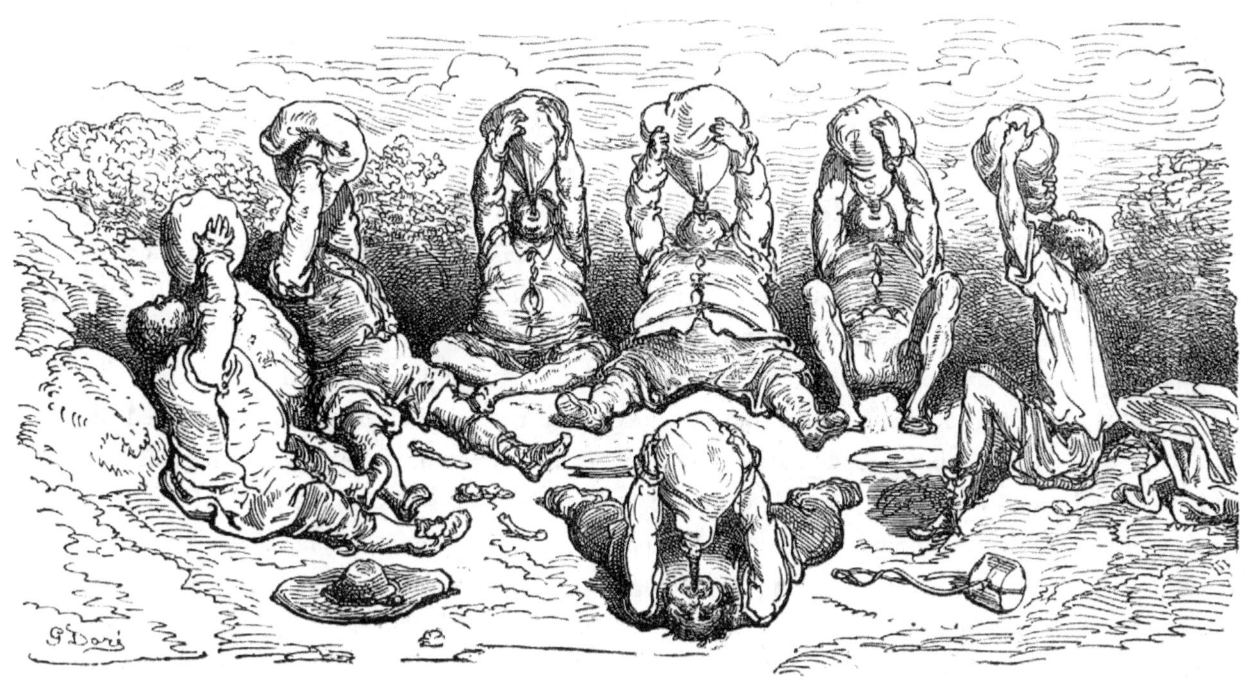

CHAPTER LIV.

WHICH TREATS OF MATTERS THAT RELATE TO THIS HISTORY, AND NO OTHER.

THE duke and duchess resolved that Don Quixote's challenge against their vassal should not be ineffectual; and the young man being fled into Flanders, to avoid having Donna Rodriguez to his mother-in-law, they made choice of a Gascoin lackey, named Tosilos to supply his place, and gave him instructions how to act his part. Two days after, the duke acquainted Don Quixote that within four days his antagonist would meet him in the lists, armed at all points like a knight, to maintain that the damsel lied through the throat, and through the beard, to say that he had ever promised her marriage. Don Quixote was mightily pleased with this news, promising himself to do wonders on this occasion, and esteeming it an extraordinary happiness to have such an opportunity to show, before such noble spectators, how extensive were his valour and his strength. Cheered and elevated with these hopes, he waited for the end of these four days, which his eager impatience made him think so many ages.

Well, now letting them pass, as we do other matters, let us a while attend Sancho, who, divided betwixt joy and sorrow, was now on his Dapple, making the best of his way to his master, whose company he valued more than the government of all the islands in the world. He had not gone far from his island, or city, or town (or whatever you will please to call it, for he never troubled himself to examine what it was), before he met upon the road six

U U

pilgrims, with their walking staves, foreigners as they proved, and such as used to beg alms, singing. As they drew near him they placed themselves in a row, and fell a-singing all together, in their language, something that Sancho could not understand, unless it was one word, which plainly signified alms; by which he guessed that charity was the burden and intent of their song. Being exceedingly charitable, as Cid Hamet reports him, he opened his wallet, and, having taken out the half loaf and half cheese, gave them these, making signs withal that he had nothing else to give them. They took the dole with a good will, but yet not satisfied, they cried, "Guelte, guelte."

"Good people," quoth Sancho, "I do not understand what you would have."

With that one of them pulled out a purse that was in his bosom, and showed it to Sancho, by which he understood that it was money they wanted. But he, putting his thumb to his mouth, and wagging his hand with his four fingers upwards, made a sign that he had not a cross; and so, clapping his heels to Dapple's sides, he began to make way through the pilgrims; but, at the same time, one of them, who had been looking on him very earnestly, laid hold on him, and throwing his arms about his middle, "Bless me!" cried he, in very good Spanish, "what do I see? Is it possible? Do I hold in my arms my dear friend, my good neighbour Sancho Panza? Yes, sure it must be he, for I am neither drunk nor dreaming."

Sancho, wondering to hear himself called by his name, and to see himself so lovingly hugged by the pilgrim, stared upon him without speaking a word; but, though he looked seriously in his face a good while, he could not guess who he was.

The pilgrim observing his amazement, "What!" said he, "friend Sancho, do not you know your old acquaintance, your neighbour Ricote the Morisco, that kept a shop in your town?"

Then Sancho looking wistfully on him again, began to call him to mind; at last, he knew him again perfectly, and clasping him about the neck, without alighting, "Ricote," cried he, "who could possibly ever have known thee, transmogrified in this mumming dress? Pr'ythee, who has franchified thee at this rate? And how durst thou offer to come again into Spain? Shouldst thou come to be known, I would not be in thy coat for all the world."

"If thou dost not betray me," said the pilgrim, "I am safe enough, Sancho; for nobody can know me in this disguise. But let us get out of the road, and make to yonder elm-grove; my comrades and I have agreed to take a little refreshment there, and thou shalt dine with us. They are honest souls, I will assure thee. There I shall have an opportunity to tell thee how I have passed my time, since I was forced to leave the town in obedience to the king's edict, which, as thou knowest, so severely threatens those of our unfortunate nation."

Sancho consented, and Ricote having spoken to the rest of the pilgrims, they went all together to the grove, at a good distance from the road. There they laid by their staves, and, taking off their pilgrims' weeds, remained in jackets; all of them young handsome fellows, except Ricote, who was somewhat stricken in years. Every one carried his wallet, which seemed well furnished, at least with savoury and high-seasoned bits, the provocative to the turning down good liquor. They sat down on the ground, and making the green grass their table-cloth, presently there was a comfortable appearance of bread, salt, knives, nuts, cheese, and some bacon bones, on which there were still some good pickings left, or which at least might be sucked. They also had a kind of black meat called *caviar*, made of the roes of fish, a certain charm to keep thirst awake. They also had a good store of olives, though none of the moistest; but the chief glory of the feast was six leathern bottles of wine, every pilgrim exhibiting one for his share; even honest Ricote himself was now transformed from a Morisco to a German, and clubbed his bottle, his quota making as good a figure as the rest. They began to eat like men that liked mighty well their savoury fare; and as it was very relishing, they went leisurely to work, to continue the longer, taking but a little of every one at a time on the point of a knife. Then all at once they lifted up their arms, and applying their own mouths to the mouths of the bottles, and turning up their bottoms in the air, with their eyes fixed on heaven, like men in an ecstacy, they remained in that posture a good while, transfusing the blood and spirit of the vessels into their stomachs, and shaking their heads, as in rapture, to express the pleasure they received. Sancho admired all this extremely; he could not find the least fault with it; quite contrary, he was for making good the old proverb, "When thou art at Rome, do as they do at Rome;" so he desired Ricote to lend him his bottle, and taking his aim as well as the rest, and with no less satisfaction, showed them he wanted neither method nor breath. Four times they caressed the bottles in that manner, but there was no doing it the fifth, for they were quite exhausted, and the life and soul of them departed, which turned their mirth into sorrow. But while the wine lasted all was well. Now and then one or other of the pilgrims would take Sancho by the right hand, Spaniard and German all one now, and cried, "*Bon campagno.*"

"Well said, i' faith," answered Sancho; "*bon campagno, perdie.*" And then he would burst out a-laughing for half an hour together, without the least concern for all his late misfortunes or the loss of his government; for anxieties use to have but little power over the time that men spend in eating or drinking. In short, as their bellies were full, their bones desired to be at rest, and so five of them dropped asleep; only Sancho and Ricote, who had indeed eaten more, but drank less, remained awake, and removed under the covert of a beech at a small distance, where, while the others slept, Ricote, in good Spanish, spoke to Sancho to this purpose:—

"Thou well knowest, friend Sancho Panza, how the late edict, that enjoined all those of our nation to depart the kingdom, alarmed us all; at least, me it did; insomuch, that the time limited for our going was not yet expired, but I thought the law was ready to be executed upon me and my children. Accordingly, I resolved to provide betimes for their security and mine, as a man does that knows his habitation will be taken away from him, and so secures another before he is obliged to remove. So I left our town by myself, and went to seek some place beforehand, where I might convey my family, without exposing myself to the inconvenience of a hurry, like the rest that went; for the wisest among us were justly apprehensive that the proclamations issued out for the banishment of our Moorish race were not only threats, as some flattered themselves, but would certainly take effect at the expiration of the limited time. I was the rather inclined to believe this, being conscious that our people had very dangerous designs; so that I could not but think that the king was inspired from Heaven to take so brave a resolution, and expel those snakes out of the bosom of the kingdom: not that we were all guilty, for there were some sound and real Christians among us; but their number was so small, that they could not be opposed to those that were otherwise, and it was not safe to keep enemies within doors. In short, it was necessary we should be banished; but though some might think it a mild and pleasant fate, to us it seems the most dreadful thing that could befall us. Wherever we are, we bemoan with tears our banishment from Spain; for, after all, there we were born, and it is our native country. We find nowhere the entertainment our misfortune requires; and even in Barbary, and all other parts of Africa, where we expected to have met with the best reception and relief, we find the greatest inhumanity, and the worst usage. We did not know our happiness till we had lost it; and the desire which most of us have to return to Spain is such, that the greatest part of those that speak the tongue as I do, who are many, come back hither, and leave their wives and children there in a forlorn condition, so strong is their love for their native place; and now I know by experience the truth of the saying, 'Sweet is the love of one's own country. For my part, having left our town, I went into France, and though I was very well received there, yet I had a mind to see other countries; and so passing through it, I travelled into Italy, and from thence into Germany, where methought one might live with more freedom, the inhabitants being a good-humoured, sociable people, that love to live easy with one another, and everybody follows his own way; for there is liberty of conscience allowed in the greatest part of the country. There, after I had taken a dwelling in a village near Augsburg, I struck into the company of these pilgrims, and got to be one of their number, finding they were some of those who make it their custom to go to Spain, many of them every year, to visit the places of devotion, which they look upon as their Indies, their best market, and surest means to get money. They travel almost the whole kingdom over; nor is there a village where they are not sure to get meat and drink, and sixpence at least in money. And they manage matters so well, that at the end of their pilgrimage they commonly go off with about a hundred crowns clear gain, which they change into gold, and hide either in the hollow of their staves or patches of their clothes, and either thus or some other private way, convey it usually into their own country, in spite of all searches at their going out of the kingdom. Now, Sancho, my design in returning hither is to fetch the treasure that I left buried when I went away, which I may do with the less inconveniency, by reason it lies in a place quite out of the town. That done, I intend to write or go over myself from Valencia to my wife and daughter, who I know are in Algiers, and find one way or other to get them over to some port in France, and from thence bring them over into Germany, where we will stay, and see how Providence will dispose of us. For I am sure my wife Francisca and my daughter are good Catholic Christians; and though I cannot say I am as much a believer as they are, yet I have more of the Christian than of the Mahometan, and make it my constant prayer to the Almighty to open the eyes of my understanding, and let me know how to serve him. What I wonder at is, that my wife and daughter should rather choose to go for Barbary than for France, where they might have lived like Christians."

"Look you, Ricote," answered Sancho, "mayhaps that was none of their fault; for to my knowledge, John Tiopieyo, thy wife's brother, took them along with him, and he, belike, being a rank Moor, would go where he thought best. And I must tell thee further, friend, that I doubt thou wilt lose thy labour in going to look after thy hidden treasure; for the report was hot among us that thy brother-in-law and thy wife had a great many pearls and a deal of gold taken away from them, which should have been interred."

"That may be," replied Ricote; "but I am sure, friend of mine, they have not met with my hoard, for I never would tell them where I had hidden it, for fear of the worst; and, therefore, if thou wilt go along with me, and help me to carry off this money, I will give thee two hundred crowns, to make thee easier in the world. Thou knowest I can tell it is but low with thee."

"I would do it," answered Sancho, "but I am not at all covetous. Were I in the least given to it, this morning I quitted an employment, which, had I but kept, I might have got enough to have made the walls of my house of beaten gold, and, before six months had been at an end, I might have eaten my victuals in plate. So that, as well for this reason as because I fancy it would be a piece of treason to the king, in abetting his enemies, I would not go with thee, though thou wouldst lay me down twice as much."

"And pr'ythee," said Ricote, "what sort of employment is it thou hast left?"

"Why," quoth Sancho, "I have left the government of an island, and such an island as, i' faith, you will scarce meet with the like in haste within a mile of an oak."

"And where is this island?" said Ricote.

"Where!" quoth Sancho, "why, some two leagues off, and it is called the island of Barataria."

"Pr'ythee, do not talk so," replied Ricote; "islands lie a great way off in the sea, there are none in the mainland."

"Why not?" quoth Sancho. "I tell thee, friend Ricote, I came from thence but this morning; and yesterday I was there governing it at my will and pleasure, like any dragon; yet, for all that, I even left it; for this same place of a governor seemed to me but a ticklish and perilous kind of an office."

"And what didst thou get by thy government?" asked Ricote.

"Why," answered Sancho, "I have got so much knowledge as to understand that I am not fit to govern anything, unless it be a herd of cattle; and that the wealth that is got in these kinds of governments costs a man a deal of labour and toil, watching and hunger; for in your islands governors must eat next to nothing, especially if they have physicians to look after their health."

"I can make neither head nor tail of all this," said Ricote; "it seems to me all madness, for who would be such a simpleton as to give thee islands to govern? Was the world quite bare of abler men, that they could pick out nobody else for a governor? Pr'ythee, say no more, man, but come to thy senses, and consider whether thou wilt go along with me, and help me to carry off my hidden wealth, my treasure, for I may well give it that name, considering how much there is of it; and I will make a man of thee, as I have told thee."

"Hark you me, Ricote," answered Sancho; "I have already told thee my mind. Let it suffice that I will not betray thee, and so, in Heaven's name, go thy way, and let me go mine; for full well I wot that 'what is honestly got may be lost, but what is ill got will perish," and the owner too."

"Well, Sancho," said Ricote, "I will press thee no further. Only, pr'ythee, tell me, wert thou in the town when my wife and daughter went away with my brother-in-law?"

"Ay, marry was I," quoth Sancho, "by the same token thy daughter looked so woundy handsome, that there was great crowding to see her, and everybody said she was the finest creature on God's earth. She wept bitterly all the way, poor thing! and embraced all her female friends and acquaintance, and begged of all those that flocked about her to pray for her, and that in so earnest and piteous a manner, that she even made me shed tears, though I am none of the greatest blubberers. And now, honest neighbour, I must bid thee good bye, for I have a mind to be with my master, Don Quixote, this evening."

"Then Heaven be with thee, Sancho," said Ricote; "I find my comrades have finished their naps, and it is time we should make the best of our way."

With that, after a kind embrace, Sancho mounted his Dapple, Ricote took his pilgrim's staff, and so they parted.

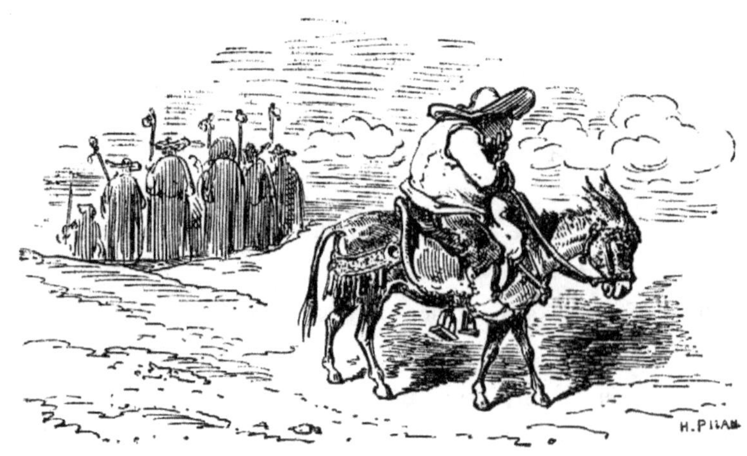

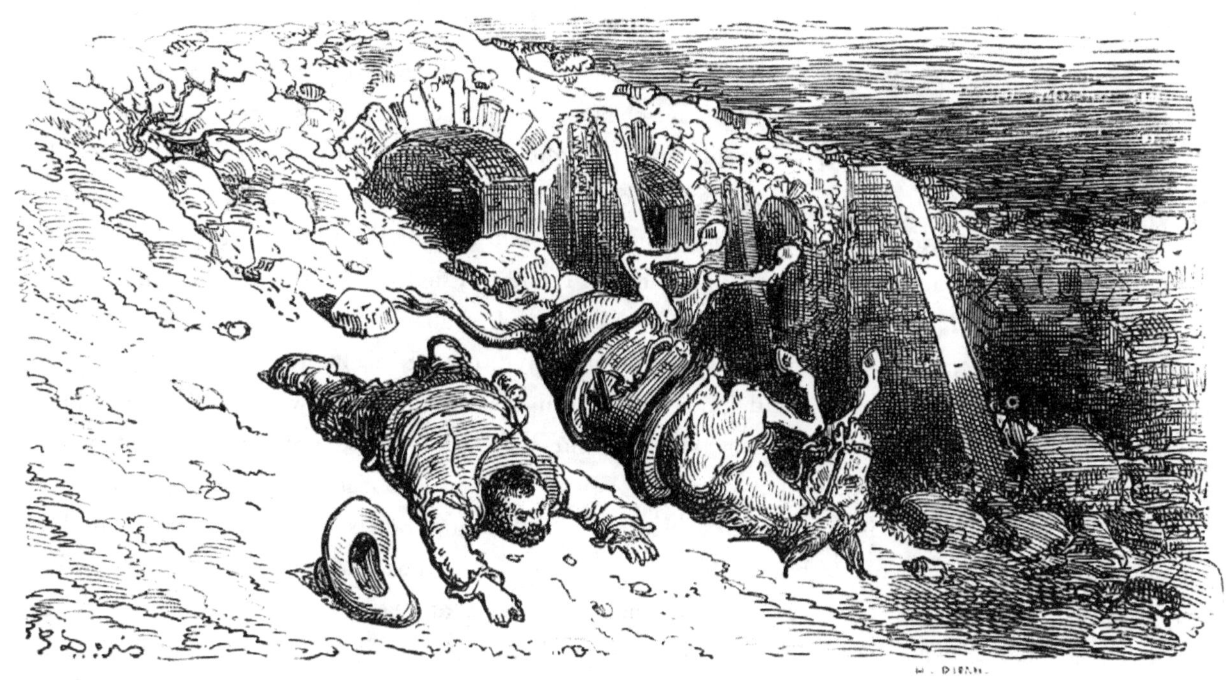

CHAPTER LV.

WHAT HAPPENED TO SANCHO BY THE WAY, WITH OTHER MATTERS WHICH YOU WILL HAVE NO MORE TO DO THAN TO SEE.

SANCHO stayed so long with Ricote, that the night overtook him within half a league of the duke's castle. It grew dark. However, as it was summer-time, he was not much uneasy, and chose to go out of the road, with a design to stay there till the morning. But, as ill-luck would have it, while he was seeking some place where he might rest himself, he and Dapple tumbled of a sudden into a very deep hole, which was among the ruins of some old buildings. As he was falling, he prayed with all his heart, fancying himself all the while sinking down into some fearful pit; but he was in no such danger, for by the time he had descended somewhat lower than eighteen feet, Dapple made a full stop at the bottom, and his rider found himself still on his back, without the least hurt in the world. Presently Sancho began to consider the condition of his bones, held his breath, and felt all about him, and finding himself sound, wind and limb, and in a whole skin, he thought he could never give Heaven sufficient thanks for his wondrous preservation; for at first he gave himself over for lost, and broken into a thousand pieces. He groped with both hands about the walls of the pit, to try if it were possible to get out without help; but he found them all so plain and so steep, that there was not the least hold or footing to get up. This grieved him to the soul; and, to increase his sorrow, Dapple began to raise his voice in a very doleful manner, which pierced his master's very heart: nor did the poor beast make such moan without reason, for, to say the truth, he was but in a woful condition. "Woe's me!" cried Sancho; "what sudden and unthought-of mischances every foot befall us poor wretches that live in this miserable world! Who would have thought that he who but yesterday saw himself seated on the throne of an island-governor, and had servants and vassals at his beck, should to-day find himself buried in a pit, without the least soul to help him or come to his relief? Here we are likely to perish with deadly hunger, I and my ass, if we do not die before; he of his bruises, and I of grief and anguish. At least, I shall not be so lucky as was my master, Don Quixote, when he went down into the cave of the enchanter Montesinos. He found better fare there than he could have at his own house; the cloth was laid, and his bed made, and he saw nothing but pleasant visions; but I am like to see nothing here but toads and snakes. Unhappy creature that I am! What have my foolish designs and whimsies brought me to? If ever it is Heaven's blessed will that my bones be found, they will be taken out of this dismal place, bare, white, and smooth, and those of my poor Dapple with them; by which, perhaps, it will be known whose they are, at least by those who shall have taken notice that Sancho Panza never stirred from his ass, nor his ass from Sancho Panza. Unhappy creatures that we are, I say again! Had we died at home among our friends, though we had missed of relief, we should not have wanted pity, and some to close our eyes at the last gasp. Oh! my dear companion and friend," said he to his ass, "how ill have I requited thy faithful services! Forgive me, and pray to fortune the best thou canst, to deliver us out of this plunge, and I here promise thee to set a crown of laurel on thy head, that thou mayest be taken for no less than a poet-laureate, and thy allowance of provender shall be doubled." Thus Sancho bewailed his misfortune, and his ass hearkened to what he said, but answered not a word, so great was the grief and anguish which the poor creature endured at the same time.

At length, after a whole night's lamenting and complaining at a miserable rate, the day came on; and its light having confirmed Sancho in his doubts of the impossibility of getting out of that place without help, he set up his throat again, and made a vigorous outcry, to try whether anybody might not hear him. But, alas! all his calling was in vain, for all around there was nobody within hearing; and then he gave himself over for dead and buried. He cast his eyes on Dapple, and seeing him extended on the ground, and sadly down in the mouth, he went to him, and tried to get him on his legs, which, with much ado, by means of his assistance, the poor beast did at last, being hardly able to stand. Then he took a luncheon of bread out of his wallet, that had run the same fortune with them, and giving it to the ass, who took it not at all amiss, and made no bones of it, "Here," said Sancho, as if the beast had understood him, "'a fat sorrow is better than a lean.'" At length he perceived on one side of the pit a great hole, wide enough for a man to creep through stooping. He drew to it, and having crawled through on all fours, found that it led into a vault that enlarged itself the further it extended, which he could easily perceive, the sun shining in towards the top of

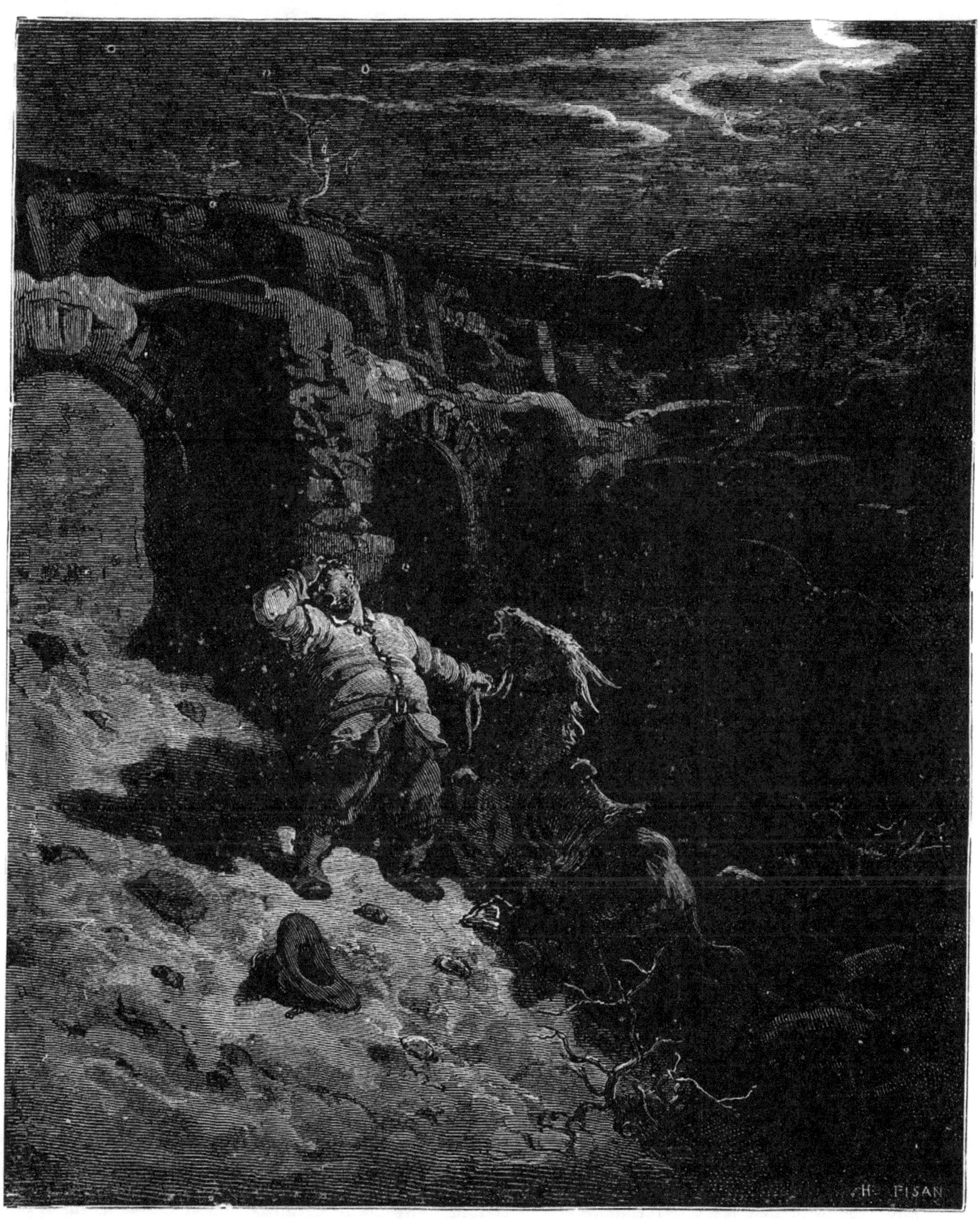

"'Oh! my dear companion and friend,' said he to his ass, 'how ill have I requited thy faithful services!'"

the concavity. Having made this discovery, he went back to his ass, and, like one that knew what belonged to digging, with a stone he began to remove the earth that was about the hole, and laboured so effectually that he soon made a passage for his companion. Then, taking him by the halter, he led him along fair and softly through the cave, to try if he could not find a way to get out on the other side. Sometimes he went in the dark, and sometimes without light, but never without fear. "Heaven defend me!" said he to himself; "what a heart of a chicken have I! This now, which to me is a sad disaster, to my master, Don Quixote, would be a rare adventure. He would look upon these caves and dungeons as lovely gardens and glorious palaces, and hope to be led out of these dark, narrow cells into some fine meadow; while I, luckless, helpless, heartless wretch that I am, every step I take, expect to sink into some deeper pit than this, and go down I do not know whither. Welcome, ill luck, when it comes alone." Thus he went on, lamenting and despairing, and thought he had gone somewhat more than half a league, when, at last, he perceived a kind of confused light, like that of day, break in at some open place, but which, to poor Sancho, seemed a prospect of a passage into another world.

But here Cid Hamet Benengeli leaves him a while, and returns to Don Quixote, who entertained and pleased himself with the hopes of a speedy combat between him and the defamer of Donna Rodriguez's daughter, whose wrongs he designed to see redressed on the appointed day.

It happened one morning, as he was riding out to prepare and exercise against the time of battle, as he was practising with Rozinante. the horse, in the middle of his manage, pitched his feet near the brink of a deep cave; insomuch, that if Don Quixote had not used the best of his skill, he must infallibly have tumbled into it. Having escaped that danger, he was tempted to look into the cave without alighting, and, wheeling about, rode up to it. Now, while he was satisfying his curiosity, and seriously musing, he thought he heard a noise within, and thereupon listening, he could distinguish these words, which, in a doleful tone, arose out of the cavern: "Ho! above there! is there no good Christian that hears me?—no charitable knight or gentleman, that will take pity of a sinner buried alive—a poor governor without a government?"

Don Quixote fancied he heard Sancho's voice, which did not a little surprise him; and for his better satisfaction, raising his voice as much as he could, "Who is that below?" cried he; "who is it that complains?"

"Who should it be, to his sorrow," cried Sancho, "but the most wretched Sancho Panza, governor, for his sins and for his unlucky errantry, of the island of Barataria, formerly squire to the famous knight, Don Quixote de la Mancha?"

These words redoubled Don Quixote's admiration, and increased his amazement, for he presently imagined that Sancho was dead, and that his soul was there doing penance. Possessed with that fancy, "I conjure thee," said he, "by all that can conjure thee, as I am a Catholic Christian, to tell me who thou art; and, if thou art a soul in pain, let me know what thou wouldst have me to do for thee; for since my profession is to assist and succour all that are afflicted in this world, it shall also be so to relieve and help those who stand in need of it in the other, and who cannot help themselves."

"Surely, sir," answered he from below, "you that speak to me should be my master, Don Quixote; by the tone of your voice it can be no man else."

"My name is Don Quixote," replied the knight, "and I think it my duty to assist not only the living, but the dead, in their necessities. Tell me, then, who thou art, for thou fillest me with astonishment."

"Why, then," replied the voice, "by whatever you will have me swear by, I make oath that I am Sancho Panza, your squire, and that I never was dead yet in my life. But only having left my government, for reasons and causes which I have not leisure yet to tell you, last night unluckily I fell into this cave, where I am still, and Dapple with me, that will not let me tell a lie; for, as a farther proof of what I say, he is here."

Now, what is strange, immediately, as if the ass had understood what his master said, to back his evidence, he fell a-braying so obstreperously, that he made the whole cave ring again.

"A worthy witness," cried Don Quixote: "I know his bray, as if I were the parent of him; and I know thy voice too, my Sancho. I find thou art my real squire; stay, therefore, till I go to the castle, which is hard by, and fetch more company to help thee out of the pit into which thy sins, doubtless, have thrown thee."

"Make haste, I beseech you, sir," quoth Sancho, "and, for Heaven's sake, come again as fast as you can, for I can no longer endure to be here buried alive, and I am even dying with fear."

Don Quixote went with all speed to the castle, and gave the duke and duchess an account of Sancho's accident, whilst they did not a little wonder at it, though they conceived he might easily enough fall in at the mouth of the cave, which had been there time out of mind. But they were mightily surprised to hear he had abdicated his government before they had an account of his coming away.

In short, they sent ropes and other conveniences by their servants to draw him out, and at last, with much trouble and labour, both he and his Dapple were restored from that gloomy pit to the full enjoyment of the light of the sun. At the same time, a certain scholar standing by, and seeing him hoisted up, "Just so," said he, "should all bad governors come out of their governments; just as this wretch is dragged out of this profound abyss, pale, half-starved, famished, and, as I fancy, without a cross in his pocket."

"Hark you, good Slander," replied Sancho; "it is now eight or ten days since I began to govern the island that was given me, and in all that time I never had my bellyful but once. Physicians have persecuted me, enemies have trampled over me, and bruised my bones, and

I have had neither leisure to take bribes nor to receive my just dues. Now, all this considered, in my opinion I did not deserve to come out in this fashion. But 'man appoints, and God disappoints.' Heaven knows best what is best for us all. We must take time as it comes, and our lot as it falls. Let no man say, 'I will drink no more of this water.' 'Many count their chickens before they are hatched; and where they expect bacon, meet with broken bones.' Heaven knows my mind, and I say no more, though I might."

"Never trouble thyself, Sancho," said Don Quixote, "nor mind what some will say, for then thou wilt never have done. So thy conscience be clear, let the world talk at random, as it uses to do. One may as soon tie up the winds as the tongues of slanderers. If a governor returns rich from his government, they say he has fleeced and robbed the people; if poor, then they call him an idle fool, and ill husband."

"Nothing so sure, then," quoth Sancho, "but this bout they will call me a shallow fool; but for a fleecer or a robber, I scorn their words—I defy all the world."

Thus discoursing as they went, with a rabble of boys and idle people about them, they at last got to the castle, where the duke and duchess waited in the gallery for the knight and squire. As for Sancho, he would not go up to see the duke till he had seen his ass in the stable, and provided for him, for he said the poor beast had but sorry entertainment in his last night's lodging. This done, away he went to wait on his lord and lady; and, throwing himself on his knees, "My lord and lady," said he, "I went to govern your island of Barataria, such being your will and pleasure, though it was your goodness more than my desert. Naked I entered into it, and naked I came away. I neither won nor lost. Whether I governed well or ill, there are those not far off can tell; and let them tell, if they please, that can tell better than I. I have resolved doubtful cases, determined law-suits, and all the while ready to die for hunger. Such was the pleasure of Doctor Pedro Rezio of Tirteafuera, that physician in ordinary to island governors. Enemies set upon us in the night, and after they had put us in great danger, the people of the island say they were delivered, and had the victory by the strength of my arm; and may Heaven prosper them as they speak truth, say I. In short, in that time I experienced all the cares and burdens this trade of governing brings along with it, and I found them too heavy for my shoulders. I was never cut out for a ruler, and I am too clumsy to meddle with edge tools; and so, before the government left me, I even resolved to leave the government; and, accordingly, yesterday I quitted the island as I found it, with the same streets, the same houses, and the same roofs to them, as when I came to it. I have asked for nothing by way of loan, and have made no hoard against a rainy day. I designed, indeed, to have issued out several wholesome orders, but did not, for fear they should not be kept; in which case it signifies no more to make them than if one made them not So, as I said before, I came away from the island without any company but my Dapple. I fell into a cave, and went a good way through it, till this morning, by the light of the sun, I spied my way out, yet not so easy; but had not Heaven sent my master, Don Quixote, to help me, there I might have stayed till doomsday. And now, my lord duke, and my lady duchess, here is your governor, Sancho Panza, again, who, by a ten days' government, has only picked up so much experience as to know he would not give a straw to be a governor, not only of an island, but of the 'versal world. This being allowed, kissing your honours' hands, and doing like the boys, when they play, who cry, 'Leap you, and then let me leap,' so I leap from the government to my old master's service again. For, after all, though with him I often eat my bread with bodily fear, yet still I fill my belly; and, for my part, so I have but that well stuffed, no matter whether it be with carrots or with partridges."

Thus Sancho concluded his long speech, and Don Quixote, who all the while dreaded he would have said a thousand impertinences, thanked Heaven in his heart, finding him end with so few. The duke embraced Sancho, and told him he was very sorry he had quitted his government so soon; but that he would give him some other employment that should be less troublesome, and more profitable. The duchess was no less kind, giving orders he should want for nothing, for he seemed sadly bruised and out of order.

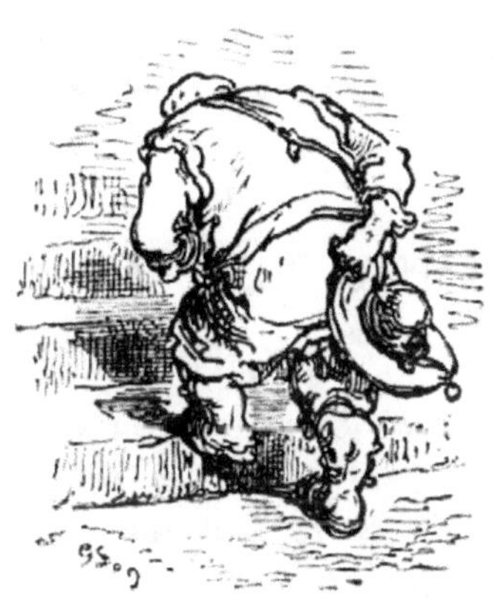

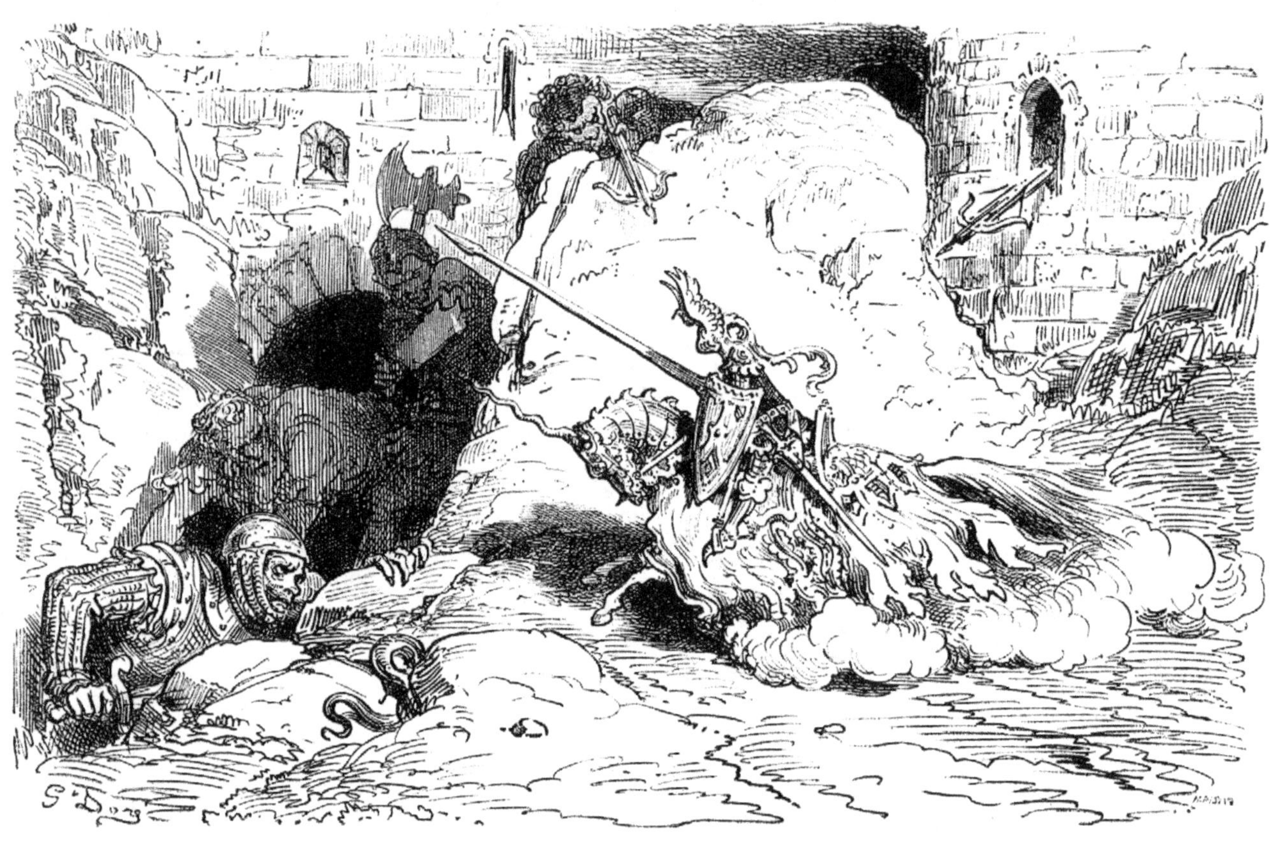

CHAPTER LVI.

OF THE EXTRAORDINARY AND UNACCOUNTABLE COMBAT BETWEEN DON QUIXOTE DE LA MANCHA AND THE LACKEY TOSILOS, IN VINDICATION OF THE MATRON DONNA RODRIGUEZ'S DAUGHTER.

THE duke and duchess were not sorry that the interlude of Sancho's government had been played, especially when the steward, who came that very day, gave them a full and distinct account of everything the governor had done and said during his administration, using his very expressions, and repeating almost every word he had spoken, concluding with a description of the storming of the island, and Sancho's fear and abdication, which proved no unacceptable entertainment.

And now the history relates that the day appointed for the combat was come, nor had the duke forgotten to give his lackey, Tosilos, all requisite instructions how to vanquish Don Quixote, and yet neither kill nor wound him; to which purpose he gave orders that the spears, or steel heads of their lances, should be taken off, making Don Quixote sensible that Christianity, for which he had so great a veneration, did not admit that such conflicts should so much endanger the lives of the combatants, and that it was enough that he granted him free lists in his territories, though it was against the decree of the holy council, which forbids such challenges; for which reason he desired them not to push the thing to the utmost rigour. Don Quixote replied that his grace had the disposal of all things, and it was his duty to obey.

And now, the dreadful day being come, the duke caused a spacious scaffold to be erected for the judges of the field of battle, and for the matron and her daughter, the plaintiffs.

An infinite number of people flocked from all the neighbouring towns and villages to behold the wonderful new kind of combat. The first that made his entrance at the barriers was the marshal of the field, who came to survey the ground, and rode all over it, that there might be no foul play, nor private holes, nor contrivance to make one stumble or fall. After that entered the matron and her daughter, who seated themselves in their places, all in deep mourning, their veils close to their eyes, and over their breasts, with no small demonstration of sorrow. Presently, at one end of the listed field, appeared the peerless champion, Don Quixote de la Mancha; a while after, at the other, entered the grand lackey, Tosilos, attended with a great number of trumpets, and mounted on a mighty steed that shook the very earth. The vizard of his helmet was down, and he was armed *cap-a-pie* in shining armour of proof. His courser was a flea-bitten horse, that seemed of Friesland breed, and had a quantity of wool about each of his fetlocks. The valorous combatant came on, well tutored by the duke, his master, how to behave himself towards the valorous Don Quixote de la Mancha, being warned to spare his life by all means; and therefore, to avoid a shock in his first career that might otherwise prove fatal, should he encounter him directly, Tosilos fetched a compass about the barrier, and at last made a stop right against the two women, casting a leering eye upon her that had demanded him in marriage. Then the marshal of the field called to Don Quixote, and, in presence of Tosilos, asked the mother and the daughter whether they consented that Don Quixote de la Mancha should vindicate their right, and whether they would stand or fall by the fortune of their champion. They said they did, and allowed of whatever he should do in their behalf as good and valid. The duke and duchess by this time were seated in a gallery that was over the barriers, which were surrounded by a vast throng of spectators, all waiting to see the vigorous and never-before-seen conflict. The conditions of the combat were these—That if Don Quixote were the conqueror, his opponent should marry Donna Rodriguez's daughter; but if the knight were overcome, then the victor should be discharged from his promise, and not bound to give her any other satisfaction. Then the marshal of the field placed each of them on the spot whence he should start, dividing equally between them the advantage of the ground, that neither of them might have the sun in his eyes. And now the drums beat, and the clangour of the trumpets resounded through the air; the earth shook under them, and the hearts of the numerous spectators were in suspense—some fearing, others expecting, the good or bad issue of the battle. Don Quixote, recommending himself with all his soul to Heaven, and his Lady Dulcinea del Toboso, stood expecting when the precise signal for the onset should be given. But our lackey's mind was otherwise employed, and all his thoughts were upon what I am going to tell you.

It seems, as he stood looking on his female enemy, she appeared to him the most beautiful woman he had ever seen in his whole life; which being perceived by the little blind archer, to whom the world gives the name of Love, he took his advantage, and, fond of improving his triumphs, though it were but over the soul of a lackey, he came up to him softly, and, without being perceived by any one, he shot an arrow two yards long into the poor footman's side, so smartly, that his heart was pierced through and through—a thing which the mischievous boy could easily do; for love is invisible, and has free ingress or egress where he pleases, at a most unaccountable rate. You must know then that when the signal for the onset was given our lacquey was in an ecstasy, transported with the thoughts of the beauty of his lovely enemy, insomuch that he took no manner of notice of the trumpet's sound; quite contrary to Don Quixote, who no sooner heard it than, clapping spurs to his horse, he began to make towards the enemy with Rozinante's best speed. At the same time, his good squire, Sancho Panza, seeing him start, "Heaven be thy guide," cried he aloud, "thou cream and flower of chivalry errant! Heaven give thee the victory, since thou hast right on thy side." Tosilos saw Don Quixote come towards him; yet, instead of taking his career to encounter him, without leaving the place, he called as loud as he could to the marshal of the field, who thereupon rode up to him to see what he would have. "Sir," said Tosilos, "is not this duel to be fought that I may marry yonder young lady, or let it alone?"

"Yes," answered the marshal.

"Why, then," said the lacquey, "I feel a burden upon my conscience, and am sensible I should have a great deal to answer for should I proceed any further in this combat; and therefore I yield myself vanquished, and desire I may marry the lady this moment."

The marshal of the field was surprised; and, as he was privy to the duke's contrivance of that business, the lacquey's unexpected submission put him to such a nonplus that he knew not what to answer. On the other side, Don Quixote stopped in the middle of his career, seeing his adversary did not put himself in a posture of defence. The duke could not imagine why the business of the field was at a stand; but the marshal having informed him, he was amazed, and in a great passion.

In the meantime, Tosilos, approaching Donna Rodriguez, "Madam," cried he, "I am willing to marry your daughter; there is no need of law-suits or of combats in the matter; I had rather make an end of it peaceably, and without the hazard of body and soul."

"Why, then," said the valorous Don Quixote, hearing this, "since it is so, I am discharged of my promise; let them even marry in God's name, and Heaven bless them, and give them joy."

At the same time, the duke coming down within the lists, and applying himself to Tosilos, "Tell me, knight," said he, "is it true that you yield without fighting, and that, at the instigation of your timorous conscience, you are resolved to marry this damsel?"

"Yes, if it please your grace," answered Tosilos.

"Marry, and I think it the wisest course," quoth Sancho; "for what says the proverb? 'What the mouse would get give the cat, and keep thyself out of trouble.'"

In the meanwhile, Tosilos began to unlace his helmet, and called out that somebody might help him off with it quickly, as being so choked with his armour that he was scarcely able to breathe. With that they took off his helmet with all speed, and then the lacquey's face was plainly discovered. Donna Rodriguez and her daughter, perceiving it presently, "A cheat! a cheat!" cried they; "they have got Tosilos, my lord duke's lacquey, to counterfeit my lawful husband; justice of Heaven and the king! This is a piece of malice and treachery not to be endured."

"Ladies," said Don Quixote, "do not vex yourselves; there is neither malice nor treachery in the case; or, if there be, the duke is not in the fault. No, these evil-minded necromancers that persecute me are the traitors who, envying the glory I should have got by this combat, have transformed the face of my adversary into this, which you see is the duke's lacquey. But take my advice, madam," added he to the daughter, "and, in spite of the baseness of my enemies, marry him; for I dare engage it is the very man you claim as your husband."

The duke, hearing this, angry as he was. could hardly forbear losing all his indignation in laughter. "Truly," said he, "so many extraordinary accidents every day befall the great Don Quixote, that I am inclinable to believe this is not my lacquey, though he appears to be so. But, for our better satisfaction, let us defer the marriage but a fortnight, and, in the meanwhile, keep in close custody this person that has put us into this confusion; perhaps by that time he may resume his former looks: for doubtless the malice of those mischievous magicians against the noble Don Quixote cannot last so long, especially when they find all these tricks and transformations of so little avail."

"Alack-a-day! sir," quoth Sancho, "those plaguy tormentors are not so soon tired as you think; for where my master is concerned they are used to form and deform, and chop and change this into that, and that into the other. It is but a little while ago that they transmogrified the Knight of the Mirrors, whom he had overcome, into a special acquaintance of ours, the bachelor Samson Carrasco, of our village; and as for the Lady Dulcinea del Toboso, our mistress, they have bewitched and altered her into the shape of a mere country blowze; and so I verily think this saucy fellow here is like to die a footman, and will live a footman all the days of his life."

"Well," cried the daughter, "let him be what he will, if he will have me I will have him. I ought to thank him, for I had rather be a lacquey's wife than a gentleman's cast-off mistress; besides, he that deluded me is no gentleman neither."

To be short, the sum of the matter was that Tosilos should be confined, to see what his transformation would come to. Don Quixote was proclaimed victor, by general consent; and the people went away, most of them very much out of humour because the combatants had not cut one another to pieces to make them sport, according to the custom of the young rabble, to be sorry, when, after they have stayed in hopes to see a man hanged, he happens to be pardoned, either by the party he has wronged or the magistrate. The crowd being dispersed, the duke and duchess returned with Don Quixote into the castle ; Tosilos was secured, and kept close. As for Donna Rodriguez and her daughter, they were very well pleased to see, one way or another, that the business would end in marriage; and Tosilos flattered himself with the like expectation.

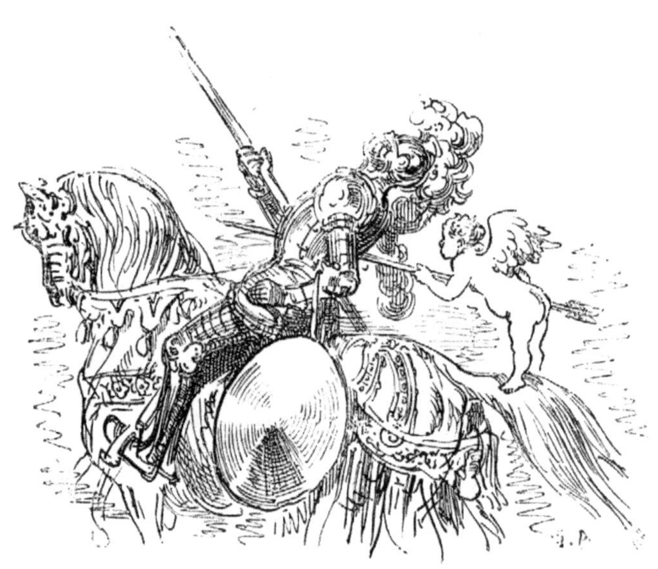

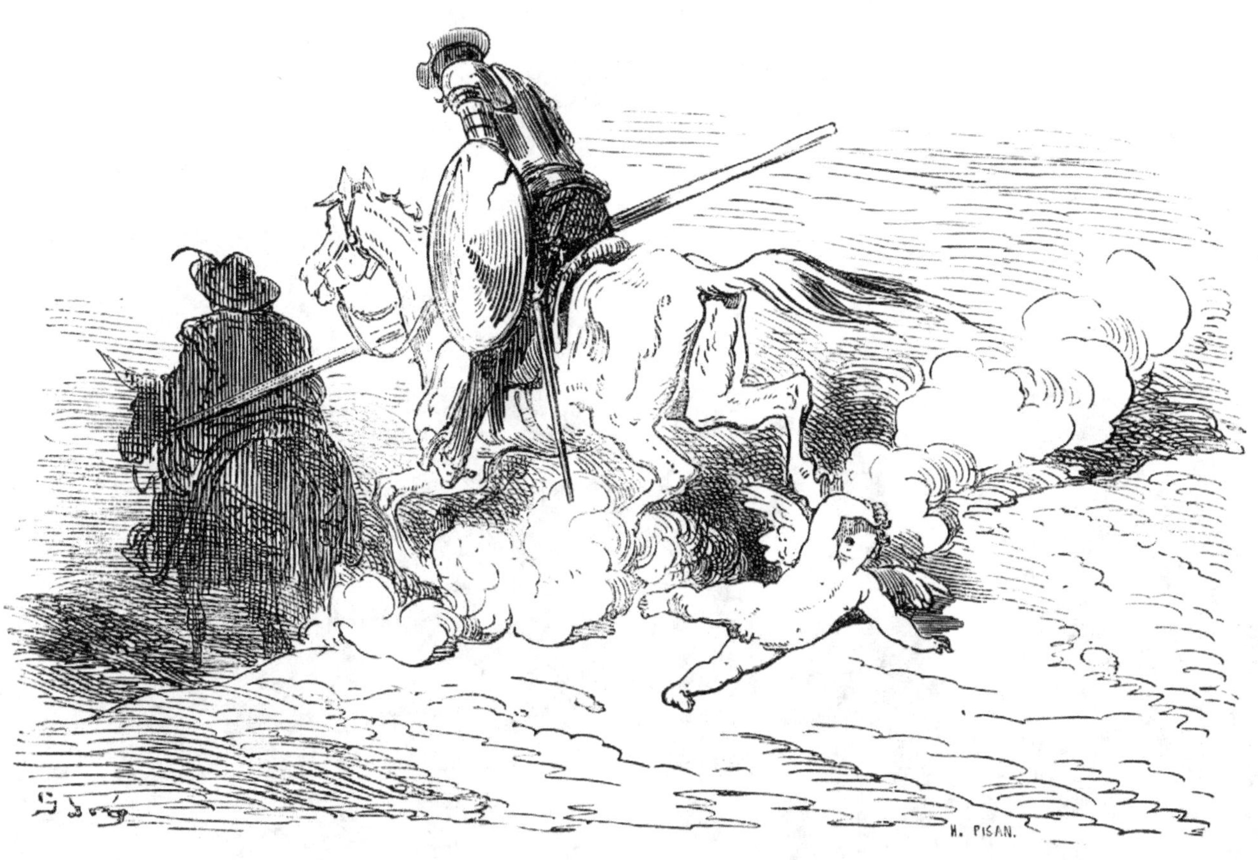

CHAPTER LVII.

HOW DON QUIXOTE TOOK HIS LEAVE OF THE DUKE, AND WHAT PASSED BETWEEN HIM AND THE WITTY WANTON ALTISIDORA, THE DUCHESS'S DAMSEL.

DON QUIXOTE thought it now time to leave the idle life he had led in the castle, believing it a mighty fault thus to shut himself up and indulge his sensual appetite among the tempting varieties of dainties and delights which the lord and lady of the place provided for his entertainment as a knight-errant; and he thought he was to give a strict account to Heaven for a course of life so opposite to his active profession. Accordingly, one day he acquainted the duke and duchess with his sentiments, and begged their leave to depart. They both seemed very unwilling to part with him, but yet at last yielded to his entreaties. The duchess gave Sancho his wife's letters, which he could not hear read without weeping. "Who would have thought," cried he, "that all the mighty hopes with which my wife swelled herself up at the news of my preferment should come to this at last, and how I should be reduced again to trot after my master, Don Quixote de la Mancha, in search of hunger and broken bones! However, I am glad to see my Teresa was like herself in sending the duchess the acorns,

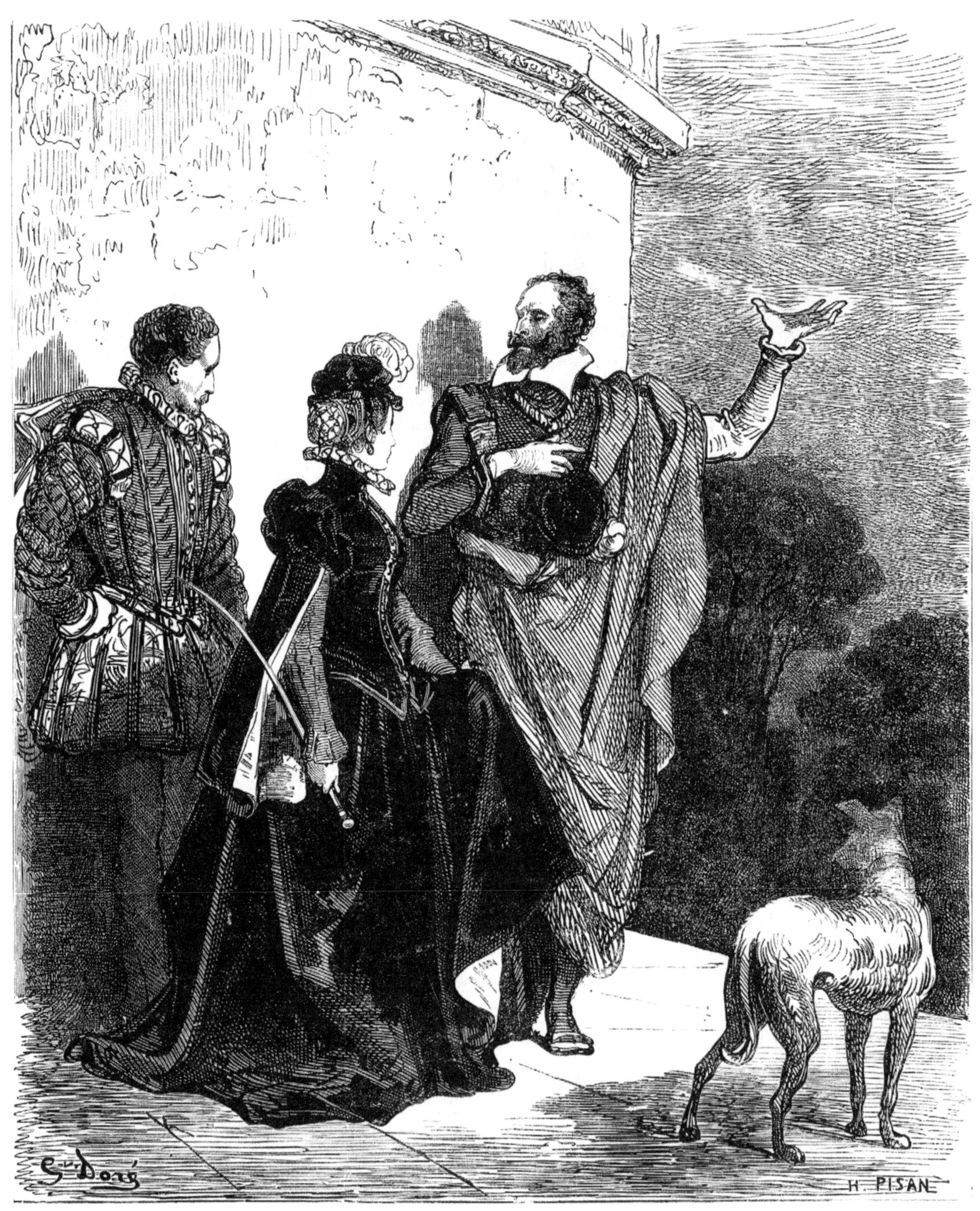

"He acquainted the duke and duchess with his sentiments, and begged their leave to depart."

which, if she had not done, I should have been confounded mad with her. My comfort is, that no man can say the present was a bribe, for I had my government before she sent it; and it is fit those who have a kindness done them should show themselves grateful, though it be with a small matter. In short, naked I came into the government, and naked I went out of it: and so I may say, for my comfort, with a safe conscience, naked I came into the world, and naked I am still: I neither won nor lost; that is no easy matter, as times go, let me tell you." These were Sancho's sentiments at his departure.

Don Quixote, having taken his solemn leave of the duke and duchess over night, left his apartment the next morning, and appeared in his armour in the court-yard, the galleries all round about being filled at the same time with the people of the house; the duke and duchess being also got thither to see him. Sancho was upon his Dapple, with his cloak-bag, his wallet, and his provision, very brisk and cheerful; for the steward that acted the part of Trifaldi had given him a purse, with two hundred crowns in gold, to defray expenses, which was more than Don Quixote knew at that time. And now, when everybody looked to see them set forward, on a sudden, the arch and witty Altisidora started from the rest of the duchess's damsels and attendants that stood by among the rest, and, in a doleful tone, addressed herself to him in the following doggerel rhymes:—

THE MOCK FAREWELL.

I.

Stay, cruel Don,
Do not be gone,
Nor give thy horse the rowels;
For every jag
Thou giv'st thy nag,
Does prick me to the bowels.

Thou dost not shun
Some butter'd bun,
Or wench without a rag on:
Alas! I am
A very lamb,
Yet love like any dragon.

Thou didst deceive,
And now dost leave
A lass, as tight as any
That ever stood
In hill or wood,
Near Venus and Diana.

Since thou, false fiend,
When nymph's thy friend,
Æneas-like dost bob her,
Go, rot and die,
Boil, roast, or fry,
With Barabbas the robber.

II.

Thou tak'st thy flight,
Like ravenous kite,
That holds within his pounces
A tender bit,
A poor tom-tit,
Then whist! away he flounces.

The heart of me,
And night-coifs three,
With garters twain you plunder,
From legs of hue
White, black, and blue,
So marbled o'er, you'd wonder.

Two thousand groans,
And warm ahones,
Are stuff'd within thy pillion,
The least of which,
Like flaming pitch,
Might have burn'd down old Ilion.

Since thou, false fiend,
When nymph's thy friend,
Æneas-like dost bob her,
Go, rot and die,
Boil, roast, or fry,
With Barabbas the robber.

III.

As sour as ink,
Against thy pink,
May be thy Sancho's gizzard:
And he ne'er thwack
His brawny back,
To free her from the wizard.

May all thy flouts,
And sullen doubts,
Be scored upon thy dowdy;
And she ne'er freed,
For thy misdeed,
From rusty phiz, and cloudy.

May fortune's curse
From bad to worse,
Turn all thy best adventures;
Thy joys to dumps,
Thy brags to thumps,
And thy best hopes to banters.

Since thou, false fiend,
When nymph's thy friend,
Æneas-like dost bob her,
Go, rot and die,
Boil, roast, or fry,
With Barabbas the robber.

IV.

May'st thou incog
Sneak like a dog,
And o'er the mountains trudge it;
From Spain to Cales,
From Usk to Wales,
Without a cross in budget.

If thou'rt so brisk
To play at whisk,
In hopes of winning riches;
For want of pelf
Stir even thyself,
And lose thy very breeches.

May thy corns ache,
Then pen-knife take,
And cut thee to the raw-bone:
With tooth-ache mad,
No ease be had,
Though quacks pull out thy jaw-bone

Since thou, false fiend,
When nymph's thy friend,
Æneas-like, dost bob her,
Go, rot and die,
Boil, roast, or fry,
With Barabbas the robber.

Thus Altisidora expressed her resentments, and Don Quixote, who looked on her seriously all the while, would not answer a word; but, turning to Sancho, "Dear Sancho," said he, "by the memory of thy forefathers I conjure thee to tell me one truth: say, hast thou any night-coifs, or garters, that belong to this love-sick damsel?"

"The three night-coifs I have," quoth Sancho; "but as for the garters, I know no more of them than the man in the moon."

The duchess, being wholly a stranger to this part of Altisidora's frolic, was amazed to see her proceed so far in it, though she knew her to be of an arch and merry disposition. But the duke, being pleased with the humour, resolved to carry it on. Thereupon, addressing himself to Don Quixote, "Truly, Sir Knight," said he, "I do not take it kindly, that, after such civil entertainment as you have had here in my castle, you should offer to carry away three night-coifs, if not a pair of garters besides, the proper goods and chattels of this damsel here present. This was not done like a gentleman, and does not make good the character you would maintain in the world; therefore, restore her garters, or I challenge you to a mortal combat, without being afraid that your evil-minded enchanters should alter my face, as they did my footman's."

"Heaven forbid," said Don Quixote, "that I should draw my sword against your most illustrious person, to whom I stand indebted for so many favours. No, my lord; as for the night-coifs, I will cause them to be restored, for Sancho tells me he has them; but as for the garters, it is impossible, for neither he nor I ever had them, and if this damsel of yours will look carefully among her things I dare say she will find them. I never was a pilferer, my lord; and, while Heaven forsakes me not, I never shall be guilty of such baseness. I beg you will be pleased to entertain a better opinion of me, and once more permit me to depart."

"Farewell, noble Don Quixote," said the duchess; "may Providence so direct your course, that we may always be blessed with the good news of your exploits; and so Heaven be with you, for the longer you stay the more you increase the flames in the hearts of the damsels that gaze on you. As for this young, indiscreet creature, I will take her to task so severely she shall not misbehave herself so much as in a word or look for the future."

"One word more, I beseech you, oh, valorous Don Quixote!" cried Altisidora; "I beg your pardon for saying you had stolen my garters, for, on my conscience, I have them on; but my thoughts ran a wool-gathering, and I did like the countryman, who looked for his ass while he was mounted on his back."

Then Don Quixote bowed his head, and, after he had made a low obeisance to the duke, the duchess, and all the company, he turned about with Rozinante; and Sancho following him on Dapple, they left the castle, and took the road for Saragosa.

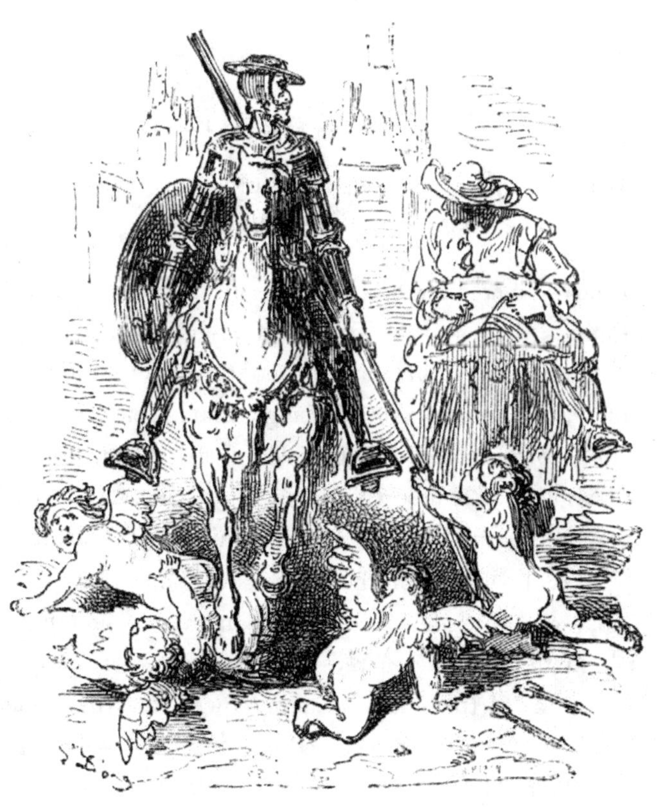

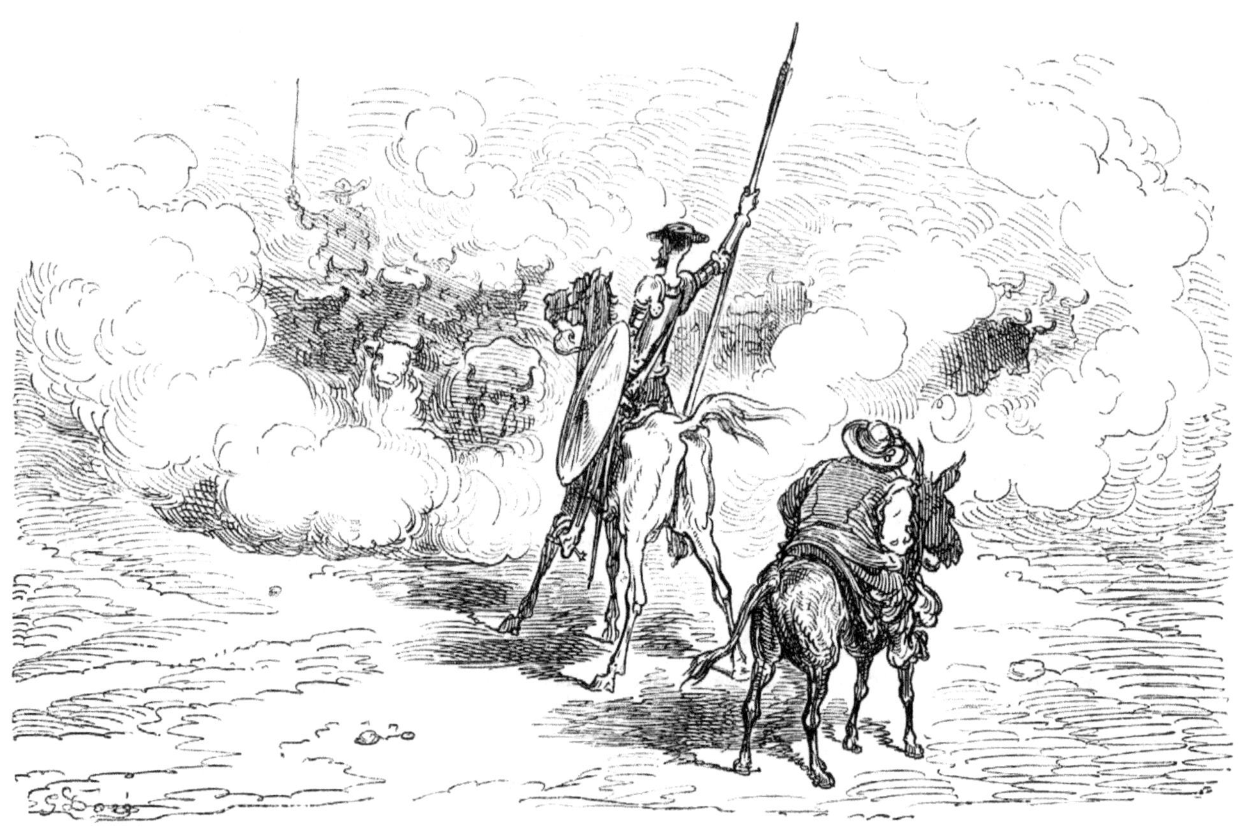

CHAPTER LVIII.

HOW ADVENTURES CROWDED SO THICK AND THREEFOLD ON DON QUIXOTE, THAT THEY TROD UPON ONE ANOTHER'S HEELS.

DON QUIXOTE no sooner breathed the air in the open field, free from Altisidora's amorous importunities, than he fancied himself in his own element; he thought he felt the spirit of knight-errantry reviving in his breast, and turning to Sancho, "Liberty," said he, "friend Sancho, is one of the most valuable blessings that Heaven has bestowed upon mankind. Not all the treasures concealed in the bowels of the earth, nor those in the bosom of the sea, can be compared with it. For liberty a man may—nay, ought, to hazard even his life, as well as for honour, accounting captivity the greatest misery he can endure. I tell thee this, my Sancho, because thou wert a witness of the good cheer and plenty which we met with in the castle; yet, in the midst of those delicious feasts, among those tempting dishes, and those liquors cooled with snow, methought I suffered the extremity of hunger, because I did not enjoy them with that freedom as if they had been my own; for the obligations that lie upon us to make suitable returns for kindnesses received are ties that will not let a generous mind be free. Happy the man whom Heaven has blessed with bread, for which he is obliged to thank kind Heaven alone!"

"For all these fine words," quoth Sancho, "it is not proper for us to be unthankful for two good hundred crowns in gold, which the duke's steward gave me in a little purse, which I have here and cherish in my bosom, as a relic against necessity, and a comforting cordial, next my heart, against all accidents; for we are not like always to meet with castles where we shall be made much of."

The wandering knight and squire had not ridden much more than a league ere they espied about a dozen men, who looked like country fellows sitting at their victuals, with their cloaks under them, on the green grass, in the middle of a meadow. Near them they saw several white cloths or sheets, spread out and laid close to one another, that seemed to cover something. Don Quixote rode up to the people, and, after he had civilly saluted them, asked what they had got under that linen.

"Sir," answered one of the company, "they are some carved images that are to be set up at an altar we are erecting in our town. We cover them lest they should be sullied, and carry them on our shoulders for fear they should be broken."

"If you please," said Don Quixote, "I should be glad to see them; for, considering the care you take of them, they should be pieces of value."

"Ay, marry are they," quoth another, "or else we are fearfully cheated; for there is never an image among them that does not stand us more than fifty ducats; and, that you may know I am no liar, do but stay and you shall see with your own eyes."

With that, getting up on his legs, and leaving his victuals, he went and took off the cover from one of the figures that happened to be St. George on horseback, and under his feet a serpent coiled up, his throat transfixed with a lance, with the fierceness that is commonly represented in the piece; and all, as they use to say, spick and span new, and shining like beaten gold. Don Quixote having seen the image, "This," said he, "was one of the best knights-errant the divine warfare or church-militant ever had; his name was Don St. George, and he was an extraordinary protector of damsels. What is the next?"

The fellow having uncovered it, it proved to be St. Martin on horseback.

"This knight, too," said Don Quixote at the first sight, "was one of the Christian adventurers, and I am apt to think he was more liberal than valiant; and thou mayst perceive it, Sancho, by his dividing his cloak with a poor man: he gave him half, and doubtless it was winter time, or else he would have given it him whole, he was so charitable."

"Not so neither, I fancy," quoth Sancho; "but I guess he stuck to the proverb, 'To give and keep what is fit requires a share of wit.'"

Don Quixote smiled, and desired the men to show him the next image, which appeared to be that of the Patron of Spain on horseback, with his sword bloody, trampling down Moors, and treading over heads.

"Ay, this is a knight indeed!" cried Don Quixote, when he saw it; "one of those that fought in the squadrons of the Saviour of the world. He is called Don St. Jago Mata

Moros, or Don St. James the Moor-killer, and may be reckoned one of the most valorous saints and professors of chivalry that the earth then enjoyed, and heaven now possesses."

Then they uncovered another piece, which showed St. Paul falling from his horse, with all the circumstances usually expressed in the story of his conversion, and represented so to the life, that he looked as if he had been answering the voice that spoke to him from heaven.

"This," said Don Quixote, "was the greatest enemy the church-militant had once, and proved afterwards the greatest defender it will ever have. In his life a true knight-errant, and in death a steadfast saint; an indefatigable labourer in the vineyard of the Lord, a teacher of the Gentiles, who had heaven for his school, and Christ himself for his master and instructor."

Then Don Quixote, perceiving there were no more images, desired the men to cover those he had seen. "And now, my good friends," said he to them, "I cannot but esteem the sight that I have had of these images as a happy omen; for these saints and knights were of the same profession that I follow, which is that of arms. The difference only lies in this point, that they were saints, and fought according to the rules of holy discipline; and I am a sinner, and fight after the manner of men."

All this while the men wondered at Don Quixote's figure, as well as his discourse, but could not understand one half of what he meant; so that, after they had made an end of their dinner, they got up their images, took their leave of him, and continued their journey.

Sancho remained full of admiration, as if he had never known his master. He wondered how he came to know all these things, and fancied there was not that history or adventure in the world but he had at his fingers' ends. "Faith and troth, master of mine," quoth he, "if what has happened to us to-day may be called an adventure, it is one of the sweetest and most pleasant we ever met with in all our rambles, for we are come off without a dry basting, or the least bodily fear."

"Thou sayest well, Sancho," said Don Quixote; "but I must tell thee, that seasons and times are not always the same, but often take a different course; and what the vulgar call forebodings and omens, for which there are no rational grounds in nature, ought only to be esteemed happy encounters by the wise. One of these superstitious fools, going out of his house betimes in the morning, meets a friar of the blessed order of St. Francis, and starts as if he had met a griffin, turns back, and runs home again. Another wiseacre happens to throw down the salt on the table-cloth, and thereupon is sadly cast down himself, as if nature were obliged to give tokens of ensuing disasters by such slight and inconsiderable accidents as these. A wise and truly religious man ought never to pry into the secrets of Heaven. Scipio, landing in Africa, stumbled and fell down as he leaped ashore. Presently his soldiers took this for an ill omen; but he, embracing the earth, cried, 'I have thee fast, Africa: thou shalt not escape me.' In this manner, Sancho, I think it a very happy accident that I met these images."

"I think so, too," quoth Sancho; "but I would fain know why the Spaniards call upon that same St. James, the destroyer of Moors; just when they are going to give battle they cry, 'St. Jago, and close Spain!' Pray, is Spain open, that it wants to be closed up? What do you make of that ceremony?"

"Thou art a very simple fellow, Sancho," answered Don Quixote. "Thou must know that Heaven gave to Spain this mighty champion of the Red Cross for its patron and protector, especially in the desperate engagements which the Spaniards had with the Moors; and therefore they invoke him, in all their martial encounters, as their protector; and many times he has been personally seen cutting and slaying, overthrowing, trampling, and destroying the Hagarene squadrons, of which I could give thee many examples, deduced from authentic Spanish histories."

Thus discoursing, they got into a wood quite out of the road; and on a sudden Don Quixote, before he knew where he was, found himself entangled in some nets of green thread that were spread across among the trees. Not being able to imagine what it was, "Certainly, Sancho," cried he, "this adventure of the nets must be one of the most unaccountable that can be imagined. Let me die now if this be not a stratagem of the evil-minded necromancers that haunt me, to entangle me so that I may not proceed, purely to revenge my contempt of Altisidora's addresses. But let them know, that though these nets were adamantine chains, as they are only made of green thread, and though they were stronger than those in which the jealous god of blacksmiths caught Venus and Mars, I would break them with as much ease as if they were weak rushes or fine cotton yarn." With that the knight put briskly forwards, resolving to break through and make his words good; but in the very moment there sprung from behind the trees two most beautiful shepherdesses; at least, they appeared to be so by their habits, only with this difference, that they were richly dressed in gold brocade. Their flowing hair hung down about their shoulders in curls, as charming as the sun's golden rays, and circled on their brows with garlands of green baize and red-flower-gentle interwoven. As for their age, it seemed not less than fifteen, nor more than eighteen years. This unexpected vision dazzled and amazed Sancho, surprised Don Quixote, made even the gazing sun stop short in his career, and held the surprised parties awhile in the same suspense and silence; till at last one of the shepherdesses opening her coral lips, "Hold, sir," she cried; "pray do not tear those nets which we have spread here, not to offend you, but to divert ourselves; and because it is likely you will inquire why they are spread here, and who we are, I shall tell you in few words.

"About two leagues from this place lies a village where there are many people of quality and good estates; among these, several have made up a company—all of friends, neighbours, and relations—to come and take their diversion in this place, which is one of the most delightful in these parts. To this purpose we design to set up a new Arcadia. The young men have put on the habit of shepherds, and ladies the dresses of shepherdesses. We have got two eclogues by heart; one out of the famous Garcilasso, and the other out of Camoens, the most excellent Portuguese poet; though, the truth is, we have not yet repeated them, for yesterday was but the first day of our coming hither. We have pitched some tents among the trees, near the banks of a large brook that waters all these meadows. And last night we spread these nets to catch such simple birds as our calls should allure into the snare. Now, sir, if you please to afford us your company, you shall be made very welcome and handsomely entertained; for we are all disposed to pass the time agreeably."

"Truly, fair lady," answered Don Quixote, "Actæon could not be more lost in admiration and amazement at the sight of Diana bathing herself than I have been at the appearance of your beauty. I applaud your design, and return you thanks for your obliging offers; assuring you that, if it lies in my power to serve you, you may depend on my obedience to your commands; for my profession is the very reverse of ingratitude, and aims at doing good to all persons, especially those of your merit and condition; so that, were these nets spread over the surface of the whole earth, I would seek out a passage throughout new worlds rather than I would break the smallest thread that conduces to your pastime. And that you may give some credit to this seeming exaggeration, know that he who makes this promise is no less than Don Quixote de la Mancha, if ever such a name has reached your ears."

"Oh, my dear," cried the other shepherdess, "what good fortune is this! You see this gentleman before us: I must tell you he is the most valiant, the most amorous, and the most complaisant person in the world, if the history of his exploits, already in print, does not deceive us. I have read it, my dear; and I hold a wager that honest fellow there by him is one Sancho Panza, his squire, the most comical creature that ever was."

"You have nicked it," quoth Sancho; "I am that comical creature, and that very squire you wot of; and there is my lord and master, the self-same historified and aforesaid Don Quixote de la Mancha."

"Oh, pray, my dear," said the other, "let us entreat him to stay; our father and our brothers will be mighty glad of it. I have heard of his valour and his merit as much as you now tell me; and, what is more, they say he is the most constant and faithful lover in the world; and that his mistress, whom they call Dulcinea del Toboso, bears the prize from all the beauties in Spain."

"It is not without justice," said Don Quixote, "if your peerless charms do not dispute her that glory. But, ladies, I beseech you do not endeavour to detain me; for the indispensable duties of my profession will not suffer me to rest in one place."

At the same time came the brother of one of the shepherdesses, clad like a shepherd, but in a dress as splendid and gay as those of the young ladies. They told him that the gentleman whom he saw with them was the valorous Don Quixote de la Mancha, and that other Sancho

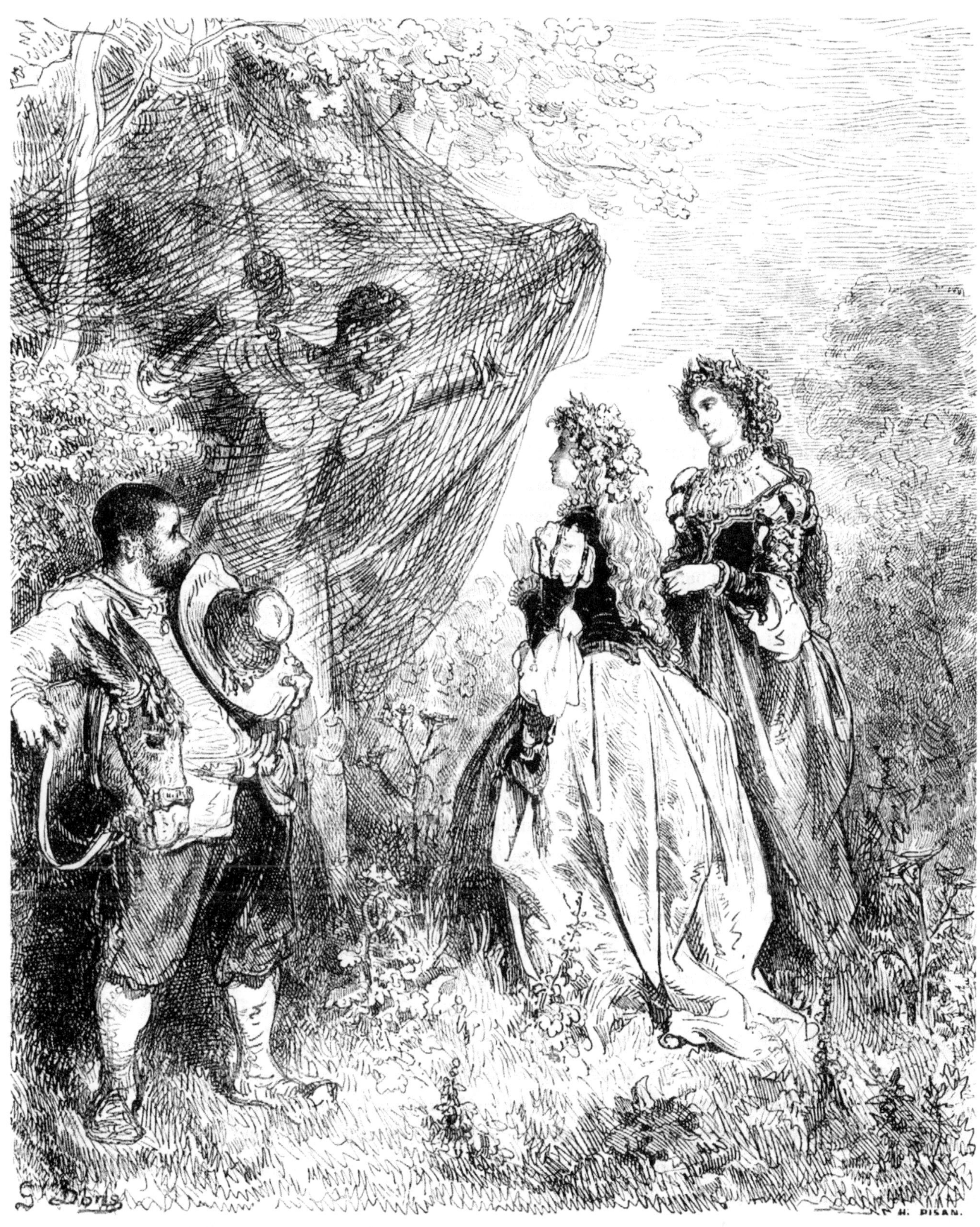

"Now, sir, if you please to afford us your company, you shall be made very welcome."

Panza, his squire, of whom he had read the history. The gallant shepherd having saluted him, begged of him so earnestly to grant them his company to their tents, that Don Quixote was forced to comply, and go with them.

About the same time the nets were drawn and filled with divers little birds, who, being deceived by the colour of the snare, fell into the danger they would have avoided. Above thirty persons, all gaily dressed like shepherds and shepherdesses, got together there, and being informed who Don Quixote and his squire were, they were not a little pleased, for they were already no strangers to his history. In short, they carried them to their tents, where they found a clean, sumptuous, and plentiful entertainment ready. They obliged the knight to take the place of honour; and while they sat at table there was not one that did not gaze on him, and wonder at so strange a figure.

At last, the cloth being removed, Don Quixote, with a great deal of gravity, lifting up his voice, "Of all the sins that men commit," said he, "none, in my opinion, is so great as ingratitude, though some think pride a greater; and I ground my assertion on this, that hell is said to be full of the ungrateful. Ever since I had the use of reason I have employed my utmost endeavours to avoid this crime; and if I am not able to repay the benefits I receive in their kind, at least I am not wanting in real intentions of making suitable returns; and, if that be not sufficient, I make my acknowledgments as public as I can; for he that proclaims the kindnesses he has received, shows his disposition to repay them if he could; and those that receive are generally inferior to those that give. The Supreme Being, who is infinitely above all things, bestows his blessings on us so much beyond the capacity of all other benefactors, that all the acknowledgments we can make can never hold proportion with his goodness. However, a thankful mind in some measure supplies its want of power, with hearty desires and unfeigned expressions of a sense of gratitude and respect. I am in this condition as to the civilities I have been treated with here; for I am unable to make an acknowledgment equal to the kindnesses I have received. I shall, therefore, only offer you what is within the narrow limits of my own abilities, which is to maintain, for two whole days together, in the middle of the road that leads to Saragosa, that these ladies here, disguised in the habits of shepherdesses, are the fairest and most courteous damsels in the world, excepting only the peerless Dulcinea del Toboso, sole mistress of my thoughts; without offence to all that hear me, be it spoken."

Here Sancho, who had, with an uncommon attention, all the while given ear to his master's compliment, thought fit to put in a word or two. "Now, in the name of wonder," quoth he, "can there be anybody in the world so impudent as to offer to swear or but to say this master of mine is a madman? Pray, tell me, ye gentlemen shepherds, did you ever know any of your country parsons, though never so wise or so good scholars, that could deliver themselves so finely? Or is there any of your knights-errant, though never so famed for prowess, that can make such an offer as he has here done?"

Don Quixote turned towards Sancho, and, beholding him with eyes full of fiery indignation,

"Can there be anybody in the world," cried he, "that can say thou art not an incorrigible blockhead, Sancho—a compound of folly and knavery, wherein malice also is no small ingredient? Who bids thee meddle with my concerns, fellow, or busy thyself with my folly or discretion? Hold your saucy tongue, scoundrel! Make no reply, but go and saddle Rozinante, if he is unsaddled, that I may immediately perform what I have offered."

This said, up he started, in a dreadful fury and with marks of anger in his looks, to the amazement of all the company, who were at a loss whether they should esteem him a madman or a man of sense. They endeavoured to prevail with him to lay aside his challenges, telling him they were sufficiently assured of his grateful nature, without exposing him to the danger of such demonstrations; and as for his valour, they were so well informed by the history of his numerous achievements, that there was no need of any new instance to convince them of it. But all these representations could not dissuade him from his purpose; and, therefore, having mounted Rozinante, braced his shield, and grasped his lance, he went and posted himself in the middle of the highway, not far from the verdant meadow, followed by Sancho on his Dapple, and all the pastoral society, who were desirous to see the event of that arrogant and unaccountable resolution.

And now the champion, having taken his ground, made the neighbouring air ring with the following challenge:—

"Oh, ye, whoever you are, knights, squires, on foot or on horseback, that now pass, or shall pass this road within these two days, know that Don Quixote de la Mancha, knight-errant, stays here to assert and maintain that the nymphs who inhabit these groves and meadows surpass, in beauty and courteous disposition, all those in the universe, setting aside the sovereign of my soul, the Lady Dulcinea del Toboso; and he that dares uphold the contrary, let him appear, for here I expect his coming."

Twice he repeated these lofty words, and twice they were repeated in vain, not being heard by any adventurer. But his old friend Fortune, that had a strange hand at managing his concerns, and always mended upon it, showed him a jolly sight; for by-and-by he discovered on the road a great number of people on horseback, many of them with lances in their hands, all trooping together very fast. The company that watched Don Quixote's motions no sooner spied such a squadron, driving the dust before them, than they got out of harm's way, not judging it safe to be so near danger; and as for Sancho, he sheltered himself behind Rozinante's crupper. Only Don Quixote stood fixed, with an undaunted courage. When the horsemen came near, one of the foremost, bawling to the champion, "So hey!" cried he, "get out of the way, and be hanged. Mischief is in the fellow! stand off, or the bulls will tread thee to pieces."

"Go to, you scoundrels," answered Don Quixote; "none of your bulls are anything to me, though the fiercest that ever were fed on the banks of Xarama. Acknowledge, hang-dogs, all in a body, what I have proclaimed here to be truth, or else stand combat with me."

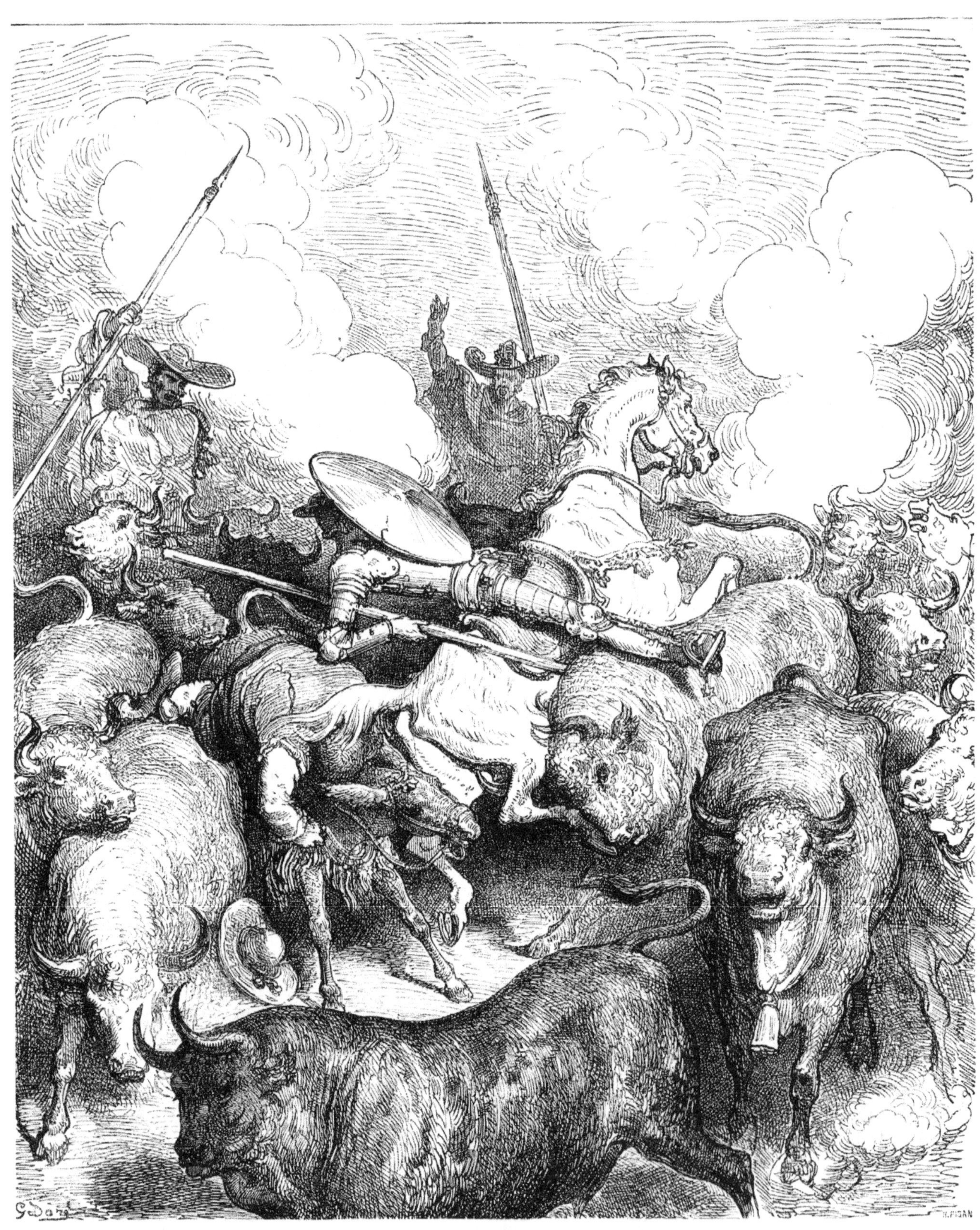

"They trampled them under foot at an unmerciful rate."

But the herdsmen had not time to answer, neither had Don Quixote any to get out of the way, if he had been inclined to it; for the herd of wild bulls were presently upon him, as they poured along, with several tame cows, and a huge company of drivers and people, that were going to a town where they were to be baited the next day. So, bearing all down before them, knight and squire, horse and man, they trampled them under foot at an unmerciful rate, There lay Sancho mauled, Don Quixote stunned, Dapple bruised, and Rozinante in very indifferent circumstances. But for all this, after the whole party of men and beasts were gone by, up started Don Quixote, ere he was thoroughly come to himself, and staggering and stumbling, falling and getting up again, as fast as he could, he began to run after them.

"Stop, scoundrels, stop!" cried he aloud; "stay, it is a single knight defies you all, one who scorns the humour of making a golden bridge for a flying enemy."

But the hasty travellers did not stop, nor slacken their speed, for all his loud defiance, and minded it no more than the last year's snow.

At last weariness stopped Don Quixote; so that, with all his anger, and no prospect of revenge, he was forced to sit down on the road, till Sancho came up to him with Rozinante and Dapple. Then the master and man made a shift to re-mount; and, ashamed of their bad success, hastened their journey, without taking leave of their friends of the new Arcadia.

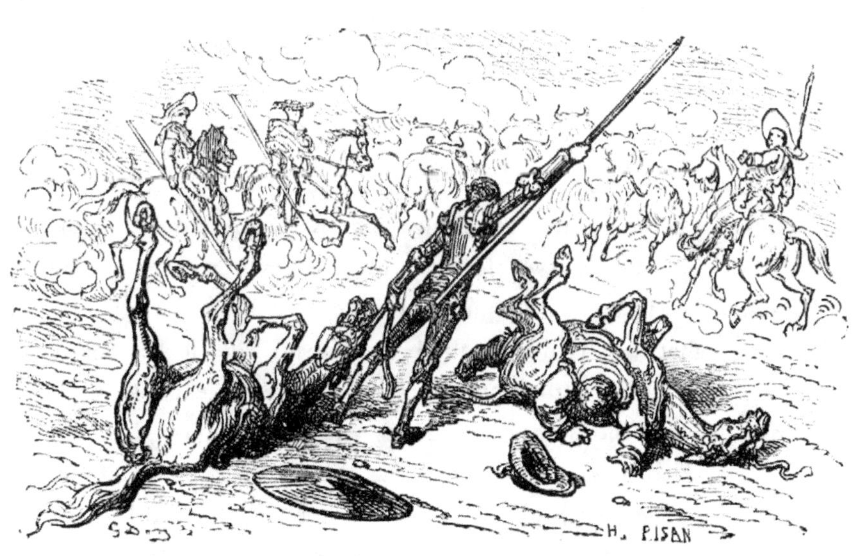

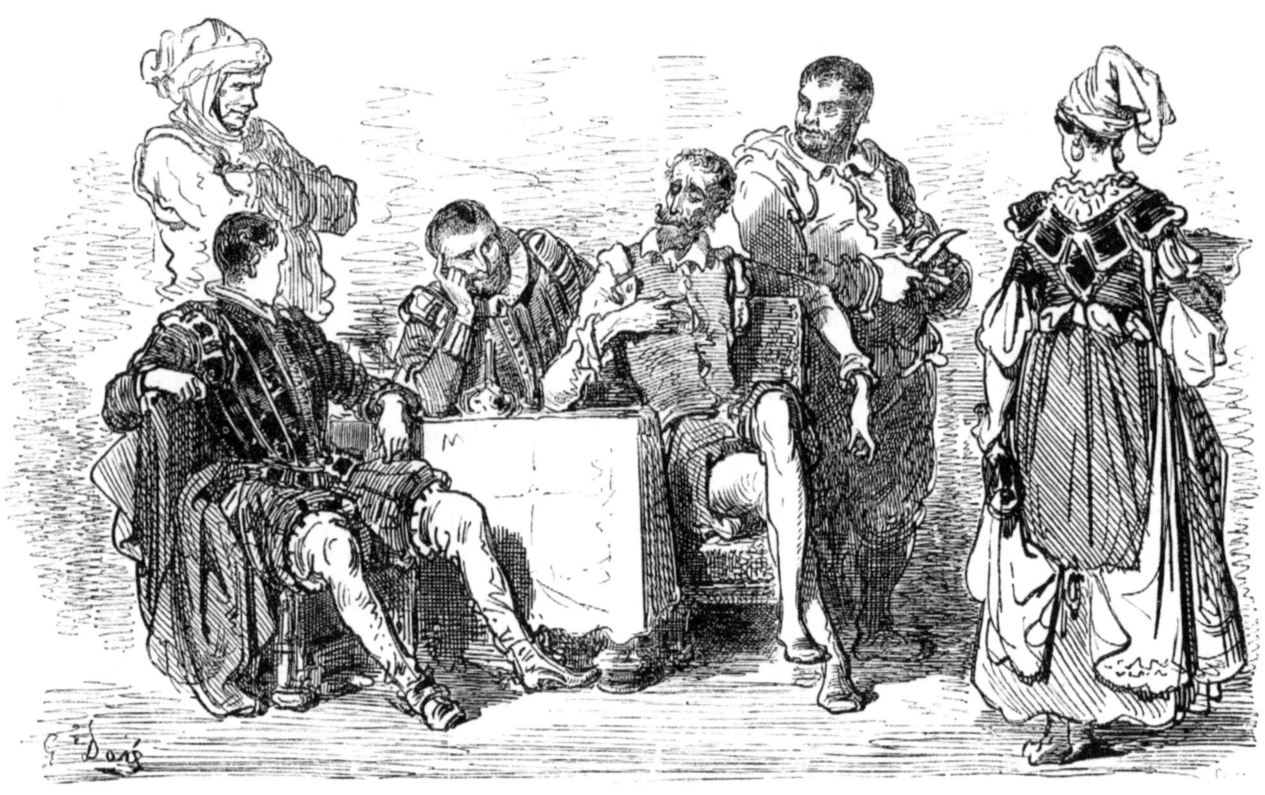

CHAPTER LIX.

OF AN EXTRAORDINARY ACCIDENT THAT HAPPENED TO DON QUIXOTE, WHICH MAY WELL PASS FOR AN ADVENTURE.

A CLEAR fountain, which Don Quixote and Sancho found among some verdant trees, served to refresh them, besmeared with dust and tired as they were, after the rude encounter of the bulls. There, by the brink, leaving Rozinante and Dapple, unbridled and unhaltered, to their own liberty, the two forlorn adventurers sat down. Sancho washed his mouth, and Don Quixote his face. The squire then went to his old cupboard, the wallet, and having taken out of it what he used to call belly-timber, laid it before the knight. Don Quixote gave him thanks, ate a little, and Sancho a great deal; and then both betook themselves to their rest, leaving those constant friends and companions, Rozinante and Dapple, to their own discretion, to repose or feed at random on the pasture that abounded in that meadow.

The day was now far gone, when the knight and the squire waked. They mounted, and held on their journey, making the best of their way to an inn, that seemed to be about a league distant.

Being got thither, they asked the innkeeper whether he had got any lodgings.

"Yes," answered he, "and as good accommodation as you could expect to find even in the city of Saragosa."

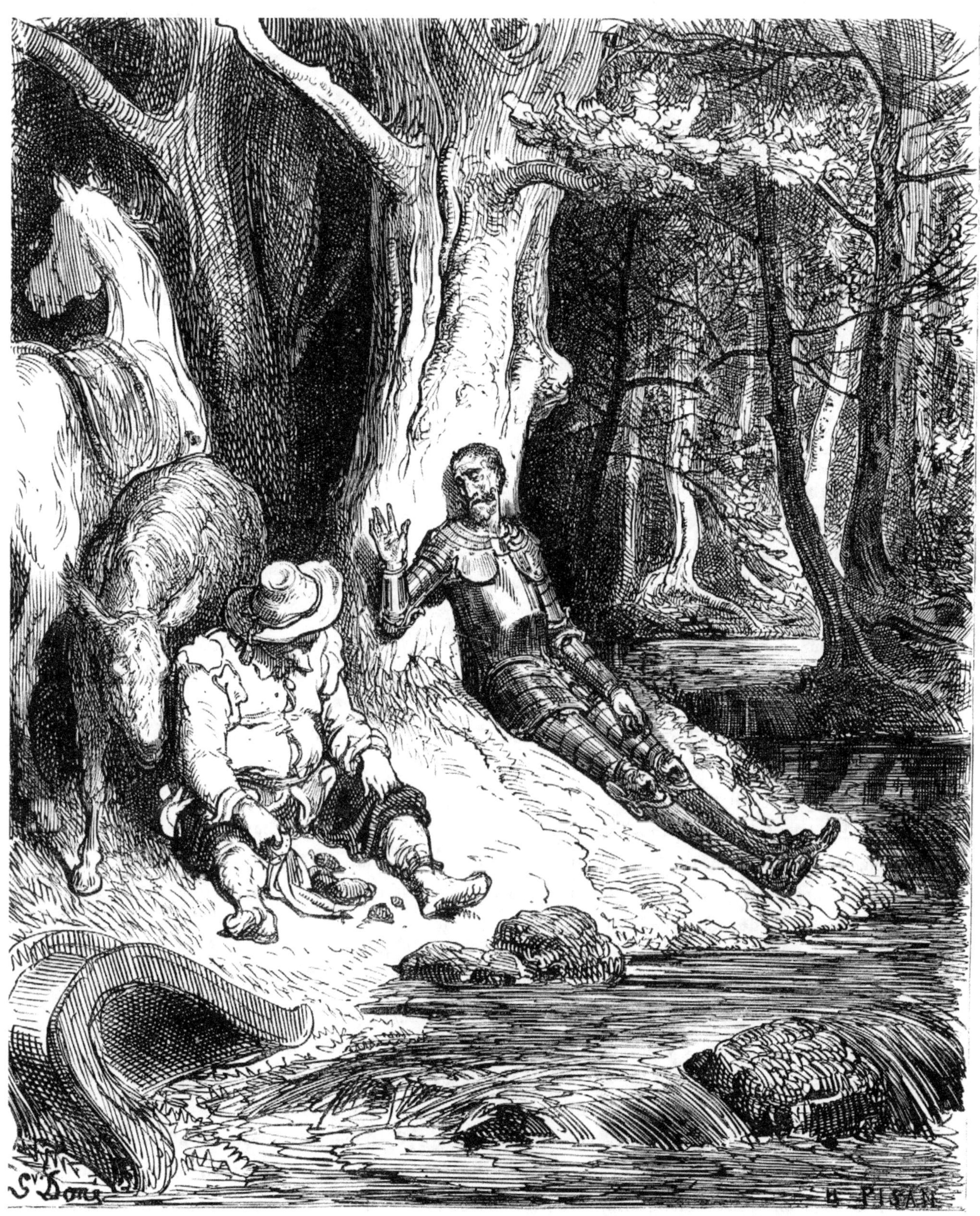

"A clear fountain, which Don Quixote and Sancho found among some verdant trees, served to refresh them."

They alighted, and Sancho put up his baggage in a chamber, of which the landlord gave him the key; and, after he had seen Rozinante and Dapple well provided for in the stable, he went to wait on his master, whom he found sitting upon a seat made in the wall, the squire blessing himself more than once that the knight had not taken the inn for a castle. Supper-time approaching, Don Quixote retired to his apartment, and Sancho, staying with his host, asked him what he had to give them for supper.

"What you will," answered he. "You may pick and choose: fish or flesh, butcher's meat or poultry, wild fowl, and what not. Whatever land, sea, and air afford for food, it is but ask and have; everything is to be had in this inn."

"There is no need of all this," quoth Sancho; "a couple of roasted chickens will do our business, for my master has a nice stomach, and eats but little; and as for me, I am none of your unreasonable trencher men."

"As for chickens," replied the innkeeper, "we have none, for the kites have devoured them."

"Why, then," quoth Sancho, "roast us a good handsome pullet, with eggs, so it be young and tender."

"A pullet, master!" answered the host; "faith and troth, I sent above fifty yesterday to the city to sell; but, setting aside pullets, you may have anything else."

"Why, then," quoth Sancho, "even give us a good joint of veal or kid."

"Cry you mercy!" replied the innkeeper; "now I remember me, we have none left in the house; the last company that went cleared me quite; but by next week we shall have enough, and to spare."

"We are finely holped up," quoth Sancho. "Now will I hold a good wager, all these defects must be made up with a dish of eggs and bacon."

"Hey day!" cried the host, "my guest has a rare knack at guessing, i' faith. I told him I had no hens nor pullets in the house, and yet he would have me to have eggs! Think on something else, I beseech you, and let us talk no more of that."

"Bless me!" cried Sancho, "let us come to something; tell me what thou hast, good Mr. Landlord, and do not put me to trouble my brains any longer."

"Why, then, do you see," quoth the host, "to deal plainly with you, I have a delicate pair of cow-heels, that look like calves' feet, or a pair of calves' feet that look like cow-heels, dressed with onions, pease, and bacon—a dish for a prince; they are just ready to be taken off, and by this time they cry, 'Come, eat me; come, eat me.'"

"Cow-heels!" cried Sancho; "I set my mark on them; let nobody touch them. I will give more for them than any other shall. There is nothing I love better."

"Nobody else shall have them," answered the host; "you need not fear, for all the guests I have in the house, besides yourselves, are persons of quality, that carry their steward, their cook, and their provisions along with them."

"As for quality," quoth Sancho, "my master is a person of as good quality as the proudest he of them all, if you go to that, but his profession allows of no larders nor butteries. We commonly clap us down in the midst of a field, and fill our bellies with acorns or medlars."

This was the discourse that passed betwixt Sancho and the innkeeper; for as to the host's interrogatories concerning his master's profession, Sancho was not then at leisure to make him any answer.

In short, supper-time came, Don Quixote went to his room, the host brought the dish of cow-heels, such as it was, and set him down fairly to supper. But at the same time, in the next room, which was divided from that where they were by a slender partition, the knight overheard somebody talking.

"Dear Don Jeronimo," said the unseen person, "I beseech you, till supper is brought in let us read another chapter of the second part of 'Don Quixote.'" The champion no sooner heard himself named than up he started, and listened, with attentive ears, to what was said of him; and then he heard that Don Jeronimo answer, "Why would you have us read nonsense, Signor Don John? Methinks any one that has read the first part of 'Don Quixote' should take but little delight in reading the second."

"That may be," replied Don John; "however, it may not be amiss to read it, for there is no book so bad as not to have something that is good in it. What displeases me most in this part is, that it represents Don Quixote no longer in love with Dulcinea del Toboso."

Upon these words, Don Quixote, burning with anger and indignation, cried out, "Whoever says that Don Quixote de la Mancha has forgotten or can forget Dulcinea del Toboso, I will make him know, with equal arms, that he departs wholly from the truth; for the peerless Dulcinea del Toboso cannot be forgotten, nor can Don Quixote be guilty of forgetfulness. *Constancy* is his motto; and to preserve his fidelity with pleasure, and without the least constraint, is his profession."

"Who is he that answers us?" cries one of those in the next room.

"Who should it be?" quoth Sancho, "but Don Quixote de la Mancha his own self, the same that will make good all he has said and all he has to say, take my word for it; for a good paymaster never grudges to give security."

Sancho had no sooner made that answer than in came the two gentlemen (for they appeared to be no less), and one of them, throwing his arms about Don Quixote's neck, "Your presence, Sir Knight," said he, "does not belie your reputation, nor can your reputation fail to raise a respect for your presence. You are certainly the true Don Quixote de la Mancha, the north star and luminary of chivalry-errant, in despite of him that has attempted to usurp your name and annihilate your achievements, as the author of this book, which I here deliver into your hands, has presumed to do." With that he took the book from his friend and gave it to Don Quixote.

The knight took it, and, without saying a word, began to turn over the leaves; and then, returning it a while after, "In the little I have seen," said he, "I have found three things in this author that deserve reprehension. First, I find fault with some words in his preface. In the second place, his language is Arragonian, for sometimes he writes without articles. And the third thing I have observed, which betrays most his ignorance, is, he is out of the way in one of the principal parts of the history; for there he says that the wife of my squire, Sancho Panza, is called Mary Gutierrez, which is not true, for her name is Teresa Panza; and he that errs in so considerable a passage may well be suspected to have committed many gross errors through the whole history."

"A pretty impudent fellow is this same history-writer!" cried Sancho. "Sure he knows much what belongs to our concerns, to call my wife Teresa Panza, Mary Gutierrez! Pray, take the book again, if it like your worship, and see whether he says anything of me, and whether he has not changed my name too."

"Sure, by what you have said, honest man," said Don Jeronimo, "you should be Sancho Panza, squire to Signor Don Quixote."

"So I am," quoth Sancho, "and I am proud of the office."

"Well," said the gentleman, "to tell you the truth, the last author does not treat you so civilly as you seem to deserve. He represents you as a glutton and a fool, without the least grain of wit or humour, and very different from the Sancho we have in the first part of your master's history."

"Heaven forgive him!" quoth Sancho; "he might have left me where I was, without offering to meddle with me. 'Every man's nose will not make a shoeing horn.' Let us leave the world as it is. 'St. Peter is very well at Rome.'"

Presently the two gentlemen invited Don Quixote to sup with them in their chamber, for they knew there was nothing to be got in the inn fit for his entertainment. Don Quixote, who was always very complaisant, could not deny their request, and went with them. Sancho stayed behind with the flesh-pot, and placed himself at the upper end of the table, with the innkeeper for his messmate, who was no less a lover of cow-heels than the squire.

While Don Quixote was at supper with the gentlemen, Don John asked him when he heard of the Lady Dulcinea del Toboso. With that he told the gentlemen the whole story of her being enchanted, what had befallen him in the cave of Montesinos, and the means that the sage Merlin had prescribed to free her from enchantment, which was Sancho's penance of three thousand three hundred lashes. The gentlemen were extremely pleased to hear from Don Quixote's own mouth the strange passages of his history, equally wondering at the nature of his extravagances and his elegant manner of relating them. One minute they looked upon him to be in his senses, and the next they thought he had lost them all, so that they could not resolve what degree to assign him between madness and sound judgment.

They asked him which way he was travelling. He told them he was going to Saragosa, to make one at the tournaments held in that city once a year, for the prize of armour. Don John acquainted him that the pretended second part of his history gave an account how Don

Quixote, whoever he was, had been at Saragosa, at a public running at the ring, the description of which was wretched and defective in the contrivance, and mean and low in the style.

"For that reason," said Don Quixote, "I will not set a foot in Saragosa; and so the world shall see what a notorious lie this new historian is guilty of, and all mankind shall perceive I am not the Don Quixote he speaks of."

"You do very well," said Don Jeronimo; "besides, there is another tournament at Barcelona, where you may signalise your valour."

"I design to do so," replied Don Quixote; "and so, gentlemen, give me leave to bid you good night, and permit me to go to bed, for it is time; and pray place me in the number of your best friends, and most faithful servants."

"And me too," quoth Sancho, "for mayhap you may find me good for something."

Having taken leave of one another, Don Quixote and Sancho retired to their chamber, leaving the two strangers fully satisfied that these two persons were the true Don Quixote and Sancho, and not those obtruded upon the public by the Arragonian author.

Early in the morning Don Quixote got up, and, knocking at a thin wall that parted his chamber from that of the gentlemen, took his leave of them. Sancho paid the host nobly, but advised him either to keep better provisions in his inn or to commend it less.

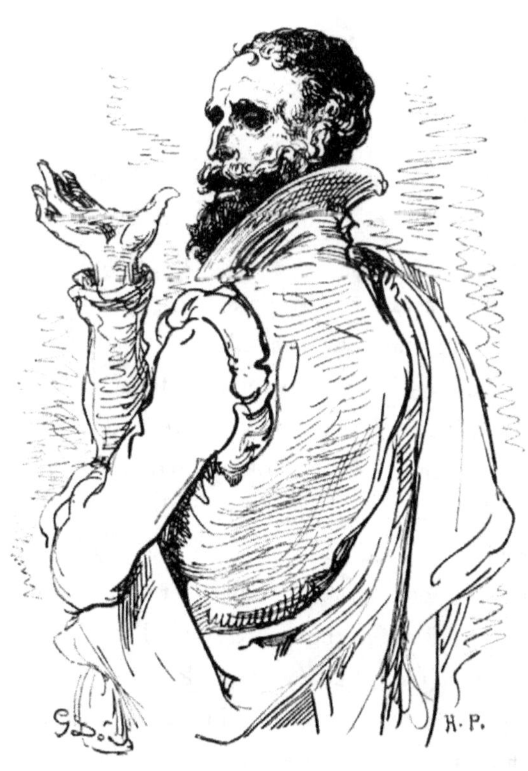

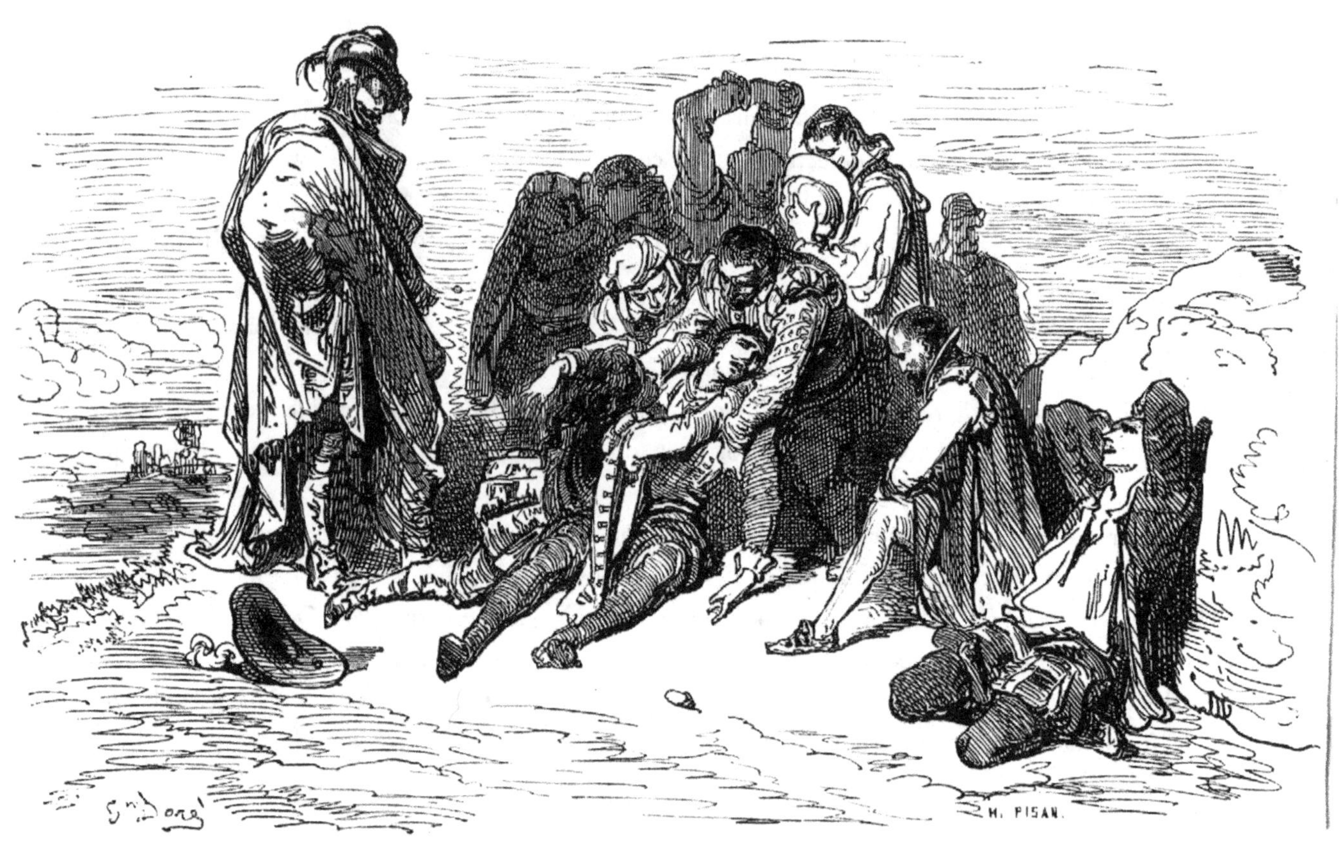

CHAPTER LX.

WHAT HAPPENED TO DON QUIXOTE GOING TO BARCELONA.

THE morning was cool, and seemed to promise a temperate day, when Don Quixote left the inn, having first informed himself which was the readiest way to Barcelona; for he was resolved he would not so much as see Saragosa, that he might prove that new author a liar, who, as he was told, had so misrepresented him in the pretended second part of his history. For the space of six days he travelled without meeting any adventure worthy of memory; but the seventh, having lost his way, and being overtaken by the night, he was obliged to stop in a thicket, either of oaks or cork-trees, for in this Cid Hamet does not observe the same punctuality he has kept in other matters. There both master and man dismounted, and laying themselves down at the foot of the trees, Sancho, who had handsomely filled his belly that day, easily resigned himself into the arms of sleep. But Don Quixote, whom his chimeras kept awake much more than hunger, could not so much as close his eyes, his working thoughts being hurried to a thousand several places. This time he fancied himself in the cave of Montesinos, imagining he saw his Dulcinea, perverted as she was into a country hoyden, jump at a single leap upon her ass colt. The next moment he thought he heard the sage Merlin's voice—heard him in awful words relate the means required to effect her disen-

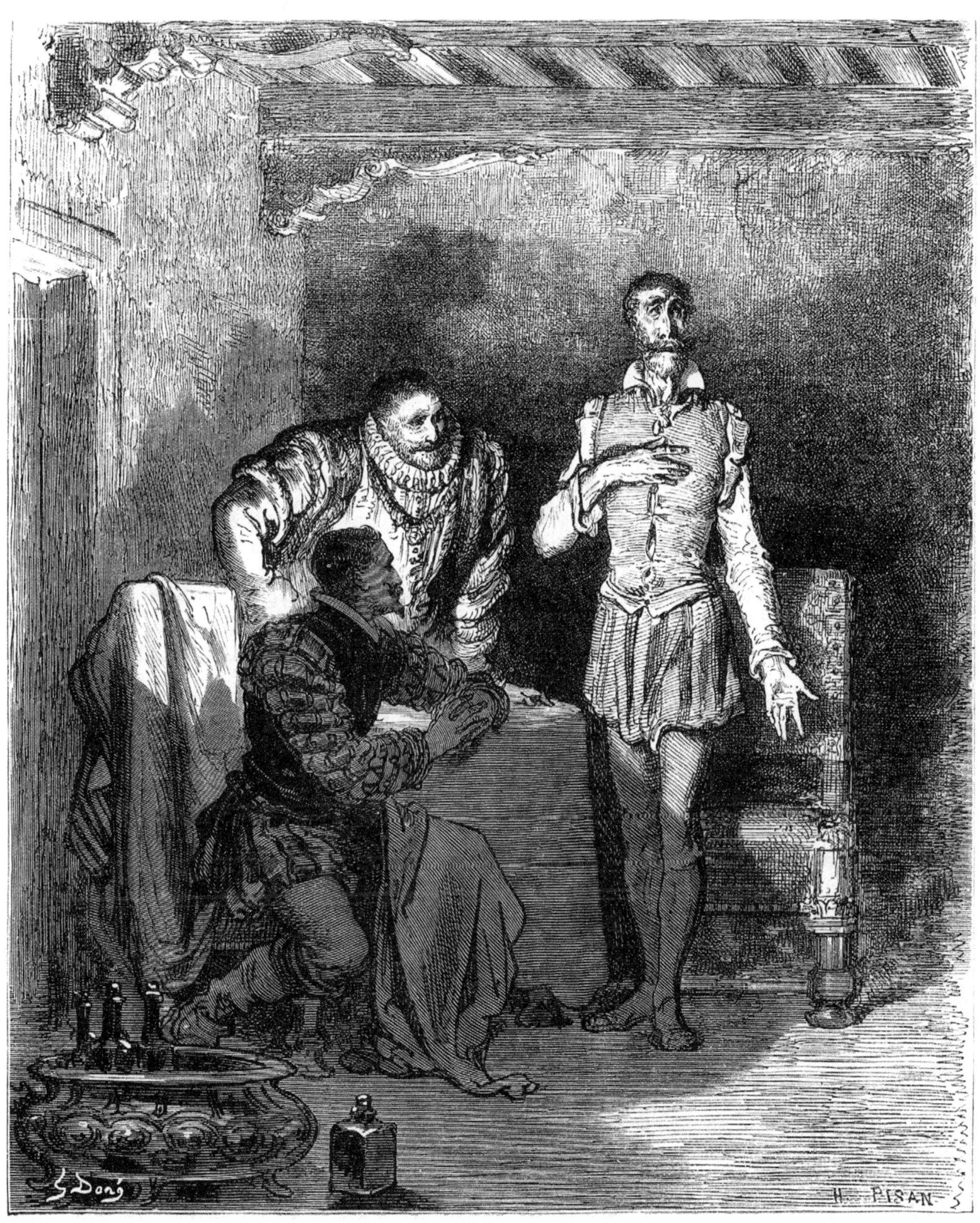

"He told the gentlemen the whole story of her being enchanted."

chantment. Presently a fit of despair seized him; he was stark mad to think on Sancho's remissness and want of charity, the squire having not given himself above five lashes, a small and inconsiderable number, in proportion to the quantity of the penance still behind. This reflection so nettled him, and so aggravated his vexation, that he could not forbear thinking on some extraordinary methods. "If Alexander the Great," thought he, "when he could not untie the Gordian knot, said, 'It is the same thing to cut or to undo,' and so slashed it asunder, and yet became the sovereign of the world, why may not I free Dulcinea from enchantment by whipping Sancho myself, whether he will or no? For, if the condition of this remedy consists in Sancho's receiving three thousand and odd lashes, what does it signify to me whether he gives himself those blows, or another gives them him, since the stress lies upon his receiving them, by what means soever they are given?" Full of that conceit, he came up to Sancho, having first taken the reins of Rozinante's bridle, and fitted them to his purpose of lashing him with them. He then began to untruss Sancho's points; but he no sooner fell to work than Sancho started out of his sleep, and was thoroughly awake in an instant. "What is here?" cried he.

"It is I," answered Don Quixote; "I am come to repair thy negligence, and to seek the remedy of my torments. I am come to whip thee, Sancho, and to discharge, in part at least, that debt for which thou standest engaged. Dulcinea perishes, while thou livest careless of her fate, and I die with desire. Untruss, therefore, freely and willingly, for I am resolved while we are here alone in this recess, to give thee at least two thousand stripes."

"Hold you there," quoth Sancho; "pray be quiet, will you? Bless me! let me alone, or I protest deaf men shall hear us. The jerks I am bound to give myself are to be voluntary, not forced; and at this time I have no mind to be whipped at all. Let it suffice that I promise you to scourge myself when the humour takes me."

"No," said Don Quixote, "there is no standing to thy courtesy, Sancho, for thou art hard-hearted; and, though a clown, yet thou art tender of thy flesh;" and so saying, he strove with all his force to untie the squire's points; which, when Sancho perceived, he started up on his legs, and, setting upon his master, closed with him, tripped up his heels, threw him fairly upon his back, and then set his knee upon his breast, and held his hands fast, so that he could hardly stir, or fetch his breath. Don Quixote, overpowered thus, cried, "How now, traitor! what! rebel against thy master—against thy natural lord—against him that gives thee bread!"

"I neither mar king nor make king," quoth Sancho; "I do but defend myself, that am naturally my own lord. If your worship will promise to let me alone, and give over the thoughts of whipping me at this time, I will let you rise, and will leave you at liberty; if not, here thou diest, traitor to Donna Sancho."

Don Quixote gave his parole of honour, and swore by the life of his best thoughts not to touch so much as a hair of Sancho's coat, but entirely leave it to his discretion to whip

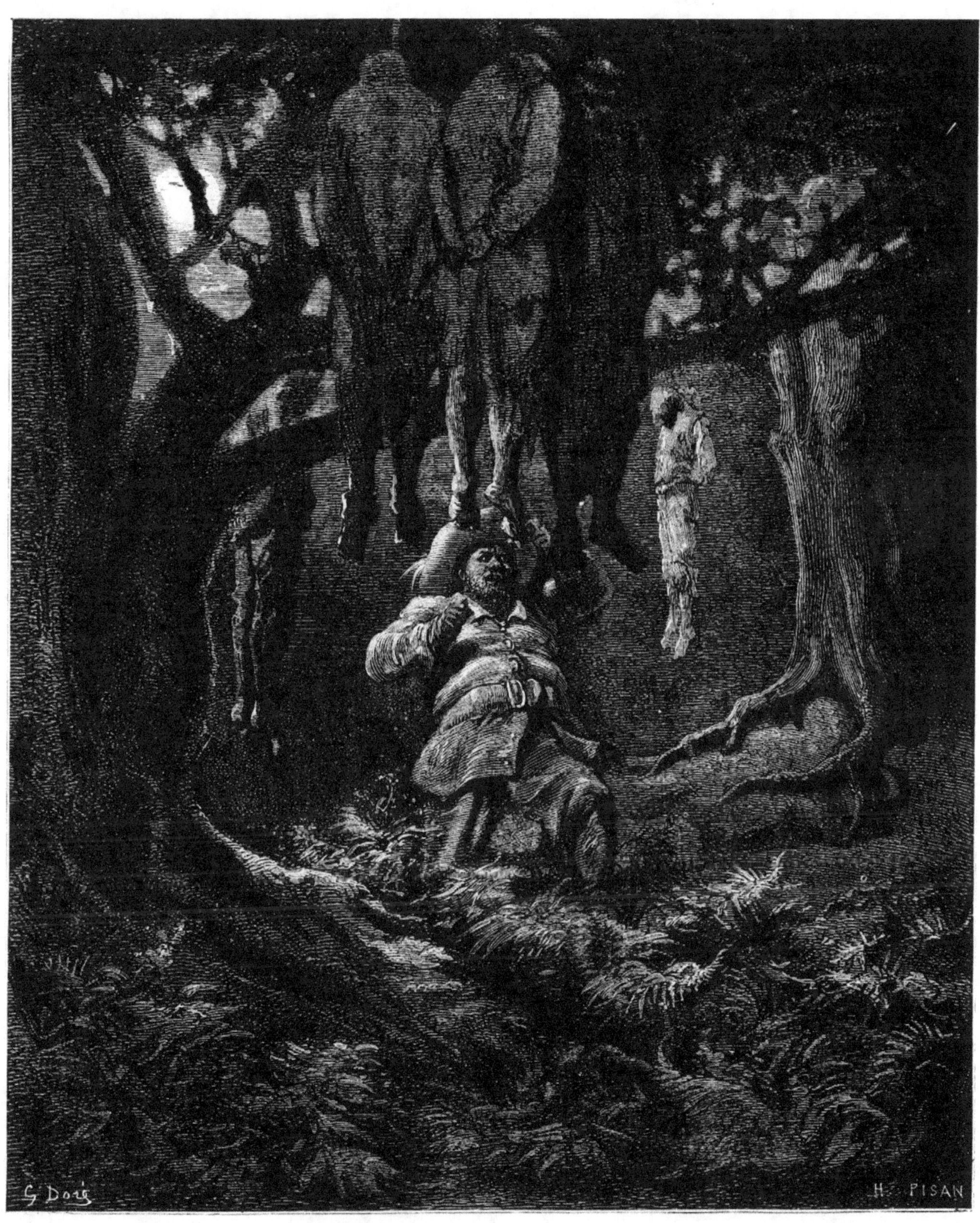

"He called out to Don Quixote for help."

himself when he thought fit. With that Sancho got up from him, and removed his quarters to another place at a good distance; but as he went to lean against a tree he perceived something bobbing at his head, and, lifting up his hands, found it to be a man's feet, with shoes and stockings on. Quaking for fear, he moved off to another tree, where the like impending horror dangled over his head. Straight he called out to Don Quixote for help, Don Quixote came, and inquired into the occasion of his fright. Sancho answered, that all those trees were full of men's feet and legs. Don Quixote began to search and grope about, and falling presently into the account of the business, "Fear nothing, Sancho," said he, "there is no danger at all; for what thou feelest in the dark are certainly the feet and legs of some banditti and robbers that have been hanged upon those trees, for here the officers of justice hang them up by twenties and thirties in clusters, by which I suppose we cannot be far from Barcelona;" and indeed he guessed right.

And now, day breaking, they lifted up their eyes, and saw the bodies of the highwaymen hanging on the trees. But if the dead surprised them, how much more were they disturbed at the appearance of above forty live banditti, who poured upon them, and surrounded them on a sudden, charging them in the Catalan tongue to stand till their captain came!

Don Quixote found himself on foot, his horse unbridled, his lance against a tree at some distance, and, in short, void of all defence; and, therefore, he was forced to put his arms across, hold down his head, and shrug up his shoulders, reserving himself for a better opportunity. The robbers presently fell to work, and began to rifle Dapple, leaving on his back nothing of what he carried, either in the wallet or the cloak-bag; and it was very well for Sancho that the duke's pieces of gold, and those he brought from home, were hidden in a girdle about his waist; though, for all that, those honest gentlemen would certainly have taken the pains to have searched and surveyed him all over, and would have had the gold, though they had stripped him of his skin to come at it; but by good fortune their captain came in the interim. He seemed about four-and-thirty years of age, his body robust, his stature tall, his visage austere, and his complexion swarthy. He was mounted on a strong horse, wore a coat of mail, and no less than two pistols on each side. Perceiving that his squires (for so they call men of that profession in those parts) were going to strip Sancho, he ordered them to forbear, and was instantly obeyed; by which means the girdle escaped. He wondered to see a lance reared up against a tree, a shield on the ground, and Don Quixote in armour, and pensive, with the saddest, most melancholy countenance that despair itself could frame. Coming up to him, "Be not so sad, honest man," said he; "you have not fallen into the hands of some cruel Busiris, but into those of Roque Guinart, a man rather compassionate than severe."

"I am not sad," answered Don Quixote, "for having fallen into thy power, valorous Roque, whose boundless fame spreads through the universe, but for having been so remiss as to be surprised by thy soldiers with my horse unbridled; whereas, according to the order of chivalry-errant, which I profess, I am obliged to live always upon my guard, and at all hours be my own sentinel; for, let me tell thee, great Roque, had they met me mounted on my steed, armed with my shield and lance, they would have found it no easy task to make me yield; for know, I am Don Quixote de la Mancha, the same whose exploits are celebrated through all the habitable globe."

Roque Guinart found out immediately Don Quixote's blind side, and judged there was more madness than valour in the case. Now, though he had several times heard him mentioned in discourse, he could never believe what was related of him to be true, nor could he be persuaded that such a humour should reign in any man; for which reason he was very glad to have met him, that experience might convince him of the truth. Therefore, addressing himself to him, "Valorous knight," said he, "vex not yourself, nor tax fortune with unkindness; for it may happen that what you look upon now as a sad accident may redound to your advantage.

Don Quixote was going to return him thanks, when from behind them they heard a noise like the trampling of several horses, though it was occasioned but by one; on which came, full speed, a person that looked like a gentleman, about twenty years of age. He was clad in green damask, edged with gold galloon, suitable to his waistcoat, and a hat turned up behind; straight wax-leather boots; his spurs, sword, and dagger, gilt; a light bird-piece in his hand, and a case of pistols before him. Roque, having turned his head to the noise, discovered the handsome apparition, which, approaching nearer, spoke to him in this manner—"You are the gentleman I looked for, valiant Roque; for with you I may perhaps find some comfort, though not a remedy in my affliction. In short, not to hold you in suspense (for I am sensible you do not know me), I will tell you who I am. My name is Claudia Jeronima; I am the daughter of your particular friend, Simon Forte, sworn foe to Clauquel Torrelas, who is also your enemy, being one of your adverse faction. You already know this Torrelas had a son whom they called Don Vincente Torrelas; at least, he was called so within these two hours. That son of his, to be short in my sad story, I will tell you in four words what sorrow he has brought me to. He saw me, courted me, was heard, and was beloved. In short, he made me a promise of marriage, and I the like to him. Now, yesterday I understood that, forgetting his engagements to me, he was going to wed another, and that they were to be married this morning; a piece of news that quite distracted me, and made me lose all patience. Therefore, my father being out of town, I took the opportunity of equipping myself as you see, and, by the speed of this horse, overtook Don Vincente about a league hence, where, without urging my wrongs, or staying to hear his excuses, I fired at him, not only with this piece, but with both my pistols, and, as I believe, shot him through the body. This done, there I left him to his servants, who neither dared nor could prevent the sudden execution, and came to seek your protection, that by your means I may be conducted into France, where I have relations to entertain me; and withal to beg of you to defend my father from Don Vincente's party, who might otherwise revenge his death upon our family."

Roque, admiring at once the resolution, agreeable deportment, and handsome figure of the beautiful Claudia, "Come, madam," said he, "let us first be assured of your enemy's death, and then consider what is to be done for you."

"Hold!" cried Don Quixote, who had hearkened with great attention to all this discourse; "none of you need trouble yourselves with this affair; the defence of the lady is my province. Give me my horse and arms, and stay for me; I will go and find out this knight, and, dead or alive, force him to perform his obligations to so great a beauty."

Roque was so much taken up with the thoughts of Claudia's adventure, that, ordering his squires to restore what they had taken from Dapple to Sancho, and to retire to the place where they had quartered the night before, he went off upon the spur with Claudia, to find the expiring Don Vincente. They got to the place where Claudia met him, and found nothing but the marks of blood newly spilt; but, looking round about them, they discovered a company of people at a distance on the side of a hill, and presently judged them to be Don Vincente carried by his servants either to his cure or burial. They hastened to overtake them, which they soon effected, the others going but slowly; and they found the young gentleman in the arms of his servants, desiring them, with a spent and fainting voice, to let him die in that place, his wounds paining him so that he could not bear going any farther. Claudia and Roque dismounting, hastily came up to him. The servants were startled at the appearance of Roque, and Claudia was troubled at the sight of Don Vincente; and, divided between anger and compassion, "Had you given me this, and made good your promise," said she to him, laying hold of his hand, "you had never brought this misfortune upon yourself." The wounded gentleman, lifting up his languishing eyes, and knowing Claudia, "Now do I see," said he, "my fair deluded mistress, it is you that has given me the fatal blow, a punishment never deserved by the innocent, unfortunate Vincente, whose actions and desires had no other end but that of serving his Claudia."

"What! sir," answered she presently, "can you deny that you went this morning to marry Leonora, the daughter of wealthy Belvastro?"

"It is all a false report," answered he, "raised by my evil stars to spur up your jealousy to take my life, which, since I leave in your fair hands, I reckon well disposed of; and, to confirm this truth, give me your hand, and receive mine, the last pledge of love and life, and take me for your husband. It is the only satisfaction I have to give for the imaginary wrong you suspect I have committed." Claudia pressed his hand, and being pierced at once to the very heart, dropped on his bloody breast into a swoon, and Don Vincente fainted away in a deadly trance.

Roque's concern struck him senseless, and the servants ran for water to throw on the faces of the unhappy couple; by which at last Claudia came to herself again, but Don Vincente never woke from his trance, but breathed out the last remainder of his life. When Claudia perceived this, and could no longer doubt but that her dear husband was irrecoverably dead, she burst the air with her sighs, and wounded the heavens with her complaints. She tore

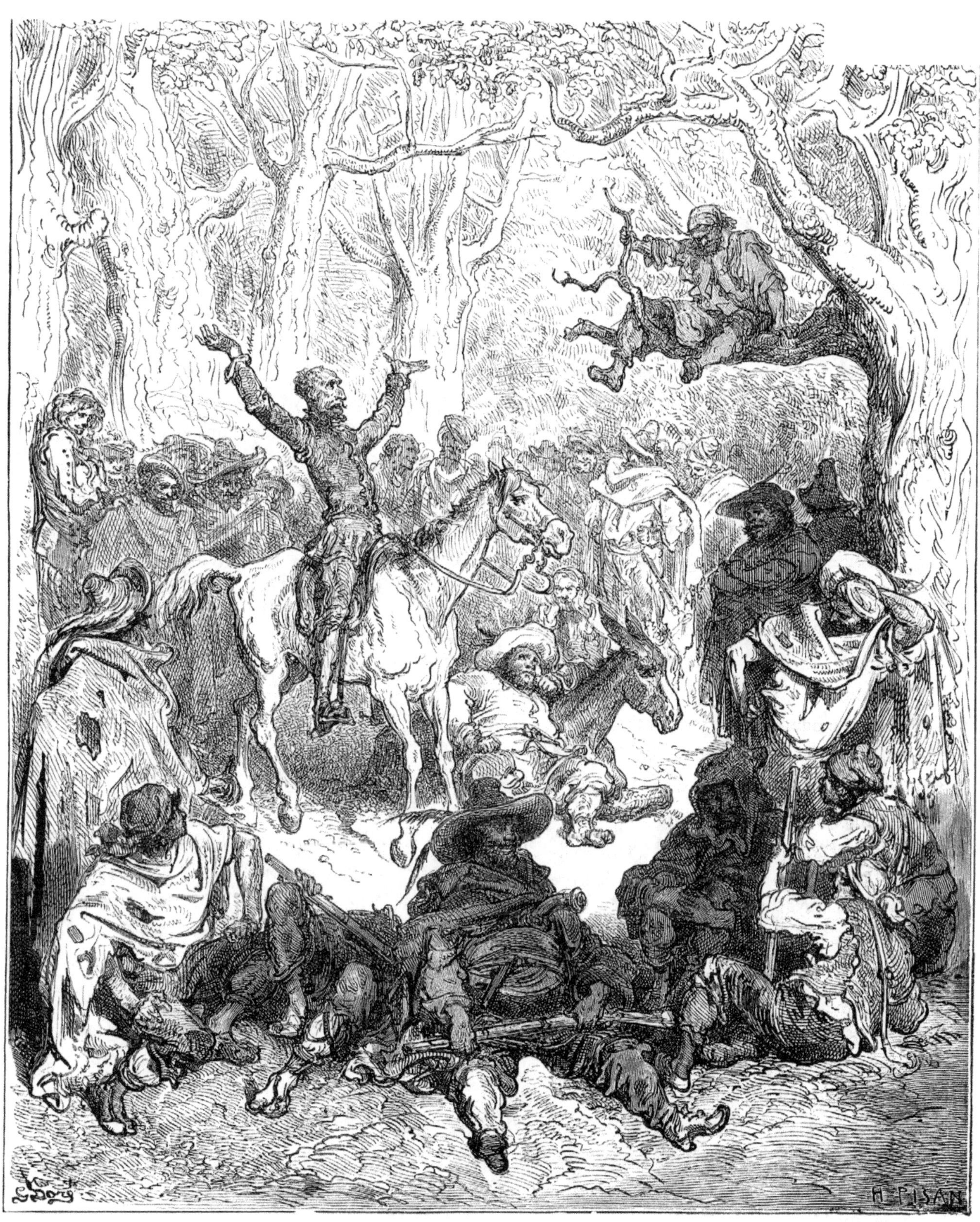

"Don Quixote, mounted on Rozinante, declaiming very copiously against their way of living."

her hair, scattered it in the wind, and with her merciless hands disfigured her face, showing all the lively marks of grief that the first sallies of despair can discover.

"Oh, cruel and inconsiderate woman!" cried she; "how easily wast thou set on this barbarous execution! Oh, maddening sting of jealousy, how desperate are thy motions, and how tragic the effects! Oh, my unfortunate husband, whose sincere love and fidelity to me have thus brought him to the cold grave!"

Thus the poor lady went on in so sad and moving a strain, that even Roque's rugged temper now melted into tears, which on all occasions before had been strangers to his eyes. The servants wept and lamented; Claudia relapsed into her swooning as fast as they found means to bring her to life again; and the whole appearance was a most moving scene of sorrow. At last Roque Guinart bid Don Vincente's servants carry his body to his father's house, which was not far distant, in order to have it buried. Claudia communicated to Roque her resolution of retiring into a monastery, where an aunt of hers was abbess, there to spend the rest of her life, wedded to a better and an immortal bridegroom. He commended her pious resolution, offering to conduct her whither she pleased, and to protect her father and family from all assaults and practices of the most dangerous enemies. Claudia made a modest excuse for declining his company, and took leave of him weeping. Don Vincente's servants carried off the dead body, and Roque returned to his men. Thus ended Claudia Jeronima's amour, brought to so lamentable a catastrophe by the prevailing force of a cruel and desperate jealousy.

Roque Guinart found his crew where he had appointed, and Don Quixote in the middle of them, mounted on Rozinante, and declaiming very copiously against their way of living, at once dangerous to their bodies and destructive to their souls; but his auditory being chiefly composed of Gascoigners, a wild, unruly kind of people, all his morality was thrown away upon them. Roque, upon his arrival, asked Sancho if they had restored him all his things.

"Everything, sir, but three night-caps, that are worth a king's ransom."

"What says the fellow?" cried one of the robbers; "here they be, and they are not worth three reals."

"As to the intrinsic value," replied Don Quixote, "they may be worth no more; but it is the merit of the person that gave them me that raises their value to that price."

Roque ordered them to be restored immediately, when one or two of their scouts that were posted on the road informed their captain that they had discovered a great company of travellers on the way to Barcelona.

"Are they such as we look for?" asked Roque, "or such as look for us?"

"Such as we look for, sir," answered the fellow.

"Away then," cried Roque, "all of you, my boys, and bring them me hither straight; let none escape."

Obeying the word of command, the squires left Don Quixote, Roque, and Sancho, to wait

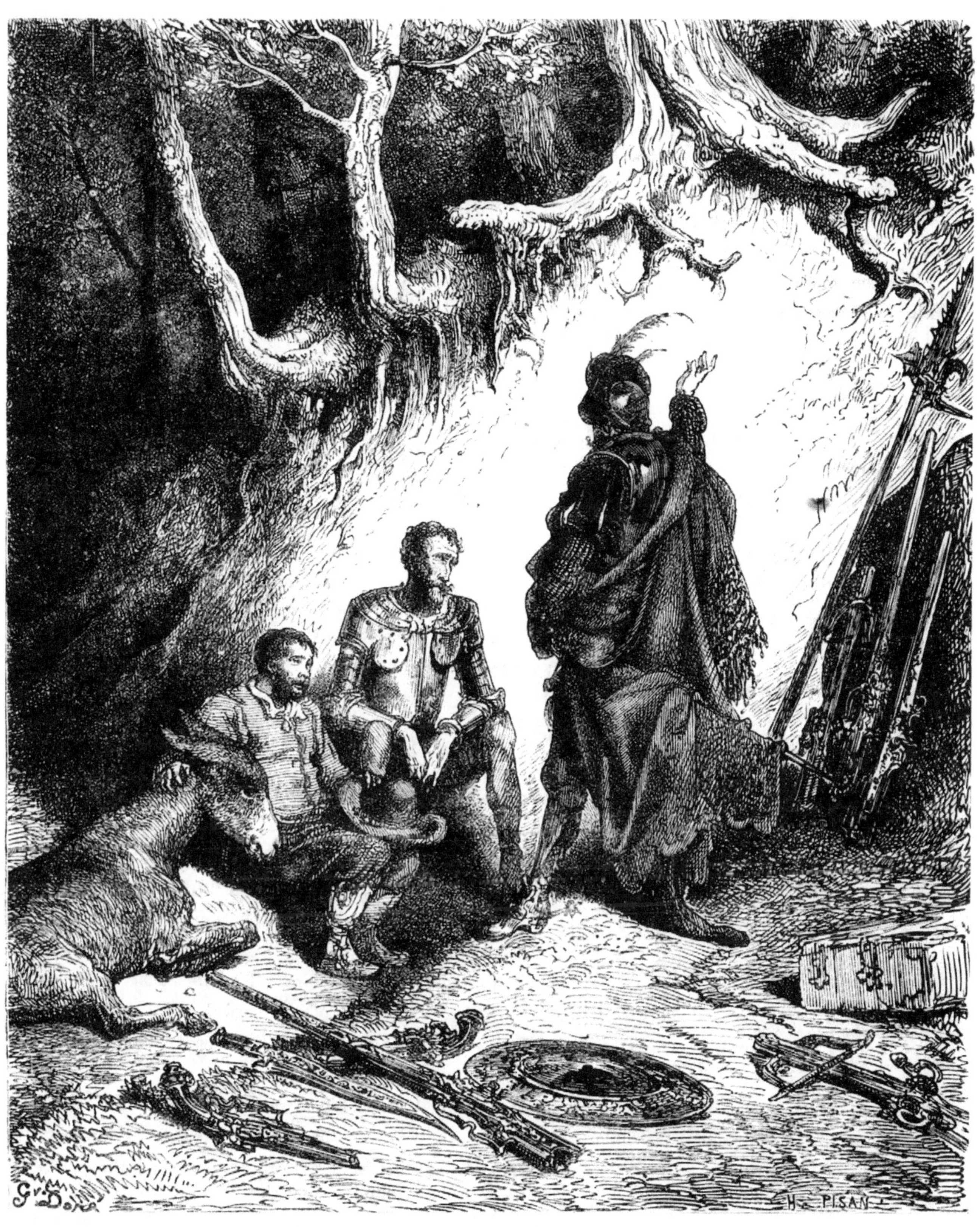

"The squires left Don Quixote, Roque, and Sancho to await their return."

their return, and in the meantime Roque entertained the knight with some remarks on his way of living.

When Roque's party had brought in their prize, they found it consisted of two gentlemen on horseback and two pilgrims on foot, and a coach full of women attended by some half-dozen servants on foot and on horseback, besides two muleteers that belonged to the two gentlemen. They were all conducted in solemn order, surrounded by the victors, both they and the vanquished being silent, and expecting the definitive sentence of the grand Roque. He first asked the gentlemen who they were, whither bound, and what money they had about them. They answered that they were both captains of Spanish foot, and their companies were at Naples; they designed to embark on the four galleys which they heard were bound for Sicily; and their whole stock amounted to two or three hundred crowns, which they thought a pretty sum of money for men of their profession, who seldom used to hoard up riches. The pilgrims, being examined in like manner, said they intended to embark for Rome, and had about threescore reals between them both. Upon examining the coach, he was informed by one of the servants that my Lady Donna Guiomar de Quinonnes, wife to a judge of Naples, with her little daughter, a chambermaid, and an old duenna, together with six other servants, had among them all about six hundred crowns.

"So then," said Roque, "we have got here in all nine hundred crowns and sixty reals. I think I have got about threescore soldiers here with me. Now, among so many men, how much will fall to each particular share? Let me see, for I am none of the best accountants. Cast it up, gentlemen."

The officers looked simply, the lady was sadly dejected, and the pilgrims were no less cast down, thinking this a very odd confiscation of their little stock. Roque held them a while in suspense, to observe their humours, which he found all very plainly to agree in that point, of being melancholy for the loss of their money. Then turning to the officers, "Do me the favour, captains," said he, "to lend me threescore crowns; and you, madam, if your ladyship pleases, shall oblige me with fourscore, to gratify these honest gentlemen of my squadron. It is our whole estate and fortune; and you know, the abbot dines on what he sings for. Therefore I hope you will excuse our demands, which will free you from any more disturbance of this nature, being secured by a pass, which I shall give you, directed to the rest of my squadrons that are posted in these parts, and who, by virtue of my order, will let you go unmolested; for I scorn to wrong a soldier, and I must not fail in my respects, madam, to the fair sex, especially to ladies of your quality."

The captains, with all the grace they could, thanked him for his great civility and liberality for so they esteemed his letting them keep their own money. The lady would have thrown herself out of the coach at his feet, but Roque would not suffer it, rather excusing the presumption of his demands, which he was forced to, in pure compliance with the necessity of his fortune. The lady then ordered her servant to pay the fourscore crowns; the officers disbursed

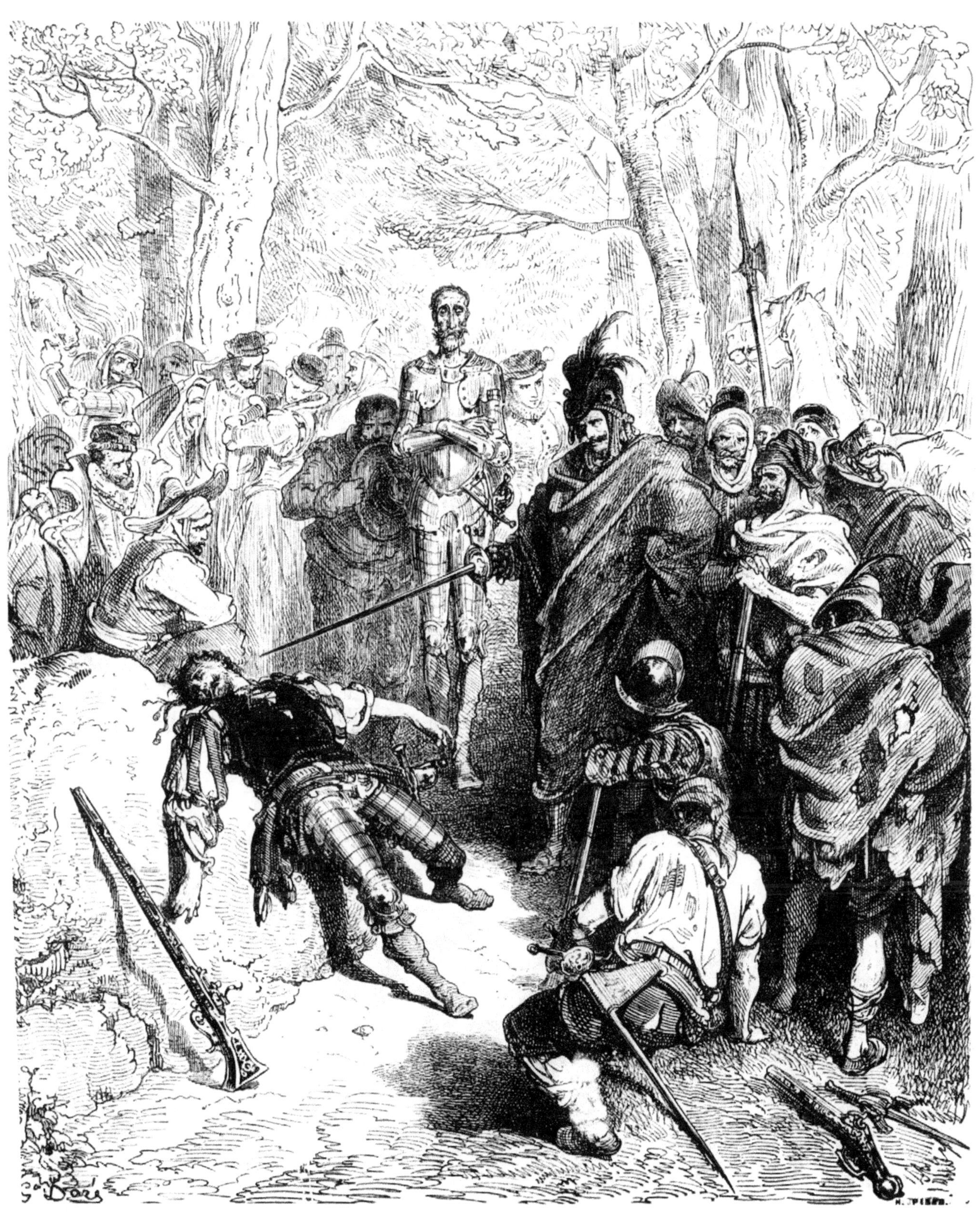

"'Thus it is I punish mutiny,' said he."

their quota, and the pilgrims made an oblation of their mite. But Roque ordering them to wait a little, and turning to his men, "Gentlemen," said he, "here are two crowns a-piece for each of you, and twenty over and above. Now let us bestow ten of them on these poor pilgrims, and the other ten on this honest squire, that he may give us a good word in his travels." So, calling for pen, ink, and paper, of which he always went provided, he wrote a passport for them, directed to the commanders of his several parties, and taking his leave, dismissed them ; all wondering at his greatness of soul, that spoke rather an Alexander than a professed highwayman. One of his men began to mutter in his Catalan language, "This captain of ours is plaguy charitable ; he would make a better friar than a pad ; come, come, if he has a mind to be so liberal, forsooth, let his own pocket, not ours, pay for it." The wretch spoke not so low but he was overheard by Roque, who, whipping out his sword, with one stroke almost cleft his skull in two. "Thus it is I punish mutiny," said he. All the rest stood motionless, and durst not mutter one word, so great was the awe they bore him.

Roque then withdrew a little, and wrote a letter to a friend in Barcelona, to let him know that the famous knight-errant, Don Quixote, of whom so many strange things were reported, was with him ; that he might be sure to find him on Midsummer-day on the great quay of that city, armed at all points, mounted on Rozinante, and his squire on an ass ; that he was a most pleasant, ingenious person, and would give great satisfaction to him and his friends, the Niarros, for which reason he gave them this notice of the Don's coming ; adding, that he should by no means let the Cadells, his enemies, partake of this pleasure, as being unworthy of it : but how was it possible to conceal from them, or anybody else, the folly and discretion of Don Quixote, and the buffoonery of Sancho Panza ? He delivered the letter to one of his men, who, changing his highway clothes to a countryman's habit, went to Barcelona, and gave it as directed.

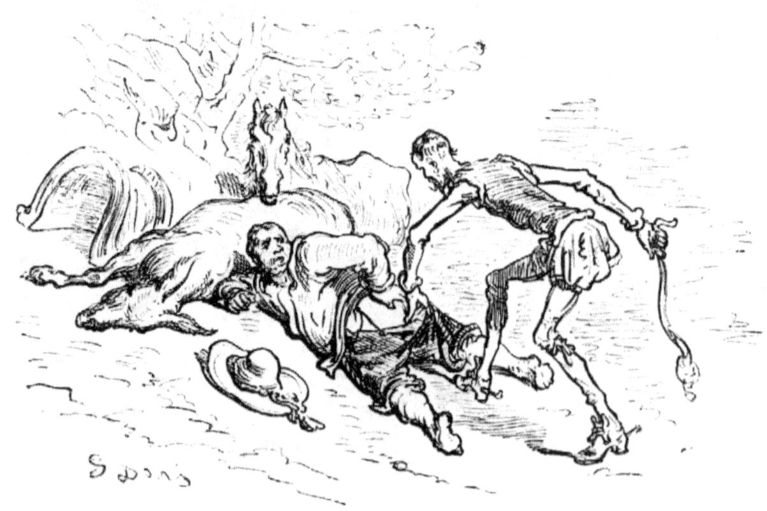

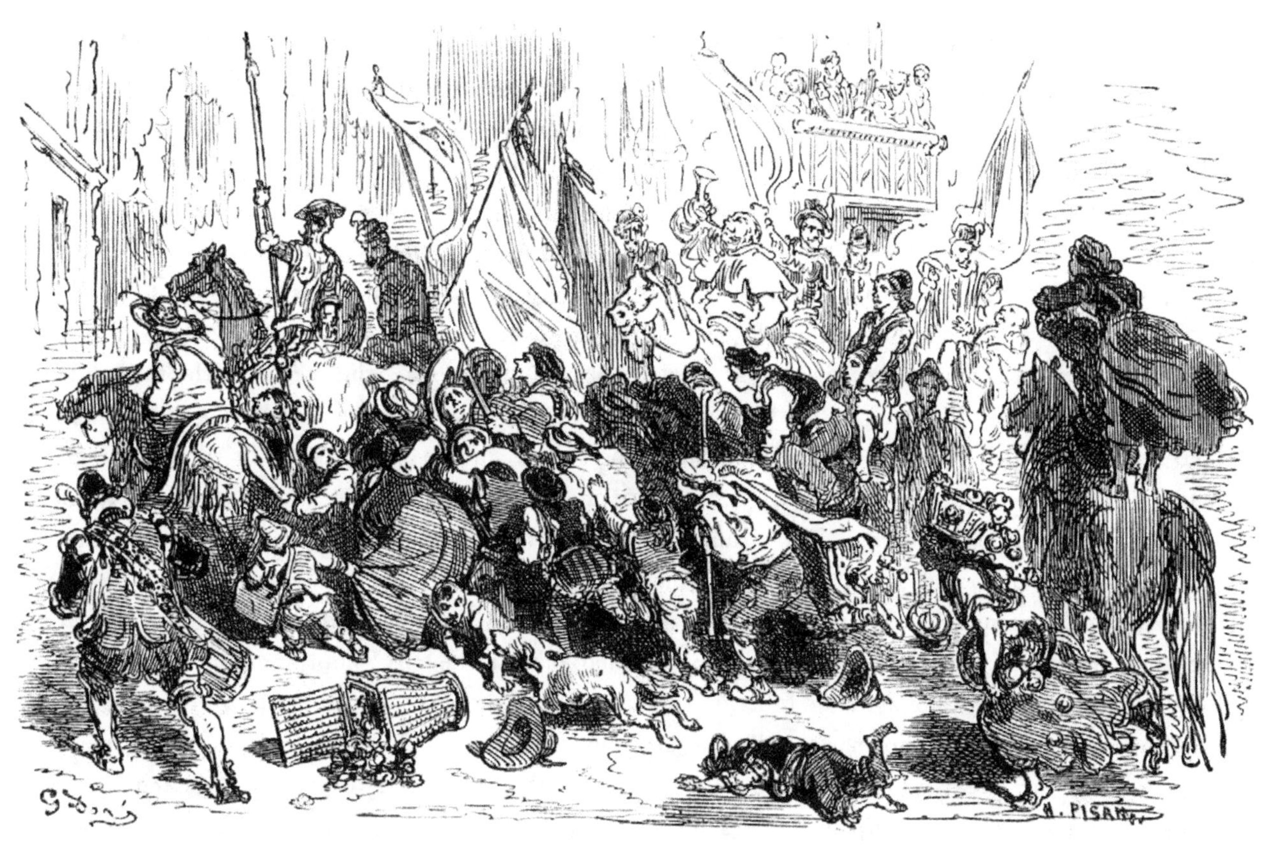

CHAPTER LXI.

DON QUIXOTE'S ENTRY INTO BARCELONA, WITH OTHER ACCIDENTS THAT HAVE LESS INGENUITY THAN TRUTH IN THEM.

DON QUIXOTE stayed three days and three nights with Roque, and had he tarried as many hundred years he might have found subject enough for admiration in that kind of life. They slept in one place, and ate in another, sometimes fearing they knew not what, then lying in wait for they knew not whom; sometimes forced to steal a nap standing, never enjoying a sound sleep; now in this side the country, then presently in another quarter; always upon the watch, spies hearkening, scouts listening, carbines presenting; though of such heavy guns they had but few, being armed generally with pistols. Roque himself slept apart from the rest, making no man privy to his lodgings; for so many were the proclamations against him from the Viceroy of Barcelona, and such were his disquiets and fears of being betrayed by some of his men for the price of his head, that he durst trust nobody—a life most miserable and uneasy.

At length, by cross-roads and bye-ways, Roque, Don Quixote, and Sancho, attended by six other squires, got to the strand of Barcelona on Midsummer Eve, at night; where Roque, having embraced Don Quixote, and presented Sancho with the ten crowns he had promised him, took his leave of them both, after many compliments on both sides. Roque returned to his company, and Don Quixote stayed there, waiting the approach of day, mounted as Roque left him. Not long after, the fair Aurora began to peep through the balconies of the east, cheering the flowery fields, while at the same time a melodious sound of hautboys and kettledrums cheered the ears, and presently was joined with jingling of morrice-bells and the trampling and cries of horsemen coming out of the city. Now Aurora ushered up the jolly sun, who looked big on the verge of the horizon, with his broad face as ample as a target. Don Quixote and Sancho, casting their looks abroad, discovered the sea, which they had never seen before. To them it made a noble and a spacious appearance, far bigger than the lake Ruydera, which they saw in La Mancha. The galleys in the port, taking in their awnings, made a pleasant sight with their flags and streamers that waved in the air, and sometimes kissed and swept the water. The trumpets, hautboys, and other warlike instruments that resounded from on board, filled the air all round with reviving and martial harmony. A while after, the galleys moving, began to join on the calm sea in a counterfeit engagement; and at the same time a vast number of gentlemen marched out of the city, nobly equipped with rich liveries, and gallantly mounted, and in like manner did their part on the land to complete the warlike entertainment. The marines discharged numerous volleys from the galleys, which were answered by the great guns from the battlements of the walls and forts about the city, and the mighty noise echoed from the galleys again by a discharge of the long pieces of ordnance on their forecastles. The sea smiled and danced, the land was gay, and the sky serene in every quarter but where the clouds of smoke dimmed it a while; fresh joy sat smiling in the looks of men, and gladness and pomp were displayed in their glory. Sancho was mightily puzzled though to discover how these huge bulky things that moved on the sea could have so many feet.

By this time the gentlemen that maintained the sports on the shore, galloping up to Don Quixote with loud acclamations, the knight was not a little astonished. One of them amongst the rest, who was the person to whom Roque had written, cried aloud, "Welcome, the mirror, the light, the north star of knight-errantry! Welcome, I say, valorous Don Quixote de la Mancha; not the counterfeit and apocryphal shown us lately in false histories, but the true, legitimate, and identic he described by Cid Hamet, the flower of historiographers!"

Don Quixote made no answer, nor did the gentleman stay for any; but wheeling about with the rest of his companions, all prancing round him in token of joy, they encompassed the knight and squire. Don Quixote, turning about to Sancho, "It seems," said he, "these gentlemen know us well. I dare engage they have read our history, and that which the Arragonian lately published."

The gentleman that spoke to the knight, returning, "Noble Don Quixote," said he, "we entreat you to come along with the company, being all your humble servants, and friends of Roque Guinart."

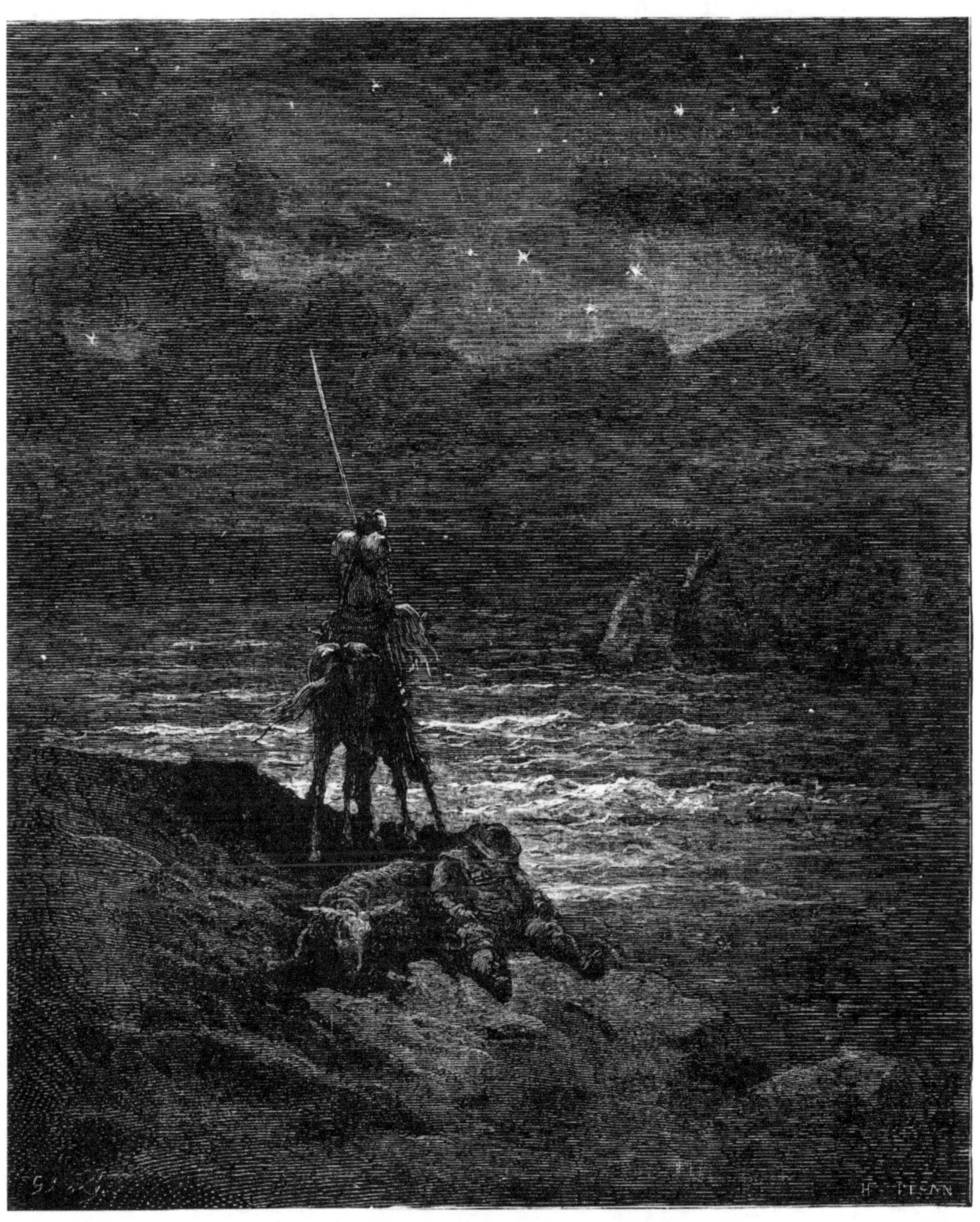

"Don Quixote stayed there, waiting the approach of day."

"Sir," answered Don Quixote, "your courtesy bears such a likeness to the great Roque's generosity, that, could civility beget civility, I should take yours for the daughter or near relation of his; I shall wait on you where you please to command, for I am wholly at your devotion."

The gentleman returned his compliment; and so all of them enclosing him in the middle of their brigade, they conducted him towards the city, drums beating, and hautboys playing before them all the way. But, as ill luck would have it, two young fellows made a shift to get through the crowd of horsemen, and one lifting up Rozinante's tail, and the other that of Dapple, they thrust a handful of briars under each of them. The poor animals, feeling such unusual spurs applied to them, clapped their tails close, which increased their pain, and began to wince and flounce, and kick so furiously, that at last they threw their riders, and laid both master and man sprawling in the street. Don Quixote, out of countenance, and nettled at his disgrace, went to disengage his horse from his new plumage, and Sancho did as much for Dapple, while the gentlemen turned to chastise the boys for their rudeness. But the young rogues were safe enough, being presently lost among a huge rabble that followed. The knight and squire then mounted again, and the music and procession went on till they arrived at their conductor's house, which, by its largeness and beauty, bespoke the owner master of a great estate, where we leave him for the present, because it is Cid Hamet's will and pleasure it should be so.

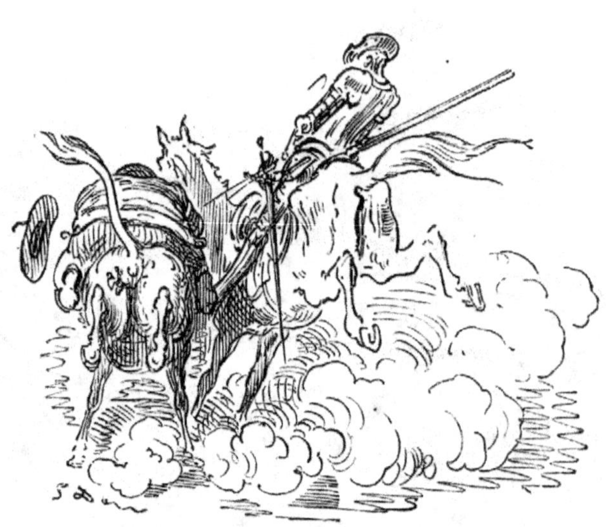

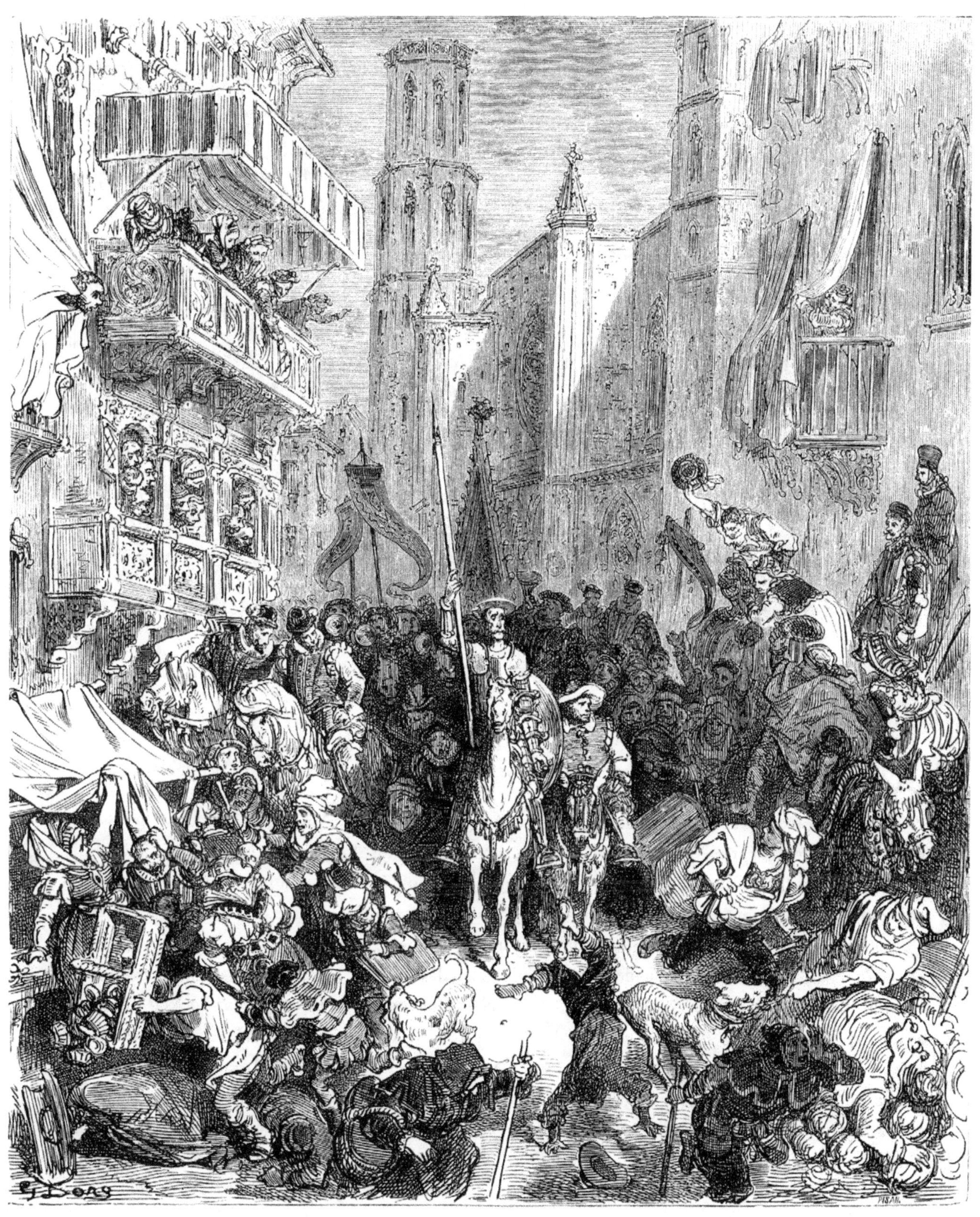

"Enclosing him in the middle of their brigade, they conducted him towards the city."

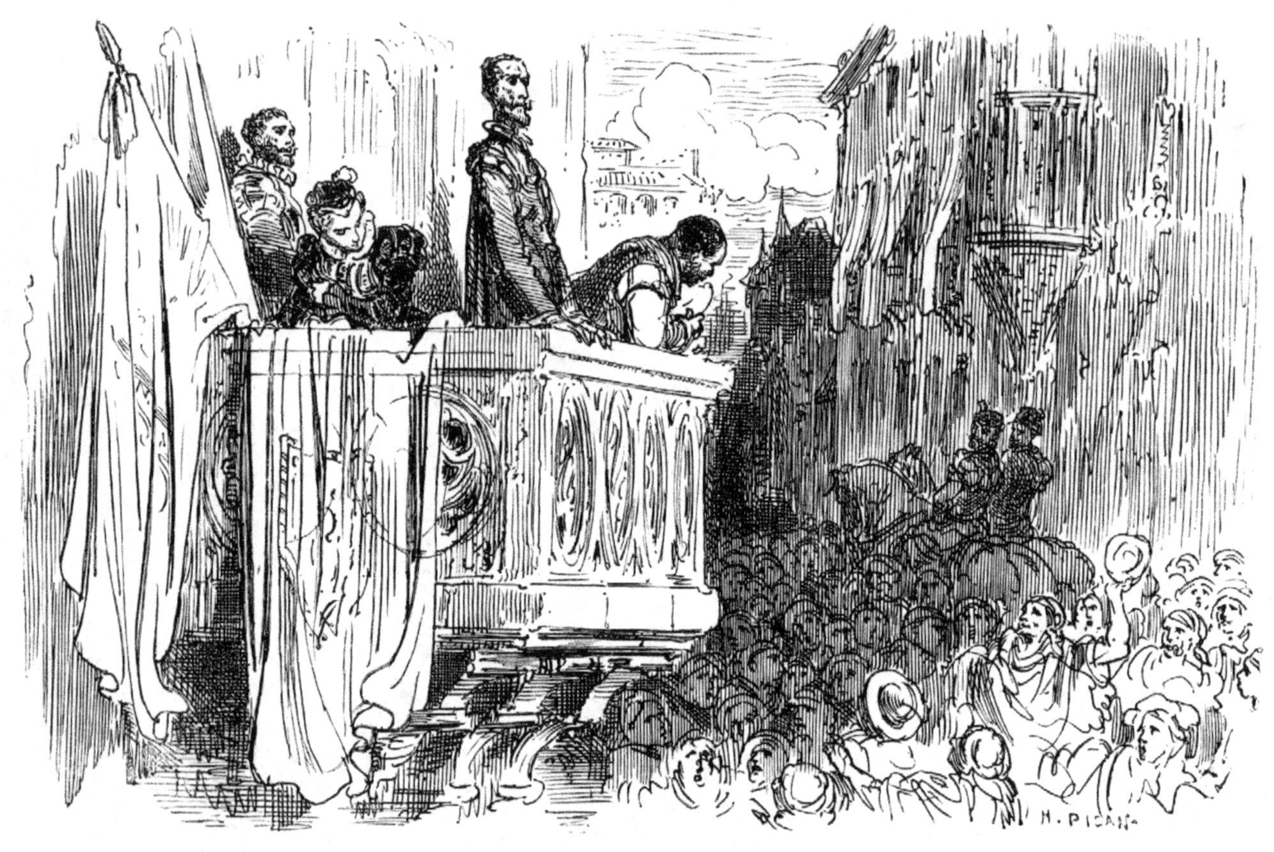

CHAPTER LXII.

THE ADVENTURE OF THE ENCHANTED HEAD, WITH OTHER IMPERTINENCES NOT TO BE OMITTED.

THE person who entertained Don Quixote was called Don Antonio Moreno, a gentleman of good parts and plentiful fortune, loving all those diversions that may innocently be obtained without prejudice to his neighbours, and not of the humour of those who would rather lose their friend than their jest. He therefore resolved to make his advantage of Don Quixote's follies without detriment to his person.

In order to this, he persuaded the knight to take off his armour, and, in his strait-laced chamois clothes (as we have already shown him), to stand in a balcony that looked into one of the principal streets of the city, where he stood exposed to the rabble that were got together, especially the boys, who gaped and stared on him as if he had been some overgrown baboon. The several brigades and cavaliers in their liveries began afresh to fetch their careers about him, as if the ceremony were rather performed in honour of Don Quixote than any solemnity of the festival. Sancho was highly pleased, fancying he had chopped upon another Camacho's wedding, or another house like that of Don Diego de Miranda, or some castle like the duke's.

Several of Don Antonio's friends dined with him that day; and all of them honouring and respecting Don Quixote as a knight-errant, they puffed up his vanity to such a degree, that he could scarce conceal the pleasure he took in their adulation. As for Sancho, he made such sport to the servants of the house, and all that heard him, that they watched every word that came from his mouth. Being all very merry at table, "Honest Sancho," said Don Antonio, "I am told you admire capons and sausages so much that you cannot be satisfied with a bellyful, and when you can eat no more, you cram the rest into your breeches against the next morning."

"No, sir, if it like you," answered Sancho, "it is all a story; I am more cleanly than greedy, I would have you to know; here is my master can tell you that many times he and I use to live for a week together upon a handful of acorns and walnuts. The truth is, I am not over nice; in such a place as this I eat what is given me; for 'a gift-horse should not be looked in the mouth.' But whosoever told you I was a greedy-gut and a sloven, has told you a fib; and, were it not for respect to the company, I would tell him more of my mind, so I would."

"Verily," said Don Quixote, "the manner of Sancho's feeding ought to be delivered to succeeding ages on brazen monuments, as a future memorial of his abstinence, and cleanliness, and an example to posterity. It is true, when he satisfies the call of hunger, he seems to do it somewhat ravenously; indeed, he swallows apace, uses his grinders very notably, and chews with both jaws at once. But, in spite of the charge of slovenliness now laid upon him, I must declare he is so nice an observer of neatness, that he ever makes a clear conveyance of his food. When he was governor, his nicety in eating was remarkable, for he would eat grapes, and even pomegranate-seeds, with the point of his fork."

"How!" cried Antonio, "has Sancho been a governor?"

"Ay, marry has he," answered Sancho, "governor of the island of Barataria! Ten days I governed, and who but I? But I was so broken of my rest all the time, that all I got by it was to learn to hate the trade of governing from the bottom of my soul; so that I made such haste to leave it, I fell into a deep hole, where I was buried alive, and should have lain till now, had not Providence pulled me out of it."

Don Quixote then related the circumstances of Sancho's government; and, the cloth being taken away, Don Antonio took the knight by the hand, and carried him into a private chamber, wherein there was no kind of furniture, but a table that seemed to be of jasper, supported by feet of the same, with a brazen head set upon it, from the breast upwards, like the effigies of one of the Roman emperors. Don Antonio having walked with Don Quixote several turns about the room, "Signor Don Quixote," said he, "being assured that we are very private, the door fast, and nobody listening, I shall communicate to you one of the most strange and wonderful adventures that ever was known, provided you treasure it up as a secret in the closest apartment of your breast."

"I shall be as secret as the grave," answered the knight, "and will clap a tombstone over your secret for further security; besides, assure yourself, Don Antonio," continued he, for by this time he had learned the gentleman's name, "you converse with a person whose ears are open to receive what his tongue never betrays; so that whatever you commit to my trust shall be buried in the depths of bottomless silence, and lie as secure as in your own breast."

"In confidence of your honour," said Don Antonio, "I doubt not to raise your astonishment, and disburden my own breast of a secret which has long lain upon my thoughts, having never found hitherto any person worthy to be made a confidant in matters to be concealed."

This cautious proceeding raised Don Quixote's curiosity strangely; after which Don Antonio led him to the table, and made him feel and examine all over the brazen head, the table, and jasper supporters. "Now, sir," said he, "know that this head was made by one of the greatest enchanters or necromancers in the world. If I am not mistaken, he was a Polander by birth, and the disciple of the celebrated Escotillo, of whom so many prodigies are related. This wonderful person was here in my house, and, by the intercession of a thousand crowns, was wrought upon to frame me this head, which has the wonderful property of answering in your ear to all questions. After long study, erecting of schemes, casting of figures, consultations with the stars, and other mathematical operations, this head was brought to the aforesaid perfection; and to-morrow (for on Fridays it never speaks) it shall give you proof of its knowledge; till when you may consider of your most puzzling and important doubts, which will have a full and satisfactory solution."

Don Quixote was amazed at this strange virtue of the head, and could hardly credit Don Antonio's account; but, considering the shortness of the time that deferred his full satisfaction in the point, he was content to suspend his opinion till next day, and only thanked the gentleman for making him so great a discovery. So out of the chamber they went; and, Don Antonio having locked the door very carefully, they returned into the room, where the rest of the company were diverted by Sancho's relating to them some of his master's adventures.

That afternoon they carried Don Quixote abroad without his armour, mounted, not on Rozinante, but on a large easy mule, with genteel furniture, and himself dressed after the city fashion, with a long coat of tawny-coloured cloth, which, with the present heat of the season, was enough to put frost itself into a sweat. They gave private orders that Sancho should be entertained within doors all that day, lest he should spoil their sport by going out. The knight being mounted, they pinned to his back, without his knowledge, a piece of parchment, with these words written in large letters, "This is Don Quixote de la Mancha." As soon as they began their walk, the sight of the parchment drew the eyes of everybody to read the inscription, so that the knight, hearing so many people repeat the words, "This is Don Quixote de la Mancha," wondered to hear himself named and known by every one that saw him. Thereupon, turning to Don Antonio, who rode by his side, "How great," said he, "is this single prerogative of knight-errantry, by which its professors are known and distinguished through all

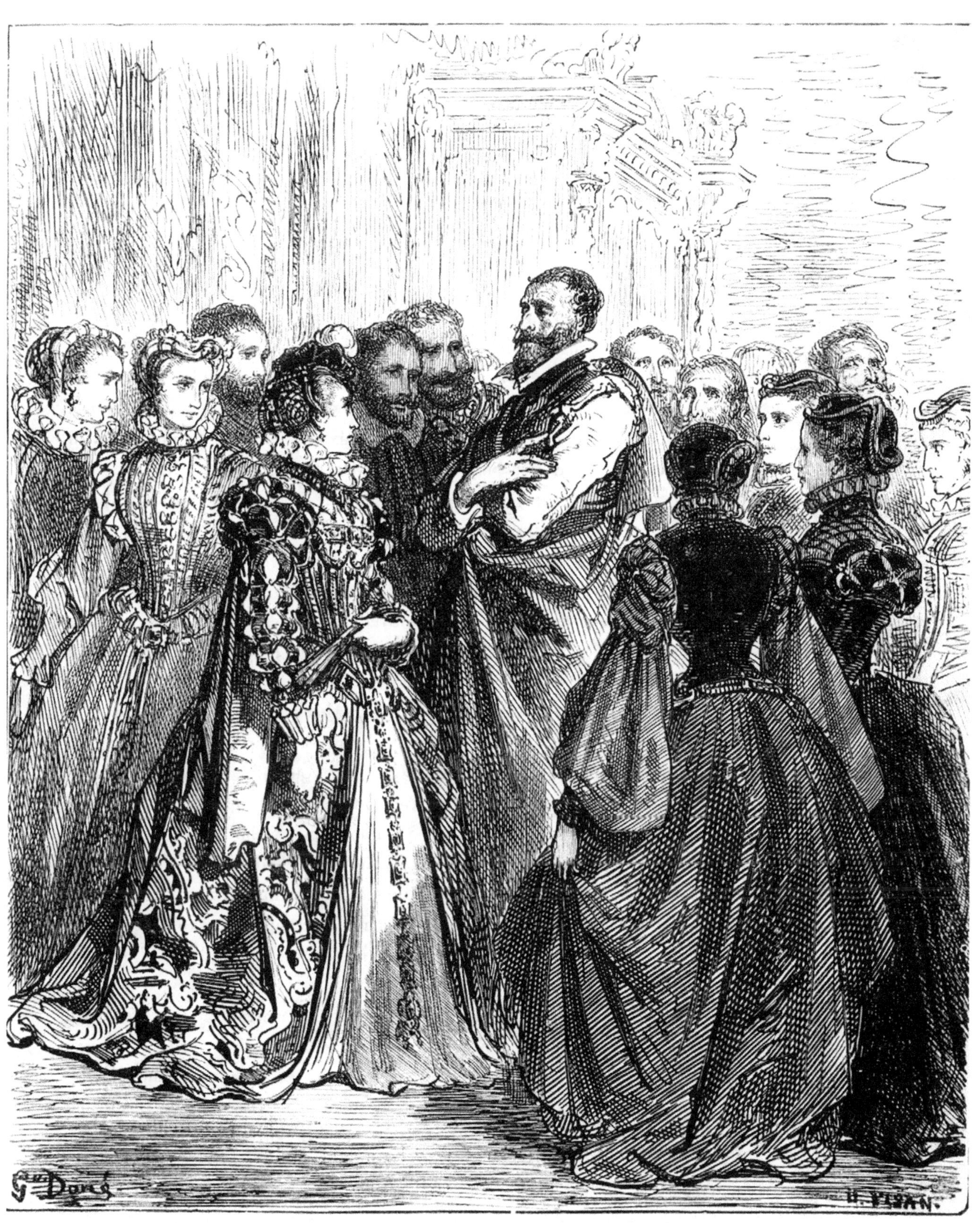

"Don Antonio's wife had invited several of her friends to a ball, to honour her guest."

the confines of the universe! Do not you hear, sir," continued he, "how the very boys in the street, who have never seen me before, know me?"

"It is very true, sir," answered Don Antonio; "like fire, that always discovers itself by its own light, so virtue has that lustre that never fails to display itself, especially that renown which is acquired by the profession of arms."

So the cavalcade continued; but presently the rabble pressed so very thick to read the inscription, that Don Antonio was forced to pull it off, under pretence of doing something else.

Upon the approach of night, they returned home, where Don Antonio's wife, a lady of quality, and every way accomplished, had invited several of her friends to a ball, to honour her guest, and share in the diversion his extravagances afforded. After a noble supper, the dancing began about ten o'clock at night. Among others were two ladies of an airy, waggish disposition, who made their court chiefly to Don Quixote, and plied him so with dancing, one after another, that they tired not only his body, but his very soul. But the best was to see what an unaccountable figure the grave Don made as he hopped and stalked about, a long, sway-backed, starved-looked, thin-flanked, two-legged thing, wainscot-complexioned, stuck up in his close doublet. At last, being almost teased to death, "*Fugite, partes adversæ,*" cried he aloud, "and avaunt, temptation! Pray, ladies, play your pranks with somebody else; leave me to the enjoyment of my own thoughts, which are employed and taken up with the peerless Dulcinea del Toboso, the sole queen of my affections;" and, so saying, he sat himself down on the ground, in the midst of the hall, to rest his wearied bones.

Don Antonio gave order that he should be taken up and carried to bed; and the first who was ready to lend a helping hand was Sancho, saying, while lifting him up, "By our lady, sir master of mine, you have shook your heels most facetiously! Do you think we, who are stout and valiant, must be caperers, and that every knight-errant must be a snapper of castenets? If you do, you are woundily deceived, let me tell you. I know those who would sooner cut a giant's wind-pipe than a caper. Had you been for the shoe-jig, I had been your man, for I slap it away like any jer-falcon; but, as for regular dancing, I cannot work a stitch at it." This made diversion for the company, till Sancho led out his master in order to put him to bed, where he left him covered over head and ears, that he might sweat out the cold he had caught by dancing.

The next day, Don Antonio, resolving to make his intended experiment on the enchanted head, conducted Don Quixote into the room where it stood, together with Sancho, a couple of his friends, and the two ladies that had so teased the knight at the ball; and having carefully locked the door, and enjoined them secrecy, he told them the virtue of the head, and that this was the first time he ever made proof of it; and, except his two friends, nobody knew the trick of the enchantment, and, had not they been told of it before, they had been drawn into the same error with the rest; for the contrivance of the machine was so artful, and so cunningly managed, that it was impossible to discover the cheat Don Antonio himself

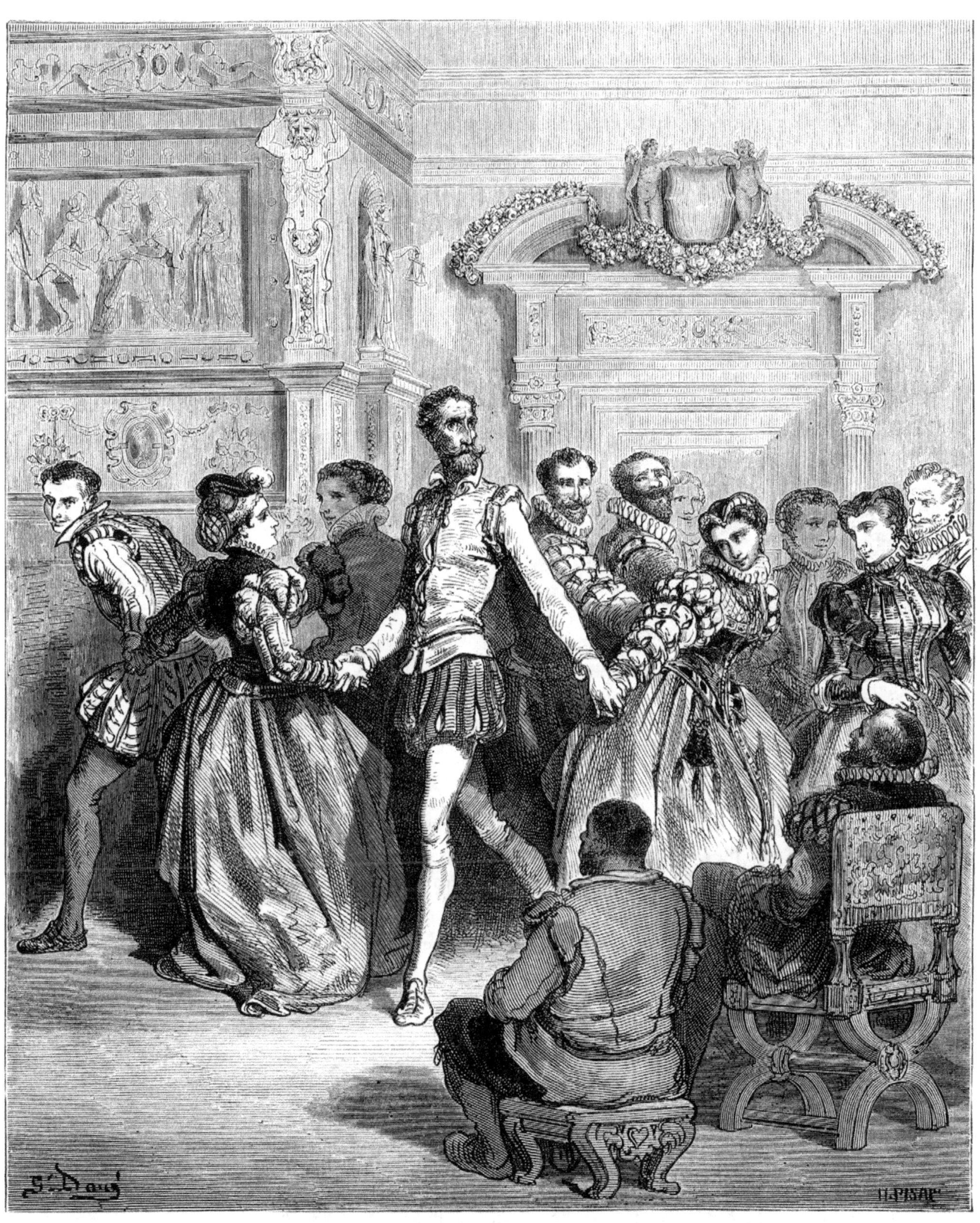

"Two ladies made their court chiefly to Don Quixote."

was the first that made his application to the ear of the head, close to which, speaking in a voice just loud enough to be heard by the company, "Tell me, oh head," said he, "by that mysterious virtue wherewith thou art endued, what are my thoughts at present?"

The head, in a distinct and intelligible voice, though without moving the lips, answered, "I am no judge of thoughts."

They were all astonished at the voice, being sensible nobody was in the room to answer. "How many of us are there in the room?" said Don Antonio again.

The voice answered, in the same key, "Thou, and thy wife, two of thy friends, and two of hers, a famous knight, called Don Quixote de la Mancha, and his squire, Sancho Panza by name."

Now their astonishment was greater than before; now they wondered, indeed, and the hair of some of them stood on end with amazement. "It is enough," said Don Antonio, stepping aside from the head; "I am convinced it was no impostor sold thee to me, sage head, discoursing head, oraculous, miraculous head! Now, let somebody else try their fortune."

As women are generally most curious and inquisitive, one of the dancing ladies, venturing up to it, "Tell me, head," said she, "what shall I do to be truly beautiful?"

"Be honest," answered the head.

"I have done," replied the lady.

Her companion then came on, and, with the same curiosity, "I would know," said she, "whether my husband loves me or no."

The head answered, "Observe his usage, and that will tell thee."

"Truly," said the married lady to herself as she withdrew, "that question was needless; for, indeed, a man's actions are the surest tokens of the dispositions of his mind."

Next came up one of Don Antonio's friends, and asked, "Who am I?"

The answer was, "Thou knowest."

"That is from the question," replied the gentleman; "I would have thee tell me whether thou knowest me."

"I do," answered the head; "thou art Don Pedro Norris."

"It is enough, oh head;" said the gentleman, "thou hast convinced me that thou knowest all things." So, making room for somebody else, his friend advanced, and asked the head what his eldest son and heir desired.

"I have already told thee," said the head, "that I was no judge of thoughts; however, I will tell thee that what thy heir desires is to bury thee."

"It is so," replied the gentleman; "what I see with my eye I mark with my finger: I know enough."

Don Antonio's lady asked the next question. "I do not well know what to ask thee," said she to the head; "only tell me whether I shall long enjoy my dear husband."

"Thou shalt," answered the head; "for his healthy constitution and temperance promise length of days, while those who live too fast are not like to live long."

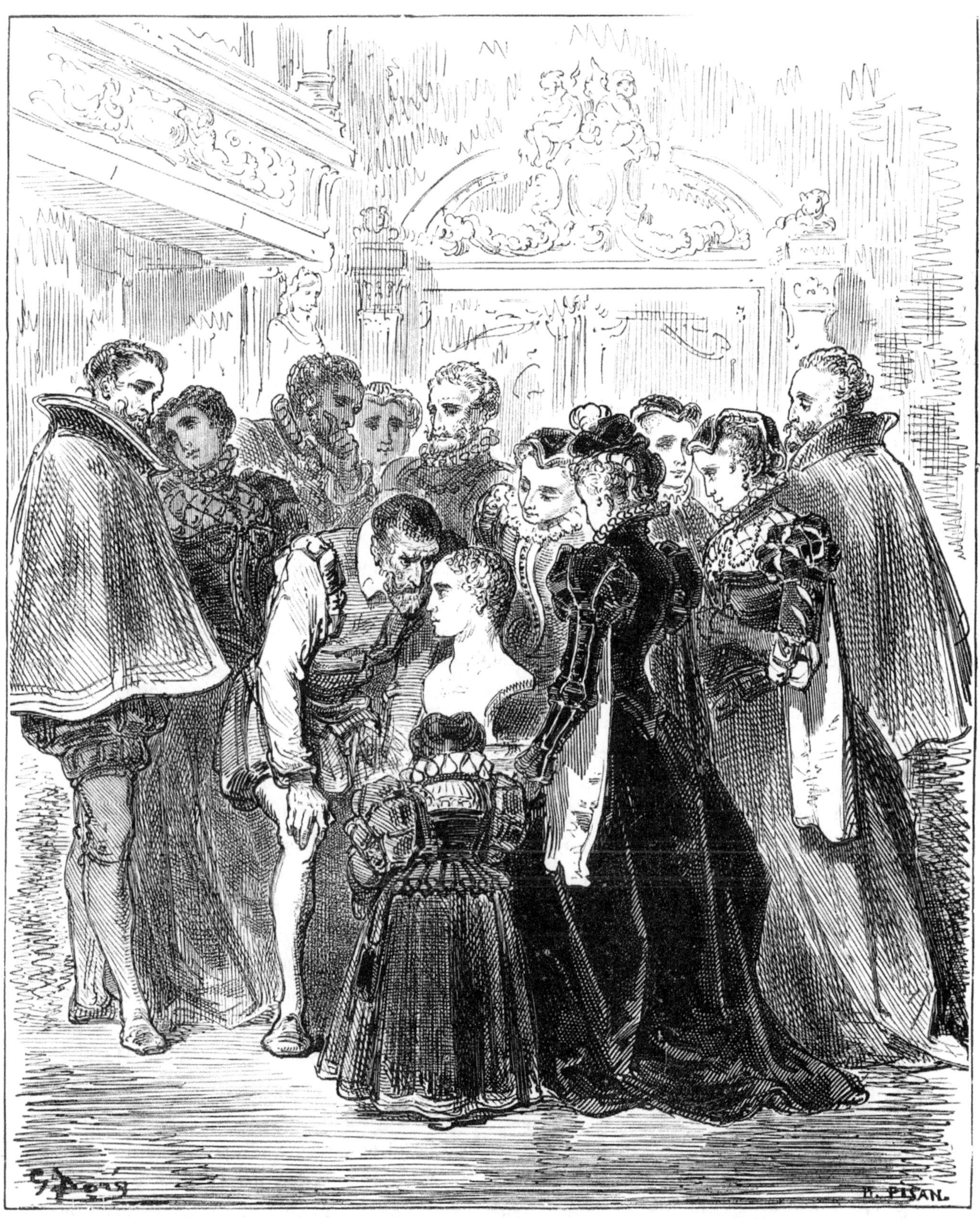

"'Tell me, thou oracle,' said he, 'was what I reported of my adventures in the cave of Montesinos a dream or reality?'"

Y Y

Next came Don Quixote. "Tell me, thou oracle," said he, "was what I reported of my adventures in the cave of Montesinos a dream or reality? will Sancho, my squire, fulfil his promise, and scourge himself effectually? and shall Dulcinea be disenchanted?"

"As for the adventures in the cave," answered the head, "there is much to be said—they have something of both; Sancho's whipping shall go on but leisurely; however, Dulcinea shall at last be really freed from enchantment."

"That is all I desire to know," said Don Quixote; "for the whole stress of my good fortune depends on Dulcinea's disenchantment."

Then Sancho made the last application. "If it please you, Mr. Head," quoth he, "shall I chance to have another government? shall I ever get clear of this starving squire-erranting? and shall I ever see my own fireside again?"

The head answered, "Thou shalt be a governor in thine own house; if thou goest home, thou mayest see thy own fireside again; and if thou leavest off thy service, thou shalt get clear of thy squireship."

"Bless me!" cried Sancho, "that is a very good one, I vow! A horse-head might have told all this; I could have prophesied thus much myself."

"How now, brute!" said Don Quixote; "what answers wouldst thou have but what are pertinent to thy questions?"

"Nay," quoth Sancho, "since you will have it so, it shall be so; I only wish Mr. Head would have told me a little more concerning the matter."

Thus the questions proposed and the answers returned were brought to a period; but the amazement continued among all the company, except Don Antonio's two friends, who understood the mystery, which Benengeli is resolved now to discover, that the world should be no longer amazed with an erroneous opinion of any magic or witchcraft operating in the head. He therefore tells you that Don Antonio Moreno, to divert himself and surprise the ignorant, had this made, in imitation of such another device which he had seen contrived by a statuary at Madrid.

The manner of it was thus: the table, and the frame on which it stood, the feet of which resembled four eagles' claws, were of wood, painted and varnished like jasper. The head, which looked like the bust of a Roman emperor, and of a brass colour, was all hollow, and so were the feet of the table, which answered exactly to the neck and breast of the head, the whole so artificially fixed that it seemed to be all of a piece; through this cavity ran a tin pipe, conveyed into it by a passage through the ceiling of the room under the table. He that was to answer set his mouth to the end of the pipe in the chamber underneath, and, by the hollowness of the trunk, received their questions and delivered his answers in clear and articulate words, so that the imposture could scarcely be discovered. The oracle was managed by a young, ingenious gentleman, Don Antonio's nephew, who, having his instructions beforehand from his uncle, was able to answer readily and directly to the first questions, and, by conjectures or evasions, make a return handsomely to the rest, with the help of his ingenuity.

Cid Hamet informs us further, that, during ten or twelve days after this, the wonderful machine continued in mighty repute; but, at last, the noise of Don Antonio's having an enchanted head in his house, that gave answers to all questions, began to fly about the city; and, as he feared this would reach the ears of the watchful sentinels of our faith, he thought fit to give an account of the whole matter to the reverend inquisitors, who ordered him to break it to pieces, lest it should give occasion of scandal among the ignorant vulgar. But still the head passed for an oracle and a piece of enchantment with Don Quixote and Sancho; though, the truth is, the knight was much better satisfied in the matter than the squire.

The gentry of the city, in complaisance to Don Antonio, and for Don Quixote's more splendid entertainment, or rather, to make his madness a more public diversion, appointed a running at the ring about six days after; but this was broken off upon an occasion that afterwards happened.

Don Quixote had a mind to take a turn in the city on foot, that he might avoid the crowd of boys that followed him when he rode. He went out with Sancho, and two of Don Antonio's servants, who attended him by their master's order; and, passing through a certain street, Don Quixote looked up, and spied, written over a door, in great letters, these words, "Here is a printing-house." This discovery pleased the knight extremely, having now an opportunity of seeing a printing-press—a thing he had never seen before—and therefore, to satisfy his curiosity, in he went, with all his train. There he saw some working off the sheets; others correcting the formes; some in one place, picking of letters out of the cases; in another, some looking over a proof,—in short, all the variety that is to be seen in great printing-houses. He went from one workman to another, and was very inquisitive to know what everybody had in hand, and they were not backward to satisfy his curiosity. At length, coming to one of the compositors, and asking him what he was about, "Sir," said the printer, "this gentleman here"—showing a likely sort of a man, something grave, and not young—"has translated a book out of Italian into Spanish, and I am setting some of it here for the press."

"What is the name of it, pray?" said Don Quixote.

"Sir," answered the author, "the title of it in Italian is "Le Bagatele.''

"And pray, sir," asked Don Quixote, "what is the meaning of that word in Spanish?

"Sir," answered the gentleman, "'Le Bagatele' is as much as to say 'Trifles;' but though the title promises so little, yet the contents are matters of importance."

"I am a little conversant in the Italian," said the knight, "and value myself upon singing some stanzas of Ariosto; therefore, sir, without any offence, and not doubting of your skill, but merely to satisfy my curiosity, pray, tell me, have you ever met with such a word as *pignata* in Italian?"

"Yes, very often, sir," answered the author.

"And how do you render it, pray, sir?" said Don Quixote.

"How should I render it, sir," replied the translator, "but by the word 'porridge-pot?'"

"Bless me!" cried Don Quixote, "you are master of the Italian idiom. I dare hold a good wager that where the Italian says *piace* you translate it 'please;' where it says *piu* you render it 'more;' *su*, 'above;' and *giu*, 'beneath.'"

"Most certainly, sir," answered the other, "for such are their proper significations."

"What rare parts," said Don Quixote, "are lost to mankind, for want of their being exerted and known! I dare swear, sir, that the world is backward in encouraging your merit. But it is the fate of all ingenious men. How many of them are cramped up and discountenanced by a narrow fortune! and how many, in spite of the most laborious industry, discouraged! Though, by the way, sir, I think this kind of version from one language to another, except it be from the noblest of tongues, the Greek and Latin, is like viewing a piece of Flemish tapestry on the wrong side, where, though the figures are distinguishable, yet there are so many ends and threads, that the beauty and exactness of the work is obscured, and not so advantageously discerned as on the right side of the hangings. Neither can this barren employment of translating out of easy languages show either wit or mastery of style, no more than copying a piece of writing by a precedent; though, still, the business of translating wants not its commendations, since men very often may be worse employed. As a further proof of its merits, we have Doctor Christoval de Figuero's translation of Pastor Fido, and Don Juan de Xaurigui's Aminta—pieces so excellently well done, that they have made them purely their own, and left the reader in doubt which was the translation and which the original. But tell me, pray, sir, do you print your book at your own charge, or have you sold the copy to a bookseller?"

"Why, truly, sir," answered the translator, "I publish it upon my own account, and I hope to clear at least a thousand crowns by this first edition: for I design to print off two thousand books, and they will go off at six reals a-piece in a trice."

"I am afraid you will come short of your reckoning," said Don Quixote; "it is a sign you are still a stranger to the tricks of these booksellers and printers, and the juggling that is among them. I dare engage you will find two thousand books lie heavy upon your hands, especially if the piece be somewhat tedious, and wants spirit."

"What! sir," replied the author, "would you have me sell the profit of my labour to a bookseller for three maravedis a sheet? for that is the most they will bid, nay, and expect, too, I should thank them for the offer. No, no, sir; I print not my works to get fame in the world; my name is up already: profit, sir, is my end, and without it what signifies reputation?"

"Well, sir, go on and prosper," said Don Quixote; and with that, moving to another part of the room, he saw a man correcting a sheet of a book called "The Light of the Soul." "Ay, now this is something," cried the knight; "these are the books that ought to be printed, though there are a great many of that kind; for the number of sinners is prodigious in this age, and there is need of an infinite quantity of lights for so many dark souls as we have among us." Then passing on, and inquiring the title of a book of which another man was correcting a sheet, they told him it was the second part of that ingenious gentleman, "Don Quixote de la Mancha," written by a certain person, a native of Tordesillas. "I have heard of that book before," said Don Quixote, "and really thought it had been burnt, and reduced to ashes, for a foolish, impertinent libel; but all in good time. 'Execution-day will come at last.' For made stories are only so far good and agreeable as they are profitable and bear the resemblance of truth, and true history the more valuable the farther it keeps from the fabulous." And, so saying, he flung out of the printing-house in a huff.

That very day Don Antonio would needs show Don Quixote the galleys in the road, much to Sancho's satisfaction, because he had never seen any in his life. Don Antonio, therefore, gave notice to the commander of the galleys that in the afternoon he would bring his guest, Don Quixote de la Mancha, to see them; the commander and all the people of the town being by this time no stranger to the knight's character. But what happened in the galleys must be the subject of the next chapter.

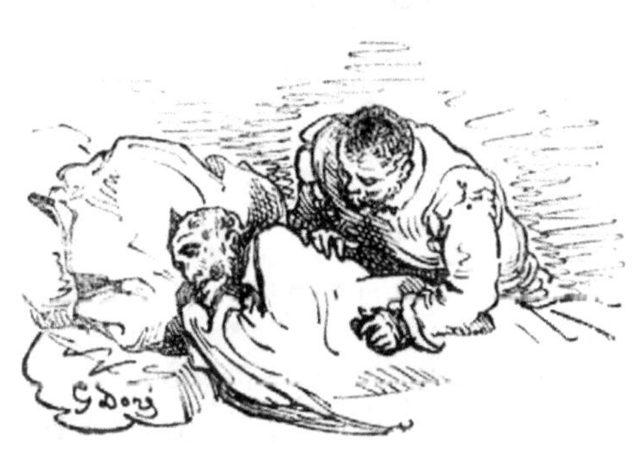

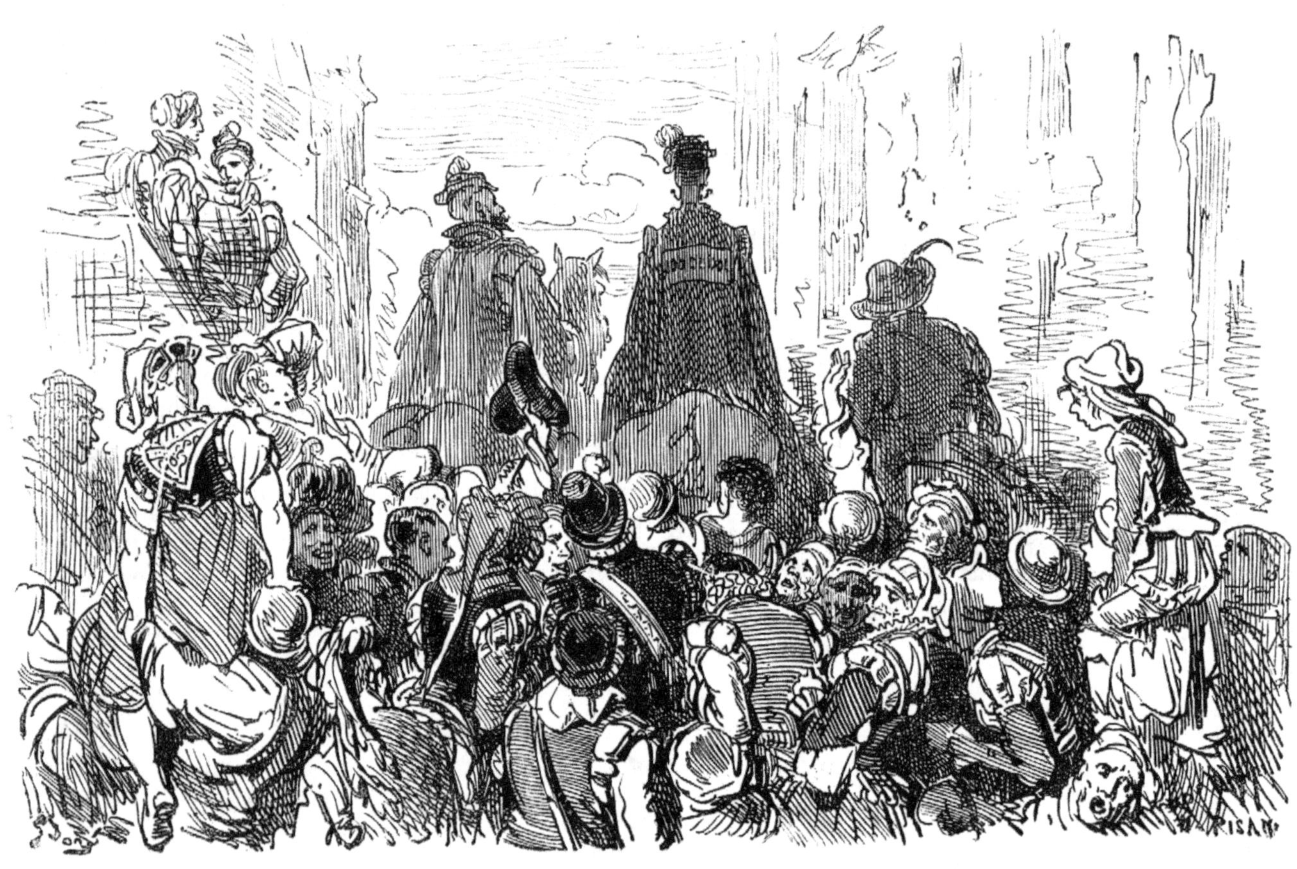

CHAPTER LXIII.

OF SANCHO'S MISFORTUNES ON BOARD THE GALLEYS, WITH THE STRANGE ADVENTURE OF THE BEAUTIFUL MORISCA (MOORISH) LADY.

MANY and serious were Don Quixote's reflections on the answer of the enchanted head, though none hit on the deceit, but centred all in the promise of Dulcinea's disenchantment; and, expecting it would speedily be effected, he rested joyfully satisfied. As for Sancho, though he hated the trouble of being a governor, yet still he had an itching ambition to rule, to be obeyed, and appear great; for even fools love authority.

In short, that afternoon Don Antonio, his two friends, Don Quixote, and Sancho set out for the galleys. The commander, being advertised of their coming, upon their appearance on the quay, ordered all the galleys to strike sail; the music played, and a pinnace, spread with rich carpets and crimson velvet cushions, was presently hoisted out, and sent to fetch them on board. As soon as Don Quixote set his foot into it, the admiral's galley discharged her forecastle piece, and the rest of the galleys did the like. When Don Quixote got over the gunnel of the galley, on the starboard side, the whole crew of slaves, according to their custom of saluting persons of quality, welcomed him with three hu, hu, huz, or huzzas. The general (for so we must call him), by birth a Valencian, and a man of quality, gave him his hand, and embraced him. "This day," said he, "will I mark as one of the happiest I can expect to see in all my life, since I have the honour now to behold Signor Don Quixote de la Mancha; this day, I say, that sets before my eyes the summary of wandering chivalry collected in one person." Don Quixote returned his compliment with no less civility, and appeared overjoyed to see himself so treated like a grandee. Presently they all went into the state-room, which was handsomely adorned, and there they took their places. The boatswain went to the forecastle, and with his whistle or call gave the sign to the slaves to strip, which was obeyed in a moment. Sancho was scared to see so many fellows in their naked skins, but most of all when he saw them hoist up the sails so incredibly fast, as he thought could never have been done but by so many conjurers. He had placed himself a-midship, next the aftmost rower on the starboard side, who, being instructed what to do, caught hold of him, and, giving him a hoist, handed him to the next man, who tossed him to a third; and so the whole crew of slaves, beginning on the starboard side, made him fly so fast from bench to bench, that poor Sancho lost the very sight of his eyes. Nor did the slaves give over bandying him about till they had handed him in the same manner over all the larboard side; and then they set him down where they had taken him up, but strangely disordered, out of breath, in a cold sweat, and not truly sensible what it was that had happened to him.

Don Quixote, seeing his squire fly at this rate without wings, asked the general if that were a ceremony used to all strangers aboard the galleys; for, if it were, he must let him know that, as he did not design to take up his residence there, he did not like such entertainment, and vowed that, if any of them came to lay hold on him to toss him at that rate, he would spurn their souls out of their bodies; and with this, starting up, he lays his hand on his sword.

At the same time they lowered their sails, and, with a dreadful noise, let down the mainyard, which so frightened Sancho, who thought the sky was coming off its hinges, and falling upon him, that he ducked, and thrust his head between his legs for fear. Don Quixote was a little out of sorts, too; he began to shiver, and shrug up his shoulders, and changed colour. The slaves hoisted the mainyard again with the same force and noise that they had lowered it withal; but all this with such silence on their parts, as if they had neither voice nor breath. The boatswain then gave the word to weigh anchor, and, leaping a-top of the forecastle among the crew, with his whip, he began to dust and fly-flap their shoulders, and, by little and little, to put off to sea.

When Sancho saw so many coloured feet moving at once (for he took the oars to be such), "Bless my heart!" quoth he, "here is enchantment in good earnest; all our adventures and witchcrafts have been nothing to this. What have these poor wretches done that their hides must be curried at this rate? And how dares this plaguy fellow go whistling about here by himself, and maul thus so many people?"

Don Quixote, observing how earnestly Sancho looked on these passages, "Ah! dear

Sancho," said he, "what an easy matter now were it for you to strip to the waist, and clap yourself among these gentlemen, and so complete Dulcinea's disenchantment; among so many companions in affliction, you would not be so sensible of the smart; and, besides, the sage Merlin, perhaps, might take every one of these lashes, being so well laid on, for ten of those which you must certainly one day inflict on yourself."

The general of the galleys was going to ask what he meant by these lashes and Dulcinea's disenchantment, when a mariner cried out, "They make signs to us from Monjoui that there is a vessel standing under the shore to the westward."

With that the general, leaping upon the coursey, cried, "Pull away, my hearts! let her not escape us; this brigantine is an Algerine, I warrant her." Presently the three other galleys came up with the admiral to receive orders, and he commanded two of them to stand out to sea, while he, with the other, would keep along the shore, that so they might be sure of their prize.

The rowers tugged so hard that the galleys scudded away like lightning, and those that stood to sea discovered, about two miles off, a vessel with fourteen or fifteen oars, which, upon sight of the galleys, made the best of her way off, hoping by her lightness to make her escape; but all in vain, for the admiral's galley, being one of the swiftest vessels in those seas, gained so much way upon her that the master of the brigantine, seeing his danger, was willing the crew should quit their oars, and yield, for fear of exasperating their general. But fate ordered it otherwise; for, upon the admiral's coming up with the brigantine so near as to hail her and bid them strike, two Toraquis, that is, two drunken Turks, among twelve others that were on board the vessel, discharged a couple of muskets, and killed two soldiers that were upon the prow of the galley. The general, seeing this, vowed he would not leave a man of them alive; and coming up with great fury to grapple with her, she slipped away under the oars of the galley. The galley ran ahead a good way, and the little vessel, finding herself clear for the present, though without hopes to get off, crowded all the sail she could, and, with oars and sails, began to make the best of its way, while the galley tacked about. But all their diligence did not do them so much good as their presumption did them harm; for the admiral coming up with her, after a short chase, clapped his oars in the vessel, and so took her, and every man in her alive.

By this time the other galleys were come up, and all four returned with their prize into the harbour, where great numbers of people stood waiting, to know what prize they had taken. The general came to an anchor near the land; and, perceiving the viceroy was on shore, he manned his pinnace to fetch him on board, and gave orders to lower the main-yard, to hang up the master of the brigantine, with the rest of the crew, which consisted of about six-and-thirty persons, all proper lusty fellows, and most of them Turkish musketeers. The general asked who commanded the vessel; whereupon one of the prisoners, who was afterwards known to be a Spaniard, and a renegado, answered him in Spanish. "This was our master, my lord," said he, showing him a young man, not twenty years of age, and one of the handsomest persons that could be imagined.

"You inconsiderate dog!" said the general, "what made you kill my men, when you saw it was not possible for you to escape? Is this the respect due to an admiral? Do not you know that rashness is no courage? While there is any hope, we are allowed to be bold, but not to be desperate."

The master was offering to reply, but the general could not stay to hear his answer, being obliged to go and entertain the viceroy, who was just come on board with his retinue, and others of the town.

"You have had a lucky chase, my lord," said the viceroy; "what have you got?"

"Your excellency shall see presently," answered the general; "I will show them you immediately hanging at the main-yard arm."

"How so?" replied the viceroy.

"Because," said he, "they have killed, contrary to all law of arms, reason, and custom of the sea, two of the best soldiers I had on board; for which I am sworn to hang them every mother's son, especially this young rogue, the master." Saying this, he showed him a person with his hands already bound, and the halter about his neck, expecting nothing but death.

His youth, beauty, and resignation began to plead much in his behalf with the viceroy, and made him inclinable to save him. "Tell me, captain," said he, "art thou born a Turk or a Moor, or art thou a renegado?"

"None of all these," answered the youth, in good Spanish.

"What then?" said the viceroy.

"A Christian woman," replied the youth; "a woman, and a Christian, though in these clothes, and in such a post; but it is a thing rather to be wondered at than believed. I humbly beseech you, my lords," continued the youth, "to defer my execution till I give you the history of my life; and I can assure you, the delay of your revenge will be but short."

This request was urged so piteously, that nobody could deny it; whereupon the general bade him proceed, assuring him, nevertheless, that there were no hopes of pardon for an offence so great as that of which he was guilty. Then the youth began:—

"I am one of that unhappy and imprudent nation whose miseries are fresh in your memories. My parents being of the Morisco race, the current of their misfortunes, with the obstinacy of two uncles, hurried me out of Spain into Barbary. In vain I professed myself a Christian, being really one, and not such a secret Mahometan as too many of us were: this could neither prevail with my uncles to leave me in my native country, nor with the severity of those officers that had orders to make us evacuate Spain, to believe that it was not a pretence. My mother was a Christian; my father, a man of discretion, professed the same belief; and I sucked the Catholic faith with my milk. I was handsomely educated, and never betrayed the least mark of the Morisco breed, either in language or behaviour. With these endowments, as I grew up, that little beauty I had, if ever I had any, began to increase; and for all my retired life, and the restraint upon my appearing abroad, a young gentleman, called Don Gasper Gregorio, got a sight of me: he was son and heir to a knight that lived in the next town. It were tedious to relate how he got an opportunity to converse with me, fell desperately in love, and affected me with a sense of his passion. I must be short, lest this halter cut me off in the middle of my story. I shall only tell you that he would needs bear me company in my banishment; and accordingly, by the help of the Morisco language, of which he was a perfect master, he mingled with the exiles, and getting acquainted with my two uncles that conducted me, we all went together to Barbary, and took up our residence at Algiers.

"My father, in the meantime, had very prudently, upon the first news of the proclamation to banish us, withdrawn to seek a place of refuge for us in some foreign country, leaving a considerable stock of money and jewels hidden in a private place, which he discovered to nobody but me, with orders not to move it till his return.

"The King of Algiers, understanding I had some beauty, and also that I was rich, which afterwards turned to my advantage, sent for me, and was very inquisitive about my country, and what jewels and gold I had got. I satisfied him as to the place of my nativity, and gave him to understand that my riches were buried in a certain place, where I might easily recover them, were I permitted to return to where they lay.

"This I told him, that in hopes of sharing in my fortune, his covetousness should divert him from injuring my person. In the midst of these questions, the king was informed that a certain youth, the handsomest and loveliest in the world, had come over in company with us. I was presently conscious that Don Gregorio was the person, his beauty answering so exactly their description. The sense of the young gentleman's danger was now more grievous to me than my own misfortunes, having been told that those barbarous Turks are much fonder of a handsome youth than the most beautiful woman. The king gave immediate orders he should be brought into his presence, asking me whether the youth deserved the commendations they gave him. I told him, inspired by some good angel, that the person they so much commended was no man, but of my own sex and withal begged his permission to have her dressed in a female habit, that her beauty might shine in its natural lustre, and so prevent her blushes, if she should appear before his majesty in that unbecoming habit. He consented, promising withal to give orders next morning for my return to Spain, to recover my treasure. I spoke with Don Gasper, represented to him the danger of appearing a man, and prevailed with him to wait on the king that evening in the habit of a Moorish woman. The king was so much pleased with his beauty, that he resolved to reserve him as a present for the Grand Seigneur; and, fearing the malice of his wives in the seraglio, he gave her in charge to some of the principal ladies of the city, to whose house she was immediately conducted.

"This separation was grievous to us both, for I cannot deny that I love him. Those who have ever felt the pangs of a parting love can best imagine the affliction of our souls. Next morning, by the king's order, I embarked for Spain in this vessel, accompanied by these two Turks that killed your men, and this Spanish renegado that first spoke to you, who is a Christian in his heart, and came along with me with a greater desire to return to Spain than go back to Barbary. The rest are all Moors and Turks, who serve for rowers. Their orders were to set me on shore, with this renegado, in the habits of Christians, on the first Spanish ground we should discover; but these two covetous and insolent Turks would needs, contrary to their order, first cruise upon the coast, in hopes of taking some prize, being afraid that, if they should first set us ashore, some accident might happen to us, and make us discover that the brigantine was not far off at sea, and so expose them to the danger of being taken, if there were galleys upon the coast. In the night we made this land, not mistrusting any galleys lying so near, and so we fell into your hands.

"To conclude, Don Gregorio remains in woman's habit among the Moors, nor can the deceit long protect him from destruction; and here I stand, expecting, or rather fearing, my fate, which yet cannot prove unwelcome, I being now weary of living. Thus, gentlemen, you have heard the unhappy passages of my life; I have told you nothing but what is true; and all I have to beg is, that I may die as a Christian, since I am innocent of the crimes of which my unhappy nation is accused." Here she stopped, and, with her story and her tears, melted the hearts of many of the company.

The viceroy, being moved with a tender compassion, was the first to unbind the cords that manacled her fair hands; when an ancient pilgrim, who came on board with the viceroy's attendants, having, with a fixed attention, minded the damsel during her relation, came suddenly, and, throwing himself at her feet,

"Oh! Anna Felix," cried he, "my dear unfortunate daughter! Behold thy father Ricote, that returned to seek thee, being unable to live without thee, who art the joy and support of my age."

Upon this, Sancho, who had all this while been sullenly musing, vexed with the usage he had met with so lately, lifting up his head, and staring the pilgrim in the face, knew him to be the same Ricote he had met on the road the day he left his government, and was likewise fully persuaded that this was his daughter, who, being now unbound, embraced her father, and joined with him in his joy and grief. "My lords," said the old pilgrim, "this is my daughter, Anna Felix, more unhappy in fortune than in name, and famed as much for her beauty as for her father's riches. I left my country to seek a sanctuary for my age, and, having fixed upon a residence in Germany, returned in this habit, with other pilgrims, to dig up and regain my wealth, which I have effectually done; but I little thought thus unexpectedly to have found my greatest treasure, my dearest daughter. My lords, if it can consist with the integrity of your justice to pardon our small offence, I join my prayers and tears with hers to implore your mercy on our behalf, since we never designed you any injury, and are innocent of those crimes for which our nation has justly been banished."

"Ay, ay," cried Sancho, putting in, "I knew Ricote as well as the beggar knows his dish; and so far as concerns Anna Felix being his daughter, I know that is true, too; but for all the story of his goings out and comings in, and his intentions, whether they were good or whether they were bad, I will neither meddle nor make, not I."

So uncommon an accident filled all the company with admiration; so that the general, turning to the fair captive, "Your tears," said he, "are so prevailing, madam, that they compel me now to be foresworn. Live, lovely Anna Felix; live as many years as Heaven has decreed you; and let those rash and insolent slaves, who alone committed the crimes, bear the punishment of it." With that he gave orders to have the two delinquent Turks hanged up at the yard-arm; but at the intercession of the viceroy, their fault showing rather madness than design, the fatal sentence was revoked; the general considering, at the same time, that their punishment in cold blood would look more like cruelty than justice.

Then they began to consider how they might retrieve Don Gasper Gregorio from the danger he was in; to which purpose Ricote offered to the value of above a thousand ducats, which he had about him in jewels, to purchase his ransom. But the readiest expedient was thought to be the proposal of the Spanish renegado, who offered, with a small barque and half a dozen oars, manned by Christians, to return to Algiers and set him at liberty, as best knowing when and where to land, and being acquainted with the place of his confinement. The general and the viceroy demurred to this motion, through a distrust of the renegado's fidelity, since he might perhaps betray the Christians that were to go along with him. But Anna Felix engaging for his truth, and Ricote obliging himself to ransom the Christians, if they were taken, the design was resolved upon.

The viceroy went ashore, committing the Morisca and her father to Don Antonio Moreno's care, desiring him at the same time to command his house for anything that might conduce to their entertainment; such sentiments of kindness and good nature had the beauty of Anna Felix infused into his breast.

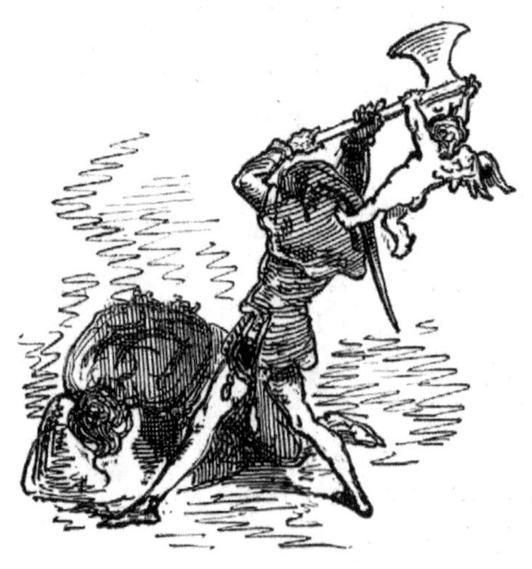

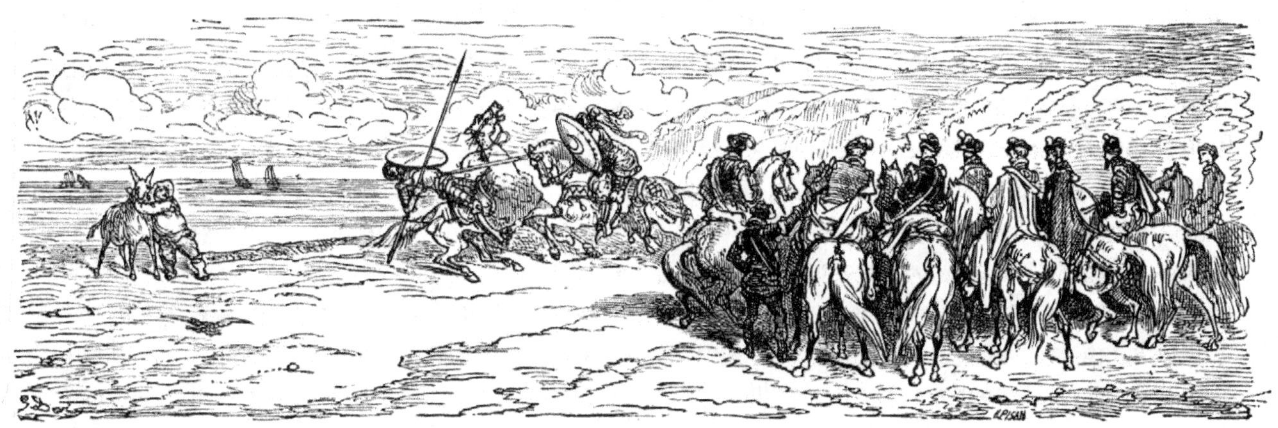

CHAPTER LXIV.

OF AN UNLUCKY ADVENTURE, WHICH DON QUIXOTE LAID MOST TO HEART OF ANY THAT HAD YET BEFALLEN HIM.

DON ANTONIO'S lady was extremely pleased with the company of the fair Morisca, whose sense being as exquisite as her beauty, drew all the most considerable persons in the city to visit her. Don Quixote told Don Antonio that he could by no means approve the method they had taken to release Don Gregorio, it being full of danger, with little or no probability of success; but that their surest way would have been to set him ashore in Barbary, with his horse and arms, and leave it to him to deliver the gentleman, in spite of all the Moorish power, as Don Gayferos had formerly rescued his wife Melisandra.

"Good, your worship," quoth Sancho, hearing this; "look before you leap. Don Gayferos had nothing but a fair face for it on dry land, when he carried her to France. But here, if it please you, though we should deliver Don Gregorio, how shall we bring him over to Spain across the broad sea?"

"'There is a remedy for all things but death,'" answered Don Quixote; "it is but having a barque ready by the sea-side, and then let me see what can hinder our getting into it."

"Ah! master, master," quoth Sancho, "there is more to be done than a dish to wash. Saying is one thing, and doing is another; and, for my part, I like the renegado very well; he seems to me a good, honest fellow, and cut out for the business."

"Well," said Don Antonio, "if the renegado fails, then the great Don Quixote shall embark for Barbary."

In two days the renegado was dispatched away in a fleet cruiser of six oars on each side, manned with brisk, lusty fellows; and two days after that the galleys, with the general, left the port, and steered their course eastward; the general having first engaged the viceroy to give him an account of Don Gregorio's and Anna Felix's fortune.

Now it happened one morning that Don Quixote, going abroad to take the air upon the sea-shore, armed at all points, according to his custom—his arms, as he said, being his best attire, as combat was his refreshment—he spied a knight riding towards him, armed, like himself, from head to foot, with a bright moon blazoned on his shield, who, coming within hearing, called out to him,—

"Illustrious and never-sufficiently extolled Don Quixote de la Mancha, I am the Knight of the White Moon, whose incredible achievements, perhaps, have reached thy ears. Lo! I am come to enter into combat with thee, and to compel thee, by dint of sword, to own and acknowledge my mistress, by whatever name and dignity she be distinguished, to be, without any degree of comparison, more beautiful than thy Dulcinea del Toboso. Now, if thou wilt fairly confess this truth, thou freest thyself from certain death, and me from the trouble of taking or giving thee thy life. If not, the conditions of our combat are these: If victory be on my side, thou shalt be obliged immediately to forsake thy arms and the quest of adventures, and to return to thy own house, where thou shalt engage to live, quietly and peaceably, for the space of one whole year, without laying hand on thy sword, to the improvement of thy estate and the salvation of thy soul. But if thou comest off conqueror, my life is at thy mercy, my horse and arms shall be thy trophy, and the fame of all my former exploits, by the lineal descent of conquest, be vested in thee as victor. Consider what thou hast to do, and let thy answer be quick, for my despatch is limited to this very day."

Don Quixote was amazed and surprised, as much at the arrogance of the Knight of the White Moon's challenge, as at the subject of it; so, with a solemn and austere address,—"Knight of the White Moon," said he, "whose achievements have as yet been kept from my knowledge, it is more than probable that you have never seen the illustrious Dulcinea; for, had you ever viewed her perfections, you had there found arguments enough to convince you that no beauty, past, present, or to come, can parallel hers; and therefore, without giving you directly the lie, I only tell thee, knight, thou art mistaken; and this position I will maintain, by accepting your challenge on your conditions, except that article of your exploits descending to me; for, not knowing what character your actions bear, I shall rest satisfied with the fame of my own, by which, such as they are, I am willing to abide. And, since your time is so limited, choose your ground, and begin your career as soon as you will, and expect to be met with. 'A fair field, and no favour:' to whom God shall give her, St. Peter give his blessing."

While these two knights were thus adjusting the preliminaries of combat, the viceroy, who had been informed of the Knight of the White Moon's appearance near the city walls, and his parleying with Don Quixote, hastened to the scene of battle, not suspecting it to be anything but some new device of Don Antonio Moreno, or somebody else. Several gentlemen, and Don Antonio among the rest, accompanied him thither. They arrived just as Don Quixote was wheeling Rozinante to fetch his career; and, seeing them both ready for the onset, he interposed, desiring to know the cause of the sudden combat. The Knight of the White Moon told him

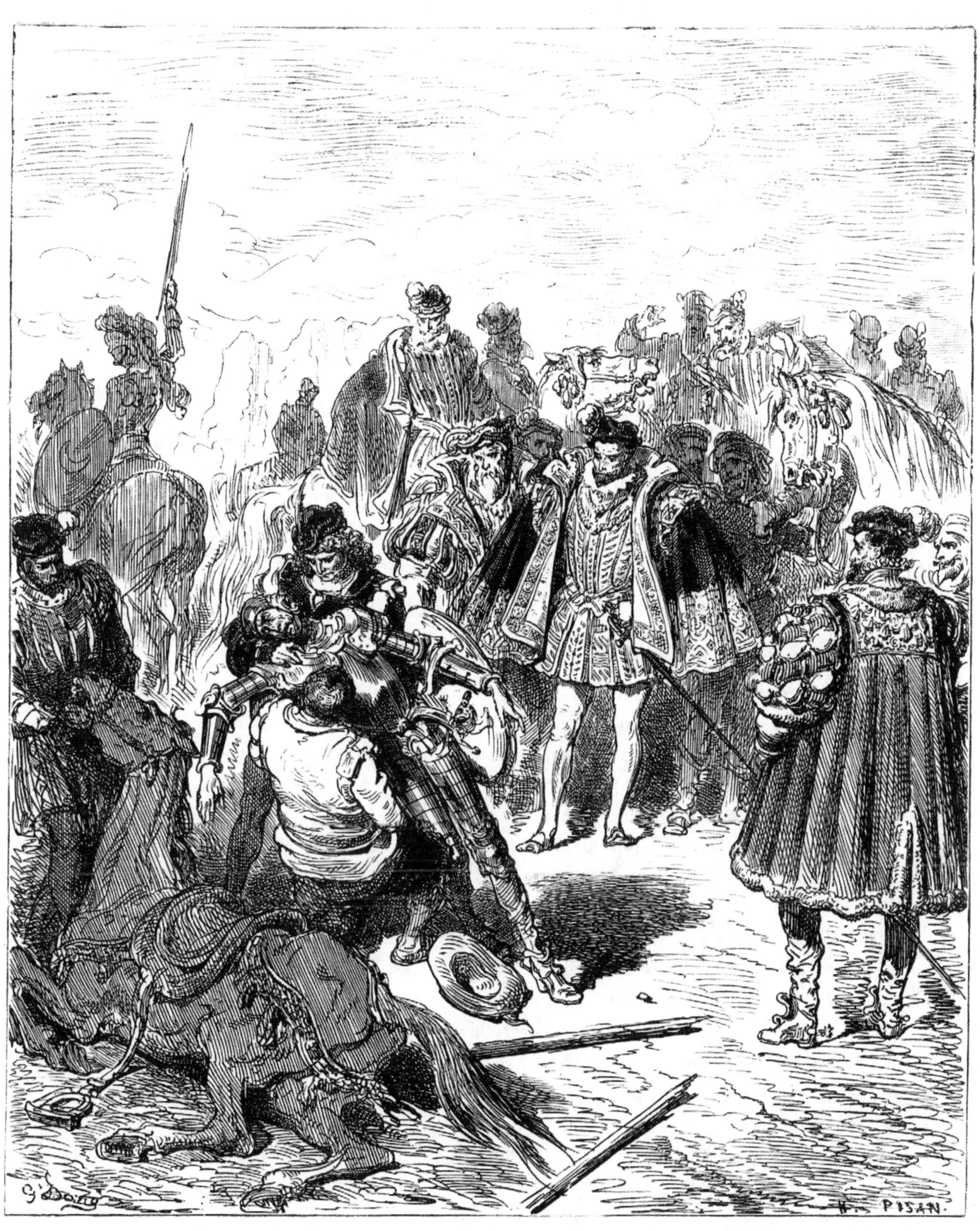

"They found him pale, and in a cold sweat."

there was a lady in the case, and briefly repeated to his excellency what passed between him and Don Quixote. The viceroy whispered to Don Antonio, and asked him whether he knew that Knight of the White Moon, and whether their combat was not some jocular device to impose upon Don Quixote. Don Antonio answered positively that he neither knew the knight nor whether the combat were in jest or earnest. This put the viceroy to some doubt whether he should not prevent their engagement; but, being at last persuaded that it must be a jest at the bottom, he withdrew.

"Valorous knights," said he, "if there be no medium between confession and death, but Don Quixote be still resolved to deny, and you, the Knight of the White Moon, as obstinately to urge, I have no more to say; the field is free, and the Lord have mercy on you!"

The knights made their compliments to the viceroy for his gracious consent; and Don Quixote, making some short ejaculations to Heaven and his mistress, as he always used upon these occasions, began his career, without either sound of trumpet or any other signal. His adversary was no less forward; for, setting spurs to his horse, which was much the swifter, he met Don Quixote, before he had run half his career, so forcibly, that, without making use of his lance, which it is thought he lifted up on purpose, he overthrew the Knight of La Mancha and Rozinante, both coming to the ground with a terrible fall.

The Knight of the White Moon got immediately upon him, and, clapping the point of his lance to his face, "Knight," cried he, "you are vanquished, and a dead man, unless you immediately fulfil the conditions of your combat."

Don Quixote, bruised and stunned with his fall, without lifting up his beaver, answered in a faint hollow voice, as if he had spoken out of a tomb, "Dulcinea del Toboso is the most beautiful woman in the world, and I the most unfortunate knight upon the earth. It were unjust that such perfection should suffer through my weakness. No, pierce my body with thy lance, knight, and let my life expire with my honour."

"Not so rigorous neither," replied the conqueror; "let the fame of the Lady Dulcinea del Toboso remain entire and unblemished; provided the great Don Quixote return home for a year, as we agreed before the combat, I am satisfied."

The viceroy and Don Antonio, with many other gentlemen, were witnesses to all these passages, and particularly to this proposal; to which Don Quixote answered, that, upon condition he should be enjoined nothing to the prejudice of Dulcinea, he would, upon the faith of a true knight, be punctual in the performance of everything else. This acknowledgment being made, the Knight of the White Moon turned about his horse, and, saluting the viceroy, rode at a hand-gallop into the city, whither Don Antonio followed him, at the viceroy's request, to find who he was, if possible.

Don Quixote was lifted up, and upon taking off his helmet, they found him pale, and in a cold sweat. As for Rozinante, he was in so sad a plight, that he could not stir for the present. Then, as for Sancho, he was in so heavy a taking, that he knew not what to do nor what to say:

he was sometimes persuaded he was in a dream—sometimes he fancied this rueful adventure was all witchcraft and enchantment. In short, he found his master discomfited in the face of the world, and bound to good behaviour, and to lay aside his arms for a whole year. Now he thought his glory eclipsed; his hopes of greatness vanished into smoke; and his master's promises, like his bones, put out of joint by that cursed fall, which he was afraid had at once crippled Rozinante and his master. At last the vanquished knight was put into a chair, which the viceroy had sent for that purpose, and they carried him into town, accompanied likewise by the viceroy, who had a great curiosity to know who this Knight of the White Moon was, that had left Don Quixote in so sad a condition.

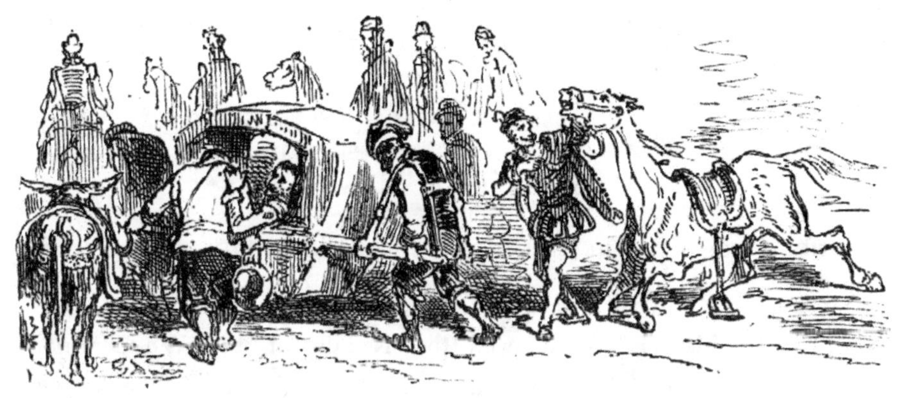

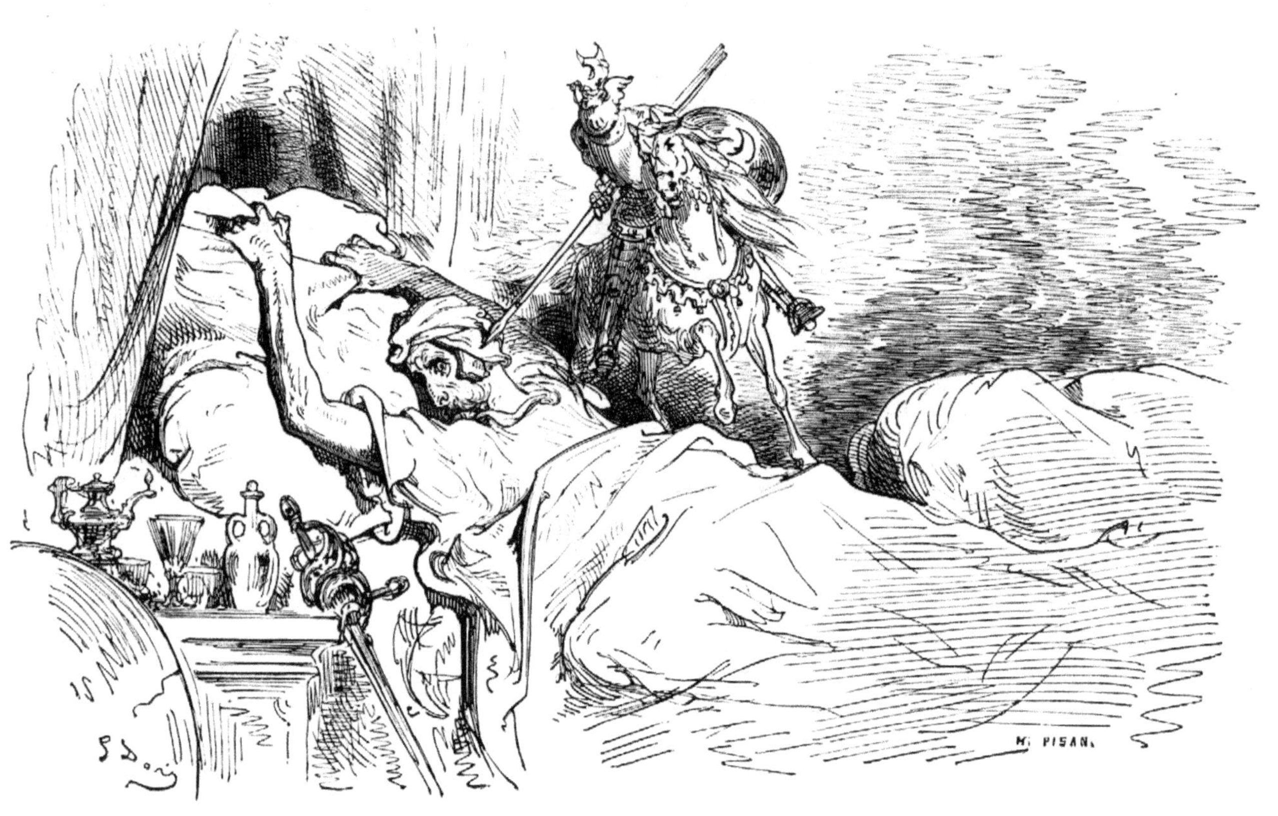

CHAPTER LXV.

AN ACCOUNT OF THE KNIGHT OF THE WHITE MOON, DON GREGORIO'S ENLARGEMENT, AND OTHER PASSAGES.

DON ANTONIO MORENO followed the Knight of the White Moon to his inn, whither he was attended by a troublesome rabble of boys. The knight being got to his chamber, where his squire waited to take off his armour, Don Antonio came in, declaring he would not be shook off till he had discovered who he was. The knight finding that the gentleman would not leave him, "Sir," said he, "since I lie under no obligation of concealing myself, if you please, while my man disarms me, you shall hear the whole truth of the story.

"You must know, sir, I am called the bachelor Carrasco. I live in the same town with this Don Quixote, whose unaccountable frenzy has moved all his neighbours, and me among the rest, to endeavour, by some means, to cure his madness; in order to which, believing that rest and ease would prove the surest remedy, I bethought myself of this present stratagem, and, about three months ago, in all the equipage of a knight-errant, under the title of the Knight of the Mirrors, I met him on the road, fixed a quarrel upon him, and the conditions of our combat were as you have heard already. But fortune then declared for him, for he unhorsed and vanquished me, and so I was disappointed; he prosecuted his adventures, and I returned home shamefully, very much hurt with my fall. But, willing to retrieve my credit, I made this second attempt, and now have succeeded; for I know him to be so nicely punctual in whatever his word and honour is engaged for, that he will undoubtedly perform his promise. This, sir, is the sum of the whole story; and I beg the favour of you to conceal me from Don Quixote, that my project may not be ruined the second time, and that the honest gentleman, who is naturally a man of good parts, may recover his understanding."

"Oh! sir," replied Don Antonio, "what have you to answer for, in robbing the world of the most diverting folly that ever was exposed among mankind? Consider, sir, that his cure can never benefit the public half so much as his distemper. But I am apt to believe, Sir Bachelor, that his madness is too firmly fixed for your art to remove; and, Heaven forgive me! I cannot forbear wishing it may be so, for by Don Quixote's cure we not only lose his good company, but the drolleries and comical humours of Sancho Panza too, which are enough to cure melancholy itself of the spleen. However, I promise to say nothing of the matter, though I confidently believe, sir, your pains will be to no purpose."

Carrasco told him, that having succeeded so far, he was obliged to cherish better hopes; and, asking Don Antonio if he had any further service to command him, he took his leave, and, packing up his armour on a carriage-mule, presently mounted his charging horse, and, leaving the city that very day, posted homewards, meeting no adventure on the road worthy a place in this faithful history.

Six days did Don Quixote keep his bed, very dejected, sullen, and out of humour, and full of severe and black reflections on his fatal overthrow. Sancho was his comforter, and, among other his crumbs of comfort,—

"My dear master," quoth he, "cheer up; come, pluck up a good heart, and be thankful for coming off no worse. Why, a man has broken his neck with a less fall, and you have not so much as a broken rib. Consider, sir, that they that game sometimes must lose: we must not always look for bacon where we see the hooks. Come, sir, cry a fig for the doctor, since you will not need him this bout; let us jog home fair and softly, without thinking any more of sauntering up and down, nobody knows whither, in quest of adventures and broken noses. Why, sir, I am the greatest loser, if you go to that, though it is you that are in the worst pickle. It is true I was weary of being a governor, and gave over all thoughts that way, but yet I never parted with my inclination of being an earl; and now, if you miss being a king, by casting off your knight-errantry, poor I may go whistle for my earldom."

"No more of that, Sancho," said Don Quixote; "I shall only retire for a year, and then re-assume my honourable profession, which will undoubtedly secure me a kingdom, and thee an earldom."

"Heaven grant it may!" quoth Sancho, "and no mischief betide us: 'Hope well and have well,' says the proverb."

Don Antonio coming in, broke off the discourse, and with great signs of joy, calling to Don

Quixote, "Reward me, sir," cried he, "for my good news. Don Gregorio and the renegado are safe arrived: they are now at the viceroy's palace, and will be here this moment."

The knight was a little revived at this news. "Truly, sir," said he to Don Antonio, "I could almost be sorry for his good fortune, since he has forestalled the glory I should have acquired in releasing, by the strength of my arm, not only him, but all the Christian slaves in Barbary. But whither am I transported, wretch that I am! Am I not miserably conquered, shamefully overthrown, forbidden the paths of glory for a whole long, tedious year? What should I boast, who am fitter for a distaff than a sword?"

"No more of that," quoth Sancho. "To-day for thee, and to-morrow for me. Never lay this ill fortune to heart; 'he that is down to-day may be up to-morrow,' unless he has a mind to lie a-bed. Hang bruises; so rouse, sir, and bid Don Gregorio welcome to Spain, for, by the hurry in the house, I believe he is come."

And so it happened; for Don Gregorio, having paid his duty to the viceroy, and given him an account of his delivery, was just arrived at Don Antonio's with the renegado, very impatient to see Anna Felix. He had changed the female habit he wore when he was freed, for one suitable to his sex, which he had from a captive who came along with him in the vessel, and appeared a very amiable and handsome gentleman, though not above eighteen years of age. Ricote and his daughter went out to meet him, the father with tears, and the daughter with a joyful modesty. Their salutation was reserved, without an embrace, their love being too refined for any loose behaviour; but their beauties surprised everybody. Silence was emphatical in their joys, and their eyes spoke more love than their tongues could express. The renegado gave a short account of the success of his voyage, and Don Gregorio briefly related the shifts he was put to in his confinement, which showed his wit and discretion to be much above his years. Ricote gratified the ship's crew very nobly, and particularly the renegado, who was once more received into the bosom of the Church, having, with due penance and sincere repentance, purified himself from all his former uncleanness.

Some few days after, the viceroy, in concert with Don Antonio, took such measures as were expedient to get the banishment of Ricote and his daughter repealed, judging it no inconvenience to the nation that so just and orthodox persons should remain among them. Don Antonio, being obliged to go to court about some other matters, offered to solicit in their behalf, hinting to him that, through the intercession of friends, and more powerful bribes, many difficult matters were brought about there, to the satisfaction of the parties.

"There is no relying upon favour and bribes in our business," said Ricote, who was by; "for the great Don Bernardo de Velasco, Count de Salazar, to whom the king gave the charge of our expulsion, is a person of too strict and rigid justice to be moved either by money, favour, or affection; and though I cannot deny him the character of a merciful judge in other matters, yet his piercing and diligent policy finds the body of our Moriscan race to be so corrupted, that amputation is the only cure. He is an Argus in his ministry, and by his watchful eyes has discovered the most secret springs of their machinations, and resolving to prevent the danger which the whole kingdom was in from such a powerful multitude of inbred foes, he took the most effectual means; for, after all, lopping off the branches may only prune the tree, and make the poisonous fruit spring faster, but to overthrow it from the root proves a sure deliverance. Nor can the great Philip the Third be too much extolled; first, for his heroic resolution in so nice and weighty an affair, and then for his wisdom in entrusting Don Bernardo de Velasco with the execution of this design."

"Well, when I come to court," said Don Antonio to Ricote, "I will, however, use the most advisable means, and leave the rest to Providence. Don Gregorio shall go with me to comfort his parents, who have long mourned for his absence. Anna Felix shall stay here with my wife, or in some monastery; and as for honest Ricote, I dare engage the viceroy will be satisfied to let him remain under his protection till he see how I succeed."

The viceroy consented to all this, but Don Gregorio, fearing the worst, was unwilling to leave his fair mistress; however, considering that he might return to her after he had seen his parents, he yielded to the proposal, and so Anna Felix remained with Don Antonio's lady, and Ricote with the viceroy.

Two days after, Don Quixote, being somewhat recovered, took his leave of Don Antonio, and having caused his armour to be laid on Dapple, he set forwards on his journey home, Sancho thus being forced to trudge after him on foot. On the other side, Don Gregorio bid adieu to Anna Felix; and their separation, though but for a while, was attended with floods of tears and all the excess of passionate sorrow. Ricote offered him a thousand crowns, but he refused them, and only borrowed five of Don Antonio, to repay him at court.

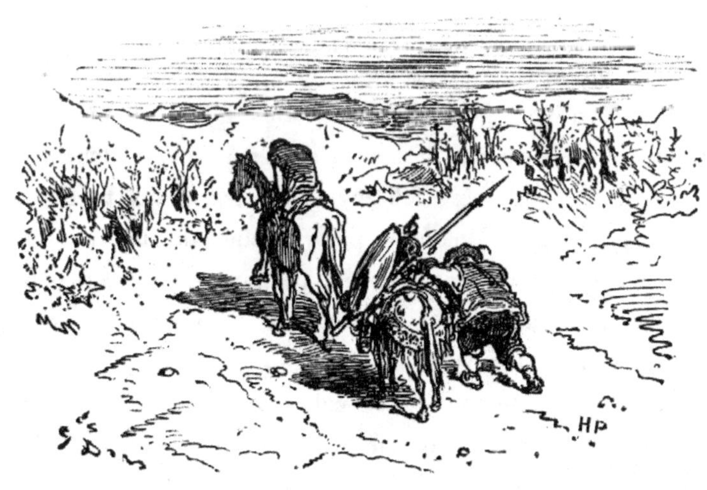

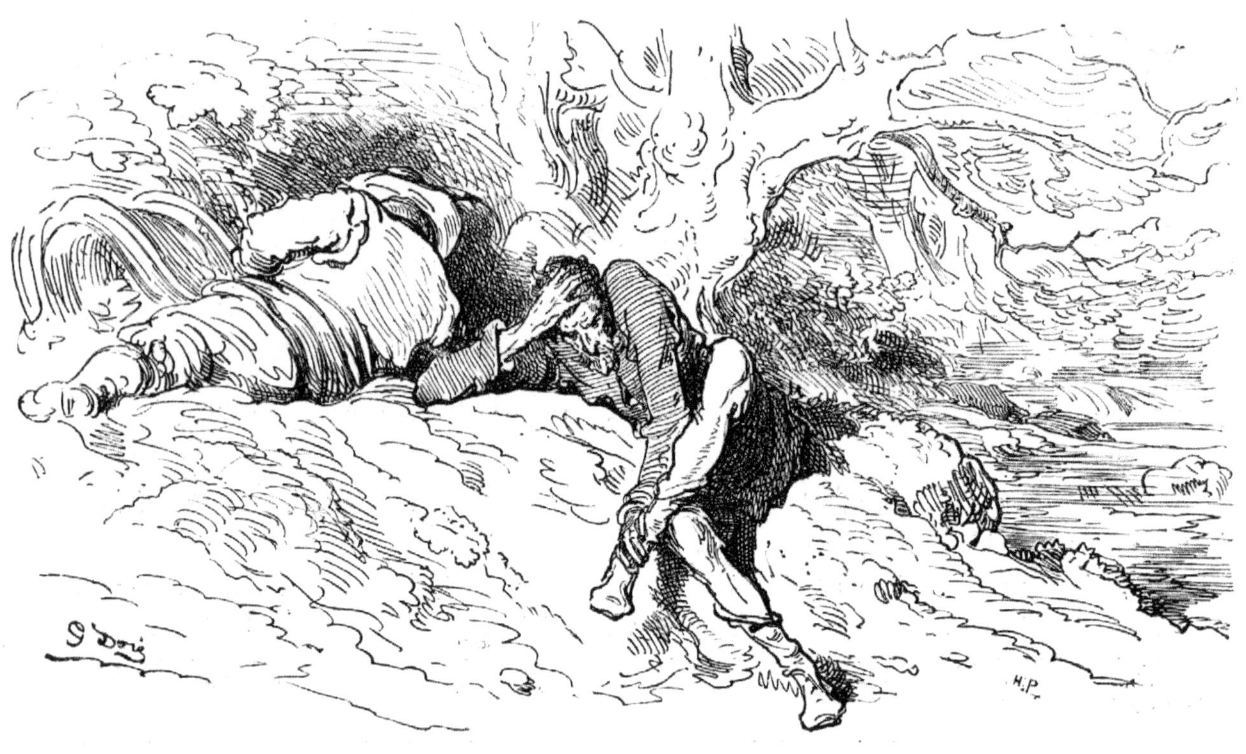

CHAPTER LXVI.

WHICH TREATS OF THAT WHICH SHALL BE SEEN BY HIM THAT READS IT, AND HEARD BY HIM THAT LISTENS WHEN IT IS READ.

DON QUIXOTE, as he went out of Barcelona, cast his eyes on the spot of ground where he was overthrown. "Here once Troy stood," said he; "here my unhappy fate, and not my cowardice, deprived me of all the glories I had purchased. Here Fortune, by an unexpected reverse, made me sensible of her inconstancy and fickleness. Here my exploits suffered a total eclipse; and, in short, here fell my happiness, never to rise again."

Sancho, hearing his master thus dolefully paraphrasing on his misfortunes, "Good sir,' quoth he, "it is as much the part of great spirits to have patience when the world frowns upon them, as to be joyful when all goes well. And I judge of it by myself: for if when I was a governor I was merry, now I am but a poor squire a-foot I am not sad; and, indeed, I have heard say that this same she thing they call Fortune is a whimsical, freakish, drunken person, and blind into the bargain; so that she neither sees what she does nor knows whom she raises nor whom she casts down."

"Thou art very much a philosopher, Sancho," said Don Quixote; "thou talkest very sensibly. I wonder how thou camest by all this; but I must tell thee there is no such thing as fortune in the world, nor does anything that happens here below of good or ill come by

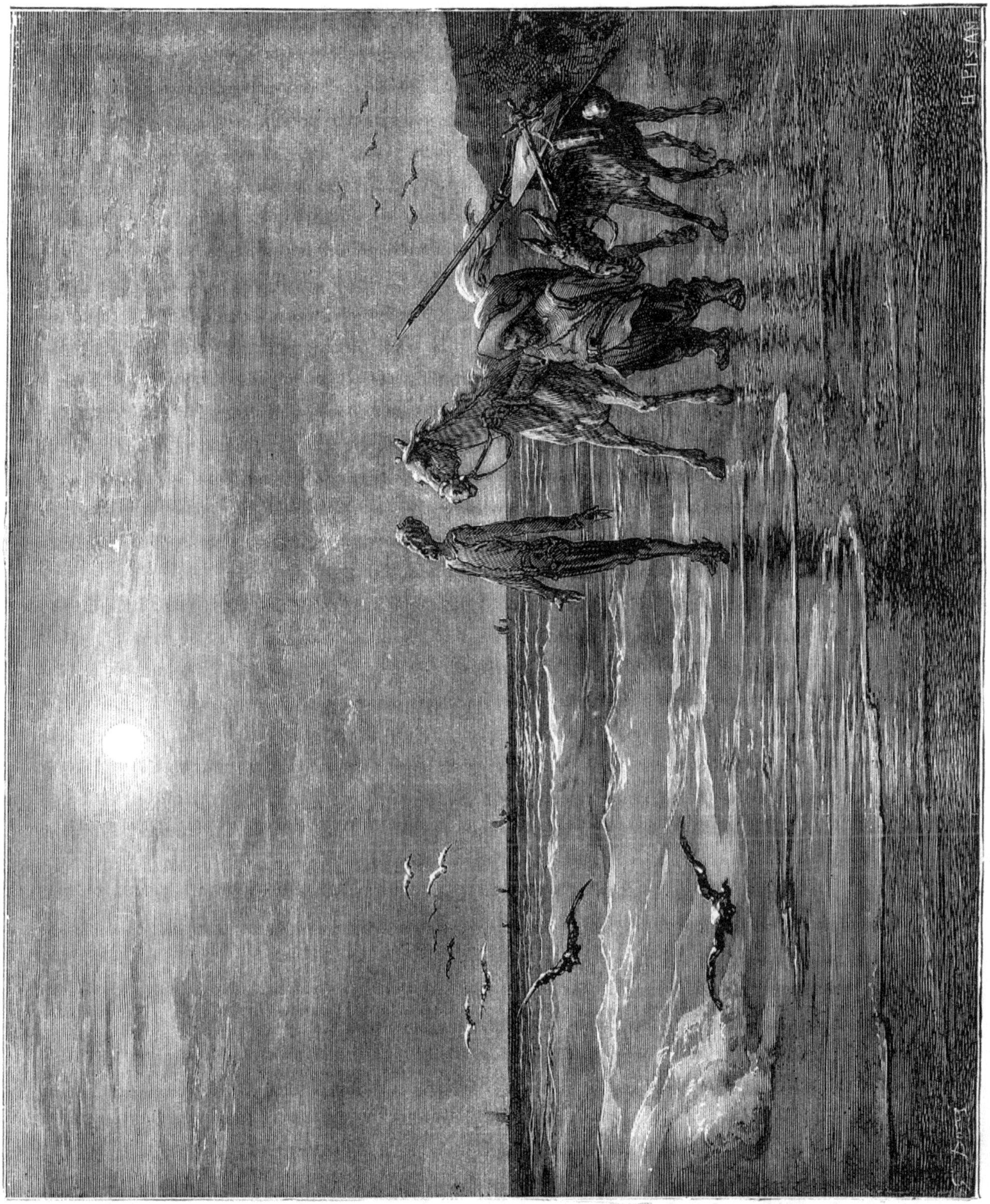

"Here fell my happiness, never to rise again."

chance, but by the particular providence of Heaven; and this makes good the proverb, that every man may thank himself for his own fortune. For my part, I have been the maker of mine; but for want of using the discretion I ought to have used, all my presumptuous edifice sunk, and tumbled down at once. I might well have considered that Rozinante was too weak and feeble to withstand the Knight of the White Moon's huge and strong-built horse. However, I would needs adventure; I did the best I could, and was overcome. Yet, though it has cost me my honour, I have not lost, nor can I lose, my integrity to perform my promise. When I was a knight-errant, valiant and bold, the strength of my hands and my actions gave a reputation to my deeds; and now I am no more than a dismounted squire, the performance of my promise shall give a reputation to my words. Trudge on, then, friend Sancho, and let us get home, to pass the year of our probation. In that retirement we shall recover new vigour to return to that which is never to be forgotten by me—I mean, the profession of arms."

They passed that day, and four more after that, in such kind of discourse, without meeting anything that might interrupt their journey; but on the fifth day, as they entered into a country town, they saw a great company of people at an inn door, being got together for pastime, as being a holiday. As soon as Don Quixote drew near, he heard one of the countrymen cry to the rest, "Look ye, now, we will leave it to one of these two gentlemen that are coming this way; they know neither of the parties; let either of them decide the matter."

"That I will with all my heart," said Don Quixote, "and with all the equity imaginable, if you will but state the case right to me."

"Why, sir," said the countryman, "the business is this: one of our neighbours here in this town, so fat and so heavy that he weighs eleven arrobas, or eleven quarters of a hundred (for that is the same thing), has challenged another man of this town, that weighs not half so much, to run with him a hundred paces, with equal weight. Now he that gave the challenge, being asked how they should make equal weight, demands that the other, who weighs but five quarters of a hundred, should carry a hundred and a half of iron, and so the weight, he says, will be equal."

"Hold, sir," cried Sancho, before Don Quixote could answer, "this business belongs to me, that came so lately from being a governor and judge, as all the world knows; I ought to give judgment in this doubtful case."

"Do, then, with all my heart, friend Sancho," said Don Quixote, "for I am not fit to give crumbs to a cat, my brain is so disturbed and out of order."

Sancho having thus got leave, and all the countrymen standing about him, "Brothers," quoth he, "I must tell you that the fat man is in the wrong box—there is no matter of reason in what he asks; for if, as I always heard say, 'he that is challenged may choose his weapons,' there is no reason that he should choose such as may encumber him, and hinder him from getting the better of him that defied him. Therefore it is my judgment, that he who gave the challenge, and is so big and so fat, shall cut, pare, slice, or shave off a hundred and fifty pounds

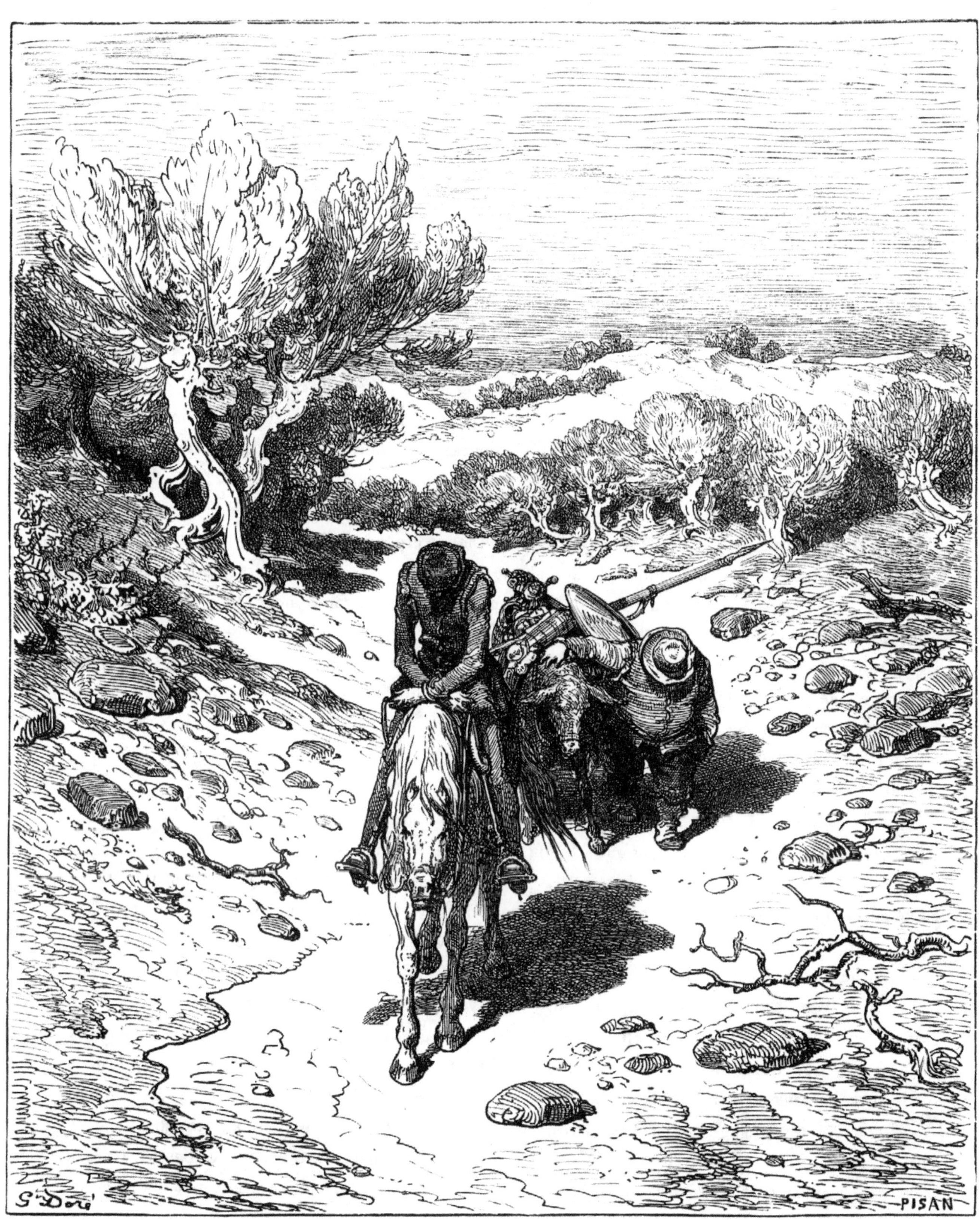

"They passed that day, and four more after that, in such kind of discourse."

of his flesh, here and there, as he thinks fit, and then, being reduced to the weight of the other, both parties may run their race upon equal terms."

"Before George," quoth one of the country people that had heard the sentence, "this gentleman has spoken like one of the saints in heaven; he has given judgment like a casuist; but I warrant the fat squab loves his flesh too well to part with the least sliver of it, much less will he part with a hundred and a half."

"Why, then," quoth another fellow, "the best way will be not to let them run at all, for then Lean need not venture to sprain his back by running with such a load, and Fat need not cut out his pampered sides into collops. So let half the wager be spent in wine, and let us go to the tavern that has the best, and lay the cloak upon me when it rains."

"I return you thanks, gentlemen," said Don Quixote, "but I cannot stay a moment, for dismal thoughts and disasters force me to appear unmannerly, and to travel at an uncommon rate;" and, so saying, he clapped spurs to Rozinante, and moved forwards, leaving the people to descant on his strange figure, and the rare parts of his groom.

That night the master and the man took up their lodging in the middle of a field, under the roof of the open sky; and the next day, as they were on their journey, they saw coming towards them a man a-foot, with a wallet about his neck, and a javelin or dart in his hand, just like a foot-post. The man mended his pace when he came near Don Quixote, and, almost running, came with a great deal of joy in his looks, and embraced Don Quixote's right thigh, for he could reach no higher. "My Lord Don Quixote de la Mancha," cried he, "oh! how heartily glad my lord duke will be when he understands you are coming again to his castle, for there he is still with my lady duchess."

"I do not know you, friend," answered Don Quixote; "nor can I imagine who you should be, unless you tell me yourself."

"My name is Tosilos, if it please your honour; I am my lord duke's footman, the same who would not fight with you about Donna Rodriguez's daughter."

"Bless me!" cried Don Quixote; "is it possible you should be the man whom those enemies of mine, the magicians, transformed into a lackey, to deprive me of that combat?"

"Softly, good sir," replied the footman; "there was neither enchantment nor transformation in the case. I was as much a footman when I entered the lists as when I came out; and it was because I had a mind to marry the young gentlewoman that I refused to fight. But I was sadly disappointed; for, when you were gone, my lord duke had me soundly banged for not doing as he ordered me in that matter; and the upshot was this: Donna Rodriguez is packed away to seek her fortune, and the daughter is shut up in a nunnery. As for me, I am going to Barcelona with a parcel of letters from my lord to the viceroy. However, sir, if you please to take a sip, I have here a calabash full of the best. It is a little hot, I must own, but it is neat, and I have some excellent cheese that will make it go down."

"I take you at your word," quoth Sancho; "I am no proud man; 'leave ceremonies to the church;' and so let us drink, honest Tosilos, in spite of all the enchanters in the Indies."

"Well, Sancho," said Don Quixote, "thou art certainly the veriest glutton that ever was, and the silliest blockhead in the world, else thou wouldst consider that this man thou seest here is enchanted, and a sham lackey. Then stay with him, if thou thinkest fit, and gratify thy voracious appetite; for my part, I will ride softly on before."

Tosilos smiled, and, laying his bottle and his cheese upon the grass, he and Sancho sat down there, and, like sociable messmates, never stirred till they had quite cleared the wallet of all that was in it fit for the belly, and this with such an appetite, that, when all was consumed, they licked the very packet of letters, because it smelt of cheese.

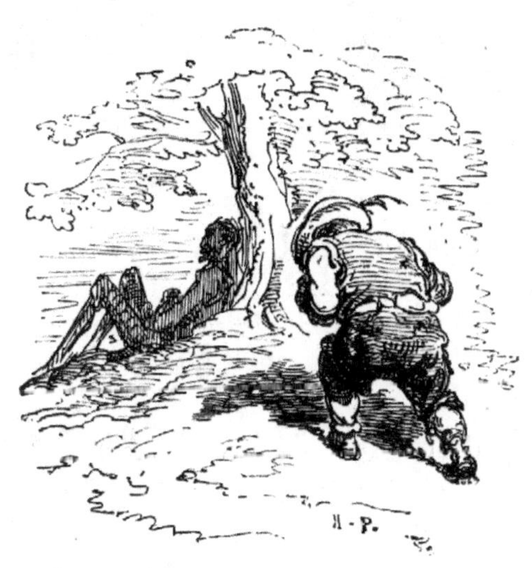

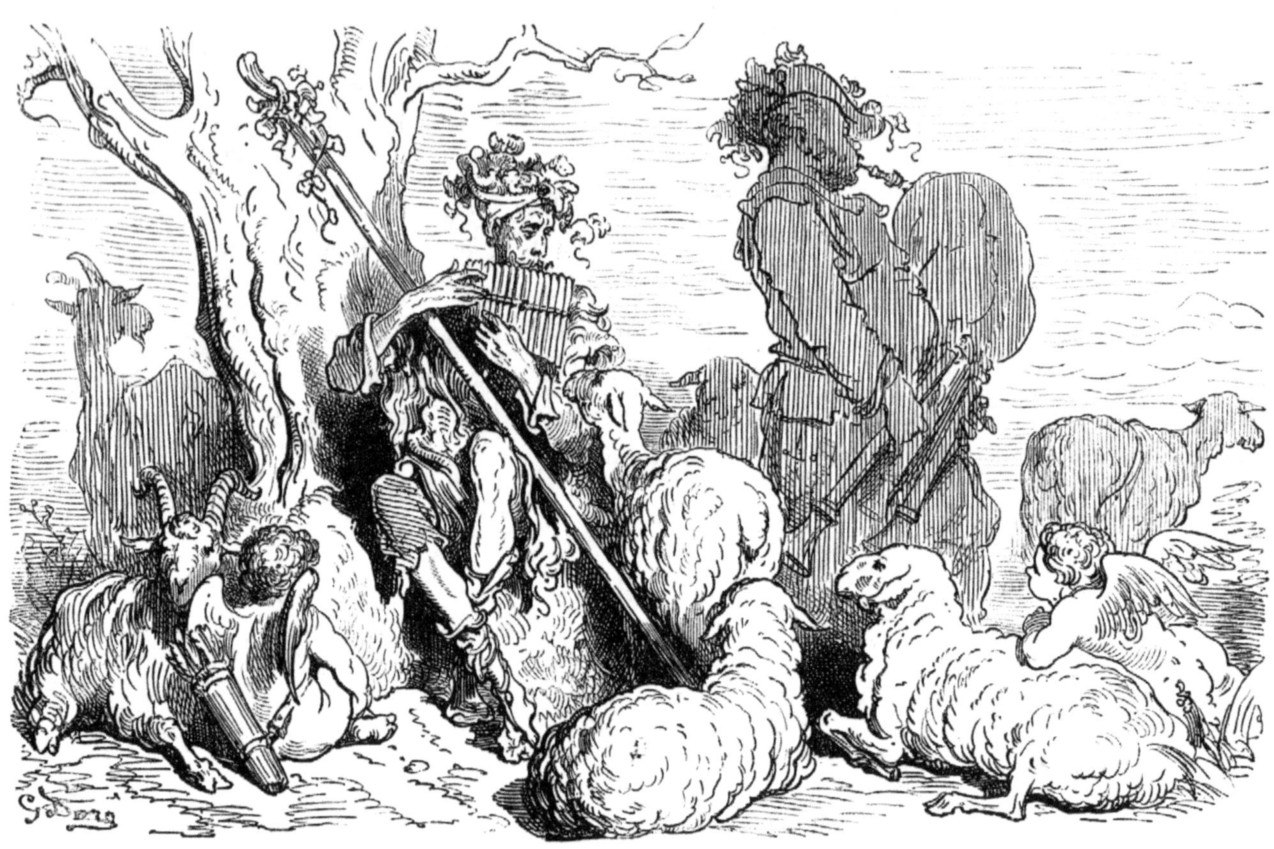

CHAPTER LXVII.

HOW DON QUIXOTE RESOLVED TO TURN SHEPHERD, AND LEAD A RURAL LIFE FOR THE YEAR'S TIME HE WAS OBLIGED NOT TO BEAR ARMS; WITH OTHER PASSAGES TRULY GOOD AND DIVERTING.

IF Don Quixote was much disturbed in mind before his overthrow, he was much more disquieted after it. While he stayed for his squire under a tree, a thousand thoughts crowded into his head, like flies in a honey-pot; sometimes he pondered on the means to free Dulcinea from enchantment, and at others on the life he was to lead during his involuntary retirement. In this brown study Sancho came up to him, crying up Tosilos as the honestest fellow, and the most gentleman-like footman in the world.

"Is it possible, Sancho," said Don Quixote, "thou shouldst still take that man for a real lackey? Hast thou forgotten how thou sawest Dulcinea converted and transformed into the resemblance of a rustic wench, and the Knight of the Mirrors into the bachelor Carrasco, and all this by the necromantic arts of those evil-minded magicians that persecute me? But, laying this aside, pr'ythee, tell me, didst thou not ask Tosilos what became of Altisidora?—whether she bemoaned my absence, or dismissed from her breast those amorous sentiments that disturbed her when I was near her?"

"Faith and troth," quoth Sancho, "my head ran on something else, and I was too well employed to think on such foolish stuff. Bless me, sir! are you now in a mood to ask about other folks' thoughts, especially their love-thoughts too?"

"Look you," said Don Quixote, "there is a great deal of difference between those actions that proceed from love and those that are the effect of gratitude. It is possible a gentleman should not be at all amorous; but, strictly speaking, he cannot be ungrateful. It is very likely that Altisidora loved me well; she presented me with three nightcaps; she wept when I went away, cursed me, abused me—all tokens that she was deeply in love with me, for the anger of lovers commonly vents itself in curses. It was not in my power to give her any hopes, nor had I any costly present to bestow on her, for all I have is reserved for Dulcinea, and the treasures of a knight-errant are but fairy gold, and a delusive good; so all I can do is only to remember the unfortunate fair, without prejudice, however, to the rights of my Dulcinea, whom thou greatly injurest, Sancho, by delaying the accomplishment of the penance that must free the poor lady from misery. And, since thou art so ungenerously sparing of that pampered hide of thine, may I see it devoured by wolves, rather than see it kept so charily for the worms."

"Sir," quoth Sancho, "to deal plainly with you, it cannot, for the blood of me, enter into my head that jerking my back will signify a straw to the disenchanting of the enchanted. Sir, it is as if we should say, 'If your head aches, anoint your shins.' At least, I dare be sworn that, in all the stories of knight-errantry you have thumbed over, you never knew flogging unbewitched anybody. However, when I can find myself in the humour, do you see, I will about it: when time serves, I will chastise myself, never fear."

"I wish thou wouldst," answered Don Quixote; "and may Heaven give thee grace at least to understand how much it is thy duty to relieve thy mistress! for, as she is mine, by consequence she is thine, since thou belongest to me."

Thus they went on talking, till they came near the place where the bulls had run over them; and Don Quixote knowing it again,—

"Sancho," said he, "yonder is that meadow where we met the fine shepherdesses and the gallant shepherds, who had a mind to renew or imitate the pastoral Arcadia. It was certainly a new and ingenious conceit. If thou thinkest well of it, we will follow their example, and turn shepherds too, at least for the time I am to lay aside the profession of arms. I will buy a flock of sheep, and everything that is fit for a pastoral life; and so, calling myself the shepherd Quixotis, and thee the shepherd Pansino, we will range the woods, the hills, and meadows, singing and versifying. We will drink the liquid crystal, sometimes out of the fountains, and sometimes from the purling brooks and swift-gliding streams. The oaks, the cork-trees, and chesnut-trees will afford us both lodging and diet; the willows will yield us their shade, the roses present us their inoffensive sweets, and the spacious meads will be our carpets, diversified with colours of all sorts; blest with the purest air, and unconfined alike, we shall breathe that and freedom. The moon and stars, our tapers of the night, shall light our evening walks. Light hearts will make us merry, and mirth will make us sing. Love will inspire us with a theme and wit, and Apollo with harmonious lays. So shall we become famous, not only while we live, but make our loves eternal as our songs.'

"As I live," quoth Sancho, "this sort of life nicks me to a hair; and I fancy that, if the bachelor Samson Carrasco and Master Nicholas have but once a glimpse of it, they will even turn shepherds too; nay, it is well if the curate does not put in for one among the rest, for he is a notable joker, and merrily inclined."

"That was well thought on," said Don Quixote; "and then, if the bachelor will make one among us, as I doubt not but he will, he may call himself the shepherd Samsonino or Carrascon, and Master Nicholas, Niculoso, as formerly old Boscan called himself Nemoroso. For the curate, I do not well know what name we shall give him, unless we should call him the shepherd Curiambro. As for the shepherdesses, with whom we must fall in love, we cannot be at a loss to find them names—there are enough for us to pick and choose—and, since my mistress's name is not improper for a shepherdess any more than for a princess, I will not trouble myself to get a better; thou mayest call thine as thou pleasest."

"For my part," quoth Sancho, "I do not think of any other name for mine than Teresona; that will fit her fat sides full well, and is taken from her Christian name too. So, when I come to mention her in my verses, everybody will know her to be my wife, and commend my honesty. As for the curate, he must be contented without a shepherdess, for good example's sake. As for the bachelor, let him take his own choice, if he means to have one."

"Bless me!" said Don Quixote, "what a life shall we lead! What a melody of oaten reeds and Zamora bagpipes shall we have resounding in the air! what intermixture of tabors, morrice-bells, and fiddles! And if to all the different instruments we add the albogues, we shall have all manner of pastoral music."

"What are the albogues?" quoth Sancho; "for I do not remember I have seen or ever heard of them in my life."

"They are," said Don Quixote, "a sort of instruments made of brass plates, rounded like candlesticks: the one shutting into the other, there arises through the holes or stops, and the trunk or hollow, an odd sound, which, if not very grateful or harmonious, is, however, not altogether disagreeable, but does well enough with the rusticity of the bagpipe and tabor. You must know the word is Moorish, as indeed are all those in our Spanish that begin with *Al*—as Almoasa, Almorsar, Alhombra, Alguasil, Alucema, Almacen, Alcanzia, and the like, which are not many. And we have also but three Moorish words in our tongue that end in *i*, and they are Borcequi, Zaquicami, and Maravedi; for as to Alheli and Alfaqui, they are as well known to be Arabic, by their beginning with *Al*, as their ending in *i*. I could not forbear telling thee so much by the bye, thy query about albogue having brought it into my head. There is one thing more, that will go a great way towards making us complete in our new kind of life, and that is poetry. Thou knowest I am somewhat given that way, and the bachelor Carrasco is a most accomplished poet, to say nothing of the curate, though, I will hold a wager, he is a dabbler in it too; and so is Master Nicholas, I dare say, for all your barbers are notable scrapers and songsters. For my part, I will complain of absence; thou shalt celebrate thy own loyalty and constancy; the shepherd Carrascon shall expostulate on his shepherdess's disdain; and the pastor Curiambro choose what subject he likes best; and so all will be managed to our hearts' content."

"Alas!" quoth Sancho, "I am so unlucky, that I fear me I shall never live to see these blessed days. How shall I lick up the curds and cream! I will never be without a wooden spoon in my pocket! Oh, how many of them will I make! What garlands and what pretty pastoral fancies will I contrive! which, though they may not recommend me for wisdom, will make me pass at least for an ingenious fellow."

They then made a slender meal, as little to Sancho's liking as his hard lodging, which brought the hardships of knight-erranting fresh into his thoughts, and made him wish for the better entertainment he had sometimes found, as at Don Diego's, Camacho's, and Don Antonio's houses. But he considered, after all, that it could not be always fair weather, nor was it always foul; so he betook himself to his rest till morning, and his master to the usual exercise of his roving imaginations.

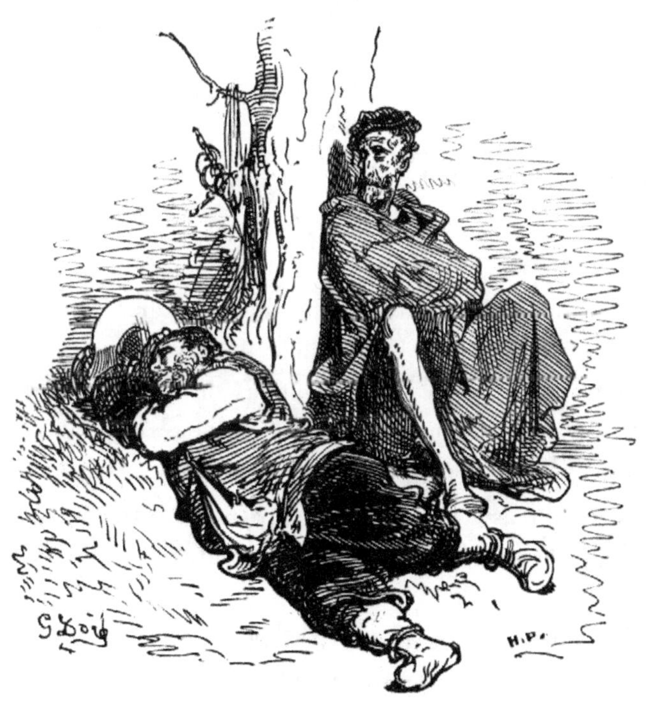

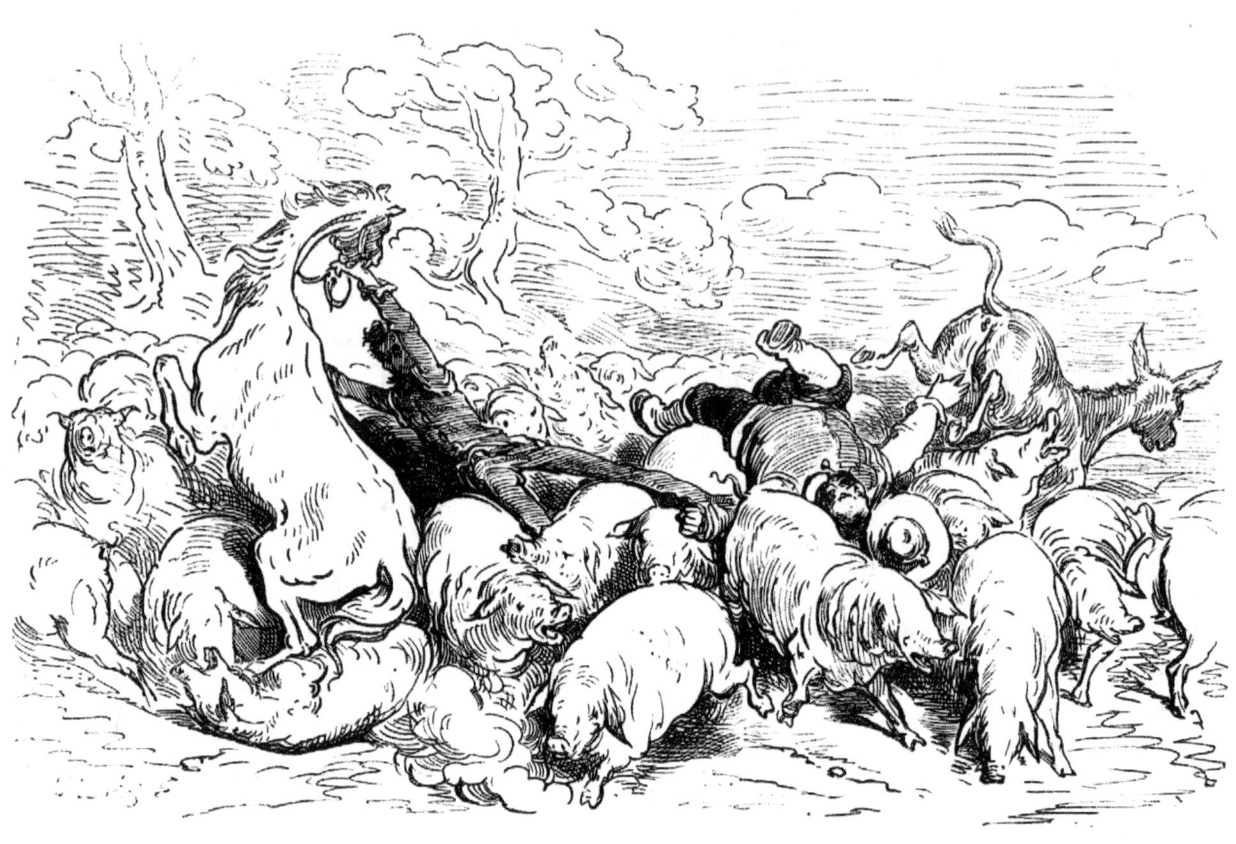

CHAPTER LXVIII.

THE ADVENTURE OF THE HOGS.

THE night was pretty dark, though the moon still kept her place in the sky, but it was in such a part as obliged her to be invisible to us; for now and then Madam Diana takes a turn to the Antipodes, and then the mountains in black and the valleys in darkness mourn her ladyship's absence. Don Quixote, after his first sleep, thought nature sufficiently refreshed, and would not yield to the temptations of a second. Sancho, indeed, did not enjoy a second, but from a different reason; for he usually made but one nap of the whole night, which was owing to the soundness of his constitution, and his inexperience of cares, that lay so heavy upon Don Quixote.

"Sancho," said the knight, after he had pulled the squire till he had waked him too, "I am amazed at the insensibility of thy temper. Thou art certainly made of marble or solid brass, thou liest so without either motion or feeling. Thou sleepest while I wake; thou singest while I mourn; and while I am ready to faint for want of sustenance, thou art lazy and unwieldy with mere gluttony. It is the part of a good servant to share in the afflictions of his master. Observe the stillness of the night, and the solitary place we are in. It is a pity

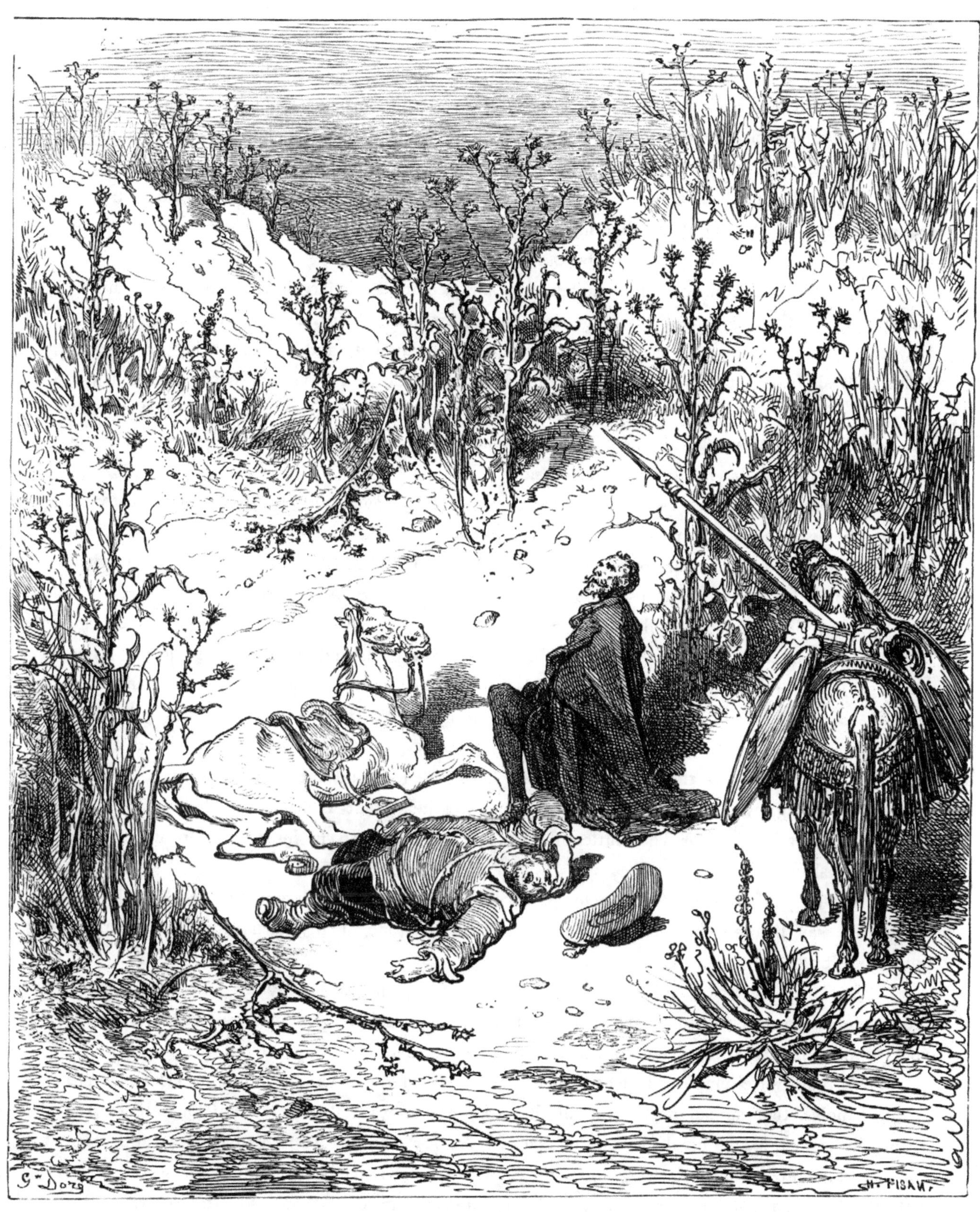

"'Sleep, Sancho,' cried Don Quixote; 'sleep, for thou wert born to sleep.'"

such an opportunity should be lost in sloth and inactive rest; rouse for shame, step a little aside, and, with a good grace and a cheerful heart, score me up some three or four hundred lashes upon thy back, towards the disenchanting of Dulcinea. This I make my earnest request, being resolved never to be rough with thee again upon this account, for I must confess thou canst lay a heavy hand on a man upon occasion. When that performance is over we will pass the remainder of the night in chanting, I of absence, and thou of constancy, and so begin those pastoral exercises which are to be our employment at home."

"Sir," answered Sancho, "do you take me for a monk or friar, that I should start up in the middle of the night and discipline myself at this rate? Or do you think it such an easy matter to scourge and clapperclaw my back one moment, and fall a-singing the next? Look you, sir, say not a word more of this whipping; for as I love my flesh, you will put me upon making some rash oath or other that you will not like; and then, if the bare brushing of my coat would do you any good you should not have it, much less the currying of my hide; and so let me go to sleep again."

"Oh, obdurate heart!" cried Don Quixote; "oh! impious squire! Oh, nourishment and favours ill bestowed! Is this my reward for having got thee a government, and my good intentions to get thee an earldom, or an equivalent at least, which I dare engage to do when this year of our obscurity is elapsed? for, in short, *post tenebras spero lucem*."

"That I do not understand," quoth Sancho; "but this I very well know, that while I am asleep I feel neither hope nor despair; I am free from pain, and insensible of glory. Now, blessings light on him that first invented this same sleep! it covers a man all over, thoughts and all, like a cloak; it is meat for the hungry, drink for the thirsty, heat for the cold, and cold for the hot. It is the current coin that purchases all the pleasures of the world cheap, and the balance that sets the king and the shepherd, the fool and the wise man, even. There is only one thing, which somebody once put into my head, that I dislike in sleep; it is, that it resembles death; there is very little difference between a man in his first sleep and a man in his last sleep."

"Most elegantly spoken!" said Don Quixote. "Thou hast much outdone anything I ever heard thee say before, which confirms me in the truth of one of thy own proverbs, 'Birth is much, but breeding more."

"Bless me, master of mine!" cried Sancho, "I am not the only he now that threads proverbs, for you tack them together faster than I do, I think. I see no difference, but that yours come in season, mine out of season; but for all that, they are all but proverbs."

Thus they were employed, when their ears were alarmed with a kind of a hoarse and grunting noise, that spread itself over all the adjacent valleys. Presently Don Quixote started up on his legs, and laid his hand on his sword. As for Sancho, he immediately set up some entrenchments about him, clapping the bundle of armour on one side, and fortifying the other with the ass's pack-saddle; and then, gathering himself up of a heap, squatted down under

Dapple's belly, where he lay panting, as full of fears as his master of surprise, while every moment the noise grew louder, as the cause of it approached, to the terror of the one at least; for, as for the other, it is sufficiently known what his valour was.

Now, the occasion was this: some fellows were driving a herd of above six hundred swine to a certain fair; and, with their grunting and squeaking, the filthy beasts made such a horrible noise, that Don Quixote and Sancho were almost stunned with it, and could not imagine whence it proceeded. But at length, the knight and squire standing in their way, the rude bristly animals came thronging up all in a body, and, without any respect of persons, some running between the knight's legs, and some between the squire's, threw down both master and man, having not only insulted Sancho's entrenchments, but also thrown down Rozinante; and, having thus broken in upon them, on they went, and bore down all before them, overthrowing pack-saddle, armour, knight, squire, horse, and all, crowding, treading, and trampling over them all at a horrid rate.

Sancho was the first that made a shift to recover his legs; and having by this time found out what the matter was, he called to his master to lend him his sword, and swore he would stick at least half a dozen of those rude porkers immediately.

"No, no, my friend," said Don Quixote, "let them even go. Heaven inflicts this disgrace upon my guilty head; for it is but a just punishment that dogs should devour, hornets sting, and vile hogs trample on a vanquished knight-errant."

"And belike," quoth Sancho, "that Heaven sends the flies to sting, the gnats to bite, and hunger to famish us poor squires, for keeping these vanquished knights company. If we squires were the sons of those knights, or any way related to them, why, then something might be said for our bearing a share of their punishment, though it were to the third and fourth generation. But what have the Panzas to do with the Quixotes? Well, let us to our old places again, and sleep out the little that is left of the night. To-morrow is a new day."

"Sleep, Sancho," cried Don Quixote—"sleep, for thou wert born to sleep; but I, who was designed to be still waking, intend, before Aurora ushers in the sun, to give a loose to my thoughts, and vend my conceptions in a madrigal that I made last night unknown to thee."

"Methinks," quoth Sancho, "a man cannot be in great affliction when he can turn his brain to the making of verses. Therefore, you may versify on as long as you please, and I will sleep it out as much as I can."

This said, he laid himself down on the ground, as he thought best, and hunching himself close together, fell fast asleep, without any disturbance from any debts, suretyships, or any care whatsoever. On the other side, Don Quixote, leaning against the trunk of a beech or a cork-tree (for it is not determined by Cid Hamet which it was), sung, in concert with his sighs, the following composition:—

A SONG TO LOVE.

Whene'er I think what mighty pain
The slave must bear who drags thy chain,
O Love! for ease to death I go,
The cure of thee—the cure of life and woe

But when, alas! I think I'm sure
Of that which must by killing cure,
The pleasure that I feel in death
Proves a strong cordial to restore my breath.

Thus life each moment makes me die,
And death itself new life can give;
I hopeless and tormented lie,
And neither truly die nor live.

Now day came on, and the sun, darting his beams on Sancho's face, at last awakened him; whereupon, rubbing his eyes, and yawning and stretching his drowsy limbs, he perceived the havoc that the hogs had made in his baggage, which made him wish not only the herd, but somebody else too, elsewhere for company. In short, the knight and squire both set forward on their journey, and about the close of the evening they discovered some half a score horsemen, and four or five fellows on foot, making directly towards them. Don Quixote, at the sight, felt a strange emotion in his breast; Sancho fell a-shivering from head to foot; for they perceived that these strangers were provided with spears and shields, and other warlike instruments: whereupon the knight, turning to the squire—

"Ah! Sancho," said he, "were it lawful for me at this time to bear arms, and had I my hands at liberty, and not tied up by my promise, what a joyful sight should I esteem this squadron that approaches! But, perhaps, notwithstanding my present apprehensions, things may fall out better than we expect."

By this time the horsemen, with their lances advanced, came close up to them without speaking a word; and encompassing Don Quixote in a menacing manner, with their points levelled to his back and breast, one of the footmen, by laying his finger upon his mouth, signified to Don Quixote that he must be mute; then taking Rozinante by the bridle, he led him out of the road, while the rest of the footmen secured Sancho and Dapple, and drove them silently after Don Quixote, who attempted twice or thrice to ask the cause of this usage; but he no sooner began to open, than they were ready to run the heads of their spears down his throat. Poor Sancho fared worse yet; for, as he offered to speak, one of the foot-guards gave him a jag with a goad, and served Dapple as bad, though the poor beast had no thought of saying a word.

As it grew night they mended their pace, and then the darkness increased the fears of the captive knight and squire, especially when every minute their ears were tormented with these or such-like words—

"On, on, ye Troglodytes; silence, ye barbarian slaves; vengeance, ye Anthropophagi; grumble not, ye Scythians; be blind, ye murdering Polyphemes, ye devouring lions."

"Bless us!" thought Sancho, "what names do they call us here! Trollopites, barber's slaves, and Andrew Hodge-podge, City-cans, and Burframes: I do not like the sound of them. Here is one mischief on the neck of another. When a man is down, down with him. I would compound for a good dry beating, and glad to escape so too."

Don Quixote was no less perplexed, not being able to imagine the reason either of their hard usage or scurrilous language, which hitherto promised but little good. At last, after they had ridden about an hour in the dark, they came to the gates of the castle, which Don Quixote presently knowing to be the duke's where he had so lately been—

"Heaven bless me!" cried he, "what do I see? Was not this the mansion of civility and humanity? But thus the vanquished are doomed to see everything frown upon them."

With that the two prisoners were led into the great court of the castle, and found such strange preparations made there, as increased at once their fear and amazement, as we shall find in the next chapter.

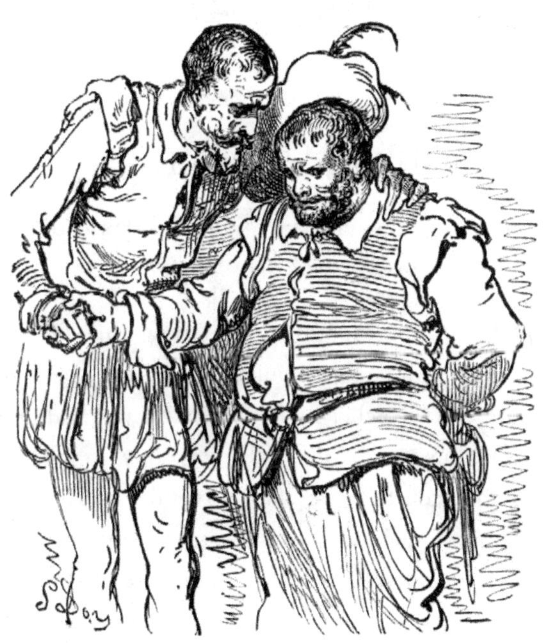

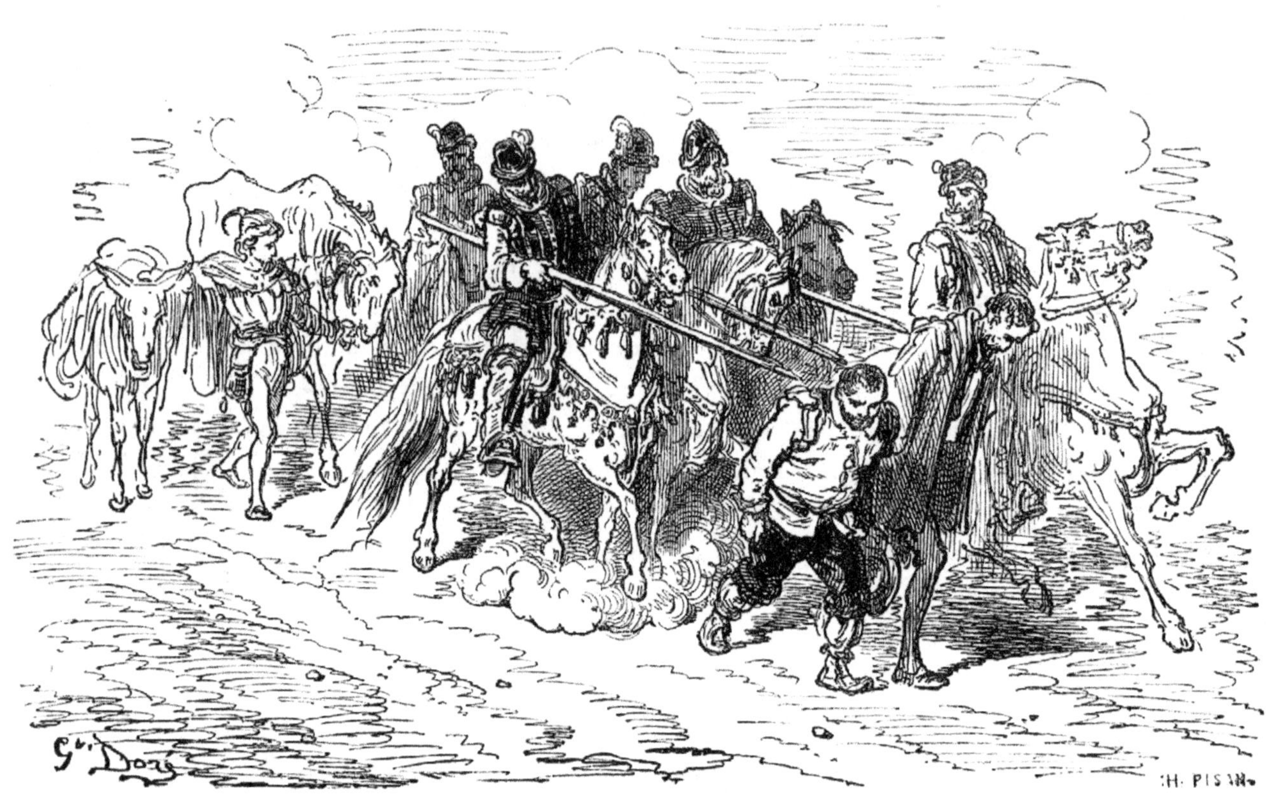

CHAPTER LXIX.

OF THE MOST SINGULAR AND STRANGE ADVENTURE THAT BEFELL DON QUIXOTE IN THE WHOLE COURSE OF THIS FAMOUS HISTORY.

ALL the horsemen alighted, and the footmen, snatching up Don Quixote and Sancho in their arms, hurried them into the court-yard, that was illuminated with above a hundred torches fixed in huge candlesticks, and about all the galleries round the court were placed above five hundred lights, insomuch that all was day in the midst of the darkness of the night. In the middle of the court there was a tomb, raised some two yards from the ground, with a large pall of black velvet over it, and round about it a hundred tapers of virgin wax stood burning in silver candlesticks. Upon the tomb lay the body of a young damsel, who, though to all appearance dead, was yet so beautiful, that death itself seemed lovely in her face. Her head was crowned with a garland of fragrant flowers, and supported by a pillow of cloth of gold; and in her hands, that were laid across her breast, was seen a branch of that yellow palm that used of old to adorn the triumphs of conquerors. On one side of the court there was a kind of a theatre erected, on which two personages sat in chairs, who, by the crowns upon their heads and sceptres in their hands, were, or at least appeared to be, kings. By the side of the theatre, at the foot of the steps by which the kings ascended, two other chairs were placed, and thither Don Quixote and Sancho were led, and caused to sit down, the guards that conducted them continuing silent all the while, and making their prisoners understand, by awful signs, that they must also be silent. But there was no great occasion for that caution, for their surprise was so great that it had tied up their tongues without it.

At the same time two other persons of note ascended the stage with a numerous retinue, and seated themselves on two stately chairs by the two theatrical kings. These Don Quixote presently knew to be the duke and duchess, at whose palace he had been so nobly entertained. But what he discovered as the greatest wonder was, that the corpse upon the tomb was the body of the fair Altisidora.

As soon as the duke and duchess had ascended, Don Quixote and Sancho made them a profound obeisance, which they returned with a short inclination of their heads. Upon this a certain officer entered the court, and, coming up to Sancho, he clapped over him a black buckram frock, all figured over with flames of fire, and, taking off his cap, he put on his head a kind of mitre, such as is worn by those who undergo public penance by the Inquisition; whispering him in the ear at the same time that if he did but offer to open his lips, they would put a gag in his mouth, or murder him outright. Sancho viewed himself over from head to foot, and was a little startled to see himself all over in fire and flames; but yet, since he did not feel himself burn, he cared not a farthing. He pulled off his mitre, and found it pictured over with imps; but he put it on again, and bethought himself, that since neither the flames burned him, nor the imps ran away with him, it was well enough. Don Quixote also steadfastly surveyed him, and, in the midst of all his apprehensions, could not forbear smiling to see what a strange figure he made. And now in the midst of that profound silence, while everything was mute, and expectation most attentive, a soft and charming symphony of flutes, that seemed to issue from the hollow of the tomb, agreeably filled their ears. Then there appeared, at the head of the monument, a young man extremely handsome, and dressed in a Roman habit, who, to the music of a harp, touched by himself, sung the following stanzas with an excellent voice:—

ALTISIDORA'S DIRGE.

While slain, the fair Altisidora lies
  A victim to Don Quixote's cold disdain;
Here all things mourn, all pleasure with her dies,
  And weeds of woe disguise the graces' train.

I'll sing the beauties of her face and mind,
  Her hopeless passion, her unhappy fate;
Not Orpheus' self, in numbers more refin'd,
  Her charms, her love, her suff'rings could relate.

Now shall the fair alone in life be sung,
  Her boundless praise is my immortal choice;
In the cold grave, when death benumbs my tongue,
  For thee, bright maid, my soul shall find a voice.

When from this narrow cell my spirit's free,
  And wanders grieving with the shades below,
Even o'er oblivion's waves I'll sing to thee;
  And hell itself shall sympathise in woe.

"Enough," cried one of the two kings; "no more, divine musician; it were an endless task to enumerate the perfections of Altisidora, or give us the story of her fate. Nor is she dead, as the ignorant vulgar surmises; no, in the mouth of fame she lives, and once more shall revive, as soon as Sancho has undergone the penance that is decreed to restore her to the world. Therefore, O Rhadamanthus! thou who sittest in joint commission with me in the opacous shades of Dis, tremendous judge of hell! thou to whom the decrees of fate, inscrutable to mortals, are revealed! in order to restore this damsel to life, open and declare them immediately, nor delay the promised felicity of her return to comfort the drooping world!"

Scarce had Minos finished his charge, when Rhadamanthus started up. "Proceed," said he, "ye ministers and officers of the household, superior and inferior, high and low; proceed one after another, and mark me Sancho's chin with twenty-four twitches, give him twelve pinches, and run six pins into his arms and back, for Altisidora's restoration depends on the performance of this ceremony."

Sancho, hearing this, could hold out no longer, but bawling out, "Bless me!" cried he, "I will as soon turn Turk as give you leave to do all this. You shall put no chin or countenance of mine upon any such mortification. What can the spoiling of my face signify to the restoring of the damsel? Dulcinea is bewitched, and I forsooth must flog myself to free her from witchcraft! And here is Altisidora, too, drops off of one distemper or other, and presently poor Sancho must be pulled by the handle of his face, his skin filled with oiled holes, and his arms pinched black and blue, to save her from the worms! No, no; you must not think to put tricks upon travellers! 'An old dog understands trap.'"

"Relent!" cried Rhadamanthus, aloud, "thou tiger; submit, proud Nimrod; suffer and be silent, or thou diest. No impossibility is required from thee, and therefore pretend not to expostulate on the severity of thy doom. Thy face shall receive the twitches, thy skin shall be pinched, and thou shalt groan under the penance. Begin, I say, ye ministers of justice, execute my sentence, or, as I am an honest man, ye shall curse the hour ye were born."

At the same time six old duennas, or waiting-women, appeared in the court, marching in a formal procession one after another, four of them wearing spectacles, and all with their right hands held aloft, and their wrists, according to the fashion, about four inches bare, to make their hands seem the longer. Sancho no sooner spied them than, roaring out like a bull, "Do with me what you please," cried he; "let a sackful of mad cats lay their claws on me, as they did on my master in this castle, drill me through with sharp daggers, tear the flesh from my bones with red-hot pincers, I will bear it with patience, and serve your worships, but the conjurers shall run away with me at once before I will suffer old waiting-women to lay a finger upon me."

Don Quixote, upon this, broke silence: "Have patience, my son," cried he, "and resign thyself to these potentates, with thanks to Heaven for having endowed thy person with such a gift as to release the enchanted, and raise the dead from the grave."

By this time the waiting-women were advanced up to Sancho, who, after much persuasion, was at last wrought upon to settle himself in his seat, and submit his face and beard to the female executioners. The first that approached gave him a clever twitch, and then dropped him a courtesy. "Less courtesy, and less sauce, good Mrs. Governante," cried Sancho; "for, by the life of Pharaoh, your fingers stink of vinegar." In short, all the waiting-women, and most of the servants, came and twitched and pinched him decently, and he bore it all with unspeakable patience; but when they came to prick him with pins he could contain no longer, but, starting up in a pelting chafe, snatched up one of the torches that stood near him, and, swinging it round, put all the women and the rest of his tormentors to their heels. "Avaunt!" he cried, "ye imps! do ye think my back is made of brass, or that I intend to be your master's martyr?"

At the same time Altisidora, who could not but be tired with lying so long upon her back, began to turn herself on one side, which was no sooner perceived by the spectators, than they all set up the cry, "She lives, she lives! Altisidora lives!" And then Rhadamanthus, addressing himself to Sancho, desired him to be pacified, for now the recovery was effected. So Don Quixote, seeing Altisidora stir, went and threw himself on his knees before Sancho.

"My dear son," cried he, "for now I will not call thee squire, now is the hour for thee to receive some of the lashes that are incumbent upon thee for the disenchanting of Dulcinea. This, I say, is the auspicious time, when the virtue of thy skin is most mature and efficacious for working the wonders that are expected from it."

"'Out of the frying-pan into the fire!'" quoth Sancho. "I have brought my hogs to a fair market truly: after I have been twinged and tweaked by the nose and everywhere, and stuck all over and made a pin-cushion of, I must now be whipped like a top, must I? If you have a mind to be rid of me, cannot you as well tie a good stone about my neck, and tip me into a well? Better make an end of me at once than have me loaded so every foot like a pack-horse, with other folks' burdens. Look ye: say but one word more to me of any such thing, and all the fat shall be in the fire."

By this time Altisidora sat on the tomb, and presently the music struck up, all the instruments being joined with the voices of the spectators, who cried aloud, "Live, live! Altisidora, live!" The duke and duchess got up, and with Minos and Rhadamanthus, accompanied by Don Quixote and Sancho, went all in a body to receive Altisidora, and hand her down from the tomb. She pretended to faint, bowed to the duke and duchess, and also to the two kings; but, after looking askew upon Don Quixote,—

"Heaven forgive that hard-hearted, lovely knight!" said she, "whose barbarity has made me an inhabitant of the other world, for aught I know, a thousand years. But to thee," said she, turning to Sancho—"to thee, the most compassionate squire that the world contains, I return my thanks for my change from death to life; in acknowledgment of which, six of the best smocks I have shall be changed into shirts for thee, and if they are not spick and span new, yet they are all as clean as a penny."

Sancho pulled off his mitre, put his knee to the ground, and kissed her hand. The duke commanded that they should return him his cap, and, instead of his flaming frock, give him his gaberdine; but Sancho begged of his grace that he might keep the frock and mitre, to carry into his own country, as a relic of that wonderful adventure. The duchess said he should have them, for he knew she was always one of the best of his friends. Then the duke ordered the company to clear the court, and retire to their respective lodgings, and that Don Quixote and Sancho should be conducted to their apartments.

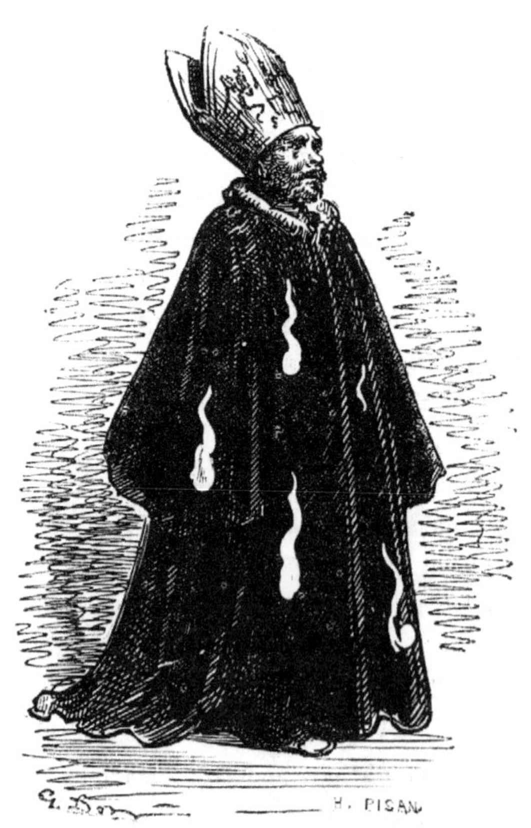

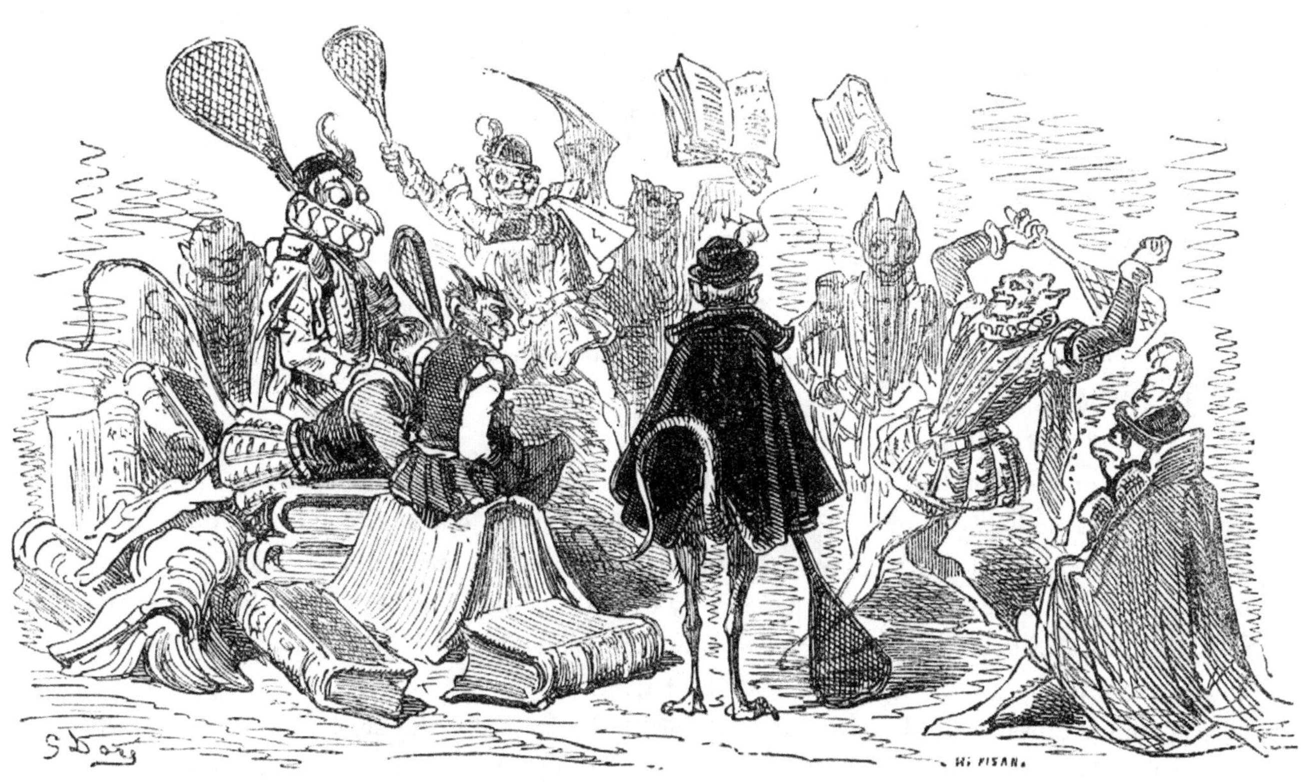

CHAPTER LXX.

WHICH COMES AFTER THE SIXTY-NINTH, AND CONTAINS SEVERAL PARTICULARS NECESSARY FOR THE ILLUSTRATION OF THIS HISTORY.

THAT night Sancho lay in a truckle-bed in Don Quixote's chamber, a lodging not greatly to the squire's liking, being very sensible that his master would disturb him with impertinent chat all night long. And this entertainment he found himself not rightly disposed for, his late penance having taken him quite off the talking-pin; and a hovel, with good sound sleep, had been more agreeable to his circumstances than the most stately apartments in such troublesome company. And, indeed, his apprehensions proved so right, that his master was scarcely laid when he began to open.

"Sancho," said he, "what is your opinion of the night's adventure? Great and mighty is the force of love when heightened by disdain, as the testimony of your own eyes may convince you in the death of Altisidora. It was neither a dart, a dagger, nor any poison that brought her to her end, but she expired through the mere sense of my disdain of her affection."

"I had not cared a pin," answered Sancho, "what she might have died of, so she had but let me alone; I never courted her nor slighted her in my born days; and, for my part, I must still think it strange that the life and well-doing of Altisidora, a whimsical, old gentlewoman, should depend upon the plaguing of Sancho Panza. But there are such things as enchanters and witchcrafts, that is certain, from which good Heaven deliver me! for it is more than I can do myself. But now, sir, let me sleep, I beseech you; for if you trouble me with any more questions, I am resolved to leap out of the window."

"I will not disturb thee, honest Sancho," said Don Quixote; "sleep, if the smart of thy late torture will let thee."

"No pain," answered Sancho, "can be compared to the abuse my face suffered, because it it is done by the worst of ill-natured creatures—I mean, old waiting-women: confusion take them, say I; and so, good night. I want a good nap to set me to rights; and so, once again, pray let me sleep."

"Do so," said Don Quixote; "and Heaven be with thee!"

Thereupon they both fell asleep; and while they are asleep Cid Hamet takes the opportunity to tell us the motives that put the duke and duchess upon this odd compound of extravagances that has been last related. He says that the bachelor Carrasco, meditating revenge for having been defeated by Don Quixote when he went by the title of the Knight of the Mirrors, resolved to make another attempt, in hopes of better fortune; and therefore, having understood where Don Quixote was by the page that brought the letters and present to Sancho's wife, he furnished himself with a fresh horse and arms, and had a white moon painted on his shield; his accoutrements were all packed upon a mule; and, lest Thomas Cecil, his former attendant, should be known by Don Quixote or Sancho, he got a country fellow to wait on him as a squire. Coming to the duke's castle, he was informed that the knight was gone to the tournament at Saragosa; the duke giving the bachelor an account also how pleasantly they had imposed upon him, with the contrivance for Dulcinea's disenchantment, to be effected at the expense of Sancho's body. Finally, he told him how Sancho had made his master believe that Dulcinea was transformed into a country wench by the power of magic, and how the duchess had persuaded Sancho that he was deluded himself, and Dulcinea enchanted in good earnest. The bachelor, though he could not forbear laughing, was nevertheless struck with wonder at this mixture of cunning and simplicity in the squire, and the uncommon madness of the master. The duke then made it his request, that if he met with the knight he should call at the castle as he returned, and give him an account of his success, whether he vanquished him or not. The bachelor promised to obey his commands; and, departing in search of Don Quixote, he found him not at Saragosa, but travelling farther, met him at last, and had his revenge as we have told you. Then taking the duke's castle in his way home, he gave him an account of the circumstances and conditions of the combat, and how Don Quixote was repairing homewards, to fulfil his engagement of returning to and remaining in his village for a year, as it was incumbent on the honour of chivalry to perform; and in this space, the bachelor said, he hoped the poor gentleman might recover his senses, declaring withal that the concern he had upon him to see a man of his parts in such a distracted condition, was the only motive that could put him upon such an attempt. Upon this he returned home, there to expect Don Quixote, who was coming after him. This information engaged the duke, who was never to be tired with the humours of the knight and the squire, to take this occasion to make more sport with them; he ordered all the roads thereabouts, especially those that Don Quixote was most likely to take, to be watched by a great many of his servants, who had orders to bring him to the castle, right or wrong.

They met him accordingly, and sent their master an account of it; whereupon, all things being prepared against his coming, the duke caused the torches and tapers to be all lighted round the court, and Altisidora's tragi-comical interlude was acted, with the humours of Sancho Panza, the whole so to the life that the counterfeit was hardly discernible. Cid Hamet adds, that he believed those that played all these tricks were as mad as those they were imposed upon; and that the duke and duchess were within a hair's breadth of being thought fools themselves, for taking so much pains to make sport with the weakness of two poor silly wretches.

To return to our two adventurers: the morning found one of them fast asleep, and the other broad awake, transported with his wild imaginations. They thought it time to rise, especially the Don, for the bed of sloth was never agreeable to him, whether vanquished or victorious.

Altisidora, whom Don Quixote supposed to have been raised from the dead, did that day (to humour her lord and lady) deck her head with the same garland she wore upon the tomb, and in a loose gown of white taffeta, flowered with gold, her dishevelled locks flowing negligently on her shoulders, she entered Don Quixote's chamber, supporting herself with an ebony staff.

The knight was so surprised and amazed at this unexpected apparition, that he was struck dumb; and, not knowing how to behave himself, he slunk down under the bed-clothes, and covered himself over head and ears. However, Altisidora placed herself in a chair close by his bed's head, and, after a profound sigh, "To what an extremity of misfortune and distress," said she, in a soft and languishing voice, "are young ladies of my quality reduced, when they are forced to give their tongues a loose, and betray the secrets of their hearts! Alas! noble Don Quixote de la Mancha, I am one of those unhappy persons overruled by my passion, but yet so reserved and patient in my sufferings, that silence broke my heart, and my heart broke in silence. It is now two days, most inexorable and marble-hearted man, since the sense of your severe usage and cruelty brought me to my death, or something so like it, that every one that saw me judged me to be dead; and, had not love been compassionate, and assigned my recovery on the sufferings of this kind squire, I had ever remained in the other world."

"Truly," quoth Sancho, "love might even as well have made choice of my ass for that service, and he would have obliged me a great deal more. But pray, good mistress, tell me one thing now, and so Heaven provide you a better-natured sweetheart than my master: what did you see in the other world?—what sort of folks are there in hell? for there, I suppose, you have been; for those that die of despair must needs go to that summer-house."

"To tell you the truth," replied Altisidora, "I fancy I could not be dead outright, because I was not got so far as hell; for, had I been once in, I am sure I should never have been allowed to have got out again. I got to the gates, indeed, where I found a round dozen of imps in their breeches and waistcoats, playing at tennis with flaming rackets. They wore flat bands, with scolloped Flanders lace and ruffles of the same; four inches of their wrists bare, to make their hands look the longer, in which they held rackets of fire. But what I most wondered at was, that, instead of tennis-balls, they made use of books that were every whit as light, and stuffed with wind and flocks, or such kind of trumpery. This was, indeed, most strange and wonderful; but, what still amazed me more, I found that, contrary to the custom of gamesters, among whom the winning party at least is in good humour, and the losers only angry, these hellish tossers of books, of both sides, did nothing but fret, fume, stamp, curse, and swear most horribly, as if they had been all losers."

"That is no wonder at all," quoth Sancho; "for your devils, whether they play or no, win or lose, they can never be contented."

"That may be," said Altisidora; "but another thing that I admire (I then admired, I would say) was, that the ball would not bear a second blow, but at every stroke they were obliged to change books, some of them new, some old, which I thought very strange. And one accident that happened upon this I cannot forget: they tossed up a new book, fairly bound, and gave it such a smart stroke that the very inside flew out of it, and all the leaves were scattered about. Then cried one of the devils to another, 'Look! look! what book is that?' 'It is the second part of the history of Don Quixote,' said the other; 'not that which was composed by Cid Hamet, the author of the first, but by a certain Arragonian, who professes himself a native of Tordesillas.' 'Away with it!' cried the first devil; 'down with it! plunge it where I may never see it more!' 'Why, is it such sad stuff?' said the other. 'Such intolerable stuff,' cried the first devil, 'that if I and all the devils in hell should set their heads together to make it worse, it were past our skill.' The devils continued their game, and shattered a world of other books; but the name of Don Quixote, that I so passionately adored, confined my thoughts only to that part of the vision which I have told you."

"It could be nothing but a vision, to be sure," said Don Quixote; "for I am the only person of the name now in the universe; and that very book is tossed about here at the very same rate, never resting in a place, for everybody has a fling at it. Nor am I concerned that any phantom assuming my name should wander in the shades of darkness or in the light of this world, since I am not the person of whom that story treats. If it be well written, faithful, and authentic, it will live for ages; but if it be bad, it will have a quick journey from its birth to the grave of oblivion."

Altisidora was then going to renew her expostulations and complaints against Don Quixote, had he not thus interrupted her:

"I have often cautioned you, madam," said he, "of fixing your attentions upon a man who is absolutely incapable of making a suitable return. It grieves me to have a heart obtruded upon me, when I have no better entertainment to give it than bare, cold thanks. I was only born for Dulcinea del Toboso, and to her alone the Destinies (if such there be) have devoted my affection; so it is presumption for any other beauty to imagine she can displace her, or but share the possession she holds in my soul. This, I hope, may suffice to take away all foundation from your hopes, to recall your modesty, and reinstate it in its proper bounds; for impossibilities are not to be expected from any creature upon earth."

Their discourse was interrupted by the coming in of the harper, singer, and composer of the stanzas that were performed in the court the night before. "Sir Knight," said he to Don Quixote, making a profound obeisance, "let me beg the favour of being numbered among your most humble servants; it is an honour which I have long been ambitious to receive, in regard of your great renown and the value of your achievements."

"Pray, sir," said Don Quixote, "let me know who you are, that I may proportion my respects to your merits."

The spark gave him to understand he was the person that made and sung the verses he heard the last night.

"Truly, sir," said Don Quixote, "you have an excellent voice, but I think your poetry was little to the purpose; for what relation, pray, have the stanzas of Garcilasso to this lady's death?"

"Oh, sir, never wonder at that," replied the musician; "I do but as other brothers of the quill. All the upstart poets of the age do the same, and every one writes what he pleases, how he pleases, and steals from whom he pleases, whether it be to the purpose or no; for, let them write and set to music what they will, though never so impertinent and absurd, there is a thing called poetical licence that is our warrant, and a safeguard and refuge for nonsense among all the men of jingle and metre."

Don Quixote was going to answer, but was interrupted by the coming in of the duke and duchess, who, improving the conversation, made it very pleasant for some hours; and Sancho was so full of his odd conceits and arch words, that the duke and duchess were at a stand which to admire most, his wit or his simplicity. After that Don Quixote begged leave for his departure that very day, alleging that knights, in his unhappy circumstances, were rather fitter to inhabit a humble cottage than a kingly palace. They freely complied with his request, and the duchess desired to know if Altisidora had yet attained to any share of his favour.

"Madam," answered Don Quixote, "I must freely tell your grace that I am confident all this damsel's disease proceeds from nothing else in the world but idleness; so nothing in nature can be better physic for her distemper than to be continually employed in some innocent and decent things. She has been pleased to inform me that bone-lace is much worn; and since, without doubt, she knows how to make it, let that be her task, and I will engage the tumbling of her bobbins too and again will soon toss her love out of her head. Now this is my opinion, madam, and my advice."

"And mine, too," quoth Sancho, "for I never knew any of your bone-lace makers die for love, nor any other young wench that had anything else to do. I know it by myself. When I am hard at work, with a spade in my hand, I no more think of my own dear wife than I do of my dead cow, though I love her as the apple of my eye."

"You say well, Sancho," answered the duchess; "and I will take care that Altisidora shall not want employment for the future; she understands her needle, and I am resolved she shall make use of it."

"Madam," said Altisidora, "I shall have no occasion for any remedy of that nature, for the sense of the severity and ill-usage that I have met with from that vagabond monster will, without any other means, soon raze him out of my memory. In the meantime I beg your grace's leave to retire, that I may no longer behold, I will not say his woful figure, but his ugly and abominable countenance."

"These words," said the duke, "put me in mind of the proverb, 'After railing comes forgiving.'"

Altisidora, putting her handkerchief to her eyes, as it were, to dry her tears, and then making her honours to the duke and duchess, went out of the room.

The discourse ended here. Don Quixote dressed, dined with the duke and duchess, and departed that afternoon.

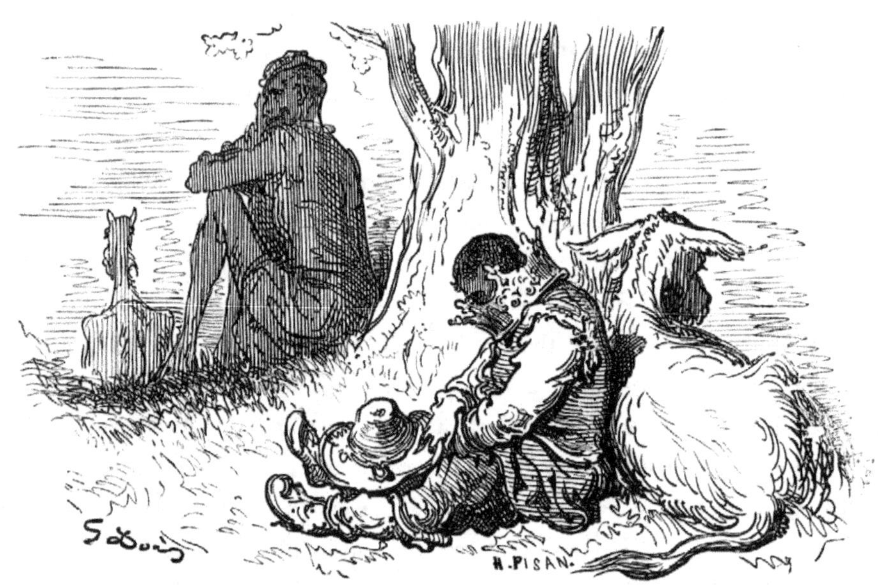

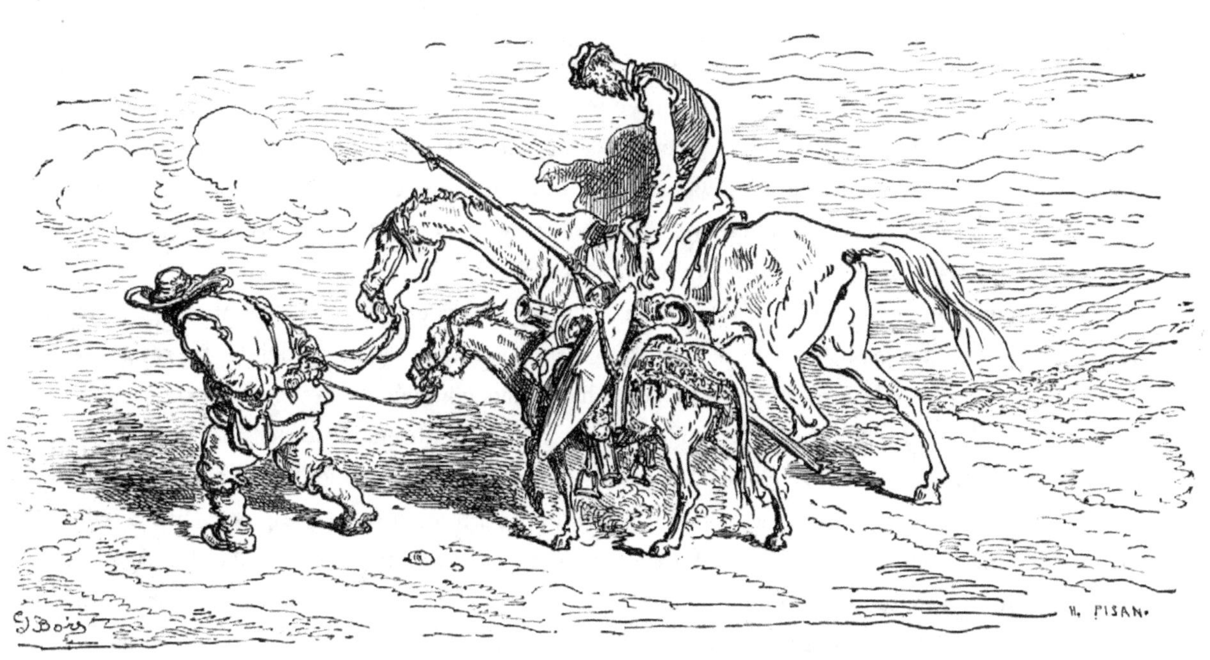

CHAPTER LXXI.

WHAT HAPPENED TO DON QUIXOTE AND HIS SQUIRE ON THEIR WAY HOME.

THE vanquished knight-errant continued his journey, equally divided between grief and joy. As for Sancho, his thoughts were not at all of the pleasing kind; on the contrary, he was mightily upon the sullen because Altisidora had bilked him of the smocks she promised him; and his head running upon that, "Faith and troth, sir," quoth he, "I have the worst luck of any physician under the cope of heaven. Other doctors kill their patients, and are paid for it, too, and yet they are at no further trouble than scrawling two or three cramp words for some physical slip-slop which the apothecaries are at all the pains to make up. Now here am I, that save people from the grave at the expense of my own hide, pinched, clapper-clawed, run through with pins, and whipped like a top, and yet not a cross do I get by the bargain. But if ever they catch me a-curing anybody in this fashion, unless I have my fee beforehand, may I be served as I have been, for nothing. Yes, indeed! they shall pay sauce for it; no money, no cure."

"You are in the right, Sancho," said Don Quixote, "and Altisidora has done unworthily in disappointing you of the smocks; though you must own that the virtue by which thou workest these wonders was a free gift, and cost thee nothing to learn, but the art of patience. For my part, had you demanded your fees for disenchanting Dulcinea, you should have received them already; but I am afraid there can be no gratuity proportionable to the greatness of the cure, and therefore I would not have the remedy depend upon a reward, for who knows whether it might hinder the effect of the penance? However, since we have more so far, we will put it to a trial. Come, Sancho, first pay your hide, then pay yourself out of the money of mine that you have in your custody."

Sancho, opening his eyes and ears above a foot wide at this fair offer, leaped presently at the proposal. "Ay, ay, sir, now, now you say something," quoth he; "I will do it with a jerk now, since you speak so feelingly. I have a wife and children to maintain, sir, and I must mind the main chance. Come, then, how much will you give me by the lash?"

"Were your payment," said Don Quixote, "to be answerable to the greatness and merits of the cure, not all the wealth of Venice, nor the Indian mines, were sufficient to reward thee. But see what cash you have of mine, and set what price you will on every stripe."

"The lashes," quoth Sancho, "are in all three thousand three hundred and odd, of which I have had five; the rest are to come. Let these five go for the odd ones, and let us come to the three thousand three hundred. At a quartillo, or three-halfpence a-piece (and I will not bate a farthing, if it were to my brother), they will make three thousand three hundred three-halfpences. Three thousand three-halfpences make fifteen hundred threepences, which amounts to seven hundred and fifty reals or sixpences. Now the three hundred remaining three-halfpences make a hundred and fifty threepences, and threescore and fifteen sixpences; put that together, and it comes just to eight hundred and twenty-five reals, or sixpences, to a farthing. This money, sir, if you please, I will deduct from yours that I have in my hands, and then I will reckon myself well paid for my jerking, and go home well pleased, though well whipped. But that is nothing, something has some savour; he must not think to catch fish who is afraid to wet his feet. I need say no more."

"Now blessings on thy heart, my dearest Sancho!" cried Don Quixote. "Oh! my friend, how shall Dulcinea and I be bound to pray for thee and serve thee while it shall please Heaven to continue us on earth! Speak, dear Sancho; when wilt thou enter upon thy task?"

"I will begin this very night," answered Sancho; "do you but order it so that we may lie in the fields, and you shall see how I will lay about me."

Don Quixote longed for night so impatiently, that, like all eager, expecting lovers, he fancied Phœbus had broken his chariot-wheels, which made the day of so unusual a length; but at last it grew dark, and they went out of the road into a shady wood, where they both alighted, and, being sat down upon the grass, they went to supper upon such provisions as Sancho's wallet afforded.

And now having satisfied himself, he thought it time to satisfy his master, and earn his money; to which purpose he made himself a whip of Dapple's halter, and, having stripped himself to the waist, retired farther up into the wood at a small distance from his master. Don Quixote, observing his readiness and resolution, could not forbear calling after him.

"Dear Sancho," cried he, "be not too cruel to thyself neither. Have a care, do not hack thyself to pieces. I mean, I would not have thee kill thyself before thou gettest to the end of the tally; and that the reckoning may be fair on both sides, I will stand at a distance, and keep an account of the strokes by the help of my beads; and so, Heaven prosper thee!"

"He is an honest man," quoth Sancho, "who pays to a farthing. I only mean to give myself a handsome whipping, for do not think I need kill myself to work miracles." With that he began to exercise the instrument of penance, and Don Quixote to tell the strokes; but by the time Sancho had applied seven or eight lashes on his bare back, he felt the jest bite him so smartly, that he began to repent him of his bargain. Whereupon he called to his master, and told him that he would be off with him; for such lashes as these were modestly worth threepence a-piece of any man's money, and truly he could not afford to go on at three-halfpence a lash.

"Go on, friend Sancho," answered Don Quixote; "take courage and proceed; I will double thy pay, if that be all."

"Say you so?" quoth Sancho; "then have at all. I will lay it on thick and threefold. Do but listen."

With that, slap went the scourge; but the cunning knave left persecuting his own skin, and fell foul of the trees, fetching such dismal groans every now and then, that one would have thought he had been giving up the ghost. Don Quixote, who was naturally tender-hearted, fearing he might make an end of himself before he could finish his penance, and so disappoint the happy effects of it—

"Hold!" cried he; "hold, my friend! as thou lovest thy life, hold, I conjure thee! no more at this time. This seems to be a very sharp sort of physic; therefore, pray do not take it all at once; make two doses of it. Come, come, all in good time; 'Rome was not built in a day.' If I have told right, thou hast given thyself above a thousand stripes; that is enough for one beating; for, to use a homely phrase, 'The ass will carry his load, but not a double load;' ride not a free horse to death."

"No, no," quoth Sancho; "it shall never be said of me, 'The eaten bread is forgotten,' or that I thought it working for a dead horse because I am paid beforehand. Therefore stand off, I beseech you; get out of the reach of my whip, and let me lay on the other thousand, and then the heart of the work will be broken."

"Since thou art in the humour," replied Don Quixote, "I will withdraw; and Heaven strengthen and reward thee!"

With that Sancho fell to work afresh, and beginning upon a new score, he lashed the trees at so unconscionable a rate, that he fetched off their skins most unmercifully. At length, raising his voice, seemingly resolved to give himself a sparing blow, he lets drive at a beech-tree with might and main—"There!" cried he, "down with thee, Samson, and all that are about thee!" This dismal cry, with the sound of the dreadful strokes that attended it, made Don Quixote run presently to his squire; and, laying fast hold on the halter, which Sancho had twisted about and managed most dexterously,—

"Hold!" cried he; "friend Sancho, stay the fury of thy arm. Dost thou think I will have thy death, and the ruin of thy wife and children, to be laid at my door? Forbid it, Fate! Let Dulcinea stay a while, till a better opportunity offer itself."

"Well, sir," quoth Sancho, "if it be your worship's will and pleasure it should be so, so let it be, quoth I. But, for goodness' sake, do so much as throw your cloak over my shoulders, for I am all in a sweat, and I have no mind to catch cold."

With that Don Quixote took off his cloak from his own shoulders, and putting it over those of Sancho, chose to remain *in cuerpo;* and the crafty squire, being lapped up warm, fell fast asleep, and never stirred till the sun waked him.

In the morning they went on their journey, and after three hours' riding alighted at an inn; for it was allowed by Don Quixote himself to be an inn, and not a castle, with moats, towers, portcullises, and drawbridges, as he commonly fancied; for now the knight was mightily off the romantic pin to what he used to be, as shall be shown presently at large. He was lodged in a ground room, which, instead of tapestry, was hung with a coarse painted stuff such as is often seen in villages. One of the pieces had the story of Helen of Troy, when Paris stole her away from her husband Menelaus, but scrawled out after a bungling rate by some wretched dauber or other. Another had the story of Dido and Æneas, the lady on the top of a turret, waving a sheet to her fugitive guest, who was in a ship at sea crowding all the sail he could to get from her. Don Quixote made this observation upon the two stories—that Helen was not at all displeased at the force put upon her, but rather leered and smiled upon her lover; whereas, on the other side, the fair Dido showed her grief by her tears, which, because they should be seen, the painter had made as big as walnuts.

"How unfortunate," said Don Quixote, "were these two ladies that they lived not in this age, or rather how much more unhappy am I, for not having lived in theirs! I would have met and stopped those gentlemen, and saved both Troy and Carthage from destruction; nay, by the death of Paris alone, all these miseries had been prevented."

"I will lay you a wager," quoth Sancho, "that before we be much older, there will not be an inn, a hedge tavern, a blind victualling-house, nor a barber's shop in the country, but will have the story of our lives and deeds pasted and painted along the walls. But I could wish with all my heart, though, that they may be done by a better hand than these."

"Thou art in the right, Sancho; for the fellow that drew these puts me in mind of Orbaneja, the painter of Uveda, who, as he sat at work, being asked what he was about, made answer, 'Anything that comes uppermost;' and if he chanced to draw a cock, he underwrote, 'This is a cock,' lest the people should take it for a fox. Just such a one was he that painted, or that wrote (for they are much the same) the history of this new Don Quixote, that has lately peeped out, and ventured to go a-strolling, for his painting or writing is all at random, and anything that comes uppermost. I fancy he is also not much unlike one Mauleon, a certain poet, who was at court some years ago, and pretended to give answers

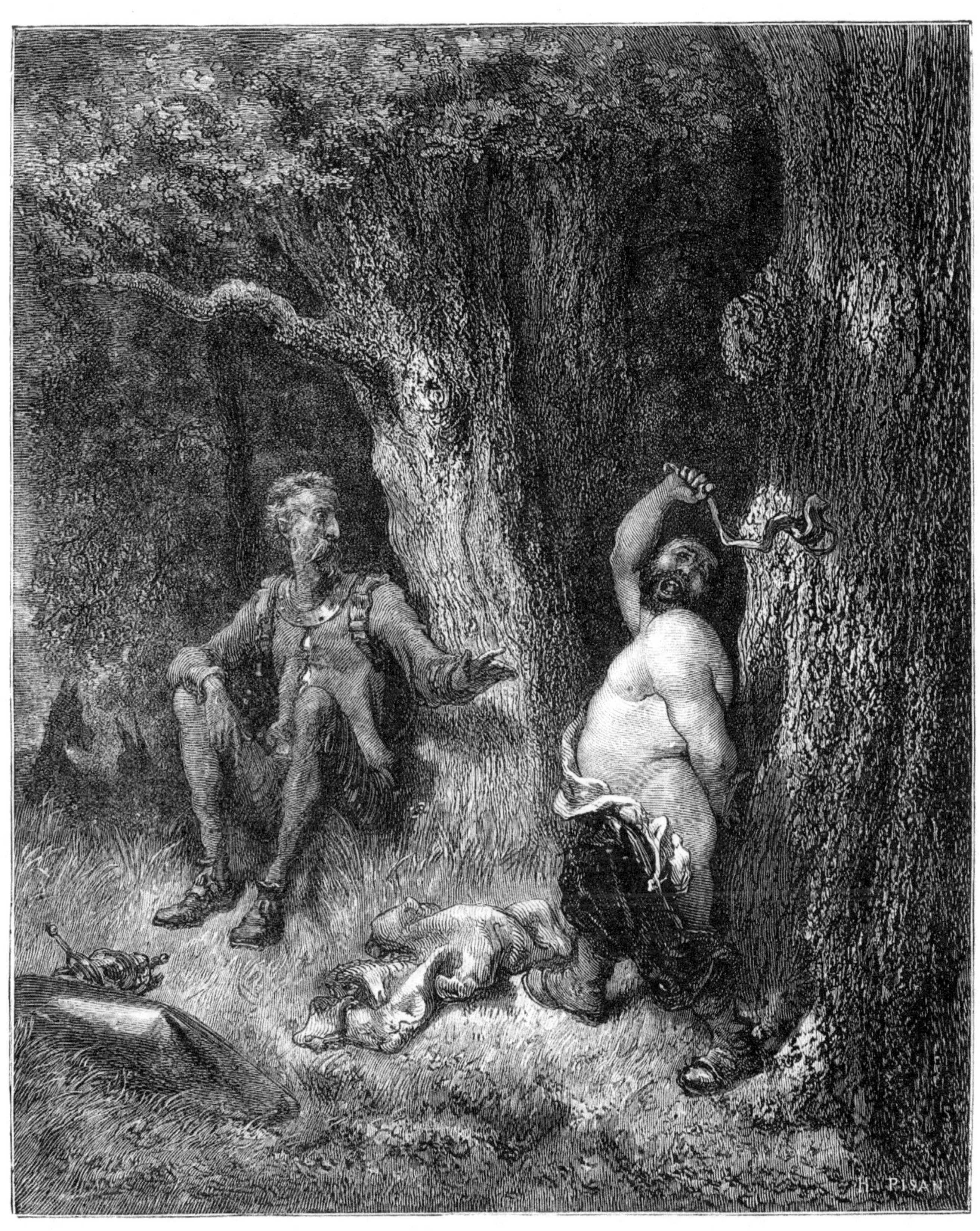

"'Hold!' cried he, 'friend Sancho · stay the fury of thy arm.'"

extempore to any manner of questions. But to come to our own affairs. Hast thou an inclination to have the other brush to-night? What think you of a warm house? would it not do better for that service than the open air?"

"Why, truly," quoth Sancho, "a whipping is but a whipping, either abroad or within doors, and I could like a close warm place well enough, so it were among trees; for I love trees hugely, do ye see; methinks they bear me company, and have a sort of fellow-feeling of my sufferings."

"Now I think on it," said Don Quixote, "it shall not be to-night, honest Sancho; you shall have more time to recover, and we will let the rest alone till we get home; it will not be above two days at most."

"Even as your worship pleases," answered Sancho; "but, if I might have my will, it were best making an end of the job now my hand is in, and my blood up. There is nothing like striking while the iron is hot, for 'delay breeds danger.' 'It is best grinding at the mill before the water is past.' 'Ever take while you may have it.' 'A bird in hand is worth two in the bush.'"

"For Heaven's sake, good Sancho," cried Don Quixote, "let alone thy proverbs; if once thou goest back to *Sicut erat,* or, as it was in the beginning, I must give thee over. Canst thou not speak as other folks do, and not after such a roundabout manner? How often have I told thee of this? Mind what I tell you; I am sure you will be the better for it."

"It is an unlucky trick I have got," replied Sancho; "I cannot bring you in three words to the purpose without a proverb, nor bring you any proverb but what I think to the purpose; but I will mend if I can."

And so, for this time, their conversation broke off.

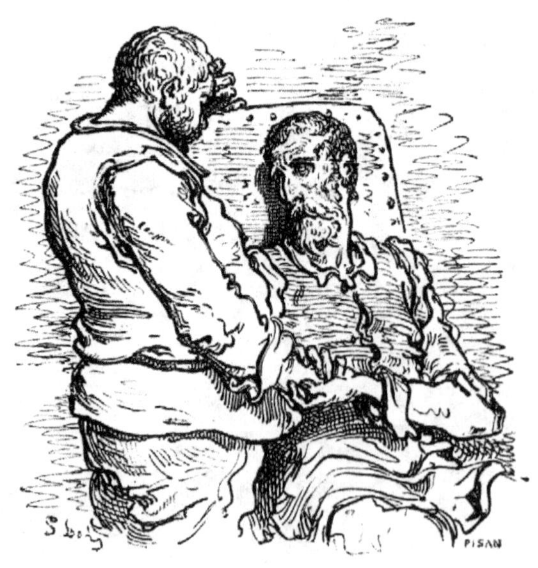

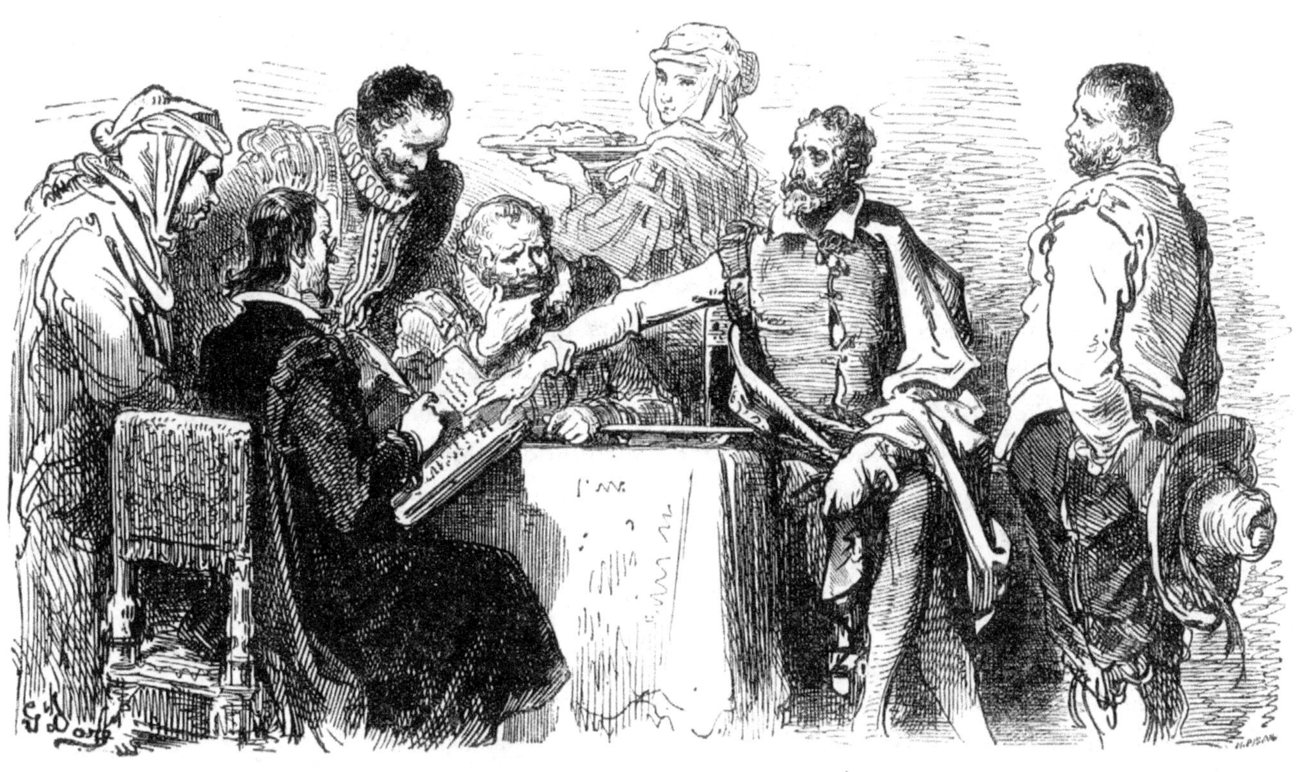

CHAPTER LXXII.

HOW DON QUIXOTE AND SANCHO GOT HOME.

THAT whole day Don Quixote and Sancho continued in the inn, expecting the return of night, the one to have an opportunity to make an end of his penance in the fields, and the other to see it fully performed, as being the most material preliminary to the accomplishment of his desires.

In the meantime a gentleman, with three or four servants, came riding up to the inn, and one of them calling him that appeared to be the master by the name of Don Alvaro Tarfe, "Your worship," said he, "had as good stop here till the heat of the day be over. In my opinion the house looks cool and cleanly."

Don Quixote overhearing the name of Tarfe, and presently turning to his squire, "Sancho," said he, "I am much mistaken if I had not a glimpse of this very name of Don Alvaro Tarfe in turning over that pretended second part of my history."

"As likely as not," quoth Sancho; "but first let him alight, and then we will question him about the matter."

The gentleman alighted, and was shown by the landlady into a ground room that faced Don Quixote's apartment, and was hung with the same sort of coarse painted stuff. A while after the stranger had undressed for coolness, he came out to take a turn, and walked into the porch of the house, that was large and airy. There he found Don Quixote, to whom addressing himself, "Pray, sir," said he, "which way do you travel?"

"To a country town not far off," answered Don Quixote, "the place of my nativity. And pray, sir, which way are you bound?"

"To Grenada, sir," said the knight, "the country where I was born."

"And a fine country it is," replied Don Quixote.

"But pray, sir, may I beg the favour to know your name? for the information, I am persuaded, will be of more consequence to my affairs than I can well tell you."

"They call me Don Alvaro Tarfe," answered the gentleman.

"Then, without dispute," said Don Quixote, "you are the same Don Alvaro Tarfe whose name fills a place in the Second Part of Don Quixote de la Mancha's History, that was lately published by a new author."

"The very man," answered the knight; "and that very Don Quixote, who is the principal subject of that book, was my intimate acquaintance. I am the person that enticed him from his habitation, so far, at least, that he had never seen the tournament at Saragosa had it not been through my persuasions, and in my company; and, indeed, as it happened, I proved the best friend he had, and did him a singular piece of service, for had I not stood by him, his intolerable impudence had brought him to some shameful punishment."

"But pray, sir," said Don Quixote, "be pleased to tell me one thing: am I anything like that Don Quixote of yours?"

"The farthest from it in the world, sir," replied the other.

"And had he," said our knight, "one Sancho Panza for his squire?"

"Yes," said Don Alvaro, "but I was the most deceived in him that could be; for, by report, that same squire was a comical, witty fellow, but I found him a very great blockhead."

"I thought no less," quoth Sancho, "for it is not in everybody's power to crack a jest, or say pleasant things; and that Sancho you talk of must be some paltry ragamuffin—some guttling mumper, or pilfering crack-rope, I warrant him; for it is I that am the true Sancho Panza; it is I that am the merry-conceited squire, that have always a tinker's budget full of wit and waggery, that will make gravity grin in spite of its teeth. If you will not believe me, do but try me; keep my company for a twelvemonth or so, you will find what a shower of jokes and notable things drop from me every foot. Ah! I set everybody a-laughing many times, and yet I wish I may be hanged if I designed it in the least. And then for the true Don Quixote de la Mancha, here you have him before you—the staunch, the famous, the valiant, the wise, the loving Don Quixote de la Mancha, the righter of wrongs, the punisher of wickedness, the father to the fatherless, the bully-rock of widows, the protector of damsels and maidens; he whose only dear and sweetheart is the peerless Dulcinea del Toboso; here he is, and here am I his squire. All other Don Quixotes, and all Sancho Panzas, besides us two, are but shams, and tales of a tub."

"Now, by the sword of St. Jago, honest friend," said Don Alvaro, "I believe as much, for the little thou hast uttered now has more of the humour than all I ever heard come from the other. The blockhead seemed to carry all his brains in his stomach; there is nothing a jest with him but filling his belly, and the rogue is too heavy to be diverting. For my part, I believe the enchanters that persecute the good Don Quixote sent the bad one to persecute me too. I cannot tell what to make of this matter; for though I can take my oath I left one Don Quixote under the surgeon's hands at the nuncio's house in Toledo, yet here starts up another Don Quixote quite different from mine."

"For my part," said our knight, "I dare not avow myself the good, but I may venture to say I am not the bad one; and, as a proof of it, sir, be assured that in the whole course of my life I never saw the city of Saragosa; and, so far from it, that hearing this usurper of my name had appeared there at the tournament, I declined coming near it, being resolved to convince the world that he was an impostor. I directed my course to Barcelona, the seat of urbanity, the sanctuary of strangers, the refuge of the distressed, the mother of men of valour, the redresser of the injured, the residence of true friendship, and the first city in the world for beauty and situation. And though some accidents that befell me there are so far from being grateful to my thoughts that they are a sensible mortification to me, yet, in my reflection of having seen that city, I find pleasure enough to alleviate my misfortune. In short, Don Alvaro, I am that Don Quixote de la Mancha whom fame has celebrated, and not the pitiful wretch who has usurped my name, and would arrogate to himself the honour of my designs. Sir, you are a gentleman, and I hope will not deny me the favour to depose before the magistrate of this place that you never saw me in all your life till this day, and that I am not the Don Quixote mentioned in that Second Part, nor was this Sancho Panza, my squire, the person you knew formerly."

"With all my heart," said Don Alvaro; "though I must own myself not a little confounded to find at the same time two Don Quixotes, and two Sancho Panzas, as different in their behaviour as they are alike in name. For my part, I do not know what to think of it; and I am sometimes apt to fancy my senses have been imposed upon."

"Ay, ay," quoth Sancho, "there has been foul play, to be sure. The same trick that served to bewitch my Lady Dulcinea del Toboso has been played you; and if three thousand and odd lashes laid on by me on my body would disenchant your worship as well as her, they should be at your service with all my heart; and what is more, they should not cost you a farthing."

"I do not understand what you mean by those lashes," said Don Alvaro.

"Thereby hangs a tale," quoth Sancho, "but that is too long to relate at a minute's warning; but if it be our luck to be fellow-travellers, you may chance to hear more of the matter."

Dinner-time being come, Don Quixote and Don Alvaro dined together; and the mayor, or bailiff of the town, happening to come into the inn with a public notary, Don Quixote desired him to take the deposition which Don Alvaro Tarfe there present was ready to give, confessing and declaring that the said deponent had not any knowledge of the Don Quixote there present, and that the said Don Quixote was not the same person that he, this deponent, had seen mentioned in a certain printed history, entitled or called 'The Second Part of Don Quixote de la Mancha,' written by Avellaneda, a native of Tordesillas. In short, the notary drew up and engrossed the affidavit in due form; and the testimonial wanted nothing to make it answer all the intentions of Don Quixote and Sancho, who were as much pleased as if it had been a matter of the greatest consequence, and that their words and behaviour had not been enough to make the distinction apparent between the two Don Quixotes and the two Sanchos.

The compliments and offers of service that passed after that between Don Alvaro and Don Quixote were not a few; and our knight of La Mancha behaved himself therein with so much discretion, that Don Alvaro was convinced he was mistaken; for he thought there was some enchantment in the case, since he had thus met with two knights and two squires of the same names and professions, and yet so very different.

They set out towards the evening, and about half a league from the town the road parted into two; one way led to Don Quixote's habitation, and the other to that which Don Alvaro was to take. Don Quixote in that little time let him understand the misfortune of his defeat, with Dulcinea's enchantment, and the remedy prescribed by Merlin, all which was new matter of wonder to Don Alvaro, who, having embraced Don Quixote and Sancho, left them on their way, and he followed his own.

Don Quixote passed that night among the trees, to give Sancho a fair occasion to make an end of his discipline, when the cunning knave put it in practice just after the same manner as the night before. The bark of the trees paid for all, and Sancho took such care of his back that a fly might have rested there without any disturbance.

All the while his abused master was very punctual in telling the strokes, and reckoned that, with those of the foregoing night, they amounted just to the sum of three thousand and twenty-nine. The sun, that seemed to have made more than ordinary haste to rise and see this human sacrifice, gave them light, however, to continue their journey; and as they went on they descanted at large upon Don Alvaro's mistake, and their own prudence, in relation to the certificate before the magistrate, in so full and authentic a form.

Their travels all that day and the ensuing night afforded on occurrence worth mentioning, except that Sancho that night put the last hand to his whipping work, to the inexpressible joy of Don Quixote, who waited for the day with as great impatience, in hopes he might light on his Lady Dulcinea in her disenchanted state; and all the way he went he made up to every woman he spied, to see whether she was Dulcinea del Toboso or not; for he so firmly relied on Merlin's promises, that he did not doubt of the performance.

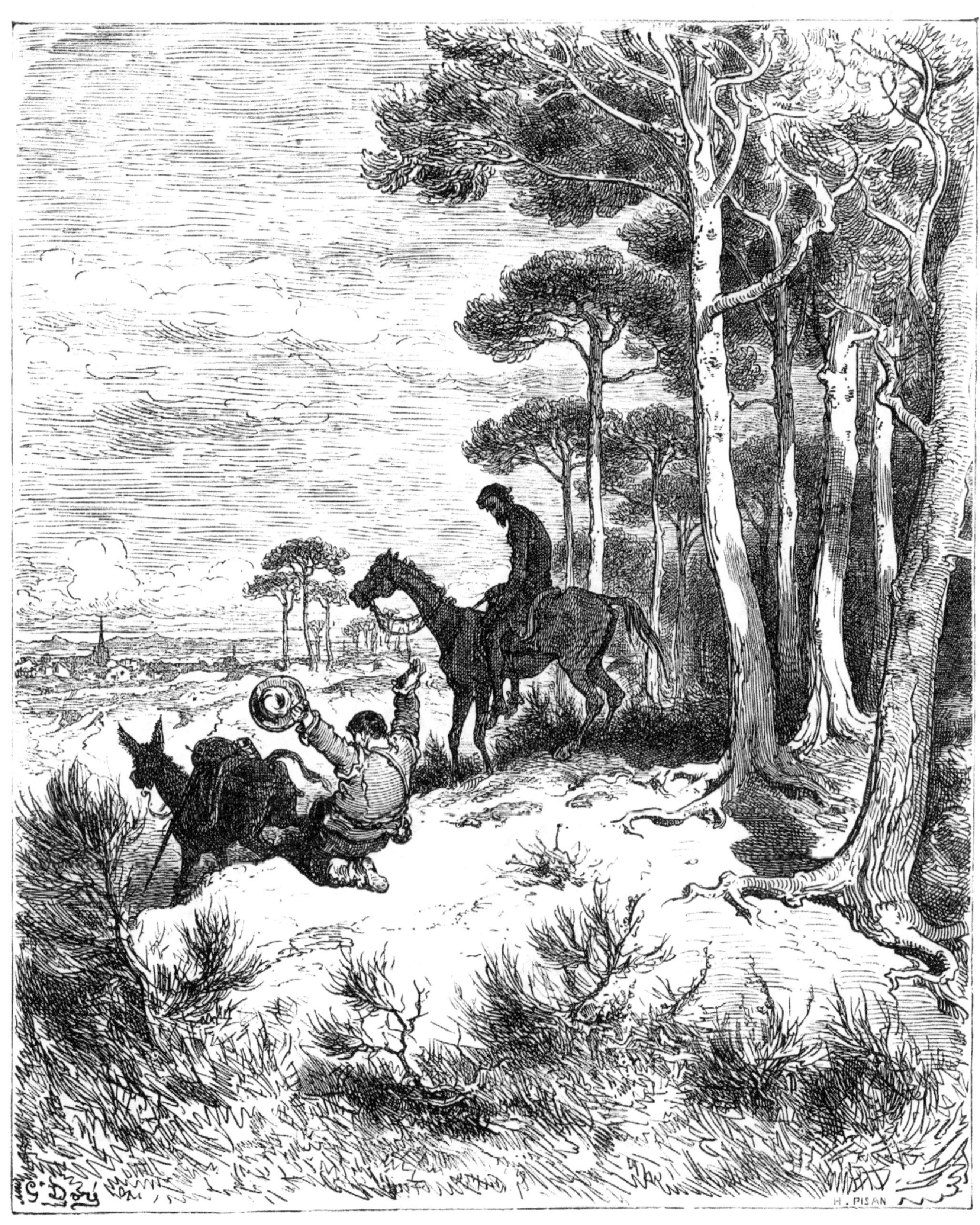

"'Oh, my long-wished for home!'"

He was altogether taken up with these hopes and fancies, when they got to the top of a hill that gave them a prospect of their village. Sancho had no sooner blessed his eyes with the sight, than down he fell on his knees. "Oh, my long-wished-for home!" cried he, "open thy eyes, and here behold thy child Sancho Panza come back to thee again, if not very full of money, yet very full of whipping. Open thy arms, and receive thy son Don Quixote too, who, though he got the worst of it with another, nevertheless got the better of himself, and that is the best kind of victory one can wish for; I have his own word for it. However, though I have been swingingly flogged, yet I have not lost all by the bargain, for I have whipped some money into my pocket."

"Forbear thy impertinence," said Don Quixote, "and let us now, in a decent manner, make our entry into the place of our nativity, where we will give a loose to our imaginations, and lay down the plan that is to be followed in our intended pastoral life." With these words they came down the hill, and went directly to their village.

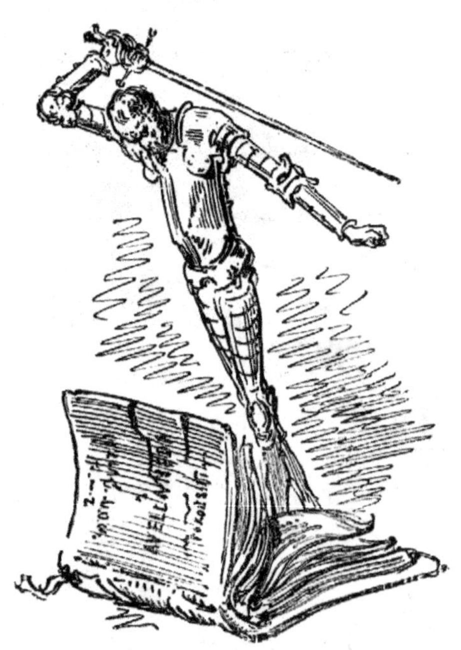

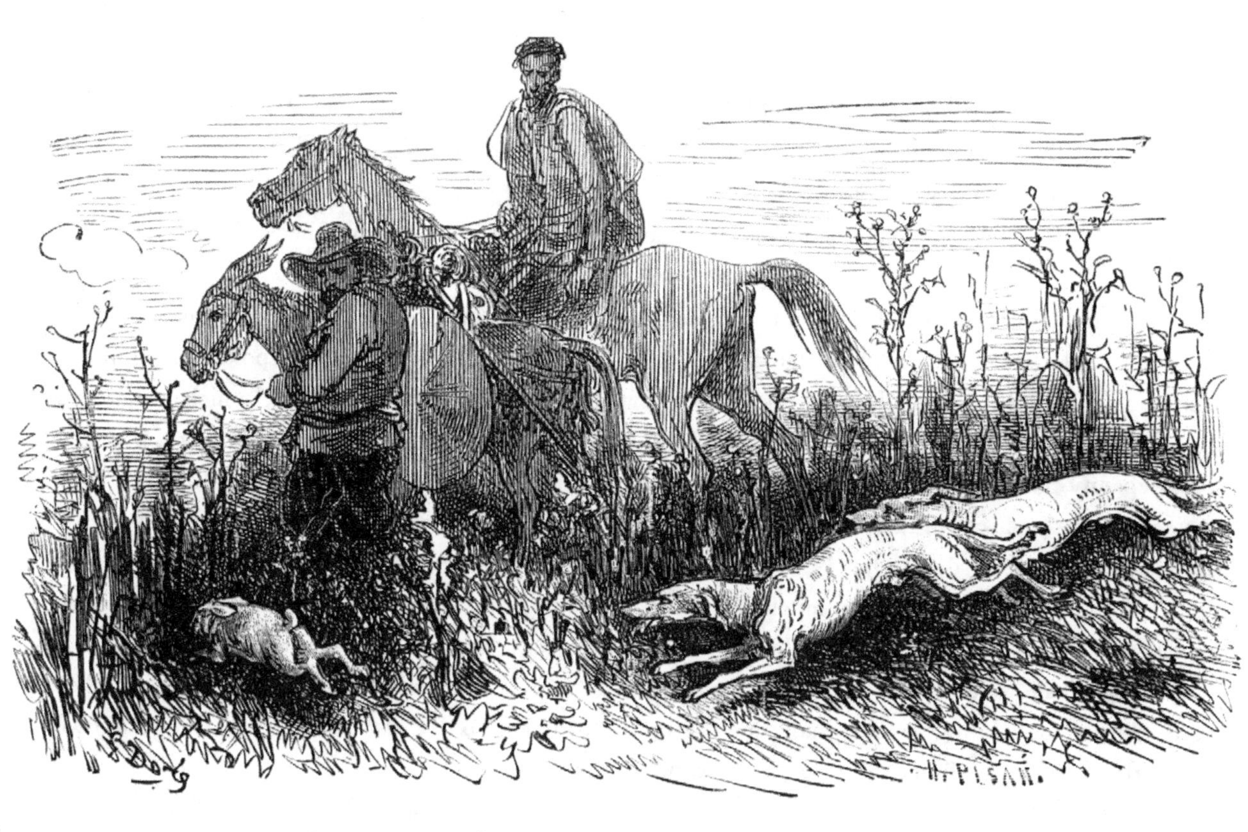

CHAPTER LXXIII.

OF THE OMINOUS ACCIDENTS THAT CROSSED DON QUIXOTE AS HE ENTERED HIS VILLAGE, WITH OTHER TRANSACTIONS THAT ILLUSTRATE AND ADORN THIS MEMORABLE HISTORY.

WHEN they were entering into the village, as Cid Hamet relates, Don Quixote observed two little boys contesting together in an adjoining field; and says one to the other, "Never fret thy gizzard about it, for thou shalt never see her whilst thou hast breath in thy body." Don Quixote overhearing this, "Sancho," said he, "did you mind the boy's words, 'Thou shalt never see her while thou hast breath in thy body?'"

"Well," answered Sancho, "and what is the great business though the boy did say so?"

"How!" replied Don Quixote; "dost thou not perceive that, applying the words to my affairs, they plainly imply that I shall never see my Dulcinea?"

Sancho was about to answer again, but was hindered by a full cry of hounds and horsemen pursuing a hare, which was put so hard to her shifts that she came and squatted down for shelter just between Dapple's feet. Immediately Sancho laid hold of her without difficulty, and presented her to Don Quixote; but he, with a dejected look, refusing the present, cried out aloud, "*Malum signum! malum signum!* ("an ill omen! an ill omen!") a hare runs away, hounds pursue her, and Dulcinea is not started."

"You are a strange man," quoth Sancho; "cannot we suppose, now, that poor puss here is Dulcinea, the greyhounds that followed her are those dogs the enchanters, that made her a country lass; she scours away, I catch her by the scut, and give her safe and sound into your worship's hands? And pray make much of her now you have her; for my part, I cannot for the blood of me see any harm, nor any ill-luck in this matter."

By this time the two boys that had fallen out came up to see the hare; and Sancho having asked the cause of their quarrel, he was answered by the boy that spoke the ominous words, that he had snatched from his play-fellow a little cage full of crickets, which he would not let him have again. Upon that Sancho put his hand into his pocket, and gave the boy a threepenny-piece for his cage; and, giving it to Don Quixote, "There, sir," quoth he, "here are all the signs of ill-luck come to nothing. You have them in your own hands; and, though I am but a dunderhead, I dare swear these things are no more to us than the rain that falls at Christmas. I am much mistaken if I have not heard the parson of our parish advise all sober Catholics against heeding such fooleries; and I have heard you yourself, my dear master, say that all such Christians as troubled their heads with these fortune-telling follies were neither better nor worse than downright numskulls; so let us even leave things as we found them, and get home as fast as we can."

By this time the sportsmen were come up, and, demanding their game, Don Quixote delivered them their hare. They passed on, and, just at their coming into the town, they perceived the curate and the bachelor Carrasco at their devotions in a small field adjoining. But we must observe, by the way, that Sancho Panza, to cover his master's armour, had, by way of a sumpter-cloth, laid over Dapple's back the buckram-frock, figured with flames of fire, which he wore at the duke's the night that Altisidora rose from the dead; and he had no less judiciously clapped the mitre on the head of the ass, which made so odd and whimsical a figure that it might be said never four-footed ass was so bedizened before. The curate and the bachelor, presently knowing their old friends, ran to meet them with open arms; and, while Don Quixote alighted and returned their embraces, the boys, who are ever so quick-sighted that nothing can escape their eyes, presently spying the mitred ass, came running and flocking about them. "Oh, la!" cried they to one another, "look you there, boys! here is Gaffer Sancho Panza's ass as fine as a lady! and Don Quixote's beast leaner than ever." With that they ran whooping and hallooing about them through the town, while the two adventurers, attended by the curate and the bachelor, moved towards Don Quixote's house, where they were received at the door by his housekeeper and his niece, who had already got notice of their arrival. The news having also reached Teresa Panza, Sancho's wife, she came running, half dressed, with her hair about her ears, to see him; leading by the hand all the way her daughter Sanchica, who hardly wanted to be tugged along. But when she found that her husband looked a little short of the state of a governor, "Mercy on me!" quoth she, "what is the meaning of this, husband? You look as though you had come all the way on foot, and tired off your legs, too. Why, you have come home more like a shark than a governor."

"Mum, Teresa," quoth Sancho; "'it is not all gold that glisters,' and every man was not born with a silver spoon in his mouth. First, let us go home, and then I will tell thee wonders. I have taken care of the main chance. Money I have, old girl, and I came honestly by it, without wronging anybody."

"Hast got money, old boy? Nay, then, it is well enough, no matter which way; let it come by hook or by crook, it is but what your betters have done before you."

At the same time Sanchica, hugging her father, asked him what he had brought her home, for she had gaped for him as the flowers do for the dew in May. Thus Sancho, leading Dapple by the halter on one side, his wife taking him by the arm on the other, and his daughter following, away they went together to his cottage, leaving Don Quixote at his own house, under the care of his niece and housekeeper, with the curate and bachelor to keep him company.

That very moment Don Quixote took the two last aside, and, without mincing the matter, gave them a short account of his defeat, and the obligation he lay under of being confined to his village for a year, which, like a true knight-errant, he was resolved punctually to observe. He added, that he intended to pass that interval of time in the innocent functions of a pastoral life; and, therefore, he would immediately commence shepherd, and entertain his amorous passion solitarily in fields and woods, and begged, if business of greater importance were not an obstruction, that they would both please to be his companions, assuring them he would furnish them with such a number of sheep as might entitle them to such a profession. He also told them that he had already in a manner fitted them for the undertaking, for he had provided them all with names the most pastoral in the world. The curate being desirous to know the names, Don Quixote told him he would himself be called the shepherd Quixotis; that the bachelor should be called the shepherd Carrascone; the curate, pastor Curiambro; and Sancho Panza, Panzino the shepherd.

They were struck with amazement at this new strain of folly; but, considering this might be a means of keeping him at home, and hoping, at the same time, that, within the year, he might be cured of his mad knight-errantry, they came into his pastoral folly, and, with great applause to his project, freely offered their company in the design.

"We shall live the most pleasant life imaginable," said Samson Carrasco; "for, as everybody knows, I am a most celebrated poet, and I will write pastorals in abundance. Sometimes, too, I may raise my strain, as occasion offers, to divert us, as we range the groves and plains. But one thing, gentlemen, we must not forget: it is absolutely necessary that each of us choose a name for the shepherdess he means to celebrate in his lays; nor must we forget the ceremony used by the amorous shepherds, of writing, carving, notching, or engraving on every tree the names of such shepherdesses, though the bark be ever so hard."

"You are very much in the right," replied Don Quixote; "though, for my part, I need not be at the trouble of devising a name for any imaginary shepherdess, being already captivated by the peerless Dulcinea del Toboso, the nymph of these streams, the ornament of these meads, the primrose of beauty, the cream of gracefulness, and, in short, the subject that can merit all the praises that hyperbolical eloquence can bestow."

"We grant all this," said the curate; "but we, who cannot pretend to such perfections, must make it our business to find out some shepherdesses of a lower form."

"We shall find enough, I will warrant you," replied Carrasco; "and though we meet with none, yet will we give those very names we find in books, such as Phyllis, Amaryllis, Diana, Florinda, Galatea, Belisarda, and a thousand more. Besides, if my shepherdess be called Anne, I will name her in my verses Anarda; if Frances, I will call her Francenia; and, if Lucy be her name, then Lucinda, and so forth. And if Sancho Panza will make one of our fraternity, he may celebrate his wife Teresa by the name of Teresania."

Don Quixote could not forbear smiling at the turn given to that name. The curate again applauded his laudable resolution, and repeated his offer of bearing him company all the time that his other employment would allow him; and then they took their leave, giving him all the good advice that they thought might conduce to his health and welfare.

No sooner were the curate and bachelor gone, than the housekeeper and niece, who, according to custom, had been listening to all their discourse, came both upon Don Quixote. "Bless me, uncle!" cried the niece, "what is here to do? What new maggot is got into your head? When we thought you were come to stay at home, and live like a sober, honest gentleman in your own house, are you hankering after new inventions, and running a wool-gathering after sheep, forsooth? By my troth, sir, you are somewhat of the latest."

"Oh, sir," quoth the housekeeper, "how will you be able to endure the summer's sun and the winter frost in the open fields? And then the howlings of the wolves, Heaven bless us! Pray, good sir, do not think of it; it is a business fit for nobody but those that are bred and born to it, and as strong as horses. Let the worst come to the worst; better be a knight-errant still, than a keeper of sheep. Troth, master, take my advice; I am neither drunk nor mad, but fresh and fasting from everything but sin, and I have fifty years over my head. Be ruled by me; stay at home, do good to the poor; and, if aught goes ill with you, let it lie at my door."

"Good girls," said Don Quixote, "hold your prating: I know best what I have to do: only let me go to bed, for I find myself somewhat out of order. However, do not trouble your heads; whether I be a knight-errant or an errant-shepherd, you shall always find that I will provide for you."

The niece and housekeeper, who, without doubt, were good-natured creatures, then brought him something to eat, and tended him with all imaginable care.

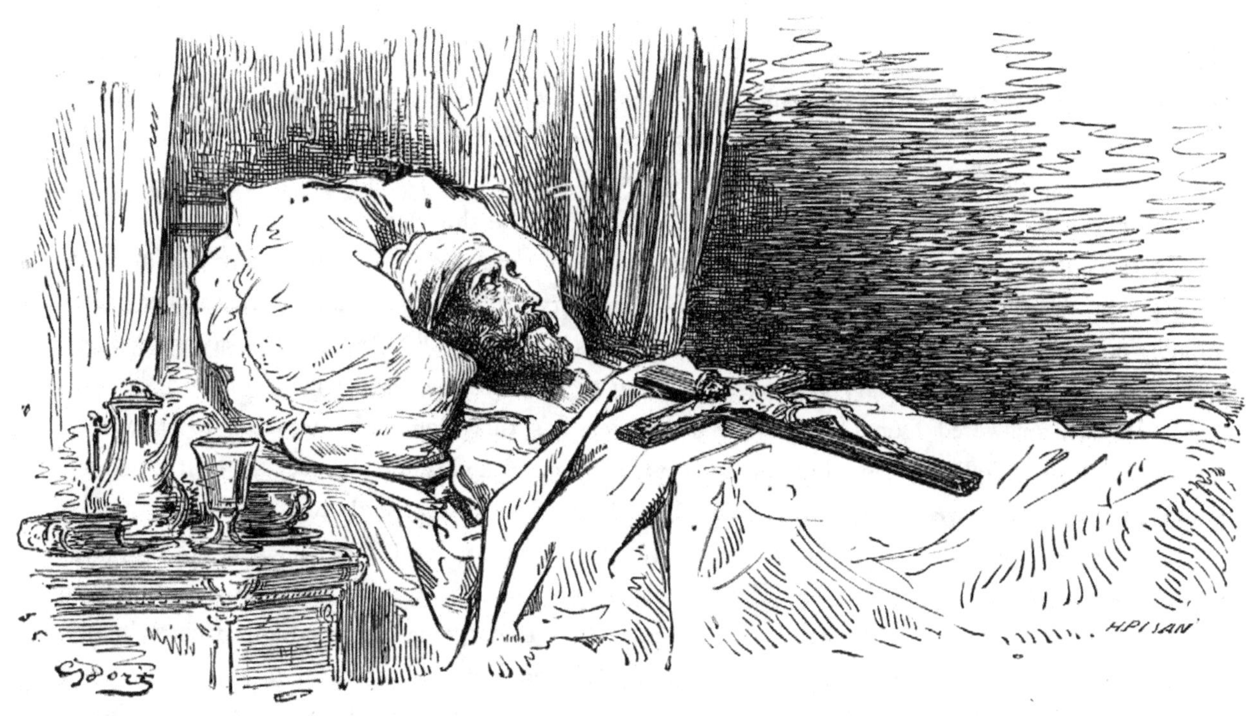

CHAPTER LXXIV.

HOW DON QUIXOTE FELL SICK, MADE HIS LAST WILL, AND DIED.

AS all human things, especially the lives of men, are transitory, their very beginnings being but steps to their dissolution, so Don Quixote, who was no way exempted from the common fate, was snatched away by death when he least expected it. Whether his sickness was the effect of his melancholy reflections, or whether it was so pre-ordained by Heaven, most certain it is, he was seized with a violent fever that confined him to his bed six days.

All that time his good friends, the curate, bachelor, and barber, came often to see him, and his trusty squire Sancho Panza never stirred from his bed-side.

They conjectured that his sickness proceeded from the regret of his defeat, and his being disappointed of Dulcinea's disenchantment; and accordingly they left nothing unessayed to divert him. The bachelor begged him to pluck up a good heart, and rise, that they might begin their pastoral life, telling him that he had already written an eclogue to that purpose, not inferior to those of Sanazaro, and that he had bought, with his own money, of a shepherd of Quintanar, two tearing dogs to watch their flock, the one called Barcino, and the other Butron; but this had no effect on Don Quixote, for he still continued dejected. A physician was sent for, who, upon feeling his pulse, did not very well like it; and therefore desired him of all things to provide for his soul's health, for that of his body was in a dangerous condition. Don Quixote heard this with much more temper than those about him; for his niece, his housekeeper, and his squire fell a-weeping as

CCC

bitterly as if he had been laid out already. The physician was of opinion that mere melancholy and vexation had brought him to his approaching end. Don Quixote desired them to leave him a little, because he found himself inclinable to rest; they retired, and he had a hearty sleep of about six hours, which the housekeeper and niece were afraid had been his last.

At length he awoke, and, with a loud voice, "Blessed be the Almighty," cried he, "for this great benefit he has vouchsafed to do me! Infinite are his mercies! they are greater and more in number than the sins of men." The niece hearkening very attentively to these words of her uncle, and finding more sense in them than there was in his usual talk, "What do you say, sir?" said she; "has anything extraordinary happened? What mercies are these you mention?"

"Mercies," answered Don Quixote, "that Heaven has this moment vouchsafed to show me, in spite of all my iniquities. My judgment is returned clear and undisturbed, and that cloud of ignorance is now removed which the continual reading of those foolish books of knight-errantry had cast over my understanding. Now I perceive their nonsense and impertinence, and am only sorry the discovery happens so late, when I want time to make amends, by those studies that should enlighten my soul, and prepare me for futurity. I find, niece, my end approaches; but I would have it such, that though my life has got me the character of a madman, I may deserve a better at my death. Dear child," continued he, "send for my honest friend the curate, the bachelor Carrasco, and Master Nicholas the barber, for I intend to make my confession and my will."

His niece was saved the trouble of sending, for they all three came in; which Don Quixote perceiving, "My good friends," said he, "I have happy news to tell you; I am no longer Don Quixote de la Mancha, but Alonzo Quixano, tne same whom the world, for his fair behaviour, has been formerly pleased to call *the Good.* I now declare myself an enemy to Amadis de Gaul, and his whole generation; all profane stories of knight-errantry, all romances, I detest. I have a true sense of the danger of reading them, and of all my past follies; and, through Heaven's mercy and my own experience, I abhor them."

His three friends were not a little surprised to hear him talk at this rate, and concluded some new frenzy had possessed him. "What now?" said Samson to him: "what is all this, Signor Don Quixote? We have just had the news that the Lady Dulcinea is disenchanted; and now we are upon the point of turning shepherds, to live like princes, you are dwindled down to a hermit!"

"No more of that, I beseech you," replied Don Quixote; "all the use I shall make of these follies at present is to heighten my repentance; and though they have hitherto proved prejudicial, yet, by the assistance of Heaven, they may turn to my advantage at my death: I find it comes fast upon me; therefore, pray, gentlemen, let us be serious. I want a priest to receive my confession, and a scrivener to draw up my will. There is no trifling at a time like this; I must take care of my soul; and therefore, pray let the scrivener be sent for, while Mr. Curate prepares me by confession."

Don Quixote's words put them all into such admiration, that they stood gazing upon one another; they thought they had reason to doubt of the return of his understanding, and yet they could not help believing him. They were also apprehensive he was near the point of death, considering the sudden recovery of his intellects; and he delivered himself after that with so much sense, discretion, and piety, and showed himself so resigned to the will of Heaven, that they made no scruple to believe him restored to his perfect judgment at last. The curate thereupon cleared the room of all the company but himself and Don Quixote, and then confessed him. In the meantime the bachelor ran for the scrivener, and presently brought him with him; and Sancho Panza, being informed by the bachelor how ill his master was, and finding his niece and housekeeper all in tears, began to make wry faces and fall a-crying. The curate, having heard the sick person's confession, came out and told them that the good Alonzo Quixano was very near his end, and certainly in his senses; and therefore they had best go in, that he might make his will. These dismal tidings opened the sluices of the housekeeper's, the niece's, and the good squire's swollen eyes, so that a whole inundation of tears burst out of those flood-gates, and a thousand sighs from their hearts; for, indeed, either as Alonzo Quixano, or as Don Quixote de la Mancha, as it has been observed, the sick gentleman had always showed himself such a good-natured man, and of so agreeable a behaviour, that he was not only beloved by his family, but by every one that knew him.

The scrivener, with the rest of the company, then went into the chamber; and the preamble and former part of the will being drawn, and the testator having recommended his soul to Heaven, and bequeathed his body to the earth, according to custom, he came to the legacies, as follows:—

"Item, I give and bequeath to Sancho Panza, whom in my madness I made my squire, whatever money he has or may have of mine in his hands. And, whereas there are reckonings and accounts to be adjusted between us for what he has received and disbursed, my will and pleasure is, that whatever may remain due to me, which can be but small, be enjoyed by him as my free gift, without any let or molestation, and much good may it do him. And as, when I was mad, he was through my means made governor of an island, I would now, in my right senses, give him the government of a kingdom, were it in my power, in consideration of his integrity and faithfulness. And now, my friend," said he, turning to Sancho, "pardon me that I have brought upon thee, as well as myself, the scandal of madness, by drawing thee into my own errors, and persuading thee that there have been and still are knights-errant in the world."

"Woe's me, my dear master's worship!" cried Sancho, all in tears; "do not die this bout, but even take my counsel, and live on a many years; it is the maddest trick a man can ever play in his whole life, to let his breath sneak out of his body without any more ado, and without so much as a rap over the pate, or a kick in the body; to go out like the snuff of a farthing candle, and die merely of the mulligrubs or the sullens. For shame, sir! do not give way to sluggishness, but get out of your doleful dumps, and rise. Is this a time to lie honing and groaning a-bed, when we should be in the fields in our shepherds' clothing, as we had resolved? Ten to one but behind some bush, or under some hedge, we may find the Lady Madam Dulcinea, stripped of her enchanted rags, and as fine as a queen. Mayhaps you take it to heart that you were unhorsed, and a little crupper-scratched the other day; but if that be all, lay the blame upon me, and say it was my fault in not girting Rozinante tight enough. You know, too, there is nothing more common in your errantry-books than for the knights to be every foot jostled out of the saddle. There is nothing but ups and downs in this world, and he that is cast down to-day may be up to-morrow."

"Even so," said Samson; "honest Sancho has a right notion of the matter."

"Soft and fair, gentlemen," replied Don Quixote; "'never look for birds of this year in the nests of the last;' I was mad, but now I am in my right senses. I was once Don Quixote de la Mancha, but I am now (as I said before) the plain Alonzo Quixano; and I hope the sincerity of my words and my repentance may restore me to the same esteem you have had for me before; and so, Mr. Scrivener, pray go on."

"Item, I constitute and appoint Antonia Quixano, my niece here present, sole heiress of all my estate real and personal, after all my just debts and legacies, bequeathed by these presents, shall have been paid, satisfied, and deducted, out of the best of my goods and chattels; and the first of that kind to be discharged shall be the salary due to my housekeeper, together with twenty ducats over and above her wages, which said sum I leave and bequeath her to buy her mourning.

"Item, I appoint Mr. Curate, and Mr. Samson Carrasco, the bachelor, here present, to be the executors of this my last will and testament.

"Item, It is my will, that if my niece Antonia Quixano be inclinable to marry, it be with none but a person who, upon strict inquiry, shall be found never to have read a book of knight-errantry in his life; and in case it appears that he has been conversant in such books, and that she persists in her resolution to marry him, she is then to forfeit all right and title to my bequest, which, in such a case, my executors are hereby empowered to dispose of to pious uses, as they shall think most proper.

"Item, I entreat the said executors that if at any time they happen to meet with the author of a book now extant, entitled 'The Second Part of the Achievements of Don Quixote de la Mancha,' they would from me most heartily beg his pardon, for my being undesignedly the occasion of his writing such a parcel of impertinences as is contained in that book, for it is the greatest burden to my departing soul that ever I was the cause of his making such a thing public."

Having finished the will, he fell into a swooning fit, and extended his body to the full length in the bed. All the company were troubled and alarmed, and ran to his assistance; however, he came to himself at last, but relapsed into the like fits almost every hour for the space of three days that he lived after he had made his will.

The whole family was in grief and confusion; and yet, after all, the niece continued to

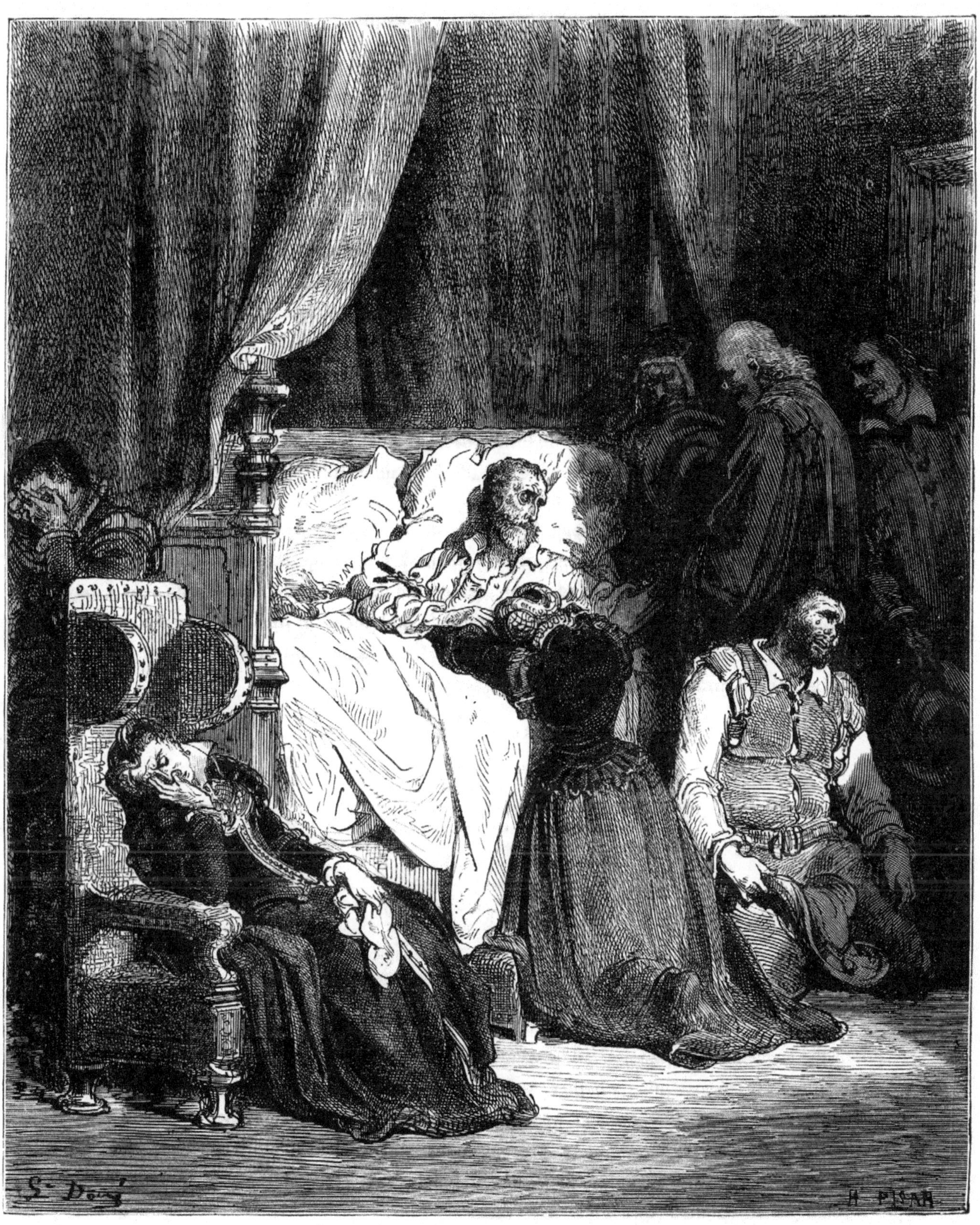

DEATH OF DON QUIXOTE.

eat; the housekeeper drank, and washed down sorrow; and Sancho Panza made much of himself; for there is a strange charm in the thoughts of a good legacy, or the hopes of an estate, which wondrously removes, or at least alleviates, the sorrow that men would otherwise feel for the death of friends.

In short, Don Quixote's last day came, after he had made those preparations for death which good Christians ought to do, and, by many fresh and weighty arguments, showed his abhorrence of books of knight-errantry. The scrivener, who was by, protested he had never read in any books of that kind of any knight-errant who ever died in his bed so quietly, and like a good Christian, as Don Quixote did. In short, amidst the tears and lamentations of his friends, he gave up the ghost, or, to speak more plainly, died; which, when the curate perceived, he desired the scrivener to give him a certificate how Alonzo Quixano, commonly called *the Good*, and sometimes known by the name of Don Quixote de la Mancha, was departed out of this life into another, and died a natural death. This he desired, lest any other author but Cid Hamet Benengeli should take occasion to raise him from the dead, and presume to write endless histories of his pretended adventures.

Thus died that ingenious gentleman, Don Quixote de la Mancha, whose native place Cid Hamet has not thought fit directly to mention, with design that all the towns and villages in La Mancha should contend for the honour of giving him birth, as the seven cities of Greece did for Homer. We shall omit Sancho's lamentations, and those of the niece and the housekeeper, as also several epitaphs that were made for his tomb, and will only give you this, which the bachelor Carrasco caused to be put over it:—

DON QUIXOTE'S EPITAPH.

The body of a knight lies here,
  So brave, that, to his latest breath,
Immortal glory was his care,
  And made him triumph over death.

His looks spread terror every hour;
  He strove oppression to control;
Nor could all hell's united power
  Subdue or daunt his mighty soul.

Nor has his death the world deceived
  Less than his wondrous life surprised;
For if he like a madman lived,
  At least he like a wise one died.

Here the sagacious Cid Hamet, addressing himself to his pen, "Oh, thou, my slender pen!" says he, "thou, of whose nib, whether well or ill cut, I dare not speak my thoughts! suspended by this brass wire, remain upon this spit-rack where I lodge thee! There mayest thou claim a being many ages, unless presumptuous and wicked historians take thee down to profane thee! But, ere they lay their heavy hands upon thee, bid them beware. and, as well as thou canst, in their own style, tell them—

'Avaunt, ye scoundrels, all and some!
  I'm kept for no such thing:
Defile me not; but hang yourselves;
  And so, God save the king.

'For me alone was the great Quixote born, and I alone for him. Deeds were his task, and to record them mine.' We two, like tallies for each other struck, are nothing when apart. In vain the spurious scribe of Tordesillas dared, with his blunt and bungling ostrich-quill, invade the deeds of my most valorous knight: his shoulders are unequal to the attempt; the task is superior to his frozen genius.

"And thou, reader, if ever thou canst find him out in his obscurity, I beseech thee advise him likewise to let the wearied bones of Don Quixote rest quiet in the earth that covers them. Let him not expose them in Old Castile against the sanctions of death, impiously raking him out of the vault where he really lies stretched out beyond a possibility of taking a third ramble through the world. The two sallies that he has made already (which are the subject of this volume, and have met with such universal applause in this and other kingdoms) are sufficient to ridicule the pretended adventures of knights-errant. Thus advising him for the best, thou shalt discharge the duty of a Christian, and do good to him that wishes thee evil. As for me, I must esteem myself happy to have been the first that rendered those fabulous nonsensical stories of knight-errantry the object of the public aversion. They are already going down, and I do not doubt but they will drop and fall all together in good earnest, never to rise again. Adieu."

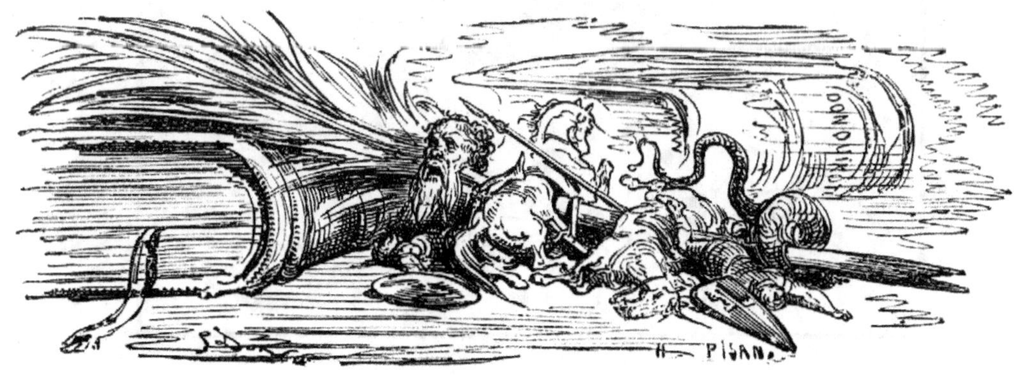

Part 1
Restored Special Edition

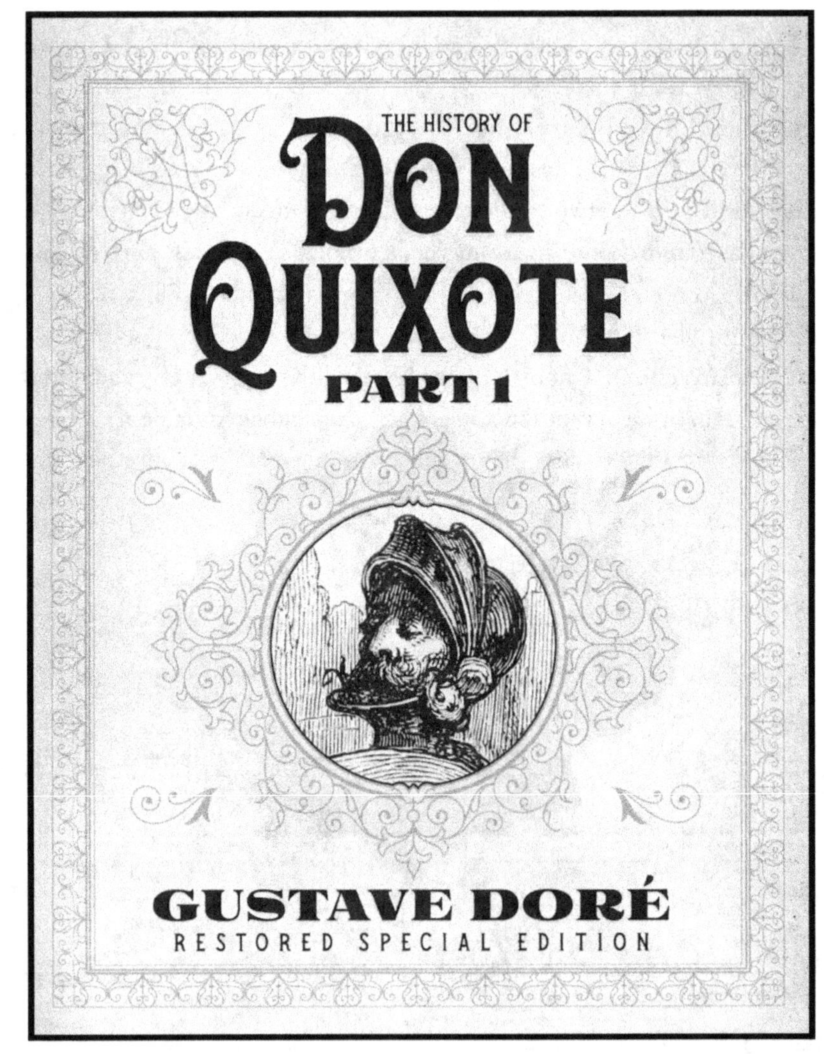

More Doré from CGR Publishing at www.CGRpublishing.com

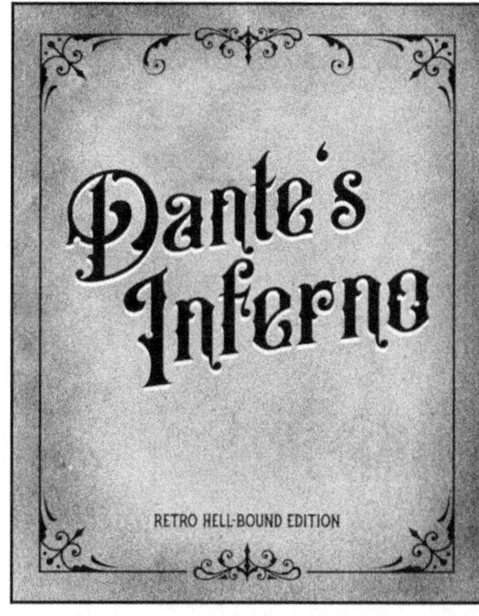

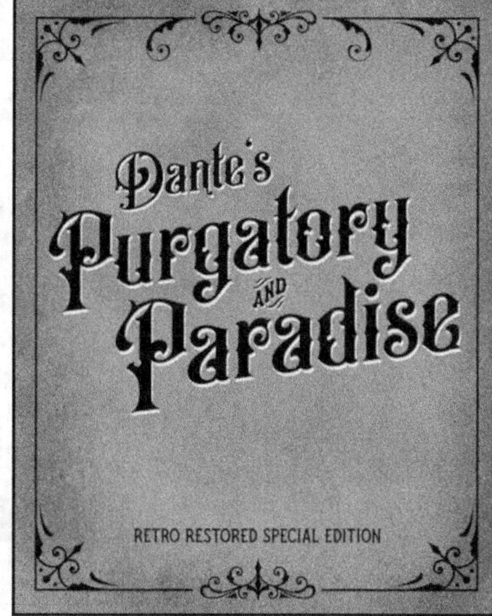

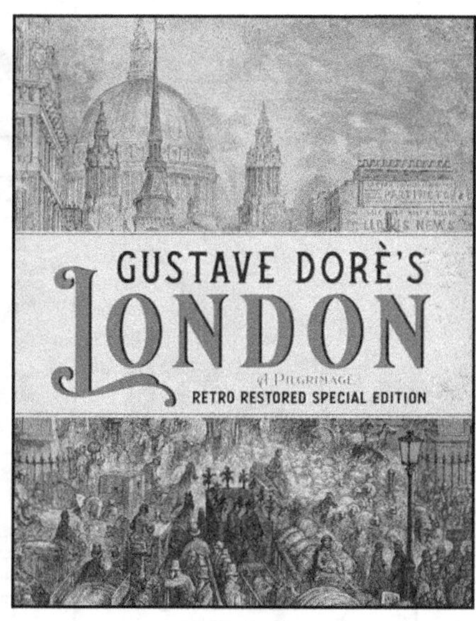

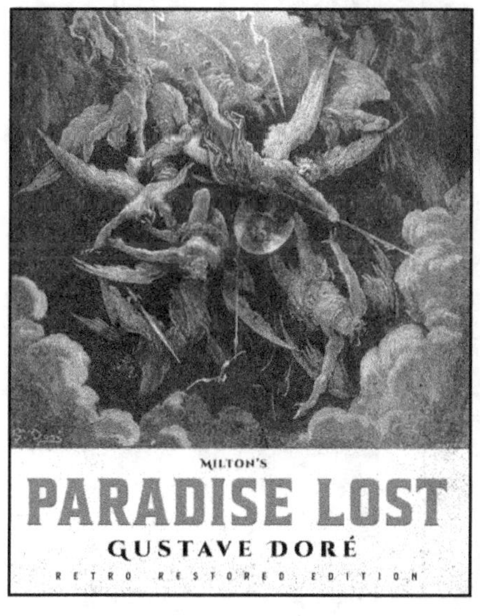

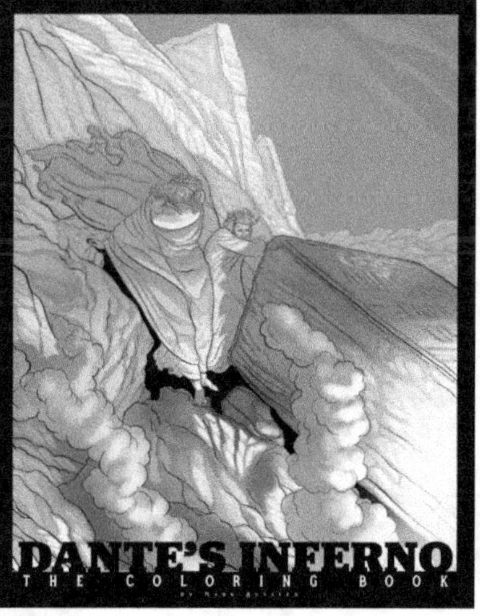

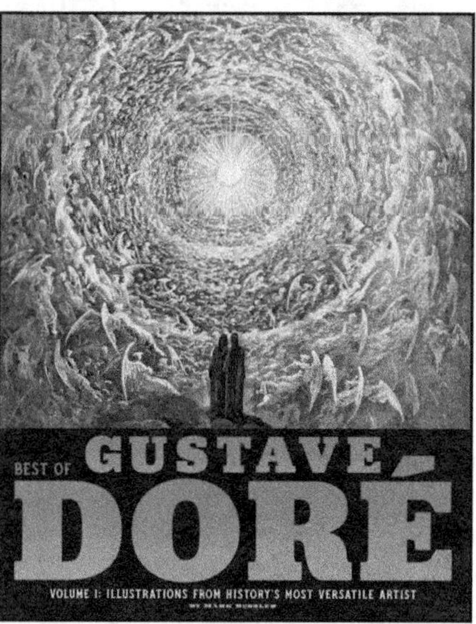

OTHER BOOKS FROM CGR PUBLISHING AT CGRPUBLISHING.COM

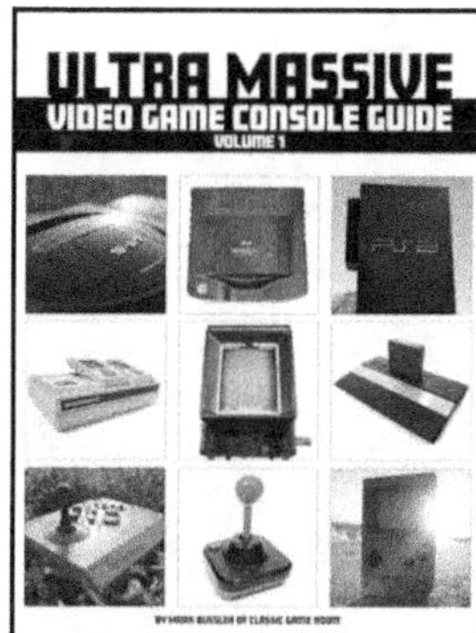

Ultra Massive Video Game Console Guide Volume 1

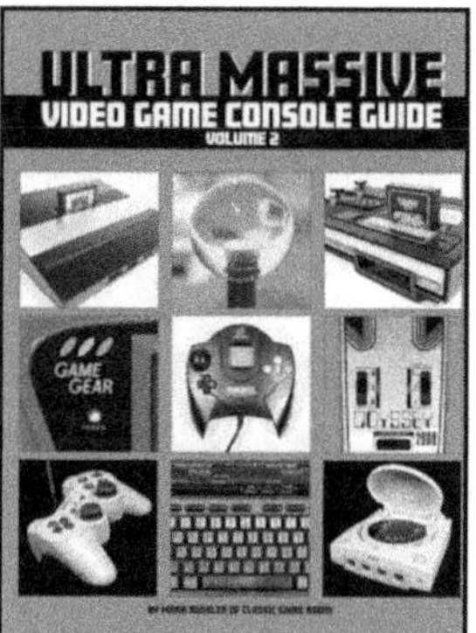

Ultra Massive Video Game Console Guide Volume 2

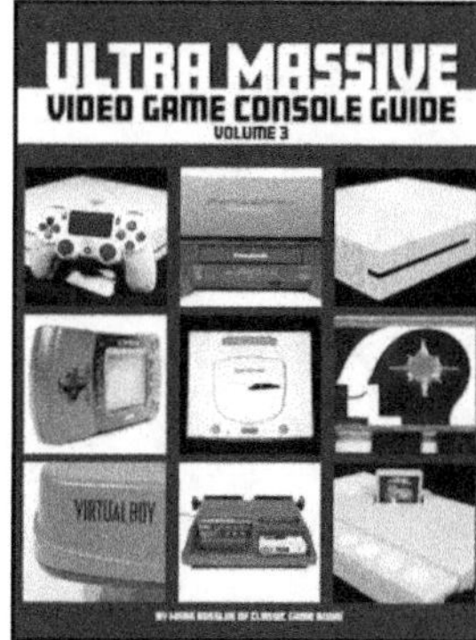

Ultra Massive Video Game Console Guide Volume 3

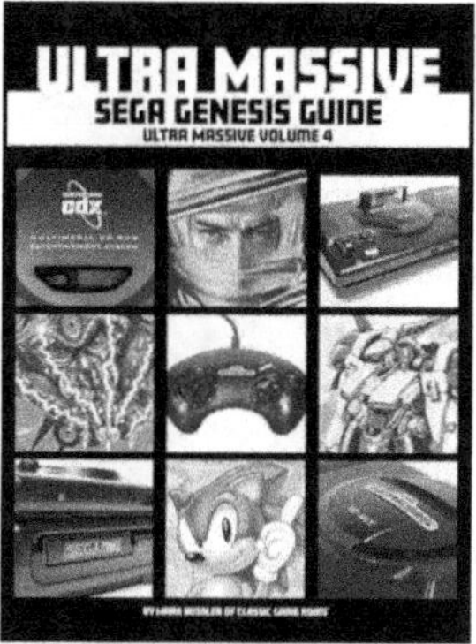

Ultra Massive Sega Genesis Guide

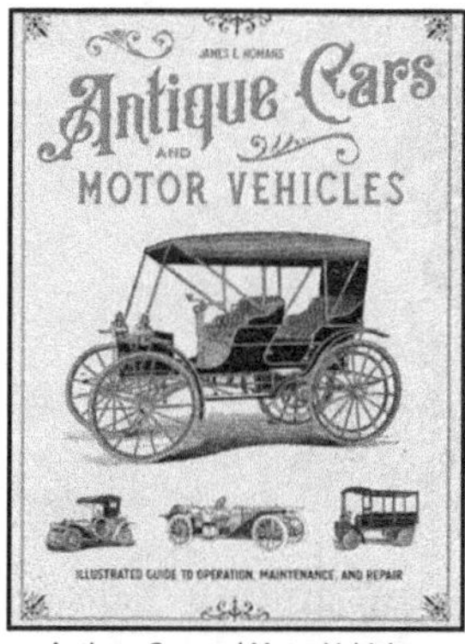

Antique Cars and Motor Vehicles: Illustrated Guide to Operation...

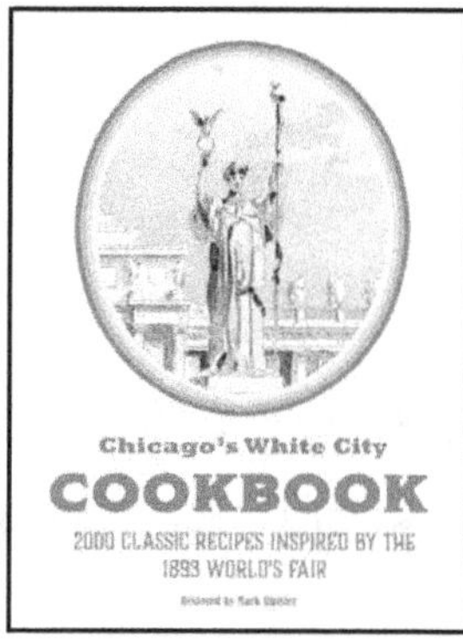

Chicago's White City Cookbook

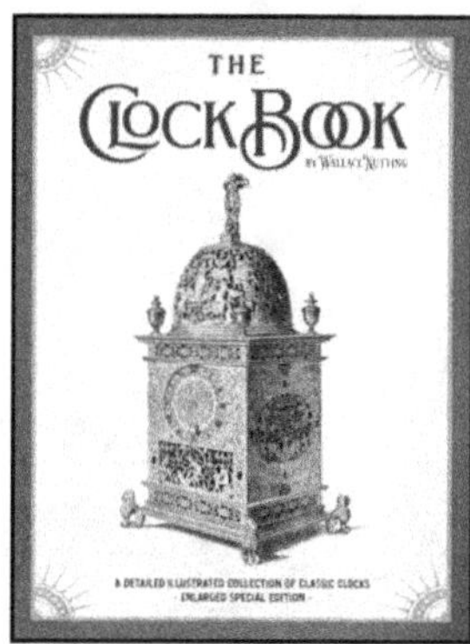

The Clock Book: A Detailed Illustrated Collection of Classic Clocks

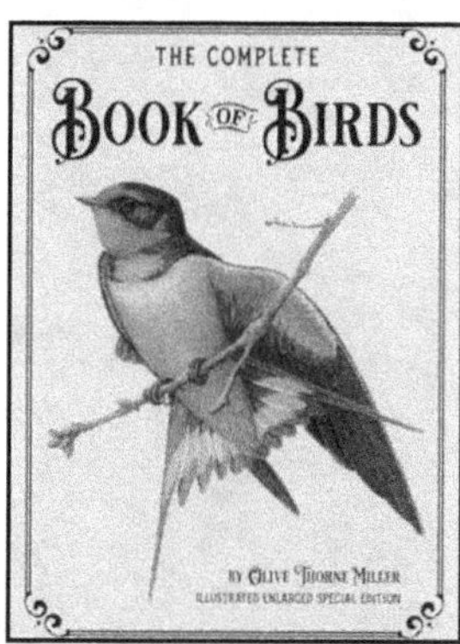

The Complete Book of Birds: Illustrated Enlarged Special Edition

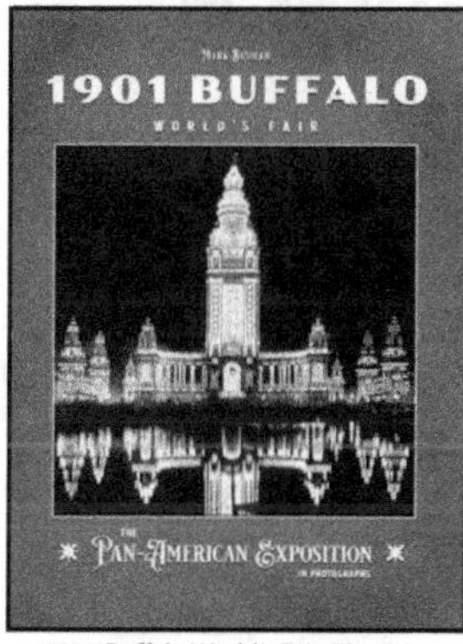

1901 Buffalo World's Fair: The Pan-American Exposition in Photographs

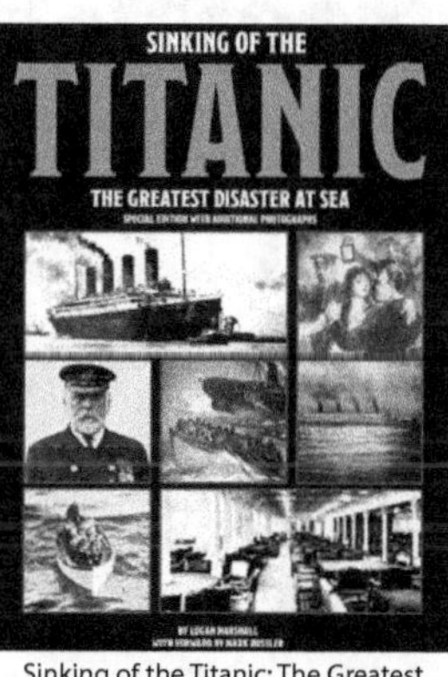

Sinking of the Titanic: The Greatest Disaster at Sea

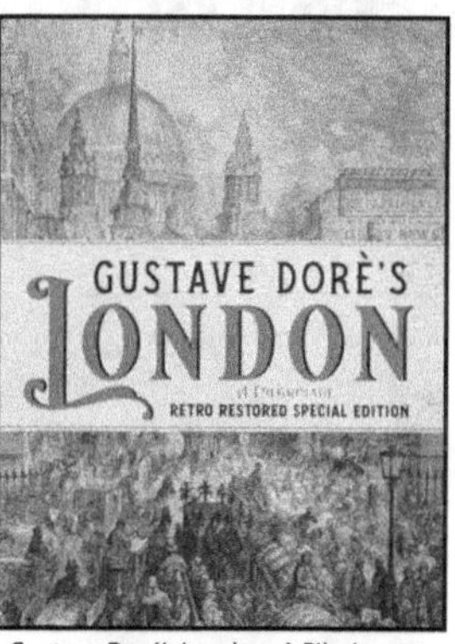

Gustave Doré's London: A Pilgrimage: Retro Restored Special Edition

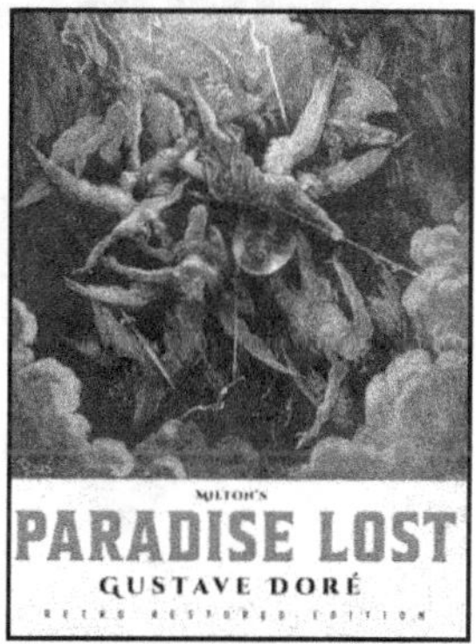

Milton's Paradise Lost: Gustave Doré Retro Restored Edition

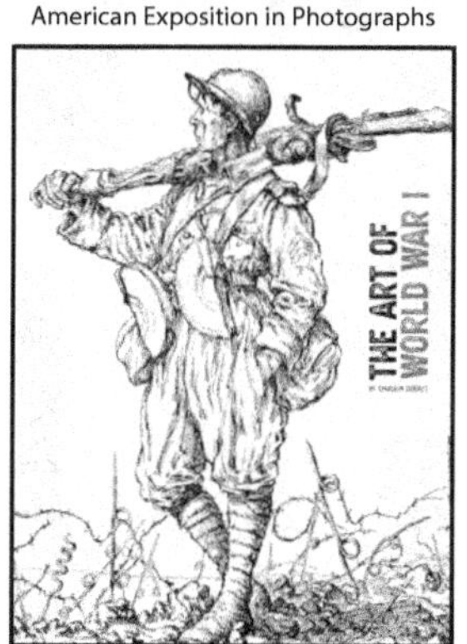

The Art of World War 1

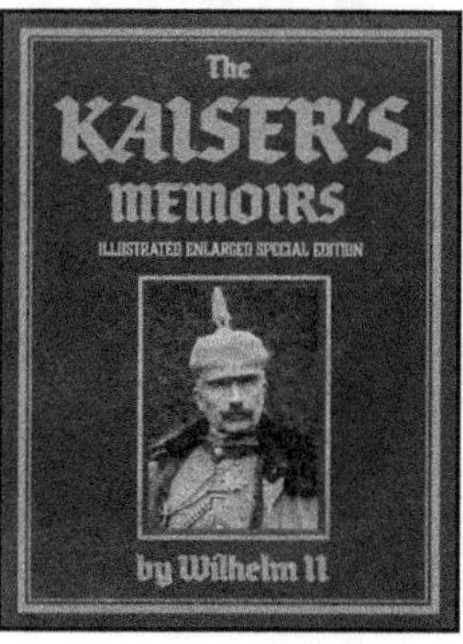

The Kaiser's Memoirs: Illustrated Enlarged Special Edition

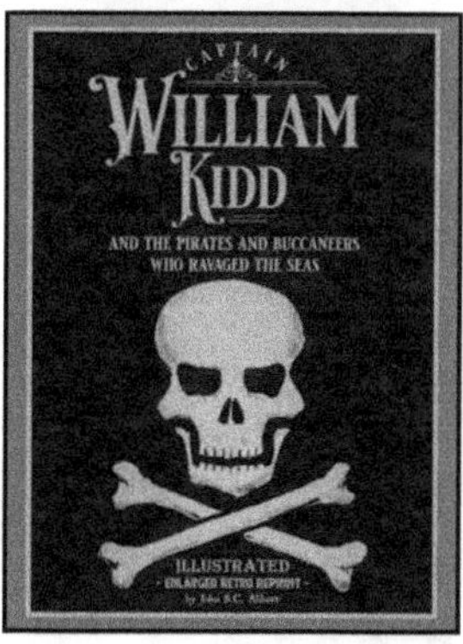

Captain William Kidd and the Pirates and Buccaneers Who Ravaged the Seas

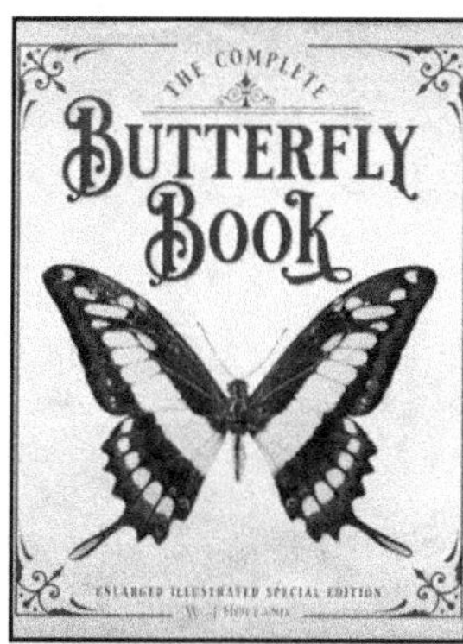

The Complete Butterfly Book: Enlarged Illustrated Special Edition

- MAILING LIST -
JOIN FOR EXCLUSIVE OFFERS

www.CGRpublishing.com/subscribe

www.ingramcontent.com/pod-product-compliance
Lightning Source LLC
LaVergne TN
LVHW061235100826
845148LV00008B/963

* 9 7 8 1 5 9 2 1 8 0 9 4 3 *